I0608953

Smugglers of Gor

Gorean Saga

Smugglers of Gor

John Norman

OPEN ROAD

INTEGRATED MEDIA

NEW YORK

All rights reserved, including without limitation the right to reproduce this book or any portion thereof in any form or by any means, whether electronic or mechanical, now known or hereinafter invented, without the express written permission of the publisher.

This is a work of fiction. Names, characters, places, events, and incidents either are the product of the author's imagination or are used fictitiously. Any resemblance to actual persons, living or dead, businesses, companies, events, or locales is entirely coincidental.

Copyright © 2012 by John Norman

978-1-4976-4868-5

This edition published in 2014 by Open Road Integrated Media, Inc.
345 Hudson Street
New York, NY 10014
www.openroadmedia.com

Smugglers of Gor

Chapter One

How helpless one is, when one is tied!

His foot turned me over. I was then on my back.

"A half tarsk," he said.

I did not understand what he meant.

I had been warned that I was not to speak.

Such as I, I gathered, must be given permission before we might speak.

I did not wish to be whipped, as had the other girl, who had dared to speak. She was now quiet, absolutely so. No longer did she dare to speak.

It was hard to conjecture what the whip might feel like, on my bare body. All of us had been stripped. I gathered that such as we might be kept in such a fashion. We had been laid side by side, in four lines. There were three aisles amongst us. It was as though we were not persons, but tethered animals. We were all females. As we lay there, the size of males, and their strength, and how different we were from them, impressed me as I think it hadn't before.

Too, the males about were standing, or walking about.

We were at their feet, literally.

I did not understand how they were dressed. They wore some sort of tunics. Their feet were shod in sandal-like boots, open somewhat, but with leather straps about the leg. Some wore headbands. Two carried whips.

I did not understand what was going on. I did know that I, as the others, were naked, and bound, hand and foot.

A fellow was moving amongst us, from one to the other. He

carried a coiled whip. He would crouch down, hold the whip to one's lips, and say, "Kiss it, and say 'La kajira'."

He was then close to me. I was on my back. I pulled at the bonds, futilely. Then he was beside me, and the heavy, snakelike coil of the whip was held before me. "Kiss it," he said, "and say 'La Kajira'."

I lifted my head a little, and kissed the whip. "La Kajira," I said. I did not know what it meant.

"The capsules are ready," called a fellow.

I did not understand that either.

A second fellow was following the first, and he, in a moment, was beside me. I caught sight of a large, thick square of soft, damp, folded, white cloth. One hand was placed behind the back of my head, holding me in place, and the other hand held the cloth, firmly, over my nose and mouth. I struggled a little, but was helpless. The cloth was damp. There was an unusual odor. I did not recognize the odor. It was pungent. It was irresistible. I looked up, and saw the ceiling of the large building, like a warehouse, and the lights, not now on. The light was dim. I tried to move my face beneath the thick folds of cloth, but they were held firmly over my nose and mouth. I squirmed. I tried to struggle. My wrists were crossed and tied behind my back; my ankles were crossed, and lashed together. I tried to pull against the bonds, but was helpless. Things began to go black. There was only the odor. I lost consciousness.

Chapter Two

There were several reasons I turned her over with my foot. First, most were supine, so it seemed suitable, more aesthetic, if the merchandise, in this wholesale lot, was positioned uniformly. Secondly, supine, they were more conveniently positioned for their first lesson, namely, that they were subject to discipline, symbolized by kissing the whip, and, second, enunciating their first words in what would be their new language, appropriate words. Too, of course, in that position, they were ready to be quickly and systematically sedated, for the voyage.

When the merchandise had been secured, each item had been placed in the bara position, though they did not know the name for the position as yet, each on her stomach, head facing to the left, her wrists crossed behind her and her ankles crossed, as well. In this position, they are easily bound, hand and foot. Some of the items had struggled, and must be forced into position, wrists and ankles held, while being bound. Later they would not do so, as they would learn that the least resistance would bring the switch or lash. They would fear then only that the position had not been assumed swiftly enough, and gracefully enough, for such as they were to be are not permitted awkwardness or clumsiness. The strugglers then, and many of the others, had later turned to their back, or side. It made little difference at this point in their new life. The primary point now was merely that they should understand themselves helpless, totally so. The item I had turned over with my foot, as some others, had remained, until then, in the bara position. I took that as an excellent sign, that they were highly intelligent. They recognized that they had been placed in a given position, and realized they had not been given permission to alter that position. Too, given their stripping and binding, they had doubtless begun to sense something of their new condition, and something of the life which would now be theirs. Similarly, several of them, including she whom I had turned over with my foot, when originally placed in the bara position, had maintained the position, docilely, while waiting for their tethering, sometimes Ehn later. All these things are indications of high intelligence in merchandise, and perhaps of something else, as well, something related, perhaps a welcoming, a readiness, a relief, an understanding, such things. Perhaps they had been waiting for years to be so bound.

But there was a third reason, as well, that I had turned her over. It was to better look upon her.

I had found of her interest, of course, weeks ago, when I had encountered her as a clerk in a large store. How startled she had been when I had looked upon her. Her lips had trembled, as with some question, possibly as to an earlier acquaintance. We had not, of course, known one another before. Yet there seemed some sort of recognition, on her part. That pleased me. Then she had backed away, embarrassed. That, I suppose, was to retreat from my regard. I did not lower my gaze, and she seemed suddenly frightened, and turned away, hurrying into another aisle. She was, of course, being assessed. I was conjecturing what she might look like, naked, exhibited on a slave block, responsive to the deft touches of the auctioneer's whip, what she might look like, barefoot, in a tunic, hurrying through the streets, avoiding free women, her neck fastened in a light, close-fitting, locked, metal collar. Did she sense such things? I do not know. Perhaps. In any event, I placed her, tentatively, on the initial manifest, and arranged for the usual inquiries, looking into her habits, her background, her interests, her tastes, her familiar itineraries, and such. She was also, unbeknownst to herself, videotaped several times, in various garments and against various backgrounds, which tapes were suitably reviewed. As I had anticipated, she was found acceptable for acquisition, or harvesting. Accordingly, I placed her on the final manifest. In education and quickness she was clearly superior. It was conjectured, as well, from a diversity of

subtle cues, physical and psychological, that she had unusual
sexual latencies, which might, in time, acknowledged and
stimulated, enfurnace her belly in such a way that she would be
not only excellently responsive but, far beyond that, helplessly,
beggingly needful. She suffered from the usual confusions and
deprivations common to young women of her milieu. As with
so many others, she seemingly found her life largely a round of
banalities. Her life was largely boring, empty, and meaningless.
She was restless, ill at ease, and unhappy. What she should be,
and do, and think, and try to feel, was largely set before her by
a culture of idiosyncratic stereotypes, the opinions she was to
hold were prescribed for her, and the values she was to maintain,
or pretend to maintain, brooked neither question nor deviation.
Every culture has its simple scions, naive and unquestioning,
dogmatic without inquiring into the credentials of dogmatisms,
mindlessly righteous in one of a thousand ways of being
mindlessly righteous, each contradictory to the other. On the
other hand, some, the highly intelligent, or, perhaps, simply, the
more cognitively alive, or aware, in the secret castles of their
own mind, ask questions, wonder about alternatives, think for
themselves, however secretly, as is prudential in any tyranny,
one of edged weapons or edged ideologies, capable of drawing
their own blood, and slaying their own millions.

She looked up at me.

I do not think she recognized me from the store, weeks ago.
Too, the light was not bright, and I was not now dressed in the
cumbersome, barbarous garments in which she had first seen me.

How tiresome, and confining, are such garments! At least
they had been removed.

I looked down on her, naked, bound at my feet.

She was beautiful, of course, else she would not have been
entered on the acquisition list, but so, too, were the others. And
many were doubtless more beautiful. I thought that, in a first
sale, she might bring something like a half tarsk. She was, in
measurements with which those of her background would be
familiar, some five feet five inches in height, and something
like one hundred and eighteen pounds in weight. She was a
brunette, with brown eyes, a common linkage, nothing special.
She did have an excellent figure, but there was nothing special

7

in that, either. One selects them with such things in mind. It was trim, well-turned, exciting, and slender.

I regarded her, more carefully.

She looked up at me. She squirmed a little. She realized herself well tied.

I found her personally of interest, but I doubted if, in a first sale, she would bring more than a half tarsk.

Perhaps if she had been strikingly beautiful? Several were. Still, a woman often becomes more beautiful. That is not unusual. It has to do, one supposes, with the life, with admission, with openness, with honesty, with fulfillment, with happiness.

Yes, I thought, in time she might become truly beautiful.

I recalled how she had kissed the whip, frightened, to be sure, but, too, seemingly gratefully. She had placed her soft lips upon it, gently, truly, fully, and had kissed it tenderly, deferently. In short, she had kissed it well. She had then completed the small ceremony, as instructed, saying "La kajira." She had said this softly, obediently. She would not know what it meant. In time she would learn.

Perhaps she suspected its meaning. One does not know. She was extremely intelligent and, latently, despite the indoctrinations and conditionings of her unusual culture, profoundly, biologically feminine.

Chapter Three

I soon learned to call men 'Master' and, shortly thereafter, free women 'Mistress'. The gulf between free and slave is profound and momentous, and such as I were brought, at least on the whole, to this unbelievably fresh and beautiful world, so bracing and green, as goods, no more than livestock, to be disposed of in markets. I was soon branded, that there would be no mistaking me, for what I was. How that simple mark transformed me! I was then different, radically so, from what I had been! And I knew myself so, and, yes, gratefully. Oh, I cried with pain, of course, helpless in the iron grip of the vise, my wrists fastened behind me, in the snug, unslippable metal bracelets, and sobbed, but, in my tears, did they know this, I sobbed, as well, with joy. At last it had been done to me. At last I was free! In a thousand dreams, had this not been done to me? Had I not, in a thousand dreams, been so marked, so designated, so proclaimed, so identified?

Am I terrible?

Perhaps, perhaps not.

Is it so strange that I, then humbled, then reduced, then subject to chains, the whip, the collar, was now free, at last free!

It was a freedom in which I had had no decision, but one forced upon me, and I would not have had it otherwise.

I was grateful to have been taken in hand, and simply treated as what I was, routinely, a female, only that, and gloriously so.

They would have of me what they wanted, and this was what I, too, wanted.

Since puberty I had sensed the radical difference between women and men, and had resented, but dared not rebel against, the lies, the pervasive, insisted-upon, venerated falsities with which I was regaled, and the pretentious, uncomfortable, alien roles which I was expected to assume.

I do not presume to speak for a sex, but I trust I may speak for an individual, myself. Doubtless women are quite different. One may wish for something which another does not. One may envy men, and another may find this emotion incomprehensible. One may hope to be served, and another to serve. One may hate, and another love. There are many things I have never understood, and how ignorant and stupid seem the ideologues, the tyrants, and fools, who see complexity in terms of conditioned, programmed simplicities. Who are the social engineers? Who appoints them? What shall be engineered? Who reviews their work? Need anything be engineered? Why should anything be engineered? Who will engineer a flower, or truth? Whose fingers draw the secret strings? How gross, narrow, and transparently self-serving, are so many manufactured values, principles, and injunctions. What are the credentials of a dictatorship which would review thought, circumscribe belief, and capture the coercive powers of a state in order to protect and propagate a favored orthodoxy? Yet, to be sure, such crimes are muchly precedent in the history of a world; they are perennially familiar to the troubled biography of a species. How many oppressions have been enforced, heresies persecuted, beliefs proscribed, truths denied, absurdities proclaimed! Behind the glistening veils may crouch an unnatural beast.

How naive I am, how unpolitical I am.

Why does the chain lure me? Why does the sight of the whip, and the knowledge that it may be used upon me, thrill me?

I wonder if my feelings are unique.

I do not think so.

How pathological the world from which I have been derived!

How many extend the hand of welcome, a knife clenched behind the back!

How is one to judge what brings about happiness, other than by the test of living, that of life consequences?

I wonder if I speak only for myself.

Perhaps, perhaps not.

But I will, at last, speak.

For years I have wanted to be at the feet of men, to kneel

naked, collared, subservient and submitted, before them, to put my head down and lick and kiss their feet, to be bound at their pleasure, to squirm helplessly in their grasp, to serve them in all ways, instantly and unquestioningly, to be commanded, to be owned, to be mastered.

The mark is placed high on the left leg, on the thigh, just beneath the hip. I have also been fastened, from time to time, in a variety of collars. My mark is the cursive kef, the common kajira mark, worn by most slaves. It is sometimes called the staff and fronds, beauty subject to discipline. It is a lovely mark. It looks well on me, and on others. It is, of course, only one of many marks. It is natural that not every property should be marked identically. But it is recommended that each property be marked. That is prescribed in Merchant Law. In the training house, a heavy metal collar, of rounded iron, was hammered about my neck. That is temporary, but it has its effect on us. When I was once displeasing, foolishly, this was replaced with a heavy, iron, point collar, which was very unpleasant. I do not know why I was displeasing. Perhaps I thought it required of me, to comply with some image, alien to my deepest self, which, on my former world, I had been expected to project. Perhaps I was merely curious to see what might occur, if I failed to comply in some particular, if I might hazard some show of resistance or recalcitrance. Certainly I learned, quickly enough. Perhaps I merely wished to ascertain certain perimeters or limits, the length of a leash, so to speak. I speak metaphorically, but it is not unusual that we are leashed. Often we are promenaded publicly. Our masters are often proud of us, and enjoy showing us off. Would it not be the same with horses and dogs, animals of my former world? We must hold our head up, and walk well. Sometimes our hands are free. In any event, these boundaries, the length of a leash, and such, so to speak, were expeditiously brought to my attention. Interestingly, I was not chagrined by the consequences of my small experiment, but, rather, reassured, even heartened. And I was very grateful when I earned my first, more typical, collar, light, flat, and close-fitting. How relieved and proud I was, when, graduated from training, it was first locked on my neck. I knew myself, and I wanted it there. I knew I belonged in a collar. I had suspected that, even on my former world, Earth.

Chapter Four

Clearly she had never been sold before. It is not hard to tell a new girl. It is not that they struggle, or scream, for that sort of thing is done with after the second or third day in their training. It is not acceptable. Those who behave so deplorably, so stupidly and futilely, so foolishly, are usually those who are only a day or so off the marching chain, who have not been in the houses, but in the camps, those who lack instruction, those as yet deprived of training.

A stroke or two of the whip and they are silent, and obedient. Another stroke or two and they are on their bellies, extending their hands to the buyers, begging to be purchased.

The difference, rather, in most cases, is various, wonder, uncertainty, hesitation, timidity, inertness, woodenness, a lack of grace, a lack of presentation, of readiness, of eagerness.

Some are clearly in misery, frightened. Some cannot hold their water. Some retch. The bowels of some are involuntarily, uncontrollably evacuated. It is not for no reason that they are ankle deep in sawdust.

How damp and foul may be the sawdust for subsequent items!

To be sure, such things are rare, probably because the sales have been rehearsed. In that way the items are aware of what will be expected of them. They are not fully informed, of course. There is always room for surprise, and spontaneity. One does not inform a new item of everything which may be done with them on the block.

I would suppose the items are not likely to forget their first sale. For most, I would suppose, as well, the first sale is the most difficult. This is not always the case, of course, for much can depend on the house, the auctioneer, the market, the mood of the buyers, and such. If it is learned that a given item was once a free woman of an enemy city, even a third or fourth sale may be terrifying.

Many, of course, are frightened, even overcome, shamed and humiliated, at their exposure, and that, interestingly, despite their training. What would they expect? Who would buy a clothed slave? Perhaps they did not expect the thing to be done so blatantly; perhaps they did not expect to be handled, and presented, in the way they are. Perhaps, too, it has to do with the whole of the thing, its reality, its newness, the sensations, the torchlight, the auctioneer, the cries of the men, the bidding.

Some of the items seem numb, almost in shock.

That makes it difficult for the auctioneer.

Are they even aware of the deft touches of his whip, that a chin be lifted, an arm raised, a body turned, a leg extended?

I am not sure that all of the items, at first, even understand, at least fully, what is being done to them. This is strange, given the training, the rehearsals. Perhaps they do not care to believe it. It cannot be being done to them. Surely it is a dream. But it is not a dream. It is real. Then they understand. They are being sold.

They move as directed.

They are merchandise, being displayed.

The item is well illuminated, while the auditorium is not. Many of the cries come from unseen bidders, obscure in the crowd, unseen in the darkness. Often the item is not even aware to whom it has been sold, only that it has been sold.

Perhaps they are still unfamiliar with the weight of chains, with their shackling.

Yet, how beautiful they are, even so!

Things are much different, of course, with the slave who knows her collar, who has knelt and kissed a dozen whips. After a time her belly burns. Men have seen to it. She is no longer hers; she is then men's. It is common, time permitting, the market conditions appropriate, to isolate such items, in their boxes or cages, for some days before their sale. Their needs are made clear by their scratching at the walls of kennels, their pressings against the bars of cages, their sobbings and entreaties before the guards, who will ignore them. They are well ready then, when brought to the block.

How piteously they strive to elicit interest.

It is natural, of course, for an item to wish to sell well. A well-presented item, other things being equal, is likely to bring a better price, and a richer master, with the likelihood of an easier life, less work, and greater prestige. Too, vanity courses brightly, rushing unobstructed, amongst such goods, familiar with such things, and each desires to win a fine price, and, particularly, one better than that garnered by rivals, or others of the house. Who does not wish to be the most beautiful, the most desirable? How proud is a top-price item! It is little wonder then that experienced items will compete on the block to excite buyers and outdo one another. How well they display the house's merchandise, sometimes subtly, so cleverly, sometimes brazenly, so boldly, invitingly, seductively! Many men who lack the coin to make a realistic bid frequent the emporia, the selling wagons, the shelves, the cages, the platforms, the camps, and barns, to gather the foods on which dreams will live. Yet many items are cheap, and not just pot girls or kettle-and-mat girls, and might be afforded even within the means of a light purse.

Sometimes a rich man adjudges the performance of an arrogant, vain, marvelously beautiful item to be intrinsically meretricious, to be hollow, and hypocritical, even fraudulent. It may call forth moans of anguish from some men in the crowd but the connoisseur recognizes its duplicity. Yet the slave is quite beautiful. Perhaps something might be made of her, if she is taught her collar, and suitably humbled. How smug she is, to be taken from the block by so generous a bid! But at his villa she is cast a rag and put to the tending of verr or tarsk. Perhaps months later, now understanding that she is a slave, and no more, she is permitted to crawl, begging, to the foot of his couch.

Though it was late I lingered at the sales, though why I am not sure.

Toward the end of the evening, I noted that a short, widely-hipped, nicely bodied brunette was conducted to the block. I scrutinized her, from the middle tiers. I recalled her. She was one of those I had first scouted on the slave world, several weeks ago. She was not particularly beautiful, as such things go, but there was clearly a subtle attractiveness about her. I had not been fully sure of her, but my colleagues had confirmed my initial impression. She was suitable collar meat. One can see certain women, and see that they belong in a collar. She was such a woman.

I recalled her bound, well tethered, and turning her over with my foot, in the warehouse, putting her to her back. I do not think she remembered me, from the large store. Prior to my turning her she had remained in the bara position, and, as some others, had held that position when placed in it, even prior to her fastening. Such things are indicative of intelligence, and even more so, perhaps, of understanding.

Some women obey because they must, and others because they must, and wish to do so, and hope to do so, and long to do so.

The selection criteria are stringent.

And they exceed those beauties which might be captured by a mechanical painter. There are the beauties of movement and expression, subtle, evanescent, and lovely, like the movement of a brook between its banks, of grass bending in the wind, of rustling leaves. Each particle is alive and precious. And there are the beauties of the vitality of consciousness, of thought, of emotion, of need, of readiness, of hope, of desire, of latent passion.

Few are deemed worthy of a Gorean collar.

It is important that they should be suitable, of course, as one intends to sell them.

And so she came to the block.

I stayed to watch.

She was thrust forward, into the torchlight.

She seemed to me then more beautiful than I had remembered her.

Of course, it had been easy to remember that she was attractive, not at all bad looking.

But now, somehow, she seemed more so.

Had she lost some small register of weight; was her waist narrower, her figure trimmer?

Before a sale, a house tries to bring its goods to ideal block

15

measurements, customized to the item, differing from item to item.

Beyond this, was she softer now, more lithe, more alive? Had she come now more to a sense of herself?

I decided she was beautiful. I wondered if she knew that.

I had the sense, beyond that, that she would be responsive, and, in time, needfully, helplessly, beggingly responsive.

Doubtless she did not now understand what could be done with her.

It is amusing, to do this to them.

In a tunic, barefoot, on the streets, I did not doubt but what men would turn, to look after her.

Something seemed special about her. I was not sure what it might be. Surely she was only another lovely beast, another bead on the slaver's chain, another vendible item, one of more than a hundred already presented before us, but there seemed something special about her. Perhaps only to me. I noticed no special interest, or particular ripple of anticipation about me. We were used to excellent merchandise, of course. Plenty of it had already been before us. Much of it had sold well. Bids were now less forthcoming. Was it, I wondered, simply that she was so unusually feminine, so clearly feminine, and this so early in her bondage, despite the culture from which she was derived? Or was it, rather, simply, that she was, and was so obviously, a slave? Much that is subtle goes into these things, much which it would be difficult to articulate.

The first time I looked upon her, of course, I saw her as fittingly collared.

Such as she belonged on the block.

Clearly she had never been sold before. It is not hard to tell a new girl.

She obeyed well, but they all do, almost all. The lash is not pleasant. Clearly she feared to excite buyers. In the house she had learned something of what it is to be a woman, and on Gor. Gor has its laws, its customs, its principles, its conventions, its proprieties, and its sensitivity, sometimes acute, to points of honor; but, to a woman brought from the slave world, it is likely to appear, at first, little more than a lawless savagery, a chaos of will and mastery, an unpredictable jungle, a threatening ferocity, a country of dangers and barbarities. To me that seems strange, given the heartless, barbaric complexities of her world with its scramblings for wealth and power, the competitions to control the weaponry of states, that one may apply such ugly resources, under the pretense of legality, to the ends of one's own aggrandizement, a world of deceit, glitter, propaganda, hypocrisy, falsity, greed, and cruelty, a world not loved, but threatened, by a thousand ignorances, neglects, lies, and poisons. What strange beast would defecate in its own lair, or foul its own nest, ruin the soil from which it hopes to harvest, defile the seas in which it would cast its nets, contaminate the very air which it must breathe? Barbarians, they do not know that they are barbarians.

What are its women worth, save to be slaves?

Collar them, master them.

Little, I fear, has prepared the unguarded slave fruit, so carefully and easily plucked from the orchards of Earth, for the world of Gor. Perhaps the major difference between these worlds is that in one nature is feared and rejected, with the result that civilization is essentially a denial of nature, almost its antithesis, a war conducted against a suspect nature, as though nature was an enemy, to be suppressed at all costs, rather than the foundation of one's very being. On Gor, civilization is not a flight from nature, but its acceptance, refinement, and enhancement. Gorean culture is built on nature, and within it, not against it, and apart from it. Unhappiness and misery is a high cost to pay for the denial of nature; it is well, I suppose, at least, that the victims are encouraged to think well of themselves, taking their unease, grief, and wretchedness as badges of rectitude. You may teach a bird that flight is evil, and break its wings, but its heart will always remember the sky.

The auctioneer had begun taking bids on the barbarian.

I would not bid.

The taverns would be open until shortly before dawn.

Some of the fellows had brought their slaves with them, these kneeling, head down, at the left knee of their seated masters, their wrists braceleted behind them. They were briefly tunicked, as is common with the slaves of men. Most were leashed, the strap of the leash lying across the master's lap, or wound, loosely, about his left wrist. Some of these slaves might have been close enough to the raised sales platform, and its torches, to be visible to the items being vended. Perhaps the items being vended might wonder if, sometime, they, too, might be brought so to an auction. The usual reason a slave is brought to an auction is merely that their masters enjoy having them at hand, relish them, and do not wish to leave them at home, caged, kenneled, chained to a couch ring, or such; on the other hand, many masters enjoy being seen with slaves whom others might envy, the ownership of a beautiful slave accruing them attention and prestige, rather as might the exhibition of a splendid kaiila or fine sleen; and others, I fear, bring them either to alarm the slave, reminding her that she, too, could easily be sold, or even, occasionally, to offer them, in a private sale.

It was late, and several had left the tiers.

Clearly the barbarian feared to excite the men.

That was comprehensible, at least now.

On Gor nature, as suggested, is respected. For example, men are not divided against themselves, shamed, diminished, reduced, ridiculed, castigated, and taught to suspect their most natural feelings and impulses. Guilt is more cruel than the sword, for one turns the knife in one's own stomach. What animal other than a human being is so stupid as to torture itself? Who sells the knife, and who collects its rent? It is a strange physician whose livelihood depends on placing poultices on wounds which, were it not for him, would not have existed. Many are the ways in which a living may be made. Some are difficult to understand, if one seeks reasons, and not causes.

Many crimes have no names.

And what of women on such a world?

Not knowing men, how can they know themselves? How should we understand day without night, summer without winter, here without there, this without that? How shall we understand women without men? There can be bodies without men, but can there be women?

Clearly she feared to excite the buyers.

Doubtless she knew how small, how weak, how defenseless, how helpless, she was. Too, by now, she had some sense of the nature of Gorean men. Little on her world had prepared her for this, for such men, their health and hardiness, their naturalness, their openness, innocence, and honesty, their unity, power, strength, possessiveness, and aggression, how they would look upon her and, without a second thought or reservation, see her as a female, and treat her as a female.

How different from her world!

Was she not as a vulnerable tabuk doe amongst larls?

"Excellent," said a fellow beside me.

The item had been placed in the slave bow, bent backwards, the auctioneer's hand in her hair.

I agreed with the fellow beside me. Her line was excellent.

I thought the auctioneer was doing a good job, particularly with a new girl. Some auctioneers work in different markets, even in different cities. Most, on the other hand, will contract to a particular house, or market. A skilled auctioneer is expensive. Some receive a percentage of the sale.

The bids were desultory. It was late. Many buyers had left. I feared the strings of many purses were now knotted tight. The goods had been exhibited in exposition cages this afternoon, prior to the sale. Her lot was 119. I had seen her in one of the cages, with several others. Some were kneeling, some sitting, some standing, some moving about. There were pans of food, slave gruel, and water in the cage, and a wastes bucket. It was easy to see the slaves who had been sold before, perhaps more than once. They wanted masters. They needed masters. There was no mistaking their glances, the positioning of their bodies. Their needs were obvious, from their faces, glimpsed behind the bars. Their eyes would plead. Some clutched the bars, pressing their face between them, as they could. Others pretended indifference, even insolence. That sometimes provokes a fellow to bid, if only to have the pleasure of having such a bold, pretentious animal cowering at his feet, lifting her lips to his whip. When a girl is called to the bars she must approach her summoner, posing and displaying herself as he might suggest. Her lot number is prominent, drawn on her left breast in grease pencil. I had called one to me, a brunette, who seemed lost, and timid, naked, locked in the cage, but did not ask her to perform. I merely wished to ascertain the lot number. Amidst all the others, near the cages and in the vicinity, I do not think she recognized me. I was not in the barbarous garments with which I had disguised myself on her crowded, polluted, misguided, hapless world, nor in the work tunic I had worn in the warehouse. I was in robes suitable for my caste, dark, with the small blue and yellow chevrons low on the left sleeve. Within them was concealed the gladius. I dismissed her with a gesture, as a slave is dismissed. She hurried back into the cage, to conceal herself, amongst the others.

There are many strategies for organizing a sale. In this market, the Jewels of Brundisium, not to be confused with the paga tavern of the same name near the wharves, one usually, as tonight, divides the evening into five segments; the first and second segments, save for a special item or two, to encourage early attendance, are intended to set the stage for the third and fourth segments. By then late comers are seated and the crowd is warmed, has found its mood, and is ready for, and eager for, the more competitive bidding. Normally that merchandise adjudged the most likely to bring high prices will then be offered. We were now in the early portion of the fifth phase. Interestingly, some unusual buyers, of a garb and sort with which I was unfamiliar, had made a number of purchases in the first and second phases of the sale. Their purses seemed deep. Certainly they had silver, and, in the third and fourth segment, even gold to spare. I do not think that one item, to this point, had gone unsold, fortunately for the item, for otherwise it might be whipped, though several, in the first and second segments, had gone cheaply, for copper, from twenty to eighty tarsks, copper tarsks. In Brundisium 100 copper tarsks is commonly valued at a silver tarsk. None had sold for less than twenty-forty copper, namely twenty copper tarsks, forty tarsk-bits. In Brundisium there are 100 tarsk-bits to the copper tarsk. In many cities, Ar, Besnit, Thentis, Ko-ro-ba, and such, the tarsk-bit is more valuable, there being most often eight or ten to a copper tarsk. I do not know the rates in Turia, nor in the islands. In Brundisium a day's wages, for a docksman, is usually twenty to forty tarsk-bits. A free oarsman will usually command more. Some alleged the unusual buyers were Tuchuks, but others denied this. The shading of their skin and the cast of their eyes suggested Tuchuk blood, but they were not armed as Tuchuks, and seemed, too, in so far as such things might be ascertained, unfamiliar with bosk, kaiila, and the terrains of the south. Some said, too, they were taller than Tuchuks, and were more spare, more sedate, more studied, more formal, more withdrawn, more graceful, and perhaps more latently intense. Some, crossed in the streets, had proved more than capable of defending themselves, with their unusual softly curved blades, one long, one short. They had attracted attention, for their apparent wealth, for buying slaves and hiring ships, and taking men into fee, many of them refugees, armed mercenaries, escaped from Ar, given the sudden, devastating, bloody restoration of Marlenus, Ubar of Ar, sometimes spoken of as the Ubar of Ubars. These ships, it was said, would coast north. Their purpose was obscure. Some ships, returned, had disembarked supplies, soldiers, and slaves on the stony beaches bordering the northern forests.

The tiers were now half emptied. Men brushed past me, to climb the steps to the exits. Attendants, below and to the sides, waited to extinguish the torches. I could see four or five figures below, and at the side of the block, the left, as we faced it, at the foot of its stairs. These would be the last to be sold.

"Twenty, twenty, twenty?" called the auctioneer.

The item had been clearly identified as a first-sale barbarian. She was brown-haired and brown-eyed. Nothing special there. Auburn hair is usually prized in the markets. Had she been auburn she would doubtless have been placed in the third or fourth segment of the sale. Her measurements had been publicized. Such measurements include not only those for hips, waist, and bosom, but those for ankle, wrist, and throat, these relevant to wrist rings, ankle rings, and collar. Her progress in Gorean, to date, was proclaimed to be excellent. I was pleased. This bespoke high intelligence. Intelligence is a major criterion in terms of which we select slaves. Who would wish a stupid slave? The intelligent slave learns her master's language quickly, learns swiftly how to please him, and perfectly, in all ways, and, being intelligent, is more likely to be in tune with her basic femaleness, and its profound needs. She is the first to lick and kiss the chains which bind her.

"Twenty, twenty, yes, twenty-five," called the auctioneer. "Thirty, thirty?"

Not unexpectedly the slave was red-silk. Sometimes white-silkers cost more, though for no reason that seems clear. Who cares about such things in the case of a slave? Is the virginity of a tarsk or verr of interest? Who cares who is first to open them?

Then casually, unexpectedly, the auctioneer, behind the slave, his left hand in her hair, holding her head back a bit, gently, but firmly, with the blades of the coiled whip, subjected her to the "slaver's caress."

She shrieked with misery, and twisted, and leaped.

"Stop, stop!" she cried.

But the gentle touch, firm and implacable, was relentless. She rose to the tips of her toes, as though she would withdraw from the touch. Then she kicked out, wildly, protestingly, and would have lost her footing was it not for the hand in her hair. She tried to turn and face the auctioneer, but, as she was held, could not do so. She was then held before the tiers, facing them, squirming, helpless, sobbing. "No, no, no!" she begged. There was laughter from those remaining in the tiers.

"Please, no!" she begged.

"'Please, no', what?" asked the auctioneer.

"Please, no, Master!" she cried. "Please, no, Master! Master!"

He released her and she, her body a wracked, scarlet, sobbing hue, went to her knees in the sawdust, shaking her head, covering her face with her hands.

Several of those remaining in the tiers laughed at the discomfiture of the slave.

As I had conjectured, the item was excellently responsive. Such things raise a girl's price. It was interesting to speculate what she might be like, once well in a collar.

"Thirty-five!" called a man.

"Thirty-six!" called another.

I was pleased the auctioneer had not punished her for her lapse. The slave, of course, addresses all free men as 'Master', all free women as 'Mistress'.

She was on her knees on the block, sobbing.

Surely a slave must realize that a potential buyer is interested in all a slave's properties.

Why was she upset, that she had been shown to be healthy, and vital?

I then recalled she came from a world in which frigidity and inertness were esteemed, at least publicly, in which formality, withdrawal, hesitation, reticence, fear, and an inability to feel were reckoned matters of merit. So might a kaiila be praised for lameness, a sleen for the inability to track even a wounded tabuk, a tarn for not daring to spread its wings and fly.

"Forty-five!" called a fellow from the tiers, below me and to my right.

She finally went for forty-eight, forty-eight copper tarsks. I had conjectured that she would bring, as a first sale girl, and a barbarian, a half tarsk, half a silver tarsk. She had fallen short of this by two full copper tarsks, but I was not disappointed. Markets vary. She might just as well have brought a tarsk plus two, two copper tarsks over a silver tarsk. When she had been presented, many buyers had left, and, of those remaining, the purses of several might have been earlier lightened. Professional buyers, speculators, tavern keepers, camp suppliers, and such, often buy more than one item.

She was purchased by an agent, one bidding on behalf of those strangely garbed fellows who had apparently been mistaken, by some, for Tuchuks.

I climbed the stairs, and exited the emporium.

I recalled that her lot number had been 119.

Chapter Five

How could he think I would not recognize him!

Had I never forgotten him, even from Earth, when I saw him, in the aisle, but a few feet away? I feared it was he, he of my dreams. I felt myself small and helpless, and what I was, female, radically and only female, weakly female, helplessly female, and I knew myself incomparably less than he. Who would want to relate otherwise to a man? And who could relate otherwise to such a man? Why had I never felt this way before other men? I felt him different from the men I had known, so different! I was suddenly aware, as I had not been before, of the radical centrality of sex to the human condition, the mighty division and chasm which separates the sexes. How real it was! How simple it was to see, once looked upon, once dared to be looked upon. I felt as though the lies of my acculturation were collapsing about me. Would he find me of interest? I feared so. What would he do with me? I feared I knew. He had turned. Our eyes had met. I had felt myself not merely seen, but considered, appraised. I felt myself looked upon not simply as a female, even one small, weak, and helpless, but as what I had so often thought myself to be, beyond that, a slave. Surely he could not know my secret thoughts, the nature of my most inadmissible, my most fearful, and fulfilling, dreams. Never had I known a man who had so looked upon me. Under his glance I felt seen, truly seen, for the first time. I felt stripped by that look. How different we are from men, from such men! How he was seeing me! Did he conjecture me naked, frightened, crouching at his feet, at a ring, bound for whipping, on a platform, exhibited before buyers? I fought the mad impulse to kneel before him, lowering my head. I feared to be punished. I strove to study him, but was not well able to do so. I was trembling. I knew I could not have spoken to him, without faltering, without stammering, even if I had wished to do so. And perhaps I would not have been permitted to do so, not without permission. As our eyes had met, I should have smiled, approached him, and, as we are trained to do, asked if I might be of service. "May I help you, sir?" I could not do so. I felt as though it was improper, somehow, to be standing in his presence. That might be acceptable, even, appropriate, for some women, but, I suspected, not for me, not for a woman such as I. I tried to break this odd spell in which I felt myself bound. Should it not be easy enough to do? Was he not merely another modern man, another approved man, another permitted man, another joke on masculinity, another travesty on, and betrayal of, what might have been? How many bodies looked like those of men, and proved no more than a facade, behind which lay a shambles, pusillanimity or nothing. Surely many men would be as tall, as large, as narrow-waisted and broadly shouldered, as muscular, as darkly handsome, as large handed, as he. What then was different about him? He appeared agile, and strong, but do not many? How might he make his living? What skills might he have? I wondered about that. He seemed misplaced in this time, in this place. I thought he might seem one less familiar with escalators than mountains, less at home with engines and calculators than with horses and falcons, than with fire, bows, and steel. There seemed something about him of a foreign flavor. Had he spoken I would not have been surprised if I had detected the trace of an accent, but he did not speak. I tried to be amused that he wore his clothing awkwardly. It seemed tailored, and yet, somehow, ill-fitting. He did not seem at ease in it, certainly. Perhaps he would have preferred something less confining, something in which a man might move freely, with speed, and assurance.

He looked upon me.

I sensed he saw me as other men had not.

I sensed that he saw the slave within my garments.

How frightening it was to be so seen, so recognized, for what I was!

Surely I had misunderstood.

It could not be!

Then, at last, frightened, I had turned, broken away, and hurried, indeed fled, between the counters, the goods, the shoppers, to the other side of the store. My haste, I fear, attracted attention. I gasped for breath. That fearful moment, the interval of our interaction, brief but seemingly prolonged, which had seemed oddly fixed in time and space, must be swept away, and forgotten as soon as possible.

But I had been unable to forget.

How could I forget those keen, dark, quiet eyes which had so surveyed me, seeing me as I had sensed I had never been seen before?

Did he seem amused, that I might stand in his presence, presenting myself as though I might be a free woman?

I suspected he knew better.

Days I had spent, uneasy, distracted, ill at ease, remembering, struggling to brush aside the cruel insistencies of recollection; how often I censured myself for my misunderstandings, my foolishness. How easy it is to misconstrue and magnify the smallest incidents, the most meaningless things! Yet, too, somehow, I sensed the matter was not done. I had the odd sensation, from time to time, that I might be the subject of inquiries, that I might be under surveillance. Perhaps photos had been taken. Perhaps somewhere, in one place or another, I had been filmed, perhaps more than once. I dismissed, as I could, such apprehensions as unfounded, even absurd. But, too, at the same time, I found that my curiosity was engaged, and my vanity piqued. Might it be true that I was watched? I did not think so, but I thought I would play a game, one which might be amusing, one which might show me the absurdity of my fears. I would meet the matter directly, and pretend to myself that I was truly under surveillance, that I was beautiful enough and desirable enough to be subjected to such scrutiny. Accordingly, I began to give more attention to my appearance than was customary. I purchased new outfits and shoes. I was attentive to my movements and my expressions. It is a simple thing to sit and rise, to stand, turn, and walk with grace. Certainly I would not dare do otherwise now, here. And I probably could not, even if I wished it, given the training. It becomes a part of one, as one is changed. It is a simple thing, too, of course, to smile, to speak clearly, and listen attentively. And so, I thought, in a variety of ways, I would act a part, and thus diminish, and then dismiss, my concerns. What could not be I would pretend was. If I were not truly beautiful, I would act as though I was, even to insolence and defiance; if I was not desirable, I would act as though I was, even to arousing interest and then, mockingly, frustrating it. And so I gave attention to my figure, with diet and exercise, gave attention to my hair, improved my makeup, enlarged my wardrobe, and made it a point to dress flatteringly. I was careful now with respect to my posture, my speech, and demeanor, and carried my head high, as might a lofty, frigid free woman. How meretricious that was, as I knew myself, in my heart, a slave. My head should have been bowed! And I should have feared the lash! But it was a game, a form of acting, you must understand. Was I not legally free! I was free! I behaved so, as I did, you must understand, merely in order to mitigate my fears, to face, taunt, defy, and deny them, to ridicule them, to prove them groundless, only that. How horrifying then if, despite my intentions, so well-meaning and innocent, it might have been this very charade which has brought me to my chains, in a Gorean dungeon, awaiting shipment, with others, we know not where. I do know we are near the docks, for I can hear waves washing against pilings, and smell the sea. We are naked, the chains are heavy. They are on our necks, our wrists and ankles. But forgive me, Masters. Forgive my vain heart. What have I done? I know I am not permitted to lie. Free women may lie, but not I. Why, truly, had I behaved as I did, so blatantly, so insolently, so provocatively? I wished, of course, as I now understand, to interest and intrigue possible watchers. I wanted to impress them. Did they know that? I suspect they did. Perhaps they were amused. Surely slave dispositions are important in being a slave. Should not those who should be slaves make the best slaves? Why should we fight our slave dispositions? Why should we pretend to be other than we are, better than we are? I suppose it is clear then why I acted as I did. I did not truly act in order to confront and overcome fear, but, rather, to display myself. If I were under surveillance, truly, and it might be so, I could hope that I wished to be found pleasing. I wished the report to be favorable. Even the pretense to freedom, arrogance, contempt, inaccessibility, frigidity, and such, was intended to be provocative. I supposed some men might enjoy taking such a woman in hand, and turning her into a stripped, collared, humbled, aroused, begging slave.

I think I played my role well.

But how alien it was to my needs.

How strange that I, lonely, lost in my uncaring world, aching for the touch of a man, should have pretended to indifference, disdain, and contempt!

I think I was closer to myself than many, and nearer to the feet of a master.

For several days I continued the game, growing, for no reason I clearly understood at the time, ever less hopeful, and more despondent. Surely I should be much pleased. Surely I had been successful. I had shown to myself that there was nothing to fear, that my apprehensions and concerns had been groundless. How relieved, and pleased, I should be! Did I understand then what I had truly been doing, what I really wanted? I do not think so. I understand now. Then, one night, clutching my pillow, bursting into tears, I ended the game, realizing its meaninglessness and futility, and accepted, sorrowing, the drabness, the boredom, the pointlessness, the impoverishment, the emptiness, the reality of my life.

How pathetic that I, a forlorn, wandering slave, should find myself on a world without masters. How was it that one such as I had been born here, in this place, in this time? Must it not be a mistake? I was not, and did not wish to be, an identical, a neuter, an artifact, a product, a role, an adversary, an enemy, a foe. I had striven to be these things, what I was not, what I was told to be, what was prescribed for me, but I had failed. I found myself exiled in my native land.

Surely the commands were clear.

My body obeyed them, my heart could not.

I truly believe he did not think I recognized him.

Did he think me stupid?

I am not stupid. I am intelligent, I think quite intelligent. Do they not want us so?

Surely an intelligent woman should bring a higher price, should be worth more in a collar, a slave collar.

Several days after ending my "game," after dismissing, as I could, the incident of the store which had so unaccountably stirred, troubled, and startled me, which had so foolishly stimulated and intrigued me, I returned, reconciled and resigned, to my old life, with its habits, predictabilities, and routines. From time to time, of course, I recalled the incident. It was not easy to forget. It idled its way through daydreams, and, more than once, recurred in my dreams, from which I, seemingly rooted in place and unable to flee, would abruptly waken.

I wondered how such dreams might have continued, had I dared to permit them to do so.

One night, I returned home, a Wednesday evening in November, a cool night, late from the store, for we had been open later than usual, for a sale, prepared a small supper, and then, weary from the day, retired. I am not clear what occurred then. It was perhaps the following morning that I awakened, but I am not sure. It may have been days later. It no longer seemed fall, or the same clime. I do not know. In some cases it is apparently days later. Similarly, transportation must be involved, of one extent or another. In any event I was awakening. I was half conscious. I stirred uneasily. Something, it seemed, was quite different. "This one is awakening," said a voice, in English. I was startled for it was a man's voice. I supposed myself still dreaming. Then I was not sure. Then I realized I was not dreaming. I was naked, and on my stomach, lying on a hard, wooden floor. I half cried out, a tiny, frightened noise, and went to rise, but a foot on my back pressed down, pinning me to the floor. "Be silent," said a voice. I was held in place, the boot on my back. Then, after a moment, it was removed. I did not move. I remained still, terrified. I sensed that I was not alone on the floor. There were other bodies about, some supine, some prone. All were female, and all were unclothed, as I, wholly. Some were clearly bound. "Cross your ankles," said the voice, "and cross your wrists, behind your back, and look to your left." I did so. I heard one girl scream, and begin to cry out, and then I heard an unmistakable sound, though one I had not heard before, the snapping of a lash on flesh, twice. There was then silence. I understood nothing of what was occurring. I remained in the position in which I had been placed. I must have remained in that position for several minutes, and then I sensed a man crouching near me. Loops of a light, silken cord, like lightning, were whipped about my wrists, and they were tethered together, and, a moment later, my ankles were similarly served. It had all been done with a swiftness, security, and assurance which must have betokened an almost thoughtless familiarity with such matters. Then the fellow was away, attending to another. I tested my bonds. I was helpless, absolutely helpless. Later, I was turned to my back by a man's foot, shod in one of those thong-wound, sandal-like boots. He looked down upon me, naked, supine, and bound, at his feet. "A half tarsk," he said, absently, in English. I did not understand him. Then he looked away. It was he, he from the store, from weeks earlier. I recognized him, of course. Had I not seen him a thousand times, in recollections, in casual reveries, in dreams? But I had not before lain at his feet, naked and bound. A bit later, a small ceremony, or what I took to be a small ceremony, was enacted. A coiled whip was placed to my lips. I was told to kiss the whip, and say, 'La kajira', with which instructions I readily complied. Had I not earlier heard the snapping of a whip? I feared it, and did not wish to feel it. Yet, too, and more importantly, and interestingly, though I hardly dared admit it to myself at the time, I was thrilled to place my lips, tenderly, submissively, on that imperious, stern leather. I was frightened, but, too, I felt somehow privileged to do so. I suspected the whip was held to the lips of few. The whip, clearly, was an image of, a symbol of, the mastery. Might a slave then not appropriately express and acknowledge her submission, her deference, her gratitude, her acceptance of, her celebration of, the unqualified, uncompromised might of the mastery, for which she had for so long yearned? Had I not waited years, surely since puberty, for such an opportunity? So I kissed the whip for the first time, lying on my back, naked and bound, lifting my head, kissed it tenderly, gratefully, submissively. Commonly the whip is kissed while one kneels. I did not know the meaning of the words 'La kajira', but it was not difficult, under the circumstances, to speculate on their nature. They would be, incidentally, the first words I would learn in my new language, Gorean, the language of my masters. Both 'Lo kajirus' and 'La kajira' may be translated "I am a slave." 'Lo kajirus' is masculine; 'La kajira' is feminine. Accordingly, the first would be understood as "I am a male slave," and the second as "I am a female slave." Perhaps the best translation into English of 'La kajira', considering the contempt in which we are held, as we are vendible work and pleasure animals, might be "I am a slave girl."

When I awakened on the wooden floor, in the high-ceilinged, spacious room, naked amongst others, and was positioned so that I might be conveniently bound, I realized that I, and these others, had been selected. Thus, having been selected, I supposed, as well, that we had been assessed, and, assessed, had been found acceptable.

But for what had we been found acceptable?

When the cords were knotted about my wrists and ankles there could be little doubt about the matter.

Then I had been turned to my back, and looked up at him. I lay before him, supine at his feet, naked, tethered.

It was he from the store!

I had never forgotten him.

How different was this interview, from that of the store!

"A half tarsk," he had said, and turned away.

I wondered if he remembered me. Perhaps, perhaps not. I did not know. There were several on the floor, in their lines.

He must remember me, I have often thought. Sometimes I am extremely angry. How dare he not remember me! How could he forget? Was it not he who did this to me? Was it not he who brought me to my chains? Was it not he who is responsible for this radical transformation in my fortunes, my condition, and status, for my reduction and degradation? Should I not hate him! Should I not deplore my state, one so helpless, so without recourse, even on another world! I clutch my chains and shake them. But probably he has brought others, as well, perhaps hundreds, routinely, to similar straits, and plights. I am not special. I have now learned that. He may not remember me. Am I not only another meaningless "collar slut," as I have been informed? But, yes, it is true. I am that, only that. Why should I be remembered?

Is the expression 'collar slut' not informative? I think so. Well does it tell me what I am, and what I am for.

How different are the men of this world from my former male acquaintances, co-workers, and such! I suppose there must be true men on Earth, many perhaps. But where were they? Why did I never meet them? I suppose the answers to such questions are obvious. On Earth the acculturation is arranged to humble, cripple, reduce, subdue, and diminish manhood. Manhood is to be repudiated and overcome, as it constitutes an impediment to the success of militant pathologies. Why should a man be ashamed of his feelings, and desires, and why should a woman be ashamed of her feelings and desires? Did it truly take ten thousand generations to discover that nature was a mistake? Is it not surprising to be taught the subversion of one's nature, to be ashamed of, deny, and fight manhood, or womanhood? What is so attractive about a crippled lion, or a poisoned rose?

The men of Gor are, in many ways, much like those of Earth, for they are clearly of the same species, if not variety. Statistically, they may be larger, stronger, quicker, more supple, more intelligent, and such, this having to do, I suppose, with those brought to this world, but there are many men of Earth, I am sure, as large, as strong, as quick, as supple, as intelligent as those of Gor. The great difference then, I think, lies in other matters, presumably cultural. Gorean civilization is not at war with nature, but allied with her. The Gorean male tends to be confident, imaginative, self-reliant, ambitious, aggressive, possessive, and dominating. No one tells him it is wrong to be himself. On Gor, for example, as opposed to the social technologies of Earth, no point is served by blurring, identifying, diminishing, or repudiating sexualities. Culture does not prescribe, in the interests of unusual minorities, alienated from their own bodies, the falsification of nature.

The room is large. Straw is strewn about. Several stairs lead up to a barred door. There are rings, iron rings, set here and there in the wall. Some of us are fastened to them.

I am stripped. So, too, are the others. Why should animals be given clothing?

The chains are heavy. They would hold men. Lighter chains are quite sufficient for such as we.

I have been branded. It is a lovely mark. It is in me, high on my left thigh, below the hip. There will be no mistaking me on this world. I have been clearly marked. No, there will be no mistaking me on this world, or perhaps on any other.

They will soon serve the gruel.

I am hungry.

I have long known myself a woman who longed to submit, to belong, to be owned, to be mastered, to serve, to strive to please, to be subject to discipline. I have long known myself a natural, and rightful, slave.

Is this so terrible?

Is it wrong to be oneself?

Perhaps, perhaps not.

I do not claim to speak for others. Why then should they speak for me?

I have never wanted to relate to a man to whom I am an equal. Or more, what woman would? How pathetic that would be, how one would despise such a man, such a betrayer of his nature, or one lacking the nature of man, but rather to one who is incomparably superior to myself, naturally powerful, commanding, and virile, one who would see me as I am, and do with me as he wished, one to whom I could be only a slave.

But I never, on Earth, expected to meet such a man, a man strong enough to see me for what I was, and do with me what he should. Once I did not know such men could exist. Here, fearfully, I have found men who will take such as I in hand, and brand, collar, and train us as thoroughly and thoughtlessly as any other animal, which we are. I now kneel before such men and know myself a slave, and fittingly and rightfully so. They give me no choice. I want none. They bring me to my true self. I am fulfilled.

Why then do they so despise me, I in their collar, so weak and helpless?

Can I help it, if I am not one of their glorious free women?

Am I so different from them, I wonder? Or beneath those robes is another slave hidden?

I was sold last night.

I suppose many women, at least on my former world, do not understand that they can be sold. That is interesting, considering the fact that we have been sold, bartered, and exchanged for millennia, and doubtless for millennia before the records of such transactions were scratched on bark, or incised into tablets of moist clay. Is it so unusual to be exchanged for barley, or cattle, or sheep, or pigs, or bars of iron, or a jingling handful of metal disks? Have not women served often enough as loot, to be allotted amongst victors, to be auctioned in foreign capitals? In kingdoms have not princesses been bartered for land, for alliances and power? Have not the daughters of the rich often served as seals upon bargains? And have we ourselves not unoften sought to sell ourselves, for our own gain? Have we not sought avidly for the golden bed, and the highest bidder?

It is one thing, of course, to sell ourselves as goods for our own profit, while denying this, and quite another to find ourselves explicitly recognized as goods, undeniably so, openly and objectively so, and being sold for the profit of another.

It is a strange feeling, at first, to realize that one has been sold, that one now belongs to another, as much as a pig or shoe.

I am told, however, that one grows used to such things. Would it not be a rare girl who has been sold but once? One is then concerned less with the fact that one is sold, for one knows one is a slave, than the quality of the market, the category in which one is sold, say, a pot girl or a pleasure slave, the price one may bring, particularly in comparison with that of others, and, of course, the nature of the buyer, say, a private individual, for which one hopes, or a farm, a business, a municipality, or such. Sometimes one is bought to be kept, sometimes to be resold. A girl cheaply purchased in one market may be sold in another for a handsome profit. Markets are apparently scouted and information conveyed and exchanged. I am told the great merchant houses have sources of information which might be the envy of warring Ubars.

I sold for forty-eight copper tarsks. I gather that this is not a great deal of money but I also know that some sold for less, although many sold for more. I am not familiar with what forty-eight copper tarsks might buy, other than it might buy one such as I. The face value of a coin is meaningless. The coin is worth only what it will buy. This is obvious, but many on my former world, oddly enough, seem unaware of this. They demand a hundred coins and think themselves ten times advanced for they formerly had but ten, and refuse to notice that their hundred today buys only what five bought once.

I remember little about my sale, until near the last, the straw, the block, the torches to the left and right, the darkness in the house, the sense of faces and bodies, the calls of the auctioneer, the occasional responses from the house, the touches of the whip, helping me, guiding me, turning me, lifting my chin, and such. I was too frightened, too tense, I fear, to smile, to display myself well. But he did not whip me. How understanding he was, how kind! Then he grasped me by the hair, and held my head back. I did not understand. Then he touched me! It was quick, and smooth, and then firm, implacable! The coils of the whip! I was helpless! I cried out, and twisted about, held, unable to escape. I fought the touch, the feeling, but it owned me! I squirmed, and sobbed, and begged. My body was wild, and spasmodic. He must desist, but he did not! I could not control myself. I heard laughter. Then he released me, a thousand times more naked than I had been before, a revealed slave! I went to my knees in the sawdust, and wept, and, bent over, my body shaking, covered my face with my hands.

How shamed I was. I heard laughter.

How faraway then was the store, the men I had known!

I was ordered away from the block, and was carried down the stairs, for my legs would not support me.

I had been sold.

I have wondered, sometime, if the glorious free women of these men, so arrogant and remote, so lofty and proud, so secure, so serene, so abundantly and beautifully robed and veiled, so regal, so majestic, so concealed from head to toe, if stripped and sold, if so caressed, would not also have cried out, squirmed, and leapt as obediently, as helplessly, as revealingly, as spasmodically, as I? How we are nothing in a rag before them! But are they, when all is said and done, any different? Might we not all be slaves?

Gorean men are patient.

I hear the gate at the head of the stairs being undone. Soon the gruel will be in the troughs, or, for those chained at the sides, to the heavy rings, in the bowls.

We are not permitted, as yet, to use our hands.

Chapter Six

There are a thousand roads.

Why does one take one road, and not another? Sometimes curiosity, sometimes adventure, sometimes because it is a new road, on no familiar map. And yet, truly, one does not know, really, where even the most familiar and prosaic road may lead. Are there not a hundred roads leading to Ar, at the end of which Ar is not found? In the distance there is the stirring of fog, into which the road leads. Do not all roads lead into the fog? When the wind rises and the fog dissipates, one is not unoften surprised at the country within which one finds oneself.

My purse was heavy enough, early, at any rate. Why did its weight not content me?

The venture had been productive. Each capsule had been filled. Why did I not book passage for Daphne, where the spring rendezvous was to take place? The gray sky ship does not linger long, even in that remote place. Whence came the craftsmen, I wondered, who might have fashioned such a ship. It was said there were islands in the night, even beyond the moons.

I thought of another world, wondering why fools would hasten its ruin, scorning and defiling it, contaminating its soil and darkening its skies, polluting its seas and poisoning its air, felling its forests and gouging its surface. Do they hate it so? If not, why do they neglect and injure it? Have they another world at hand, a secret one, better and more convenient? Would they not insult and despoil it, as well? What is so terrible about trees and grass, white clouds and blue skies? Perhaps they do not care for such things. Perhaps they want a world such as they have made theirs, one crowded and smoky, odorous, and filthy. Perhaps they desire such a world, and deserve it.

It is good to be again on Gor.

The sky ships pay well.

Too, we are often given our pick of the stock.

It is not unusual for a fellow to reserve to himself a particular item, usually on a temporary basis, usually one he may have found arrogant or annoying, that he may have the pleasure of introducing her to the collar. A few days later, she, now well apprised of her bondage, may be led, back-braceleted, hooded, and leashed, sobbing, begging to be kept, to the market. I was thinking of reserving to myself, temporarily, one who had been meticulously, expensively, overbearingly, and pretentiously dressed, as is sometimes the case with slave stock, who had presented herself as aloof, superior, haughty, and frigid, but I did not do so. They are quick enough, at one's feet, incidentally, to beg a strip of cloth, a rag. I was actually puzzled about her, for when I had initially noticed her she had been quite different, modestly and tastefully garbed, given the season, in a simple sweater, blouse, and skirt, diffident and needful, muchly aware of her sex and perhaps slightly fearing it, aware of how she might appear to men, as a woman suitable to be appropriated, exquisitely female, clearly waiting and ready. Our eyes had met, and it had not been difficult to see her, standing there, startled and apprehensive, as the slave she was, though not yet in the encircling band, locked on her throat. I had half expected her to kneel, and bow her head.

She was not strikingly, even startlingly, beautiful, like many of the women we bring to Gor, but there was something, at least to me, arresting about her. Certainly my colleagues had agreed. She was, in her way, an excellent choice for a Gorean block.

I recalled her.

She was the sort of woman whom it is difficult to think of, save as barefoot, in a slave tunic.

Clearly, some women belong in such, a particularly revealing tunic, which makes it clear to the occupant and the observer, casual or otherwise, precisely what she is, and only is.

I wanted to get her out of my mind.

Why then did I occasionally visit the capsule chamber, and

regard her, in her capsule, naked and sedated, the identificatory steel anklet, inscribed with its legend, locked on her left ankle? It is commonly removed before they are revived. Two hoses enter the capsule, one at the head, one at the feet, the first to supply oxygen, the second to withdraw carbon dioxide.

I often, to my annoyance, thought of her. I tried to dismiss her from my mind, but it was not easy to do.

Surely she was not that beautiful.

Or was she?

I remembered her.

Why her?

There are so many, and one puts the lash to them, as needed. It would be the same with her, if she dared to be displeasing. She had doubtless felt it in her training. Thereafter they are muchly concerned to please.

Paga was of little assistance, or the belled sluts of the taverns. The turning wheels and the cards, the dice tumbling on the felt, were of little assistance, save in lightening my purse.

I did attend her sale. She did not do well on the block, as a whole. It was clearly her first sale. She was, however, obviously eager to please the auctioneer. I suppose that is understandable. He, after all, held the whip. On the other hand, I had gathered, from the reports of instructors and guards, as I had expected, that she was a woman who understood that she was a woman, and accordingly, in the order of nature, wished to defer to men, and be pleasing to them. These inclinations are obvious consequences of the nature of the hereditary coils. Despite the distortions, the curbs, and obstacles, of a pathological acculturation, stunting minds and shortening lives, nature, embedded in each cell in the human body, persists. Nature, like a living plant, may be crippled, stunted, denied, poisoned, and, if necessary, uprooted and destroyed, but it returns again, patient, latent, ready, alive, in each new child, in each new seed.

The most interesting aspect of her sale occurred late in the sale, when the auctioneer chose to display her slave reflexes.

As I had anticipated, they proved excellent.

How startled and distressed she was!

How foolish, did she still think herself free?

It was interesting to consider what might be her nature later, once her slave fires had been ignited.

I could conceive of her crawling on her belly to a master, tears in her eyes, begging to be touched.

It is pleasant to own such a woman.

What man does not want one?

I wondered if she would be domestically suitable, say, could she sew, or cook, such things. Some attention to such things is commonly involved in their training. To be sure, the principal object of a slave's training is to teach her to give inordinate sexual pleasure to a master.

It is primarily what she is for.

I did not wonder about her heat. She would be a hot slave. Periodically, recurrently, helplessly, she would find herself in desperate sexual need. She would soften and oil at a casual glance. Her need would run down her thighs. She would proffer a master a juicy pudding, bubbling and delicious. She would be a pleasant confection, a delightful candy, a moaning, gasping tasta squirming on its stick.

And I wondered, again, if she could sew, or cook, such things.

If her efforts were unsatisfactory in such ways, or others, her grooming, her posture and grace, the care of a domicile, her shopping, or such, one might reduce, or deny her, the touch of the master, of which touch, at that time, she would be in desperate need.

The slave must learn, of course, to please the master, unquestioningly, and instantaneously, in all ways.

His satisfaction is paramount, not hers.

Still, a hot slave is a precious possession. It is one of the great pleasures of the mastery to play with his toy, to patiently lick, kiss, and caress his property, it perhaps helplessly bound or chained, to turn it into a writhing, pleading, sobbing, subdued, owned, gasping, bucking, lovely, helpless, ecstatic beast.

She went for forty-eight copper tarsks, which was about what I thought she would bring, something in the nature of a half tarsk, of silver.

Some weeks before, as I had been given to understand, the forces of Cos, Tyros, and their allies, and hirelings, most in mercenary bands, had withdrawn from Ar. The accounts of this were various. It was claimed by some that the work of the occupying forces was done, that Ar had been taught her lesson, her walls razed and her coffers looted, that she was now impoverished, docile, and subdued, and was no longer a threat to the civilized cities. Accordingly, the occupying forces had executed an orderly withdrawal, one supposedly scheduled for months aforehand. Others claimed that the troops of Cos and Tyros, and the others, had marched from the city, over streets carpeted with blossoms, amidst shouts of joy and flung garlands, the tribute of a grateful populace, freed from the gross despotisms and tyrannies of the past. And some said that like a storm at sea, one without warning, the red waves of revolt had surged into the streets, pouring forth from hovels and sewers, from taverns and stables, from cellars and insulae, that thousands of citizens, many armed only with clubs and stones, had rushed forth, intent upon the blood of invaders and traitors. Marlenus, Ubar of Ubars, it was said, had returned to Ar.

In any event, several of the coastal cities and towns, and, in particular, Brundisium, were now filled with what might, I suppose, be accounted refugees. It was claimed by some that the retreat from Ar had been a rout, precipitous and disorderly, and, in some cases, even disciplined troops had cast aside their shields and fled for their lives. Were it not for the ruination of her walls, thousands might have been unable to escape the city, to the open fields beyond. Countless dead would have been heaped at the gates. As it was, men of Ar tried to prevent the remnants of the occupying forces fleeing and hundreds of sympathizers and collaborators from leaving the city. Bands of mercenaries not quartered outside the city often had to fight their way to the countryside. Even in the open fields they were pursued and hunted, sometimes from the sky by tarnsmen of Ar, no longer enrolled in the sorry task of protecting uniformed looters and policing a sullen, resentful citizenry with which they shared a Home Stone. For pasangs about the city the fields were littered with feasting for scavenging jards. Within the city long proscription lists were posted, and traitors and traitresses were hunted down, house to house. Hundreds of impaling spears were adorned with writhing victims. Few free traitresses, or traitresses who long remained free, escaped the city. The common price for their license to accompany armed, fleeing men, unwilling to accept the burden of conducting free women, was their stripping and the collar. Many were currently being offered in the markets of Brundisium and other coastal cities. Some of those vended in the recent sale I had attended were former high women of Ar, now naked properties worth only what men were willing to pay for them. Many of the refugees still flooding into Brundisium were ragged, exhausted, and half-starved. Some had sold even their swords. Others had formed larger or smaller outlaw bands and prowled the roads, producing a realm of peril and anarchy for a hundred pasangs about. Passage to Tyros or Cos was costly, and many of Brundisium's newcomers were destitute. Some, armed with clubs, hunted urts by the wharves. Two men had been killed for stealing a fish. It was said, too, that various towns and cities, even villages, in the island ubarates themselves were not enthusiastic about the turn of events, that they were less than willing to welcome the return of defeated, penurious veterans. Could honor be retained in the face of defeat, even rout? If the stories were true, of triumph, and such, where was their wealth, their spoils? Surely, for whatever reason, or reasons, justified or unjustified, an inhospitable reception not unoften awaited them. Some, even regulars managing to return to the islands, found themselves isolated and despised, denied work and a post. "Where is your shield," they might be asked, "where is your sword?" In Brundisium, on the other hand, a busy port, with access to the northern and southern coastal trade, and an access to the major island ubarates westward, Cos and Tyros, there was considerable prosperity, for the coin that leaves one purse will soon find a home in another.

But beyond the influx of refugees, more streaming in each day, the crowding, the begging, the closing of hiring tables, the raiding of garbage troughs, the sleeping in cold, damp, dangerous streets, the discordant accounts of doings to the south and east, the racing about of rumors, it was clear that something different and unusual was occurring in Brundisium, something apart from refugees, apart from remote dislocations, apart from proscriptions and impaling spears, apart from tumult and flight, apart from red grass and bloodied stones, apart from hazard and vengeance, apart from political rearrangements, apart from exchanges of power wherein, as it is said, the "streets run with blood."

This had to do with those spoken of as the Pani.

There must be two or three hundred of them in Brundisium, and perhaps many more in the north, in their unusual garb, with their dark, keen eyes, their black hair drawn back and knotted behind their head, men lithe and graceful, like panthers, taciturn, not mingling, avoiding the taverns, equipped with their unfamiliar weaponry.

It was not clear from whence these strange warriors, and their cohorts and partisans, were derived. Some, from the eyes, said they were Tuchuks, but others who had had the fortune, or misfortune, of encountering Tuchuks, as some looted, ransomed merchants, survivors of raided caravans, and such, denied this. Surely none wore the colorful, ritual, exploit scarring of the Tuchuks. Some said they came from the World's End, but, as is known, the world ends at the farther islands, and beyond them is nothing. It was alleged they came from the Plains of Turia, far south of Bazi and Schendi, or from the Barrens to the east, but, if such things are so, why was there no heralding of their approach, no records of their passage?

In any event many are in Brundisium.

They speak a comprehensible dialect of Gorean, one with which I am not familiar. They work largely through agents. They have gold, apparently much gold. Some serious project is afoot. Their agents are hiring ships, and recruiting men, many ships, many men. Some ships, with crews, and complements of armed men, have already left port, bound north. They are laying in extensive supplies. Guarded compounds near the wharves are stacked with boxes, barrels, bales, clay vessels, like blunt-bottomed amphorae, tied together by the handles, bulging sacks, and weighty crates. It is as though some great voyage was contemplated, but the ships are small coasters, many of which one might not even risk to Temos or Jad, and they seem to move north. What might be in the northern forests, or Torvaldsland, to warrant this mighty movement of men and supplies? Do they think to found a city at the mouth of some far river, say, the Laurius or the remote Alexandra? Such locations would seem remote and inauspicious. Too, interestingly, many of the supplies seem to be war supplies, and naval stores. Why would one require naval stores to found a city, or even a village? Other goods, one supposes, would suggest trading, or the raid. There are bundles of silk, coils of wire, brass lamps, jars of ointment and salve, flat boxes of cosmetics; and poles on which are strung shackles and slave chain. Do they truly think there is that much slave fruit in the north? And, besides, they are already buying slaves. They are buying them from the shelves, from the wharf cages, the dock markets, and the house markets. Agents of Pani, for example, had purchased several of the girls in the recent sale I had witnessed, including the one whom I had found of some negligible interest, whom I had originally seen in a large emporium on another world. She would not remember me, though it was I who brought her to the collar and whip, where she, and such as she, belong. Some were even purchased at the gates, off their rope coffles, as bandits, or refugees, had brought them in. It was not fully clear why these purchases, or so many of them, had been made. If they were to be resold there seemed little point in taking them north. Better markets were elsewhere. Perhaps they were for gifts or trade goods. But to whom, and where? Certainly a lovely female makes a splendid gift, and, in many situations, can be bartered to one's advantage. But who is, say, to buy them in the north, and so many? To be sure, many men were taking ship north, and they might be intended for them, if not for outright purchasing, for brothels, slave houses, or taverns. Men will want their slaves. Many of the purchased slaves were being held in the vicinity of the docks, in holding areas, the basements of warehouses, and such. In some places, through the high, narrow, barred windows in the walls, through which light may filter, they would hear the calls of longshoremen, their loading chants, the rumble of wheels on the planks, the creak of timbers, the stirring of slack canvas on a round ship, the water washing against the pilings.

I am familiar with such places as I have brought slaves to them. How they moan and cry out, and sob, when herded down the stairs to the straw, and rings! It is not pleasant to be confined in such a place, for they are often dark, cold, and damp, the straw soiled, the chains heavy. It was to such a place that a particular slave might have been brought.

I did not know.

How pleased they are then to be brought into the light, and the keeping of masters!

As I have mentioned, the agents of the Pani were recruiting. One might have supposed then, under the current circumstances in Brundisium, with the business to the southeast, the accompanying influx of refugees, and such, that the misery in Brundisium, the crowding and hunger, would have been muchly relieved, as men were taken into fee, but, unfortunately, that was only partly the case. For better or for worse, the agents of the Pani had not set up hiring tables, but conducted matters discreetly, if not secretly. They made inquiries, as they could, and seemed to scout men. They frequented the taverns and the lower dock areas, and would approach a prospect, two or three at a time, often in the darkness. Sometimes swords crossed. They seemed most interested in men who had retained their weaponry, and their pride. On the other hand, honor, the allegiance to a Home Stone, the promise of loyalty, and such, did not seem a requirement for the service contemplated. Some prospects they bought from prison for gold, some waiting execution. They seemed particularly interested in strong, agile, savage, dangerous men. I had the impression they were intent to fee men who could handle blades well and ask few questions with respect to their unsheathing. It was my impression that in some respects they were very little particular in their choices. They were not reluctant, it seems, to recruit vagabonds, likely bandits, rogue mercenaries, cutthroats, boasters, liars, gamblers, and thieves. Such men could be kept in line, I was sure, only by paga, gold, the promise of women, and an uncompromised discipline as swift and merciless as the strike of an ost. Accordingly, many who were approached, even when starving, refused to be wooed even by the golden staters of Brundisium when it became clear to them the likely nature of many of their companions. One does not wish to have a foe at one's back or side. Others declined service when their would-be recruiters refused to reveal to them the length and nature of the service intended, and even its location. Indeed, I think that many, perhaps most, of the recruiters did not know the answers to such questions themselves. It was known that the first leg of their journey would take them north, somewhere north. What might occur there, or thereafter, was unclear. More frighteningly, at least to many, was the level of weapon skills which were being sought. Many potential recruits were put to the test of arms, pitted against one another, only the winner to be accepted. Some men killed more than one man to win their place.

"The cards have been unkind to you," said a voice.

"That is not unusual, of late," I said.

"More paga?" she asked.

"He has had enough," said the voice.

"Where are you from?" I asked.

"Asperiche," she said.

"How came you here?" I asked.

"I was taken in my village," she said, "by raiding corsairs from Port Kar, and later sold south."

"How much did you bring?" I asked.

"Two silver tarsks," she said.

"Here?" I asked.

"Yes, Master," she said.

"When?" I asked.

"The last passage hand," she said.

"Summon the proprietor's man, and a whip," I said.

"Master?" she asked.

"In the current market you would bring no more than thirty-five, copper," I said.

Trembling, she knelt, tears in her eyes. "Forgive me, Master," she said.

I motioned her away, impatiently, clumsily.

"Thank you, Master," she said, and leapt up and fled, with a flash of bells, from the small, round table, at which I sat, cross-legged.

"Are you weak?" asked the voice. "Why did you not have her lashed?"

"Do you think I am weak?" I asked.

He regarded me, for a moment. "No," he said.

"I am unarmed," I said.

"But weapons are checked at the door," he said.

"They are entitled to their vanity," I said.

I looked after her. The bells were on her left ankle. They were all she wore, other than her collar. It was not a high tavern.

"How did you know she was lying?" he asked.

"The market, the season," I said.

"It seems you are an excellent judge of such things," he said.

"Of such things?" I asked.

"The likely price of collar-meat," he said.

"I am of the Merchants," I said.

"The Slavers," he said.

I shrugged.

"The Slavers," he said.

"Very well, the Slavers," I said. We regard ourselves as a subcaste of the Merchants. Do we not acquire, and buy, and sell? What difference is there, other than the nature of the goods handled?

"Slavers," said he, "are cunning, and skilled with weapons."

"Much like the scarlet caste," I said.

"Or the black caste," he said.

"I am not an assassin," I said. I wondered if he were.

"Slavers must plan, and raid, and seize," he said. "Often they must fight their way into a house, or pleasure garden, and fight their way free."

"I have met men on the bridges," I said. To be sure, there seemed little danger on the ships, the sky ships, save at departure and arrival, leaving or re-entering the atmosphere. There seemed little danger, too, on the slave world. They did not, it seemed, protect their women. Perhaps they did not realize their value.

"You have had too much to drink," he said.

"You followed me from the gambling house," I said.

"You lost heavily," he said. "Perhaps tonight you will feed from the garbage troughs."

"Perhaps," I said. "Who are you?"

"One who places a golden stater on a table," he said.

I looked at the small, round, golden disk. The staters of Brundisium are prized on the Streets of Coins in a hundred cities. They constitute one of Ar's most coveted coinages.

"I am not an assassin," I said.

"I, and others," he said, "are seeking blades, armsmen."

"For the strange men," I said.

"The Pani," he said, "yes."

"Such," I said, "or most, seem themselves warriors."

"Additional men, many, are sought," he said.

"There are many in Brundisium," I said.

"Not all will do," he said.

I looked at the coin lying on the table. It was interesting how such small, inert objects could move men, and ships, cavalries, and armies.

"Some men have never seen such a coin," I said.

"Laborers, common laborers, peasants, verr tenders," he said. "And this golden friend is not without his fellows," he said.

"What must I do?" I asked.

"Ships move north," he said.

"Each day?" I asked.

"One every two or three days," he said, "sometimes two or more together."

"For what purpose, to what end?" I asked.

"In time," said he, "all will become clear."

"I would have it clear now," I said.

"The pay is good," he said, touching the stater lightly, at the edge, as though he might move it toward me.

"Berths are won by the sword, I understand," I said.

"Sometimes," he said.

"And if berths were limited?" I asked.

"Then, surely," he said.

"I am cognizant of the fellows you seek," I said.

"Men such as you," he said.

"I have no wish to feel a knife in my back," I said.

"Such an assailant," he said, "would be dealt with summarily, and unpleasantly."

"That would do me little good," I said.

"Discipline is rigorous," he said.

"Among such men it must be," I said.

"Surely," said he.

"Men such as I?" I asked.

"I fear so," he said.

It was now too late to make the rendezvous to the west, on

Daphne, even were a vessel to leave this night, even had I the wherewithal to book passage. For some reason I had lingered too long in Brundisium. Why was that? But, too, I had voyaged on the sky ships, and more than once. I did not know if I would choose to so voyage again. I would leave it, like much else, to the future. There are many roads. I had taken such service for the pay, but, too, for the difference, the danger, the adventure. Too, for the pleasure of knotting cords on the wrists and ankles of slave fruit, on luscious, bipedalian, barbarian cattle.

But now I was again on Gor, and now, at least for the time, was content. There are many roads.

And surely there were enough Earth women here, if one's tastes ran in such directions.

I thought of Earth stock, now familiar in Gorean markets.

How exciting, and beautiful, so often, was such stock! To be sure, we, and others, were selective, very selective.

Doubtless that made a difference, a great difference.

How little the men of Earth valued it. Why did they not better protect it? It can be worth a man's life to try to take a free woman from a Gorean city, even a slave. We strive to protect our free women, and even our properties, our verr, our kaiila, our slaves. Did the men of Earth not prize their females? Did they not realize how attractive, how exciting, how valuable, how wonderful, how desirable, they were? Was that so hard to see?

Then I thought of true free women, our own women.

How different were the women of Earth from them, those of Earth lacking Home Stones, with their brazenly unveiled features, their openly displayed ankles, the pleading silk of their secret lingerie, so fit for slaves. They were not Gorean free women. They belonged on the block, being bidden for. I could not understand why the men of their world did not see this, why they did not realize how valuable their females were, and what might be done with them. Certainly it was clear enough to us. Could they not see what they were, what they needed, what they wanted? Did they not understand them? Why did they deny them the ownership and domination without which they could not be fulfilled, without which they could not be women? Why did they not kneel them, and inform them that they were women, and now, owned, would be treated as such? Did they think they were not women, that they were something else, neuters, sexless creatures, or such, inert cultural contrivances? Did they not realize what it might be, to have one at their feet, collared, owned, trained to their tastes, hoping to be found pleasing?

It is very pleasant.

It is also pleasant, of course, to take a Gorean free woman and teach her the collar, and kindle her slave fires, until she crawls to you, begging, indistinguishable from a barbarian, and then like them, forever then a slave.

They are all women.

There is no real difference.

They are all women.

The golden stater was thrust toward me.

I thrust it back.

"No?" he asked.

"No," I said.

He replaced the coin in his wallet.

"It is men such as you," he said, "which we want, and will have."

"I think not," I said.

"Do you know who I am?" he asked.

"No," I said.

"Tyrtaios," he said.

"I do not know the name," I said.

"Let it be known that you have refused Tyrtaios," he said.

"Why?" I asked.

"It may explain much later," he said.

"And serve as a lesson to others?" I asked.

"Perhaps," he said.

"Weapons are at the door," I said. "Do you wish to meet outside?"

"I wish you well," he said, and, rising, turned about, and left. I saw two others rise, as well, and follow him through the portal.

A proprietor's man approached, and lingered by the table, looking toward the portal through which the three men had exited. He did not look at me. He said, softly, "Beware."

"Paga," I said.

"I will send a girl," he said.

"Master," she said, a moment later, kneeling. It was the same woman, she from Asperiche.

"Knees," I said.

She widened them, reddening.

Did she not know how to kneel before a man?

"Paga," I said.

"Yes, Master," she said, rose, and, with an angry jangle of bells, withdrew.

She seemed to me insufficiently deferential.

She had lied before, and I had not had her lashed.

Did she still think she was a free woman? Had she not yet learned she was a slave?

Lying is permitted to the free woman, not the slave.

I supposed she was the sort of slave who would misinterpret a forbearance as weakness, the sort of slave who would abuse a lenience.

That is unwise on their part, for it is easy enough to remind them of their bondage, fiercely, and with unmistakable clarity.

I thought of another woman, one first seen in a large emporium, on the world Earth. I recalled that she, in the warehouse on Earth, had looked well at my feet, stripped, on her back, as I had turned her, looking up at me, bound hand and foot, clearly ready for processing.

I trusted she would not be so foolish.

If she were, the whip would quickly instruct her in deportment.

Yet vanity in a woman is charming, even endearing. Let them lie about their sales price, the wealth and position of their master, the loftiness of their former station, and such.

But it is quite another thing to be in the least bit displeasing.

It is interesting to see how carefully some, at first, will tread a line, flirting with a master's patience, practicing a deference akin to insolence, and then to note their dismay when they discover that the line has been moved by the master in such a way that they find themselves clearly on its wrong side, the whip side. Informed that their games are done, they then strive to be wholly pleasing, as the slave they now know themselves to be.

It is so much easier for all concerned then.

Perhaps they merely wished to be taught their collar.

If so, their wish is granted.

The slave is not a free woman. She is a property, a belonging, an animal one owns. One expects total pleasingness from her, deference, and subservience, instant and unquestioning obedience, and, at a word or the snapping of fingers, the provision of ecstatic gratification.

"Fellow," I called to the proprietor's man.

He came to the table. He seemed uneasy. One notes such things. At his belt hung the coin sack.

"Who is Tyrtaios?" I asked.

"I have heard the name," he said. "Beware."

"I have refused him," I said.

"That has been gathered," he said.

"Do you let your girls touch coins?" I asked.

"No," he said. He rustled the coin sack at his belt.

I looked beyond the fellow, to the back of the room, on the left, several yards away, where the slave from Asperiche was waiting, to dip the goblet in the vat. The proprietor, a coarse, swollen fellow in a soiled apron, was himself tending the vat. It was a low tavern. The coin box, with its slot, and lock, was behind him.

"Do you think I have had too much to drink?" I asked the proprietor's man.

"Perhaps," he said.

"I have the ostrakon here," I said, "with its number. Bring me my weapons."

"I fear they are missing," he said, not looking at me.

"Why is that?" I asked.

"Forgive us, Master," he said. "We wish to live."

"There is a back exit from the tavern," I said.

"I fear it is watched," he said.

The slave had now dipped the goblet in the vat, and had turned about.

"I see," I said.

"It is your service they want," he said, "not your life."

I supposed that was true. A crossbow bolt loosed in the darkness would handle such a matter, conveniently, before a shadow could be noted, a blade drawn.

"What lies in the north?" I asked.

"I do not know," he said.

"Remain at hand," I said.

"Master," said the girl, kneeling.

Under my scrutiny, she widened her knees. She placed the goblet on the low table, behind which I sat, cross-legged.

"You seem displeased to be in a collar," I said.

"I am in a collar," she said. "What more is there to say?"

"Perhaps you have not yet learned it," I said.

She was silent.

"Perhaps you do not yet realize you belong in one," I said.

"May I withdraw?" she asked.

"Position," I said.

She went to position, kneeling back on her heels, her back straight, her belly in, her shoulders back, her head up, the palms of her hands down on her thighs. One does not break "position" without permission.

I reached into my wallet. There was little left. I removed a Brundisium tarsk-bit, which is a large coin, the size perhaps intended to compensate for the slightness of its value.

"Open your mouth," I said.

"I am not permitted to touch money," she said.

I placed the coin in her mouth. "Do not drop it," I said. The coin was far too large to swallow, and, held in her mouth, she could not speak. She was effectively, and embarrassingly, silenced.

She cast a wild, piteous glance at the proprietor's man.

"I think," I said, "it is true, that I have had too much to drink." I then dashed the contents of the goblet on the startled, recoiling slave. She shook her head, and, blinking and twisting, tried to free herself of the paga. It was in her hair, and had drenched her face, and upper body. It ran down her body to her belly and thighs. She stank then of the drink. She shivered. I looked to the proprietor's man. "She has been found displeasing," I said.

"She will be lashed," he said.

"Later," I said.

"Master?" he said.

I removed my cloak. "You will put this on," I said, "and draw the hood, and precede me through the door."

"Certainly not," he said.

"I thought you wished to live," I said.

He donned the cloak, and drew the hood about his features.

"What is going on?" asked the proprietor, come from the vat.

"Do not interfere," I said. Men about regarded us. Some rose up, but none approached.

"Now," I said to the proprietor's man. "You will exit the tavern, and walk to the left, toward the wharves."

He bent down, and, drawing the hood and cloak more closely about him, exited the tavern.

I would let him precede me by a few yards. He left the tavern, and I remained behind for a bit, back, within the threshold. Then I, too, exited. As I had expected, very shortly, figures emerged from the shadows, two, though I had expected three, following the proprietor's man, which two figures I followed. The lights of the tavern were soon behind us, and the wharf streets, in this section of the city, are narrow, crooked, and dark. Normally men carry their own light in such streets, or have it carried for them, often with guards or retainers in attendance.

As I had expected the two figures soon rushed forward and seized the proprietor's man. I heard scuffling, and heavy blows, presumably of clubs. Intent on their work, presumably to beat their victim senseless and convey him, bound, to some predesignated location, the fellows were oblivious of my approach.

It was short work.

"What did you do to them?" asked the proprietor's man.

"They will be all right," I said. "You will not lose two customers." I had not broken the neck of the first, nor the back of the second. It did seem pertinent to render them unconscious, which I did by taking each by the hair, when they were down, stunned, and yanking their heads together. Two clubs were somewhere on the pavement, but I did not know where they were.

"What are you doing?" asked the proprietor's man.

It was dark.

"Making this worth our while," I said. "You played your part very well."

"My part?" he asked.

"Of course," I said.

I pressed one of the wallets into his hands, and retained the other.

"Is there a garbage trough nearby?" I asked.

"Yes," he said, "several, the nearest down the street, toward the water."

"My cloak," I said. "It will be chilly by the water."

After a bit, we had deposited the two ruffians in a trough.

"How will this be explained?" asked the proprietor's man.

"They were set upon in the darkness, and robbed," I said.

"I do not think their principal will be pleased," said the proprietor's man.

"I suspect he will be more pleased than you realize," I said.

"You have exceeded his expectations?" asked the proprietor's man.

"I expect so," I said.

"You are then a two-stater hire?" he asked.

"I would think so," I said.

"I must return to the tavern," said the proprietor's man.

"We will go together," I said. "I trust my weapons will be available."

"Certainly," he said.

On what ship, I wondered, would I take passage? Certainly I had lingered about the docks frequently enough, in the early morning, watching, not really knowing why. Observing, waiting, for what?

I recalled her lot number had been 119, not that it mattered.

She was a slave.

Chapter Seven

I, and certain others, had been kept in that basement, or dungeon, at the foot of the stairs, with the damp, soiled straw, and the dim light, filtering in from above, in its narrow, dust-sprinkled shaft of illumination, for days. After four days I had been removed from the sirik. I could then freely move my hands and feet, and the linkage was not on my neck. How helpless we are in the sirik, and perhaps beautiful. But I was then, two days later, as some others had been, fastened to the wall. They do with us what they please. This was done by means of a collar and chain, which ran to a heavy ring, dangling from a plate, anchored in the wall. I felt even more helpless than when in the sirik, for in the sirik one may move about, with its small steps, and lift one hands to one's mouth, to feed oneself, when permitted to use one's hands. Now, with a rustle of chain, I could move no more than a two or three feet from the wall. And the collar was heavy on my neck. Doubtless the room, or dungeon, with its heavy, thick walls, was quite enough to keep us in place. Within it we were helpless enough, were we not, considering the walls, the barred gate at the top of the narrow stone stairs, our nudity, the men about, and such, but, one supposes, our chaining, of one sort or another, must have had its purpose, or purposes; perhaps it was intended to be mnemonic or advisory, or perhaps instructive, to leave us in no doubt that we were slaves, and only that, or, perhaps, it was merely because men enjoyed seeing us that way, so vulnerable and helpless in such impediments, impediments of their choice. I suppose I should have resented my nudity, and such constraints, and being exposed to frequent, open, public, appraisive scrutiny, as the men might wish, as the animals we now knew ourselves to be, and, sometimes, being forced to take food and water on all fours, from pans, not permitted to use one's hands and such, but I found it, somehow, this helplessness, this subjection to complete, uncompromised masculine domination appropriate for me, fitting, reassuring, and thrilling. Here, as I had not on Earth, I felt myself a woman, and, for the first time, radically and basically female, far beyond anything I had experienced on Earth. Here, in a way, I had learned what I was, basically, and naturally. No longer needed I pretend to be something else, some sort of imitation man, a pseudoman, or a facsimile man, or something advised to be manlike, or a creature to which sex should be unimportant or irrelevant, or a neuter of some sort, or, worse, a nothing, something meaningless, no more than a societally contrived artifact. I was now what I was, myself, and wholly so, though I was ankle-deep in straw, nude, on another world. Doubtless this had something to do not simply with my needs, and the unhappiness I had known on Earth, but, too, with the men of this world, dominant, powerful, virile men, who would see me as a woman, and slave, and treat me as such, men so natural, so astonishing and mighty, that before them I knew myself a slave, and could be but a slave.

Women came and went in this place, some introduced, some removed. Sometimes men in rich robes, muchly different from the simple tunics of the guards, came to review us. Notes were taken, and lists made. I strove, desperately, as I had in the training house, to improve my Gorean. It would be the language of my masters. I had felt the monitory switch frequently enough in the house, from my branded, collared instructresses, when I erred in grammar, or ventured a poorly chosen or inept word. Here, in the basement, or dungeon, it was much easier; here my mistakes brought only amusement, ridicule, or contempt. I bartered portions of my rations for instructions. Several times, a few of us would be aligned, and examined, our feet widely spread, our hands clasped at the back of our neck, or at the back of our head. This was done with me, twice. Sometimes a slave was taken to the side, and made use of, in the straw. Some of us spoke Gorean natively, for we were not all outworlders, cattle brought from the slave world. These often wheedled the guards for information, calling up from the bottom of the stairs, for we were not permitted on the stairs, save to be entered into the place or removed from it. We learned little, I fear. We did know we were near the water. We could hear it, outside. After a time, I could follow much of the Gorean about me. It seemed that this building, which I took to be large, judging from the size of the basement, or dungeon, was some sort of depot, from which supplies, and such, at least currently, would be taken north. So much had been gathered from chance remarks overheard. It was apparently not clear even to the guards what lay to the north. I began to dream in Gorean.

I often thought of the man whom I had first seen in the store, before whom, for the first time, I had felt myself viewed as what I had secretly taken myself to be, a slave.

I could not forget him, of all the others.

I recalled him from the warehouse, when he had turned me to my back before him. Nude, and helpless, bound, lying at his feet, I had looked up at him. I had recognized him instantly. I suspect he did not remember me. I wondered if, when he had first seen me in the store, in my skirt, blouse, and sweater, he had considered what I might have looked like, as I then was, helpless, bound, slave naked, at his feet. I had had the strangest, shocking sense, when our eyes had first met, not only that I, a suitable slave, was before a master, perhaps for the first time, but that I might be before my master. My knees had been weak, my breath had become short. I feared I might fall. I had felt the strangest inclination to kneel before him, my head lowered, in suitable submission. Then I turned about, and fled away, amongst startled shoppers, and puzzled fellow clerks. After our encounter in the warehouse, in which he failed to recognize me, or it seems so, I did not see him again until the afternoon before my sale, in the exposition cage. During my training, how often I had sneaked little glances about me, at the guards, the visitors, prospective buyers, trainers, physicians, and attendants, hoping to see him! I knew myself too poor a slave to be of interest to such a man, perhaps one of skills, position, and wealth, but, still, I hoped to see him. I was sure it was he who had brought me to the iron, and the collar. At least that much I must have pleased him!

But I did not see him again until the afternoon in the exposition cage. The cage serves an important purpose. It makes it possible for prospective buyers to inspect the merchandise before the sale, take notes, make comparisons, and such. The exposition cage is very different from the common slave cage. The common slave cage is designed for a single occupant. It is small. In it, commonly, the slave may not stand, or stretch her body to its full extent. Too, it is closely barred. The slave, for the closeness of the bars, cannot be well seen within it. The smallness of the cage makes it possible for several cages to be stored in a given area. Some are designed in such a way that they may be fastened together, even stacked. The exposition cage is quite different. It is quite large. In it a slave may stand, and move about with ease. The bars, too, are widely spaced, though not so widely spaced that a girl may slip between them, to enable customers, passers-by, and others, to enjoy a relatively unimpeded view of the goods to be offered later in the day. A girl may be called to the bars, for a closer inspection, and she must, if commanded, smile, pose, assume various positions, and such, that she may be the better assessed. A girl dares not demur. The lash is always at hand. Some of the girls try to attract the attention of various fellows, usually young, handsome fellows, or those in richer robes, with presumably heavier purses. Occasionally a fight breaks out in the cage, as one slave may have, perhaps inadvertently, obstructed a possible buyer's view of another, or have thrust another aside, to present herself in her stead, or such. The slaves are to speak little in the cage, either to one another or to the men outside the bars. We may answer questions, as to our training, our origin, our fluency in Gorean, and such things. The standard phrase we are permitted is the ritual phrase, "Buy me, Master." Each of us is marked, her lot number inscribed in grease pencil on her left breast. I was told that my number was 119. Barbarian slaves are commonly kept illiterate. There were several of us in the cage, perhaps more than was appropriate for suitable viewing, but the sale, I had gathered, was a large one, which would last several Ahn. Apparently many slaves were being purchased for transportation beyond Brundisium, by one or more mysterious buyers to whom, it seemed, price was not a matter of particular concern. Accordingly, the various houses represented in the sale were anxious to participate in so attractive a market. Many slaves, too, had been brought to Brundisium as a consequence of political events which, it seems, had taken place in the south. An unusual market situation had accordingly come about, one in which goods were relatively abundant while prices, interestingly, remained relatively stable, this apparently because of buyers rich in coin who wished to conduct their affairs with dispatch, and be on their way.

He had called me to the bars of the exposition cage.

It was he!

For a moment it was hard to breathe. I could barely move. For days, weeks, I had hoped to see him, sought to see him, and now I had been summoned to the bars! I feared I might grow weak, and fall. It was hard to breathe. It was almost like the first time I had seen him, but now I was on his world, not mine, and I, nude, a young kajira, viewed him through the bars of an exposition cage. It seemed I could not move, but then I approached the bars, not well, I feared. I wanted to throw myself to my belly, and reach through the bars, and touch him, and beg him to purchase me. Did he not know I was his slave, from the first moment I had seen him? But to my dismay I saw he did not recognize me. He did not know me! I meant nothing to him! Surely he must once have found me of interest, or I would not have been brought here, or the kef would not have been burned into my thigh, but he might have found hundreds of similar interest. What was I to him but another item in a ledger, another small, sleek beast, another piece of meat, slave meat?

I wanted to speak to him, but the words had not come.

Perhaps I should have cried out in bitterness, denounced him, and shaken the bars in helpless, futile rage, but I did not.

Was it not he who had looked upon me, and had seen fit to bring me to bondage?

Should I not have hated him for this?

Rather I wanted to kneel before him.

I wanted to be his, his belonging.

I wanted to live for him, to love him and serve him, wholly, and selflessly. But I was unworthy even to fetch his sandals in my teeth.

I do not think I even stood well before him, slender, soft, head down, submitted.

I closed my eyes, and tears pressed between the lids, and I opened my eyes, and he was gone.

He had not even remembered me.

I was to be sold. Shortly, I would belong to another.

I had fallen to my knees beside the bars, and had put my head in my hands, and wept.

The gate at the head of the stairs had been opened.

I looked up, the heavy collar on my neck. The chain, too, is heavy, dependent from its ring. I had little doubt that the collar and chain, as the others, was originally intended for men, perhaps criminals, perhaps prisoners of war, bound for the quarries or galleys. This basement, or dungeon, I supposed, had been rented, or commandeered, for female slaves, perhaps because of our numbers, unusual in this place, or season. I understood little or nothing of what was going on. We are not informed. We are kajirae. Curiosity, supposedly, is not becoming to us. Would herders inform verr or kaiila of their plans? I preferred the chains, the bracelets, and restraints of the slave house, where I had been trained. They are light, lovely, tasteful, attractive, and feminine. They, like the brand and collar, are intended to enhance our beauty, for a woman's bonds, like her garmenture, if she is permitted garmenture, are intended to set her off nicely. In them she is to be framed, presented, and displayed, excitingly and attractively, purchasable goods. I suppose it only needs be added that in them, as well, as lovely and feminine as they are, we are helpless; they confine us with perfection.

It must be early in the morning.

Three fellows were descending the stairs; one held some short lengths of cord, and some strips of dark cloth, and another several loops of rope. The last, who wore blue, carried a marking board, and pencil.

Slaves shrank away from them.

If I had not lost count, this was my eleventh day in the

basement, or dungeon. I had seen these fellows before, perhaps four or five times. They were the guards, or attendants, who brought girls down the steps, or escorted them upward, and beyond the gate.

Without a command, or the accompaniment of guards, we were not permitted on the stairs, those high, narrow, rail-less stairs, a wall at one side, at the height of which, giving access to the lower holding area, was the barred gate.

We knew the purpose of the cords, the strips of cloth, the long rope.

In the house, and here, as the girls spoke, I had heard of lovely Ko-ro-ba, busy Harfax, mighty Ar, and even vast, remote, Turia.

Why could we not be purchased for such places?

But we recognized the cords, the strips of cloth, the long rope.

"Be silent," said the fellow in blue.

We all knelt, for we were in the presence of free men.

On this world a chasm separates the slave and the free. I suspect that few on my former world could even begin to comprehend the nature of this chasm. Certainly I had not. Then I found myself a slave. The free individual is a person; the slave is not; she is an animal, and is usually marked and collared as such. As any other animal, she may be bought and sold, and dealt with as her masters might please. The free individual has caste, clan, and Home Stone. The slave has nothing, and is herself owned. The free person knows himself free, and conceives of himself as such. The slave knows herself slave, and conceives of herself as such. She exists for the master, and hopes to please him.

The men surveyed us.

We knelt in the straw, naked, waiting, viewed.

We were frightened. It would be done with us as men pleased. We were slaves.

"Recall your lot numbers," said the fellow in blue, with the marking board and pencil.

We had no names. We had not yet been named. When we were named, if we were named, they would be slave names, put on us, and taken away, at a master's pleasure. Do verr and tarsk have names?

"You will form a line, standing, facing me, head down, wrists crossed behind your back," said the fellow in blue, with the marking board, and pencil.

In the times before, the line had consisted of as few as ten girls, and as many as twenty.

"Sixty-eight," called the fellow in blue, with the marking board, and pencil.

"Master," responded a red-head.

She rose to her feet, with a rustle of chain. She was siriked. This impediment was removed, and cast to the side of the stairs.

She then crossed her wrists behind her back, took her place, and lowered her head.

She was a tall girl, perhaps five feet nine or so. Normally the line proceeds from the tallest to the shortest girl.

"Forty-one, twenty-two, one hundred and six," called the fellow in blue. "Master," said each, identifying herself.

They took their places, two being first relieved of physical constraints, one a sirik and one a wall collar.

"Eighteen," said the fellow in blue.

"No, no, no!" screamed a girl.

She leaped to her feet, darted with a scattering of straw past the fellow in blue, and, scrambling, sobbing, stumbling, falling once, leaping up again, fled toward the stairs, at the top of which, high above, was the dark, barred gate. Then she screamed with misery, several feet from the stairs, caught by the hair, and yanked back, that by the fellow who carried the loops of rope. He twisted her rudely, abruptly, about, and downward, and she was then at his feet, he crouching over her, his hand in her hair. He then straightened up, angrily, and, she crying out in pain, jerked her to her feet, and held her beside him, bent over at the waist, her head tight against his hip, her head down, facing the floor, she then in leading position. In a moment, she had been conducted to the side of the fellow in blue. Her small hands were on the wrists of the fellow who held her. She was whimpering. As she was held, she could only look down, into the straw. She held her head still, extremely still, to avoid more agony, for the guard's hand was tight in her hair.

"I am disappointed, Eighteen," said the fellow in blue.

"Forgive me, Master," she whispered.

"You moved awkwardly," he said gently, chidingly. "You were

clumsy. Indeed, you fell. Free women may move awkwardly, clumsily, stiffly, however they please, but you, you must keep in mind, are no longer a free woman. You are now kajira. Surely you know that you are to move beautifully, with loveliness and grace, and, in a situation such as this, only with permission."

"Yes, Master," she wept.

"I trust you did not injure yourself," he said.

"No, Master," she said.

"You must not do so, as you are another's property," he said. "Your master would not be pleased if you lowered your value."

"Yes, Master," she said.

I did not think she knew her master, no more than the rest of us. We did not know by whom we had been purchased, or for what reason. We had gathered we were to be shipped north, to some point on the coast.

"Release her," said the fellow in blue.

She went to her knees, her head down, to the feet of the fellow in blue.

"I was of the Merchants," she wept, "the high Merchants!"

"No longer," said the fellow in blue.

"No, Master," she said.

"You are now yourself goods," he said.

"Yes, Master," she said.

"It is fortunate that in your brief, foolish, and ill-advised flight you did not reach the stairs," he said.

"Yes, Master," she said.

"Otherwise you would have been punished."

"Yes, Master," she said. "Thank you Master. Forgive me, Master."

"Do you not think it would be appropriate to express your gratitude to he who saved you from a beating?" he asked.

"Yes, Master," she said, and crawled to the fellow who had halted her in her precipitate flight.

"Thank you, Master," she whispered, and, head down, with her soft lips and tongue, for several moments, addressed herself to his feet.

The licking and kissing of the master's feet is a familiar behavior on the part of a slave girl. It is a ritual, like kissing the whip, which is symbolic of submission. But these behaviors, or rituals, are often rich and complex. For example, we are taught the licking and kissing of a man's whip in such a way that he may be driven mad with passion. Too, of course, it has its effect on the slave, as well. The kissing of the feet is also, obviously, symbolic of submission, and is rich in significance. For example, it indicates that the slave is her owner's animal. It is often a placatory behavior. It may also express contrition, gratitude, and a slave's love. Too, it is a way in which to place oneself before the master, and plead for attention. I had sometimes begun to sense how one's needs might sometimes be much upon us. How frightening to be so at a man's mercy, to be so needful, and dependent upon him! How she hopes and begs that he may be disposed to show her a mercy and kindness. She is only a slave. I resolved that I must fight such things. But I did not want to fight them; rather I wanted to so belong to my master, to be that much his. It was my hope that he would be kind to me. This sort of behavior, the kissing and licking of feet, is sometimes commanded by the free woman, in her hatred of the slave, who thereby recalls to the slave that she is a slave, and no more than a property, a negligible chattel.

"You may now, Eighteen," said the fellow in blue, "take your place in line."

"Thank you, Master," she said, and rose, and stood in place, in line, her wrists crossed behind her back, her head down.

It is a beautiful posture, and one suitable for slaves. Too, in it, one may be conveniently coffled, and bound.

I thought that she had gotten off quite easily. To be sure, she had not managed to reach the stairs. I do not think that I, or the others, would have minded, or much minded, if she had received a lashing. Indeed, however deplorably, we might have enjoyed that. Eighteen was not popular, given her pride, her airs, her pretensions to superiority. Let her weep under the leather! Subject to the lash, we are all equal. Let her learn that! And, too, she had had a lower number than mine, and most of the rest of us, as well, and had been offered earlier in the sales, quite early, in fact. That, too, one supposes, did not endear her to us. To be sure, the best might be offered later in the marketing. And, in the house, I had gathered that the finest jewels on the "necklace" are usually distributed throughout the afternoon and evening. Supposedly this brightens and freshens the sales, whets anticipation and capitalizes on the delights of surprise, such strategies theoretically keeping the buyers alert and attentive. Why had the men not lashed her? She was quite beautiful, of course. I wondered if masters were more lenient with beautiful slaves. No, I thought, they are Gorean. Why had they not lashed her? Then I recalled she had not reached the stairs. I found myself wishing that she might have reached the stairs. I wondered if her punishment might have been measured to the number of stairs climbed. Sometimes a piquant arithmetic seems to be involved in such matters. Then I supposed not. In any event, she had not reached the stairs.

Lashings are quite unpleasant.

I had been lashed once, in my training, to inform me of the experience. I did not care to again feel the caress, however briefly, of that implement, the five-stranded Gorean slave lash, designed for the improvement of slaves without leaving a permanent marking, which might lower their value. Having felt it I feared it, and would do anything to avoid it. Yet, too, I felt an indescribable excitement and thrill, a sense of reassurance and security, and even identity, and reality, knowing myself subject to its attention, knowing it would be used upon me if I failed to be pleasing. I was thereby well reassured I was a slave.

"One Hundred and Nineteen," said the fellow in blue.

"Master!" I responded, suddenly, frightened.

How naturally that word came to me!

On my former world, in my employments, on the streets, it had never occurred to me that I would be so reduced and degraded, that I would be made a slave, this so fulfilling me. I had never expected to kneel before men, owned, and utter to them, in full significance and reality, that telling word, "Master."

But it was so on this world.

How naturally that word had come to me!

A key was thrust into the collar lock, and the bolt moved. The weight was then removed from my neck, and I was free of the wall.

I took my place in the line, head down, wrists crossed behind my back.

The girl before me had been, I had earlier gathered, of the

Merchant caste, even of the high Merchants, whatever that might be. Surely she had boasted amongst us that she was of the high Merchants. Her vaunted declaration, however, had brought her only derision and mockery from her chain sisters. "Where are your robes and veils?" she was asked. "Did I not see you well-siriked of late?" asked another. "I thought, two days ago," said another, "I saw you chained by the neck, naked, to the wall." "If she has caste," said another, "her thigh will be bare." "See her thigh!" exclaimed another. "It is marked!" said another. "Ah, my dear," said another. "Then you are only a lying slave." "Slave girls may not lie," said another. "I fear you must be punished," said another. "Please, no!" the girl had cried, but the others had then seized her, thrown her to the straw, and beaten her. Thereafter she spoke no more as though she might still be free. I had gathered that many might resent the Merchants, envying their wealth. It was said they raised nothing, and made nothing, but were brigands without lairs, bandits who looted without risk, men who drew blood with knives of gold. Membership in the Merchants, of course, might range from itinerant peddlers to the masters of great houses, dealing with a dozen cities. The Merchants regard themselves, with justification I would think, as a high caste, but few Goreans number them amongst the high castes, which, traditionally, are taken to be five in number, the Initiates, Builders, Physicians, Scribes, and Warriors. None, I suppose, would dispute with the Warriors that they are a high caste. If the Merchants are not a high caste, it is clear they are an important caste. It is said they own councils and sway law, that their gold hides and whispers behind thrones, that cities heed their words, that Ubars are often in their debt. Doubtless amongst the Merchants, as amongst other men, one will find the astute and honorable, the honest and diligent, the noble and loyal, as well as the corrupt and greedy, the cruel and callous, the venal and heartless. The girl before me might once, I supposed, if of the high Merchants, or such, as she claimed, have been wealthy. But now she was a portion, a negligible portion I would suppose, of the wealth of another. How lost she was amongst us, so isolated and alone, reduced from her former status, and despised by her sister slaves. No wonder, I thought, that she might have broken in the strain, and irrationally, so foolishly, tried to run toward the stairs. Did she expect to ascend them, and thrust her hands through the bars of the gate, and elicit pity; did she think the gate would be opened, and she would be released?

Did she not know that there was no escape for the Gorean slave girl, and that that was now what she was?

Did she think she had been branded to be freed?

She had been branded to be purchased, and put to use.

Certainly there was no escape for me. Where was there to escape to? And certainly my body, with its mark, proclaimed me a slave. And, I supposed, sooner or later, I would wear a collar.

I did not fear the collar. I knew I belonged in one.

It would be locked on me, and I could not remove it. It would publicly, and appropriately, proclaim me slave, and, most often, would identify a master, whose property I was. Sometimes, if one is given a name, the name, too, will appear on the collar. "I am so-and-so, the slave of so-and-so." "I am so-and-so, so-and-so owns me." "I am so-and-so, the property of so and-so." Sometimes the collar is quite simple, as in "I am owned by so-and-so," "I am the property of so-and-so," or merely "Return me to so-and-so," or such.

Had I a choice, I knew whose collar I would beg to wear. But I would have no choice; I was a slave.

The typical collar was practical and informative, light and comfortable, and attractive. I wondered sometimes if free women did not envy us our collars. They much enhanced the beauty of a woman, aesthetically, and, of course, in their significance. They arouse men, and have their effect on the woman, as well. Do they not inform her of what she is, and what she is for?

I knew that I was different from some, at least, of the other girls. Unlike some of them, I had known I was a slave, even on Earth. Doubtless, in time, they, too, would come to understand that they were slaves, and had always been slaves, lacking only the master and the collar. They would come home to themselves, in being owned and mastered. What hormonally normal woman does not wish to kneel before a master? Is this not clear enough from their dreams, and their feelings? Who does not wish to be a man's belonging?

Who does not wish to feel his bonds, his lips and hands on one's body, owning it, possessing it, subduing it, treating it as he wishes, so casually, so thoughtlessly, so imperiously, caressing it into submission, forcing it to yield to him the pleasures of the master, and forcing us, as well, to endure, should it please him, whether we will or no, unspeakable, spasmodic ecstasies of rapture, ecstasies which we will beg to yield, again and again, as his ravished slave?

"What was your caste?" I had been asked.

"I had no caste," I said.

"She is a barbarian, can you not tell?" had said another girl.

"Listen to her," said another. "You can tell from her speech."

"She cannot even speak the language properly," said another.

"Barbarians do not have caste," said another.

"Barbarians are stupid," said another.

"I am not stupid," I had said.

The fellow in blue continued to call lot numbers.

Seventeen girls were called forth; five had been siriked, four, including myself, had been chained at the wall. The rest, unencumbered, had been at liberty to move about the room as they wished, saving that they might not, without permission, as noted, ascend the stairs leading to the barred gate.

We stood in line, waiting, positioned as required, head down, wrists crossed behind our back.

We had seen the use of the long rope, the cords, the strips of cloth, before. We were to be taken from the holding area. The double loop of cord was put about my left wrist and jerked tight, and, a moment later, my wrists were secured in place. A bit after that a length of the long rope was knotted about my neck, and then the two fellows proceeded forward, one fastening the wrists of the girl before me together, she who had claimed to have been of the high Merchants, and the other adding her to the coffle. Shortly thereafter the fellow with the strips of cloth was behind me. "Look up," he said. I was then blindfolded. I felt a moment of panic, bound, tethered, and unable to see. How utterly helpless we are! This is done, commonly, from the rear forward. Supposedly this helps to keep the line tranquil, lessening the possibility of bolting. I remembered the unwise flight of the girl before me. I heard her whimper in terror, as she was blindfolded. We are so helpless! It is said that curiosity is not becoming to a kajira. It is not unusual to keep us in ignorance. Doubtless that helps to control us. Often we are not informed of where we are to be taken, and what is to be done with us. We are slaves. When we had been brought to this place we had been bound, coffled, and blindfolded, as well. We would not be able to recognize the inside of the building, its outside, the streets about, or such. We did know that we were in Brundisium, apparently a large city, and a port. Too, from the sounds, and the smells, it was clear that we were in the vicinity of water. Too, as noted earlier, we were familiar, at least with rumors, that we were to be taken north.

I felt a slight movement on the rope, and then felt it pull at the back of my neck, and I moved forward.

"Be careful of the stairs," said a male voice.

Chapter Eight

"May I speak?" she asked.

"Yes," I said.

She was kneeling beside me, on the boards, in a white tunic, of the wool of the bounding hurt, her wrists braceleted behind her, her leash of common brown leather looping up to my hand.

"Why are we here?" she asked.

"Are you curious?" I asked.

"Forgive me, Master," she said.

It was early morning.

The air was fresh, and keen. The wharves were crowded. Men came and went. Pennons fluttered from halyards. Large eyes were painted on each side of bows, that the ships might see their way.

One could smell fish. The early boats had come in. Grunt and parsit were strung between poles. Crabs were sold from baskets.

It was from such wharves that the small ships, mostly coasting vessels, not round ships, one every two or three days, had been plying north.

Why should I be interested in them?

Surely it was a foolishness.

I recalled her lot number had been 119, not that it mattered.

She was a slave.

Who can understand the motivations of men, of oneself?

I was angry with her, she no more than another marked collar slut. Still she had looked well at my feet in the warehouse. Were her bound curves that different from those of other helplessly trussed beauties? What had been in her eyes, as she had looked up at me? She did not even recognize me, I who had brought her to rope and iron! How uncertain she had been, how trembling and frightened, and dismayed, on the block, naked, routinely turned about, presented for the perusal of buyers. I recalled the first time I had seen her, in her quaint, concealing, barbarous garments, and how our eyes had met, and her eyes had widened, and her lips parted, and it seemed she might fall, and she was so frightened, was so much like a startled, wide-eyed, helpless tabuk doe finding herself beneath the gaze of a larl. She had turned about and fled, as though she might have escaped, if we had found her of interest. I had entered her on the list as a possible acquisition, and she was put under surveillance. Shortly thereafter she was entered on the acquisition list, and, from that point forward, though not yet marked and collared, and all unwitting of the fact, she was a Gorean slave girl.

I recalled the first time we had met.

She had seemed so startled, so frightened. In seeing me, did she somehow sense what it might be to be a slave? Had she sensed, even then, what it might be to be owned, to kneel before a man, stripped, chained, marked, and collared, his? Had she understood herself a slave, even then, suddenly, unexpectedly, perhaps for the first time, in the presence of a master?

If I could see her again, I felt I could forget her. I wanted to see her again, if only to force her from my mind, to remove her memory from my blood. Surely she was no different from thousands of others, and less than most.

Surely she was less, even, than the slut kneeling at my thigh.

If I could see her again, I was sure I could put her from me.

Perhaps I could laugh at her, spit upon her, strike her, and then contentedly dismiss her, sending her on her way, a meaningless slave, to whatever fate might await her.

She was worthless. She had not even brought a half silver tarsk off the block. Why then did I remember her?

Last night there had been a fracas in the vicinity of a local tavern. Two men, it seems, had been set upon and robbed. But such things were not uncommon in Brundisium, even in calmer times.

I had not forgotten the offer of the golden stater.

I had inquired and learned that the offer to most was in

copper tarsks, to the equivalent of a silver stater. But I had been offered a golden stater. I did not think my sword was worth that much more than that of others. In what way then might I have such value, that others might not? Too, I was curious about the ships, the smaller ships, not the round ships, which were coasting north.

What lay in the north?

Who were the mysterious Pani?

Their agents seemed well supplied with gold, gold at a time when even copper would go far. Ships were being hired, and men recruited, not merely shipsmen, pilots, helmsmen, oarsmen, and such, but men-at-arms, as well, hundreds, mercenaries, many lacking Home Stones, many perhaps indistinguishable from ruffians, vagabonds, brigands, thieves, and cutthroats.

Surely there were no great cities, no wars, in the north.

Of what use would be shipsmen, or soldiers, a small army, in the north?

Her lot number, I recalled, had been 119. The marking, if not cleansed, or washed off, lasts several days. It would probably still be on her, and the others. The slaves, doubtless, would be accounted for, marked off, in terms of their numbers, when put aboard.

Records are kept in such matters.

Many men were going north. Accordingly, slaves, as food and drink, as other utilities and necessities, would be supplied to the camps, the forts, the villages, the towns, or shelters. Gorean men will have their slaves; they will not do without them. It is what women are good for. Let free women take note.

"May I speak?" asked the girl kneeling beside me.

"No," I said.

She was from Asperiche originally, had been taken by corsairs of Port Kar, and sold south. I had purchased her from a local tavern. "Do not sell me to him!" she had begged. The proprietor's man, with one of the ruffian's wallets in his belt, had been most congenial. She had shrunk back in her cage, terrified, when the light of the lantern fell upon her. There was a rustling in the other cages, as well, as other slaves stirred, or knelt at the bars, grasping them, to watch. She, and the others, had had the ankle bells removed, for they are worn, usually, only on the floor and in the alcoves. Many men enjoy a belled slave, whose tiniest motion will be marked by the bells. She clutched the light blanket about her slender shoulders. The proprietor, who held the lantern, was at our side. "This is the one," I said, indicating the illuminated girl. "She was earlier displeasing." "Please, no, Master!" she said. "Before leaving the tavern, you may recall," I said to the proprietor's man, "I left instructions that she was to be lashed." "Yes, later," he said. "Now?" he asked. "Yes," I said. "Please, no, Master!" she cried. "I have a business to conduct," said the proprietor. "You must learn to be pleasing!" "I will be pleasing," she exclaimed, "I will be pleasing!" "No, no!" she wept, as the two locks on the cage's gate were opened. There was laughter from several of the other cages, and I gathered that the girl from Asperiche was not popular with her chain sisters. "Crawl, slut!" called more than one, as the slave was gestured from the tiny cage and, on all floors, head down, made her way to the floor ring, before which she was knelt, and to which her small hands were fastened. The proprietor's man removed a whip from its nearby peg, on the wall, on the right, as one entered the cage area. "Strike her well!" called one of the slaves. "Two-silver-tarsk girl!" laughed another. "Five copper tarsks, I would say," called another. The girl, now fastened by the wrists to the ring, turned about, kneeling, and regarded me, wildly. "You did not have me beaten when I misspoke my sales price," she said. "When you lied," I said. "You are not like the others," she said. "You are sweet, gentle, kind, sensitive, and understanding. You will not have a poor, helpless girl struck. You cannot do so! You will not! You cannot!" "Ten strokes," I said to the proprietor's man. "No!" she shrieked. There was much laughter from the other cages. "It will not be necessary for her to count the strokes," I said, "as she may find that difficult after the third or fourth stroke, nor need she thank you once you are finished. It is possible she might not be genuinely grateful." "I hate you, I hate you!" she wept. Then she cried out as the first stroke was administered. "Please, no more!" she wept. "I will be pleasing, I will be pleasing!" "That is our hope," said the proprietor, nodding to his man. "Aii!" she wept. The next blows were soon done, and she now lay on her belly, her hands stretched before her, fastened to the ring.

She shuddered, in misery, sobbing, and twisted a little.

Muchly had she writhed and shrieked under the fiery rain of leather. The proprietor's man had done his work well. She had not been pleasing. She now lay at the ring, a miserable, punished slave.

There was laughter from the other cages about.

"Beat her more!" called one of the other slaves.

"More!" called another.

"No, please," she cried.

Insolence, rudeness, disrespect, impudence, incivility, slovenliness, temper, impatience, carelessness, clumsiness, and such are not acceptable in a slave. The slave is not a free woman, who may be as she wishes. The slave is owned, and is to be as her master wishes. She is in a collar. Accordingly, she is to be deferent, obedient, attentive, softly spoken, graceful, and submissive.

"Perhaps now you will be more concerned to be pleasing?" inquired the proprietor, holding the lantern.

"Yes, Master!" she said.

There was more laughter from the other girls.

She had learned much. She was now well aware of what it might be to be a slave, and that she was a slave.

The proprietor's man returned the whip to its peg. He then returned and freed her wrists from the ring.

"You may now return to your cage," said the proprietor, "on all fours."

"Yes, Master," she said.

At the gate to her cage, she turned about, on all fours, and lifted her head to me, her eyes bright with tears, tears running down her cheeks.

"You had me whipped," she said.

"Certainly," I said. "You were to some extent displeasing."

"I hate you," she said, "I hate you!"

"Beware," I said.

"I hate you!" she hissed, and turned about, to enter the cage.

"Ai!" she cried, for my hand in her hair had arrested her progress. I drew her backward, up, and off balance, and threw her on her back before me, at my feet, and turned to the proprietor. "What do you want for her?" I asked.

"No, no!" she cried.

"How much?" I asked.

"Do not sell me to him!" she wept.

"Three silver tarsks!" cried the proprietor.

"One," I said. It was well over what I conjectured he had paid for her. With a silver tarsk he might, in the current market, buy two of her. She was not worth a silver tarsk, but one does not always buy, or sell, with purely economic considerations in mind. I had been annoyed. Besides, at the moment, money did not much matter to me. I had recently, in the street outside, acquired additional resources.

"Done!" he said.

"No, no," she wept.

There was much laughter from the other cages.

"Beat her well!" called a slave. "Sell her for sleen feed!" called another.

I drew a silver tarsk from the ruffian's wallet, and tossed it to the proprietor, who caught it, neatly, in his left hand.

"I am staying the night," I said to the proprietor.

After the business of the street, a quarter of an Ahn past, I was not sure what might lurk in the darkness.

I thought nothing, but it is a long walk toward the center of the city and the inn of Tasdron where I had left my things.

"The tavern is closed," he said.

I slapped the hilt of the blade at my left hip, for I had regathered weapons upon my return to the tavern. The proprietor's man had not chosen to question me in this matter. It reposed in its greased scabbard, slung from its across-the-body strap, from, as I was right-handed, the right shoulder to the left hip. I had a knife, as well, in its sheath, fixed laterally on my waist belt, behind my back. In this way it is not obvious, from the front, that it is there. It is quickly and easily drawn with the right hand.

"Very well," said the proprietor.

"I will visit your kitchen, as I will need some supper," I said.

"As you wish," said the proprietor, looking from the large coin in his hand to the blade at my hip.

I looked at the supine, trembling slave. Her left knee was raised.

The proprietor's man removed her collar. She had been sold.

"Bell her," I said to the proprietor's man, "and chain her, to await me, in the first alcove."

"It will be done," he said.

"I trust the alcove is well furnished," I said, "with various instruments, a switch, a whip, such things."

"Of course," he said.

The slave looked at me, frightened, over her shoulder, her dark hair about her back, as she was conducted, by the left arm, from the room.

"There was an altercation in the street," said the proprietor. "I heard so from my man."

"Have no fear," I said to the proprietor. "None know I am here. Reprisals are unlikely. I will leave before dawn. If any inquire after me, tell them I may be found at the wharves, and will be armed."

"May I speak?" had asked the girl kneeling beside me.

"No," I had said.

I had had her for a silver tarsk.

She was then silent, in the brief white tunic, kneeling beside me, on my leash. She had slender ankles, and nicely turned calves. It was clear why the corsairs had not left her behind in her village square, naked and bound, contemptuously rejected. It is no coincidence that most slaves are "slave beautiful," for, if they were not, it is not likely that they would be made slaves. Suppose one were interested in the capture of wild kaiila. Would one not choose, as far as possible, to herd only the finest to the sales pens? It is much the same with women. Being made a slave is, in its way, a tribute to the beauty and desirability of a woman. Sometimes a free woman is spoken of, if not to her face, as "slave beautiful," namely, that she is beautiful enough to be a slave. Supposedly this is quite insulting to a free woman, and would result in cries of rage and protest, but, should this lamentable assessment come to her attention, she is likely, secretly, to be profoundly pleased. What woman would not wish to be "slave beautiful?" To be sure, given the robes of concealment, the veilings, and such, it is often difficult to know whether or not a free woman is "slave beautiful." This is a difficulty one seldom encounters with slaves, of course, given the garmenture in which men place them. I had picked up my things, in the small pack, at the inn of Tasdron, as I commonly did in the morning, in case I might wish them. One did not know when the long poles might thrust one ship or another from the wharves, the sail take the wind, or the low-banked oars enter the water, and rise again, shedding their sparkling showers in the early morning light. Sometimes it seems that the blades have lifted rainbows from the water.

I saw nothing of much interest about.

I feared another morning might be lost.

Perhaps she had already been shipped north.

I felt the girl's head lean toward me, and I felt her lips, soft, on my thigh. How timid, and humble, was that kiss! Did she fear to be cuffed to the planks? I recalled her startled, begging cries toward morning, and how she had clutched me. She had entered the alcove an enslaved woman; she had left it a slave.

"You may speak," I said.

"I do not know my name," she said. "I do not know my master's name; I do not even know what is on my collar."

"Be content," I said. "I am watching."

"Was Master pleased?" she asked.

"'Pleased'?" I said.

"—In the alcove," she said.

"More so toward morning, than before," I said.

"Master well knows how to subdue a slave," she said.

"I needed a slave," I said.

"A slave hopes that she was pleasing to her master," she said.

Certainly she had been zealous to please.

"A slave was pleasing," I said.

"Then a slave is pleased," she said.

Before we had left the tavern I had removed her bells, leaving them behind in the alcove.

As it had been chilly in the gray light, in the vicinity of the wharves, I had wrapped my cloak about me, and she had heeled me, hurrying behind me, unbidden, to the inn of Tasdron.

She had been pleasant in the bells. I wondered if a master would place bells on the other slave, the Earth slut, who had sold for forty-eight copper tarsks. What would an Earth slut make of being naked, and belled? Any woman, I supposed, would understand such things, what sort of woman would be belled, and the meaning of being belled.

In the dining hall of the inn of Tasdron, I had knelt her beside my table. As my resources had been considerably replenished the previous evening, I had breakfasted well, on larma, vulo eggs, fried sul, roast bosk, sa-tarna, and even black wine, the beans for which, I supposed, derived from the far slopes of the Thentis mountains, and may have been brought west at some risk. For the girl I ordered a bowl of slave gruel, to be placed on the floor beside the table, from which she would feed, head down, without the use of her hands. At two of the other tables, slaves, kneeling beside the table, were also given slave gruel. Their masters did permit them to hold the bowl with both hands, but were not otherwise permitted to use their hands. One of them smiled at me, over the rim of the bowl, but then lowered her eyes, and then lowered her head, to feed, shyly, humbly. Had her indiscretion been noted, I had little doubt but what she would have been cuffed. A slave must be careful with her smiles, for masters are often particular about such things. The girl is to keep well in mind to whom she belongs. Only one is her master. The other two slaves were tunicked, briefly, of course, as they were the slaves of men.

I glanced at my slave, as she fed, obediently. I supposed that she might have, the previous night, objected to such an arrangement. This morning she took it as a matter of course. She had learned much in the alcove. I wondered how a certain Earth-girl slave might appear, so feeding. As any other slave, I supposed. Interestingly, I suspected that the Earth-girl slave would welcome the opportunity to feed so beside her master. It would excite, reassure, and fulfill her. From the first moment I had seen her, her shocked, trim, well-turned, exciting, slender body seemingly arrested in motion, then uncertain, wavering, and the startled, vulnerable expression in her eyes, her suddenly paled, sensitive, exquisite features, the parted, ready, inviting, kissable lips, in that large, strange emporium, I had sensed she belonged at a man's feet. Had I gestured imperiously to my feet, I had the sense she might have crawled to me and placed her lips upon them. But then she half cried out, and fled away. I thought she might do. Yes, I thought. Put her on a chain, and train her, and she might do very nicely. She would respond well to male domination, to command, to being collared, to being helplessly owned. Her fulfillment would be to be a man's possession. The judgment of my colleagues, too, had borne me out. She would need little breaking to the collar. She had, I suspected, worn one, so to speak, since puberty. Yes, I thought, she would feed well beside a man's table, or from his hand. She would be incomplete and miserable without a master. She was a slave, a lovely slave. I must forget her!

Several others, some with slaves, had then entered the dining hall. Some were free women who, naturally, regarded the slaves with satisfaction and contempt. Two approached my table.

I had not invited them.

"Put her in a collar," said one of them to me, of my slave.

"She has been recently purchased," I said. "That omission will be soon rectified."

I supposed that some of the metal workers' shops would now be open.

"Animals look well in collars," said the other.

"True," I said. I wondered how she might look in a collar. Given the veiling, it was hard to tell.

"Clothe her," said the first woman.

Tears formed in the eyes of the girl from Asperiche.

Few things can so reduce and humiliate a female slave as the withering, contemptuous glance of a free woman.

There would be little to protect them from free women, if it were not for masters.

"I will consider the matter," I said.

I supposed that one or another of the cloth workers' shops would be open, or soon open.

"Apparently you cannot afford to clothe her," said the first woman.

"Or are too cheap to do so," said the second.

"Here is a tarsk-bit," said the first woman. "It should be enough for a tunic."

"Or a rag," said the other.

I stood up, and slipped the coin in my wallet.

"You are both thoughtful and generous, kind, noble ladies," I said to them, "and doubtless you are both as beautiful as you are beneficent."

"Perhaps," said one, provocatively.

"Let us see," I said.

"What?" they cried.

I seized them both, and flung them on their bellies across the small table, with a clatter, amidst the dishes, and the residue of food.

It was a simple matter, then, to keep them in place.

I jerked back their hoods, and tore away their veils.

"Behold!" laughed a fellow. "Two are face-stripped!"

Some of the free women, at the other tables, stood. One had screamed, two gasped. "Interfere!" said one of them to a fellow, standing, watching, he presumably her companion. "Not at all!" he laughed, striking his left shoulder twice with the flat of his right hand. "Beast!" she cried to him. "Do something!" said another free woman to her escort, or companion. "I am," he said. "I am watching." "Take me home," she said. "Later," said he, "after breakfast." "Now!" she said. "I would not hazard the streets of Brundisium alone," he said. She remained standing beside him, and seemed pleased enough to be doing so.

"Remove their sandals," I ordered my slave, "and give me the straps."

"Stop!" cried one of the free women, and then the other.

I tied the hands of each behind her back.

Each had long hair, and, by the hair, I fastened them together, knotting them, head to head, close to one another.

"No!" they cried, as my knife parted garment after garment.

"Have no fear," I said. "I will stop with the last garment."

"Sleen!" cried one.

"Perhaps I will not stop with the final garment," I said.

"We are free women!" cried the other. "Free women!"

"Have mercy," cried one, "mercy!"

"Ah, silk," I said, "and not overly long."

"Beast, monster!" said the other.

"Have no fear," I said.

I pulled them by the hair to their feet. They were now face-stripped, barefoot, and bound.

I regarded them.

"I find both of you inferior to my slave," I said.

"Sleen, sleen!" hissed one.

"Ah," I said, "a sleen! Here are your purses. If you wish them, you may carry them in your mouth, as might a pet sleen."

"Never!" cried one.

"Then you will leave them here," I said.

"No!" cried the other.

"Open your mouths," I said.

Each bit on her purse.

"I will now permit you to leave," I said. "If you should crave succor, from some fellow outside, it is likely your purse will fall. Perhaps the best thing would be to kneel down before one fellow or another, and put your head down, and release the purse, thereby keeping it near. You might then beg, head down, to be untied. To be sure, the purse might be taken and you left on your knees, barefoot and bound."

"I would say that is extremely likely," said a bystander.

It was true that times were hard in Brundisium.

"Now," I said to the free women, "be away, lest I call for a switch, and have you switched like slaves from the inn."

Weeping, awkwardly, pulling one another's hair as they stumbled forth, the two free women left the inn.

"It is a joke worthy of a Ubar," said one of the fellows about.

"How long do you think they will keep their purses?" asked a fellow.

"Not long," I said.

"Guardsmen will pick them up, supposing them to be slaves," said another, "as they are barefoot and, essentially, slave-garbed."

"It may be an Ahn, or better, before a free woman may be found to discreetly examine their bodies," said another.

"Before then," said another, "they may be whipped and put in cages, for claiming."

"You may be sure that guardsmen will be annoyed, having been inconvenienced," said another.

"They will see it as a merry jest," said another.

It was true that many Gorean males found the pride and pretensions of free women annoying. Certainly it was easier to deal with women in their place, at one's feet, in collars.

I would not have behaved as I did, of course, if my Home Stone had been that of Brundisium.

Had that been the case, it would have been expected that I would endure uncomplainingly, and graciously, the contumely of the women, however prolonged and unpleasant it might be, for they were free, and a Home Stone would have been shared. Anything else would be not only improper, but, I supposed, unconscionable. On the other hand, not all Gorean males are patient with women, even those with whom a Home Stone might be shared. I wondered, sometimes, why free women occasionally so hazarded themselves before men. Were they exploiting their freedom, or testing its limits? Did they not know that they were women, and in the presence of men? Perhaps, as the saying is, they were "courting the collar."

"More black wine," I said to the waiter.

Most Gorean shops, particularly those of the lesser trades, open at dawn. The proprietors and workers commonly live on the premises, above or behind the shop, and breakfast is commonly taken in the shop itself, while waiting for business. One does not care to miss a possible customer.

I finished the black wine, rose, and dropped a silver tarsk on the table, a rather insolent gesture, I suppose, as it would have purchased half a hundred such breakfasts, save for the black wine. But then I had come by the money easily, the night before. I included, as well, one copper tarsk-bit. I then left the shop, heeled by the slave.

I must make some small purchases.

By the time I reached the wharves she was tunicked and leashed. Her hands looked well, braceleted behind her. On her neck, close-fitting, and locked, was a collar.

She was kneeling beside me.

"I am grateful to be permitted to speak," she said.

I did not respond to her.

"We have been here for an Ahn," she said. "I have heard the bars."

I feared another morning was lost.

"You are watching?" she said.

"Yes," I said.

"For what is Master watching?" she asked.

"Cargo," I said.

"Shapely cargo?" she asked.

"Yes," I said.

"I feared so," she said.

Two men passed, drawing a dock cart, laden with weights of cheese, cradled in tur-pah. Shortly thereafter two fellows passed, bearing a pole between them, from which hung gutted, salted harbor eels. Four docksmen passed, each bearing on his shoulder a bulging, porous, loosely woven sack of reddish suls. At least two ships, coasters, were preparing for departure.

A small flock of verr, some twelve or so, were herded by, conducted by a small boy with a stick. Some coasters, as well as round ships, have pens for livestock. The coaster, being shallow keeled, will usually have its pens on the open deck. Most round ships, given the dangers of weather and the distance of the voyage, keep livestock below, in the first or second hold. Coasters and long ships will commonly beach at night, the crew cooking and sleeping ashore. Indeed, most Gorean mariners, when practical, like to keep in sight of land. The moods of Thassa are capricious, and the might of her winds and waves prodigious.

Some small groups of armsmen, probably mercenaries, drifted past us. There was no discipline, no formation. Some carried spears on their shoulders, and others crossbows.

All seemed wary, dangerous men.

As I had scouted this portion of the dockage in the past, I knew that gear of war, as well as bundles of other supplies, whatever they might contain, had been put aboard one ship or another, sometimes in abundance. One could see how several had rested lower in the water. Sometimes it had been easy enough to identify the goods, as tools, such as axes, adzes, planes, wedges, clamps, and saws, or materials such as tar, turpentine, canvas, paint, and cable. One might have supposed them bound not for the northern beaches and forests but a shipyard, such as the arsenal of Port Kar.

"Ho!" I said, suddenly, softly.

"May I see?" she said.

"Remain on your knees," I said.

From the yard of a dark building, behind the wharves, through a double wooden gate, wide enough to exit a wagon, a scribe, in his blue work tunic, carrying a tablet, had emerged. As I had expected, for I had seen this before, he was followed by a coffle of stripped slaves, fastened together by the neck on a single rope. Their hands were tied together behind their back, and they were blindfolded.

The coffle would be halted outside the building, where it would wait, until it was met by an officer from one of the ships.

Three guards were with the coffle, one on one side, two on the other, the two on the side facing the approach to the wharves.

I looped the leash about the neck of my slave, and tucked in the strap.

"Master?" she asked.

I approached the coffle, as I had the others, to place myself between it and the ships. In this way, I could, with others, survey its components.

I was followed by my slave.

Doubtless she was grateful for her tunic. I had arranged with the cloth worker that it be "slave short." She had nice legs. Why should a master not display them? As with the common slave tunic it was sleeveless, and, naturally, as most slave garments, lacked a nether closure. This helps the slave to better realize that she is a slave, that she is always at the convenience of the master.

Several men, mercenaries, docksmen, and others, had gathered in the vicinity of the coffle.

"Good!" I said.

"Master?" asked the slave.

I was sure it was she.

Men, as is their wont, were examining the slaves, and commenting on them. Slaves, unless new to bondage, are accustomed to being publicly viewed, and spoken of, as the goods they are. Verr, kaiila, tharlarion, and such, do not object to this, so why should slaves?

"I wager that one is hot," said a fellow.

"Ten Ehn and I could make this one weep, buck, and beg," said a fellow.

"Consider the flanks of the tall brunette," said another. She was first in the coffle.

"The ankles of the redhead," said another.

"Excellent," said another, "I would like to see them shackled."

"There is a pudding that would juice at a touch," said another.

"Pretty vulos," commented a man.

"Tastas, each of them," said a fellow, "a confectioner's delight."

"Put them on their sticks," said another.

Remarks, as well, suggestions, and such, were addressed to the slaves, but they could not speak, as they were forbidden speech in coffle. I did see some tears run below the blindfolds on more than one slave. The lips of two or three trembled. Did they not know they were slaves?

I went to the one in which I was interested.

Sensing someone near her she stood more straightly, more beautifully. She may have supposed it a guard, and did not wish to invite the instructive stroke of a switch.

One expects much of slaves. They are not free women.

As I had expected, I could still see the residue of her lot number, now much faded, as was that of the others, on her left breast.

It was 119.

I went a bit to the side, to examine her small wrists, crossed, corded together, closely, behind her back. The opaque cloth of the blindfold had been wrapped twice, snugly, about her head, and knotted in place, behind her head. She could see nothing. She could feel the planks of the walk with her feet, and the breeze on her body. She was on the same long rope as the others. It is looped about the neck and knotted, and then taken ahead to the next girl. The loop was loose, but it could not be slipped.

I regarded her.

The beast was beautiful, quite beautiful.

I was annoyed.

She was more beautiful than I remembered her. I had wanted to find her less beautiful. But she was more beautiful. To be sure, she had now had some training, had learned to kneel, and obey men.

I was angry.

I had hoped to cast her image from me, to rid myself of her

memory. I should not have come to the docks! I should not have watched, and waited, for days. I might have taken ship for Daphne days ago, but I had lingered in Brundisium. I was a fool.

"Master?" asked my slave, timidly.

I did not respond to her.

Surely the slave in the coffle could not be as beautiful as she seemed. I looked at the others, and was reassured. They were all lovely, and surely she on whose breast was inscribed the faded number, 119, was no better than most of them, and less than several of them.

Why then did she seem as she did to me?

I moved close to her, a bit back and on the right side, and breathed, softly, on the side of her neck, below the right ear. "Oh!" she said, softly, startled, and jerked at the cords on her wrists, but, too, inadvertently or not, she had also lifted her head. She had responded, as a slave, to the caress of a man's breath.

"Not so close," said one of the guards.

I moved back.

It had been a simple test, but it had told me what I wanted to know. She was a slave, no more than a slave, and should be a slave.

I smiled to myself.

She was a worthless piece of collar meat, no different from tens of thousands of others.

She belonged in a collar, and chains, at a man's feet.

That was indisputable.

Two fellows, officers, were approaching from one of the ships. Behind them I could see several armsmen were boarding. One of the officers carried a tablet.

I would soon be rid of the troublesome slave. How pleased I was! I had never forgotten her, but now it would be easy to do so, for she would be carried to the north, and I should never see her again.

I had not remembered her as beautiful as she was. To be sure, she had now been in bondage for a time. Being in her natural place does much to enhance the beauty of a woman.

I must forget her.

What would it be to own her, I wondered, for such a woman must be owned. They must be treated with firmness, and never permitted to forget that they are mere slaves. They are to be mastered, uncompromisingly and utterly.

I looked back to the coffle. Papers were being exchanged between the officer and the scribe. Much is done with notes.

Men need slaves.

The coffle would soon be boarded, climbing the narrow plank to the ship.

I would never see her again.

I could then forget her.

How pleased I was.

I considered how she might look on all fours, crawling to me, bringing me the whip, it held between her small, fine, white teeth, the slave whip. I considered how she might look, kneeling before me, the coiled whip now in my hand, addressing to it the attentions of the female slave, caressing it with her lips and tongue, humbly, and at length, well aware that if I were not satisfied, it would be used upon her.

"Master," said my slave, "might we not now return to the inn of Tasdron?"

Again I did not answer her.

"She is not so beautiful, is she?" asked my slave.

"No," I said.

The coffle had now begun to move toward the nearest of the two small ships. Docksmen stood at mooring cleats, ready to loose the ropes and fling them to fellows aboard the ship. A mariner stood at the bow, amidships, and stern, each with his harbor pole. Four mariners stood ready to hoist the small yard, with the now-folded sail. Oars were still inboard. The two helmsmen were at their posts.

I would wait until the ship departed, and see it disappear, a bright speck, outside the farther breakwater. That would be the last of it, and of her. The matter would then be done.

The coffle was conducted up the planking onto the deck. There they were knelt, and relieved of the neck rope. They would remain bound and blindfolded until Brundisium was no longer visible. Curiosity is not becoming in a kajira. After the vessel was well underway, it seemed likely they would be taken to the base hold, the ceiling of which is waist high, which is floored with ballast sand, and there chained together by the neck, after which they would be freed of the wrist cords and blindfolds. A coffle from a different building was already stowed in that fashion in the base hold of the second ship. The base hold is usually dark, and the ballast sand is damp. Verr are sometimes penned in a base hold, but, more commonly, on the open deck.

The second ship, I noted, was also making ready for departure. It had been ready yesterday, but, seemingly, was waiting for the first ship. The cargos were very similar, and I had seen armsmen divided between the two ships. Two ships, together, are accounted safer than two ships, taken singly. Round ships are the preferred prey of the "sleen of the sea," but the sleen, when hungry, do not disdain smaller prey. I had had some interaction, in a tavern, with the fellow who seemed to be the high officer of the armsmen on the second vessel.

The first ship, now, freed of its mooring, was thrust from the dock with the harbor poles. I saw the yard being raised, foot by foot, tackle creaking, followed, foot by foot, by its increasing expanse of unfolding canvas.

As docksmen were at the mooring ropes, I assumed the second vessel was ready to clear the harbor.

The first ship was already a hundred yards from the wharf.

I looked at the second ship.

"Let us return to the inn of Tasdron," said my slave.

"You are fond of its gruel?" I asked.

"I am afraid on the wharves," she said, "the men, how they look at me."

"You must accustom yourself to that," I said. "You are a desirable slave."

"Sometimes," she said, "slaves, even free women, disappear from the wharves."

"You heard that in the tavern," I said.

"Yes," she said, uneasily.

"They would be safe enough," I said, "on a chain somewhere."

I looked after the first ship. I remembered the slender barbarian. At last I was rid of her. I could now put her from my mind.

The matter was now done.

I unlooped the leash from the neck of my slave, and gave

it a jerk, that she might feel it pull at the back of her neck. She looked at me. She was now again the captive of the leash.

The first ship was now near the breakwater.

The matter was over. It must be over. It must be done!

I cried out, angrily.

"Master?" inquired the slave, frightened.

I turned about.

"Master," she said, "that is not the way to the inn of Tasdron!"

I strode to the second ship.

"Tal," I said, to he whom I remembered from the tavern. He was near the boarding plank, to the second ship. It was he, Tyrtaios, who had proffered the golden stater.

He turned about. "Tal," he said.

"Do you still want swords for the north?" I asked.

"Such as yours, yes," he said.

"I might take ship," I said.

"I had expected to have you aboard," he said, "bound and gagged, in the hold."

"Is my sword so valuable?" I asked.

"You, and your kind," he said, "may be more valuable than you suspect."

"Men who ask few questions?" I said.

"Assassins, slavers, and such," he said, "men who are open to unusual opportunities, who will do much for gold, and ask no questions."

My slave, as we were stopped, knelt at my thigh, her head down, as was appropriate. The leash looped up to my left hand.

Tyrtaios regarded her. "Your slave is lovely," he said.

"She is not yet fully trained," I said.

"Different men train them differently," he said.

"True," I said.

"She is from the inn, is she not?" he asked.

"Yes," I said.

"She seems much different now," he said.

"She is," I said.

"Would you like several like her, or better?" he asked.

"Perhaps," I said. Some men reckon wealth in terms of tarn disks, others kaiila, others bosk, and some in terms of slaves.

"I sent two messengers to recruit you," he said, "but they failed in their mission."

"Oh?" I said.

"They were set upon in the darkness," he said, "pummeled, and robbed, by a dozen assailants."

"It must be difficult to determine the number in the dark," I said.

"A great number," he said.

"Interesting," I said.

"I offered you a golden stater," he said.

"I am a two-stater hire," I said.

"Excellent," he said.

He drew from his purse two golden staters and, one after the other, placed them in my hand. I placed them in my pouch.

"What is doing in the north?" I said. "Where are you bound?"

He regarded me. His eyes, oddly, reminded me of those of a snake.

"Forgive me," I said.

"Welcome aboard," he said.

Chapter Nine

The voyage to the north, I gather from Brundisium, had taken several days, and for us, kept most of the time in a lower portion of the ship, in darkness, on damp sand, unable even to stand upright, was unspeakably miserable. We were also put in collars and chained together by the neck, seventeen of us. We lived for the moments when the hatch would be opened, and we would be allowed to climb the ladder and emerge on the open deck. There was another ship, like ours, astern. We had several soldiers aboard, as well as mariners. We were too small and weak to be put to the great levers drawn by the oarsmen. The time is kept by a drum. Mostly we proceeded under sail. Several nights the ship was beached and the crew and soldiers went ashore to sleep and cook, and, I suppose, to hunt, take on water, and such. We were kept in the hold. Watches were doubtless kept. If there is an alarm, the ship may be launched in a matter of Ihn. I know this, for a drill was done twice. Each man knows where he is to be, and what he is to do. Perhaps that is why we were not taken ashore. Certainly, given our chaining, there was no possibility that we could have slipped away, perhaps to starve or be eaten in the wild. In some places, farther south, there are women in the forest who do not belong to men. They are free women and hate us, for we belong to men. If they capture us they beat us and sell us. But if they are captured, it is said that they, too, quickly, learn they belong to men. Apparently they sell well.

Once we were brought to the deck, and placed at the rail. There, one by one, our hands were tied behind us. A third ship, low in the water, was abeam, parallel to us.

Our captain had a glass of the Builders and was surveying the third ship. "She flies the pennons of Brundisium," said one of his officers. "I do not think she is of Brundisium," said the captain, soberly. "Port Kar?" asked the officer. "I do not know," said the captain. "Fly the code flags. We shall await the countersign." Pennons were raised on a halyard. "No response," said the officer. "She is thinking of closing," said the captain. "Keep the armsmen out of sight." "If she closes," said the officer, "it will be the end of her." "Yes," said the captain. "That is the purpose of the slaves," said the officer, "to lure her in?" "Rather," said the captain, "to seem to lure her in. That will make them wary. Too, we have a fellow astern, so there would be two ships to one. I think she is merely scouting us." "It is, then, a corsair," said the officer. "Yes," said the captain. "I think so. At least she is not of Brundisium, despite her pennons." "Do you anticipate an engagement?" asked the officer. "No," said the captain. We remained, neck-chained, and back-bound, for nearly an Ahn at the rail. Then the strange ship turned away.

At last we reached some point on the northern coast, in the vicinity of the great forests. We were brought to the deck, and then, when the ship had the beach abeam, and was a few yards from shore, we were plunged over the rail, and found ourselves awash in the surf. My head went under water for a moment, and the roaring of the sea thundered in my ears. I was for a moment terrified, and disoriented. But the weight of the chain oriented me, and, struggling, I got my legs under me and, sputtering, coughing, my eyes half blinded with salt water, I stood up. The water was not deep, but it was cold. It came only to my waist. We were waded to the shore and knelt there, in the surf, it washing up about our knees and calves. I shivered, and wiped the water from my eyes. I could see the beach before me, which was a mix of sand and rock. It seemed rough, cold, and forbidding. But beyond it I could see the forest, which seemed lonely and beautiful. There was no one about that I could see, and I wondered how this place, which might be no different from ten thousand others, had been selected for our landfall. There must have been a signal of some sort. Naturally I had no idea where we were, other than on some remote beach, in the north. We were days from our port of departure.

"Position," called a fellow, himself descending from the ship, splashing, and wading to shore.

So, cold, wet, and shivering, miserable, we went to "position," kneeling back on our heels, our backs straight, our heads up, looking ahead, our knees spread, as the slaves we were, the palms of our hands down on our thighs.

It seemed then that the men forgot about us.

And it is well-known that kajirae are curious.

Much of the material cargo was being put to shore. Several men were in the water, being handed boxes, sacks, and bales, and some sealed vessels, even craters and amphorae. Some of the larger boxes were cast overboard, and, thrust, were floated to shore. Two large boxes, which had been lashed down on deck, and covered with greased canvas, were lowered over the side on ropes, with great care, to several men. I had no idea what the content of these boxes might be.

"Ai!" I cried, in misery, lashed at the side of the neck by a switch. He had come up behind me, from having brought a small barrel to shore.

"Are you not to be in position, your eyes forward?" he inquired.

"Yes, Master!" I said. "Forgive me, Master!"

I had twisted about, just a little, from time to time, to watch the men.

"Ha!" he said. "And you two, your eyes are now forward!"

"Yes, Master!" they said. Then they cried out, "Forgive me, Master!" I heard their cries, to my right, as the switch struck twice.

I was not the only one, it seemed, who had been curious.

The side of my neck stung. I had been reminded that a lapse from position, however slight, is not acceptable.

I was grateful, of course, that the men had not seen fit to lash us.

Looking ahead, I saw a figure emerging from the forest, in the green which I would come later to recognize as that of the foresters.

He lifted his hand, and said, "Tal," and approached us. He conferred, briefly, with the chief of our armsmen. I had the sense that signs and countersigns might have been exchanged.

The newcomer seemed particularly interested in the two large boxes which had been lowered carefully on ropes over the ship's side, and then carried to shore. He then came before us, and examined us, one by one. "That one is a barbarian," he was told, while I knelt as beautifully as I could before him. I was careful not to meet his eyes. Some masters do not allow their girls to meet their eyes. "No matter," he said. "They all sweat and squeak the same." He then drew back, and passed his eye over us once more. "Good," he said. I could sense the relief which went through the chain. Certainly I felt it. We wish desperately to be found pleasing by men. It can be fearful for us if we are not.

Off in the forest we heard the roar of a beast.

We looked at one another, frightened.

Then, to my surprise, we were freed of the collars and chain. "You may stand," we were told. We then stood in the surf, the water washing about our ankles. I held my arms about myself, as I was cold.

The collars and chain were then carried back to the ship. The mariners were busying themselves, apparently for departure. Oars emerged from the oar ports. The yard was being raised. The bow of the ship was turning about. I wondered why the ship had not been beached. One gathered that the captain and his officers were uneasy in this place. I suspected they had made more than one journey north. The collars and chains, doubtless, on a return trip, would grace new occupants, new beasts, such as I.

"Approach," we were told, and, gratefully, we then stood on the beach, beside the disembarked cargo of the small vessel.

"Be in line, in order of descending height," he said.

We so arranged ourselves.

We were then, from the back to the front, being put in a rope coffle, the rope to be knotted about our necks, as it had been when we had exited the holding area in our port of departure. We were not being blindfolded. I supposed one part of the beach and one part of the forest was not much different from other parts. Our hands were not being tied behind us. I soon discovered why.

Then the rope was knotted about my neck, and taken forward,

to the next girl. I was then, again, a part of a coffle. Coffles are sometimes spoken of as "the slaver's necklace." I hoped I would be an attractive bead on such a necklace. It is a slave's hope that men will find her pleasing. Much depends on it. Too, I found that I wanted to be found pleasing to men, and a slave, the slave I was.

"You are at the edge of the great forest," we were told. "It is roamed by beasts."

In the distance, we again heard a roar, and shuddered.

"That is a forest panther," he said.

It was perhaps the same beast, or one responding to it. I supposed such beasts somehow adjudicated territory amongst themselves.

"Men," said the newcomer, addressing the armsmen. "We will trek to a place called Tarncamp. Most of you will work and train there. Some may go east, to another camp. Its name you need not now know."

"Work?" asked an armsman.

"Heavy labor, in the forest," said the newcomer. "Felling trees, shaping and smoothing timbers, transporting them to the east, such things."

"My tool is the sword," said the armsman.

"It will find its work soon enough," said the newcomer.

"I decline such service," said the armsman.

"You are far from Brundisium," said the newcomer.

The ship was departing. It was now more than a hundred yards from shore. I saw no sign of the second ship. I did not know what had become of it. Considering that the coast is generally kept in view, it seemed unlikely it would have been lost at sea; considering how long it had been with us it seemed unlikely it would have encountered difficulties of which we would have been unaware; and now, considering our position, and how far north we were, it seemed unlikely it would have fallen afoul of a corsair; the "sleen of the sea" would find little to feed upon in waters so lonely and remote.

"I shall await another ship," said the armsman.

"You would be put to death as a deserter," said the newcomer.

"One need only follow the coast south," he said.

"You would be dead within ten yards," said the newcomer.

The armsman looked warily toward the trees.

"Yes," said the newcomer, "there are bowmen in the forest."

At this point there was another roar in the forest, but this one seemed mighty, as though it might have torn leaves from the trees.

"That is no forest panther!" said a man.

"No," said the newcomer, "it is a larl."

"Larls are not this far north," said a man.

"They do not range so," said another.

"It is a trained beast, brought north," said the newcomer. "There are others, as well. It will accompany us to Tarncamp. Tarncamp has its established perimeter, marked by wands. One must not, without authorization, pass beyond the wands. Yesterday two deserters were torn to pieces."

"You have deserters?" said a man.

"Occasionally," said the newcomer.

"What manner of service is this?" inquired the reluctant armsman.

"One which is unusually well paid," said the newcomer. "Did not each of you receive the equivalent in copper tarsks of a silver stater of Brundisium?"

There was assent to this amongst the men.

"Be of good cheer," said the newcomer. "In time, you will receive the opportunity to wash your blade in the blood of foes."

"Of course," said a fellow, "we are to train here, secretly, and then sweep south!"

"But why so far north?" asked a man, uneasily.

The newcomer did not respond.

I turned about and looked west, out to sea.

I did not see the second ship.

There must have been a signal from the forest, a particular signal, I thought, to bring us to shore here. It then occurred to me that there might have been another signal, a different signal, possibly, to bring the second ship to the shore, or would be such a signal. In this way, if nothing else, armsmen could not convene with others until Tarncamp was reached, until they were within the wands. I knew little of larls. Certainly I had never seen one. I did know they were beasts of prey, apparently large beasts of prey. I had seen, in the training house, a sleen, a restless, vicious, agile, six-legged, carnivorous, sinuous, snake-like mammal. It is apparently an extraordinary tracker. In the wild, it commonly burrows. Trained sleen are used for a large number of purposes, one of which was made clear to us, particularly to those of us who were barbarians being trained, the hunting of fugitive slaves.

The newcomer turned about and lifted his arm, toward the forest.

I heard the snap of a whip coming from the forest. It is a sound well known to, and much feared by, the female slave. The coffle stirred, apprehensively.

"Ah!" said more than one man.

A line of slaves, perhaps twenty, with ropes and poles, emerged from the forest. They were not coffled. And they were, I was pleased to note, tunicked. It is said that a free woman might perish of shame if placed in a slave tunic, but, to a slave, such a garment, which she knows need not be accorded to her, may be a treasure, more precious to her than some assemblage of robes and veils to a free woman. Indeed, amongst slaves a tunic, in its way, constitutes a symbol of status. Certainly tunicked slaves commonly look down upon naked slaves. Whereas a slave might prefer to be naked before her master, that she might know herself the more his slave, almost any slave wishes to be clothed in public. To be sent naked about one's errands, one's shopping and such, is usually regarded as an instruction, if the slave is new, or, if she is not, as a sign that she is out of favor with her master, perhaps having failed to be fully pleasing in some way. In many ways may a slave be praised or rewarded, punished or disciplined. Among these ways clothing or its lack, as the nature of bonds, food, quarters, and such, may figure.

I suppose I am vain, but I never objected to the slave tunic. I thrill to see myself in it, displayed for perusal, exhibited as a slave. I think I have an excellent figure for such a scrap of cloth, such a mockery of a garment, my legs and such, though perhaps I am a little slender. But I do not think the men mind. I think I would rather be naked at the feet of my master, but, in public, I delight in the tunic. Perhaps free women would switch me across the calves, but I would still be pleased. Indeed, I do not think they would strike me, if they were not envious of me.

Perhaps they, too, would like to be so exhibited, so proudly and shamelessly, for the perusal of men.

I suppose that many women, on my old world, were uncertain as to their desirability. That is probably to be expected, on such a world. I know I was. But then I found myself brought to Gor. I knew then that in the opinion of some men, at least, and those dealers in, and connoisseurs of, women, I was desirable. They bring us here to sell us. How desirable I am I do not know, but I know I must have met at least some basic criteria, criteria for marketability. I would hate for men to kill for me, but it pleases me that they would pay for me. It is nice to know that one has some value, if only a handful of copper coins. Free women may be priceless, but, too, I suspect some would not bring a tarsk-bit. Many Goreans believe that all women are natural slaves. I do not know if that is true or not, for who knows all women, but I know that I am a natural slave. I cannot be fulfilled without the collar. I belong at a master's feet. I want to love and serve, choicelessly, in sweet abasement. We hope to be well treated. But we will be treated as the master sees fit, for we are slaves.

Are we so different from free women?

I do not know.

Surely the culture marks great differences between us. The free woman is a person, a citizen, and may possess a Home Stone; we are animals and properties, marked and collared as such, and we lack Home Stones, for such are denied to beasts. And surely our clothing, when we are permitted clothing, contrasts with that of free women, as a revealing tunic, or camisk, differs from colorful swirls of fine robes and veils. It is sometimes said that the free woman dresses to please herself, whereas the slave is dressed to please her master, and this is true, but, I think, overly simple. For example, if the free woman were to dress as a slave, she might soon be collared, and if the master were to dress his slave as a free woman, he would be jeopardizing her life. Custom and tradition, and sometimes law, are involved in these matters. The free woman may dress to please herself, but, too, it seems she is well advised to please herself by conforming, and strictly, to a variety of canons, canons of taste, custom, convention, and sometimes of law. In some respects, societally, she is less free than the slave. The culture does deem it important, and free women insist upon this, that a clear distinction be drawn between the free woman and the slave. The most obvious way to mark this distinction publicly and conveniently is the collar, or its absence, and garmenture, say, the robes of concealment as against a tunic, or camisk. One supposes that the slave might be dressed in a drab, form-concealing, shapeless sack, but men will not have it so. They are proud of their slaves, and wish to see them, and display them. If one had a beautiful kaiila, would one throw a blanket over it? So the brief tunic is a common slave garment. Men will have it so. Then, as might be expected, free women denounce the tunic as a shameful garment, and attempt, in terms of it, to shame its occupant. This is sometimes effective, for a time, with a new slave, but, sooner or later, the slave, at least when no free women are present, comes to revel in the lightness and freedom of such a garment, and its flattering betrayal of her beauty, as opposed to the hobbling impediments of cumbersome robes and veils, however resplendent, well-layered, and colorful. An additional point might be mentioned, relevant to slave garmenture, particularly with respect to its revealing nature, aside from the preferences of men, which is the supposed protection it affords to free women. The notion here seems to be that a roving tarnsman, a raider, a slaver, a girl hunter, and such, given the choice between a prey of obvious interest, say, a scantily clad slave girl, and one of an unknown quality, say, a free woman in the robes of concealment, given the risks involved, and such, is more likely to drop the slave loop about the slave than her exalted free sister. Who, it is said, would wish to risk his life for a tarsk? On the other hand, there is little doubt that the capture of a free woman, given the care with which they are guarded, the glory of capturing one, and such, is usually considered an estimable coup. A common test for a young tarnsman is to steal a free woman from an enemy city, bring her home, brand and collar her, and have her serve and dance before his family and friends at his victory feast. And the first wine at the feast, following her public licking and kissing of his whip, before which time no one may eat or drink, will be served to him by his new slave. Too, of course, one may always hope that the prey, when brought to the camp and stripped, may prove a prize. Most slaves, of course, were once free women, free insofar as a woman may be regarded as free, as not yet collared.

"Behold these slaves," said the newcomer, gesturing to the tunicked slaves recently emerged from the forest. "Are they not of interest?"

Only too obviously were they of interest, judging from the responses of the men.

"Such, and many others," said the newcomer, "serve in Tarncamp. They exist for your service and pleasure. You may buy them, or rent them, or visit them in one or another of the slave houses. The Pani, who are your employers, are generous with such meaningless baubles."

Some of the men smote their left shoulders in approbation.

"And," he said, "you know of the changes in Ar. Indeed, I am sure we owe the presence of some of you here to such changes."

Several of the men looked uneasily at one another.

"We all know of defeat and flight," he said, "the sorry fate of the occupational forces, of the rising of the men of Ar, of screaming crowds, diversely armed, of fires, of the decimation and disruption of troops, the desertion of officers, the stranding of units, of frequent withdrawals under fire, the confused retreats of mercenary prides, the breaking apart and scattering of free companies, of men, hungry and disorganized, hunted down and slaughtered like urts in the field."

This account ignited protest, and an angry muttering, amongst some of the men, perhaps mercenaries, and perhaps some regulars, lost from their units, unable to rejoin them. Tears coursed down the cheeks of more than one man.

"Well," said the newcomer, "you doubtless know as well of the proscription lists and the flight, where possible, of hundreds of traitors and collaborators from Glorious Ar. Many fled toward the coast, to arrive at length, as many soldiers, as well, haggard and starving, destitute, in Brundisium. Indeed, some of you here may have been amongst such unfortunate, needful wretches, then only scattered refugees."

Some fellows exchanged glances.

"But if so, as you are here, if you are men, welcome, and rejoice, for it is your good fortune, as that of your fellows, armsmen or not, to have sold your swords north. Riches and glory await you!"

This aroused the attention of the men, all of the men, visibly.

"But many lovely free women of Ar," he said, "profiteers, traitresses, collaborators, conspirators, betrayers of their Home Stones, fleeing, taken in hand, had their hair cropped and were collared."

There was assent amongst the men, and laughter.

"And many of the most beautiful of these," he said, "will kneel to you in Tarncamp, and fear only that you will not find them pleasing."

"Of high caste?" asked a fellow.

"Many," said the newcomer, "for what women, if not of high caste, would be in a position to secure coin and power by serving the enemy, to reveal secrets, to supply information, to corner, manage, and horde goods, to wheedle concessions and arrange clandestine sources of supply and private markets, to profit from the occupation?"

I supposed there would always be such, in any city.

Women of lower caste could do little more than consort with the enemy. From what I had heard there were few of the lower castes on the proscription lists. Perhaps they were less important, or less visible, or would be less readily denounced, being less hated. Or perhaps they had less to offer the enemy, and thus were of less interest to them. Or perhaps they were stronger than their betters, more willing to suffer and wait, and endure.

"And so," said the newcomer, "women who once would not have consented to speak to you through the curtains of their palanquins, women who would have scorned you in Ar, who held themselves so superior, who would have regarded you as less than the dust beneath their slippers, now, if sufficiently beautiful, naked and collared, will carry buckets of hot water to your baths."

"Excellent," said a fellow.

Many of those women, I supposed, would have been apprehended by fellow fugitives and sold in Brundisium.

One would make a coin where one could, and, I suppose, the

making of some coins, more than others, can be exceedingly pleasant.

I supposed few such women were sold as virgins.

"But," said the newcomer, examining us, recently, rudely disembarked from the vessel, examining us as a Gorean examines slaves, "I do not find your own cargo inferior."

The girl next to me, Eighteen, trembled.

Some of the slaves brought from the forest shrugged. They were tunicked. Why, I wondered, should they be so superior? I supposed they might well have been brought to the beach, earlier, as we, in no more than collars and chains.

As the burdens were arranged, I soon realized why our hands had not been tied behind our backs. I put my hands up, over my head, and steadied the box. It was not heavy. In the house, I had been taught to balance and carry objects in this fashion, generally bundles or baskets. A corollary of this manner of carrying an object is it immobilizes the hands and accentuates the figure, rather like the fastening of a girl's hands behind the back of her neck.

Most of the heavier objects would be slung from the poles brought by the tunicked slaves. Many others would be borne on the backs of the armsmen.

There was no longer any sign of the ship.

I supposed it was returning to Brundisium. Perhaps it would first manage a rendezvous with the second ship, but I did not know.

Interestingly the two large boxes, which had been covered with canvas on the open deck, concerning which the mariners had been so careful, were consigned to four men each, who managed them, each box, by lashings and two poles. They were transported rather in the fashion of a palanquin.

"Gently, gently!" warned the newcomer.

One of the boxes wavered, and he rushed to it, steadying it. As the box had moved, it sounded as if objects of iron or steel might be enclosed. Its contents, I gathered, if not fragile, were of considerable importance. I did not understand its importance. Perhaps it contained tools, or materials to which tools might be pertinent. As nearly as I could tell, in any event, it was an unusual form of cargo.

The box I was carrying was not heavy.

Men do not overburden slaves, no more than they would overburden any animal of the size or weight of a slave. It would be impractical, and foolish, to do so.

"May I speak, Master?" I asked the newcomer, who stood near me.

"You are a bold slave," he said.

"Forgive me, Master," I said. At least I had not been cuffed.

"You may speak," he said.

"There was a second ship," I said.

"Its landing would be different, its route would be different," he said.

"I feared," I said, "it might have encountered some misfortune."

"That is unlikely," he said. "What is your interest?"

"Nothing," I said.

I suddenly tensed, beneath his gaze. "Forgive me, Master," I said. "I am only a barbarian. There was a man, a master. I saw him in the barbarian lands. I think it was he who brought me to civilization and the collar."

"When did you last see him?" asked the newcomer.

"Before my sale, in Brundisium," I said, "I enclosed in an exposition cage."

"Did you see him at your sale?" he asked.

"No," I said, "but there were torches about the block. I could not well see into the tiers. They were muchly dark."

"But you heard the bidding," he said. "Surely you sensed the restlessness of the men, their interest."

"Yes, Master," I said.

"Would you recognize his voice?" he asked.

"I think so," I said. How could he think that I could not tell that voice, though he had said but a few words in my presence?

"Did you hear him bid?" he asked.

"No, Master," I said.

"Forget about him," he said.

I was silent.

"That will be difficult for you to do, I gather," he said.

"It was at his feet that I lay bound and naked, in a warehouse, a large building, in the barbarian lands."

"They have buildings in the barbarian lands?" he asked.

"Yes, Master," I said.

"Interesting," he said. "I thought you might live in huts, or tents, or wagons, as the Kataii, or Paravachi."

"Most of us do not," I said, "Master."

"I looked up at him, as I lay before him, and he looked down upon me," I said.

"And he saw you in the exposition cage," he said.

"Yes, Master," I said.

"But he neither bought you, nor even bid upon you?"

"No, Master," I said.

"Forget about him," he said.

I was again silent.

"He was a slaver, I take it," he said.

"I gather so," I said.

"Then," said he, "dismiss him from your mind. To him, I assure you, you and such as you are worthless, naught but meaningless collar meat. You are no more important to such a man than one vulo amongst others, one verr amongst others, one tarsk amongst others."

"Yes, Master," I said. Tears formed in my eyes.

"Have no fear," he said, "you will change hands many times, and have many masters."

"Yes, Master," I whispered.

"You will be muchly handled, and well used," he said, "and as the worthless slave you are."

"Yes, Master," I said.

"And you will strive to serve each with perfection," he said, "each with all the perfections of the female slave."

"Yes, Master," I said.

"You should hate him," he said.

"Master?" I said.

"You were deprived of your freedom," he said. "It was he who brought the searing iron to your flank, marking you indisputably for all to see as mere goods. It was he who arranged it that your neck would be encircled with the metal band of bondage, closed and locked in place. It was he who put you upon the block, to be sold to the highest bidder. It was he who made it such that you must kneel to men, and hope to please them. It was he who brought you to kennels, cages, and chains. How you must hate him!"

"Forgive me, Master," I said, "but I do not."

"Surely you resent the helpless servitude and choiceless degradation in which you have been placed."

I lowered my head.

"Speak," he said.

"It is my hope," I said, "to be found pleasing by my masters."

He stepped back a bit.

I straightened my body a little, lifted my head a little.

"You are a pretty one," he said.

"Thank you, Master," I said.

"What is your name?" he said.

"I have not been named," I said. "I have been identified by my lot number, one hundred and nineteen."

"Slaves should have names," he said.

"It will be as masters wish," I said.

He turned about. "Ho!" he called.

We then began to leave the beach, and approach the trees. Before we entered the trees, I looked back, briefly, at the cold beach, and the restless, shimmering expanse of Thassa, and the horizon beyond it.

As we entered the trees, I saw two fellows. They wore tunics of a mottled green and brown. As they stood very still, I did not even notice them until we were almost at their side. Each held a strung, but not drawn, bow, a large bow, with an arrow, a long arrow, light at the string, as though it might be ready for flight.

A few moments later, I heard again, this time far to my right, the mighty roar which I had heard before, that roar which seemed it might have taken leaves from the trees. It had been said to be that of a larl. Occasionally I would hear it again during the next few days, as we trekked to Tarncamp. The beast, somewhere, off in the forest, was apparently accompanying our march.

Chapter Ten

I had expected the two ships to beach together, but they had not. Indeed, our vessel did not even beach at this point, but turned about, and rocked in place, parallel to the shore, some yards from the beach.

I had some sense of the cargo of the first ship, tools, supplies, slaves, and such, but our vessel was clearly a transport for armsmen. I kept the girl from Asperiche muchly in the first hold, as I did not wish trouble on the deck. In this decision Tyrtaios, whom I took to be first amongst the armsmen, though not amongst the mariners, concurred. "It is well," he said, "not to lose men." He had said this looking toward the coast, said it rather as one might have preferred not to lose pieces in a game. In Tyrtaios I sensed intelligence and power, and a prudential sense of instrumentality, unqualified by extraneous considerations. In a way he was far less dangerous to his men than an idealist or fanatic, who would sacrifice armies and continents to pursue a face in the clouds, a goal he does not even understand, an end which, if achieved, would betray the dreams in terms of which it was sought. Let the idealist and the fanatic curse the inevitable fruits of his success, the brass he took for gold, the unexamined shadow he took for substance, the bright illusion he took for reality; he does not lament the downfall of peoples and states, the carts of bones and the lakes of blood; his grief, rather, is for himself, as the innocent victim of alleged lies and treasons which, had he opened his eyes, would have been as obvious as a cliff's edge. But Tyrtaios was neither an idealist nor fanatic; he was well aware of the balance between means and ends, between resources and their limitations. I was sure he would shepherd his men, and nourish them, but, as a dark player might, regarding not only the board, and a particular victory, but the larger game, a different game, one not played on a board. Tyrtaios would be a practical commander, whose expenditure of men and supplies would be rational, and judicious, and cold. I wondered if Tyrtaios was an Assassin. Assassins are not blinded by dreams. They do not draw their weapons irresponsibly, in righteousness, in drunkenness, in rage. They consider matters, bide their time, and, when ready, paint the dagger. They do not kill for ideals, or dreams. They kill for coin.

Unaccountably I was furious at the disappearance of the first ship. Why should that be?

What was it to me?

It was not even clear to me why I had ventured north. Ah, yes, two golden staters!

I wondered how Tyrtaios saw me. I suspected that my hire had not been purchased for the quickness of a blade, the edge of a sword, not for two staters of gold. How, I wondered, did he understand the Merchants, the Slavers? What was his caste? Was he an Assassin? I was not. I had told him so. Did he believe me? How did he understand me? I feared he saw me in terms of himself, as one might look into a dark glass.

"There," said Tyrtaios, pointing.

"That is the signal?" I asked.

"I have it so from the captain," said Tyrtaios.

"You were not informed?" I asked.

"We will disembark," said Tyrtaios.

"It is a banner of sorts," I said. I had never seen such a banner, which was narrow, and rectangular.

"It is a Pani banner," he said.

The common military ensign is a metal standard, raised on its pole or staff, bearing its device, and, usually, identifying a unit, whether it be an army, a division, or a company. Commands may be given by means of the standards, and their motions. They may function much as drums or battle horns. On the other hand, by their means, too, one may, as in the early dawn, after a forced march, marshal and deploy troops silently. Men will die to protect their standards. If a general falls, it is expected that his standard bearer will be at his side. Wars have been fought to regain a lost standard.

"Prepare to disembark," called Tyrtaios to the more than a hundred men on the vessel.

"I shall free a slave, and fetch her to the deck," I said.

Several of the armsmen did not know she was on board.

Except on a round ship, and even on many of those, mariners do not welcome the presence of a free woman. Such, it is said, sow discord. Such are to be respected, but, in time, men grow hungry. It is a strain, even on a well-trained sleen, to circle meat it is forbidden to touch. The matter worsens, of course, if the free woman insists on the privileges of the deck, or, say, if she is careless of how she stands when the wind whips her robes, and matters may become intolerable indeed should she delight herself with certain pleasures not unknown to occasionally appertain to her sex, usually harmlessly, flirting with, or teasing, taunting, and tormenting men, confident in the inviolability of her freedom, perhaps in the possession of a shared Home Stone, and such. It is one thing, of course, to engage in such games in a theater, a street, or plaza, and quite another on a ship at sea, far from taverns, the relief of paga girls, and such. More than one woman began a voyage free and concluded it being sold in a distant port. Sometimes a round ship will carry slaves for the men, ship slaves. These are at the pleasure of the crew. The long ships, of course, the armed war knives of the sea, seldom depart with slaves aboard, though they may return with them.

"Master!" whispered the girl as the light of the small, shallow tharlarion-oil lamp fell upon her.

"Do not kneel," I said.

She blinked against the light, which, in the darkness, dim as it was, must have seemed bright to her.

"The ship is still," she said.

"We are disembarking," I said.

"Where are we?" she asked.

"I do not know," I said, "somewhere north of the Alexandra."

She spoke softly as she had been warned to do, days before.

"Ankle," I said.

She slid back, against the hull wall, and extended her left ankle.

I placed the small lamp on the planks and removed her shackle. "There are over a hundred men on board," I said, "not counting mariners, with their officers. You are the only slave on board. Many do not know you are here. Stay close to me."

"Surely Master can defend me, and keep me," she said.

"It would be easier," I said, "if you had the body of a tarsk and the face of a tharlarion."

She stood up, and played with her hair, annoyingly, tossing and spreading it, and then, with both hands, brushing it behind her. She then stood straight and, with her small hands, smoothed down the tunic.

"But I do not have the body of a tarsk and the face of a tharlarion," she said.

"Stay close to me," I said, "very close."

"Yes, Master," she said.

I had not put her to use in the hold, as I did not want her shared. Thus, for the days at sea, I had deemed that she would be available to none, not even to me, her master. I would be as deprived as the others. I did not wish to feast while others starved. I supposed an oddity of propriety, even honor, was involved in this, but, too, doubtless, a sense of prudence. Only a fool publicly counts his gold. Accordingly, I had taken pains to be muchly visible on deck, eating and sleeping there, taking my turn on the bench, and so on. In doing so, of course, I was acutely aware of the hunger of the men, and the danger it might pose, for I, too, shared their hunger.

"Behold!" cried a fellow, as, the hold hatch back, I drew her into the light, from the ladder to the open deck.

"Steady," warned Tyrtaios.

"A vulo!" said a fellow.

"Prepare to disembark," called the captain.

"She was loaded at Brundisium," said a fellow.

Men crowded toward us.

The slave from Asperiche shivered, concealing herself, as she might, behind me.

"Now!" called the captain.

"Ho!" called Tyrtaios. "Over the side!"

But the men did not move.

"Who is the first to disobey?" inquired Tyrtaios.

None seemed ready to claim this distinction.

"Who concealed her?" demanded a fellow, glaring at me.

"I," I said. Then I said to the slave, "Step away from me, back, to the left, and side."

Instantly she obeyed.

The fellow's blade had already departed its housing.

"I give you permission to kill him," said Tyrtaios to me.

The exchange was extremely brief, and the fellow reeled back, grasping his slashed arm, the blade lost on the deck.

"Ahh," said several of the men.

"Master," breathed the girl from Asperiche, shuddering.

"Why did you not kill him?" asked Tyrtaios, interested.

"Had his blade been more dangerous," I said, "it would have been done."

Tyrtaios turned to the men. "Who hesitates to obey?" he asked.

He received no response.

"Over the side," said Tyrtaios, and, one by one, they went to the rail, and leapt into the water.

When the fellow who had attacked me went to the rail, grasping his bleeding arm, Tyrtaios, with a brief stroke of his blade, cut the spinal column at the back of his neck.

"Why did you do that?" I asked.

"Even though a blade be weak," he said, "a knife in the dark can be dangerous."

"I suspect there was little risk of that," I said.

"I have need of you," he said. "It is a risk I chose not to take."

"You now have one less man," I said.

"But better discipline amongst the others," he said.

"You did not allow him the opportunity to defend himself," I said.

"You saw his skills," he said. "Why prolong matters?"

"I see," I said.

"In the future," he said, "do not expect me to do your work."

"I will not," I said.

Tyrtaios then sprang over the rail, plunging into the restless, waist-high water. He paused only long enough to clean his blade, and then waded ashore. Men poured over the rail after him, and about him, making their way to the shore.

I gathered the slave into my arms, stepped to the rail, and leaped into the water.

It took only a few moments to wade ashore.

Two men, Pani, in their short, unusual robes, white, with red sashes, each with two swords thrust within the silk, one with the strange banner, waited for us by the trees.

"Where are we going?" I asked one of the Pani, he who did not carry the banner.

"Tarncamp," he said.

I noted that the ship had already departed.

Chapter Eleven

From the coast, it took four days, through the forest, to reach Tarncamp.

Although my burden was not heavy, it seemed to become so, as we trekked on, Ahn after Ahn. My arms began to ache. I was sweating. I became more and more conscious of the loop of rope on my neck, holding me in place. After a time, even the tunicked slaves began to stumble.

"Burdens down, rest," was the command we longed to hear.

We were not draft tharlarion, not pack kaiila!

But slaves often function as porters, as beasts of burden. This is particularly so within cities, where distances are short. It is not unusual to see burdened slaves in the vicinity of markets, docks, loading platforms, warehouses, granaries, and stables. We are cheaper than men. Among the peasants it is not unknown for us to struggle against our harness, dragging our master's plow. As the slave is owned, she, as any other animal, may be put to any purpose the master pleases. Indeed, some men enjoy treating us so, putting us to manual labor, even when there is no need. It is useful as a discipline, and, surely, it reminds us that we are slaves. And even lighter labors may serve this purpose. What slave has not scrubbed floors, naked, in shackles?

How weary I was, in my place, carrying my burden!

Surely it was not for this that I had been taught in the house to cook, clean, launder, and sew, to tie a tunic, to move with grace, to speak as a slave, to kneel, belly, lick, and kiss, to eat and drink from pans, to gratefully receive scraps from a master's hand, to apply cosmetics, to fetch a whip or slippers in my teeth, to bedeck myself with beads and armlets, to wear bells, to beg in a hundred ways, to present myself in chains, to please men in the furs.

"Burdens down, rest," we heard.

Gratefully I lowered my burden, and sank to my side, in the fallen leaves. As I lay, I could see, on the trunk of a nearby tree, a yellowish stain, at about what would be the eye level of a large man. I recalled that, once or twice before, not thinking about it, I had seen a similar stain. I supposed it might be a form of unusual moss, or some sort of parasitic growth.

"Kneel to be watered, and fed, pretty beasts," we heard.

That came from the front of the march, near the first of the tunicked slaves. I lay as I was, for it was not our turn.

Ahead of us, too, were the men.

I wondered what might be in the large boxes, borne by four men each, as a palanquin might be carried.

There was little mystery about the other burdens.

My legs ached.

"Kneel to be watered, and fed, pretty beasts," we heard, this time closer.

We of the rope coffle struggled to our knees, wearily, put our heads back, and each grasped her left wrist behind her back with her right hand.

In my turn the stem of the bota was thrust between my teeth, and I drew in, eagerly, gratefully, my ration of water. I then, a bit later, opened my mouth, widely, and a handful of slave gruel, or moist mush, was thrust in my mouth. One swallows it a tiny bit at a time, that one not choke. It is bland, and largely tasteless, but filling, for what one gets of it, and apparently nutritious. It was a far cry from the provenders I had been taught to prepare in the house, ranging from roasted, seasoned bosk and tarsk, and fresh plate breads, with honeys and butters, to frosted pastries and decadent, creamed sauces which, in some cities, were outlawed by sumptuary laws. For what it was worth, the free men with the small caravan did not seem much better off. The rations of Gorean warriors, in the field, I am told, are often austere. A small sack of grain, commonly Sa-Tarna, the Life Daughter, is often carried in the pack, or at one's belt. Two handfuls of this, the hands cupped together, may then be dampened in a spring, or stream, and eaten. The Pani are fond of rice. It is sometimes boiled in a helmet.

Each Ahn we stopped. At night the coffle rope was tied between two trees, and our hands were tied behind us.

I was puzzled why, in this lovely, lonely forest, with no one about, or I supposed no one was about, the men lit no fires. I wondered, too, how they found their way through the forest, as it seemed trackless. Certainly there were no signs that we were following a familiar path. I saw no sign, either, of anything resembling a compass, or other form of direction finder. There had been a compass on the ship, as I had seen it when on deck, when we were being aired. It was fastened on a pedestal between the two helmsmen. There was the sun, of course, whose progression could be marked through the canopy of foliage, often far above us. I had gathered that many ships had been voyaging to the north, for whatever reason. Perhaps there were many paths to our destination, which I took to be a camp of sort, Tarncamp. Again, I was puzzled how the men found their way through the forest. Doubtless some of those with us, who had been at the shore, were guides, and familiar with such things. I trusted we were not lost.

"Up, up, burdens!" called a fellow.

I lifted my burden, and stood, and was ready to move. It does not do to dally. The rope before me looped up to Eighteen, and, behind me, looped up to Forty-Three. I was taller than she, as Eighteen was taller than I. There were seventeen in our coffle. We would be distributed variously at Tarncamp.

Suddenly, briefly, we heard a succession of thunderous snapping noises from above the canopy, and we looked up, and leaves fluttered about us, and we were cast into a flight of shadows, as though swift, fierce, jagged clouds would blot out the sun, one following another, but these shadows were cast by no clouds. Something alive was above us! A shrill scream penetrated the canopy, and several of the slaves screamed. They understood, I took it, as I did not, what might be occurring. I could utter no sound, so startled, and terrified, I was. Girls looked wildly to one another. Then there was yet another shadow, and another sound like the cracking of suddenly tightened silk, by giants, and another scream, and another body had rushed above us. By such a scream, I supposed, might one announce the march of Ubars, or claim worlds.

"That is the drover," said a fellow.

"How many?" asked another.

"I counted twenty," said a fellow.

"Twenty-two," said another.

"They are ugly brutes," said a man.

"They are beautiful," said another.

"You may have them," said another.

"Keep them at their distance," laughed a man.

"Climb to their saddle," laughed another.

"Better to sup with larls," laughed another.

One of the men looked at me. I fear I could not but shudder.

"Tarns," he said to me. "They kill men. Men fly them."

I looked up, at the canopy. A leaf or two, late, dislodged, fluttered downward. They struck me on the shoulder, and fell to the side.

The men were kind to us, but there is always the lash. A slave does not forget that. She hopes to be pleasing. Here, on this world, women, at least if they were such as I, slave, found themselves in the order of nature. Here we belonged to men. Here men would have us as they wished, and do with us as they pleased.

Here, on this world, I discovered what I had long suspected on my former world, the meaning of my smaller, softer, so different body, its slightness and curves; here I found the explanation of a thousand dispositions, needs, and hopes I had been commanded to ignore or deny on my former world.

So here, on this world, men would have us as they wished, and do with us as they pleased, at least if we were slaves. I did not object; I was grateful, as I had not been on my former world; where there were true men, I knew I would be owned; where there were true men, I knew I belonged in a collar, and would be collared; I hoped only to be well-collared, and to please my master.

I thought of my former world.

How artificial, how contrived, and false now seemed that world. How hollow its lies and pretenses. How estranged from nature it was! Was nature so fearful that it must be denied, and betrayed? In whose interest was this treason? Was the biography of a world so terrible that gates must be barred against it? Were there not green fields, bracing winds, and a warm sun outside the gates? You can burn books; you cannot burn truth. Who is accountable for the tragic routes leading to misery and want, to unhappiness and deprivation? Whence the monstrous distortions which would turn an animal against itself, and teach it to suspect, repudiate, and lacerate its own being? Who spoke to their own advantage, and proclaimed as truths self-serving inventions, concealing imperatives and demands in the cloak of statements? Who was it who, so ill-constituted and envious, jealous of health and joy, so exploited the credulity of the innocent, honest, and trusting? Will most humans not believe whatever they are told, any of a thousand inconsistent, competitive fabrics, each proclaimed as the one and only truth?

I was grateful for the men, who had weapons. The forest was dark, lonely, and beautiful. It was particularly frightening at night. What can one do to defend oneself, if one is bound, and on a rope? One might as well be a tethered verr. Indeed, sometimes bound, tethered slaves are used as bait. Watches were kept, of course. Twice panthers had prowled about the camp's periphery. Happily, most carnivores, if young, if fresh in their skills and strength, if healthy, are unlikely to attack humans, as the human is not their natural prey. They may, of course, if they are starving, or feel their territory is threatened, attack a human. In any event, the human is an unusual quarry for an animal, and is seldom its first choice for prey. If it feels threatened, intruded upon, or hunted, of course, it can be extremely dangerous. The greatest danger to a human is usually an animal which is older, or in poor health, one which is unable to, or finds it difficult to, secure its more natural prey. To be sure, there is always the unusual animal. Too, once an animal, any animal, has fed on human, it will be likely, thereafter, to include it in its prey range.

"Straighten your body," said a fellow.

"Yes Master," I said.

"Not stiffly," he said, "lithely, gracefully!"

"Yes, Master," I said.

"Do you think you are a free woman?" he asked.

"No, Master," I said.

"You are kajira," he said.

"Yes, Master," I said.

"You are a barbarian, are you not?" he asked.

"Yes, Master," I said. I hoped not to be struck.

"You are no longer permitted to be ashamed of your body," he said.

"Yes, Master," I said.

"It is acceptable," he said.

"Thank you, Master," I said.

"It has been seen fit to be collared," he said.

"Yes, Master," I said.

"So be proud," he said.

"Yes, Master," I said.

"Besides," he said, "it is no longer your business."

"Master?" I asked.

"It is no longer yours," he said. "It belongs to your master. You must display it as your masters will have it, beautifully, shamelessly, brazenly, proudly, excitingly, vulnerably."

"Yes, Master," I said.

"And even if in the presence of free women," he said, "though it means the lash."

"Yes Master," I wept.

"Show them what it is to be a woman," he said.

"Yes, Master," I said.

He then, to my relief, stepped back.

But he continued then, and was joined by two others, to regard me. I kept my head up, my eyes straight ahead.

"A pretty beast," he said.

Yes, I thought, I am a beast, but, perhaps, a pretty one.

"As the others," said another.

"That is why they are here," said the other.

How they looked upon me!

How owned I felt then!

How owned I was!

I knew myself an animal, an owned animal.

That night, in the camp, bound, and on the rope, I squirmed in the leaves. I wept. My body flamed, each inch of it.

"Be still," said a coffle sister.

"She wants a master," said another.

"So do we all," said another.

"Are we to be sold, or distributed, in Tarncamp?" asked another.

"What does it matter?" whispered another.

I could see two of the three moons through the foliage above. A few yards away a guard was crouching, bracing himself on a spear. There was another elsewhere, somewhere. One could see occasional clouds drifting past, solitary, lonely, unhurried, above, in the night.

I recalled an incident, from my former world, which had occurred in an unlikely venue, the aisle of a large, crowded emporium, when I had been seen, and looked upon, and looked upon, though I was fully clothed, as a slave might be looked upon. Had that gaze not, as though mighty hands, parted and torn away my clothing, revealing, as though for a master's consideration, what had impermissibly dared to conceal itself within? I had sensed myself more than regarded; I had sensed myself considered, appraised.

How strange how a single moment, a chance encounter, can alter a consciousness and transform a life, reordering an existence and its meaning. Even then, I supposed, somewhere, there reposed an iron by which my thigh would be marked, chains which might encircle my limbs, collars which might enclasp my throat. Was there not, even then, a large, heavy, towering block waiting, somewhere, whose sawdust my bare feet might tread, from which I might be vended?

I stirred, bound.

I recalled how I had lain at his feet, supine, stripped and tied, hand and foot, looking up at him, in something like a warehouse.

I had seen him but once more, through the bars of an exposition cage, prior to my sale, in a place called Brundisium.

I had no doubt it was he who had brought me to Gor, to bondage, and the sales block. I supposed I should have hated him, but instead I knew, rather, I wanted his collar.

Surely he had seen me as a slave.

Would that he had seen me as his slave!

He had summoned me to the bars of the exposition cage, and looked upon me, but had then dismissed me, casually, as the slave I was.

That night I had been sold.

I had not seen him since.

I would never see him again.

One of the girls had said I wanted a master. That was doubtless true. What slave does not long for her master? And what man does not long for his slave?

I had begun to sense, frequently now, stirrings in my belly, discomforts which I feared might grow intolerable and insupportable. How fearful, I suspected, are the needs of a female slave, and how helpless she is in their grasp. Surely I must resist the growing of slave fires within me! How merciless are the men to us! And how amused they are at what they have done to us. Was it not better to be a free woman of ice, refined and composed, at ease with her body, untroubled, inert, and serene? What is it about the collar, and finding oneself owned, as a beast is owned, which so transforms us, which puts us so piteously and helplessly at the feet of masters? From the school I could remember the moans and cries, the scratchings and beggings, of slaves. I must never let myself suffer so, must never permit myself to become no more than the negligible, pleading toy of an imperious brute. But, resist it as I could, and dread it as I might, I feared it could be done with me, and would be done with me. I was kajira! But, I wondered, are free women, really, so different? How many, I wondered, in their loneliness, sob and twist within their coverlets, moan, and pummel their silken, tear-dampened pillows with frustration?

It was late.

In the house I had been taught something of the pleasing of men, and the guards, under supervision, as is customary, had tried me out, testing me, and seemed pleased with my responsiveness, rudimentary and incipient though it might have been. The last time I had begged him not to leave me, but he had thrust me from him, laughing. Certainly by the time I reached the block, I had some understanding of what I was, and what would be expected of me. The guards in the dungeon were more merciful, and I, and the others, sometimes vied to please them.

I twisted about in the leaves, under the moons.

Surely my body was telling me of my need of a master. I supposed, in time, it would beg for a master.

I remembered one man beyond the others, beyond all others. But he had not put me to his pleasure.

How foolish that a girl should desire a certain master, that there should be one to whose feet she most desired to press her lips.

Does she not know she is a mere slave, an object, a utensil for a male's pleasure, for any male's pleasure?

I would never see him again.

In the exposition cage I had been dismissed. We were now somewhere, far to the north. Brundisium was far behind us. I did not know our destination, save that it was spoken of as Tarncamp.

I would never see him again.

I wept, an unwanted, neglected, barbarian slave.

I pulled a little at the ropes. It was meaningless, of course. I had been tied by a Gorean male. I was helpless, utterly so.

I heard the guard being changed, and then I fell asleep.

Chapter Twelve

I had, of course, put the thought of her from me, or, at least, intended to do so. Surely the only reason I had taken ship north was from curiosity, or an intriguing sense of possible adventure. Too, I had, somehow, not made my way to Daphne, of the farther islands, to rendezvous with one of the sky ships. I trusted it had made its departure successfully. If there is a blockade, it seems porous. It is almost as though the attention of the guardians of the clouds, if they exist, is intermittent, or differs in its severity, from time to time. It is pleasant, of course, to scout the offerings of the slave world, to consider them, and make selections, limited, of course, by the number of capsules in the slave hold. How innocent they are, and how naive, and unsuspecting. Some are vain, pretty little things. Some are unusually beautiful, and sophisticated. It is hard to be sophisticated, of course, when one is kneeling, head down, and one's throat is clasped in the slave band. I suppose that many never think of the block, though I am not sure of this, or what, turned about and exhibited, they might bring. I suppose few consider themselves as they might be, as a belonging, suitably marked, fittingly collared, though it is hard to be sure of this, as they are obviously slaves. Perhaps, being slaves, they consider such matters frequently. It is hard to know. In any event, it is pleasant to pick slave fruit, to net shapely slave beasts, and bring them to market. We commonly veil and protect our free women. Those of the slave world display them for our assessment, and acquisition. Perhaps if they realized they were slaves, they would collar them themselves, and then protect them better. It is hard to know. At any rate, I had surely not come north to track a slave, a meaningless slut, even a barbarian. That would be unthinkable. She was nothing to me. Who would want her? She was cheap goods. She had not even sold for a full tarsk. Probably I had come north for the coin, or for curiosity, or, at least, for adventure. Certainly not for a slave. Perhaps she was not even here, and, if not, what would it matter, and who would find that of interest? Why, I wondered, had I signed articles, to ply the trade in such a far place, again and again. What had I hoped to find? Why, I wondered, now, was I unconcerned, even indifferent to the matter, that my unaccountable dalliance in Brundisium had resulted in my failure to keep the rendezvous on Daphne? Usually I am reliable, even scrupulous, in such matters. One could always, again, of course, later, consider the perusal of the slave orchards, the culling of the far slave herds. Undoubtedly I would do so. There are pleasant aspects to the work, and it pays well.

But perhaps I would not do so.

I did not know.

I had seen no sign of her in Tarncamp.

I wondered if she were here. What did it matter?

Chapter Thirteen

The Pani seldom touch us, for we are inferior. I am not even sure that they respect their mercenaries, and laborers.

On the fourth day, after the shore of Thassa, we reached the large, sprawling, extensive set of buildings and shops called Tarncamp. I now wore a Tarncamp collar. To my joy I was cast a tunic which I eagerly donned. It was the first I had worn since the house. I suppose it scarcely rates the appellation of a garment, but it is precious to us. As animals we need not be permitted clothing, but, I am informed, many cities recommend the clothing of slaves in public, assuming that the clothing makes it clear that we are slaves, which injunction the masters see to, to their satisfaction. Presumably that we are attired, after a fashion, is to spare the sensibilities of free women and, perhaps, to reduce, to some extent, the accostings, encounters, provocations, and such, which might be attendant on the public exhibition of wholly bared, collared properties. To be sure, slaves, particularly formerly free Gorean women, are sometimes publicly paraded naked, saving for their locked neck bands, that they may the better understand that they are now slaves. Too, this is sometimes done for a slave who has in some way failed to be fully pleasing. We try to be fully pleasing. And one, after a time, desires to be found fully pleasing. One hopes to be a pleasing, desired slave. It is a warm, precious, beautiful thing to be. I, and the others of my rope, had been given brief, common tunics. As most such tunics, these were sleeveless and, of course, lacked a nether closure. The slave is to understand herself as always available to the master. The tunics were brown, of cheap rep-cloth. They were not wrap-around tunics, nor the sort with a disrobing loop at the left shoulder, for the convenience of a right-handed master. These slipped over the head. This did not really afford an impediment to our use, as they might be easily thrust up to our waist. I think there is little doubt that the slave tunic, in its variations, is an attractive, provocative garment. How can a woman be displayed more attractively, or be made more aware of her womanhood, than being placed in the garment of a slave? It is sometimes thought that in such a garment a woman is more naked than naked, at least in the sense that it leaves few of her charms to the imagination, invites attention, and suggests the pleasures that might await its removal. Still we were pleased, extremely pleased, that the masters had seen fit to clothe us, though, of course, fittingly, as slaves.

Shortly after having arrived at Tarncamp, after our collaring, and before we were given tunics, we were put in examination position, standing, feet spread, head back, hands clasped behind the back of our head. Aligned so, we were examined, measured, and, I fear, assessed, and also, I gather, registered in some way, as records were kept.

I, and some of the others, sometimes gasped, or whimpered, even moaned, in the course of our examination.

"Oh," I had said, suddenly. "Oh!" I had cried.

My hips had jerked. This was inadvertent. I could not help the response of my body. I had half bent over at the waist. I had almost freed my hands from the clasping behind the back of my head. Fortunately I had not done so. Otherwise I might have been lashed.

"Straighten your body," I was told. "Hold position."

"Yes, Master," I had said.

Then again my head was up, and back. Tears formed in my eyes. Again I could see little but clouds, and the blue sky. I was aware of the men about.

"How is she?" asked the fellow who stood back a bit, he who held the board, who was taking notes.

"Are you a new slave?" asked he who was my examiner, who had handled me as a slave may be handled.

"Yes, Master," I had said.

I had lost track of time, and did not understand the calendar of my masters. In my reckoning, it had been something like five or six weeks since I had been brought to this strange, fresh, unusual, beautiful world, brought as a slave.

"For a new slave, then, excellent," said my examiner.

"Good," said the fellow with the board, the marking stick.

I wanted to beg him, he closest to me, he who had touched me, as an owner of women touches women, to be again touched, but I dared not do so. I had not been given permission to speak.

"She has been well selected," said a fellow.

"They all are," commented another.

I later, in my turn, was told I might kneel, which I gratefully did. How natural it now seemed to me to kneel before a free male! It now seemed to me right that I should be so positioned. Before such men I, a slave, belonged so. I would have been considerably uneasy, even frightened, to be standing in his presence. How presumptuous, how insolent, how perilous that would have been! On my world, I had occasionally, though very, very seldom, felt an inclination to kneel before a man, one man or another, to assume before him this appropriate posture of respect and submission, appropriate for a female before a male, but, of course, I had not done so. I doubted if the men of my former world would even have understood this. Perhaps, confused, stammering, embarrassed, they would have chidingly hastened me to my feet, rather than commanding me, one submitted, to minister to theirs. Surely I remembered one man, one man encountered on my former world, though a man not of that world, one encountered in the aisle of a large emporium, before whom, startled, I could barely stand, and before whom I had felt I should kneel, head down, submitting myself to his survey and power, his authority, his manhood, but I had not done so. I had turned about, terrified, and fled. Later I had looked up at him, naked, on my back, bound hand and foot. It seems, after all, that I had been found of interest, if only as a slave, a property, a possession, a toy. In any event, there seemed few men of my former world before whom one would have been tempted to kneel, before whom it would have seemed appropriate to kneel. But then I had not realized at that time that such men as Goreans could exist. Perhaps they were such as men might once have been, on my old world, but no longer were. In any event I knew that I, at least as a slave, belonged at their feet. It was my place. They understood this, and I did, as well. It was reassuring to be so before them. I was then where I belonged.

I looked up at him, the free male.

"You have not been long in the collar," he said.

"No, Master," I said.

"You are a barbarian," he said.

"Yes, Master," I said.

"You do not have a name," he said.

"No, Master," I said.

I was as yet an unnamed animal. My name would be decided upon, and placed on me, by the free.

"How have you been known?" he asked.

"My lot number, from a market in Brundisium," I said, "was 119."

"A slave should have a name," he said.

"It will be as masters wish," I said.

"Numbers are not sensual," he said. "A female slave should have a female name, and one which makes clear that she is a slave."

"As masters wish," I said.

"Were you a slave on your former world?" he asked.

When you are a female kneeling before a male, the dominance hierarchy is quite clear, even, I suppose, if you are a free woman. It is certainly clear when you are a slave. I understand that a free woman is forced to kneel naked before a man, before she is collared.

"No," I said.

"'No'?" he said.

"I was not marked and collared," I said.

"An oversight," he said.

"Perhaps," I said.

"'Perhaps'?" he said.

"Yes, Master, an oversight, Master," I said.

"But the matter is remedied here," he said.

"Yes, Master," I said.

Surely I had known, often enough, on my former world,

despite its commands and injunctions, from my casual, unguarded thoughts, from my fantasies, and my dreams, from my longings, from my dispositions, hopes, and needs, from my yearnings, from what I had wanted from men, their force and ownership, from how I had wanted to submit myself, wholly, from my desire to be ruled by a master, to belong to him, and serve him, a vulnerable, helpless, unquestioning chattel, that I was, at least in my heart, a slave.

Now I was kneeling, my thigh marked, my throat enclasped in the collar.

"You had a name, did you not, on your barbarian world?"

"Yes, Master," I said.

"What was it?" he asked.

"Margaret Alyssa Cameron," I said.

"'Mar-gar-ret-a-liss-a-cam-er-ron',"" he said, slowly.

I thought it well to remain silent. Actually I did not think he had done badly. I was not sure I could repeat, or easily repeat, for example, a series of nine meaningless noises.

"Barbarian names are often complex," he said.

"Yes, Master," I said.

"Did you know that such names are commonly found in primitive groups, innocent of civilization?"

"No, Master," I said.

"Surely you recognized them as barbarisms," he said.

"I had not thought of it," I said.

"Of course not," he said. "You are a barbarian."

"Yes, Master," I said.

"Such a name will not do," he said.

I knew that slave names were commonly simple, as one would expect, as they are the names for animals. Common slave names, at least on the continent, were such as Tula, Bina, Lana, Leila, Lita, and such. Commonly, too, the slave has but a single name, but she may be more clearly specified as, say, Tula, the slave of Flavius, of such and such a street or district. Barbarian slaves are commonly given barbarian names, for example, Amanda, Amber, April, Beryl, Ethel, Tracy, Heather, Rose, Vivian, Victoria, Jocelyn, Stephanie, and such. Such names will mark her as barbarian, and suggest that she is born for the collar, as opposed to a Gorean woman of caste and Home Stone, and may be treated accordingly. Such names are apparently stimulatory to many Gorean males. Many Goreans delight in the mastery of barbarians. Certainly they well teach us our collars. Sometimes a barbarian name is placed on a Gorean female slave as a punishment name, to humiliate and humble her, to inform her that she is, in the master's view, no more than a barbarian, and may expect to be treated accordingly. I find it difficult, sometimes, to understand the Gorean view in these matters. How is it that there is such a difference between the free woman and the slave, and then, again, that there is no difference? A radical distinction is drawn between the Gorean free woman, with caste and Home Stone, and the slave. The free woman is lofty and noble; she is esteemed, exalted, and honored; she is respected and shown great deference. On the other hand if she, usually a capture from a foreign city, falls slave all that is behind her, and she finds herself no more than another piece of vendible collar meat, auctioned off a block as one might auction a tarsk from the pens. Moreover, many Gorean men divide women into those who are slaves with collars and those who are slaves but not yet collared. Perhaps the distinction is that between culture and biology. In any event, I dare speak only for myself. I had little doubt that I was a slave, that I wanted to be a slave, and that I could be happy only as a slave, that I could be fulfilled only as my master's slave. Some women wish to serve and love, to submit themselves selflessly, wholly, and helplessly. We are the slaves of our masters. And culturally, in my case, I encountered no problems in this respect. I was something ingredient in the culture, expected in the culture, approved in the culture, and desired in the culture. Accordingly, culturally, I was free to be what I was and wanted to be. I had no dilemma, for I was collared. As far as I can determine the men and women of Earth, my former world, and those of Gor are clearly of the same species. Indeed, legend has it that humans, some humans, were brought here long ago from my former world by unusual beings. They are often spoken of, in whispers, as Priest-Kings. I suppose this is a myth of some sort, but, myth or not, an explanation of some sort would seem to be required. Perhaps ancient humans once possessed an advanced technology, which was somehow lost. One has heard of Mu, Atlantis, and such places. In any event, it seems clear that the human female, whether Gorean or not, tends to be regarded by many Gorean men as the natural property of males. To be sure, this surmise, or conviction, is seldom expressed openly to Gorean women, particularly to those of station, high caste, and such. In any event, once collared, there would seem little to choose between us. We both learn our collars quickly. The Gorean woman may have an advantage in some ways, for she is familiar with the culture; indeed, she may have owned her own slaves, male or female. She is likely to better realize, then, as a woman of my world might not, the nature of female bondage, and what is expected of the female slave. It would seldom occur to a Gorean woman, once enslaved, to dare to be less than fully pleasing to her master. Barbarians, of course, may be less aware of this, at least at first. It is, however, quickly taught to us.

"We will need a barbarian name for you," he said, "as you are a barbarian. It would not do to waste a fine Gorean name on you."

I was silent.

"The name must be short, and simple, an obvious slave name, and one that makes clear that you are without significance or importance, that you are a mere, negligible, chattel. Yet, we want the name to be sexually stimulatory, one which will elicit masculine interest, and aggression. We want it, in effect, to say, 'Here is a helpless, vulnerable slave, is she not lovely, is she not exciting, do with her as you will.' We want it to suggest that you will be helpless and pleasant at the end of chain, or attractive, bound helplessly, a nicely tethered love bundle, in the furs. Sometimes barbarians are placed in unusually revealing tunics. Their masters often like to show them off, and help them to keep in mind that they are slaves. They do nicely on leashes."

"Yes, Master," I said.

I hoped I might stand, walk, kneel, lie, or writhe well on my leash. How natural that animals be leashed!

"Position!" he snapped.

Instantly, reflexively, I went to position, kneeling back on my heels, back straight, head up, hands palm down on thighs, looking forward, not meeting his eyes, knees spread.

My body must have reacted, somehow, when I had thought of myself on a leash.

I was now, again, in position.

How could a woman be more presented as a slave? Seeing a woman so positioned, what else could she be?

Strangely, the thought crossed my mind of myself, naked, on my former world, in the aisle of the great store, on a master's leash, and then, as he paused, kneeling at his thigh, head down, docilely. Others, moving about, fully clothed, if they noticed me, would have recognized me as a slave. I wondered if such might one day occur on my former world, that sort of thing. Clearly cultural adjustments would have taken place. Such scenes are not unprecedented on Gor, though commonly the slave would have been tunicked, revealingly, and scantily, of course, as would be appropriate for her condition and status.

The fellow backed away from me, and surveyed me, and spoke, over his shoulder, to his fellows, of which there were two, one of whom was keeping the notes, or records.

"What do you think?" he asked.

"Nice," said the fellow who was not keeping the notes, or records.

I held position, gracefully, but determinedly. It is not pleasant to be cuffed, or switched. And it is less pleasant to be put under the lash.

"What is she?" asked he who had been addressing me, of the fellow with the board, the marking stick, the papers, the notes, and such. To that fellow he seemed to defer.

"A Laura," said the fellow with the papers, and such.

"You are Laura," said the fellow who had been addressing me. "What is your name?"

"Laura," I said, "if it pleases Master."

He then went to the next girl in line. I remained in position. I had been named. I was Laura.

Chapter Fourteen

The ax bit the wood.

"Good stroke," said Tyrtaios. "Many would take three to go that deep."

"These logs," I said, "are not being dressed."

"Sawyers are elsewhere," said Tyrtaios. "They will see to the shaping and fitting, the beams and planking."

The heavy hauling was done in sturdy wagons, which left Tarncamp, and moved east by means of a narrow path through the forest. These wagons were drawn by draft tharlarion.

"At Shipcamp," I said. I had not been there.

"Perhaps," said Tyrtaios.

"Some," I said, "say these are for a fort of wood."

"In a way," he said.

"We are far from the sea," I said.

"Some days," he said.

I struck the trunk, again. The shock moves through one's whole body. After a time one's body aches. One longs for the night. I had not come north for the service of a woodsman. Nor had many others, if any. Why, I wondered, had I come north? Yes, I thought, two golden staters, adventure, and what else was to be done? Surely there could be no other reason. There was much discontent in the camp. The wood of the Tur tree is closely grained. It is much easier to fell Needle Trees. Tharlarion, by means of tackle, would draw the logs to a clearing, where, by arranged hoists and pulleys, by hooks and counterweights, they would be lifted to the wagon beds. When it rained it took double teams of tharlarion to draw the wagons, which were often mired, sunk to the axles. I had occasionally been a member of work parties, put to the east road, to repair it for passage. But they had not let us too far down the road. Perhaps work parties came from another direction, to repair the more eastern stretches of the road. As far as I knew, they were not permitted far enough west to reach Tarncamp.

"I think you know more than you say," I said.

"One must consider carefully those in whom one confides," he said.

"True," I said.

"There is a river," I said.

"The Alexandra," he said.

"You are building a fort at its head waters, for trading inland?" I asked. "There is a company? You will then barge furs down river to Thassa?"

"Perhaps," he said.

Again I struck the trunk.

Some yards away four fellows, two on each handle, were working with a large, two-handled, iron toothed saw. It is a heavy device. One saw the sawdust scatter with each clear motion of the blade. Sometimes the blade would be arrested in the wood.

I glanced at them. Then I said to Tyrtaios. "They cannot hear us," I said.

"I suppose not," he said.

"I am sure you have been to the other camp, Shipcamp," I said. "It is said you have been even to the pavilion of Lord Okimoto."

"Who said that?" he asked.

"One hears things," I said.

"One pays one's respects," he said.

Lord Okimoto was a lord, or daimyo, of the Pani, whose headquarters were at Shipcamp. At Tarncamp, the lord, or daimyo, was a Lord Nishida. I had seen Lord Nishida about, commonly on tours of inspection. He was usually accompanied by Pani warriors, in their short robes, with the two swords, their hair pulled back and knotted behind the head. In his retinue, as well, were some fellows of the sort who had been recruited in Brundisium. It was by means of some of these that he usually communicated with the common mercenaries. There seemed to be formalities involved here with which I was unfamiliar, and even amongst the Pani themselves. I knew little or nothing of the other daimyo, Lord Okimoto. I had gathered that he had some sort of precedence and that Lord Nishida was expected to defer to him. Tyrtaios, at least, it seemed, had been as far as Shipcamp. Beyond the training area, Pani guards regulated traffic on the east road.

"I do not see why armsmen, or so many, were brought here for this work," I said. "It is not work for armsmen, and you have far more than would be required to garrison a trade fort and police traffic on a river."

"It would seem so," said Tyrtaios.

"A great deal of timber has been moved eastward," I said, "perhaps more than would be needed for a local trade fort, or the construction of barges."

"Perhaps," said Tyrtaios.

"One does not enlist a small army without purpose," I said.

"Perhaps there is a purpose," he said.

"I know of no cities in the vicinity," I said, "no walls to raze, no palaces to pillage, no gold to seize, no trade routes to command, no women to collar."

"Perhaps elsewhere," he said.

"This is a wilderness," I said.

"That is why we are here," he said.

"Some venture, some project, is concealed here," I said.

"Obviously," he said.

I struck the trunk angrily, fiercely, three more times. Then I turned to face him. "What venture, what project?" I asked.

"I know little more than you," he said.

"But more," I said.

"Yes," he said.

"You stand high," I said. "It is said you have been admitted even to the pavilion of Lord Okimoto."

He shrugged.

"You were known in Brundisium," I said. "You were deeply involved in the recruiting. Seemingly you were feared. You gave me fee."

"Two golden staters," he said.

"High wages for a woodsman," I said.

"I trust," he said, "the staters will not prove to have been poorly invested."

"I have received nothing more," I said.

"Nor have the others," he said, "as yet."

"And where is the wealth, the silver, the jewels, the women, the gold?" I asked.

"Not here," he said.

"Where?" I asked.

"Elsewhere," he said.

"Stand clear," I said.

He moved to the side.

"Beware," I called, to any about.

Four more strokes, and there was a gross splintering, a breakage of wood, and the tree fell crashing to the earth, half obscured by a rising cloud of dust and leaping, shimmering leaves.

"You recruited me," I said to Tyrtaios.

"I think you may prove useful," he said.

"How so, more than another?" I asked.

"You have skills," he said.

"Many could best me in the songs of steel," I said.

"I do not think so many," he said. "I could, Tarl Cabot, the commander of the tarn cavalry could, and doubtless several others, but not so many."

I knew little of the tarn cavalry, though it had been formed, and was still being trained, in the vicinity. It did not seem to me that a large number of tarns would be necessary in patrolling a river, certainly not a cavalry of such.

"Two staters of gold," I said, "is a high price for one sword."

"Yes," he said.

"Therefore," I said, "more is involved."

"Of course," he said.

"This is the first time here," I said, "that you have seen fit to seek me out."

"I had not forgotten you," he said.

"What is my fee intended to purchase?" I asked.

"A quick eye, a swift hand, of course," he said.

"But more," I said.

"Of course," he said.

"My caste has something to do with these matters," I said.

"Yours, and perhaps some others," he said.

"I am a mere Merchant," I said.

"A Slaver," he said.

"A Merchant," I said.

"I suppose," said he, "it is merely a matter of the goods, of one sort or another, with which one deals."

"Surely," I said.

"But," said he, " I would suppose the acquisition of some goods is more perilous than the acquisition of others, and that some goods are more pleasant, once acquired, to handle, enjoy, manage, process, and sell, than others."

"Doubtless," I said.

"One supposes," he said, "one might expect courage from one of such a caste, perhaps a willingness, under certain conditions, to accept risks, perhaps serious risks, if the end in view might justify such an acceptance. One supposes one of such a caste must be able to plan, to follow through with plans, or, if it seemed wise, to depart from a plan, even suddenly, to change or alter plans, even to withdraw, and plan anew, that one such must be not only bold, but subtle and shrewd, that one such must understand the value of deception, of surprise, of patience, of discretion, of secrecy."

"Perhaps you would care to speak to me," I said.

"I may be here for such a purpose," he said.

"So, speak," I said.

"We expect loyalty," he said.

"'We'?" I asked.

"Yes," he said.

"I have taken fee," I said.

"And is not gold the best guarantor of fidelity?"

"Commonly," I said.

"And of much else," he said.

"Often," I said.

"It is our expectation," he said, "that you can guard a confidence, and might well discharge tasks to which you might be assigned."

"Perhaps," I said.

"And without demur," said he, "without requesting, or demanding, reasons."

"Perhaps," I said.

"A Merchant," said he, "is one concerned with profit."

"Commonly," I said.

"And there may be much profit," he said.

"Excellent," I said.

"I trust, of course," he said, "that you are not a fool, one who harkens to myths and lies."

"Myths and lies?" I said.

"For example," he said, "those of honor."

"It is my hope," I said, "that I am not a fool."

"You are familiar with the wands," he said, "those about the perimeter of the camp."

"Of course," I said. "Their purpose was made clear to us, on the beach, and, later, in the camp."

These were slender wands, a yard or so in height, planted in the soil, with a bit of cloth tied upon them. They occurred every several yards, or so. One was not permitted, without authorization, and accompaniment, to venture beyond the wands. The perimeter was patrolled by larls, usually released at night, which were trained to track, seek out, and fall upon any who might be so foolish or unwary as to have left the camp without authorization or accompaniment. The beasts responded to certain signals associated with food, which signals were changed from time to time. One was reasonably safe if one knew the signals. The beasts were occasionally brought in, even at night, their normal release time, if lanes were to be opened, for one reason or another. To be sure, few knew when the larls were to be released, whether during the day or at night, though, as suggested, the night release was more common, probably because desertions took place most frequently under the cover of darkness. Whereas I had heard them in the forest, on our column's march to Tarncamp, I had not seen them. In any event, as far as I knew, our column had not been threatened. To be sure, we had kept to a particular trail, one, I had gathered, of several, and had been approaching, not attempting to exit, Tarncamp.

"My superior," he said, "is troubled by one matter."

"Who is your superior?" I asked.

"It is not necessary that you know," he said.

"Lord Okimoto?" I asked.

"Perhaps," he said, "perhaps not."

"You came to speak," I said.

"My superior," he said, "has had you watched."

"And perhaps others are watched, as well?" I said.

"Doubtless," he said.

"And you amongst them?" I ventured.

"I would suppose so," he said.

Many are the strands of intrigue, and a tremor in one strand, as in the web of the urt spider, is often registered in several others. Not unoften he who presumes himself a spy, secure in station and privileged in access, reporting upon others, is himself under suspicion. Is it not often the case that the first is concerned with the second, and the second with the third, and the third with the first, and in the center of all this, attending to the strands, rather like the urt spider itself, there is something which observes and waits. But here the web is invisible, and what observes and waits is unseen.

"Should I be flattered," I asked, "that I might be watched?"

"That you are watched more than others?" he said.

"Yes," I said. I knew the camp was tense. The men brought here were mostly mercenaries, strong, rough men, many of whom were fugitives from the forces which had garrisoned and exploited Ar. They expected, and were hungry for, the prizes of war. Among them, too, were thieves, brigands, and cutthroats, some of whose names and descriptions adorned the public boards in more than one city. Some of the higher sort had been collaborators in Ar, who had fled the city to avoid impalement. Several had mocked and forsworn Home Stones. Such men were dangerous. They had not come to the wilderness to weary themselves with prolonged, arduous tasks. In almost every case, it had been supposed that the silver stater which had brought them north was the harbinger of others to follow. But none had followed. There was much discontent in the camp. A weapon unsheathed by silver, when the silver is gone, remains unsheathed, and dangerous. Squabbles were frequent, over gambling, and slaves. Some had attacked Pani warriors, and had fared badly. I had heard of several desertions. Perhaps some were successful, but the remains of bodies had been frequently dragged to the camp. The jaws of more than one larl, returning to its housing in the morning, had been stained, dark with matted, dried blood. Some days ago there had been a failed attempt on the life of Lord Nishida, which attempt had been shortly followed by a presumably coordinated, large-scale attack on the camp, one beaten away, on the ground, by Pani and mercenaries, and in the air, by Lord Nishida's tarn cavalry, commanded by the tarnsman, Tarl Cabot. I knew him only by reputation. His relationship to the Pani seemed obscure. It was said his sword was quick and his temper short. I supposed him an able officer. It was said some men would risk their life to serve under him. This made little sense to me. He was, of course, a tarnsman. Few men are such. Few dare the tarn, and, of those, many but once. It had become clear, after the attack, that this wilderness was not only a remote, miserable, dangerous venue in which we, far from civilization, were for most practical purposes incarcerated, and, under discipline, were put to manual tasks befitting the lower castes, but was, in addition, somehow involved in a project of such a nature that serious, determined forces were aligned against us, forces willing to destroy us and our work altogether. We not only did not like where we were and what we were doing, but we were at risk, as well, for no reason we understood, from the hostility of apparently numerous, formidable, skilled foes. We were in jeopardy, and knew not why. We knew not even what we were about. Two fellows had attempted to incite mutiny. They had been crucified. I had not fought in the attack on the camp, as I, with several others, in a work party, had been better than four pasangs from the camp, improving the east road, that allegedly leading to "Shipcamp," presumably named for the barges being constructed there to descend the Alexandra to the coast.

"You have scouted the wands too frequently," he said. "Perhaps you contemplate desertion."

"No," I said.

"Why do you remain?" he asked.

"Where there are two golden staters," I said, "perhaps there are more."

"Not for having taken fee, then, not for honor?" he asked.

"I fear there is little honor in this camp," I said, "little here but the hope of gain, and the fear of the forest, and of death."

"Things will change," he said, "before ice closes the Alexandra."

"I do not understand," I said.

"Much begins here," he said.

"But is not to end here," I said.

"Why do you frequent the wands?" he asked.

"Perhaps to prevent the escape of others," I said.

"The Pani will attend to that," he said, "and the beasts."

"Might I not be rewarded," I asked, "if I brought back, say, a fugitive slave?"

"The slaves are not stupid," he said. "If they were, they would not have been collared."

"Perhaps one," I said, "even one of intelligence, might not realize the impossibility of escape."

"Only a barbarian might be so naive," he said.

"A barbarian, then," I said.

"Female, marked, collared, half-naked, clad kajir?" he said.

"A possibility," I said.

"More likely she would be stolen," he said.

I supposed that so. There was, in effect, no escape for a female slave. Female slaves, recaptured, are commonly, as a matter of civility, returned to their masters for discipline. Some are doubtless picked up by others, to be sold or subjected to an even harsher slavery, as they were apprehended fugitives. There is, in effect, given the culture, nowhere to escape. It would be much the same with a strayed kaiila. The alternatives are not bondage or freedom, but what collar will be worn. Some slaves are tracked by sleen. This can be very unpleasant, particularly if she cannot reach the waiting cage in time.

"To be sure," said Tyrtaios, "such a one might manage to pass the wands."

"True," I said. And then, one supposes, they would fall to the larls, or forest panthers, or forest sleen. They might even intrude inadvertently into the territory of a shaggy forest bosk, and be trampled or gored. Perhaps some might be apprehended by Panther Girls, and exposed on the coast, bound provocatively to stakes, to be sold to the crews of passing ships. But many, too, I supposed, might perish in the forest, due to the severity of elements, the scarcity of food.

"My superior," he said, "would not consider seriously that

your frequenting of the perimeters might be so generously and eccentrically motivated."

"I like to be alone," I said, "away from the camp."

"Who would you expect to meet at the wands?" he asked.

"No one," I said.

"If you were another," he said, "you would have been killed by now."

"But I have been spared," I said.

I myself was not fully clear why I spent the time I did, not that it was that much, in the vicinity of the wands. It was good to know the land, and good to be alone, sometimes, and good, sometimes, to have time to think. And surely no one, even a barbarian, would be foolish enough to approach, let alone linger by, the wands. Certainly, in such a place, she would be in great jeopardy. Too, the camp was large, and the perimeter considerable in extent. The chances of encountering a single slave at a given time at a given point would be minimal, at best. But I had searched the camp, insofar as it was practical, and found no trace of a particular, attractive beast, even chained on her mat in one of the slave houses, not that I was interested in her, for she was no more than another course, or serving, of collar meat, though perhaps a rather nice morsel of such. I did frequent the slave houses, from time to time, however, as the mat slaves were often changed, not, of course, to look for her, which would have been absurd, but as a matter of idle curiosity. Who knew what might be found there? Might the offerings not be refreshed occasionally? Too, a slave was not infrequently bought off her chain. And then she would be replaced with another. Who knew what new morsel might be found chained there, illuminated in the light of the candle, lifted in its holder? Perhaps something interesting. Who knew? When I would venture to the slave house I would leave Asperiche behind in the hut, bound hand and foot. Such things are good for a woman, as it reminds them that they are women, that they are the properties of men, and that it will be done with them precisely as men please. In passing, one might mention that the offerings in the slave house were often flavored with former free women of Ar, often once of high caste, importance, power, and wealth. These were frequently fugitives from Ar, traitors, profiteers, collaborators, and such, many escaped from the proscription lists. Many had fallen slave following their flight from the city, females alone and defenseless in the fields, and many had purchased their conduct from the city from escaping mercenaries, at the cost of the collar itself, mercenaries unwilling to be burdened by free women. Accordingly, now, in Tarncamp, many a lowly fellow, who might have never laid eyes on one of these jewels of glorious Ar, who knew her only by reputation, who might have been beaten for lingering in the vicinity of a particular tower in which she resided, who might have been blinded for daring to part the curtains of her closed palanquin, could now find several such women on the end of a chain in the slave house, as naked and accessible as a common paga slut. Too, they learned their collars quickly, not that they were given much choice in the matter. There was soon no difference between them, and other women, at least those in collars. I supposed it was pleasant for some fellows to put such women to use, hitherto so far above them, to have her gasping, moaning, thrashing, and begging, and, as he saw fit to leave, to have her plead with him to linger, if but for a moment. Such women had now learned there was more to life than raiment and jewels; there was also the collar and the touch of a master. Some men, and I muchly disapprove of this, would occasionally bring such a helpless slave to the brink of ecstasy, and then leave, denying her the pathetically beseeched release for which every nerve in her body begged. This, I think, is cruel. Could they not forget the past, and realize that the lovely, aroused, tethered beast at their disposal is now only another slave? And one supposes, as well, that many of these women, escaped from proscription lists, and perhaps wanted in Ar, were grateful for the opportunity to slip unnoticed into the obscurity of bondage, of becoming only another negligible, vendible object. And, of course, as their masters would see to it, they would eventually become, as other slaves, the helpless prisoners of slave fires.

"It is not only the matter of the wands," he said. "You scout about too much in the camp."

"Oh?" I said.

"You ask few questions," he said, "but you look about a great deal. I think there are few who know these premises as well. Pani notice such things."

"Apparently not only Pani," I said.

"It is supposed," he said, "that you are mapping the camp, the training area, the east road, perhaps to convey a sense to others of defenses, armories, supplies, the rounds of guards, and such."

"I had not thought of such things," I said.

"Matters to be confided to others, say, at the wands," he said.

"I see," I said.

"So," said he, "you understand the concern of my superior."

"So," I asked, "why have I not been killed?"

"I think you have some other concern," he said.

"What could that be?" I asked.

"I do not think, now," he said, "that your prime motivation was pay, that you came north for gold, or gold alone."

"Oh?" I said.

"Your behavior suggests," he said, "that you are searching for something, something which, to your frustration, you have not found."

"That is an interesting thought," I said.

"Someone has come north," he said, "perhaps to escape you, a debtor, perhaps, or perhaps an enemy, or someone who has information you much desire."

"Perhaps," I said.

"But perhaps he is not here."

"Perhaps it is a she," I suggested.

"There are no free women in camp," he said.

"Some," I said, "are with the Pani, Pani women."

He smiled.

"They are sedately clothed," I said. Their robes were colorful and narrow. They moved with short, delicate steps. "One can scarcely detect their slippers."

"They have been sold," he said, "usually as children, rather with papers, deeds, or contracts. They do not contract themselves. They serve who owns their contracts."

"I see," I said.

"And contracts may be exchanged, bought and sold, such things."

"I see," I said.

"You may think of them as free, or not," he said.

"I would suppose them not free," I said.

"And I, as well," he said. "But they hold themselves a thousand times above our slaves, who are branded and collared, and publicly exhibited as the helpless, lovely animals they are."

"Too," I said, "they are clearly Pani."

"As I said," he said, "there are no free women in camp. Free women are a nuisance, an inconvenience, a bother. They crave attention, they speak when they wish, they make demands. They stand even in the presence of free men. One cannot just point to the ground and have them on their belly before you, their lips and tongue ministering to your feet."

"They are not yet mastered," I said.

"No," he said.

"Perhaps, then," I said, "I am seeking a slave."

"Do not trifle with me," he said. "Do not jest, or be foolish. Slaves are cheap. They are meaningless. They are worthless. They can be bought in a thousand places."

"True," I said.

"Perhaps," said he, "you are seeking a fellow who has information important to you, or others."

I did not respond.

"Perhaps," he said, regarding me narrowly, "you are an assassin, seeking your flighted quarry."

"I am not of the dark caste," I said.

"For that," he said, "I suspect your skills would be insufficient."

"Perhaps yours would not be," I said.

"Perhaps not," he said.

"It grows late," I said. The sun was muchly blocked by the trees. The fellows who had handled the two-handled saw had withdrawn. None were now about, save myself and Tyrtaios.

"You may not realize how late," he said.

He wore his scabbard on the left hip. The draw would be across the body. He was right-handed. I had determined that as long ago as Brundisium. This is particularly important if one is concerned with a short weapon, such as a sleeve dagger, a tunic knife, a hook knife, such things.

"Put aside the ax," said Tyrtaios.

I laid it by.

"I meant only," he said, "that it is later than many in Tarncamp realize."

"I do not understand," I said.

"The season advances," he said. "Ice will soon form in the Alexandra. Tarncamp will be abandoned."

"Our work here is finished?" I asked.

"Largely," he said.

"What then?" I asked.

He looked about himself.

"We are alone," I said. I had determined that earlier.

"Much is afoot," he said, "more than I fully understand. You have heard of Priest-Kings, and Kurii?"

"All have heard of Priest-Kings," I said. "How else would there be a world, a universe?"

"Perhaps," he said, "Priest-Kings are the children of the world, of the universe."

"They are gods," I said.

"And might not gods," he said, "be the children of the world, or universe, as much as sleen or kaiila?"

"I know little of such things," I said. "I am not an Initiate."

"Initiates," said he, "are frauds and hypocrites, living off the superstition of the lower castes."

"Beware," I said, looking about.

"Do you believe in Priest-Kings?" he asked.

"Certainly," I said.

"Do you think they concern themselves with us?" he asked.

"Of what interest might we, or urts or sleen, be to such remote and powerful beings?" I asked.

"But you believe in them?" he said.

"Certainly," I said. "There is the Flame Death. There are well-authenticated cases."

"Then they occasionally concern themselves with us," he said.

"It seems so," I said.

"What are they afraid of?" he asked.

"They are without fear," I said.

"Why, then," he asked, "the weapon and technology laws?"

"I do not know," I said.

"Their enforcement, too," he said, "appears imperfect."

"Doubtless they enforce them when, and as, they please," I said.

"Or, perhaps," he said, "they do not always detect lapses or violations."

"They would then have to be, to some extent, finite, and limited," I said.

"Precisely," he said.

"You hint at heresy," I said.

"Or truth," he said. "Suppose that Priest-Kings, wise and powerful, or cruel and powerful, or arrogant and powerful, or exotic and powerful, were in their way mortal, and vulnerable, and concerned to protect their kind and world."

"From what?" I asked.

"Others," he said.

"'Others'?" I asked.

"Kurii," he said.

"You said that word before," I said. "I do not understand the word. What are Kurii?"

"I do not know," he said, looking about. "But I think they are foes of Priest-Kings."

"Then they are foolish, indeed," I said. "Who would be so foolish as to challenge gods?"

"Gods," he said. "Other gods."

"Children of the world?" I said.

"I have not seen one," he said. "But I have heard they are large, and terrible."

"Then some have seen them," I said.

"Some, I think," he said. "But they fear to speak of them. Perhaps they are warned not to do so."

"I do not think they exist," I said.

"I found a fellow, in a marsh beside the Cartius," he said, "bitten at the shoulder, ribs and intestines torn from his body, who cried out the words, 'Kur, Kur,' and died."

"He was delirious," I said. "A larl commonly attacks in such a way, fastening on the neck or shoulder, and clawing out the belly, and organs."

"Larls are rare in the locale of the Cartius," he said.

"But you saw no sign of an unusual beast," I said.

"No," he said. "Have you ever seen a Priest-King?"

"No," I said.

"What do you think they are like?" he asked.

"Like tall, large, and handsome men," I said. "Unseen like the wind, mighty like the sea, wise as the stars, swift like the flash of lightning."

"Like men?" he said.

"Surely," I said. "Did they not create us in their image?"

"How imperfect then must they be," he mused.

"Lower your voice," I said.

"Perhaps," he said, "the ost, the sleen, the hith, the panther, the river shark, the larl, was created in their image."

"Such words might have you impaled," I said.

"Only where Ubars fear the white caste," he said.

"Priest-Kings and Kurii," I said, "have something to do with Tarncamp?"

"I do not know," he said. "It is conjecture."

"Much here is mysterious," I said.

"Consider a kaissa board," he said. "The pieces do not know they are on the board; they do not know they are pieces; they do not know there is a game; and certainly they do not know who plays the game."

"No," I said.

"Suppose now," he said, "the players are closely matched, and the board is balanced. The game is frozen, arrested, and a draw is unwelcome."

"I do not understand," I said.

"Might not the players," he asked, "seek to resolve the game, in one way or another?"

"Perhaps," I said.

"Might not even a spearman, least of the pieces, influence the outcome?"

"But the game is balanced, arrested," I said.

"But might not the players," he suggested, "free the pieces?"

"That would be to abandon the game," I said, "to forsake it, to substitute for its beauty, for its stately majesty, a sport of gambling stones, an extraction of ostraka from the urn, a casting of dice."

"Perhaps," said he, "it is another way of continuing the game, a darker, more fearful kaissa."

"I do not understand," I said.

"Suppose something were at issue," he said.

"A world?" I asked.

"Or parts of a world, a division of a world," he said.

"I understand nothing of this," I said.

"Suppose something simple was at issue," he said, "say, a slave. If the game seemed arrested, prolonged, or wearying, might not the issue of her possession be resolved easily, simply, by drawing a card or casting a die?"

"And the slut would go to the winner."

"Of course," he said, "just as anything else for which one might gamble."

"There are many men here," I said.

"And in Shipcamp," he said.

"A war is involved?" I asked.

"It seems so," he said.

"But there is no war here," I said. "Ar is free, the island ubarates are quiescent, there are, as far as I know, only the usual raids and skirmishes amongst the cities."

"A war elsewhere," he suggested.

"You have been to Shipcamp," I said.

"Yes," he said.

"A fort is being built there?" I asked.

"No," he said.

"What then?" I asked. Enormous amounts of timber, and other stores I did not recognize, many in sealed containers, had traversed the eastern road. Haulage had been taking place for weeks, almost daily.

"Something else," he said.

"What?" I asked.

"Perhaps a ship," he said.

"A ship?" I asked.

"A great ship," he said.

"Not a fort, not a hundred barges," I said.

"No," he said.

"The outcome of a war is somehow involved in this?" I asked.

"I think so," he said.

"And where is this war to be fought?" I asked.

"Not here," he said.

"Where?" I asked.

"Beyond Cos and Tyros," he said, "beyond the farther islands, at the World's End."

"There is nothing at the World's End," I said, "only the currents, the storms, and the great cliff, over which ships will be swept, to plunge forever."

"Such things are said," he said, "but you do not believe them."

I was silent.

"You are apprised, I would suppose, of the Second Knowledge," he said.

"I do know," I said, "that ships do not return from beyond the farther islands."

"Why?" he asked.

"I do not know," I said. "Thassa guards her secrets."

"Some," he said, "are curious to inquire into those secrets which Thassa guards."

"Who would be so foolish?" I asked.

"Some," he said. "Have you heard of Tersites, of Port Kar?"

"I have heard of him," I said. "He disappeared, years ago. He was a shipwright, eccentric and unreliable, driven from Port Kar. It is said he is lame, half-blind, and mad. It is said he is at war with Thassa, and would challenge her."

"It is his ship," said Tyrtaios, "and it is being built for, and outfitted for, a voyage to the World's End."

"From whence are the Pani?" I asked.

"I think," said he, "from the World's End."

"How came they here?" I asked.

"It is said," he said, "on the wings of Priest-Kings."

"Or Kurii?" I asked.

"Perhaps," he said.

"Let them return similarly," I said.

"Apparently," he said, "that is not part of the game."

"The ship," I said, "may never reach the World's End."

"That, too, I think," said Tyrtaios, "is part of the game."

"How am I involved in this?" I asked.

"I think," said Tyrtaios, "that one player, and perhaps neither, is content to resign himself in these matters to the role of a passive, uninvolved spectator."

"One or neither then would be content, despite possible

asseverations, pledges, and such," I ventured, "to leave the matter to chance."

"I think too much is involved," said Tyrtaios.

"Priest-Kings and Kurii are involved," I said.

"I think so," said Tyrtaios.

"I have seen neither," I said.

"Nor have I," he said.

"Gods battle with gods," I said.

"And we," said he, "small men, have our own projects, and interests, and wars. I am sure that the Pani suspect little of what is going on. They presumably see little beyond their own conflicts, their own foes."

"What of Lord Okimoto?" I asked.

"I think he suspects more," said Tyrtaios, "and intends to intertwine his own ambitions and prospects with these larger matters. Surely wars can be exploited for one's own ends, even a war of gods."

"And you?" I asked.

"Let each further his own projects as he may," he said.

"And what is my role here?" I asked.

"A marking of cards, the weighting of a die, the control of ostraka deposited in the urn, such things," he said.

"I trust," I said, "you will soon be more explicit."

"At Shipcamp," he said.

"It is growing cold," I said.

"Let us return to the shelters," he said.

Chapter Fifteen

I shielded my eyes, as I could, from the light of the candle. It was not bright, I suppose, but the contrast with the darkness of the slave house was painful. I half closed my eyes. I could not see who held the candle. I knew he would carry a switch. At the entrance to the slave house, that rude, long, low-ceilinged, wooden building, the visitors are given a small lamp, or a taper, in its holder, and a switch. The offerings, on their mats, are aligned on the two sides of the building, with an aisle between them.

If we are not pleasing, we are switched.

We strive to be pleasing.

"Does the light hurt your eyes, pretty kajira?" he asked.

"Yes, Master," I whispered.

"Get on your belly," he said.

I turned to my belly, with a soft rattle of the chain. I felt it pull against my collar ring. The chain runs to a heavy ring anchored in the floor, on my left, if I were on my back. The mat is thick, and coarse, and the floor is of planking. We are not coddled.

I had seldom been switched.

We hope to please the masters.

The palms of my hands were on the mat, at the sides of my head. I looked to the left, my right cheek on the mat.

I sensed that he was regarding me. We are on some four feet of chain. We are naked.

"What is your name?" he asked.

"Laura," I said, "if it pleases Master." They may name us, of course, as they please. I had been used under a variety of names. Sometimes, I fear, we stand proxy for another.

"That is a barbarian name," he said. "Are you a barbarian?"

"Yes, Master," I said. I tensed. "Please do not whip me, Master," I begged. Some men seem to feel that barbarian women, some barbarian women, from the world Earth, have exceeded their place, and they are then whipped. I did not think that I had exceeded my place. I think I had recognized what it was, since puberty.

Even on my former world, I had been curious as to what it might be, to be owned and serve a master. On Gor, I had learned. Yet each master is different, and our helplessness in the arms of one may not be identical with our helplessness in the arms of another. There are a thousand ecstasies, and a thousand yieldings, each in a sense the same, and yet each different. What is common in each is that one is slave, and one is master. Sometimes, if only from a chagrin at my lowliness, or perhaps in an attempt to recover something of my former free woman's independence and pride, I had resolved to resist the attentions to which I found myself subjected, but I had soon found myself succumbing as might any other collar slut, which I now was. How helpless we are in their hands! Initially, weeks ago, I had surrendered myself, at least in part, for fear of the consequences of a master's displeasure, or even his failure to find me fully pleasing. In my training, as brief as it was, I had been taught the lash of the switch and, once, the stroke of the whip, and would go to great lengths to avoid both. I also learned that there are infallible signs in a slave's body, signs of authentic response, which signs are easily read by Gorean males. They easily detect, and do not accept, pretense. Accordingly, after leaving the house, and having felt the switch, and, once, the lash, I had surrendered wholly, and helplessly, as I must, holding back nothing, surrendered to feeling, emotion, and radical sentience, as a yielding, worthless object, as a slave to her master, which I was. Again and again I would steel myself to resist, somehow, even despite the perils, but then I would be touched, and I would be again a slave. Too, I feared, but longed for, the growing of my needs, now multiplying, waxing, and intensifying. In my mind, and belly, I was becoming different, or, perhaps better, was becoming more and more, in my mind and belly, what I had always been, a slave. And surely I now knew at least the glimmer of slave fires. Men were seeing to it. I had no choice. I was given no choice. It was being done to me, regardless of my will. I felt helpless, but then a slave is helpless. How far I was now from the arrogance of my former self, which, while desperately desiring bondage, had sought, in accord with the mechanistic, sterile prescriptions of my world, demanded of me, to deny these desires, and drive them from my mind! No longer were such options permitted me. I could no longer help myself. I was now a slave!

"Oh!" I said, suddenly, touched.

"Excellent," he said.

I dug my fingernails into the mat.

Some weeks ago, my coffle, disembarked, marched east from the sea, had arrived at an extensive enclave termed Tarncamp. There were many buildings there, for housing, cooking, feeding, washing, sleeping, exercise, storage, and such. Amongst them we passed an impressive pavilion. It was said to be the pavilion of a Lord Nishida. He was first, I gathered, in the camp. The pavilion, palisaded, seemed to be the center of much activity. Men came and went, and slaves, as well. In passing by the open gate, with its two large panels, swung back on each side from the palisade wall, I could see the pavilion within was largely open, rather like an extensive dais. Guards were about. Did he fear attack? In passing, I heard the roar of a beast from somewhere within the palisade. I trusted that it was well secured. It reminded me of the roars, though they had been from a much greater distance, I had heard on the beach, and, twice, in my journey to this place, through the forest. I supposed they emanated from the same, or a similar, sort of beast. It soon became clear that this large enclave was a work camp of some sort, one in which, apparently, much timbering took place. We saw wagons, filled with logs, drawn by tharlarion. We also saw stables in which such beasts might be fed, watered, and sheltered. The journey here had taken some four days. We had, however, following others, including the several men bearing the two large, strange, apparently weighty boxes or crates unloaded from our galley, soon left Tarncamp, and, by a short trail, emerged onto what we learned was a training area of sorts. Here I had my first clear sight of tarns. Before, in the forest, I had known them only as large, frightening shadows overhead, rapid, monstrous darknesses overhead, storms of wings smiting the air, whose passage had torn leaves from the canopy, these then showering downward, scattering about us. Too, I had not forgotten the single wild, streaming, raucous scream I had heard. It had been said that they killed men, and that men flew them. One alighted on the training ground not ten yards from us. Dust scattered about. We crowded together, stripped, our necks in the rope coffle, instinctively. I think I cried out. I know others did. How small the rider was compared to the bird! I think it fair to call it a bird, but it was no form of life with which I was familiar. I wondered on what world such a thing might have emerged from the dark, grisly, unforgiving, demanding games of nature, certainly not on my former world, nor, I suspected, this world. Perhaps it had arisen on some larger world, perhaps a much larger world, a world on which evolution might select for such massive size and power. In this sense, I did not know if such a monster were well thought of as a bird, or not. It was, as far as I could tell, a form of life alien to both the Earth and Gor. Still it was clearly a bird, or very birdlike. It had talons, a beak, long and wicked, and mighty wings. Too, it was crested. I had heard of convergent evolution, as in a shape best fitted to negotiate an aquatic environment, examples of which might be the dolphin, the fish, the ichthyosaur, and such. Too, consider eyes, and how widely spread they are amongst diverse life forms, insects, fish, mammals, birds, and such. Considering the values of given shapes, certain appendages, diverse irritabilities, tactual, auditory, and visual sensors, and such, one would expect them to arise, sooner or later, on any world capable of sustaining complex life forms. Accordingly, I supposed, evolution might provide a place on diverse worlds for birds, or birdlike creatures, creatures of keen eyesight, creatures which might attack, grasp, and tear, creatures not bound to the earth, creatures which might negotiate and traverse the very atmosphere itself.

"Hold your coffle!" called the fellow from the saddle of the tarn, he yards from the ground.

His command was not necessary. We were terrified to move, and were crowded together.

"Burdens down!" called the coffle master. "Stand, align yourselves!" We knew how we were to stand. We stood as slaves, erect and proud, as prize goods.

"Where do you get these tarsks?" called the fellow in the saddle.

"In Brundisium!" responded the coffle master.

We were indignant, as we knew we had been carefully selected. Even a slave has her pride, though it may be no more than the pride of a slave. We must be careful, of course, to give little, or no, sign of our displeasure or annoyance. We did not wish to be cuffed, or put to our bellies and switched in the dirt. Too, we had not been given permission to speak. We could not help it if prices had been low in Brundisium. After all, there had been, I had gathered, serious difficulties in Ar, a large city, in the recent past. Indeed, at least three items in our coffle had been former free women of Ar, two of high caste.

"A copper tarsk for the lot!" said the fellow on the tarn.

"Some sold for silver!" said the coffle master.

I had sold for copper.

"Mat girls," laughed the tarnsman.

"We must on to Shipcamp," said the coffle master.

"Hold the coffle," said the tarnsman, pointing. "See the targets. An exercise is underway. A flight is behind me. I am charged to clear the field."

We looked to our right, and, in the distance, we saw specks, several specks, moving specks.

The coffle master shaded his eyes.

The specks were far, and, for a bit, it seemed they were arrested, not even moving, and then it was clear they were moving, and were larger, slightly larger. At the distance their speed was not clearly discernible, and yet I was sure, from their passage in the forest, overhead, that it was likely to be considerable.

I looked to my left and saw rows of targets, perhaps forty or fifty.

These were perhaps something in the neighborhood of a foot and a half in width, and some six feet high. Portions of the targets were colored, rather at the level of what might be a man's waist, chest, neck, and head.

When I turned back , the specks were no longer specks but clearly spread ranks of flighted creatures, at four levels, and, as I later determined, each rank was followed by its column, the ranks in these columns separated by some fifty yards, or so.

The fellow who had arrested our progress, then, with a snap of wings and a shower of dust, departed the field.

Shortly thereafter four waves, or ranks, of tarnsmen swept by, the lowest wave perhaps no more than five yards from the ground, the highest perhaps twenty or twenty-five yards from the ground. In a moment they were gone, arrows launched, but, wheeling about, they returned from the opposite direction, and again loosed their missiles, and then wheeled about, again, and, approaching from the original direction, loosed another volley of missiles, and then sped away. There had been three passes. The targets were bristling with arrows, front and back. Fellows from the margins of the field went to the targets and retrieved the arrows. I would later learn that records were kept, as each arrow could be identified as that of a given bowman. In this way, marksmanship might be evaluated, and bowmen distinguished. The bows used, though I did not realize the importance of this at the time, were short bows. Such a bow can clear the saddle, enabling its missile to be fired easily in any direction. The crossbow is well known on Gor, but its rate of fire is far exceeded by that of the straight bow, either the peasant bow or the shorter, saddle bow.

I was much frightened by what I saw. Almost every arrow fired had struck a target. How frightening, I thought, to be the quarry of such marksmen!

I would later learn that there had been, some days previous, an attack on this camp, which had been repulsed, in part by such tarnsmen.

Shortly after the exercise, the flights apparently departed for some rendezvous, the fellow who had cleared the field returned.

"May we proceed?" called our coffle master.

"Do you want to run any of your girls?" asked the tarnsmen.

"No," said the coffle master.

I did not understand this exchange. One or two of the other girls, however, must have understood, for their relief, given the negative response of the coffle master, was evident.

"Burdens up," called the coffle master, and we retrieved our burdens. I think we were all pleased to leave the training area.

Later that evening, we were camped along a road leading east from the training area, toward a place called Shipcamp. We lay in the leaves and grass, as usual, our hands bound behind us, our coffle rope tied between two trees. We could speak to one another then, though softly, that the men not be disturbed.

"I am frightened," I whispered, to Relia, who had earlier had the lot number Eighteen. It was she who had fled toward the stairs in the dungeon, but had been precluded from reaching them by one of our keepers. She had looked well on her knees, licking and kissing a man's feet, in gratitude for not having been beaten. Prior to this experience she had been insufferably proud, and arrogant, at least with some of us, though not daring this with the masters, and was certainly so with myself, for I was only a barbarian. She had apparently once been of the Merchants, perhaps the high Merchants, and had even held herself to be of high caste, despite the fact that few Goreans accepted the Merchants as a high caste. It was regarded as a rich caste, but that is not, in the eyes of many, the same as being a high caste. It was, of course, a powerful caste, given its wealth, and even Ubars might court its favor. How are men to be paid, and wars waged, if not with gold? In any event, she who had once been "Eighteen" had now changed considerably, and surely was now better aware of the meaning of the mark which had been burned into her left thigh, just under the hip. She was still reserved with me, and regarded me with condescension, but would no longer strike me, or speak to me as she had originally, perhaps if only because doing so would offer her chain sisters an excellent, and welcome, pretext for administering, given the recent past, another unpleasant lesson in civility. After they had seen her on her knees in the dungeon, a frightened slave at a master's feet, they no longer stood in awe of her. Indeed, it was not unusual now for one or the other of them to push her, trip her, strike her, or pull her hair. Even now there were bruises on her body. We policed ourselves, so to speak, as no First Girl had been set over us, who would enforce order. I thought 'Relia', which name had been given to her just before mine had been given to me, was a nice name, and it was, of course, at least, a Gorean name. Indeed, as I understood it, some free women had that name. If she was purchased by a free woman, of course, it would have been instantly changed, to something more appropriate to a slave, Lana, Tula, Lita, or such. She was quite lovely, and, I suspect, that influenced the master who had named her. Masters often prefer lovely names for slaves; mistresses are usually less indulgent. She was taller than I was as I was taller than the girl behind me in the coffle, who was Janina, another nice name, which was also Gorean. Our lot numbers were now all but indistinguishable on our left breasts. I think we had all tried to remove them, as well as we could, with the bit of precious oil we were supplied when, roped together, we were allowed to enter the shallow, washing pools. We envied the freer girls who might be permitted a wooden tub in the open air. In the house, I had learned that a slave is to keep herself clean, fresh, rested, and well groomed. A free woman may be as ill-kempt and slovenly as she pleases, but this option is not permitted to the slave. She is, after all, a property, and is to be pleasing to her master. Many masters prefer long hair in a slave, hair which is "slave long," as it is not only lovely but is often useful, as well, in the furs, for delighting and tantalizing a master. Too, she may sometimes be bound with her own hair, and certainly controlled by means of it. Some masters, too, prefer a smooth slave, and, in such a case, may have the slave depilated, or have her body hair shaved away. Sometimes the master attends to this himself. This is more common in certain cities than in others.

"Relia," I said.

She did not respond.

"Are you asleep?" I asked.

"No," she said.

"Are you angry?" I asked.

"No," she said.

"Janina is asleep," I said. I did not wish to raise my voice.

"So?" she said.

I did not want her to think that I would have been so forward as to address her first, had Janina been awake. Janina, happily, regarded slaves as pretty much of a muchness. She did not seem much concerned, at least now, that I might be a barbarian. We were all, after all, on the same rope.

"The tarnsman spoke of 'running a girl'," I said. "What does that mean?"

"We were not run," she said. "It does not matter."

"I am frightened," I said, again.

"We are all frightened," she said.

Janina, to my right, stirred.

"It could mean different things," she said. "It is a capture game. There are many such. You are the quarry. You might be pursued on foot, on kaiilaback, by a tarnsman in the saddle. Ropes might be used, or nets, or a tarn's talons. In the far south, a bola is used to entangle the legs of a running girl, and then she is bound, and returned to a starting point."

"It is cruel," I said.

"Men enjoy it," she said. "In it they also hone their capture skills."

"We might as well be animals," I said.

"We are," she said.

I felt foolish. How naive had been my remark. Did I not yet realize what I now was?

"It is a sport," she said. "Sometimes they wager on such things. A good runner can be of great value to her master."

"Doubtless it could improve her price," I said, bitterly.

"Considerably," she said.

"You spoke," I said, "of honing their capture skills."

"The ideal prize," she said, "is the free woman, of an enemy city."

"They are loot," I said.

"We are women," she said, "in the collar or out of it. We are all loot, all prizes, goods, something to be acquired, owned, bought, sold, traded."

"I was frightened by the archery," I said, "the birds, the waves, the strikes, the ferocity, the accuracy, the penetration."

"Were they not such marksmen," she said, "they would not be in their saddles; there would be no place for them in the cavalry."

"How could one escape such shafts?"

"Have no fear," she said. "Men will not fire upon you, no more than on any other domestic animal, a kaiila or verr. We are to be roped, herded together, penned, and shackled, and put to the pleasure of masters. That is for us. We are slaves."

I pulled a little at the cords which held my hands behind my back. I could feel the hemp loop knotted about my neck, which held me with the others.

"What of free women?" I said, uneasily.

"They are free," she said. "They are in considerable danger. Why else do you think they submit themselves so readily, and desperately?"

"I see," I said.

"How quickly," she said, scornfully, "they tear away their veils, and struggle to divest themselves of their robes, that they may kneel and, head deeply down between their lifted, extended arms, wrists crossed for binding, submit themselves!"

I was silent.

"How quickly," she said, "their wrists are lashed together!"

"You speak," I whispered, "as though from experience."

"Barbarian!" she hissed.

"Forgive me," I said.

"But how thrilled I was," she said, "to be bound, and led away."

"You had been found acceptable," I said.

"Yes," she said. "I was spared. I would live."

"You are very lovely," I said.

"In Brundisium," she said, "I went for a silver tarsk."

"That is a fine price," I said.

"In that market," she said, "it was quite good. What did you go for?"

"I have heard," I said, "forty-eight copper tarsks."

"That much?" she said.

"Yes," I said.

"Do not be annoyed," she said. "Much depends on the market. You might have gone for more, or less."

"I see," I said.

"Do not be upset," she said. "I have seen the eyes of masters upon you."

"Oh?" I said.

"You are not unattractive," she said. "In Brundisium, you might have found yourself sold to a tavern."

"I see," I said. I gathered this might be a compliment.

"Some men," she said, "might bid heatedly to have you at their feet."

"I would hope to be found pleasing," I said.

"You had better be, and perfectly, if you know what is good for you."

"I understand," I said.

"Are you still afraid?" she asked.

"Yes," I said.

"Do not be afraid of the archers," she said. "Your tunic, if you are permitted one, will guarantee your safety. Even free women, in the sacking of a city, often affect tunics, to be taken for slaves. Apprehended, they are often lashed for deceit, a most unpleasant whipping, and then swiftly shackled, collared, and marked."

"I hope they will give us tunics," I said.

"In Shipcamp," she said. "I heard a guard speak."

"Good," I said.

"Do you want a tunic?" she asked.

"Of course," I said.

"You are modest?" she asked.

"Certainly," I said.

"But you are not permitted modesty," she said.

"Surely in public," I said.

"Perhaps a little," she said, "if it is permitted by masters."

"Yes," I said, "if it is permitted by masters."

"But you are a barbarian," she said.

"No matter," I said.

"What do you know of modesty?" she said. "You were never a free woman."

"I was!" I said.

"As free as women on your world can be free!" she scoffed.

"Perhaps," I said.

"You do not know what it is to be free," she said, "for you were never a Gorean free woman. You cannot know the freedom we have, the pride, the nobility, the splendor, the power, the raiment, the veiling, the dignity! Men defer to us. They step aside. They make way for us. They will not sit in our presence without permission. We have Home Stones! Did you have a Home Stone?"

"No," I said.

"I thought not," she said.

"Not everyone has a Home Stone," I said.

"Beasts, misfits, vagabonds, exiles, repudiated men, scoundrels, outlaws, and such," she said, and then, lowering her voice, whispered, "and perhaps Priest-Kings."

I felt it wise to refrain from speaking, as she had spoken of Priest-Kings.

"How can you think of modesty on your world," she said. "It is my understanding that there are places on your world where women bare their faces, even on the streets."

"I have heard of some Gorean free women, unveiled, on the wharves," I said.

"Of low caste," she said. "And on work days, not holidays."

A Gorean free woman is likely to fear the stripping of her face more than the stripping of her body. Although I found this surprising at first, upon reflection, it seemed reasonable. Bodies, however lovely, are relatively similar, and relatively anonymous, whereas the face is likely to be unique, individual, personal, distinct, and special. Moreover, it is revealing, in its thousand mixtures, and subtleties, of expression. Surely a woman is a thousand times more revealed in her features, these revealing her thousand whims, moods, and secrets, than in her body, however exciting and marvelous it may be. And Gorean men savor and relish, and own, and master, the whole. In the face of the woman men read the slave. It is the whole woman, inside and outside, face, body, mind, thoughts, needs, emotions, which is wanted, which is desired, which is collared. Accordingly, the first thing that is done with a captured free woman, unless she is to be held for ransom, or delivered veiled to another for the pleasure, is to face-strip her. After this, so shamed, many women, of their own volition, kneel to be collared. Many, it seems, have waited their entire life to be collared. How often the happiness and radiance of the slave, caressed and mastered, outrages the free woman.

* * * *

161

"Please do not touch me," I begged.

"You writhe well," he said.

I scratched at the coarse fibers of the mat.

"I cannot help myself," I protested.

"You are not permitted to do so," he informed me.

"Stop, Master!" I begged.

"Very well," he said.

"No, no, no!" I begged. "Do not stop! Please, please, do not stop!"

"You beg that I should continue?" he asked.

"Yes, Master!" I said.

"As a slave?" he asked.

"Yes, Master," I said, squirming in shame, in conflict, and need.

"We will see what we can do here," he said.

"Be merciful," I begged.

"You are a new slave, are you not?" he asked.

"Yes, Master," I whispered, intensely.

"Clearly you feel pleasure," he said, "whether or not you wish to do so."

"Forgive me," I said. How could a man respect a woman who is no more than a helpless, spasmodic toy in his grasp, squirming and begging? Where was refinement, sophistication, self-control, dignity, pride, personhood, and respect? How could a woman respect herself when she reveals herself as no more than a helpless, uncontrollable, pleasure animal, a slave?

What is she good for then, but love, service, and submission?

"Your body lubricates nicely," he said. "It has welcomed me, and clasped me. Too, though it is early, it has rewarded me with a number of spasmodic responses."

"'Early'?" I said.

"Yes," he said.

"There is more?" I said.

"Of course," he said.

"I do not understand," I said.

"Certainly you are aware that you juice readily, and nicely," he said.

"Let me alone," I begged.

"I think, in time," he said, "you will prove to be a hot little urt."

162

"No, no!" I said.

"Perhaps not so much now," he said. "But later."

"Be merciful," I begged. "Please, be merciful!"

"It is easy to see," he said, "even at this point, why they have chained you in a slave house."

"When will you be done with me?" I wept.

"You are afraid, are you not?" he said.

"Yes!" I said.

"Let us try this caress," he said.

"Ai!" I wept.

"Subside," he said. "Lie still, relax. Let there be a calm before the storm, little vulo."

How mighty was the ship!

How tiny we were on the dock, bearing our burdens, coming and going, serving the workmen, carrying supplies, and food and water, in the shadow of that curved, towering structure rearing above us.

"See," called Relia, pointing.

"What?" I said.

"Ice," she said, "ice in the river."

"It was washed down from a tributary," said Janina, shading her eyes. "At this time of year there is already ice farther north."

"It is warm enough here," I said. We were still tunicked. I supposed it must have been a large piece of ice, broken free, that it would be in the river, here in the Alexandra, this far south.

"Soon the season will change," said Janina.

"Masters hasten," said Relia. "The Alexandra will freeze, and the ship will be trapped. She might be crushed."

"It is still warm," I said.

"Now," said Janina.

Clearly colder weather was anticipated. We had been issued woolen materials, woven from the fleece of the bounding hurt, with awls and string, from which we were to fashion winter garmenture for ourselves. The nature of this projected garmenture, as might have been anticipated, was clearly specified. A cloth worker measured us and cut the patterns, as we were not permitted scissors. Under his supervision we sewed the garments. The awls were allotted, counted, and returned. Our work must be approved by the cloth worker. I had to remove stitches twice, and resew them. In any event, we, though slaves, would be well bundled. When we were finished we each had trousers and a jacket. The jackets, belted, came to our thighs, and had hoods. We also had a shawl and blanket. Our feet were wrapped in thick cloths, and our legs, over the trousers, boot-like, were similarly swathed.

"Look at me," I had laughed, so clad, the cloth worker not about, and had said to Janina, turning about, "I am a free woman!"

She, too, ascertaining the cloth worker was not about, had laughed. There were no free women in Shipcamp, unless they might be of the Pani.

Even to joke about being a free woman might garner a slave a lashing. Surely she should know better.

But today was warm, and we were tunicked.

Our necks were encircled with light metal collars. We could not remove these, as they were locked on us. They were "dock collars," which indicated the sphere of our activities and where we would be chained at night.

I looked across the Alexandra which, at this point, was some one hundred yards in width. The fragment of ice was downstream, turning in the current. I did not know for certain what lay across the Alexandra, but I did know there were two or three buildings there, and something which was palisaded. Occasionally longboats crossed the Alexandra, to and fro. It was said supplies were kept there, across the river, and that, within the palisade, in log kennels, certain special prisoners, or special slaves, were kept. I knew little of this. It did seem clear that they, sooner or later, if there, would be boarded on the ship. One conjecture had it that they were female slaves of such astounding beauty that it would be inappropriate to house them with more common stock. Others said that they were kept separate because they were so beautiful that their presence would cause disruption in the camp, that men would kill one another for them. I found this hard to believe. It was hard to suppose that there would be women there more beautiful than, say, Relia, and some of the others about.

I looked up, at the mighty ship.

It must have been long in the making. It was already in the water, moored against the wharf, when I arrived. Some of the other girls had seen the chocks smote away, and witnessed its descent to the water. Much of the building dock within which it had been constructed had been dismantled, but one could note, here and there, several remaining ribs of what had been the supporting framework and some timbers of the slide leading to the river.

Workmen busied themselves near me. One fellow carried coils of rope on his shoulder.

I looked up, again, at the ship.

There was apparently still much to do, matters having to do with interior work, and decking, the hanging of the giant rudder, the fixture of masts.

"There is water to be fetched," said Janina.

"Yes," I said, and adjusted the strap of the flattened bota on my shoulder.

Shipcamp was a large enclave. It lay at the eastern end of what was usually called the "Eastern Road," though, I think, it tends to veer southeast. I do not think it as large as Tarncamp. Certainly not as many men were housed here. Tarncamp housed a small army. Too, it had its nearby training field, where I and others had witnessed the exercise in which waves of tarn riders had flown against an array of targets. Shipcamp, though garrisoned with its mercenaries, was less a training and housing facility than a shipyard. It contained several workshops and open-sided sheds. Carpenters were here, and sawyers, rope weavers, sail makers, fitters, riggers, and smiths. Mariners, too, were about. The camp was mostly on the northern shore of the Alexandra. The larger, northern camp was narrow, some half of a pasang in length, along the river, and probably no more than two hundred yards in width, extending back toward the forest. There was very little on the southern bank of the Alexandra, some two or three buildings, and the mysterious palisaded area.

I had been here several days.

The journey from the cold, stony beach of Thassa, brushed by the wind, to Tarncamp had taken the better part of four days, and the similar journey from Tarncamp to Shipcamp had been much the same. One supposes unencumbered men might have made the journey in less time, but women, and wagons, would take longer.

I know little or nothing of what is being done here. I suppose that is appropriate, and to be expected, as I am kajira. Curiosity, we are informed, is not becoming to us. Yet, it is my distinct impression that many here, even the masters, do not understand what is being done here, its purpose, and its destiny. Doubtless some know; perhaps the ponderous Lord Okimoto, the camp commander, whom I had seen four times; perhaps the strange, lame, twisted little man they call Tersites, who was much about, whom I had often seen. He, I take it, is the master of these works and the yard. It seems little escapes him. He speaks with authority, impatiently, often shrilly, petulantly. Men strive to please him. They obey him without question. I suppose him to be a shipwright. One speculates, of course. The ship is very large. It is much larger than a river ship. I am sure there are many points on the Alexandra where it could not be brought about. Too, as nearly as I can determine, it is deeply keeled, and there might well be difficulties in even bringing it to the sea, depths varying, and given many bars, which may shift, and rocks. Too, I would suppose the channel is sometimes narrow, and twisting. Doubtless the masters are well aware of such things, and the route seaward has been sounded and scouted with care. It seems clear the ship is a deep-water ship. It is intended, then, to negotiate Thassa. Perhaps it is intended to trade with Cos and Tyros, or various island ports. But the harbors might be too shallow for it. Would not a variety of galleys be more practical? For what is so large a vessel required? It is much larger, many times larger, I am told, than even the largest of common round ships, or cargo vessels, which, too, are apparently very different from the long, low, knifelike vessels of war. Until Shipcamp, I had known only the two Gorean vessels which had been en route to the north, and the one other, seen during the voyage, when I, with the others, had been permitted on the deck. I had gathered, of course, earlier, that the harbor at Brundisium was large, crowded, and busy, but I, as the others, had been blindfolded when we were boarded.

I again considered the great ship.

It was too large to be propelled by oars. It would supposedly have six masts. They were not yet in place. Not even the great rudder was hung. What was the meaning of such a ship? For what work, what voyage, might it be intended? It was not a warship in any common sense; yet, interestingly, it nested six galleys, three to a side, which might be independently launched, and those galleys, I gathered, given their rams and large, crescent-like blades at their bows, suggested aggression and menace.

One thing seemed clear; when the ship was ready, which should be soon, we were to be joined by the armsmen and work crews from Tarncamp. Indeed, the tarn cavalry, trained toward the west, close to Tarncamp, was also to join us before we embarked. Why would tarns be needed? What purpose might they serve? Too, even though the vessel was large, it would carry hundreds of times the men required to manage it. Better to transport troops, I thought, would be smaller ships, a fleet of such. Who would care to risk an army, perhaps a war, by entrusting it to a single mount, to but one vehicle, to but one vessel? But Thassa, I supposed, vast Thassa, might lift her hand, and smash a fleet as well as a single vessel, and, I suspected, a mighty vessel might brave her wrath where a hundred common barks might perish in the sea. Too, what an enormous store of supplies might be housed in so mighty a vessel, supplies which might last years. Would it not be an island of wood, a world of sorts, sufficient onto itself, indefinitely scorning land, cresting indefinitely the dark turbulence of proud, dreadful, beautiful Thassa?

"Kneel," said a stern voice, and I instantly knelt. I felt the boards of the dock on my knees. I kept my head down, and clutched the bota.

"Head up," he said, and I was permitted to lift my head. When the head is lifted, one may commonly meet the eyes of the master.

"Tal, Laura," he said.

"Tal, Master," I said. All free males are Master; all free women are Mistress.

The men knew the names of several of us, who were commonly about the docks. We were often accosted in our work, called to, summoned, teased, commented upon, and such. Familiarities were often taken with us. I had often been sped on my way with a smack below the small of my back. It was common to be delayed in our duties, to be embraced, fondled, and kissed. We were, after all, slaves. It was more difficult for some former free women of Ar who were hooted at, cuffed, and jeered. The memories of men were long, particularly those who were veterans of the former occupational forces in Ar, and they wished to well impress upon the women that they were no longer proud, free, noble, and untouchable, but were now mere properties and animals, slaves.

"What have you in your bota?" he inquired.

"It is empty," I said. Surely that was clear.

"You will replenish it," he said.

"Yes, Master," I said.

"I saw you sold," he said.

I had been purchased, as had many others, by agents of the Pani. There were private slaves in Tarncamp and Shipcamp, but I, like most, was one of the public slaves.

"I hope Master found me pleasing," I said.

"I bid on you," he said, "twenty tarsks. What did you go for?"

"Forty-eight," I said.

"That would be about right, at the time," he said.

"Master was seeking a bargain," I suggested.

"Of course," he said. "You would go for more now."

"Master?" I asked.

"You are trimmer now," he said, "sleeker, better toned, more alive, more beautiful, more slave."

"I have been longer in the collar, Master," I said.

"Doubtless you are more helpless now," he said, "more responsive."

I put my head down.

"One can tell such things," he said.

I bent down and kissed his right foot, softly, and then his left. It pleased me to do this, for such a male, so strong, so powerful.

"Now," he said, "you might go for close to a silver tarsk."

I then knelt up. "A slave is grateful," I said, "if Master is pleased."

I did not dare meet his eyes. How attractive were so many

Gorean men! I knew their eyes had often been upon me, and more so in the last weeks, but I, too, often cast my glances shyly, unnoticed I trust, upon them. I did not think this was different from other slaves. There are, after all, men, and there are women, and it is natural that each should feel desire, the man the desire of the master, and the woman the desire of the slave. How marvelous, I had thought, to be owned by one of them, to be the slave of just one man, to be his alone, to be his to be done with as he pleased. And often, at night, in the long, low kennel, chained with others, I would think of one particular man, one whom I recalled from long ago. Never had I forgotten him. His memory was ever with me. I did not even know his name. I had first seen him in an emporium on a far world. I had once lain at his feet, bound. I had seen him through the bars of an exhibition cage, prior to my sale. I had no doubt that he had been somehow instrumental in my transition to Gor, in my collaring. He had not recognized me in the cage. He had not even remembered me. I was nothing to him, only another beast to be acquired, to be herded about, to be bought and sold.

"And with what," he asked, "will you replenish your bota?"

"With water, surely, Master," I said.

He looked about, as though warily. "Mix in paga," he said.

"It is early," I said.

"Nonetheless," he said.

"There is to be no paga on the dock," I said.

"Just a little," he said.

"There is to be no paga on the dock," I said.

I dared to look up at him, and then quickly turned my eyes away, down. I feared he was not pleased. I was not a paga girl. This was not a tavern. I could be lashed for even approaching a paga vat. "We are not to be used on the dock," I whispered.

"Fear not, pretty tasta," he said.

"Forgive me, Master," I begged.

"Will you try?" he asked.

I was terribly afraid.

"Well?" he asked.

"I will try," I whispered.

"It seems you should be lashed," he said.

"Master?" I said.

"Do you not know that there is to be no paga on the dock?" he said.

"Yes, Master," I said, confused.

"Then why would you fetch some?" he asked.

"I do not understand," I said.

"Do you want to be lashed?" he asked.

"No, Master!" I said.

He slapped his knee, and laughed, uproariously. I now saw two other men about, and they, too, were amused.

I reddened.

"On your way!" he laughed.

I sprang up, tears in my eyes, and fled down the dock, away from the men. I heard them laughing behind me.

I later, in anger, in acute frustration and chagrin, recounted this incident, in all its humiliation, to Relia and Janina. "Do not be concerned," said Relia. "You are becoming more attractive. The men are noticing you. I have seen heads turn as you pass." "It is a joke," said Janina. "We are poor kajirae. The men make sport of us; they frighten us, they tease us." "They mean no harm," said Relia. "They cannot use you. It is a way of having to do with you. It is a way of flirting."

I wondered if he whom I well remembered, he who had so obviously dismissed and forgotten me, that mighty figure, would have behaved so. I supposed so. Doubtless he, too, the handsome, virile, monster, would have laughed. Doubtless he, too, would think nothing of using me, a poor, kneeling, frightened, half-clad kajira, for his amusement. Perhaps he, too, might have designed so cruel a jest, or even one more amusing. We were so utterly helpless. We were slaves. Relia had suggested that they were flirting with me. I wondered if that were true. If they had owned me, they would not have bothered with such things. They would have merely put me to their purposes. I wondered if I were truly becoming more attractive. If it were so, I certainly did not object. Certainly the more appealing, the more beautiful, the more pleasing a slave is, the better is likely to be her life and lot. Certainly she hopes to be pleasing to her master, and strives to be so. She hopes to be a good slave. Too, she does not wish to be lashed.

Two days later, I was halted in my work, and knelt, on the

dock, in the presence of a stately fellow with blue robes, who carried a clipboard. He was of the caste of Scribes. He was followed by two men at arms.

"Your lot number, in Brundisium," he said, scanning the board, with its attached papers, "was 119."

"Yes, Master," I said.

"You are Laura," he said.

"Yes," I said, "if it pleases Master."

"Barbarian," he said.

"Yes, Master," I said.

"Stand," he said, "and cross your wrists behind you."

One complies.

In a moment my wrists were tied together, behind my back. This accentuates the figure, more than a frontal tie. Too, it is stimulatory, as the captive is more helpless, and more vulnerably displayed. The free end of the rope was then brought about, and looped twice and knotted about my throat. Enough rope, some five or six feet was left, to serve as a leash.

I did not understand what was occurring. I was frightened.

"May I speak?" I asked.

"No," I was told.

"Take her to the end of the dock and back," the Scribe said.

In our journey we passed several workmen, and some slaves. Some of the workmen struck their left shoulder with their right hand. Others grinned. "Nice," said one. "Excellent," said another. Some of the slaves seemed amused, and then turned away, again, to their tasks.

At last, I was returned to where I had originally been knelt, near the eastern end of the long dock. The scribe and the other armsmen were there.

"Master," I begged the Scribe, "may I speak?"

"No," he said. Then he said to the armsman who had the care of my rude leash. "Take her to the slave house."

"No!" I had begged. "No! Please, no!"

"She is a shapely slut," he said. "Let it be done."

I was then led on my leash from the dock.

How aware I then was of the collar on my neck!

* * * *

171

"Gently," he said, "gently."

"Master!" I protested.

His hands were strong, and I knew myself slave, only slave. How faraway now was my former world, my former self!

I must reassert myself, I thought, wildly. I cannot be this! I cannot be here, in the darkness, on a chain! How strong his hands were! How helpless I was in his grasp!

No, no, I thought, and then yes, yes, please.

We are removed, from time to time, we are changed. Even since I was here, girls had come and gone.

"Oh!" I said.

"Good," he said.

I wanted to resist, and I did not want to resist.

I cannot be this, I thought, but I knew it was what I was. My thigh was marked, clearly, incisively. Clearly there was no mistaking that. I wore a heavy metal collar, to which was attached a chain, fixed to a stout ring, anchored at the side of my mat. Beneath that collar was a light, close-fitting metal collar. It was there, visible, locked, even when I might be up and about the camp, being summoned, fetching and carrying, cleaning, laundering, ironing, digging roots, picking berries, tidying, being about whatever duties might be given me. And there would be the tunic, so exciting to men, in which I felt so exposed, and so vulnerable! Well was I displayed for their perusal! I scratched at the mat, tears in my eyes. And how exciting were such things to me, as well, the mark, the collar, the tunic! How right they seemed to me! How female I felt, marked, collared, and tunicked, how much then a distinctive, lovely part of nature, so different from men!

How could I have felt more woman?

And how thrilled I was, so set forth. Never on my world had I felt so female, so woman! Here I was what I was, at last, gladly, rightfully, woman, owned, helpless, slave!

No, I thought, no! I must escape. I must escape!

"Oh, oh!" I said.

"Easy, little vulo," he said.

"Ai!" I said.

"We are going to fly, are we not, little vulo?" he asked.

"You have done enough to me," I said. "Let me subside!"

"I am curious to see what you are," he said.

I felt myself lifted, turned about, and thrust down, on my back, for his convenience, as the meaningless object, and animal, I was.

"I will show you what I am!" I cried, angrily, rearing up.

I was thrust back, rudely.

I was given three strokes of the switch. I recoiled beneath them, turned to my side, and tried to make myself small.

"Forgive me, Master!" I begged.

He laid aside the switch, but it was at hand.

"Let us see what may be done with you," he said.

He was patient, and his hands were strong. His touch was sure. Gorean, he was well practiced in the handling of slaves. He had perhaps had hundreds of helpless slaves at his mercy, as I was now. How could we help ourselves, even if it were permitted?

I whimpered a little, and then, suddenly, gasped.

"Yes," he said, "someday you will be a hot little urt."

A whimper escaped me.

"One day," he said, "you will crawl to men, begging, the bondage knot in your hair."

Surely not, surely not, I thought.

"You are not a fine, noble, proud, free Gorean woman," he said. "You are only a barbarian."

Did he think Gorean women any different, I wondered. Did he not know we were all women? Did he not understand that in this very slave house almost all the slaves, perhaps all but I, writhing, bucking, begging, crying out, pleading, had been such "fine, noble, proud, free Gorean women"? Doubtless he meant free women, women not yet collared. There, I supposed, was a dramatic difference. I had had no encounters with Gorean free women, but I had been much apprised by my instructresses, and many fellow slaves, of their alleged nature. These putative informants had entertained what I supposed to be not only a dim, but a radically distorted, and, I hoped, a certainly extreme view, of Gorean free women, regarding them to be haughty, short-tempered, impatient, supercilious, rigid, demanding, unbending, arrogant, boastful, pretentious, hostile, suspicious, cruel, severe, unhappy, unfulfilled, egotistical, and self-centered.

Perhaps this evaluation, insofar as it might pertain to anyone, pertained only to certain free women of the high cities, and, perhaps then, of the higher castes. I did not know. I did think it likely that Gorean free women, given the culture, were probably far more conscious of their position and status, of their freedom, their exalted station, and such, than those of my former world. Consequently their reduction to slavery, a condition alleged to be universally despised, would seem to constitute, culturally, a cataclysmic reversal in fortune, one likely to be particularly traumatic and devastating. On the other hand, many, it is said, "court the collar," and it seems to be the case that "free captures," in their hundreds or thousands, as in the wars, the raids of slavers, the seizures of caravans, the depredations of pirates, the fall of cities, and such, once collared, once owned, find fulfillments until then no more than suspected. In any event, Gorean or barbarian, we were all women, and once collared, once owned, it seemed there was little to choose between us. Certainly we went for similar prices.

"Yes," he said, "you will crawl to men."

I suddenly feared I might.

Were slave fires growing in me? Surely not! What if they should begin to rage? I would be their victim, and prisoner! How helpless I would be! I recalled slaves pleading for the touch of a guard, begging to be brought soon to the block.

At the first opportunity, I thought, before it is too late, while I yet retain a shred of my former self, I must attempt to escape! But who would want to escape, I thought. What had freedom to offer, which might compare with the fulfillments of belonging to, of being possessed by, a master? I had heard of slaves, pathetic collared animals, mere properties, who had undertaken long journeys, undergone terrible hardships, and braved fearful dangers, to find their way back to the feet of a master.

I suddenly, unexpectedly, moaned.

I felt my hips lift, pathetically.

"Steady," he said. "Wait."

"Oh," I said. "Please, now!"

"Soon," he said, softly, soothingly.

I began to whimper, pleadingly.

"What shall we do with you?" he asked.

I was about to speak, to cry out, to beg, but his hand cupped itself over my mouth. I looked up at him, in the light of the taper. My eyes must have been wild, pleading, over his hand. "Beware," he said. "Think before you speak." He then removed his hand from over my mouth. "You may now speak," he said. "What is your wish?"

"That it be done with me as master pleases," I whispered.

"Only that?" he asked.

"Yes, Master!" I sobbed. "Yes, Master!"

I was sweating, and quivering, in expectation. My body was alive, my belly begging.

I tensed.

He must not leave me so! Please, Master, I thought. Do not leave me so!

I did not know him, save that he was now my master. I knew him not, not from the market, not from the dungeon, not from the ship, not from the camp, not from the dock.

He could be anyone, and I could be any slave.

Surely it was not he for whom I longed in whose power I was. It was not he whose voice it seemed I had heard a hundred times, only to discover myself mistaken, not he whose image I had conjured up so often, he before whom I had hastened to kneel in my dreams. It was not he in whose power I longed to lie helpless, whose voice and image had so often figured in my hopes and heart. I recalled him from the emporium on my former world, from a warehouse, from an exposition cage! It was on his chain that I longed to yield; it was in his ropes that I yearned to find myself cast on the altar of his lust, a helpless offering to his mightiness.

No, no, I thought. I must hate them all, all, even he whom I had unsuccessfully attempted to banish from my least thoughts. How I must hate him, I thought. Was it not he who brought me choiceless to this world, on which I was marked, collared, and sold! Was it not he who had brought me even to this chain, to this degradation, to this rude, primitive place, on a far world?

What fate is this, I asked myself.

How could one such as I, intelligent, educated, refined, sensitive, proud, be here?

"You are ready," he said.

"Yes, Master," I whispered. Be merciful, Master, I thought. Do not leave me like this!

"I wonder if you think yourself a free woman," he said.

"Master?" I said.

"I wonder if you think yourself a free woman," he said.

"No, Master," I said.

"We shall see," he said.

"Master?" I said.

"I shall now release the catch on your cage, little vulo," he said, "and you may fly."

"Master?" I said.

"Aiii!" I cried.

"Fly away," he said.

"Ai!" I cried, again, and again, and he could scarcely, with all his strength, hold me.

He stood up then, and I lay at his feet. Surely I had been the choiceless vessel of his pleasure, and he was now done with me. But surely he must know, too, even if it is of no interest to him, that the slave, too, feels, trembles, cries out, and endures the thousand raptures consequent on her condition and collar. To be sure, he had been kind, and patient, with me, if only as a matter of curiosity. In a thousand ways we may be put to use, and sometimes with little more meaning than a casual cuffing. Our feelings are nothing. We are done with as the masters please. We are slaves.

"Please, stay with me, but a moment, Master!" I begged, reaching out to him. I wanted to be held, to be kissed, to be sheltered, to be warmed by his presence, to be spoken to.

I saw the light of the taper disappear down the aisle.

I could not believe what had been done to me, what I had felt, how I was changed, my responsiveness.

"Master!" I called after him.

He was gone.

I remained behind, as I must, on the mat, a ravished slave.

No more dared I think of myself as a free woman, if I had ever done so. I knew how I had yielded. It was a slave yielding. There was no doubt in my mind now, if there ever had been. I now knew myself a slave. I was that, only that.

There had been nothing of the free woman in that yielding.

It was the yielding of worthless, meaningless slave, spasmodic and helpless, in the arms of a master.

I was angry, and miserable.

I had been abandoned, as a slave may be abandoned.

I must escape, I thought.

Never again could I be a free woman. I knew that. But I was determined to flee, not as a free woman might flee, but as a flighted slave might flee, the slave I knew myself to be. I would always be a slave, but I could, at least, be an escaped slave!

Slaves came and went in the slave house. They were brought in, and taken out. I supposed the stock was to be freshened, from time to time. Sooner or later, I would be again outside, in the camp. I would then again be assigned familiar tasks. What if I might dig roots, or venture out, to gather fire wood? It would be easy to slip between the wands and hurry away, into the forest. One could do this in the morning, before the larls are released. Commonly they are released, or most of them, at night.

I would escape!

How I hated men!

And I knew that I was owned by them.

And mostly I hated one, he who had brought me here from my own world, he who was responsible for my collaring. He had forgotten me, the virile, gross beast, not even recognizing me when I had stood before him, within the bars of the exposition cage in Brundisium, but I had not forgotten him.

At the first opportunity I would escape.

Chapter Sixteen

I had come to Shipcamp with the wagons, and something like fifteen hundred or more men. The smaller cohorts of Pani accompanied us.

The journey took the better part of four days.

Slaves were generally tied behind the wagons.

The road was muddy, and the travel difficult.

Behind us, Tarncamp was gone. The barracks, the sheds and shops, the huts, the storerooms, the workshops, the arsenals, the bath houses, the food halls, the slave houses, the pavilions, large and small, had been burned. Blackened debris had been dragged into the forest. Gray ash had been cast about. The winds would rise, and the rains come, and the winter, with its ice and snow, and the awakening, green spring, and in two or three years the insistent, patient forest would repair and cover what men had done.

I was pleased to leave Tarncamp, and so, too, were the men. Some even sang, wading in the mud. This sometimes came to the axles of the wagons, to the bellies of the smaller tharlarion. Logs and planks bridged many holes. Their packs seemed light. They were moving. Things were changing. Few of us were woodsmen. Most of us were mercenaries, some mariners, many ne'er-do-wells, some landless men, and some fugitives. Most, I supposed, were veterans of the forces which had garrisoned Ar. Our tools were the sword and spear, not the ax, the adz, the plane, the saw. An end had apparently come to the seemingly endless round of cutting and hauling, lopping, the rough shaping, and rude trimming, to the backbreaking labor in the forest, the purpose of which was never explained to us. On the morning of the fourth day, we came to a rise from which we could see the Alexandra, like a ribbon below us, and, ahead, men cried out in wonder. I hurried forward, with hundreds, thinking to see, for the first time, a great trade fort which might control the trade of the Alexandra, but I stopped, stunned, as others, at the forest's edge, for below, seemingly small in the distance, was what I knew must, from the distance, be the remains of an enormous framework, now empty, a long, wide dock, and, moored at the dock, what seemed a ship, a great ship, a ship like no other, less a ship than an island of wood, a floating city, carved in a ship's likeness.

"It is the ship of Tersites!" said a man.

"There is no such thing," said another. Surely we had all dismissed the rumors, the stories told in the taverns.

"See!" said the first man pointing. "See!"

"Move," said a Pani officer. "Move!"

The wagons began to roll, descending, their brakes clamping, grinding, against the wheels. The traces of the tharlarion, wagon after wagon, were suddenly slack, and some of the beasts squealed, frightened.

"Careful!" called the officer.

Men began to make their way down the slope. It was slippery from the rains. "Paga!" said a man. "War!" said another. "Slaves!" called another.

I remained on the crest for a time.

Shipcamp was much smaller than Tarncamp, but it contained its scattered range of structures, a hundred or more, and these were mostly north of the dock. Only a bit later did I realize the existence of a small, palisaded enclave across the river. I did not know what was housed there. I supposed it had been intentionally separated from the main camp.

Behind me, on my left, was Asperiche. She had learned to heel, appropriately. It had been pleasant to teach her the many aspects of her collar. She was now well aware it was on her, and locked.

"Perhaps," she said, "Master may now sell me."

I turned about. I examined my slave, the paga girl, the slim, lovely brunette I had named Asperiche, from her island of origin, she purchased from the tavern in Brundisium. She had been insufficiently deferential twice. Masters do not accept such things. I had spared her one lashing, the first time, perhaps foolishly, but she had later, again, been displeasing, a lapse I saw no reason to accept a second time, and I had arranged that she would be better apprised of the fact that a slave is to strive to be pleasing, invariably so. She had apparently not been long in the collar. I suppose that is why she had been less than pleasing in the first place, and, in the second place, naively thought to avert her discipline. To be sure, many slaves strive to avert their discipline, even those who should know better. The lash, it seems, is unpleasant. Let them then mind their behavior. It is interesting to see them beg, so helpless and so much in your power. How assured, how confident, she had been, so sure of the effect of her beauty. Indeed, it was considerable. Perhaps I should not have spared her the lash the first time. That was possibly a mistake, encouraging her to think she might escape a second time. In any event, I had not succumbed, no more than any master might, to her tearful blandishments, her plaintive wheedling and clever wiles, her smiles, and proffered promises. When these protestations were done, duly noted, and such, I saw to it, to her misery, that she was summarily given the lashing she deserved. After her lashing, she had not only failed to be grateful that I should be concerned that she be improved, but, incredibly, had been resentful, even to asserting that she hated me, as if that would be of interest to anyone. I was, however, annoyed, and, to her horror and dismay, purchased her. She then found herself the property of the very fellow she had been trying to disparage or disconcert. It was his collar she would then wear. Why did I purchase her? First, she was beautiful, very much so. Second, she needed to be taught her collar, a lesson she had not yet learned. And third, a man needs a slave. She would do.

"I do not understand," I said. "Why should I sell you?"

"I am not stupid, Master," she said.

"I have never thought so," I said.

"She must be here," she said.

"Who?" I asked.

"She whom you seek," she said.

"I do not understand," I said.

"She for whom you have come to this strange, terrible wilderness."

"I have come for pay," I said, "for excellent fee. I have come for adventure. I have come for curiosity."

"You have come for a slave," she said.

"I have a slave," I said.

"I was with you on the dock, day after day, in Brundisium," she said. "I saw you watch, and wait, and watch again. Only when one coffle was embarked did you take ship."

"One enjoys seeing beautiful slaves," I said.

"We speak to one another," she said. "You much examined Tarncamp. You examined the sheds, the kennels, the cook houses, the slave houses, the stables, the wagon yards. You met incoming parties. You frequented the perimeters. Twice you inquired of a lot number."

"It seems kajirae are observant," I said.

"We are often about," she said. "Little attention is paid to us. We may be unobtrusive, but we are often there. We listen. We talk to one another."

"Curiosity," I said, "is unbecoming to a kajira."

"It seems she whom you seek was not in Tarncamp," she said. "Thus, if she has not wandered into the forest, to be devoured by the beasts, or has not been fed to sleen, or traded south, or such, she must be here, somewhere."

"I have no interest in slaves," I said, "save for those natural to a fellow, their utility, as work and pleasure beasts."

"Men kill for them," she said.

"You are all collar sluts," I said. "There is little to choose from; it is merely one piece of meat or another."

"We bring different prices," she said.

"So do verr, tarsks, and kaiila," I said.

"Some slaves," she said, "have entangled the hearts of Ubars in their meshes."

"Even a Ubar," I said, "may be a fool."

"Some men have given a city for a slave," she said.

"One who is mad," I said, "may buy a paving stone with gold, barter a ship for a stick, a palace for a pebble."

"Has Master not come north seeking a slave?" she asked.

"No," I said. "Put such foolishness from your head." It was not clear to me how Asperiche, whom I regarded as an extremely intelligent slave, could utter such vaunted nonsense. It was true I recalled a slave, of course, but I recalled a thousand slaves. That slave might, or might not, be about, but it made no difference to me. My curiosity in the matter was idle, at best, if it existed at all. Asperiche was wrong. It was not possible that I had come north for a slave. One does not care for a slave. They are mere brutes, conveniences, sleek and luscious, to be dealt with as was appropriate for such brutes.

"Still," said Asperiche.

"Do you wish to be beaten?" I asked, angrily.

"No, Master," she said, putting her head down.

"Why should I sell you?" I asked. "I could not get a copper tarsk for you, as you are."

"Forgive me, Master," she said.

She was covered with mud to the thighs, and her small tunic was spattered with mud. Rain had soaked her hair, and it lay about her head and shoulders, in scattered, bedraggled, unkempt strands.

I stood near one of the halted wagons, which was waiting its turn to try the slope to the valley, beside its rear left axle. Its back was open, and the gate down, and the wagon bed contained a number of packs, including mine. Some fellows were fetching theirs out, with their smaller weapons. Most of the men had not been permitted weapons while on the trail. I, on the other hand, as several others, mostly officers, had been permitted arms. I wore my waist belt, with dagger, and the shoulder belt, with the slung sheath, and gladius. Guards, mostly Pani, had policed the journey. I pulled my pack free, from under others. At the rear of the wagon bed was a number of rings with coiled ropes. It was by means of these that slaves had been tied behind the wagon. There were usually three to five behind a wagon. Most others had been fastened in neck coffles, or wrist coffles. The neck coffles were of rope, the wrist coffles of chain. Shortly after reaching this point, to avoid the danger of a slipping or an uncontrolled wagon, the girls tied behind the wagons had been freed, and herded down the slope. Long log kennels and chains would be awaiting them, and the others, just as a variety of barracks and smaller dwellings had been arranged for the men. Designated precursors had seen to such matters, days ago. I myself had been assigned a hut. I supposed this had to do with the intervention of Tyrtaios. I did not know if it would be shared or not. I was confident it would not be shared with Tyrtaios, as he apparently stood high with the Pani. Rather as I had been permitted weapons on the trail, so, too, Asperiche had not been fastened to a wagon, or coffled, like most of the other slaves, but had been permitted to stay with me. In this Tyrtaios, too, might have been involved. I did not know. This arrangement, however, was not that unprecedented with private slaves, slaves owned by individuals. I found myself wondering, not that I was interested, if a particular slave was now a private slave, or, so to speak, a public, or camp, slave, like most. Presumably she would be a public, or camp, slave, as she had been embarked as such.

I, pack in hand, looked down to the Alexandra, lovely, wide and shimmering, in the morning light, to the huge, partially dismantled framework of mighty Tur beams, to the long dock, with its many sheds, and the broad, towering vessel which was moored there, held in place by gently, strained lines, against the current, its lofty bowsprit high, lifted, like the alert head of a living thing, one waiting to be born, one already scenting the faraway sea.

"Doubtless she is here," said Asperiche.

"Who?" I asked.

"She whom you seek," she said.

"You are less than presentable," I said.

"Master?" she said.

"You are filthy," I said.

"Doubtless there are washing sheds below," she said, "with tubs and warm water. I will be able to launder my tunic, and iron it, and care for my pelt, and be more pleasing to my master."

She lifted her head.

"You may look into my eyes," I said.

"Thank you, Master," she said.

"You may speak," I said.

"My need," she said, "is upon me."

"Doubtless the need of a free woman," I said.

"I am not a free woman," she said. "That is behind me. I can never go back. My need is a thousand times beyond that of a free woman. I am a slave. My need is slave need."

I looked down upon her.

"A slave would be caressed," she whispered. "A slave begs to be caressed, begs as a slave."

"You are very beautiful," I said.

"More beautiful than another?" she asked.

"Another?" I asked.

"She whom you seek," she said.

"I seek no other," I said. "That is unthinkable, absurd."

"But, if you did?" she said.

"I would suppose," I said, "that you are more beautiful."

"But she is different," she said. "For you she is unlike all others. She is special to you, in a way that others are not, in a way that I am not."

"Do not speak foolishly," I said. "Surely you are aware of your interest, of your attractions. Have I not put you to my pleasure often enough?"

"I have been well mastered," she said.

"So?" I said.

"As might be any slave," she said.

"So?" I said.

"I do not think I have been owned as might be your slave of slaves, the one you would die to possess. I have not seen in your eyes the unexampled, terrifying predatory lust of the approaching larl, the keen, piercing glance of the tarn. I have not felt myself as owned, as overcome and helpless, as the tabuk doe in the jaws of the larl, the young she-verr clasped in the talons of the tarn. I have not been seized, flung down, and devastated. I have not known the decisive click of the collar lock which informs me that I have been decisively, triumphantly claimed. I have not felt the ropes on me of that master of masters, by whom I would know myself possessed as the most helpless and most desired of slaves is possessed."

"You speak as a foolish slave," I said.

"I fear I am not as foolish as Master might wish," she said.

"The collar looks nice upon your neck," I said.

"As it might look upon the neck of any slave," she said.

"Or any woman," I said.

"Yes," she said, "or any woman."

She inched closer to me. How bold she was. She had not received permission to do so.

"Doubtless you wish to display your collar," I said.

"It is Master's collar, and it is locked on me," she said.

"Beware," I said.

"Master looks upon me as a slave may be looked upon," she said.

It is a way, of course, in which one would not look upon a free woman. That would be highly inappropriate. How terrified might be a free woman, to be so looked upon, to be looked upon as a slave. I wondered if they ever considered such things, what it would be to be so looked upon, to be looked upon as a slave. I trusted not, as they were free. And presumably they would never have that experience, unless they were stripped, and a collar, chains or shackles, was in the offing.

"But ela," she said, "I am not presentable."

"You are beautiful," I said.

"I am filthy," she said.

"Do you think I am fastidious?" I asked.

"Master?" she said.

"It adds to your beauty," I said.

"Master?" she said. "Oh!"

I then, pack in hand, drew her to the side, away from the trail, between the trees.

Chapter Seventeen

I saw him, on the dock! It was he! I was stunned, I was shaken, my knees were weak, I nearly fell. In that instant I could hardly breathe. My hand went to the collar on my neck. I touched the hem of my tunic. I am sure it was he. It was he! He turned about, and I instantly knelt, head down, trembling.

I heard the snap of his fingers, and I knew I must lift my head, that I might be regarded.

I looked up.

I was trembling.

Surely he remembered me. Surely he had not forgotten! He must remember me! He could not have forgotten me!

I was on my knees before him, tunicked and collared.

It was he who had brought me to this, to this strange, different, natural, beautiful, fresh world, much as Earth might once have been, a world of blue skies and white clouds, of wind and rain, of storms and sunlight, of green fields and dark forests, of bracing, uncontaminated air and clean, clear, bright, flowing water, a simple, primitive, rude, unspoiled world, a world on which such as I could be only a slave.

I looked up at him. Tears were in my eyes. My lips were parted. I was at his feet, where I belonged. Surely he must know I loved him, that I was his, his even from another world, his by all the fierce, uncompromising rights of nature. Does a slave not know her master?

Four days before I had been freed of my chain in the slave house, a new slave put in my stead. I was furious with what had been done to me, but my belly had been well heated there.

It would be hard to be again as I had been. I must now fight my body, that body to which I now seemed a stranger. How it betrayed me with its health and need, with its eagerness, its responsiveness, its helplessness, and vitality! I must be at war with it! How could I be myself in a collar? And how could I be myself other than in a collar! In my heart I knew I belonged in the collar, but I was determined to deny this reality, determined to fight it desperately, attempting to cling to the last, tattered shreds of my pride! Was I not of Earth? Did I not know, from my world, what a "true woman" was to be? And did I not know how the betrayals of the body and the forswearings of, the treacheries and disloyalties to, our deepest and most real self, these denials and depredations, were to be commended as accomplishments and adornments! To our blood, and to our hearts, we must do treason. But I feared that Gorean men would not permit this, at least if one were a slave. In the hands of a Gorean male what could a woman be but a slave? I must escape! Surely they aroused me well. How helpless I had been in their grasp! How angry I was with myself that I could not but respond as the least and most worthless of slaves! How I had leaped, and moaned, and whimpered, and begged for the least continuance of their touch! But how could this be? Was I not of Earth? And how lonely I was, to my distress, and shame, when, restless, twisting, on my mat, lying in the darkness on my chain, I had been neglected or overlooked. Why had I not rejoiced? I had tried to rejoice, and failed. Offers had been made for me I had learned, six offers. Six! How startled I was to learn this. I, of Earth, was desired, and as a Gorean slave! Naturally I had striven to find this indication of interest, this form of evaluation, distressing and humiliating. I had struggled to be dismayed. Men had wanted to buy me, and as the slave and animal I was. How deplorable, how terrible! But only one girl, I had learned, had received more offers! I did not know who had made the offers, and thus, had one been accepted, I did not know to whose feet, hooded, I would be put. Then, after a time, I had been removed from the slave house. I had been conducted to an assignment shed, from which I would be put to various tasks. As I could not read, the roster was read to me. I laundered, I worked in the kitchens, I carried water, I ran errands, I cleaned

huts. I was waiting, each day, hoping to be sent to the edge of
the camp, toward the wands, that I might search for roots, pick
berries, or gather firewood. I, like the others given such tasks,
would not be supervised. I did not understand why this was.
They seem to think we will all return to our chains. Are we all
so docile, so eager, so enamored of our collars? They did not
know me. I was different! I was of Earth! On the day of such
an assignment, which would surely be soon, I would seize my
opportunity. I would escape. I would never be caught! Why,
I wondered, is it said that there is no escape for the Gorean
slave girl? Except at night, when we are often chained, it seems
escape would be quite easy. If escape is so easy, why do so few
girls attempt it? Is it because we know ourselves slaves, and
rightfully so?

I looked up at him, as a meaningless slave to her adored
master.

No longer did I think of escape. All such thoughts fled from
me. I loved him! I wanted only to be his! I wanted to love and
serve him! I wanted to be only his helpless, loving slave!

He was here!

He must want me. Was I not his?

It was he who had brought me to this, to the bondage which
I had feared, and for which I had longed, a bondage in which I
must serve, a bondage in which I would know myself owned, a
bondage in which I would be a mere property of my master, a
bondage in which I would find my fulfillment as a woman, and
a slave.

I was at his feet, the feet of my master!

He had followed me, even from Brundisium, so far, to this
strange, remote, and wild place, to seek me for his collar!

I was his!

I looked up at him. My lips trembled. I wanted to speak, but
dared not do so.

Surely he could see the hope, the surrender, the love, in my
eyes. I forced myself to hold my hands down on my thighs, that
I not lift them piteously to him. I did not wish to be cuffed. But
I found them turned, inadvertently, so that their palms were
uppermost, their small, soft, sensitive, vulnerable expanses of
tissue exposed to him.

I am yours, I thought. Buy me, own me, I thought.

He smiled, but it was a smile of contempt. He then turned away. I remained as I was, kneeling on the rough boards of the dock.

I do not even think he recognized me. My small frame was shaken with fury. I looked after him, moving away, as though nothing had happened. Indeed, from his point of view, nothing had happened. He had merely had a brief encounter with a meaningless slave.

He had not recalled me. I was nothing to him!

Tears ran down my cheeks. On my thighs I clenched my fists. I wanted to scream with helplessness, futility, and rage.

Well then did I understand that I was marked, tunicked, and collared.

How I hated him, and all men, the masterful beasts who would take us in hand, own us, and do with us as they pleased!

I stared after him, angrily, the callous brute, so tall and strong, with that easy, unhurried walk, the proud, high gaze before which men might take pause, the broad back, the narrow waist, the sturdy legs, that indifferent, cruel, magnificent larl of a man, to whom my feelings were nothing.

I did not even know his name.

Buy me, buy me, Master, I thought.

No, no, no, I thought.

I hate him, I hate him!

All my pride of Earth welled up within me. How horrifying that I should be here, on a remote world, a marked, half-naked, collared slave!

How incomprehensible and lamentable was my fate!

I looked after him, enraged, and hated him!

It was he who had brought me to this, to the indelible marking of my body, to the shame and degradation of a collar, to the revelatory scandal of a tunic, he who had brought it about that I was now an animal, that I was now goods and merchandise, that I might now be given away, or bought and sold. How miserable I was, there, kneeling alone on the boards! How I hated him! And all men! Why could they not be like the men of Earth, sweet, understanding, sensitive, weak, confused, timid, eager to please, easily guided, suitably conditioned, manipulable, repudiators of nature, betrayers of their blood, traitors to their manhood? Why were Goreans so different, so unassuming, so thoughtless, so unpretentiously confident, so unconsciously and innocently proud, so self-satisfied, so unquestioning, so virile, so powerful, so strong, so unaware, so triumphant? Why did they look upon us, and see us as theirs, and make us theirs? I did not think the men of Earth and Gor were so different, if at all, biologically. Surely they were of the same species. The differences, I was sure, were those of enculturation. Why had those of Gor never abandoned nature; why had they never strayed from her, why had they never betrayed her, and themselves? Doubtless there were complex historical explanations for such things.

I then looked about, wildly, at the long dock on which I knelt, the heavy boards stretching before me, diminishing in the distance, the great ship ahead, uneasy at its moorings, at the broad river to the left, the sheds, shops, and forest on the right.

I must escape. I would escape.

I must be wary. No sooner would a man lay his eyes upon me than he would see me as goods, as a slave. The tunic, the collar! How different to be a slave on Gor, I had gathered, as opposed to a free woman! They were everything, we nothing. I had never even seen a Gorean free woman, though there must have been some about, say, when I was on the dock in Brundisium, coffled, blindfolded, my hands tied behind me. Perhaps some were outside the market wall, but yards away, when I was in the exposition cage. Within the wall there were only men, regarding us, considering their choices. I had heard there were male silk slaves. Perhaps there were other markets where they were exhibited and sold, markets frequented by women rich enough to buy them. Such slaves were apparently scorned by Gorean males. It was said Earth was a good source of such slaves, as its males had already learned to fear, please, and obey women. Many were silk slaves and did not know that they were silk slaves. Some were natural silk slaves and others had been raised, taught, and trained to be such. These were told they were "true men." Even their mistresses despised them. What, on Earth, did they lack but a distinctive garb, and the collar? I had not seen a Gorean free woman but I had heard much of them, particularly from my instructresses in my house of training. They spoke of them with loathing, but also fear. One of the sorriest fates of a kajira would be to find herself the serving slave of such a self-centered, regal, haughty monster. It is supposedly harrowing even to encounter one on the streets. For some reason, they hate us. I had gathered that the Gorean free woman, in the might of her liberty, possesses a standing, prestige, status, and force far beyond that of the allegedly free woman of Earth. Even Gorean males who may have a dozen servitors and own a hundred women, and be followed by a score of clients, will step from her path, and defer to her. They will listen attentively to her, even though she might speak the most arrant of nonsense. She is, after all, free. She need not kneel and humbly, as a slave, request permission to speak, a permission which may not be granted. She is said to well and shamelessly exploit the eminence and authority which the culture bestows upon her. Where all are free, at least after a fashion, there is nothing special or important about freedom. It is taken for granted, and one thinks little of it. The Gorean free woman, on the other hand, understands that she is free in a manner which might dismay, and would surely far exceed, that of the allegedly free woman of Earth. Certainly she may contrast herself with the meaningless animal, the female slave. Why then do free men court the free woman and buy the slave? Why do they yield their place in the theaters and concert halls to the free woman, and drag the slave by the hair to a tavern's alcove? When the free woman is courted, she may be uncertain if it is she, or her wealth, her influence, her familial and caste connections, or such, which are sought; when the slave is purchased, as she has nothing, she is well aware that is she herself which is desired, and for the purposes of a slave, service and pleasure, inordinate pleasure. How horrifying it must be for one of these lofty free women, hitherto so exalted, privileged, and superior, hitherto so smug, petulant, arrogant, and demanding, hitherto so incomparably, so insufferably proud, if she should, to her horror, undergo a catastrophic reversal of fortune, if she should find herself reduced to bondage, to be stripped, collared, and sold! Yet how strange, too, that these women, so many of them, seem restless, impatient, short-tempered, and miserable. Surely this is incomprehensible. Do they not have everything for which a woman might long, cultural elevation, standing, status, prestige, power, dignity, and respect, even awe? Why then are they so unhappy? And why are they so cruel to us, and hate us so? We are not interfering with their precious freedom. We could not do so if we wished. We are only helpless beasts, in our collars and tunics. Can we help it if men want us more? And why do they so often insult and taunt men? Are they angry with men, and, if so, why? What do they want from men? Do they not understand that this might annoy, or anger, the men? A slave might die of fear before risking such a thing. And why do some of them join small caravans, and risk dangerous journeys to far places, or wander dark, unguarded streets, or stroll the high bridges alone, in the bright moonlight? Are they so smug, so sure of themselves, that they do not understand the perils of such things? Do they court the collar? Do they long to be owned, and thrown naked, with a jangle of chain, to the furs of love?

I looked about myself, at the men about, the workers, several of them, a mercenary or two, a mariner in his brimless cap. These were Gorean men. Such men wanted women as slaves, and so they had them so. Such men were scions of a culture founded on nature and its fulfillment, not its denial. I wondered if such men knew we yearned for their collars.

I thrust such thoughts from my mind!

I was of Earth!

Goreans were fools! I would escape!

Chapter Eighteen

"What is wrong, Master?" inquired Asperiche.

"Nothing," I told her, angrily.

"You have seen her!" she laughed. "At long last! Here, in Shipcamp!"

"Who?" I asked.

"She whom you have sought so long," she said. "Even in Brundisium, surely in Tarncamp!"

"I have sought no one," I said.

"I think Master did not come to this remote, forlorn place for two staters," she said.

"Gold staters," I said.

"Even so," she said.

"Do you wish to be beaten?" I asked.

"Is she well-curved," she asked, "a blonde or a brunette?"

"You would look well," I said, "on all fours, bringing me the switch in your teeth, whimpering plaintively to be beaten."

"I trust she is not a barbarian," she said.

"What is wrong with barbarians?" I asked.

"I thought so," she said. "They are stupid."

"They twist, sob, and cry out, as well as any other woman," I said.

"Buy her," she said. "Does she have a private master?"

"No," I said, "she is a camp slave."

"She will be cheap then," she said. "Has she been in the slave house?"

"I do not know," I said.

"If so," she said, "she would be well heated by now."

"I do not want her," I said.

"Buy her," she said. "Get her out of your system. Get her on your chain, have her crawl about for a time in your collar, use her for slave sport, make her sob and cry, and beg, and then sell her."

"She is nothing to me," I said. "I turned my back on her. I left her on her knees, on the dock."

"What is her name?" she asked.

"I do not know, nor do I care," I said.

"Was she sold in Brundisium?" she asked.

"Yes," I said, "to agents of the Pani, who were stocking slaves for the camps."

"More likely, for trade goods," she said.

"Perhaps," I said.

"What was her lot number?" she asked.

"119," I said.

"Master has an excellent memory," she said.

"I scouted her, on the world called Earth," I said. "She owes her collar to me."

"I have heard it is a sorry world," she said.

"It has not been well kept," I said.

"Not even the urt soils its own nest," she said.

"I have no interest in her," I said.

"If you know her former lot number," she said, "it would be easy enough for you, a free man, to learn her name, and where she is housed. Records are kept. I could be beaten if I inquired."

"Curiosity," I said, "is not becoming to a kajira."

"So I have been told," she said.

"And now you have been told again," I said.

"Asperiche understands," she said. "She is not stupid. She is not a barbarian."

"We do not bring stupid slaves to Gor," I said.

"Naive slaves then, ignorant slaves," she said. "Barbarian kajirae do not even know they are women."

"They soon learn," I said.

"They are all frigid," she said.

"Not all," I said.

"Some," she said.

"The collar takes that out of them," I said.

"Slaves talk," she said. "There are only so many barbarians. Lot numbers take time to wear off. Masters are not the only ones with memories. Would you like me to find her for you, bind her hands behind her, and switch-herd her to your feet?"

"Certainly not," I said.

"You do not want her kneeling, bound before you?"

"No," I said.

"What is special about her?" she asked.

"Nothing," I said. "Where are you going?"

"To fetch food," she said. "The kitchen is open now."

Chapter Nineteen

"I have not seen you so," I said to Tyrtaios.

"I have been contacted," said Tyrtaios.

"Friends?" I asked.

"One might say so," he said.

"In the camp?" I said.

"No," he said.

"Across the river?" I asked.

He looked at me, suddenly, narrowly. "What do you know of what lies across the river?" he asked.

"Very little," I said. "I do know there is a palisaded compound there, which presumably houses special supplies, and perhaps prize slaves, too precious to be risked amongst the men of Shipcamp."

"You have access to a glass of the Builders," he said.

"No," I said. "I have heard such."

"I see," he said. His hand fell then to his side. No longer did it rest, half opened, poised like a crouching sleen at the hilt of his belt knife.

"Whatever your business," I said, "I think it must soon be brought to a conclusion, for the great ship is muchly fitted." The single great rudder had been hung yesterday. "I suspect the eyes will be soon painted."

"I think not," he said. "Tersites has forbidden it."

"Men may fear to sail," I said, "if the ship cannot see."

"Those who do not embark," he said, "will be left behind, or slain."

"Why would Tersites not permit the ship to see?" I asked.

"I do not know," he said. "Perhaps he is afraid to let it see, for what it might see."

"You intend to embark?" I said.

"Yes," he said. "Much is at stake."

"Perhaps a world," I said, "or its division."

"You need do only what you are told," he said.

"And what am I to be told?" I asked.

"There is a cargo," he said, "two large crates, heavy, with mysterious contents, now across the river, for safekeeping, which are to be secretly embarked."

"Games are afoot," I said, "in which the dice are to be judiciously weighted."

"The cargo was conveyed across the river, weeks ago," he said. "It must now be brought back, to the wharf, to be stowed aboard the great vessel."

"There are guards," I said.

"I have selected them," he said.

I wondered how it was that Tyrtaios would have had the authority to make such selections.

"Tonight," he said, "clouds are likely to conceal the moons. Boats come and go. I think there will be little difficulty in placing the cargo aboard."

"And if there is?" I asked.

"Then men will die," he said.

"What of the Pani?" I asked.

"They have their own concerns, their own projects, their own wars," he said.

"Still," I said.

"One high amongst them is involved in this," he said.

"I see," I said. I had supposed so.

"A place has been prepared for the cargo," he said. "It will be stowed, netted, and lashed down amongst objects of a similar appearance. An innocent labeling will identify it on the manifests."

"The manifests are already prepared?" I asked.

"Of course," he said.

"This business is to be transacted tonight," I said.

"Conditions permitting," he said. "Clouds, the moons obscured, darkness, an empty dock, the absence of random patrols."

"Mariners speak of a storm tonight," I said.

"So much the better," he said.

"If all is so innocent, or seemingly so," I said, "why not manage the business in the day?"

"Too many are about," he said. "Smiths, carpenters, sail makers, sawyers, docksmen, mariners, wagoners, armsmen, even slaves. Even one who might be curious, or suspicious, or ask a question, is far too many."

"Who are your friends?" I asked.

"Friends?" he asked.

"Those by whom you have been contacted," I said.

"They are in the forest," he said.

"Not across the river, with the boxes?"

"They fear to be near them," he said.

"Surely they are innocent enough, mere crates, mere boxes," I said.

"Doubtless," he said.

"Nothing in there is alive," I said.

"Not now," he said.

"If they are in the forest, if beyond the wands," I said, "they must fear the larls."

"Perhaps," he said, "it is the larls which might fear them."

"They have access to a forbidden weapon," I conjectured.

"I do not think so," said Tyrtaios.

"Then?" I said.

But Tyrtaios did not respond.

Most Goreans, I was sure, certainly those of the First Knowledge, knew little of forbidden weapons. There were rumors, whispers, stories, of course, of lightning sticks, tubes of fire, bows which cast quarrels so swift and small one could not even see them in flight, of metal rocks which burst apart like ripe pods in the Schendi death plant, and such.

"I have not seen these boxes," I said.

"They are large, and heavy, but manageable," he said. "As before, we will fashion a platform athwart two linked longboats. I anticipate no difficulty. Meet us here at the eighteenth Ahn. This should give us the time to cross the river, fetch the cargo, fasten it on the platform, come back, free it, and get it aboard."

"All by the twentieth Ahn," I said.

"Earlier, if possible," he said.

"The shore side of the dock will be clear," I said.

"It will be seen to," he said.

"What of passers-by?" I asked.

"It will be seen to," he said, "by the knife."

"The wind is rising," I said. "I think the mariners are right. There is to be a storm."

"Wear a cloak," he said, "a dark cloak."

Chapter Twenty

I tried to slip the shackle from my ankle. It was held with perfection, of course, as was doubtless the intention of the masters, the brutes and beasts who owned us.

"What are you doing?" inquired Janina, turning toward me, with a rustle of her own chain. It was muchly dark in the log kennel. The kennel was low-ceilinged, windowless, and some twenty paces, master's paces, in length. There was a small hanging lamp at each end. We are stripped in the kennel, but we have our blankets. My shackle, with its short chain, was attached to the long chain, which was fastened at each end of the kennel. "Nothing," I said, angrily.

"You will scrape your ankle doing that," she said.

"The masters will not be pleased if you mark yourself," said Relia, across the kennel, on the other long chain. "They like us smooth, to their touch."

"Do they!" I said, angrily.

But I could remember, only recently, how concerned I had been, that I would be smooth to the touch of masters. Slaves are concerned with such things. They hope to be desirable, and pleasing. After all, they are slaves.

"In the last few days," said Relia, "you have been so different, so surly, petulant, and unhappy. What is wrong?"

"Nothing," I said.

"It was after she returned from the dock," said Relia, to Janina.

"What happened?" asked Janina.

"Go to sleep," said another slave, turning in her blanket.

I wept. "You cannot slip your shackle," said Relia.

"She knows that," said Janina. "It is symbolic, if anything, something to do, frustration."

"She could still mark herself," said Relia.

"She is a barbarian," said another.

"Sleep," said the slave, who had turned away from us.

"Day after day," I said, "carrying water, back and forth, doing errands, running, fetching, cooking, serving, the kitchens, the shops, the ironing, the laundering, the sewing of rent tunics!"

"What do you expect?" asked a slave.

"She is a barbarian," said another.

"But a pretty barbarian," said another.

"They are all pretty," said another, "else they would not be brought here."

"Some are beautiful," said another.

"Not as beautiful as we," said another.

"No," said another.

"You are not in a rich man's house, a pleasure garden, the palace of a Ubar," said Relia, "with little to do but sing and play the kalika."

"More likely," said another, "with little to do until it was time to adorn your master's slave ring."

"I do not know how to sing and play the kalika," I said.

"She cannot even dance," said another slave.

"All slaves can dance," said another.

"How is that?" asked another.

"They are women," said another.

"Some are better than others," said a slave.

"Of course," said another.

"If she were more intelligent," said another, "she might be educated, to be a more interesting chattel."

"I am educated," I said.

"How many breeds of kaiila are there?" asked a slave.

"I do not know," I said.

"When do talenders bloom?" asked another.

"I do not know," I said.

"How many eggs does the Vosk gull lay?"

"I do not know," I said.

"Children know such things," said a slave.

"Surely she has more serious opinions," said another, "as

to the ranking of the nine classic poets, the values of the Turian hexameter, should prose be allowed in song drama, the historicity of Hesius, the reform of the calendar, the dark geometries, the story of the czehar, the policies of the Salarian confederation, the nature of the moons, the sumptuary laws of Ti, the history of Ar."

"Some men enjoy a conversation with a slave," said another, "until they remind her that she is in a collar, and put her to the furs where she belongs."

"I am educated on my world," I said, "not yours!"

"This is now your world," said a slave.

"And on it you are uneducated," said another.

"She is illiterate and stupid," said a slave.

"I am not stupid!" I said.

"Ignorant then," said another.

"Yes, ignorant and illiterate," said another.

"But she is pretty," said Janina.

"She might look well, roped at a man's feet," said another.

"As Earth sluts go," said another.

"So, too, might a she-tarsk," said another.

I shook my ankle, angrily, with a rattle of chain.

Two of the girls laughed.

"It is on you, little vulo," said a girl.

"Do not demean me!" I said.

"How can one demean a slave?" asked a girl.

"I am not a slave!" I cried.

"We are all slaves," said a girl.

"Not I!" I cried.

"Do you think we do not know a slave when we see one?" asked a girl. "Consider your figure, your desires, your needs, what you most want."

"A collar," said another.

"No!" I cried.

"It is obvious," said another, "even to look upon you. You are a natural slave, a slave in your very nature, a needful chattel, one miserable and unfulfilled otherwise, a needful chattel requiring a master."

"No!" I said. "No!" I pulled at the chain. How I feared what they said was true! How I feared I might be a slave! And surely

I had understood myself as, and accepted myself as, a slave, a rightful slave, even on Earth. But that was before, before!

"For days you have been different," said Relia.

"What happened?" asked Janina.

"Nothing," I said, angrily.

"You will soon feel better," said Janina.

"It is not like you had been sold from a beloved household," said another.

"Do not fret, Laura," said Relia. "You need only the proper master, and a touch of his whip."

"I am going to escape," I said.

There was at that point a great crash of thunder, and several of us cried out. I had cried out for I was startled. I suppose we all were. I, however, unlike, I am sure, several of the others, took the mighty crash, which seemed to shake the very logs of the long kennel, as no more than a natural thing, a simple, if impressive, disturbing, harsh, violent manifestation of suddenly fierce, unusual weather. Some of the girls, however, particularly those of the First Knowledge, deemed lightning, at least upon occasion, the cast, fiery missile of angered Priest-Kings, and its successor, thunder, as proclaiming, for all to understand, the fact of its terrible passage. A moment later we heard a torrent of rain beat against the low roof of the kennel.

"To where?" asked a girl.

"I do not know," I said, "to anywhere."

"When will you escape?" asked a girl.

"Sooner or later," I said, "I will be assigned away from the dock area, to root out vegetables, to pick berries, to gather firewood, something."

"Do not run," said a girl.

"There is nowhere to run," said another girl.

"You are collared," said another.

"You will be hamstrung, fed to sleen," said a girl.

"Fear the forest," said another.

"You will not be able to find your way, and what way might you try to find?"

"You are kajira. You will have no way to find."

"The only way for you is to the feet of a master."

"You will wander in circles," said another.

"You will be lost," said another.

"You will starve," said another.

"Winter is coming," said another.

"There are animals," said another. "Sleen, panthers."

"I am not afraid," I said, though I was afraid, very afraid.

"You do not want freedom," said a girl. "You want a master. You want to kneel naked before a man, and bend down and kiss his feet. You want to lift your head, and lick and kiss his whip. You want to be owned, to belong wholly, to submit, to obey, to be dominated, to be mastered, to be possessed as only a slave can be possessed, to grovel, to selflessly love and serve."

"No, no, no!" I said.

"Whatever man sees you will bring you back, or keep you," said another.

"Perhaps they will free me!" I said.

"You are too pretty to free," said another.

"You will be taken in hand, and thrown to a man's feet," said another, "where you belong."

"And where you want to be," said another.

"No, no!" I said.

"Avoid the wands," said Janina.

"There are larls," said another.

"I am not afraid of larls," I said. I would count them, in the cages, and make away, and would have so great a start that they could not catch me.

"Then you are a fool," said Relia.

"Larls are not men," said Janina. "They will not care that you are clever, or pretty. They will not ravish you or shackle you, or beat you, or sell you to another. They will eat you."

There was another crash of thunder, and the rain continued to fall heavily.

"It is a terrible night," said a girl.

"None will be about this night," said another.

"May the roof hold," said another.

A drainage ditch had been dug about the kennel, and I did not fear that water would be likely to seep into the kennel. The roof was sturdy, and caulked with ship's tar.

"It may rain for days," said a girl.

"It is the season," said another.

"Then snow," said yet another.

"Ice was in the river yesterday," said another. "I saw it."

"The great ship must soon leave," said another. "Otherwise it will be frozen fast."

"What is to be done with us?" asked a slave.

"We have served our purpose," said another, "in Tarncamp, and now in Shipcamp. They do not need us any longer."

"Perhaps they will kill us," said a slave, apprehensively.

"Do not be foolish," said another. "We will be sold south."

"We may know of secret things," said a girl. "They may kill us."

"We might talk," said another, frightened.

"Not I," said another.

"You will speak quickly enough on the rack," said another.

"True," said another.

"They will kill us then!" cried a girl, and jerked wildly at her chain.

"Men do not kill kajirae," said Relia, "no more than they would kill pretty birds or kaiila."

"What then?" asked a girl.

"Is it not obvious?" said Relia.

There were cries of misery, and consternation, in the kennel. We were all familiar with the great ship. We had seen it, often enough. It was looming, awesome, and mysterious. It was unlike other ships. It was almost a floating city. For what had it been built? For what waters had so mighty a keel been laid? What storms had it been framed to withstand? What broad, trackless, landless wildernesses might it hazard? What strange harbors might so monstrous a vessel seek, by what unfamiliar, far ports of call might it be lured?

"No, no!" cried several of the girls.

The rain continued to beat heavily on the roof. The wind began to howl. Thunder sounded again, and again.

We drew our blankets more closely about us.

"You have been to the dock, all of you," said Relia. "You have seen the loading of cargoes, the great casks, the bags of sa-tarna and suls, crates of bitter tospits, paga and ka-la-na packed in straw, medicines, salves and unguents, endless streams of supplies."

"And the objects of war," said another, "timbers, hurling stones, cordage, jars of pitch, finned darts, spears, glaives, javelins, varieties of blades, masses of shields, bucklers, wrappings in which are bound a thousand arrows."

"But, too," said Relia, "coffers which might contain pearls, gems, jewelries, golden wire, weighty coins."

"Vessels of rare metal, black- and red-figured potteries, candles and lamps, perfumes and silks," said Janina.

"I saw siriks, shackles, slave harnessing," said a slave, uneasily.

"What," asked Relia, "do you think the likely object of the projected voyage?"

"War," said a slave.

"Trade," averred another. "Consider the cargos, rep-cloth, wool of the hurt, candles, mirrors, lamps, such things."

"War with whom, trade with whom?" asked Relia.

We were silent.

"What do men prize most," asked Relia, "after gold, after victory in war, after fine kaiila, and loyal sleen?"

"Beautiful, fearful, obedient, docile slaves," said another.

"How many of you have been sold?" asked Relia.

"Everyone in the kennel has been sold," said a slave, "and some of us many times."

"What are you then?" inquired Relia.

"Slaves," said a girl.

"Articles of commerce, objects for vending, stock, properties, wares, commodities, goods, merchandise," said Relia.

"I do not understand," said a girl.

"Our role in this is clear," said Relia. "We need not fear being left behind. Dismiss such thoughts. We are cargo, as much as suls or paga, as much as would be nose-ringed kaiila, penned tarsks, or tethered verr."

"No, no!" cried a slave.

"They will take us with them," said Relia, "if not for the common purposes of slaves, the services and delights derivable from our ownership, then as goods, objects for sale, for barter, and trade."

"No!" cried another slave.

"We are cargo," said Relia, "the one cargo you wish to overlook."

"I am afraid," cried a slave.

"We all are," said Relia.

"I have heard a mariner whisper in terror," said a slave, "for he fears Tersites, the shipwright, is mad, and would do war against Thassa, would contemplate a journey to where the world is no more, where the seas, like a waterfall a thousand pasangs in width, plunge over the cliff of the world, to fall a thousand pasangs to the rocks of fire, from whence, as boiling steam, they arise until, chilled by the moons, they form clouds and fall again to the earth, as rain."

"It is true," whispered a girl.

"It is raining even now," said a slave, frightened, as the precipitation, turning like a whip in the hand of the wind, struck at the roof and then at the sides of the kennel, one side and then the other, and then, more steadily, fell again upon the roof.

"I do not want to be taken to the World's End!" cried a girl.

"Then slip your shackle," said Relia.

There was then another great crash of thunder.

"In the morning, or soon," said a girl, "when we are loose, let us all run away."

"There is nowhere to run," said a slave.

"The masters would be displeased," said another. "What would be done with us?"

"We cannot escape," said another. "We are collared. There is no escape for us. We are kajirae!"

"Relia," I said.

She turned toward me.

"The rains will wipe out scent trails, will they not?"

"For a time, yes, I think so," said Relia.

"Good," I said.

"Do not do anything foolish," said Relia.

"Stay away from the wands," said Janina.

"Perhaps," I said. I then rolled myself in the blanket, and lay down.

I listened for a time to the rain, and then fell asleep. I was awakened, from time to time, by bursts of thunder, but, each time, I went back to sleep. In the morning the day's roster would be posted, and Relia, as was customary, would read it, aloud. I was not the only one in the kennel, incidentally, who was unable to read. It is not that unusual to find individuals, particularly in what are spoken of as the "lower castes," who cannot, or do not, read. Indeed, some Goreans are too proud to read, even some of the "higher castes." Many men at arms, for example, pride themselves on their illiteracy, regarding reading as a pursuit more appropriate to merchants and scribes than to those of the "scarlet caste." Rich men, too, may hire a reader, or one to write letters for them, and such. Some of the lower scribes set up awnings, or set up shop under a trellis, near a market, or in an inn or tavern, or such places, at given times, and make themselves available to read letters, write them, and so on. Many mariners, too, incidentally, do not read, despite the fact that many are of fine mind, and are the masters of much lore and remarkable skills. It is enough, they say, when one can read the currents, the clouds, the winds, the skies, and the stars. The barks to which they trust their lives, the skies, even Thassa herself, they note, do not read.

Chapter Twenty-One

"Ai!" I cried, "What things are these!"

There were two of them. Almost as one, those two large, shaggy heads had turned, so swiftly that it seemed there had been no turning. They had been intent on the live animal bound on the spit. Then, almost as though there had been no movement, we were regarded.

"No!" said Tyrtaios to me. "Do not!" His hand stayed mine. So the bright serpent of steel remained in its housing, tense. "No," said Tyrtaios, again.

I had not seen such eyes in beasts. They were large, rounded eyes, and they suddenly flashed like burnished copper, reflecting the firelight.

They were crouched down. The legs seemed short for the body, but the body was long, and the arms were very long. There was something odd about the hands, or paws, but it did not then register with me what it might be.

We had come on two beasts, in the woods. But there was a fire. Surely beasts do not build fires.

But they were beasts.

Why had a fire been built?

A small beast squirmed, bound on a stick, or spit.

Many shadows were about. The clearing was small. Branches and trees were about. The moons were obscured. The beasts, regarding us, were deeply furred, so much so I was not immediately sure of the size or form of the actual body. Too, for an instant, only an instant, it seemed the fur had been erected, frighteningly, and then it subsided.

Tyrtaios removed his hand from mine.

"Had you drawn," said Tyrtaios, "you would now be dead, and perhaps myself as well."

"They are only beasts," I said.

"I first saw such things only days ago," said Tyrtaios.

"Beasts," I said.

"Sometimes they are the last things one sees," said Tyrtaios. "They do not always care to be looked upon by men."

"Let us circumvent this place," I said, "for I fear peril here, and continue on, to keep the rendezvous with your friends."

"These," said Tyrtaios, "are the friends."

"Beasts?" I said.

"Look more closely," said Tyrtaios.

"I see the leather bands which bind them," I said. The firelight shone on the broad straps.

"They are not bound," said Tyrtaios. "That is harnessing. Do you not observe accouterments? See, too, the metal rings on the left wrists."

"Its master has put large, golden rings in the ears of one," I said.

"It has a lord," said Tyrtaios, "somewhere, probably not here, but no master."

"They must be dull of sense," I said, "for such beasts, for they did not know of our presence until a moment ago."

"No," said Tyrtaios, "they were well aware of our presence. Their seeming unawareness, almost somnolence, was to put us at our ease."

"To lure us in?" I said.

"I think not this time," he said.

"They turned their heads quickly, only when we were almost upon them," I said.

"I doubt they could have helped that," he said. "I think it was reflexive, when a certain critical distance was reached. The beast can only control itself so far. That must be remembered. They can control themselves only so far. They are dangerous, even to friends, and allies. The ears went back against the head, at the same time. Did you notice?"

"No," I said. It was dark. Much had happened quickly. I wondered if Tyrtaios had really noticed that, about the ears, or had just realized, afterwards, that it had taken place. The ears were lifted now, and turned toward us, like large eyes which could hear sound.

"We did not come on them unawares," said Tyrtaios. "They can detect the tread of a field urt through grass at a dozen paces."

"You speak of them as though they were men," I said.

"They are similar to men, but different, very different."

"I was startled," I said. "It was fortunate I did not fall on them with my sword."

"You would have been unsuccessful," he said.

"How so?" I said. "They are not armed." The strike of the double-edged gladius would be first to the left, and then, with the backstroke, to the right, both strokes to the throat, both like a whisper, scarcely heard, but deep enough. The blade must not be impeded, no more than necessary. He who uses the gladius like a butcher, is not likely to use it long, and perhaps but once.

"The one behind you is," said Tyrtaios.

I turned about, slowly.

Behind us, a mighty ax grasped in its hands, or paws, was a third beast, larger than the others. I had not heard it behind us. For so large an animal it had moved with great stealth. To be sure, so, too, when hunting, do the sleen and larl. Had it been hunting, and what then might it have been hunting? I then had the sense that it might have been behind us, lost in the shadows, almost invisible, for some time. I would later come to understand, too, that the path toward the fire had been cleared of dried leaves, and twigs. A forester might have noted such things, the lack of sound. I had not. Apparently it had been intended, from the positioning of brush and branches, and forest debris, that we would approach the two beasts by the fire by means of this readied avenue. I suspect Tyrtaios had been aware of this, and had found it acceptable. Perhaps he felt there was no alternative.

I regarded the beast behind me. It was crouched over, grasping the enormous ax. A man would have found it difficult to have lifted, let alone wield, that mighty tool, or weapon. In its grasp it seemed little more than a stick. One blow from that huge, long-handled, broad-bladed, double-bladed device might have felled a small tree. I did not doubt it could cut a man in two. In the beast there was no sign of agitation, but, rather, of attention, of vigilance. What storm of force, I wondered, might be unleashed in such a mighty frame? Surely it was there, beneath that surface. Could lightning, waiting, conceal itself within a pelt, lie in ambush; it might seem so. I had the sense of a crossbow with its bolt loaded, the slight pressure of a finger on the trigger, that of a mountain containing fire, a seething, churning lake of molten stone, easily agitated, which might erupt. I regarded the beast. I could not well sense its mien. I could read no expression, nor intent, on its face, or muzzle; there was no wrinkled snout, no bared fangs. There was no sound, no snarl, no growl. The nostrils were slightly distended. The ears were back, against the side of the head.

"Make no sudden moves," said Tyrtaios.

I had no intention of doing so.

Tyrtaios lifted his hand to the two beasts by the fire, palm inward. "Tal," he said.

One of the beasts by the fire lifted a small metal box, which almost disappeared within its grasp. It was then I noted, uneasily, that its large hands had multiply jointed digits, or fingers, which were rather like tentacles. Moreover, there were six of these digits on each hand.

"Can they speak?" I asked.

"Gorean?" he asked.

"Of course," I said.

"Some," he said, "after a fashion. Most not."

"How any?" I asked. "They are beasts."

"Can you speak their tongue?" he asked.

"They have a tongue?" I said.

A tissue of noises which were far from human, but might rather have been the unintelligible emanations of a beast of prey, of a larl, or sleen, emerged from the throat of the beast who held the tiny box, or that which seemed tiny in its grasp.

Simultaneously the large beast behind us withdrew into the forest, perhaps to watch the path.

The beast with the box pressed a part of its surface, on the side, and, on its upper surface, rotated what seemed to be a tiny dial, rather like that by means of which one might set a chronometer.

From my time on the world Earth, and from the voyages I

had made, I was no stranger to a variety of interesting devices seldom found on Gor, devices of communication, and record keeping, and such, devices the nature of which was unknown to most Goreans, even to those who had attained to the Second Knowledge.

The beast with the box regarded Tyrtaios.

It then made a sound, a soft, guttural sound.

A mechanically produced sound came from the box. It took me an instant to realize that it was a familiar Gorean word, a greeting. It was 'Tal'.

"It is done?" asked the beast.

"Yes," said Tyrtaios.

"You are late," said the beast.

"It seemed wise to leave in darkness," said Tyrtaios. "Too, it would be well for us to soon return, in darkness, as well, lest our absence be noted."

"You have brought the certification, with its seal?" inquired the beast.

"The two objects, two great boxes," said Tyrtaios, "as instructed, have been placed on the ship, and stored as instructed, inconspicuously, amongst other cargo."

"They appear on the manifests?" asked the beast.

I noted the small animal, live, squirming on the spit, on which it was bound. It made no sound.

"Yes," said Tyrtaios, "innocently, as tools for metalwork."

"Good," said the beast.

"I am supposing you know the nature of this secret cargo," said Tyrtaios.

"I am so privileged," said the beast.

"I am not so privileged?" asked Tyrtaios.

"No," said the beast.

"I see," said Tyrtaios.

"You would not understand its nature," said the beast.

"It is to be employed at the World's End?" asked Tyrtaios.

"Precisely," said the beast.

"Assuming the voyage is successful, and one reaches the World's End," said Tyrtaios.

"I suspect," said the beast, "that the ship will never reach the World's End, for such a voyage has never been accomplished.

Ships which pass the farther islands do not return. At least none have done so. I think it is madness to essay such a voyage, to embark so, thusly tempting the cruelties of Thassa, but those above me, higher in the rings, will risk much, even the cargo itself, which on this world is unique and invaluable, on the slim chance that the voyage will be successful. And, should the voyage be successful, it is of the utmost importance, a matter dealing with worlds, that the cargo reaches the right party."

"It is so valuable?" said Tyrtaios.

"Yes," said the beast.

"Then it is gold, or silver, a great quantity, really," said Tyrtaios.

"No," said the beast. "Compared to it gold or silver, precious ointments, coffers of jewels, and such, things that you regard as of value, would be no more than a spoonful of silt, a cup of sand or dirt."

"I see," said Tyrtaios.

"But to you, greedy friend," said the beast, "it would have no value whatsoever in itself, only in its proper delivery to the selected parties. To you it would be, in itself, incomprehensible, meaningless, literally worthless, but to those who understand it, and can make use of it, it is of great value. Keep clearly in mind, it is worth gold and silver, and such, to you, only if it reaches its intended destination. You will then be well paid, with perhaps more than tharlarion weights of gold and silver, perhaps even with countries, and ubarates."

"I would be curious to see what is so worthless, and so valuable," said Tyrtaios.

The second beast, who had been following this exchange, suddenly growled, menacingly. The first beast, however, cautioned it to silence.

"You have heard of the Flame Death of the Priest-Kings?" asked the first beast of Tyrtaios.

"I have heard of it," said Tyrtaios, "but I have not seen it."

"I have seen it once," said the beast, "when a fellow of mine, brandishing a forbidden weapon, one forbidden by the laws of Priest-Kings, was suddenly torn away from me, literally from my side, in a burst of light, of flesh, of blood, and ash. The stones on which he had stood had melted."

I realized then that the beasts, who were presumably

advanced, perhaps as much as the men of Earth, or more, here, on Gor, had limited themselves to permitted weapons. They then, I thought, as men, realized the power of Priest-Kings, and feared them. How formidable, how terrible, I thought, must be Priest-Kings.

"I do not understand," said Tyrtaios.

"Should the cargo be tampered with," said the beast, "it will be destroyed, and he who would dare to tamper with it, perhaps merely desiring to apprise himself of its nature, with it. Only certain parties, properly instructed, entrusted with the codes, can open the containers with impunity."

I regarded the small animal, hairless, on the spit, writhing, cooking. Its mouth opened and closed. Its eyes stared out, wildly. It made no sound. Presumably it felt nothing.

"You have seen that?" I said to Tyrtaios, indicating the small animal on the spit.

"Of course," he said, in annoyance.

"It is alive," I said.

"Obviously," said Tyrtaios.

"It is insensible of pain," I said.

"Not at all," said Tyrtaios.

"It is silent," I said.

"I have been here before," said Tyrtaios. "It is ingenious. A small incision is made in the throat. That silences the animal."

"Its cries might annoy your friends?" I said.

"I do not think so," said Tyrtaios. "I suspect they do not concern themselves with such things. Nor should you. Perhaps they would enjoy it. I do not know. Rather, here, in the forest, one would not wish its whimperings, shrieks, or squeals to attract the attention of, say, a passing sleen or panther."

"Why do they not kill it?" I said.

"I do not know," said Tyrtaios.

"Kill it," I said.

"Do not concern yourself."

"Kill it," I said.

"We are guests here," said Tyrtaios. "Be civil."

"Have them kill it," I said.

"Why?" he asked.

Many Goreans, I suppose, might seem callous, heartless, or

cruel to many of Earth, but they commonly, as those of Earth often do not, love their world, love growing things, trees, grass, flowers, and the world itself, the day and night, the seasons, the wind and sky, the stars, the sound of water in brooks, and live animals, birds, and such. They care for their world and the living things within it. Perhaps this is foolish, but it is a common Gorean way. Who is to say which way is best? Or does it matter? But Goreans will kill for their way.

"What is the concern of your companion?" asked the beast with the device.

"The food," said Tyrtaios.

"What is wrong with it?" asked the beast. "We are preparing it for you. You commonly cook your food, do you not? We prefer a live kill, with the fresh blood."

"I think," said Tyrtaios, "he would prefer that it be killed."

"It is said that cooking it alive improves the flavor," said the beast. "I have heard so."

"Have them kill it," I said.

"It may not be their way," said Tyrtaios.

"Kill it," I said, "or I will."

"No need," said Tyrtaios. "It is dead now."

The second beast, he not with the device, slipped the small animal from the spit.

"Your companion is correct," said the beast with the device. "It is better undercooked, and best when raw, alive, with the racing of the blood, and the many secretions of terror flooding within its circulatory system."

The second beast lifted the limp, hairless, burned body toward us.

I shook my head.

"Pulling the fur out, too, bit by bit, before placing it on the spit, this producing chemical alterations associated with pain, improves the flavor, as well, or so I am told," came from the first beast, its words emerging from the device.

"You are thoughtful," said Tyrtaios.

"We hoped to please you," came from the device.

"We are grateful," said Tyrtaios. "The mighty lords are generous. The hospitality of their race is legendary. Well do I recall, aforetimes, the sumptuousness of their provender. But, alas, we have now no time to feed. We must soon return to Shipcamp, lest our absence be noted."

The beast who had offered us the food then discarded it, to the side, in the bushes. It was not, I gathered, to their taste. Or, perhaps, in its present, ruined condition it was fit only for humans.

"Do you still wish the fire?" asked the beast with the device.

"For a little time," said Tyrtaios. "Our night vision is less acute than yours."

The primary purpose of the fire then, I supposed, had been to mark the location of this rendezvous. One gathered that the large beasts, their eyes like dark moons, might easily negotiate terrains in which a human might find himself helpless. So, too, of course, could the sleen and larl.

"Can you trust your companion?" inquired the beast with the device. "If not, he need not leave this place."

"Do not fear," said Tyrtaios. "There are too few of us as it is, given your instructions. Your prescripts have been clear. Few know of these things. But some must know, else these matters cannot be pursued to fruition."

The beast made growling noises, which seemed to me laden with menace. The sounds which emerged from the device, however, were even, and noncommittal. They might have been printed on a public board. "Reliability is best guaranteed at the point of a sword."

"That is understood," said Tyrtaios.

"The certification?" asked the first beast.

Tyrtaios reached within his tunic, and handed a folded paper to the beast with the device, who put the device to one side, near the fire, and perused the paper. I saw it only briefly. To me the script, which was cursive, was unintelligible, little more than claw marks, but, affixed to the paper, there were two seals, one which seemed no more than a patch of hair, interwoven with silver thread, and the other was in the script of the Pani, in which they transcribe their Gorean, much as the tribesmen of the Tahari write their Gorean in their own unusual letters, or signs. Spoken Gorean, despite differences in accent, such as those of Ar and Cos, is widely comprehensible on Gor. It is, after all, Gorean, the Language.

On the other hand, many are the marks by which the same sounds might be represented. The paper seemed worn to me, soiled, and frayed, and I suspected its message, assuming it was a message, might have been framed and inscribed months ago, and perhaps faraway. The seal of hair on it, supposing it was a seal, which I took it to be, from its appearance and placement, seemed partly removed, or torn, and surely some of the silver threads had parted. Perhaps it had been conveyed to Shipcamp after a long journey, I supposed a secret journey, and had survived various perils and hardships. Certainly it seemed, from its appearance, its discoloration and staining, to have endured a variety of housings and weathers. On the other hand, the seal in the Pani script was fresh. I conjectured that that seal had been emplaced on the document recently, perhaps even earlier today.

"It is in order," said the beast, lifting its head.

These words came from the device, now lying to one side. I thus noted two things; first, with interest, that the device, to be effective, need not be in hand, and, second, with some apprehension, that the hands, or paws, of the beast were now free. One thing was certain. The certification, or document, had now been delivered. I was not now clear what, if anything, might ensue. I was aware, very much aware, should it charge, I would not have time to unsheathe even the dagger at my belt.

"You will require humans to guard the cargo, and deliver it to the appropriate parties," said Tyrtaios.

"Unfortunately," said the beast.

"The noble lords cannot well share the journey of the great ship," said Tyrtaios.

"Nor would we desire to do so," said the beast.

"You fear the voyage will be unsuccessful," said Tyrtaios.

"It cannot succeed," said the beast. "None reach the World's End, not so. The great ship is the folly of a madman, lame, half-blind Tersites. He dares dispute the will of Thassa, known for a thousand years, that none may venture beyond the farther islands. Those who have done so have never returned. The ship is great, but Thassa is greater. And she is not patient. She scorns Tersites, his vanity and presumption. She mocks the architecture of his delusions. She scorns the very wood with which he has framed his dreams. She will dismantle his vaunted, arrogant, floating city timber by timber."

"The cargo has been loaded," said Tyrtaios. "The certification has been delivered."

"You now wish pay?" asked the first beast.

"Others know of the cargo," said Tyrtaios. "If I do not return, it will be removed from the ship, and burned."

"You have made such an arrangement?" asked the first beast.

"Of course," said Tyrtaios.

"And you have men personally loyal to you, who will see to this?"

"Yes," said Tyrtaios.

"I wonder if that is true," came from the device.

"You cannot risk that it is not," said Tyrtaios.

"Your precaution is well understood, but unnecessary," said the beast. "You stand high in our esteem, and trust."

Tyrtaios inclined his head, slightly.

The first beast made a sign to the second, who withdrew a small, but weighty sack from a leather container which lay near the fire.

He cast it to the feet of Tyrtaios, who did not move.

"It is tarn disks, gold, of double weight," came from the device.

"We must return to Shipcamp, before we are missed," said Tyrtaios. "I wish you well." He turned, as though to leave.

"Stop, wait," came from the device.

Tyrtaios turned about.

"You have passed the test well," came from the device.

The second beast then, though I think the gesture pleased him not, bent down, and, not taking his eyes from Tyrtaios, picked up the small sack. The skin on the back of my neck seemed to rise, as I saw that small sack almost disappear in the latitudinal grasp of those long, encircling, multiply jointed six digits. It was then handed to Tyrtaios, with an understated politeness that I found disconcerting. I was confident that we might not have left that small clearing alive, were it not that we were seemingly required as elements, essential elements, in some business which eluded my comprehension.

"It is a great pleasure to do business with one so astute," said the first beast.

"I wish you well," said Tyrtaios. He slipped the small sack inside his tunic. I was surprised he did not place it in the wallet slung at his waist. Mostly, I wished to leave this place, to make away as soon as possible.

"Wait," said the first beast.

Tyrtaios turned back.

"Have you not forgotten something?" came from the device.

"Lord?" asked Tyrtaios.

"It is worth nothing to you," said the beast.

"What?" asked Tyrtaios.

"Were you not entrusted with a vessel, a small vessel, constituting a celebratory draft, a gift, a reward and pledge, placing a seal on our business?"

"Ah!" said Tyrtaios.

"Did you forget?" came from the device.

"Yes," said Tyrtaios.

"Of course," said the beast.

"Forgive me," said Tyrtaios.

"It is from a Home World," said the beast. "It is rare here. Perhaps you hoped to sell it. But, greedy friend, it is worthless to you."

"There is very little in the vessel," said Tyrtaios.

"Did you sample it?"

"No," said Tyrtaios.

"I doubt that it would be to your taste," said the beast.

"The seal is unbroken," said Tyrtaios.

"Give it to me," said the first beast.

"To me!" said the second beast.

"My superior entrusted it to me, and, I gather, his superior to him," said Tyrtaios.

"For us!" said the second beast.

"For the three of you, surely," said Tyrtaios. But the third beast was not present. It had apparently gone to watch the trail.

"We two," said the first beast. It then shut off the device, abruptly.

The two beasts then, crouched down, regarded one another, I thought balefully.

Tyrtaios reached into his wallet, and drew forth a small bottle. I feared the two beasts were to pounce upon him, given the regard in which they seemed to hold the small vessel, but they stopped suddenly, angrily, apprehensively, for, having broken the seal and removed the bottle's stopper, Tyrtaios held it, as though to spill its contents on the ground. The two backed away, a pace, eyeing one another.

Tyrtaios pointed to the first beast, that which had managed the communication device, and held the bottle toward it. We took him, I gathered, to be first amongst the three beasts. The second growled, menacingly. Tyrtaios did not relinquish his grip on the bottle, even when the first beast seized his hand in its paws and forced the bottle to his own lips. It seemed it would drain its contents, what little there was. Tyrtaios yanked back the bottle, and a bit of the beverage splashed free. A howl of rage came from the second beast, but the first regarded Tyrtaios with fury. Tyrtaios then handed the bottle to the second beast, who with one motion threw the contents down that open, dark, fanged, spread maw. Both beasts then leapt into the air, and then crouched down, eyeing one another. The long tongues moved about their jaws. The bottle lay on its side, in the dirt, empty.

"They left none for their fellow," observed Tyrtaios.

"Let us leave," I said.

"Where is the third?" asked Tyrtaios.

"Out there in the darkness, guarding the trail," I speculated.

"No matter," said Tyrtaios. He loosened his dagger in its sheath.

"We need a lamp," I said.

"There is light enough," he said. "We need only reach the river."

We then left the small clearing.

I looked behind us, and noted that the small fire had been extinguished. I gathered that it had served its purpose, marking their campsite, and that the beasts had little need of its illumination.

"When the fee was cast to the ground," I said, "it was no test."

"Certainly not," said Tyrtaios. "It was a gesture of contempt, a transparent sleight, an obvious insult."

"But the beast," I said, "then need retrieve it himself, and did so, seething with fury."

"We permitted it to save face," said Tyrtaios, "pretending to accept the matter on the leader's vaunted terms, as a test of our pride, and probity."

"Do you think he was fooled?" I said.

"Of course not," said Tyrtaios.

"He is dangerous," I said.

"They are all dangerous," said Tyrtaios.

"I do not understand the business of the certification," I said.

"It certifies," he said, "that the cargo was placed on the ship of Tersites, as was intended."

"That much I gathered," I said, "but what is involved here, what is the cargo, what is afoot?"

"I know very little about it," said Tyrtaios, "and I gather that that is for the best."

"Doubtless the messenger, he who delivered it to your superior, would know," I said.

"I think not," said Tyrtaios. "And the messenger is dead, as the others before him."

"I do not understand," I said.

"The certification, which was to be delivered only when the cargo was placed on the ship of Tersites, has come from faraway, perhaps from as far away as the Voltai range, and has passed from one messenger to another, each one of whom was killed after delivering it to the next."

"They expected nothing, and were unconnected, the one with the other?" I said.

"A useful procedure for ensuring security," said Tyrtaios.

"You delivered it boldly," I said.

"I am needed for the success of their venture, whatever may be its nature," said Tyrtaios.

He then, with his dagger, parted the strings which held the wallet to his belt, and cast the wallet into the brush.

I did not understand why he did this. He did not resheathe his dagger.

"Let us continue on," I said, uneasily.

"No," he said, "we are waiting here."

"I do not like this business," I said.

"It pays well," he said.

"Why are we waiting?" I asked.

"There is no point in going further, not now," said Tyrtaios. "It would be foolish to do so."

"I do not understand," I said.

"The fire at the campsite is out," said Tyrtaios. "That will doubtless inform our third friend that we have left the site, and are on the trail."

"So?" I said.

"So our friend will be expecting us, and, when we do not appear, he will investigate."

"I would suppose so," I said. "I am not eager to encounter him."

"Unfortunately I must do so," said Tyrtaios. "He was not with the others. I think that had not been anticipated. But no matter."

"I understand nothing of this," I said.

"You do recall," said Tyrtaios, "that the beast with the speaking machine claimed to know the contents of the cargo."

"Yes," I said.

"The other two, as well, would be likely to know," said Tyrtaios.

"I suppose so," I said.

"Our friend is approaching," said Tyrtaios.

And surely, a darkness amongst darknesses, but a moving darkness, was moving toward us, a large darkness. Then the thing was before us. It stopped. It seemed uncertain. Perhaps it was puzzled, that it had not been joined on the trail. In any event, it had now retraced its path, and it stood, looming, before us. How large the thing was, and, in its way, how terrible. It growled, softly. There was no device, no speaking machine.

"Tal," said Tyrtaios, pleasantly, and plunged his dagger into the beast's chest.

I leaped back, and the large body fell at our feet. The blow had been unhesitant, efficient, unwavering, swift, clean, firm, deep, to the hilt, exact, powerful, a blow worthy of the dark caste itself.

I did not speak my suspicions.

Tyrtaios wiped his blade clean on the beast's fur.

"You killed it," I said. "Why?"

"It was necessary," said Tyrtaios.

"What of the others?" I said.

"They are dead," said Tyrtaios.

"The beverage?" I said.

"Precisely," said Tyrtaios.

"And this one did not drink," I said.

"Precisely," said Tyrtaios.

So, I thought, there are now three fewer who know the nature of the cargo I had helped to put aboard the great ship.

"Let us return to Shipcamp," I said.

"No," said Tyrtaios. "We return to the camp of our friends."

"Why?" I asked.

"On Gor," said he, "such things are not likely to travel with an empty purse."

"I see," I said.

I accompanied Tyrtaios back to the clearing. We rekindled the fire, and he, on his knees, rummaged the packs of the beasts.

"Good," he said, from time to time.

I gathered his trip was not without profit.

I regarded the bottle, fallen to the ground, in the center of the clearing. Two large bodies, contorted, lay near it.

"Do not touch it," he said.

"I will not do so," I said.

I recalled that he had placed the tarn disks within his tunic, not within his wallet, and that later, on the trail, he had cast the wallet away. The bottle, I recalled, had been carried in the wallet. The substance must be very powerful, I thought, so little of it, yet enough to slay two such beasts, even three. Tyrtaios, who was not a timid man, had been unwilling to keep even the wallet in which the vessel, closed as it was, had been carried.

Tyrtaios cut the golden rings from the ears of the first beast. He did not concern himself with the rings on the left wrist of either beast. They were of base metal.

Tyrtaios then stood up, shouldering a large leather sack, in which he had placed a number of articles, coins, belts, buckles, accouterments, and such.

"No forbidden weapons?" I asked.

"No," said Tyrtaios, "and I would not touch them did I find them."

"Nor I," I said, looking about myself, uneasily.

He then kicked dirt over the fire, and we stood in the darkness of the forest.

"What was done here?" I asked.

"What was commanded," he said.

"Should the cargo reach the World's End," I said, "who will know to whom it is to be delivered?"

"My superior," said Tyrtaios.

"It is hard for me to think of one such as you having a superior," I said.

"For a time," said Tyrtaios. "For a time."

"Someone is waiting at the World's End to receive the cargo?" I said.

"Someone, or something," he said. "One gathers so."

"This has to do with worlds?" I said.

"I think so," he said. "Would you like a ubarate, or a country?" he asked.

"Of course," I said.

He then went to the edge of the clearing. I sensed his position in the darkness from the sound.

"What of these bodies?" I asked.

"We will leave them," he said, "for the forest, for the winter, for rain, for snow, for wind, for urts, for sleen, for panthers."

"I see," I said.

"Have no fear," he said. "I have removed the harnessing, the accouterments. I have discarded the speaking device."

"They will be taken as beasts," I said.

"They are beasts," he said.

"Much as men," I said.

"In their way," he said.

"What are they?" I asked.

"Surely you know," he said.

"I think so," I said.

"Kurii," he said.

"Yes," I said.

Chapter Twenty-Two

"Master," said Asperiche, "what is the punishment for an escaped slave?"

"Why do you ask?" I said.

"No reason," she said.

"Are you thinking of escaping?" I asked.

"To where?" she said.

"Anywhere, I suppose," I said.

"I am branded," she said, "and collared."

"So?" I said.

"No," she said. "I am not a complete fool, like some."

"Do you have anyone in mind?" I said.

"No," she said.

"Good," I said.

"I suppose the chances of escape are slight," she said.

"I gather so," I said.

"I suppose one might escape to the teeth of beasts, or to a new master," she said.

"It is dangerous to keep an escaped slave," I said, "and, having fled, she would almost certainly be kept in a far harsher bondage."

"I fear so," she said.

"It is a matter of honor to return an escaped slave to her master," I said.

"If a Home Stone is shared, or such," she said.

"Of course," I said. Slave raids, naturally, were a separate matter. But then the slave does not escape. She is simply stolen, as might be any other form of property.

"What would be her punishment?" she asked.

"For a first offense," I said, "commonly a beating, one she will never forget."

"And for a second attempt?" she asked.

"There is seldom a second attempt," I said.

"There is scarcely ever a first attempt," she said.

"True," I said.

"For Gorean girls," she said.

"True," I said. Once the collar is on a Gorean girl she realizes she is a slave. Even should she manage to return to her own city, or family, she will be scorned, and kept as a slave, and subjected to the greatest cruelties and indignities, for her bondage has stained the honor of her city, or family. Such are soon sold away, or sometimes returned in chains to the very enemies who first captured and enslaved her. The Gorean slave girl is well aware that the collar is on her. She realizes the obduracy of her condition, and her utter inability to change it. She is helpless. She is slave. "And for any girls," I added.

"Not always," she said.

"I do not understand," I said.

"Some slaves," she said, "are stupid."

"Few," I said.

"What of barbarians?"

"Most barbarian slaves are quite intelligent," I said. "They are selected, in part, for their intelligence. Who would want a stupid slave?"

"I would suppose some men," she said.

"Surely not," I said.

"What of those who might find a barbarian of interest?" she asked.

"Barbarians sell well," I said. This was so, particularly after a third or fourth sale. Some merchants bought them on speculation. Too, barbarians were selected with great care. It was not as though one seized them as they fled from buildings in a burning city, and, even there, sometimes one simply stripped them and released them, assessing them as less than collar-worthy. To be assessed as less than collar-worthy is a great insult to a woman. This may have something to do with the animosity with which the Gorean free woman commonly regards the female slave, who, obviously, has been found collar-worthy.

"It is probably true," she said, "that not all barbarians are stupid."

"Of course not," I said.

"Nor all who find them of interest either," she said, begrudgingly.

"Certainly," I said, heatedly.

"What is wrong?" she said.

"Nothing," I said.

"Shall I fetch the whip?" she asked.

"No!" I said.

"Master has not answered my question," she said.

"What question?" I said.

"What might be the punishment," she said, "for a slave's second attempt at escape?"

"There would be no second attempt," I said.

"But, if so?" she said.

"Hamstringing, disfigurement, being run for sleen or larls, the cutting off of feet, sometimes being used as live feed," I said. "Are you sure you are not thinking of escape?"

"No," she said. "I am quite content in my collar, as I have learned what it is to be in the arms of a master."

The strongest chains that bind a woman, that make her thrive and rejoice in her bondage, are not formed of metal.

"I do not understand the nature of this conversation," I said.

"The great ship, as I understand it," she said, "is due to cast off very soon, any day now."

"That is true," I said. We had delayed the loading of the two large boxes, with their mysterious contents, until the departure of the great ship was imminent.

"That may explain much," she said.

"What are you talking about?" I said.

"Do you know Axel of Argentum?" she inquired.

"No," I said. "Who is he?"

"One whom I often find in my vicinity," she said.

"You are well-shaped," I said. "There are probably a number of fellows in your vicinity, several of whom are unknown to you."

"I cannot abide him," she said.

"You are not at his feet," I said.

"He is too much about," she said.

"He may be thinking of making an offer for you," I said.

"Master would not sell me," she said.

"Why not?" I asked.

"Do not sell me to him!" she said.

"What do you think you are worth?" I asked.

"I loathe him!" she said.

"Perhaps you wish to be sold to him," I said.

"No!" she said.

"You say he is too much about?"

"Yes!" she said.

"What is this to me?" I asked.

"I heard him speaking to another," she said.

"And you were simply in the vicinity," I said.

"I was passing," she said.

"Perhaps he might find you too much about," I said.

"He is handsome in a vulgar sort of way," she said.

"Perhaps he might turn the head of a simpler girl?" I suggested.

"Perhaps," she said. "I, personally, cannot stand him."

"What you heard," I said, "was not from slaves."

"No," she said. "We would dare not speak of such things."

"Of course," I said.

"Perhaps Master would care to hear what I heard," she said.

"It seems you wish to tell me."

"I thought Master might be interested," she said.

"Proceed," I said.

I supposed that this Axel of Argentum, or whoever he was, had probably overheard the discourse of slaves. In fact, I would not have been surprised if he had overhead this matter from Asperiche herself, who had it from other slaves. Asperiche was a very intelligent woman, and in pretending shyness, a trepidation, an overt, too obvious unwillingness to speak, a fearing to speak, might have signaled her desire to speak, and, perhaps, thus call herself to the attention of a handsome fellow, if only for the nonce, as a vessel of information, a rather lovely vessel. Might he not be curious, and thus command her to speak, to which command she, as kajira, however unwillingly, however tearfully, must helplessly respond, however reluctant she might be to do so. And, in this way, once he was apprised of the matter, she might pretend to me she had the information from him. And certainly he would then know of it. Asperiche was clever. And why had she chosen him? Why not another? And why was she in the fellow's vicinity in the first place? Yes, I recalled, she was passing by. Did she want a bid made on her? How furious she would be if I let her go for a tarsk-bit.

"I am prepared to inform Master," she said.

"Do so," I said.

"A slave," she said, "has escaped."

"Fled," I said, "not escaped."

"Fled, then," she said.

"What is this to me?" I asked.

"She transgressed the wands this morning," said Asperiche.

"So, what is this to me?" I asked.

"Very little, I suppose," she said. "But it is, I think, a first offense. One thus hopes the masters will be lenient, particularly as she may have value, and the ship is soon to sail."

"I see," I said.

"I think I will be pleased, quite pleased, of course, to see her tied and beaten."

"Why?" I asked.

"No reason," she said.

"A first offense?" I asked.

"I think so," she said.

"You think that is in her favor, here?"

"I trust so," she said.

"Out here," I said, "it does not matter. The larls will take her. There will not be enough left of her to beat. Even the Pani will not pursue her."

Asperiche turned white.

"What is wrong?" I asked.

"Master must interfere!" she said.

"Why?" I asked.

"You must!" she wept.

"It is unfortunate," I said, "particularly if she is a nice piece of slave meat."

"Master!" said Asperiche.

"She knew the law," I said. "She disobeyed. She transgressed the wands. She must pay the price."

"Please, Master!" she said.

"Only a fool comes between a larl and its prey," I said.

"But it is the barbarian, Laura," she said.

"I know no barbarian named Laura," I said.

"It is she whose lot number in Brundisium was 119," she said.

"What?" I cried.

Chapter Twenty-Three

"Where have you been?" asked Relia.

"About, Mistress," I said. Relia served as First Girl in our kennel. One addresses the First Girl as "Mistress." She needed not know where I had been. I had conducted a similar inquiry each morning, following the great storm.

"There is a large stand of Tur trees, west of the dock, near the wands, well twined with Tur-Pah," said Relia. "Men with climbing tools have freed much of it. It has been drying on racks since yesterday. Fill one basket, and no more. Deliver it to our kitchen." Our kitchen was Kitchen Five. Shipcamp, as Tarncamp, was divided into various sections, each with its own administration area, officers' quarters, barracks, dojo, eating halls, kitchen, slave kennels, and such. Our kennel was Kennel Five. Some facilities were shared, such as the Slave House.

"Yes, Mistress," I said. I fear I trembled.

"How are you this morning?" asked Relia, concerned.

"Fine, Mistress," I said.

"I worried about you, the night of the great storm," she said. "Are you all right now?"

The night of the great storm was four nights ago.

This was the first morning I would be in a less-frequented area of the camp. I had been assigned so. Relia did not have control of the schedule.

"Yes, Mistress," I said. "I spoke foolishly. I am in a collar."

"What sort of collar?" she asked.

"A slave collar," I said.

"Do not forget it," she said.

"No, Mistress," I said. Did she not know that her pretty neck was locked in one as well?

"You will be in the vicinity of the wands," she said.

"Yes, Mistress," I said.

"Stay away from them," she said.

"Yes, Mistress," I said.

Shortly thereafter, I was making my way down the dock. I held the basket on my head as I had been taught. This is one of the first things a slave learns. It lifts the breasts nicely. The men like it.

I must not hurry. I must not stumble. I must give no indication of the fear, and tumult, within me.

The ground would be soft from the rains. The worst had been four nights ago, the night of the great storm. I would be near the wands, permissibly so.

The weather had turned warm the last two days. There was much humidity in the air. The planks of the dock felt warm to my bare feet. A light breeze blew my tunic back against me. One could feel the moist air through it. It was of rep-cloth, a not uncommon material for the garments of slaves. It is light, porous, loosely woven, and clinging. The garment was sleeveless, and came high on my thighs. Such tunics leave little to the imagination. The disrobing loop, for I now wore one, was at my left shoulder, where it would be convenient to the hand of a right-handed man. Such garments, too, of course, lack a nether closure. We are to be at the convenience of our masters. In such a tunic it is said that a woman is more naked than naked. This is untrue, of course, and we treasure whatever scraps of cloth we may be permitted, but the saying has a point, which is that the tunic proclaims the woman a slave. It says, in effect, "I am a slave; I am such that you may do with me as you will." Is she not then, in her way, naked before the free, more naked than naked in her tiny tunic, naked psychologically, societally, socially? The morning was bright, and my heart was beating rapidly. I could see the end of the dock before me. On Gor, a slave, tunicked and collared, I was far more aware of my surroundings and their multiple ambiences than I had been on Earth, where noise and glitter, and clutter and filth, and garments which I was beginning to feel were outlandishly barbaric, seemed to shut away the natural world. Here, muchly bared, and owned, I was keenly aware of a gentle wind, the splash of rain, the feel of wet grass on one's feet, the scent of a flower, the texture of a piece of cloth, than I had ever been on my former world. How fresh and clean was the world, this world, how rich and sensuous it was. And there were other textures, and feelings, too, the knowledge that one is owned, and must obey, and the realization that one will be punished if one is not satisfactory, and little things, like the feel of wood on one's knees as one knelt before the free, the sense of a strap cinched tight on one's body, the clasp of slave bracelets, the weight of a shackle, the fiber of cordage in which one lay, bound, and helpless.

"Tal, vulo," said a man.

"Tal, Master," I said.

"Tal, tasta," said another.

"Tal, Master," I said.

"Tal, collar-girl," said another.

"Tal, Master," I said. One of my first instructresses had told us the difference between a woman and a girl. The girl is in a collar.

I was careful not to meet the eyes of a free man. That can be presumptuous. A slave girl will usually not meet the eyes of a free man unless she is commanded to do so. And that can be frightening. We are slaves. And I am told that it can be even more frightening to meet the eyes of a free woman. I had never met a free woman, and I did not care to do so. Meeting the eyes of a free woman, uncommanded, I am told, is likely to result in the stroke of a switch, which many of them carry with them. They hate us. And we, of course, our bodies muchly bared, our necks in collars, owned, helpless animals, are much at their mercy. It is our hope that the masters will protect us.

I stopped to look up at the great ship, like a mountain of wood beside the dock. High above, I could see a man looking over the rail. He was watching a line of men, on my level, climbing a boarding plank, carrying sacks.

It was early in the morning.

The ship, in the current, tugged at its moorings. I understood that it would soon depart. If so, there was little time to lose. If I dallied until nightfall I would be chained in the kennel, and, in the morning, I might be coffled with others, and put aboard, in one of the slave holds. I must act! I had waited days for such an opportunity! The rack of Tur-Pah was near the wands, beyond the dock.

Past the ship I looked across the river. The light was bright on the water. I shaded my eyes. I could not well see the buildings there, for the glare, but I could see some of them, and there were others there, as well. I could see, a hundred man's paces or so back from the river, the closely set, pointed timbers of a palisade. This was all a portion of Shipcamp, I supposed, though across the river, apart from the main buildings. The palisade, I understood, marked the outward perimeter of a maximum security area, a holding area, one housing high slaves. Supposedly these slaves were so extraordinary that one did not dare put them amongst the men, lest discipline be lost, and sedition and chaos ensue, men killing one another to possess them. I did not believe this, but I was willing to suppose that the slaves might be of high quality, such as might do for officers, and perhaps, in some cases, might be acceptable in the pleasure gardens of a Ubar. On the other hand, I did not think they would be so different from the rest of us. Certainly here in Shipcamp, or primary Shipcamp, there were many beautiful slaves, quite beautiful slaves, which might do quite well for officers, and who might not disgrace the shackles of a Ubar.

I was now at the end of the dock, and looked back at the great ship. How strange I thought that such a vessel would be built here, in this wilderness, in this remote place, so far from the sea. Could this be madness? Some said the ship was a creation of madness. I wondered if some terrible secret was housed here, in this strange place, seemingly lost in the northern forests. I might have wondered too if the Alexandra could even offer so mighty a keel a feasible passage to the sea had I not realized that her depth and course would have been well scouted in this regard. Too, I knew of the men in small boats, coming and going so frequently, with their charts, weights, and marked ropes, mapping, testing, and sounding that lengthy, broad, twisting, flowing road of water. But even so, all was not at ease, and peril was afoot. A river is not the open sea. A river is treacherous, with its shifting channels, its differential siltings, its vagaries of current, given changes in the configuration of the shore, its varying depths depending on the rainfall upstream, the occasional impediments of floating debris, the countless ridges and bars which might form overnight and be washed away, to form themselves anew, in a matter of Ahn.

I must be away I thought, and swiftly, though I must show no haste now, not now. There would be time for that later. I feared there might be guards near the wands. Yet I had been told this was not likely to be so. I wondered why that might be. Surely what lay beyond the wands, whatever it might be, could not in itself deter the flight of one who was sufficiently resolved, and one clever enough to count the larls.

How I hated he who had brought me to the collar, who had scorned me on the dock! How I had demeaned myself before him, kneeling as though in the presence of my master, as though I, Margaret Alyssa Cameron, of Earth, might be a slave! He had not even recognized me, he who had brought me and others like cattle to this world, to chains and collars!

I hated him. I hated him! And I wanted to kneel before him, and press my lips to his feet. Could I, Margaret Alyssa Cameron, be a slave, his slave? No! No, I cried to myself. Then I realized that name was no longer mine. I was no longer Margaret Alyssa Cameron. I had been a number, 119, and I was now "Laura," because I had been so named! I felt the collar on my neck. It was there. I was then indeed "Laura," or whatever masters might choose to name me, should they give me a name. But Laura could run! She could flee! I was not such a fool as to suppose I was not now a slave, for in the perfection of the law it was so, but I could run. Laura could run!

I looked beyond the end of the dock. Somewhere out there, in the forest, within the wands, there would be racks of Tur-Pah.

My legs almost failed me. I feared I might fall. Briefly I feared I might faint. For a moment I was terribly afraid. I had heard more than one slave say she would die of fear, even to think of running. I did not understand this. Surely they knew no more than I of such things. What fools they were, such ignorant barbarians! How stupid they were. I had counted the larls. I had even had the presence of mind to put my blanket into the vat for laundering.

I looked back, again, at the ship.

It was quite different from the other Gorean vessels I had seen, which tended to be numerous, graceful, slender, and beautiful, low in the water, long in keel, and narrow in beam, even the "round ships." And the vessels of war were like knives in the water, swift, low, multiply oared, and concave prowed, armed with deck engines, rams, and crescent-like blades, which might shear away timbers and oars. Many of those were painted green, that they might be difficult to detect on the billows of Thassa, until, mast down and oar-propelled, it was perhaps too late. How different then was the ship of Tersites. Doubtless it was seaworthy, but it was broad and towering, six-masted, and single-ruddered. It would be like a city at sea, a dangerous, armed city, walled with wood, with sails which might challenge clouds. It seemed less a ship than a fortress, or castle, which might for some mad reason have chosen to disguise itself as a vessel. It could house a small army. Rumors had it that she would seek the World's End. It was easy to see why even sturdy men, harsh fellows, callous fellows, mercenaries, even seasoned mariners, might flee. Parts of some had been returned to Shipcamp, to be held, guarded, under the paws of sleeping larls, until the beasts might once again awaken, hungry. But clearly, I thought, those fellows had not been wise enough to count larls. And perhaps some had escaped. Fewer, I had gathered, had tried to escape from Shipcamp than Tarncamp. I supposed that most of the disgruntled, those which might be the soonest dismayed, had chosen to cross the wands earlier, in Tarncamp. Too, at Shipcamp, there was the river.

How imposing was the ship of Tersites! But how frightening, too, it was, in its brooding size, its vastness, darkness, and mystery. I would never be put on that ship as a slave, another coffled beast, a shapely article on an inventory! How terrified had been several of my chain sisters even to think of being embarked on such a vessel. But they would be, as the lovely, helpless animals they were! But not I! I would not be so treated. I was different. I was from Earth! So let them be chained in their stalls, or holds, to be carried away as the meaningless goods they were, but not I! I would escape!

I then left the dock. I wanted to run, my heart cried out to run, but I forced myself to move unhurriedly, gracefully. I must be only another girl, another slave girl, about the business of her masters. The ground was soft beneath my bared feet. I soon came to the racks on which Tur-Pah, harvested yesterday, had been left to dry. I looked about, carefully. There were no guards about. I then concealed my basket and darted between the wands.

Chapter Twenty-Four

"Hold!" cried Tyrtaios.

I stopped, angry.

"What is it?" he called. "Where are you going?"

"I have business to attend to," I informed him.

"Within the camp, I trust," he said.

"I fear not," I said.

"You are not to leave Shipcamp," he said. "It is unauthorized. It is forbidden. None are to leave Shipcamp."

"We left two nights ago," I told him. "Do not attempt to stop me."

"We are associated," he said. "It is daylight. You will be seen. It will arouse suspicion. Others may investigate. I might be implicated. The business might be jeopardized."

"There is something to attend to," I said.

"The departure of the ship is nearly upon us," he said. "Already bunks, quarters, are assigned. Men will soon board. Slaves from across the river are being readied. Kennel One, here in Shipcamp, may be boarded tonight. The ship could leave tomorrow, or the next day."

"It is my intention to return in time," I said.

"My blade could stop you," he said.

"Why?" I asked. "Might that not arouse suspicion, as well? Might that not provoke curiosity, and perhaps an investigation?"

"Stay," he said, menacingly.

If the ost could choose a human form I thought it might choose one much like that of Tyrtaios.

"I have no doubt you can redden your blade with my blood,"
I said. "I trust you are wise enough not to do so."

He slammed his blade, half drawn, back into the scabbard.

"You fear to take ship?" he said. "You are going to run?"

"I fear of the edge of the world, the sea beyond the farther
islands, the plunging cliff, as much as the next fellow," I said.

"But no more?" he said.

"I think no more," I said.

"You are not running?" he said.

"No," I said, angrily, "I am hunting."

"There is provender aplenty in the kitchens," he said, "forest
tarsk, long-haired bosk, even tabuk. The Pani hunters provide
well."

"That is not my prey," I said.

"Ho!" he said, suddenly, delighted. "You have found the
fellow you have sought, he who is your debtor, or he who
insulted you, he for whom you have ventured this far, even to
the northern forests!"

"Perhaps," I said.

"I commend you," he said. "How noble, how sweet, is the
flavor of vengeance."

I did not respond.

"You encountered him," he laughed, "and he cried out, and
fled!"

"Perhaps," I said.

"Would that I could have witnessed that," he said. "To see
terror on the countenance of one's prey is an exquisite pleasure."

"A pleasure, perhaps," I said, "familiar to those of the dark
caste, when the victim first sees the dagger painted on the
hunter's brow."

"Perhaps," said Tyrtaios. "I would know nothing of such
things."

"No," I said.

"Beware the larls!" he said. "They have been released."

"Already?" I said.

"A slave has fled," he said, "this morning."

"Interesting," I said.

"A barbarian, a little fool," he said.

"I must be to my hunt," I said.

"Let him go," said Tyrtaios. "The larls will find him. You could not improve upon their work."

"But it would be their work, not mine," I said.

"Ah," said Tyrtaios. "You are of the dark caste."

"No," I said.

"You are determined?" he said.

"Yes," I said.

"I do not like it," he said. "The moorings will soon be cast."

"Not for days," I said.

"Perhaps tomorrow," he said.

"I expect to return soon," I said.

"Do so," he said.

"You can understand the urgency of the matter," I said.

"If it is blade business, yes," he said. "It is blade business, is it not?"

"I am to the hunt," I said.

"It is unlikely you can apprehend your quarry before the larls," he said.

"One must attempt to do so," I said.

"Return by tomorrow morning," he said. "Boardings are scheduled. Those reluctant to board will be put to the sword."

"I understand," I said.

"When did your quarry depart?" he asked.

"This morning," I said.

"He will have too long a start on you," he said.

"The quarry," I said, "is not swift. It is small. It is likely to tire easily. It will be unacquainted with woodcraft. It may even be lost, it may unwittingly, inadvertently, wander about, even move in a circle."

"You seek the slave!" he said.

"I have some interest in her," I said. "Her flanks please me."

"Let her go," he said. "By now panthers and sleen, if not the larls, will have her."

"It is not nightfall," I said.

The sleen, in the wild, is predominantly nocturnal.

"Her remains, by now, will be the feasting of urts and forest jards," he said.

"I think," I said, "she will be safe until dark, unless for the larls."

"Let her go," he said, "and buy another, or ten others."

"She needs to be taught her collar," I said.

"She should have learned it by now," he said.

"She ran," I reminded him.

"When a woman has learned her collar, she fears to crawl from her master's feet without permission," he said.

"It is pleasant to have absolute power over a woman," I said, "to own her, to have her at your feet, naked, collared, trembling and obedient."

"And you would have this one so?" he said.

"Yes," I said, "she, or another."

"You know her from Brundisium?" he said.

"Even earlier," I said.

"Why did you not buy her in Brundisium?" he asked.

"I am fighting the wanting of her," I said.

"Then have her, and beat her, and tire of her, and sell her," said Tyrtaios.

"I shall," I said.

"She is only a slave," he said.

"I will teach her what it is to be a slave," I said.

"And then, when she has well learned her collar," he said, "and is whimpering for your least touch, cast her aside as the meaningless garbage she is."

"I shall," I said.

"Do not pursue her," he said. "The larls are out. Do not be a fool."

"The day is pleasant," I said. "I think that I shall stroll in the forest."

"Rent a sleen," he said.

"I shall," I said.

"And you will need rope." he said, "a good deal of rope."

"Of course," I said.

"And a whip," he said.

"Yes," I said.

Chapter Twenty-Five

I cried out, and pulled away from the thorn shrub, my tunic rent on the right side, at the waist. There was a scratch there, small, the width of two of my fingers, inside the tunic.

It occurred to me that the masters might not be pleased that my tunic was torn. But then, I thought, what difference does that matter now!

I continued on my way.

I had not seen the extended branch. I must be more careful.

My heart was high. I must by now be pasangs beyond the wands. I looked up, through the trees. I thought it might be the eighth Ahn, but was less than sure. Gorean children would be more adept at such estimations than I. They are taught to estimate the time of day by the position of Tor-tu-Gor, Light-Upon-the-Home-Stone, rather as they are taught to recognize fruits and blossoms, trees and flowers, and a thousand small things within their environment, things which children of my world seldom notice, and in which they are seldom interested. I was derived from that world, one in which nature was incidental, unimportant, and neglected. Goreans view themselves as within nature, perhaps as a part of nature; surely, at least, they respect her and love her, and it would never occur to them to scorn and deny her; they live with her, not against her; on the other hand, we commonly view ourselves as outside of nature, and surely, on the whole, if not against her, apart from her. She is alien to us, the home without which we could not live, and is left unnoticed.

I was buoyant.

I thought it must be the eighth Ahn, or approximately so. Midday, when Tor-tu-Gor stands highest in the sky, is the tenth Ahn. In the cities, the tenth Ahn is commonly marked by the ringing of a great bar, or bars, which may be heard from wall to wall. The bars may also mark other Ahn, depending on the city, and may serve as a signal of alarm, of sorrow, of victory, of celebration, and such. Time on Gor is most often kept by water clocks, sand clocks, sun dials, marked candles, and such. Mechanical chronometers exist but they are rare, and expensive. I have also found them confusing to read as their "clockwise movement" is opposite to that which is commonly taken to be "clockwise" on my former world.

I continued on.

Indeed, I sped amongst the trees.

I was joyful!

I was free, I thought, at last, free!

Free!

Then I paused amongst the leaves, the trees, and shade. I stood there, still, small between the trees. I put my hand to my neck. On it was a collar. My left hand strayed to my thigh. Incised there, small, and lovely, but clear, and unmistakable, was a brand. I felt my clothing. How tiny and light it was. It was scarcely there. How free women would scorn and hate me! I was naked, save for a bit of cloth, the scrap of cloth which might be allotted to a slave.

Was I truly free, I asked myself?

Then I thought to myself, no, Margaret, Laura, you are not free, but a slave. I had been duly and legally embonded. All was in order. I was legally, and indisputably, a slave.

And I was thrilled to be such, such as could be owned, and sold, and then I forced such terrible thoughts from my mind.

I knew how I was supposed to want to be, and I tried to want to be that. I must try to be, I thought, as I have been told I should be.

What I was, and what I might want, was immaterial. I did not count; other things counted.

But, I knew, however I might want to think about such things, for better or for worse, I was a slave, in all legality.

But, I told myself, I am an escaped slave!

I have fled Shipcamp.

There are no ropes or shackles on me. I am loose, and running, and I sped on, again.

How proud I was of myself. And how foolish I was! Did I not know I was a slave?

It must then have been early in the afternoon.

The sunlight was bright where it fell between the trees. There was a mottling of brightness and darkness. Sometimes the trees were separate and tall, and there was little but a leafy space between them. At other times, they were more closely set, and brush was much about them. I avoided such thickets. One did not know what might be within them. Once I was very frightened, for I thought I saw a beast's head peering at me, large, and broad, but it did not move. I dared to move to one side, and regard it with more care, and found it was no more than a mixture of brush, branches, light and shadow.

I began to grow weary, and hungry, but I did not wish to stop.

I had not dared to conceal food in the basket this morning, even had I been permitted in the vicinity of the kitchen, where I might have stolen some, and the storage sheds were chained shut. On the other hand, I had no fear of starvation, at least for many days, until the onset of winter. I knew enough of the forest within the wands to recognize many things outside them which might be eaten; leafy Tur-Pah, parasitic on Tur trees, of course, but, too, certain plants whose roots were edible, as the wild Sul; and there were flat ground pods in tangles which I could tear open, iron fruit whose shells might be broken between rocks, and autumn gim berries, purple and juicy, perhaps named for the bird, whose cast fruit lies under the snow, the seeds surviving until spring, when one in a thousand might germinate. I saw a small, purple, horned gim flutter away from the bush. It startled me, for I had not seen it there. It is strange how close things may be, and yet not be seen. Its coloring deepens at this time of year. It molts in both the spring and autumn, and in the autumn its coloring is much like that of the fruit and leaves of the bush itself. It is not truly horned, but the feathering about the sides of the head suggests horns. The berries are tasty. They do mark the tongue and, if one is not careful, the mouth. When one is sent out to pick them one is not allowed to eat them, even one. The mouth and tongue are inspected. One does not eat one, even one. The lash is not pleasant.

As the Ahn passed, I grew more and more confident.

I was sure I was now well beyond the range of the larls. And the larls, of course, nearer Shipcamp, roam about, and may, or may not, pick up a scent. They are not put on a scent, as might be a sleen. I had little fear of sleen as there were few in camp, and I had put my blanket to the laundering, so they would have no scent to follow.

How little I knew of sleen!

I had fled camp, of course, moving west, beyond the dock, along the northern bank of the Alexandra. At some point, I knew, to move south, I must cross the Alexandra. I hoped to find a small boat, and make use of it. I might steal one near a river village. If necessary, I might cling to a log and float with the current, or construct a small raft of branches, bound together with wild Tur-Pah vines. There was little to fear from river tharlarion at this latitude. Had I been on my former world, I supposed one might conveniently petition aid from some worthy, understanding fellow, a kindly sort who would be sympathetic to my situation, and might be depended upon to assist a woman in need. On this world, however, I was not sanguine about this possibility. These were not men of Earth, conditioned for years, for political purposes, into devirilized, malleable weaklings, males taught to deny their blood, taught to pride themselves on their lack of manhood. What was wrong with them? Did they not understand what was being done to them, by those who bore them no good will? Could they not hear the voices of their own blood? But males here were not males of Earth. Males here were Gorean. I would not be coddled, shielded, protected, and concealed; my flight would not be abetted. I would be looked upon as what I was, a loose animal, a possibly desirable, loose animal, to be taken in hand and dealt with as strong men might please.

I shuddered, and better hitched up the disrobing loop at my left shoulder.

I looked about.

I heard a snuffling, and grunting, to one side, and stopped. There were three small tarsks there, rooting, only a few paces away. Some tarsks are extremely large, so large that they are sometimes hunted in the open plains with lances, from tarnback, but these were no larger than verr. The boar can be dangerous, with its short temper and curved, slashing tusks, but I saw no boar here, and, in any event, they are most dangerous in the spring, when marking out territory. They were rooting, of course, and this meant food. I waited for a time, and then, when they had drifted on, rooting elsewhere, investigated their rooting place, with its turned, gouged ground. I found some small, tuberous roots which had been missed, or rejected. I did not know what they were, but from the texture of the root and its starchiness, I would have supposed some tiny variety of wild Sul. I also found another root, and carelessly bit into it, which turned out to be a most serious, even hideous, mistake, unless, perhaps, one were on the brink of dying of starvation. It was not poisonous, of course, but one could easily conceive of it being regarded as such. In a loose sense, it was edible. It had been left by the tarsks, and this was not surprising. Its bitterness was unbelievable. Recoiling, dismayed, weeping with misery, I spat it out, and then, hacking and coughing, half retching, continued to spit away whatever residue I could. I spat again and again into the ground. I knew well what it was, for I had encountered a fluid, brewed from it, long ago, in my training. I had been knelt, my hands tied behind me. Then I had cried out in pain, for my head, by the hair, had been jerked back, far back, by a guard. I saw the ceiling above me. Without releasing my hair, but keeping my head in place by means of it, he then, with his free hand, pinched shut my nostrils. I had then sensed a second guard, approaching. As he neared, and then loomed over me, I saw he carried a metal, narrow-spouted vessel. In a moment, I began to gasp. Only through my mouth could I breathe. I tried to squirm, and shake my head, but I was held in place. Then, as I opened my mouth widely, gasping, fighting for breath, I felt the spout of the metal vessel in my mouth. I could not fully close my mouth because of it. I took a deep breath, sucking the air into my lungs. Then, before I could breathe again, the vessel was tipped, and fluid began to flood into my mouth, a repellant, gross, revolting fluid, and it filled my mouth like a pool. Held as I was, I could not rid myself of it. I needed air.

My head hurt, from the strain on my tightly grasped hair. My wrists fought the cords that held them. In my oral cavity, bitter and reeking, brimming it, reposed that small, foul pool, like a tiny lake of bitter, odious filth. I wanted to force it from my mouth, but could not do so. I had no air with which to expel it. I feared I might suffocate. My lungs cried out for air. I must breathe, but to do so the beverage must first be swallowed. I did so. No, I had not forgotten slave wine. It is brewed from the sip root. Relia had told me that in the vast grasslands far to the east, the Barrens, the white slaves of red masters must chew and swallow the root raw. I spat again into the dirt. We are to be bred, of course, only as, and when, and if, the masters please. Our bodies are not our own; they are the masters'. I was then allowed to rise and return to the training room. My hands, tied behind me, would not be unbound for over an Ahn. We must not be allowed to rid ourselves of the fluid. The taste was with me for more than a day. Slave wine has been developed by the green caste, the caste of Physicians, one of the five high castes of Gor, the others being the Initiates, the Builders, the Scribes, and the Warriors. The green caste has also produced the "releaser," as it is called, which is reputedly delicious. It removes the effects of slave wine. When administered the "releaser," a girl may expect to be hooded and sent to the breeding stalls. Needless to say, free women are not subjected to the hateful and disgusting, the contemptible and demeaning, miseries of slave wine. Related potions which might be quaffed by free women, if they should choose to do so, for they are free, are reputedly mild and flavorful, as would be suited to their status. They, of course, are not animals to be bred or not bred as masters might choose. They are free. They are not owned. They are not slaves.

I continued on.

The ground became softer, and spongy, and water was about my feet. Wet grass, coarse, cut at my ankles.

The forest floor is far from uniform. It has its thousand rises and falls, its heights and valleys, its fallen timbers and rotting wood, its scarred, blackened trunks and scorched, lightning-fired wastes, its scattered boulders, its bare places, its flowered meadows and blossoming thickets, its crags and cliffs, its rills, and streams and rivers, its rock-cupped ponds, its galleries of tall trees with quiet aisles of leaves between them, its jumbled barriers of nigh-impenetrable brush, its innumerable geodesics, and textures. There are countries within it.

There had been much rain of late.

I hoped it might rain again, as that would wash scent away, clearing it from rocks and soil, obliterating trails.

I had no idea where I was, save that I was clearly north of the Alexandra.

I saw a tabuk, small, graceful, single-horned, here in the woods brown pelted, startled, lift its head from a water-filled declivity, and dart away. They are lovely animals, round-eyed, and alert. Usually there is more than one about.

It was now late afternoon, and still warm.

I climbed to a dry place, a small clearing amongst the trees, sat down, and, with grass, dried my feet and calves. I was weary, and hungry. I had been gone for Ahn. I would now be far from the range of the larls. I would rest for a moment, and then be, again, on my way. Nearby, in the grass, was a tangle of thick, stout, leafy vines, on several of which were large, pod-like growths. I had seen nothing like them in the vicinity of either Tarncamp or Shipcamp. I did not care for the look of them, and so I moved a bit away. I then lay down. I pulled the tunic down about my thighs, though there were none about to see. I knew masters sometimes enjoyed looking on sleeping slaves. I supposed they found them beautiful. I wondered if we were beautiful. I supposed some of us were. I wondered if I were. I did know that I had been brought to Gor, and collared.

I awakened suddenly, screaming, unable to separate my ankles, which seemed fastened together by some thick, living, coiling, fibrous material. And I felt it moving more about my legs. Then I shrieked with pain. "Ost!" I thought. But there were no osts here, surely, not here. The ost did not range this far north. If there were osts here they would be caged pets, or assassination devices. I looked down, with horror. Fastened in my right calf were two fibrous, fanglike thorns. These had been concealed within the pod, which had opened. I did not know if it had been attracted to me by heat, motion, or the scent of blood. I screamed, and tried to rise, and fell. More of the snakelike tendrils rustled toward me. I could see, about the two thorns deep in my calf, tiny rings of blood. My blood, I understood, was being drawn into the plant. I could see the moving darkness within the thorns. Other pods had now turned in my direction. I saw another tendril slithering toward me.

I screamed.

The growth was alive, not as a plant is alive, but as a nest of disturbed, excited snakes might be alive. There was a fierce rustling to my right, reflecting the agitation of the growth. A sucking, hissing, popping sound came from the pod, whose two thorns, fanglike, were deep in my leg. It trembled. It shook. It was like a tiny, fiercely respiring lung, a small pump, greedy and blind, a living engine without eyes or awareness, jerking and throbbing, fastened in my flesh, drawing blood from my body. I rolled away, to my left, and sat up, and tore the thorns from my leg, throwing them, and their pod and vine away. The coils on my ankles drew tighter, and I rolled to my belly and, scratching at the ground, digging into it with my fingers, dragged myself away, inch by inch, pulling at the vines until they were taut. I was sure the thing was a plant and not a free-moving animal. It would live primarily by photosynthesis, and the water and minerals it could extract from the soil. I had pulled the vines partly from the soil, perhaps a foot or so, when, suddenly, they fell away. In such a form of life certain mechanisms had doubtless been selected for. The behaviors of agitation and attack had doubtless been selected for, but so, too, I gathered, triggered by tensions likely to accompany or precede uprooting, had been a release and withdrawal. It was almost as though the plant wished to feed but not at the cost of its own demise. Doubtless these things were random at one time, but there are differences amongst behaviors; some are in the best interest of the organism, and others not. Then, statistically, over time, behaviors in the best interest of the organism, its health, longevity, replication, and survival, would tend to be favored. I slid back, away, further, from the plant. The coils which had looped about my ankles, and constricted there, withdrew into the tangle. Other tendrils stretched toward me, but, like restless, disappointed, anchored snakes, could move no further than their length, some a few feet, others some yards. I stood up, and backed away, my leg bleeding. I looked back at the restless tangle of growth, trembled, felt suddenly ill, and threw up. Fortunately, having found the thick tangle, perhaps a foot deep and some yards in width, ugly, and repellant, I had chosen to wrest away from it, but, it seemed, not far enough. Had I been closer to the tangle I do not doubt but what I would have been drawn into it, been covered by it, and, wrapped in its coils, drained of blood, and whatever other life fluids from which the growth might derive nourishment. Though I had never seen a life form of its sort before, I had little doubt what it must be. No wonder I had seen none about Tarncamp, or Shipcamp. They were such as would be cleared away from inhabited areas. I shuddered. There are many dire fates to which a displeasing slave might be subjected. One often hears of two. She might be fed alive to ravenous sleen; and sometimes she might be stripped, bound, and cast alive to leech plants. These things I had encountered were, I did not doubt, leech plants. Now I understood, better than before, why slave girls strive to be pleasing, fully pleasing, and as the slaves they are, to their masters. Yet, as I understood it, at least from my instructresses, free women do not understand, really, why slaves strive to be pleasing. Free women tend to think it is because of fear, fear of the switch or whip, of close chains, of unpleasant bindings, of restricted rations, heavy labors, enforced public nudity, and such. To be sure, one does fear such things, and they are at the disposal of the master. Else we would not be slaves. But the real reason the slave strives to be pleasing, fully pleasing, to her master, is because he is her master and she is a slave. It is profoundly rewarding to her to be a slave, to be owned, dominated, and mastered. She knows she has no choice in such matters but to be what she, in her deepest heart, most desires to be, a slave.

Why is it that we make such excellent slaves? Surely it is because it is what we want to be, and are.

Certainly I knew I wanted to kneel, and be owned, and had known this even from my former world. Being brought to Gor was thus for me, in its way, more than a dream come true; it was a restoration of human biological reality, a recovery of a rightfulness of nature, a returning of me to the path of my heart, a bringing of me to a world in which I would have no choice but to be myself. Here, I found myself at the feet of men, where I belonged; here I knew my identity as a female.

I touched my collar.

I was not displeased to be a slave.

No, no, I thought! I am a woman of Earth! I must repudiate my heart! I have been taught so! Should not biology crumble before political injunctions? What rights has she before rules, invented to thwart and subvert her? Dismiss nature. What has she to justify herself, save reality, blood, and need? I knew what I had been taught, in a thousand ways, a thousand times. Why had it seemed to me so false, and so alien, even on my former dismal, unhappy, polluted, awry world? What were its motivations, what ends did it seek, whose programs was it intended to promote? Surely not mine, surely none I recognized or found congenial. Is it appropriate that a culture be founded on division, and hate? Nature denied is nature poisoned. The weather, the tides, the circulation of the blood are without ideology; they are themselves, clean, innocent, and honest.

Would it be so wrong, I wondered, for humans, too, to be themselves?

It was now late in the afternoon.

I was no longer sure how far I might be from Shipcamp, and the Alexandra.

Let the great ship sail. I would be far away. I would be chained in no hold; I would not be penned like a verr.

I looked back at the thick tangle of vines and pods, which I was sure was a thick stand of leech plants.

I understood that it might be the fate of a displeasing slave to find herself cast, naked and bound, to such hungry, alert growths.

And I was suddenly terrified to realize that I, in my flight, might be accounted just such a displeasing slave.

No matter.

I would not be recaptured.

I was clever. I would not permit it.

I must hurry on.

Yet I was not eager to travel through the night.

What if, in the darkness, I might inadvertently stumble into another stand of such hungry, alert growths?

I was hungry, but saw nothing about to eat.

It seemed dark now, for the time of day. The wind was rising, and some leaves fell from the nearby branches. It was time, at Shipcamp, that the slaves of Kennel Five would be given their warm slave gruel, before they would be returned to their chains in the low, heavy enclosure. Usually we were permitted to feed ourselves, but sometimes we must eat on all fours, head down, not using our hands. This is useful in reminding a girl that she is a slave. Often enough we are given bread and fruit. In some kennels the girls, kneeling, feed from a trough, not using their hands, which are often tied behind them, but not in our kennel, Kennel Five. My training group had occasionally been put to a trough for our feeding. Once, to help us keep in mind what we were, we shared the trough with tarsks. Our common drink was water. Private slaves, I understand, fare much better. Some are the pets of their masters, but the whip is always on its peg. One hopes to keep it there. Occasionally we are given a handful of slave pellets. I do not know what is in them, but they are nourishing. Our diet, our exercises, our rest periods, and such, are carefully regulated, as would be expected, given that we are stock. Attention is given to our health, vitality, and desirability. Masters concern themselves with our weight, and figures, even to scales and measures. We each have our "block measurements," and are expected to keep closely to them. We are to be such that we could be brought responsibly, and plausibly, to the block, at any time, not that we are to be sold but that we are to be such as are obviously vendible. We are to keep ourselves clean and well-groomed. Our posture, our carriage, and our figures are to be such as would be likely to inspire envy and hatred in a free woman. Our bodies are commonly much exposed, and this makes it imperative to carry them well. Whereas there is a considerable variety in the figures of slaves, with respect to the presence or absence of a pound here and there, there are few, if any, obese slaves. We are not free women, who may be as unclean, unkempt, disgusting, and fat as they wish. Indeed, it is one of the transitions faced by the free woman reduced to bondage, that she must now, tunicked, even camisked, certainly well displayed, become exciting, attractive, and desirable. She might now, after all, be marketed.

To be slovenly in a collar is not acceptable. The master will not stand for it. One might also note, in passing, that a free woman can be loud, intrusive, forward, unpleasant, ill-tempered, and so on. Such things are her prerogative. The slave, on the other hand, is to be deferent and obedient. Amongst free persons she commonly kneels. When she speaks, if she is permitted to do so, she will commonly speak softly and clearly. Her diction is to be excellent. She is not a free woman. Unless her need is on her, her presence, while obvious and lovely, is unobtrusive. She is to remember that she is her master's animal. As a slave, she is expected to behave as a slave. On the other hand, let us suppose, for a moment, she is alone with her master. Her behavior then is likely to be whatever the master might wish. She might behave as before, should it be his wish, as it may be, but, too, if he wishes, he might snap his fingers, speak a simple word, point to the floor, or such, and he will have at his disposal something seemingly quite different, something free women can only enviously suspect, to their rage, a lascivious, needful pleasure object, perhaps indistinguishable from a paga girl or a brothel slut, something of the sort for which men bid heatedly. And it is at its own slave ring!

I heard thunder, which did not please me. But I supposed rain would be in my favor.

Though the day had been warm, it was late autumn. Twice I had seen ice in the Alexandra, doubtless washed down from some northern tributary. Though it was rumored that the great ship would soon cast its moorings, any day now, many had scoffed at this, speculating that it was unlikely, for the season. Certainly it was not a river ship, and, I was told, one does not take to Thassa, the sea, in the winter. Even in the summer, with her storms and moods, she is daunting, unruly, and dangerous. In the winter, I was told, it would be madness to venture amongst the swirling mountains of her waves, the cold and bitter hammers of her winds. Yet it seemed the ship was being readied. But eyes had not yet been painted on her bow. How then could she see her way? But what if eyes were not to be permitted to her, for some reason? Might not mariners be uneasy to crew a ship forbidden to see her way?

It was growing cold.

I was hungry.

It would soon be dark.

I felt a drop of rain.

I did not have my blanket. But I could not well have brought it from Shipcamp.

I cried out, as a small body, no higher than my waist when it struck the ground at my side, bounded past me. I could have touched it. It disappeared amongst the trees. I had glimpsed it only briefly, but it was a tabuk. I did not know if it were the one I had seen earlier, or not. It had paid me no attention; perhaps it had not even noticed me, or cared to notice me. I found that surprising, for it is difficult to approach a tabuk, as they are alert, skittish animals. I stepped back. There was nothing cautious or leisurely about its passage. It had been moving quickly. Yet its bounds, as it fled past, seemed erratic, unpredictable. But that is not unusual in a tabuk, if it is alarmed. Was it alarmed? Why did it not move in a straighter, more direct fashion? Then I could not move, but stood still, as though paralyzed, my hand before my mouth. Not three yards away, its motion arrested, there was a paused, crouching sleen, a wild sleen. I knew it was a sleen, as I had seen them in Shipcamp, where some are kept and trained by sleen masters. I found them frightening animals. Domestic sleen are often larger and more aggressive than sleen in the wild, for they are bred carefully and selectively for a variety of purposes, war, herding, the hunt, and such. I think the beast was as startled to see me as I was to see it. Its belly low to the ground, its shoulder was no higher than a bit above my knee. It was some five to six feet in length, its body sinuous, snakelike. It must be a young animal, I thought, as an adult sleen, even in the wild, may range from eight to ten feet in length. It reminded me of a furred reptile, viper-headed, fanged. The eyes in that triangular, fanged head were full upon me. Its tail lashed back and forth. I could not move. I could not even have cried for help. Then the beast's head dipped, sweeping, to the ground. I heard it snuffling. Then its muzzle was almost at my feet. Its body literally rubbed against my leg as it snaked past me, and it continued on its way. I knew little about sleen, but I did know it was the planet's most adept, reliable, tenacious tracker. That is why they are often used in hunting. A flaw, or virtue, of the sleen as a hunter is its single-mindedness. As a flaw, once fastened on a scent, and committed to it, it will ignore better, easier game for less desirable, more-difficult-to-obtain game; on the other hand, once committed to a scent, it is likely to pursue it relentlessly, which, if one is after a particular quarry, might be, I suppose, accounted a virtue. As noted, the sleen, in the wild, is predominantly nocturnal, usually emerging from its burrow at dusk, and returning to it in the early morning. The sleen, I gathered, was pursuing the tabuk, and, accordingly, I had been to it no more than an unexpected distraction. Still, what if another should come across my scent? I would hope it would not commit to it, but would ignore it in favor of more familiar game. But one does not know. Much depends on how hungry an animal is. The hungry sleen may attack even a larl, which is likely to kill it; in the far north I am told snow sleen will hunt in packs, rather like swarming sea sleen, but the sleen, generally, like the larl, is a solitary hunter. Older animals, of course, may be reduced to hunting slower, less-desirable prey. Where the sleen ranges, peasants, foresters, and such, commonly remain indoors at night, or, if venturing out, are likely to do so in armed groups. The hunts of wild sleen, of course, are not invariably successful, or the value of their range would be soon reduced by overhunting. In the wild, the sleen will usually return to its burrow by morning, and, after sleeping, seek a new trail the next night. Too, after a kill, many sleen, rather like certain reptiles, may remain asleep or quiescent for weeks, even months. This is not the case, however, with the domestic sleen, which are bred with different ends in view. They are restless, energetic, active, possess a rapid metabolism, sleep far less, and function well both diurnally and nocturnally. Their aggression, diverse behaviors, and such, are often triggered by private, secret, verbal signals, sometimes taken from only one person. Sometimes a bond, almost resembling affection, exists between the beast and its master.

I continued on.

Night was darkening the forest.

I would soon stop.

I knew that there were not only sleen in the forest, but panthers, as well. Larls are not indigenous to the northern forests, and I was confident I was far beyond the range of those employed for patrolling by the Pani in the vicinity of Tarncamp and Shipcamp. There was some danger of intruding into the territory of the wild bosk, but I did not much fear them. They would not be likely to seek me out. Similarly I did not fear forest urts or tarsk, though the boar can be dangerous. I had heard of Panther Girls but did not think there would be many, if any, about, this far north. Some bands, I had heard, roamed in the vicinity of the Laurius, much farther south. Too, in a few weeks winter would greet the forest. Should I encounter Panther Girls I thought I might join their band. But then I touched my neck. There was a collar on it. Panther Girls were free women. They despised slaves. Woe to the slave who fell into their hands! I did not understand the hatred of Panther Girls for slaves. What were they afraid of? Did they, in all their vaunted freedom, in their skins and necklaces, fear something in themselves? What might it be? Could it be the slave?

It was now dark.

I stood, and felt more drops of rain. One could hear its patter on leaves. I heard thunder, far off.

I was cold, and hungry.

I thought of a master, and tried to stir the heat of anger against him in my shivering body. It was he whom I had first seen, long ago, in the aisle of large, crowded, emporium on Earth. Our eyes had met. How weak I had suddenly felt. A free woman on an alien world I had almost fallen to my knees before him, my head lowered, placing myself before him, even in so public a place, in what could only be understood as a slave's submission. Is such a thing so natural to a woman, I wondered? Has it been coded in us, since the savannas, and caves? How his eyes had looked upon me! Somehow it had been clear to me that this was no man of Earth, or no common man of Earth. Under his gaze I had felt stripped. It was the first time I had ever been looked upon as what I had so often thought myself to be, a female slave. I had turned about, and fled. He had later stood over me when I had lain bound in a warehouse. He had observed me in an exposition cage in Brundisium, and turned away from me, rejecting me, doubtless, as inferior merchandise. And I had fallen to my knees before him on the dock at Shipcamp, and he had again turned away! How I despised and hated him! I had prostrated myself before him, as a tunicked, collared, marked slave, on the dock at Shipcamp, and he had again turned away. I had been scorned. I hated him. And yet, I knew, in some sense, he was my master, and I his slave.

And I did not even know his name!

Lightning, far off, suddenly broke open the sky with a wound of light, and a moment later the atmosphere cried out, rumbling, as though in pain.

I did not even know his name!

I cried out with misery as the forest was suddenly illuminated about me, and, almost simultaneously, was shaken by a great stroke of thunder. It seemed almost over my head, at the crest of the trees. I couched down, making myself tiny, my hands over my head, sobbing and cold. For better than an Ehn I could not hear. The rain was then falling heavily. The tunic I wore, of rep-cloth, was light, and obviously cut for a slave. At its best it is a mockery of a garment, the sort in which one puts collar-girls, the sort which makes it clear to the girl and the world that its occupant is owned. It is certainly not designed to protect the girl from the elements. That is done with cloaks, boots, wrappings, blankets, jackets, leggings, and such.

I shook with misery, and cold.

I was lost. I knew little more than that I was somewhere north of the Alexandra.

Chapter Twenty-Six

"You need a sleen," said the fellow.

He carried a pack, as did I.

"Who are you?" I asked.

"Axel," he said.

"Of Argentum?" I asked.

"You know of me?" he said.

"I have a slave," I said, "who knows of you."

"That would be pretty Asperiche," he said.

"I trust she has not been a nuisance," I said.

"One puts up with slaves," he said, "particularly if they are lightly clad, well collared, and beautiful."

"If she annoys you," I said, "cuff her, and well."

"I have your permission?" he asked.

"Certainly," I said.

"She fears she is not your preferred slave," he said.

"I have no other," I said.

"At present," he said.

"At present," I agreed.

"Asperiche has been much about," he said.

"I feared so," I said.

"She has made known to me your interest, however incomprehensible, in a missing slave."

"I have no interest in her," I said, "as she is a slave. I thought I might go hunting, however, simply for the sport."

"I think the larls are out," he said.

"I know they are," I said.

"It seems a less than auspicious time to go hunting," he said.

"It may enrich the sport," I said.

"By now," he said, "one of those fellows may have brought part of her back to the cages."

"It is possible," I said.

"More than likely," he said.

"You keep sleen?" I asked.

"I have one," he said.

"Is it a good tracker?" I asked.

"What sleen is not?" he asked.

"Let me rent it," I said.

"It might take off your leg," he said. "It would be best for me to accompany you."

As I did not know a great deal about sleen, and animals sometimes differ considerably in their habits and temperament, and one usually hires both a sleen and a sleen master, I was not adverse to what I took to be his offer.

"How much do you want?" I asked.

"No more than the interest and pleasure of the hunt," he said.

"Asperiche?" I asked.

"Only the hunt," he said.

"I do not understand," I said.

"Hunters do not always have the same quarry in mind," he said. "Do you know a Lord Okimoto?" he asked.

"No," I said.

"Do you know an officer, Tyrtaios?" he asked.

"I have seen him," I said, "about the dock, and camp."

"I suspect you know him better than that," he said.

"Do you know him?" I asked.

"Perhaps better than you," he said.

I thought it not well to pursue this matter, as it might lead to unwelcome inquiries. I did not know how much this Axel, allegedly of Argentum, might know of matters into which it might be dangerous to inquire.

"You have sought me out because of Asperiche?" I said.

"Perhaps," said he, "because of Lord Okimoto, and Tyrtaios."

"You are a spy then," I said, "to accompany me beyond the wands?"

"Surely you do not expect them to believe that you would cross them for a slave?"

"No," I said, "but for the pleasure of the hunt."

"I, too," he said, "have a hunt in mind."

"Me?" I asked.

"Not at all," he said. "You need not be hunted. Your location is not in doubt. Obviously you are here. If it was wished, you could be cut down where you stand."

"By you?" I asked.

"Or another," he said.

"We need not cross the wands," I said. "Draw."

"I do not choose to do so," he said.

"At present," I said.

"At least at present," he said.

"You are perhaps an Assassin," I said.

"No," he said. "Are you?"

"No," I said.

"Several in the camp," he said, "think you are of the dark caste."

"I am of the Merchants," I said.

"I have heard, the Slavers," he said.

"Very well," I said.

"A dangerous occupation," he said, "but one with its pleasures."

"You said," I said, "you had a hunt in mind."

"The quarry I have in mind," he said, "is one of interest to both Lord Okimoto and Tyrtaios."

"Surely not a fled slave," I said.

"She might be useful in their plans," he said.

"Let us fetch your sleen, and seek the scent."

"There is no hurry," he said. "If the larls have not eaten your runaway by now, she is probably safe for a time."

"Why do we delay?" I asked.

"Surely you know the larls are out," he said. "It is dangerous. They have not yet been recalled."

"I shall bargain for another sleen," I said, angrily.

"Our sleen is waiting," he said, "near a rack of drying Tur-Pah, beyond the western end of the dock. I have tied him there. He is restless. He scratches at the earth. Your slave is a stupid little fool, even a barbarian. She put her blanket to the laundry, how clever, unaware that her scent saturates her chaining place in her kennel, that it lies in pools in each footstep she takes, that it lingers in grass, mud, and brush, even for a time in the very air through which she passes."

"She may be a stupid little fool," I said, "even a barbarian, but her eyes are deep, her lips are soft, and her flanks are of interest."

"I have also heard, from the Slave House," he said, "that she juices nicely, helplessly, and uncontrollably."

"Excellent," I said.

"It is pleasant," he said, "to have a slave so much at your mercy."

"It is the same with them all, sooner or later," I said. "They are not free women."

"True," he said.

"Obviously," I said.

"You have some interest in the slave?" he asked.

"Not at all," I said.

"Asperiche thought you might," he said.

"She is mistaken," I said.

"It is only the sport of the hunt you seek," he said.

"Yes," I said.

"I see," he said.

"Let us hunt," I said.

"The larls," he said.

"Let us chance the business," I said.

"Not until the tenth Ahn," he said, "when the larls will be recalled."

"They have been hardly out," I said.

The larls were occasionally released in the morning, though commonly in the evening. I did know they had been released this morning. Earlier I did not know if that was because of the fled slave or was no more than a matter of coincidence, but now, it seemed, another reason might be involved, one which might be of interest to Lord Okimoto and Tyrtaios. Axel, I recalled, had mentioned another quarry, and, I had gathered, the larls withdrawn, this enabling the hunt of Axel, such a quarry, one apparently of interest to Lord Okimoto and Tyrtaios, might prove, eventually, to have some relationship to the fled slave. I understood little of this, at the time.

"It has to do with the word of Lord Okimoto," he said.

"And your hunt," I said.

"Yes," he said.

"What is your quarry?" I asked.

"It is suspected the camp is being scouted," he said.

"Then enemies, a spy, or spies?" I said.

"Much is obscure," he said. "Lord Okimoto wishes to inquire into the matter."

"Leave them for the larls," I said.

"Perhaps later," said Axel. "First, intelligence might be gathered."

"Should you not be accompanied, by mercenaries, by several men, by Pani?" I asked.

"Allies, from the coastal ships, certain crews, are about," he said.

"Not in Shipcamp," I said.

"No," he said, "their knowledge of Shipcamp is imperfect, speculative."

He suddenly lifted his hand, and I heard then the first stroke of the bar, beginning to signal the tenth Ahn.

"The larls are being recalled," he said.

"How do you know?" I asked.

"I have been informed," he said.

"How are they recalled?" I asked.

"It is done with whistles," he said. "Few humans can hear the notes."

I looked at Axel, closely. "Perhaps Kurii could hear the notes," I said.

"What are Kurii?" he asked.

My test, it seemed, had failed, or had been detected.

"Some sort of beasts," I said. "I have heard of them."

"Sleen can hear the notes, and panthers," he said.

"What has my hunt to do with yours?" I asked.

"I do not know, clearly, what I am looking for," he said. "Only that there is sign that the camp has been scouted, perhaps is being scouted. My hunt then is primarily one of reconnaissance. I have no scent trail on which to put our six-legged friend. Your hunt provides a convenient cover for mine. It will be thought we are on the same hunt, foolish though it may be, for a slave. Apprehension amongst the men, fear of an attack, is not welcomed."

There had already been a large-scale attack on Tarncamp. I

had been logging in the forest, and had not participated in the camp's defense.

"I need the sleen for my hunt," I said. "My sword will not accept our parting in the forest, should you decide to pursue another path, another hunt."

"Have no fear," he said. "We will do your business first."

"Why is that?" I asked.

"Asperiche," he said, "is quite pretty."

"So she has indeed been much about," I said.

"I have not objected," he said.

"Nor have you put her to use," I said.

"No," he said. "I am not a thief."

"I see you have your pack," I said.

"And you yours," he said.

"Let us be on our way," I said.

"Certainly," he said. "Even should we encounter a larl it will now ignore us. It is returning to its cage, and dinner."

Shortly thereafter, not far from the western edge of the dock, we encountered the sleen. It was a large, mottled beast, some nine feet long, brown and black. It became excited at his appearance. It began to whine, and tear at the turf, and writhe and twist about, almost like a snake.

"I do not want it to kill the slave," I said.

"It has not been given that command," he said.

Its snout was to the forest, its nostrils flared, its eyes keen, its long, sinuous body trembling.

Its tether was taut.

"Hold, hold," said Axel soothingly. He then freed the monster of its tether. The beast, though trembling, remained in place.

Axel then donned a heavy pair of gloves, and attached a chain leash to the beast's heavy, thick, spiked collar.

"Why the chain, why the gloves?" I asked.

"He cannot chew through the chain," he said. "And I do not wish to lose a hand."

"I gather he becomes excited," I said.

"That is not unusual in a hunting sleen," he said. "Easy, easy, Tiomines," he said, soothingly.

"It is unusual that it would be this agitated this early, is it not?" I asked.

"The scent is very fresh," he said.

"It must have been laid down Ahn ago," I said.

"You know little of sleen," he said.

It is not unheard of for sleen to follow a given scent for days, even one which may have been laid down weeks ago.

Axel then looped together the freed tether, and attached it to his belt. He then adjusted his pack, as did I.

Near the restless beast, lying near it, within what had been clearly the compass of its tether, were two javelins. Axel retrieved one of these, and handed me the other.

"I gather you did not fear these would be stolen?" I said.

"No," he said.

"The larls are in," I reminded him.

"Now," he said.

I hefted the javelin, it was light, supple, and smoothly, but wickedly, bladed. It was no more than five feet in length, at best. The head was fixed to the shaft, not detachable as is often the case with the military javelin, which is likely to be socketed in such a way that after a strike the missile cannot be drawn free whole, to be immediately reused, perhaps by an enemy. The head, of course, can be resocketed later. The hunting javelin, on the other hand, can be withdrawn easily from the target, whole, and used repeatedly. There is little danger that the typical target of a hunting javelin will return it to its owner. Javelins, whether intended for sport or war, are quite different from the typical Gorean war spear, which is commonly a weighty, formidable weapon, requiring considerable strength for its apt employment. It is usually thickly hafted, seven feet or more in length, and lengthily and broadly bladed, usually with bronze.

"Would this stop a larl?" I asked.

"A spear would be better," he said, "if the larl were in flat country, in open country, and anticipated, but the size and weight of the spear impairs its utility as a hunting tool. The javelin is more quickly handled, and is thus more useful at short range. A larl in undergrowth may be difficult to detect, and can come at you unexpectedly, and very quickly. Similarly, given the javelin's smaller size it is less cumbersome, and easier to take through brush and thickets. Similarly, it is lighter and, if necessary, can be carried at a run, for Ahn at a time. Try pursuing tabuk with a spear. The javelin is less tiring to bear than a spear, and more convenient, in several ways."

"Still," I said.

"Much depends on the location of the strike, and its penetration," he said. "One might kill a larl with a hand knife."

"Your animal is ready," I said.

"He has been ready for some time," he said.

"Let us be on our way," I said.

Two Pani watched us cross the line of the wands. They made no attempt to stop us.

I had heard several men had been killed near the wands, as the time of launching the great ship grew closer. The Pani did not accept deserters.

We had moved past the wands no more than a few yards when Axel held up the growling, unwilling beast.

"Look," he said, pointing.

"I see," I said.

It was a basket, apparently discarded, lying on its side in the brush.

Chapter Twenty-Seven

I looked up, into the night sky, and the pouring rain. Then, I struggled to my feet, and looked about myself. I was afraid to move, but was determined to do so. I must avoid recapture at all costs. I did not wish to die under the jaws of sleen, nor writhe bound amongst leech plants, while a thousand eager thorns drew the blood from my body.

I touched the collar on my neck. It was cold and wet. It was locked on me. I was a collared slave girl. I had heard there was no escape for the slave girl on this world, no escape for the Gorean slave girl, and I knew myself a Gorean slave girl.

But I have escaped, I told myself.

My hair was sopped, and hung about my face and neck. I brushed it back, away from my face. We are to keep ourselves well-groomed, I recalled. The masters might not be pleased, I thought. Perhaps I would be beaten.

They will never catch me, I thought.

But how could I elude the masters? I was a slave girl, a Gorean slave girl.

I stood there in the darkness, my feet in the water and leaves, cold and miserable, and now, again, hungry, very hungry, the rain streaming from my body.

I had no idea where I was.

I was fearfully disoriented.

I was frightened.

Then I thought to myself it is foolish to be afraid. Who would know where they were in this dark, cold, fearful place? I was not so lost, really.

It was foolish to be concerned.

I had escaped!

That was what counted.

I had made good my escape!

One need not know exactly where one was. It was not that important. All that was necessary was to continue to move west, away from Shipcamp. To be sure, I was now uncertain of my distance from the Alexandra, and I did hope to return to the river, sooner or later, to cross it, and thence to make my way south.

Things were going well.

I had escaped.

I put my hands out, and, in a moment, felt the bark of a tree, a Tur tree. I wanted the rain to stop, but it gave no sign of doing so.

I was sure that I was now beyond the range of the larls. Too, before I had crossed the wands, I had determined they were securely caged. That had given me an excellent start, as I had planned. I had eluded them. I had planned well. I had been clever, extremely clever. I had even placed my blanket in the laundering vat. There were many dangers in the forest, of course. A branch might break free in the storm. A boulder might slip, dislodged in the rain, and tumble down an incline. One might even fall, unaware of a ledge. But what I most feared, the animals, I had even glimpsed a sleen, would not be likely to be about in such a night. I was sure of that. Prey would be quiescent, withdrawn, unstirring, not venturing out; sign would be little deposited, if at all. If there were scent the rain would confuse it, or wash it away. Surely a long, deep burrow, or a sheltered lair, would be preferable on such a night to prowling about, futilely searching for absent quarry.

So, in the darkness, as I could, I continued my flight. I moved carefully, often putting my hands out before me. Lightning occasionally gashed the darkness, turning the night for an instant into a bright, cold, frightening noon, but then again, as quickly as a door might close, I found myself once again in darkness, as though shut in a room, the room of the forest, with no light, only rain, wind, cold, darkness, and thunder.

Once I screamed with fear when lightning, like an ax of light, split half a tree from its trunk, not yards away. Briefly there was a sudden coat of fire on the sundered wood, narrow, diagonal, to my right, but it was extinguished by the rain, only an Ihn or two after its appearance.

I continued on my way.

Though I was weary, and hungry, so hungry that I was almost faint with hunger, I forced myself to go further, and further, to put every tenth of a pasang I could between myself and the kennels and chains of Shipcamp, and the great, fearful, mysterious ship restless at its cables, the purpose of which seemed obscure, and which for some reason so many feared to board. I had escaped in time, shortly before her departure. I would not be aboard when she descended the Alexandra, and would open the wings of her canvas to the winds of Thassa, capricious, vast, turbulent Thassa, the sea.

The rain stopped after a time, I supposed somewhere in the vicinity of the twentieth Ahn.

The cloud cover was still heavy.

The moons were obscured.

I continued on, and on, in the mud, stumbling in the darkness.

Surely I walked for a very long time, and then, exhausted, unable to continue, but content with my progress, I lay down to rest, I think a little before dawn, and must have slept for better than two Ahn.

It was light when I awakened, and I drank, as might have a tabuk doe, from a puddle of clear, gathered water in a hollow, in the wet grass. Then I found a Sul plant, the golden Sul, and dug out the tuber, washed it clean in the water, and consumed it, I fear voraciously. Looking about, gathering my bearings, I noted Tur-Pah clinging about nearby Tur trees. The Tur tree is tall and hardy, and the common host to Tur-Pah, but Tur-Pah, interestingly, does not thrive on all Tur trees. The difference apparently has to do with the grades and natures of the soil in which the tree is rooted.

I washed my body with wet grass and leaves, wiping away dirt. I brushed back my hair, and, as I could, combed it with my fingers. My tunic was muchly soiled, and rent in more than one place. I had a scratch on my side, and my right calf was sore, where it had been punctured by the thorns of the leech plant.

My body ached but I was not displeased, with yesterday, and the night.

I had done well, quite well.

I located a pool of water and, kneeling and bending down, examined my reflection.

I did not think I was bad-looking, for a common slave. I thought I might even be such that some might consider me beautiful. Certainly, when permitted access to mirrors, I had thought I had become much better looking on Gor than I had been on Earth, more relaxed, more vital, glossier haired, smoother skinned, trimmer, better-postured, and more excitingly curved. In any event, I was far from Shipcamp. I had escaped. I congratulated myself on my boldness, and with the success of my flight. Surely I was not only beautiful, or, say, at least quite good looking, but I was more clever than the others, and perhaps more clever than most. Perhaps they could learn from a mere barbarian! Then, in my generally contented, admiring scrutiny of my own reflection, I stopped, suddenly, my attention arrested. Surely I could not ignore a patent feature obvious in the surface which I beheld, the reflection of an encircling metal band fastened about my neck. I was collared! I smiled in the reflection, however, and, carefully adjusted the collar, that the lock would be properly placed, at the back of my neck. I lifted my chin a bit. Yes, I thought, for whatever reason, the collar is quite attractive on a woman. Indeed, there are Gorean sayings pertinent to this sort of thing. "With the collar comes beauty," "Put her in a collar and see her become beautiful," and so on. I suspect such sayings are not popular with free women.

When I stood up, to continue my journey, I suddenly stopped, confused, and frightened.

I suddenly felt sick, very sick.

I was facing Tor-tu-Gor. It should have been behind me. Further, far off, through the trees, I could see a river which must be the Alexandra, but it was to my right, and it should have been to my left! I ran forward a little bit and saw, anchored in the soil, supple, clearly visible, easily marked in the vegetation, a path on one side of it, about a yard high, a wand, and, along that path, others, as well.

Lying in the brush to my left, not far from the wands, was a basket, apparently discarded.

I turned about with misery, and fled away, back into the forest.

Chapter Twenty-Eight

"Your little vulo has flown far," said Axel.

"She is not my vulo," I said, "merely a little beast, pursued for pleasure."

"What will you do with her, when you apprehend her?" inquired Axel.

"I assume her tunic has a disrobing loop," I said.

"I gather she will learn what it is to be caught, her neck enclasped in a collar," he said.

"Beware," I said, "there are leech plants."

"I see them," he said. "There is little danger if one is aware of them."

"Hold your sleen," I said.

"Steady, steady, Tiomines," he said. The chain leash was taut.

"Do not let him proceed," I said.

"He will not do so," said Axel. "Sleen find such things aversive."

"The trail leads here?" I said.

"Apparently," he said.

There was a rustling in the growth, and two strands, thick and fibrous, began to inch toward us, pods lifted, swaying, like the heads of snakes.

Axel backed away a little, shortening the leash.

"They are ugly things," he said.

I drew out my sword and slashed down at the vine to the right, severing it a hort behind its pod. Immediately the vine shook, and began to withdraw, trailing a fresh, light, green exudate, concealing itself amidst the leaves of its fellows.

I sheathed the sword and pried open the pod, revealing the two curved thorns.

"Blood," observed Axel.

"Steady your beast," I urged, for the sleen had lifted its head and gathered its legs under it. I feared it might lunge at me.

Axel took the opened pod, and held it near the snout of the sleen, which began to growl, and lash its tail.

"Your beast seems pleased," I said.

"The blood," he said, "is like paga, like sunrise."

"The trail leads away," I said.

"Proceed, Tiomines," said Axel, and the beast, tugging at the leash, snout to the ground, with renewed zest, addressed himself once more to his work.

How stupid, I thought, was the meaningless quarry. It did not even know enough to avoid leech plants. It was, of course, only a barbarian. But its eyes were deep, its lips soft, and its flanks of interest.

I recalled it from an emporium on another world, from long ago, where I had first seen it, arrayed in its clumsy, barbarous garments. It looked much better in a collar and slave tunic.

Chapter Twenty-Nine

I fled back, away from the wands, frantically, sobbing, keeping the Alexandra on my left. I had not run more than fifteen or twenty Ehn when I stopped, suddenly, almost falling. I heard the sound of a switch, falling on a body. It was an unmistakable sound, not unfamiliar to kajirae. I myself had seldom been switched, nor are most kajirae. There is no point in switching us. We strive to be to be pleasing to our masters. Still we know we can be switched. We are kajirae. Something was to my left in the forest, behind me, between myself and the broad ribbon of the Alexandra, now some half pasang distant. I could see four or five bodies through the trees, approaching, afoot. Shielding myself in the trees I remained absolutely still. I did not want this group, which seemed small, either behind me, following me, nor ahead of me, impeding my flight. I decided I would move north, and then west, taking care not to lose my relation to the Alexandra again. I moved back in the trees. The group was coming closer. There should be no one here, I thought, not this close to the wands. This must be something, I thought, independent of Shipcamp. I then heard, again, the stroke of the switch, this time twice. But I heard no cry of pain, no begging for forgiveness, no pleading to a master for mercy. This surprised me, for the switch is unpleasant and one will do much to avoid it, and the whip, of course, is worse. We are not free women. We strive to please our masters. It is no wonder we are so seldom punished. We do not wish to be punished. Still it is thrilling to know that one is owned, and will be punished, if one is not pleasing.

I could now see the group, clearly, some seventy to eighty feet from me. There were five in the group. To my astonishment there were no men in the group. Had I not heard the stroke of a switch? Each individual in the group, rather, was a woman, though there the similarity amongst them stopped. It was almost as if one were dealing with two different sorts of life.

The switch fell again, twice again, first on the second slave, and then on the first, hurrying them forward. "Harta!" I heard. "Hasten!" "Faster!" The two slaves were slight, and lovely, briefly tunicked, very briefly, and clearly collared. Both were such as might be well bid upon by men. Both were such, so female, so desirable, that they might expect the contempt and hatred of free women. Both, despite their beauty, were burdened, and, I suspected, excessively so. Marketable beauties, they were being utilized here as common draft slaves, as mere beasts of burden. How they must be hated, I thought. Each, in a common Gorean fashion, balanced her load, a large, canvas-covered, squarish, roped bundle, on her head. I thought they were overburdened. Their size and strength did not seem well proportioned to what they were given to bear. Each was serving as might a pack kaiila. I did not think masters would burden them so, unless as a discipline. They were roped together by the neck. And each, for some reason, was gagged. It was then obvious why I had heard no response to the striking of the switch.

The other women, there were three I saw, were quite different. The differences between the two sorts were radical, fearful, and unmistakable. The others were not burdened. They were large, strong, sturdy women. I was afraid of them for they reminded me, a little, in their stature, and power, of men. And I feared men, at least the men of this world, for they were masters, and I was not only a woman, but goods, a slave. In some respects they seemed neither male nor female, or, perhaps better, discontentedly, unwillingly, or unhappily female. Certainly they were very unlike Gorean free women. Surely they were dressed very differently. There was nothing here of layered, shimmering veils, of golden sandals, of cloaks, hoods and scarves, of jeweled purses, of the rich, flowing, colorful, intricately draped robes of concealment, common to the Gorean free woman. Too, there was nothing here of the grace, and beauty, and femininity, of the provocative softness, of the promise of secret delights, of the implicit, whispered needs, of the typical Gorean free woman, obvious even in, and perhaps even enhanced by, the robes of concealment. Yet I had little doubt that these unusual, different women, or creatures, I now looked upon were both Gorean and free. Certainly they carried themselves much as free men might, but, I thought, pretentiously so. Did they think they were men? They carried knives on a loop slung about their shoulder. They carried light spears. Their hair was bound back in talmits. On their necks there were no collars, but barbaric strings of claws. On their arms and wrists were golden bands. Two had a golden anklet. Clearly then they were women. Did they not have their vanity? They were clothed briefly, and not that differently from slaves, but they wore not rep-cloth, the wool of the bounding hurt, or silk, work silk or pleasure silk, but the skins of animals, of forest panthers. They were not dressed by men for the pleasure of men, but, perhaps, should the occasion arise, to torment and taunt men. But, too, would not such light garb be ideal for moving easily and swiftly in natural, difficult terrains, in the woods, in the jungles, in evading, hunting, attacking, and perhaps, I thought, in reconnoitering.

I recognized the large, strong, fierce women as Panther Women, or, as the men will have it, Panther Girls, for they seem to think of all women in terms of the collar, either presently or in the future. I had heard that Panther Girls, subdued and taught their collars, made excellent slaves, grateful, devoted, loving, obedient, and passionate. But I did not understand why they had to be subdued. Were they not women? Did they not long for masters? Did they war only in the hope of being conquered? I did not have to be subdued. Rather, I longed for my place in nature. On my former world I had feared it would be denied to me. Why were Panther Women, or Panther Girls, so different, so hostile to men, and to themselves? Did they hate a womanhood which they lacked, or doubted they possessed? Was this a matter of pride of some sort, of striving to realize some sort of an unusual image? Why had they fled to the wilds, to forsake civilization, and men, and live as savages, as beasts? Were they trying to be men? Did they fear the cry of their heart, the piteous, insistent pleading of their blood? But I did not understand how there could be Panther Girls this far north, certainly not in the autumn, with winter looming. Had not ice been noted in the Alexandra? One thinks of Panther Girls much farther south, perhaps in the basin and environs of the Laurius, not the Alexandra. Their presence here was certainly anomalous. What were they doing here?

The small caravan had passed, and I backed away, a step, would turn, and would resume my flight, moving to the north, and then, again, follow the Alexandra west.

"Oh!" I cried, in pain.

"Do not move, kajira," said a woman's voice. "It is a spear in your back."

The point was in my back. It had gone through the tunic, and entered my skin, enough that I could clearly feel it, but not enough to do much more than break the skin. I did feel a trickle of blood course down my back.

"Do not turn around, kajira," said the voice.

I would not have done so. I had not received permission to do so.

"Your tunic is filthy," she said.

"Forgive me, Mistress," I whispered.

"On your belly, in the dirt," said the voice. "Cross your wrists behind you."

In a moment I felt my wrists knotted together, behind me, with a light, leather thong.

"Get up," she said. "Stand up. Let me look at you. Let us see what we have here."

I struggled to my feet, and faced her.

"Nice," she said. "The men will like you."

I put down my head.

"We have two burden slaves with us," she said. "You will make another."

I kept my head down.

"You are a runaway, are you not?" she asked.

"Yes, Mistress," I said, not raising my head.

Surely, out here, in my current condition, that must be obvious. I suspected she knew of Shipcamp. How much she knew of it, I did not know. Perhaps she knew as much as I, perhaps more.

"Have no fear," she said. "We will not return you to the masters, for a capture fee."

They wish to conceal their presence in this vicinity, I thought. Again I wondered what they might be doing here, this far north.

"We will keep you for a marketing beach, on the coast," she said. Then she snapped, "Turn about, lift your head, and open your mouth, widely."

In a moment I felt a heavy leather wadding thrust into my mouth, and then its straps were buckled together behind the back of my neck.

I was then gagged, as securely and effectively as the two slaves I had seen in the small caravan.

It seemed that I, and the others, were to be kept silent. No plaintive cry, no unwelcome sound, was to be risked from us.

She then put back her head, and uttered a long, wailing, birdlike cry. A bit later a similar cry was heard, farther down the trail.

"You are pretty," she said. "I will be pleased to show you to them."

I gathered that my captor, this large, sturdy, blue-eyed, widely shouldered, blond-haired, harsh, strapping woman was first in this small contingent of Panther Girls so unaccountably in the vicinity of Shipcamp.

The point of her small, short, light spear was jabbed into my back. "Move, kajira," she said.

I preceded her through the trees.

"Faster," she said. "Run."

Again I felt the point of the spear.

I moved as rapidly as I could, my hands bound behind me, down the rough, sometimes steep, ground, toward the river.

She strode behind me.

More than once I felt the jab of her spear.

Some yards from the river, near the edge of the small camp, she said, "Stop, stand, head up."

Then she called out, "Ho, I have snared a vulo! Come see her."

Three Panther Women, carrying their spears, approached. My captor put her hand in my hair, holding my head back, exhibiting me to her companions.

"How small and weak she is," said one of the Panther Women.

I was not small, nor weak, for a typical woman, though I was far inferior in size and strength to them. Doubtless they would define womanhood, and value, as they pleased, however eccentrically.

"How pretty, how small, how slight, how feminine, she is," sneered another of the large women.

I knew myself despised.

I looked beyond the three Panther Women, and saw the two neck-roped slaves, one a blonde, like my captor, and the other a brunette, rather like myself, kneeling down, close to one another. The gags were tight and heavy in their gag-packed, swollen, distended mouths. The rope which linked them was coarse. Their hands were before them, wrists crossed. Their wrists were not bound, by cords or thongs, but by the mistress' will. One may not, without permission, separate them. It is a convenience with slaves, who dare not disobey. They looked very frightened. Their eyes met mine and I, too, was frightened. Neither dared meet the eyes of any of the Panther Women.

"Heads down," snapped one of the Panther Women, the one who had not yet spoken of me, and the two slaves lowered their heads. She then turned to me, and regarded me, slowly, appraisingly.

"A runaway," said my captor.

I suddenly realized it was this other woman, and not my captor, who was first in this tiny band of Panther Women. I should have realized that, of course. My captor would be most likely an outtrekker, a guard or scout of sorts, one who would cover the forest flank of the group's march, the river on the other side. The leader would be with the main group, where she might apprehend, direct, and command. The leader, who was also blond, with long braided hair, in two plaits, dangling to the small of her back, was the largest of the four women. Her ornaments were the gaudiest, and most abundant, her mottled skins, which would blend well with a background of bark and shadows, seemed the finest and loveliest of the four; they were light, well-worked, form-fitting, smooth, and supple, and might have won the grudging approval of an examining fellow of the caste of leather workers. Too, I had gathered that leadership in such a band was not easily purchased, but often won by the knife or spear. A defeated leader, if surviving, was banished from the group, being driven away into the forest, alone. Sometimes free women, miserable and unhappy in their lives, resentful of the conventional constraints commonly imposed on them in the cities and towns, fleeing unwanted matches, debtors hoping to escape the law, and such, attempted to join a band of Panther Girls. But membership in such a band did not come easily. Most often such candidates, particularly if slight and attractive, found themselves stripped, bound, and sold. Others, thought to have promise, were sent naked into the forest with a spear, to kill a panther, and return with the bloodied skin about their shoulders. Most, I had been told, do not return. The panther is dangerous, elusive prey; it is territorial and aggressive; and in such a situation it is seldom clear who is the hunter and who the hunted. Panther Girls are commonly filled with hatred; they commonly resent and hate men, whom it seems, oddly enough, they appear to envy and attempt to emulate, but, interestingly, perhaps even more, they commonly resent and hate typical free women, perhaps because such women are too female, and too unlike men. Whereas the Panther Woman, or Panther Girl, as other free women, commonly holds the slave in contempt, and is cruel to her, she seems to hate her less, on the whole, than she hates either the free male or the typical free female. The animus borne to the slave by the typical free woman is doubtless motivated primarily by the fact that men commonly prefer the lovely, lightly clad slave, submitted and needful, docile, obedient, and passionate, hoping to please, to the proud, exalted free woman jealous of her thousand prerogatives and determined to exploit each of them in her favor. The free woman is not concerned to please, but to be pleased. She is not to be bought and commanded, but to be solicited, wooed, and cajoled. She may be sought for prestige, position, family, influence, fortune, and such. The slave is purchased for herself. She does not even own her collar. One courts the moody, unpredictable free woman who may confuse, vacillate, misdirect, tease, and tantalize to her heart's content. One puts the slave to one's slave ring. The free woman may dangle the prospect of her couch, angling for gain, selling herself for her own profit. The slave is sold for the profit of another. The free woman is the equal of her free companion; the purchased female is the slave of her master.

The free companion wonders if his free companion will be in the mood this night; he will hope so; the master orders his slave to the furs. So the animosity of the typical free woman for the slave is largely dependent on the fact that the slave, however unworthy, is a rival, a rival men are likely to much prefer. On the other hand, the Panther Women, or Panther Girls, hating men, are less likely to see the slave as a rival. They are more likely to see her as a mere slave, as a work beast, a convenience, a beast of burden, an object which may be sold for a profit. To be sure, they, like other free women, seem to be particularly cruel to attractive slaves, so much remains obscure.

"So, Vulo," said the leader, looking upon me, "you thought to escape?" She then put her hands to my collar and patted it gently, on each side, as though sympathetically. "But, little vulo," she said, "this is a collar, is it not, and it is on your neck. I would not be surprised if it were locked. Yes, here is a nice little lock, and we find the pretty collar is well fastened on your pretty neck. You are in it. How stupid is our little vulo. And I would not doubt but what your thigh wears a pretty mark, as well." She then jerked up the tunic on my left side, to the hip. "Yes," she said, "here is a pretty mark on your pretty thigh. You are nicely marked." She then thrust the tunic down, disdainfully. "Well, pretty vulo," she said, "in your pretty tunic, in your pretty collar, with your pretty mark, where did you expect to go, what did you expect to do?"

The gag was thick and bulky in my mouth. It is unpleasant to wear such a gag. It is not attractive, but it is quite effective.

"Stupid, stupid vulo," she said.

Tears came to my eyes.

"Take her into the woods," said one of the women, "and bind her to a tree, gagged, for the beasts."

"Surely she is marketable," said my captor.

"Who would want a stupid slave," said the woman who had spoken.

"Men are stupid," said my captor.

"On your belly," snapped the leader, "your face in the dirt, as befits the garbage you are."

I then lay amongst them, prone, my hands bound behind my back, unable to plead, or speak.

"Tie her for the beasts," said the woman who had spoken before.

"We could trade her on the coast, for a vessel of ka-la-na," said one of the Panther Women.

"To the beasts," said the one who had spoken before. She had a wide, green-and-brown talmit. "Surely you know why we are here. We must complete our work and report to the employer. We have already risked much by bringing two collar sluts with us."

"Do not be concerned," said the leader. "They are fearful, obedient little beasts. Do you wish to do your own manual labor, to gather provender, to clear ground for a camp, to bring fire wood, to cook, to fetch soft boughs for our bedding, to wash talmits, and polish leather? Do you not enjoy having your feet cleaned with their tongues?"

"One would have been enough," said she who had spoken, she of the green-and-brown talmit.

"Do you wish to bear a burden yourself?" asked the leader.

"I am a free woman!" said the other, angrily.

"And what other pack animals would bear burdens for us?" said the leader.

"Two, then," she said, "are enough!"

I was then kicked in the side.

"And with three, we might travel more swiftly," said the leader.

"It is dangerous," said the other. "Tie her for the beasts."

"Consider her hair," said the leader.

"It is filthy, and dirt, and flakes of leaves, adhere within it."

"Suitably washed, groomed, and watered, she would be presentable," said my captor.

"You want her selling fee," said the other.

"I would share it," said my captor.

"Consider her lineaments," said the leader.

"Surely she is shapely goods," said my captor. "Consider her shoulders, her arms, her forearms, drawn back, the neatness of her small wrists, nicely tied together, the narrowness of her waist, the sweet flare of her hips, the pleasantries of a modest but well-turned fundament, her thighs, the rounded calves, the trimness of her ankles."

"This is not Brundisium, or Ar," said she of the green-and-brown talmit. "They do not pay much on the beach."

"They rob us," said another Panther Woman, angrily, she who had been muchly silent.

The leader then crouched beside me, and pulled my head up and back, by the hair.

"You know gag signals, do you not, Vulo?" she said.

I made a tiny, plaintive sound. I doubt that it could have been heard more than a few feet away. One sound signifies "Yes," two sounds, "No." All slaves are taught this.

"Do you wish to live?" she asked.

I made instantly a tiny, pathetic noise, a single noise, one sound.

"Do you wish to be added to the rope?" she asked.

I made my small sound again, piteously.

"Do you beg," she asked, "as the meaningless slave you are, to be added to the rope?"

Fervently, desperately, I made again a single, small, pleading sound.

"Put her on the rope," said the leader, rising.

My captor took a length of the rope which fastened the other two slaves together, by the neck, and I felt it tied, and knotted, about my neck.

"Switch her," said the leader.

Then I writhed, and squirmed, helpless and bound, on my belly, tears bursting from my eyes, muddying the dirt before me, under a lashing rain of supple leather. I could not cry out, for the cruelty of the gag, but tiny, startled, miserable sounds escaped me. I did not think they could have been heard more than a few feet away.

I was then untied.

"Kneel beside the others," I was told.

I did so, painfully.

"Head down," I was told.

I lowered my head.

"You are bound by the mistress's will," I was told.

I crossed my wrists before me.

I then knelt there, beaten, a rope on my neck, my head down, my wrists crossed.

"Welcome," said the leader, "to the band of Darla."

Chapter Thirty

"Your beast is excited," I said to Axel.

"She was here, last night," said Axel.

His beast, Tiomines, was scratching at the ground.

"What is he doing?" I asked.

"Scratching up scent, releasing it, fresh, into the air."

"Better he should be following it," I said.

"Be patient," said Axel.

"Still," I said.

"Be patient," he said. "Do not annoy him."

I had no intention, I assured myself, of annoying a sleen.

"He is playing," said Axel, "he is enjoying himself, he is relishing, he is reminding himself of what a bright, glowing thing it can be, he is taking it more deeply into himself."

The beast then lifted its head, growling.

If we came upon the prey, I trusted Axel could control the beast.

"I had expected to take her last night," I said, "before dark."

"No," said Axel. "She had a start of several Ahn."

"Sometimes," I said, "the beast seems uncertain."

"One loses the trail, one finds it," said Axel. "It is like script on a page, easy enough to read, but one must find the page."

"What if one cannot find the page?" I asked.

"The page is there," said Axel. "We know that. So it will be found, sooner or later."

"There are beasts in the forest," I said.

"Of course," said Axel.

"I would that we had had her roped yesterday," I said.

"Surely you have no interest in this slave, save for the sport of the hunt, no more than in any other, save as prey?" he said.

"Certainly not," I said.

"I think you want her crawling at your feet, on all fours, fetching your whip to you, in her teeth, the very whip with which she may be beaten."

"It seems you have been talking with Asperiche," I said. It would be easy, I thought, to be annoyed with Asperiche. She seemed to have the foolish idea that I might be interested in a particular slave, which was absurd, for are they not all the same in a collar? What difference did it make, one or another?

"Asperiche," he said, "wishes to be a preferred slave, and she fears she is not yours."

"She is the only one I have," I said.

"Now," he said.

"Yes, now," I said.

"She is pretty," he said.

"That is why one buys them," I said. "I see I must lash her for speaking to strange men."

"I accosted her," he said. "She must kneel and respond."

"I see," I said.

"Most are camp slaves," he said. "I did not realize she was privately owned."

"Doubtless you soon learned," I said.

"It is pleasant to have her on her knees before one," he said.

"As any woman," I said.

"Of course," he said.

"She is a forward slab of collar meat," I said.

"I could take that out of her," he said.

"So could I," I said.

"What do you want for her?" he asked.

"I had hoped to have our quarry in hand by now," I said. "The tracking seems slow."

"The scent is not the easiest to follow," said Axel. "The prey is furtive, and light. It is not like following clumsy, ponderous tharlarion."

"It makes for slower tracking?" I said.

"A male is larger, heavier, easier to follow," said Axel.

"I fear to lose the trail," I said.

"There is no danger," said Axel. "It is still quite fresh."

Last night had been lacerated by lightning, much thunder, and a lengthy, cold, soaking rain, to be sure, severities of a sort not that unusual in this latitude at this time of year. Axel had taken the first watch, and I the second. We had warmed ourselves with carefully measured swigs of paga, from Axel's flask. We had both brought meat and bread, and there was always the provender of the forest itself, if one can recognize it, and, in some cases, bring oneself to eat it. We had brought with us, in our packs, camp blankets and rain blankets, and so, save for the thunder, the noise, had fared rather well. Axel had shared his camp blanket and rain blanket with the beast, sleeping beside it. I would not have cared to do so. It would have been impractical to make a fire, but even had it been practical, we would not have done so. Shipcamp was within a day's march. One does not know with whom one shares the forest.

"There was a long, fierce rain last night," I said.

"It was quite cold, and windy, as well," he said.

"Yes," I said.

"Excellent," said Axel.

"How excellent?" I asked.

"A slave, Relia, acts as first girl in Kennel Five," he said. "She was the last to see our little 119 before her ill-advised departure. She informs me that she had only her tunic, nicely slave-cut, and, delightfully, only of summer rep-cloth. She had no rain blanket, not even a camp blanket. Accordingly, I expect our game, concerned that she might be pursued, well aware she was in danger from the forest, hungry and exhausted, alone, perhaps lost, lying in the cold and rain, in the mud and leaves, may not have spent a pleasant night."

"I am more concerned," I said, "with the trail. The rain may have washed it clean, washed away the scent."

"You know little of sleen," he said.

"Animals may have her by now," I said.

"What difference does it make?" said Axel. "She is a slave."

"Let us resume the hunt," I said.

"There is no hurry," he said. "Let us have breakfast first."

"Let us not," I said.

"I think it would be wise to assuage the hunger of Tiomines," he said. "She may be close. Should we soon come upon her, I would prefer that Tiomines not be ravenous."

"Yes," I said. "Let us have breakfast first."

Chapter Thirty-One

The gags had been removed from our mouths, and we had been put to all fours. A sul was thrown to the ground before each of us. We might not touch it, until we had received the order to feed.

"Feed," said Tuza, she of the green-and-brown talmit, who, I took it, was second in power in this small group of four, for the beasts do not count.

I put my head down, and fed, as did Tula and Mila.

We were not permitted to use our hands.

Such things help to remind us that we are animals.

We were then, on all fours, conducted to pools beside the river, where we were watered. We were then, on all fours, on our rope, conducted back to the clearing, where our gags were reaffixed.

I had returned inadvertently to the wands, and then fled, again. Not long after having fled from the wands, I had fallen captive to a small band of Panther Women, unaccountably in the vicinity of Shipcamp.

"We have that for which we have come," said Darla. "Little was accomplished by the raid on Tarncamp, which was repulsed, and few desire to again encounter the sky cavalry of the enemy. It is unusual and formidable. But we, unlikely informants, unsuspected women, no army to be encountered, but a small band, invisible in the woods, as elusive as panthers, have penetrated the forest, and discovered what men had not, not only that the rumored ship exists, but its actual location, and that its departure is imminent. The blow must be struck soon, before the bird spreads its wings. No longer now is the employer blind, no longer now need he sustain the expense of maintaining large numbers of men at the mouth of the Alexandra. He may now organize and dispatch a small, chosen force, perhaps only two hundred men, to move with speed, and in secrecy, to emerge from the forest, burn the ship, and then withdraw, their task completed, no battle given. It will be a raid, unanticipated and effective, over and done with before the enemy fully comprehends what has occurred, before any defense can be mounted, after which the raiders will slip away, returning to the forest, long before any pursuit can be organized. Have no doubts. The employer will be pleased."

"We will be well-paid," said Tuza.

"Already, dear friend," said Darla, "your wallet is heavy."

"I do not trust men," said another of the Panther Women, Hiza, whose dark hair was cut as closely as that of a metal worker.

"Let us move quickly," said the fourth of the Panther Women, blond, broad-shouldered Emerald, looking uneasily toward the forest. It was she who had captured me, she who had easily snared the "vulo." It surprised me that she, or any of these women, might be apprehensive. They were so different from myself, or the other slaves. It was hard to believe we were all women. We looked up at them from our knees. But we, of course, were slaves, rightful slaves. Certainly I knew myself such.

"Yes," said Hiza.

"Soon," said Darla, "perhaps by nightfall, we may build a fire."

"Good," said Hiza. "I hunger for cooked food."

"We may then free the mouths of our little friends," said Darla.

"But keep them silenced," said Tuza, "by the will of the mistress."

Tuza then, switch in hand, went to us, who were kneeling to the side, neck-roped, wrists crossed before us.

"You, Tula," she said, jabbing her on the shoulder with the implement of discipline and instruction, "would you not like to expel the heavy, bulky wad of leather strapped in your mouth?"

Tula looked up, frightened. She made a single, tiny, pathetic, pleading sound.

The switch came down, fiercely, on her small shoulder. She

almost separated her wrists, but fortunately did not do so. "How dare you speak without permission?" said Tuza.

"You inquired," said Darla, not pleasantly.

I gathered there was ill-will between the captain of this small band and she who was, I gathered, her lieutenant.

"You saw," snapped Tuza, "she raised her head, before a free person, without permission!"

"True," said Darla. "Have the burdens redistributed."

This was managed by Hiza and Emerald. One would not trust kaiila to arrange their own burdens.

"Stand up, here, in line," said Darla.

I stood behind Tula and Mila, on the rope.

"You are no longer bound by the will of the mistress," said Darla. We separated our hands. I would have preferred the mercy of cords, tying my hands together. Men, who are kinder, would almost always have used cords. We need not fear then that we might forget, or somehow, inadvertently, separate our wrists. It is much crueler, forcing us to be constantly vigilant, constantly in fear that we might find our wrists apart. But, too, I suppose, men like to look upon us bound. They find us attractive, constrained, helpless, at their mercy. But, too, how thrilling it is for us, as slaves, to know ourselves utterly helpless before males, our natural masters.

We steadied our burdens, on our heads, with our two hands.

"They are ready," said Emerald.

"You are slaves," said Darla. "Stand well."

We did so. The slave, like the dancer, is attentive to her posture, her carriage, her grace.

She is not entitled to the prerogatives of the free woman. She is owned.

"We will sell them on the coast," said Darla. "Ho! Move!"

The first stroke of Tuza's switch was across the left shoulder, and the second a lashing sting across the back of the thighs. Small sounds of pain escaped us. I was last in our small coffle, and thus the first struck, and then Mila and Tula. We hurried. Tuza would not be sparing with her switch.

"Keep our pretty pack beasts moving," said Darla.

Tuza's switch fell again.

"Harta!" said Tuza. "Harta!"

"You see, dear Tuza," said Darla, "how much more swiftly we can move with a third bearer."

"Harta!" said Tuza.

"We will cover pasangs before dark," said Darla.

"I am hungry for cooked food," said Hiza.

"Harta!" said Tuza. "Harta!"

Gagged as we were, we could not cry out for mercy. Tears streamed down our faces. Tiny sounds of pain escaped us, scarcely audible, as we were hurried on, more and more quickly, the river to our left.

Chapter Thirty-Two

"I do not understand it," said Axel.

"The trail is still clear," I said.

"Yes," said Axel.

"It turns back, toward Shipcamp," I said. One could tell this from the sun.

"Is she of the Foresters?" he asked.

"No," I said. "Why do you ask?"

"It is a bold stratagem," he said, "doubling back, to confuse the trail, though one unlikely to succeed, given sleen."

"Doubtless," I said.

"She is a bold one," he said.

"How so?" I said.

"Consider the risks involved," he said.

"True," I said.

"I have known slaves, of course," he said, "naive, ignorant, frightened slaves, who became confused, who knew little of woodcraft, who wandered about in the darkness, who became disoriented, who lost their way, and several who, amusingly, did little more than describe a great circle in their flight."

"If the trail continues in this fashion," I said, "it may reach the wands themselves."

"I should not be surprised if it does," he said.

"What then?" I asked.

"It will turn back, to the forest," he said.

"Unless she has been taken by Pani," I said.

"Yes," he said, "or others."

"Let us see," I said.

"We shall," he said.

He then shook the chain leash on the collar of Tiomines. "On, fellow," he said.

Chapter Thirty-Three

I lay at the side of the camp, with Tula and Mila. We were bound, hand and foot. We had been freed of the gags when the campsite had been determined, toward evening, but silenced by the will of the mistress, so that we might utter no sound. They did not fear that we might be heard, in such a way that their presence might be detected. Rather, this was now a convenience for the mistresses, who did not wish to hear the discourse of slaves. Would herdsmen, or drovers, care to hear the discourse of kaiila? Slaves, of course, save in critical situations, as in emergencies, may not speak without permission. To be sure, most slaves have a standing permission to speak, particularly when alone with their masters, but it is always clear to them that this standing permission is a permission, and that it may be revoked at the master's pleasure. Slaves, of course, as other women, love to speak, and suffer when not permitted to do so. They are denied one of the loveliest and most precious of their pleasures, and gifts. It is a torment to a slave to not be permitted to speak. Most masters love to hear their slave speak, are interested in her slightest thoughts, and often attend to her views. But, when all is said and done, she may be simply bound and thrown to the furs.

Naturally I had tried the knots on my wrists and ankles, but found them, as I had anticipated, of Gorean efficiency. Struggle would be futile.

In one sense, the slave is helpless and defenseless, for she may not so much as touch a weapon. In some cities it is a capital offense for her to do so. In another sense, of course, she is not wholly defenseless; she obviously has the weapons of her sex, her desirability, and beauty, and, it should be noted, as well, and not negligibly, those of her wit and tongue. How often her speech, with her submissive posture, her tearful eye, her extended hand, her trembling lip, serves to placate, to divert wrath, to enable her to escape the switch and whip! Then suppose she is denied speech. How then is she to explain herself, to supply details which may have been overlooked, to call attention to extenuating circumstances, to explain how she was misunderstood, to make clear what she truly intended, or was trying to do, to wheedle, beg, cajole, solicit indulgence or mercy, and so on?

It was toward evening when we were grateful that the mistresses would make camp. How ironic, I thought, that I had managed to escape Shipcamp, but only in this fashion. We hoped to be permitted to rest, certainly I did, but, linked together, by our neck rope, we were soon set to labors on behalf of our mistresses, and were seldom out of the sight of one or another of them. Certainly we dared not speak to one another. Do pack beasts speak?

We were first to prepare the ground for the camp, and so we gathered up forest debris from the site, stones, leaves, and sticks, and, with branches, swept the ground smooth. I did not think men would be so particular. We were also put, in the preparing of the site, to the gathering of a plenitude of soft boughs on which our mistresses, to rest more comfortably, might spread their blankets. Then, given cloths, to be fashioned into sacks, we were sent into the woods to gather gim berries, under the supervision of short-haired Hiza. We did not dare eat any. We hoped we might be permitted some. I had no thought of running away. I was on the rope, and Hiza had her small spear, or javelin. Too, as I now understood, with much misery, the forest was dangerous, formidable, and lonely, and there was really nowhere to run. Well then was I convinced of my condition, which was helpless, and slave. Too, my chances of survival were much higher here than if I were alone, here with these armed, skilled, dangerous, and mighty women, almost like creatures of the forest themselves, who could detect sign and move with stealth, whose passage would be little marked by the forest floor, who could read the sun, the moons, the growth on trees, the declivities of the Alexandra's basin, signifying the drainage of water, the seasonal flights of birds. After we had poured our berries onto the mat, Tula was removed from the rope and her ankles were fastened together, some horts apart, by rope shackles. She could walk with care, but not run. Then she was given a stick and set to the digging of a fire hole.

"Mila, Vulo," said Hiza. "Fetch water."

We were each given a pitcher, and we then went down to the shore, on our rope, filled our vessels, and returned to the camp. Hiza observed us, from the camp. It was not necessary. We would not run. We were slaves, obedient slaves.

"Mila, Vulo," said Hiza. "Gather fire wood."

This task was much less difficult than I had anticipated. Whereas last night it had rained fiercely further east on the Alexandra, it had rained less heavily in this area, and the day had been sunny and warm. The best wood would be gathered on the shore of the Alexandra, which was quite close, where debris was exposed to the sun.

Mila and I, bending over, roped together by the neck, filled our arms at the shore. We were accompanied by Hiza and Emerald.

"You can sell Mila," said Emerald to Hiza. "I will sell Vulo."

"Darla will decide," said Hiza.

"I caught Vulo," said Emerald.

"Darla will decide," said Hiza.

"It does not matter," said Emerald. "All is shared."

"I trust so," said Hiza.

"I can exhibit her better," said Emerald.

"Only men know how to exhibit a slave," said Hiza.

Mila and I could scarcely bear more wood. Hiza then, with a gesture of her javelin, indicated that we should return to the camp.

The fire hole had been dug, and soon Darla, with a fire drill and shredded tinder extracted from a pouch in one of the packs, and a number of small sticks removed from a wrapper in the same pack, had ignited a small blaze. She then, after adding some of our wood to the blaze, placed four stones about the blaze. On these stones she placed a small iron fire rack. Soon, then, a pot of sullage, tended by Tula, was bubbling over the fire. Emerald put some dried meat from her pack into the brew, and Hiza cast in two handfuls of our picked berries into the brew. When the provender was ready, Tula, with a ladle, filled four shallow, golden bowls with the sullage, and, humbly, head down, as a slave, served the mistresses. I was surprised at the golden bowls, which were, I supposed, some sort of loot. Sometimes, in concert, bands of Panther Women will attack a small caravan in the forest or an outlying trading post on the coast. On the other hand, perhaps the bowls were payment of a sort, or a token of more to come, from the mysterious "employer" Darla had mentioned.

When the mistresses had satisfied themselves with sullage, Tula was returned to the rope, and the rope shackles she had worn were removed. We then knelt to the side, hungry.

Tuza carefully returned the golden bowls to the pack.

"There are four," said Darla.

Tuza angrily thrust the fourth bowl into the pack.

Emerald then drew three shallow, porcelain cups from several others in another pack. She then dipped these into the pot, filling them with sullage, and then placed them on the ground, near the fire.

She observed us, to note our reaction. We knew enough not to move.

She then handed each of us one of the cups. Mine was chipped. I looked at it, held in my two hands. I could feel the warmth of the sullage. I was desperately hungry. I supposed we all were. We looked up at Emerald. I took it her name was from her greenish eyes. I did not regard her as bad looking. I thought there would be men who might find her acceptable as a slave. I imagined her, deprived of talmit and ornaments, briefly tunicked, with a collar on her neck. She might do, I thought. Perhaps very well.

"Feed," she said, and we gratefully lifted our cups to our mouths.

"Enjoy it," she said. "But do not hasten. It is all you will receive. We must be careful of your figures. You are, after all, to be sold."

Then she bent down, near me, and whispered. "I am going to sell you," she said. "You may speak."

"Yes, Mistress," I whispered. She then placed her finger before her lips, and I knew I had been again silenced.

I again lifted the small porcelain bowl to my lips. The meat was gone, but there were some berries left. I had had such berries, from time to time, in Kennel Five, mixed with the slave gruel. Slave gruel is not that different from some pottages I had known on my former world. As slave feed, however, it is commonly served plain and bland, served without spices, sugars, salts, or other flavors. It is apparently quite nourishing. I am told that in public eating houses, not brothels or taverns, slaves, when admitted, and not chained to rings outside, may kneel beside their master's bench, and while he eats from the plates, and such, on the table, if it be his will, may be given a bowl of slave gruel, which will be placed either on the bench beside him, or on the floor near his place. Should he bring a sleen with him it might be similarly fed, though with a different provender, one suitable to its digestive system. Some eating houses object to admitting sleen, but the matter is sensitive. Sleen are dangerous.

"Ho," said Tuza, reaching into a pack. "Now that we are safe, ka-la-na!"

Hiza uttered a sound of delight, and Emerald clapped her hands in delight. I gathered that this was a welcome surprise.

"You sly she-sleen," said Darla.

Small golden goblets, matching the bowls, emerged, and Tuza poured ka-la-na into each. I noted she was particularly generous with Darla. Perhaps she wished to mollify her. Too, of course, Darla was leader.

I had never tasted ka-la-na but I had gathered there were a great many varieties, differing much in quality. Some Ubars might barter a city or a hundred slaves for a given flask of the beverage. Others were so cheap and common that, as the joke goes, they might be mixed with the swill of tarsk. The word itself, which is generic for several wines, derives from the ka-la-na trees, or wine trees, of Gor. But wines, as is well known, may be derived not only from the clustered fruits weighting the branches of the ka-la-na tree in the autumn, but, as on my former world, from vine fruit, tree fruit, bush fruit, even from some types of leaves.

"Have more wine," said Tuza to Darla, holding the bottle toward her. "There is more."

"You are a sly she-sleen," said Darla, smiling. But she drew back her cup. "Bed the animals," she said.

Tuza corked the bottle, rose up, and loosed the switch from her belt. We kept our heads down. Our hands were on our thighs.

"Bara!" she snapped.

Instantly we turned about in the neck rope, with its three knotted double loops, and went to our stomachs, our heads to the left, our wrists crossed behind us, and our ankles, as well. It is not advisable to hesitate in responding to a command. The bara position was, I suppose, the first slave position in which I had been placed. Of course I did not at that time understand it, or know its name. I had been in that position when I had regained consciousness in what appeared to be a warehouse, long ago, on my former world. I had been in that position, tied helplessly, when a foot had turned me over, to my back, and I had seen him, the man by whom I had known myself, for the first time, looked upon as what I had always suspected myself to be, a slave. I knew nothing of Gor, save uneasy rumors I had heard whispered about in the employee's cafeteria, when men were not present, and in the female employees' locker room at the store. How I had dismissed their whisperings as absurd, and yet, at the same time, wondered if I might appeal to the slavers of such a world. What would it be, I had wondered, to stand naked on a block, and be sold? I would learn. Then I had found myself turned to my back, and, bound hand and foot, looking up at him, he from whom I had fled in consternation in the store. I knew little, if anything, of Gor, but I knew I was looking up into the eyes of a man who was a natural master of women, one to whom a woman could be but a slave.

"They are prepared," said Tuza.

One is quite helpless in the bara position. One is on one's stomach and one's hands are behind one, so one cannot use them to rise, and one's body is extended, with one's ankles crossed. One cannot easily rise from that position. Too, psychologically, one feels oneself submitted, and at the mercy of others. One knows one is at the feet of free persons, prostrate, perhaps even as a mere slave might be. Too, obviously, so positioned, one may be conveniently and easily tied.

"Hiza," said Darla, "secure our little beasts for the night."

In a few moments, with light cords, we had been bound for the night.

We lay very still, helpless, waiting, frightened.

We knew Tuza was behind us.

Then we cried out with pain as Tuza gave each of us, with her long switch, two strokes across the back of our thighs.

"Sleep well, sluts," she said. "We have a long trek ahead of us, in the morning. By the next Passage Hand you will be bound naked to selling poles on the beach, awaiting passing galleys."

She then returned to the fire.

"Have more ka-la-na," she said to Darla.

Chapter Thirty-Four

"Ho!" said Axel, pointing to the ground.

Tiomines was snuffling about, scratching at the ground.

"What is it?" I asked.

"Our little friend has been here," he said, "but so, too, has another. See, the stirred leaves, the sandal print. Excellent, excellent!"

"I do not understand," I said.

"I had hoped for such fortune," he said, "but was muchly uncertain that it might be obtained."

"I would appreciate it," I said, "if you would speak more clearly."

"It is thought the camp was under surveillance," he said. "Shadows, glimpses, the uneasiness of larls in their cages. But there was no clear trail, one of relevance, one to which to put a sleen. There are many trails, those of larl masters, of deserters, those of scouts, trails of recruits, being conducted here, such things. But if you were to find a coin in the sand, even one of modest value, you might stoop to pick it up, might you not?"

"Of course," I said.

"That was our hope," he said. "Your stupid little barbarian friend is such a coin. Our visitors, or spies, if they exist, would have the vicinity under surveillance, and thus it is not impossible that they might note the unauthorized departure of an unwise slave. She has some value, even if it is negligible. Why should they not drop their net on her, and haul her in?"

"They are greedy," I smiled.

"It is a common fault," he said. "Her trail will now lead us to them."

"There may be several," I said, "and we are only two."

"We will be wary," he said. "Our business is to locate the enemy, not engage him, or her."

"'Her'?" I said.

"See the sandal print," he said, pointing. "It is small. It is almost certainly the print of a woman's sandal."

"Panther Girls," I said.

"They might do well in matters of observation, and surveillance," he said.

"They may have men with them," I said.

"That is unlikely," he said, smiling.

"I see," I said. "But there may be several."

"Possibly," he said. "That might be better determined later. In any event, you may recall that I informed you while in camp that we have allies about, from the coastal ships, levies from some crews."

"But not from Shipcamp," I said.

"No," he said, "they know little or nothing of Shipcamp. The word of Tyrtaios may be accepted on this."

"They do not know why they have been stationed in the forest?" I said.

"No," he said. "Is it to intercept deserters, to trade, to convey departing contingents to the galleys, to take part in some action? They do not know."

"I see," I said.

"We wish to have a force on the ground, one between Shipcamp and the coast, which may be utilized in the case of an emergency. It is a precaution, I gather, on the part of Lord Okimoto."

"He who is first in Shipcamp," I said.

"Yes," he said.

"He leaves little to chance," I said.

"It is his way," he said.

"If you locate the enemy," I said, "you will utilize these allies?"

"One would attempt to do so," he said.

"How will you contact them?" I asked.

He drew from his tunic a whistle, looped on a string about

his neck. "They have a larl with them," he said. "The Pani have seen to it. This whistle will be heard only by the larl, and such beasts. The larl will then lead the contingent to the source of the sound."

"How far does it carry?" I asked.

"I do not know," he said. "But far, easily for a pasang or two. It is said some larls can hear the squeal of a wounded animal from five pasangs away."

"And if it does not hear it?" I asked.

"Then, my friend," he said, "depending on the situation, it might prove wise to withdraw with discretion."

"To return to Shipcamp and report," I said.

"Yes," he said. "Tarnsmen might be dispatched. And the tarn can outdistance the kaiila."

"Your beast," I said, "appears ready to continue the hunt."

"He has been ready," said Axel. "Let us proceed, lest he become annoyed at the delay."

Chapter Thirty-Five

I squirmed a little in my bonds. I am not sure why I had awakened. Tula and Mila were asleep. I was uneasy. I moved my neck a little in the coarse, knotted, double loop which encircled my throat, which held me to the others. We were lying as we had been placed, facing away from the fire, and the mistresses. They had been drinking for some time before retiring. They had not posted a guard. They apparently thought themselves safe. Certainly they were now far from Shipcamp. Tuza had plied Darla with ka-la-na, even more than the others. Perhaps she wished to better ingratiate herself with the leader, for I had sensed some tension, if not animus, between them. Darla, Hiza, and Emerald had, long ago, retired to their blankets, spread on the mattresses of soft boughs we had gathered for them. They, of course, were free. We, on the other hand, lay in the dirt, bound. On my former world I could have scarcely grasped the chasm which separates the slave from the free. On Gor it was easy to grasp. There was an insurmountable division, a separation into kinds. How unbridgeable is the gap which separates the free from property, from goods, from merchandise, from the owned animal, from the slave!

Why had I awakened? I did not know.

I turned to my left side, and turned about, careful not to draw on the rope, which might have awakened Mila, and Tula, beyond her. I propped myself up on my left elbow, and twisted about, to where I might see the remains of the fire, now muchly burned down. I could hear the Alexandra several yards away, soft in its banks.

I could see Hiza and Emerald, asleep. Darla, too, was asleep. I did not see Tuza. This frightened me, for if she were about, and saw me turned about, it might earn me a thrashing. Tuza was short-tempered. She was impatient. Her switch was supple and cruel. I think she enjoyed beating slaves, at least lovely slaves, for some reason. Was she jealous of us, even though she had the glory of freedom on her and we were no more than docile, servile, collared beasts? Did it have to do with the fact that men found us of interest, and would buy us, and own us? Was it our beauty, if beauty it was, which so infuriated her? Why should she be concerned with us? Did she not know we were slaves, simple beasts, and could be sold? I dreaded the morning, when I would be again at her mercy. Why did she use the switch so upon us? What if we might be attractive to men? What did it matter? We were no more than simple beasts, animals, at her mercy. Our bodies were rich with the stripes of her displeasure. Did she not know we were desperate to please her? She was so different from a man. We would hardly ever be struck by a man, unless we were somehow displeasing. To be sure, we might sometimes be lashed, if only to remind us that we were slaves. The lash well confirms our bondage upon us.

I had had the sense, from the evening, though to be sure I was facing away, my head to the left, my right cheek on the dirt, that Tuza may not have drunk as deeply as the others. I had conjectured this from various remarks, from chidings, from jokes, from laughter, protests, and such. She had seemed to be pouring wine, and pressing it on others. I was not sure she was as eager to drain her own goblet, certainly not again, and again. I had wondered about this, and even wondered if it was the case, but I had then fallen asleep. Such things were not my concern. They were the business of the mistresses. Curiosity, as I recalled, was not becoming in a kajira.

But where was Tuza? She was not in her blankets.

Perhaps, I thought, she has fled, has perhaps robbed and deserted the band. But would she not have taken one of us with her, gagged, to carry her loot? The packs seemed much to me as they had been earlier.

I then saw Tuza emerge, like a shadow, from the forest. In her hands she carried some object.

I could not have called out even had I wished to do so. It was not that I was simply afraid to speak, though I was, or because I had been silenced by the will of the mistress. It was different. I watched in horror. I could not make a sound. I was too frightened. I tried to call out. But no sound came from my throat.

Too, it was finished in an instant. Nothing would have been different, even had I managed to cry out.

Tuza had slipped to her knees beside Darla, lifted her hands over her head, grasping the dark object, which was a heavy stone, and struck downward. Darla made a small noise, and then, apparently, lapsed into unconsciousness. Tuza put the stone to one side, and drew out her knife. I realized clearly that Tuza, had she wished, might have broken open the skull of her victim, killing her instantly, but had controlled the blow, for, it seemed, she had other plans for the leader of the band of Darla.

I saw Tuza look toward me, but she did no more than smile. With her knife she cut the skins from Darla, and removed her weapons, and ornaments, one by one, with several of which she decorated her own body. She then jerked the bloody talmit from Darla's head. She then fetched some articles from one of the packs. I heard a rustle of chain. She then knelt beside the unconscious Darla, and moving her inert body about, encircled it with a waist chain, which she drew back, snugly, about Darla's belly. The chain, as is common with such chains, contained its associated slave bracelets, by means of which a slave's hands may be cuffed before her body, or behind it, in both cases being held close to her body. A slave's hands are helpless in such a constraint. For example, if she is front-cuffed, she may not even lift her hands to feed herself. But the unconscious Darla's hands were pulled back, and cuffed closely together, at the small of her back. Tuza then snapped a pair of ankle shackles on the unconscious Darla. They would permit her ankles a play of less than a foot.

Tuza then, apparently muchly satisfied with herself, stood up, stirred the fire, and threw upon it much of the fuel we had gathered earlier in the preceding evening. Soon a hardy blaze was illuminating the clearing, brightly. It was bright enough for a man's paga feast, the sort at which stripped free women must dance as slaves and, to their shame, though they are still legally free, will be put to use as sluts before their collaring and branding.

Hiza sat up in her blankets. Emerald rubbed her eyes.

"Awaken, slothful sisters!" cried Tuza. "Donna is avenged! Welcome to the band of Tuza."

Hiza leaped up, drawing her knife, but Tuza faced her, her own knife drawn, and ready. Tuza crouched like a panther, the blade of her knife at her knee, blade upward.

Emerald was now on her feet as well. She, too, had drawn her knife.

"Darla is defeated," said Tuza. "I am first. I am leader. Victory is ours. More gold for us. See the armlets, the bracelets, and anklets I have left for you. Rich booty. I share! Donna is avenged."

Hiza and Emerald stood near the fire, uncertain.

"Do you wish to do contest?" asked Tuza. "Alone, together?"

By now Tula and Mila, too, were awake, and turned about, frightened. To be sure we, as slaves, would abide the outcome.

"What Darla did to Donna," cried Tuza, "I have now done to Darla! Let it be so. Let the strongest, the fiercest, the mightiest, command the band."

"Do not speak of vengeance," said Hiza. "You had no care for Donna. You hated her, as you hated Darla. You collaborated with Darla, to oust Donna, that you should receive the gift of the lieutenancy!"

Tuza fixed her eyes on Hiza. "Do you have your blade drawn before your leader?" she asked.

Hiza thrust her dagger back into its sheath. And Tuza turned her attention to Emerald. "Well, pretty Emerald," she said, "do you care to carry an unsheathed blade before your leader?"

"No," said Emerald, and resheathed her weapon.

"Who is leader?" asked Tuza.

"You," said Hiza.

"You," said Emerald.

"Perhaps," said Hiza, "you should have fought, in the way of the Panther Women."

"I did not choose to do so," said Tuza.

"No," said Emerald. "Darla was dangerous."

"It is not our way to kill a leader in her sleep," said Hiza.

"Of course not," said Tuza. "I did not kill her."

"She lives?" said Hiza.

"Of course," said Tuza. "Killing her would not satisfy me. I have something much better in mind."

Hiza and Emerald exchanged puzzled glances.

"I do not understand," said Emerald.

"You will fetch her, both of you," said Tuza, "but first arrange the slaves. Get them up. The little beasts are already awake. Kneel the sluts, heads up, so that they see what ensues."

Shortly thereafter we were kneeling in a line, on our neck rope. Our ankles were still bound together, and our wrists, as well, behind our back.

"Lift your heads, slaves," said Hiza.

Tuza regarded us. "You are no longer silenced by the will of the mistress," she said.

We took ourselves then to be in the common modality of the slave, subject to no more than the usual restraints on our speech.

But still we did not speak, not daring to do so, not even to request permission to speak.

Masters and mistresses do not always care to hear the speech of slaves.

"Changes have occurred in the camp," said Tuza. "There is a new leader. It is Tuza. You will find her less indulgent than the former leader, who was weak. It is a long trek to the coast. You will be expected to work well for your gruel. If you are found unsatisfactory, you will be tied in the forest, and left for the beasts. If all goes well, you will be stripped and sold on the coast. Is this understood?"

"Yes, Mistress," we whispered.

Our voices trembled. It had been long since we had been permitted to speak. It seemed strange to enunciate sounds. I feared momentarily I might not be able to say words. But I had heard myself whisper, "Yes, Mistress."

"You are poor stock," said Tuza. "I am thinking of being displeased with you. What shall I do with you?" She glared at each of us, in turn. "Please do not beat us, Mistress," said Tula. "Please be kind, Mistress," said Mila. "Please be merciful, Mistress," I said. "You, Vulo," she said. "Mistress?" I said. "You writhe nicely under the switch," she said. "Men will like that."

"Please be merciful, Mistress," I said. Surely we all responded similarly under the switch, for we were all slaves. Tuza, I feared, bore me some particular animosity. That was probably, I surmised, because I had been captured by Emerald, who expected to sell me.

Tuza then spun about, and faced Hiza. "Do you question the will of the leader?" she asked.

"No," said Hiza.

She then faced Emerald. "Do you question the will of the leader?" she asked.

"No," said Emerald.

She then faced us, and said, "Do you question the will of the mistresses?"

"No, Mistress," we said.

"Good," said Tuza. She turned back to Hiza and Emerald, and gestured to the side of the camp, contemptuously, where Darla lay, unconscious and chained. "Fetch the garbage," said Tuza. "Both of you! Now!"

"She is not dead?" asked Hiza.

"No," said Tuza. "Be quick!"

Hiza and Emerald went to the side of the clearing where Darla lay. It was now morning, and fully light. It was easy to see why Hiza had been uncertain as to whether Darla was alive or not. The body was inert, and there was a considerable amount of blood about the head. The blanket, too, was dark with blood. Hiza and Emerald, half lifting, half dragging, brought the inert body of Darla to the center of the camp, and put it where Tuza indicated, at her feet. I saw a tiny movement of Darla's hands, clasped behind her back in the steel of slave bracelets, the slight opening and closing of fingers. A small sound escaped her, as though she might be stirring in her sleep.

"See," said Tuza, "she is alive. I planned it so. I want you to see her as she is, and should be. And I want her to understand what she is, and should be."

"She may die," said Hiza.

"No," said Tuza. "More is planned for her."

"Should we not wash the blood from her head and body?" asked Emerald.

"That is work for slaves," said Tuza.

"But she is free," said Hiza.

"Let her be washed by slaves, as a slave," said Tuza. "Yes, yes! Excellent! Unbind our tunic girls; have them wash the chained she-tarsk, that she be less offensive to our eyes. Then set our little beasts about their tasks, let them sweep and clean the camp, let them tidy things, let used boughs be cast aside, let them fetch water and wood, and berries, let them serve us, let us have a fine breakfast. I want our former leader to see that even tunic sluts are freer than she!"

"The rope?" inquired Emerald.

"Remove it from Tula, but put her in rope shackles," said Tuza. "She is an excellent cook. Let the other two address themselves to less demanding tasks."

"But on the rope?" said Emerald.

"Certainly," said Tuza, "for one would not wish them to stray, to be eaten by panthers."

"We shall have a splendid time," said Tuza, "before we begin the trek."

"What will be done with Darla?" inquired Hiza.

"You will see," said Tuza. "Quickly now, unbind the sluts, that they may be put to work!"

Chapter Thirty-Six

"How many are there?" I had asked.

"Not many," said Axel. "I would guess six or seven altogether."

"At least one is a slave," I said.

"Most likely more," said Axel. "Panther Women, who tend to be large and fierce for women, often hold smaller, weaker women as slaves."

"Feminine women?" I said.

"Yes," he said, "they despise feminine women, and enjoy holding them as slaves."

"How many would be armed then?" I asked.

"Four or five," he said.

"I trust we would make a determination on this matter before doing anything precipitate," I said.

"Certainly," he said. "While you seize one Panther Girl, binding her helplessly, another might drive her javelin into the back of your neck."

"It seems they touch weapons," I said.

"Certainly," he said, "until they are collared, and then it might mean their death to touch one, even inadvertently."

"Are there men with them?" I asked.

"It seems unlikely," he said, "for Panther Girls seldom league themselves with men, for before men their bravado fades, its fraudulence becomes transparent. They no longer find themselves dominant, but find themselves before the truly dominant, and then must fight their blood, as other women who long for the raptures of submission, the fulfillments of being owned and mastered."

"Still," I said, "might there not be men in the party, if only temporarily?"

"I think not," he said, "the size and depth of the prints do not suggest that."

"Some of the prints are those of small, bared feet," I said.

"Three are with bared feet," he said, "and they are probably slaves. Still, one cannot be sure. Sometimes Panther Girls trod the forest barefoot. Too, a ruse might be in play, to suggest fewer Panther Girls than are actually with the party."

"But no men," I said.

"I think not," he said, "but we shall soon know."

"How soon?" I asked.

"Quite soon," he said.

It was late in the afternoon. There were many shadows. It was hard to see the tracks. It would soon be night.

Axel held Tiomines back. "No, fellow," he said.

"You pause," I said.

"We will camp here," said Axel. "It is growing dark. The forest is dangerous."

"Panthers might lurk," I said.

"And knives, and javelins," he said.

"I see," I said.

"It would be most unwise to come upon our friends inadvertently, suddenly," he said.

"You seem to think they are quite close," I said.

"Yes," he said, "can you not smell it?"

"What?" I said.

"A campfire," he said.

Chapter Thirty-Seven

Mila and I, with dampened cloths were wiping the blood from the head, face, neck, and left shoulder of Darla.

She opened her eyes, suddenly, wildly, and jerked at her cuffed hands, held behind her, the two, narrow, snug, circular restraints attached to her waist chain. Mila and I, alarmed, leaped back. Darla struggled to her feet, crying out with rage, as a storm might rise. "What is the meaning of this?" she demanded, jerking at the restraints.

"Behold!" called Tuza, from across the site. "The mighty Darla wakes!"

"Remove these chains!" cried Darla.

"Or is it," said Tuza, approaching, "merely an escaped slave, wandered in from the forest?"

"Release me!" demanded Darla. She struggled wildly in the bracelets, linked to the snug waist chain. Did she not know her efforts were useless? Had she not, often enough, put captured free women, or free women hoping to join her band, in just such impediments, before delivering them naked to buyers? "Where are my garments!" she cried. "Give them to me! I demand to be released! I demand my clothing! Remove these constraints! Give me my weapons! Where are my ornaments?"

"Some are here," said Tuza, lifting her left arm, with its armlets and several bracelets, while, with her right hand, she lifted and fingered, exhibiting them, the strings of claws which she had looped about her throat.

Darla took an angry stride toward Tuza but, beside herself with rage, had either failed to notice, or had forgotten, the shackles which bound her ankles, and she fell into the dirt, before Tuza.

"Get up," said Tuza.

Darla struggled to her feet, and stood facing Tuza, shaking with fury.

"I wonder if men would like her," said Tuza, regarding her former leader.

"She-tarsk!" cried Darla.

"She is still filthy," said Tuza. "Mila, Vulo, clean her. I find her appearance offensive."

"Slaves!" cried. Darla. "How dare you touch me?"

Mila and I stepped back.

"Clean her," said Tuza. "As you might a shackled slave, waiting to be put upon the block."

Carefully, frightened, with our cloths, dampened in the Alexandra, we wiped away the blood and dirt which adhered to the body of the former leader. We were much afraid to do this, for she was free, and did not wish it. We trusted she would understand that we did not do this of our will, but as slaves. It is common for a slave, in her training, to be taught the bathing of masters, the sponging, the oils, the strigil, the rinsings, the towelings, and such. To be sure, we are also instructed in various ways we may please the master while bathing him, and in the manner of the slave. On the other hand, as I understand it, the matter is commonly quite different with free women. Certainly Darla did not wish to sustain our ministrations. Contact with a slave may be regarded as sullying by a free woman. She is, after all, free. In the case of the bath of a free woman, as I understand it, the slave commonly does little more than prepare the bath, test the temperature, for this may vary from mistress to mistress, place the oils, and such, scent the water, ready the towelings, lay out the after-bath gowns, and such. To be sure, she may assist her in and out of the bath, as well. Whereas I suppose a woman might have a personal serving slave of whom she is fond, being a woman's serving slave is commonly regarded as the most dreaded of bondages. Most free women despise, and hate, female slaves, and own, and treat them, accordingly. Often they will not allow them to so much as cast a glance on a male. A good female serving slave, of course, particularly one of taste and discretion, may be invaluable to a free woman. There are some free women of the upper castes, wealthy women, who from childhood have never dressed themselves, who do not even know the intricate clasps and closures of the robes of concealment they wear, let alone their blendings and drapings, the best colors for the time of day and the season, the arrangements ideally in order for receivings, visitings, promenades, attendance at the readings, the theater, the song drama, and so on. In any event, few of us are trained as women's slaves. Perhaps there are other schools, or courses, in this sort of thing. I have heard that free women, if they have a serving slave, or slaves, often purchase pretty ones, ones of a sort they particularly hate, in this way denying such a slave a master, which gratifies the free woman, and denying a master the slave, which, I suppose, gratifies her as well. It is also rumored that some free women purchase beautiful slaves in order to attract men to themselves, the fellow hoping to see more of the slave. But woe to the slave should she so much as dare to meet the eyes of the visitor. It is then, afterwards, the lash for her. The female serving slave, too, is apparently useful in the affairs of her mistress, carrying messages, arranging meetings, standing watch, and so on. Given the common loathing of the free woman for the slave, Darla's reluctance to be washed, and publicly, by two slaves, was understandable. Clearly it was intended by Tuza as an insult. Similarly, a captured free woman may be profoundly insulted by her captor, if he has her stripped and exhibited in his presence by female slaves, while he ponders her value. Is she to be kept for a time, or sold? Is she a pot girl, or a kettle-and-mat girl, or does she have the makings, suitably trained, of a pleasure slave? Perhaps, if nothing better, she might be used for sleen feed. In any event, I knew nothing of being a woman's slave. I had been trained for men.

"Get away from me!" screamed Darla, and Mila and I, disconcerted, drew back.

"Continue," said Tuza, and we resumed our ministrations, however reluctantly. Darla held her head up, angrily, proudly, and stared out, toward the Alexandra.

"Good," said Tuza. "Much better. Now brush and comb her hair."

Hiza located a brush and comb, and I brushed Darla's hair, and Mila combed it.

"Good," said Tuza, "you are almost as presentable as a naked slave."

"Free my hands, free my ankles," cried Darla, "and give me a dagger, a javelin!"

"I like you as you are," said Tuza.

"Let us do contest," cried Darla, "in the manner of the Panther Women!"

"I would not soil my javelin on you," said Tuza, "pretty Darla."

"'Pretty'!" screamed Darla.

"Now that I look upon you, better groomed," said Tuza, "I think men might find you of some interest."

"She-sleen!" cried Darla.

"If you had a collar on your neck," she said.

"She-tarsk!" cried Darla, pulling at the bracelets, with a rattle of metal.

"Look," said Tuza, "she is crying!"

"No, no, I am not!" wept Darla.

I was startled to see this, but tears ran down the cheeks of Darla. Could it be, I wondered, that she was a female, truly a female?

Tuza drew forth her dagger, and put its point to the bosom of Darla. The former leader drew back a little.

"You are afraid," said Tuza.

"No," said Darla.

But I saw she was afraid. She trembled. She turned white. Tears were in her eyes.

She looked then much less like a Panther Woman, than a woman. Darla, I conjectured, in this unexpected, and unusual situation, was suddenly coming to grips with her sex, its slightness, its softness, its helplessness, its weakness, its sensitivity, its limitations, its jeopardy, its fearful and glorious flood of rich and profound emotions, emotions over which she, to her consternation, found she could exercise not the least control, in whose grasp she found herself the lifted and transported prisoner of parts of herself a thousand times stronger than her conscious will, and its depth, its vulnerability, its dependence. Did this situation, chained before Tuza, I wondered, give her some sense of what it might be to be a woman before a man, or, say, a slave before a master?

I feared Tuza would ram the blade into the former leader, to the hilt.

"Do not kill her!" begged Hiza.

"Stand straighter," said Tuza. "Get your back straight, your belly in, your shoulders back, your head up!"

Tears in her eyes, Darla obeyed.

"Excellent," said Tuza, "you are standing almost as well as a slave."

"Please!" said Darla.

"Do you wonder what has become of you, what has been done to you?" asked Tuza. "You are now exhibited as what you are, and should be, a naked, worthless slut, no more than a chained slave!"

"I am free! Free!" cried Darla.

"I thought free women were clothed," said Tuza.

"Please, Tuza!" wept Darla.

"Do not dare to speak my name!" said Tuza.

"Do not kill her!" cried Hiza.

Tuza stepped back, and indicated Darla with the point of her knife. "There is the one you feared," she said to Hiza and Emerald. "The mighty leader! See her helpless, see her without her talmit, without her skins, her weapons, her ornaments. Is she so mighty now! See her as she is, stripped, chained, and shackled, frightened, in tears, only a woman!"

Then Tuza turned back to Darla. "Get on your knees," she said, "where you belong."

Darla knelt, and looked up at Tuza. "What are you going to do with me?" she asked. "What is to be my fate?"

"You will learn later," said Tuza. "First we will have breakfast. Busy yourself, Tula. Mila, Vulo, lay out the mats, the plates, the goblets and utensils, and then kneel, prepared to serve your mistresses. Hiza, fetch the talmit once unworthily worn by our pretty prisoner, and tie her ankles together."

"Please," said Darla.

"Will it be necessary to gag you?" asked Tuza.

"No," said Darla.

"You might look well in a gag," said Tuza, "pretty one."

"It will not be necessary to gag me," said Darla.

"You have gagged enough slaves," said Tuza. "Why should you not be gagged, and as a slave?"

"I will be silent," said Darla.

The breakfast was prolonged, doubtless by intent. It was served by Tula, returned to the rope, Mila, and myself. We were even, following the meal of the mistresses, allowed to feed ourselves with our own hands.

"Eat well, kajirae," said Tuza. "We have a long trek to the coast before us." I recalled we were to be sold on the coast. Darla knelt to the side, unable to rise, her ankles tied together. She had not been fed.

After breakfast, we cleared the mats, extinguished the fire, washed the gear of cooking and feeding in the Alexandra, and tidied the camp. Our bundles had been arranged and put to order by Hiza and Emerald.

We were standing by our burdens, I think about the eighth Ahn, awaiting the command to bear them, when Tuza drew out her knife, went to Darla, seized her by the hair, bent her head back, and put the blade of the knife to her throat.

"What is to be done with you?" asked Tuza.

"Sell me," whispered Darla.

Hiza and Emerald gasped.

"Do my ears deceive me?" laughed Tuza.

"Sell me," she said. "The sham is done. The charade is complete. The pretense is over. I am a woman, and a slave."

Tuza sheathed her dagger, slapped her thigh, and turned, laughing, to Hiza and Emerald. "Hear that," she laughed, "hear that!" But neither Hiza nor Emerald was laughing. Tula, Mila, and I stood near our burdens, frightened, mere women, feminine women, so unlike the mighty Panther Women, so unlike that we could be to them as naught but despised slaves, women of the sort which men immediately think of in terms of a brand and tunic, women of the sort which men think little of enslaving, and seek for their chains, their cords, their ropes, and straps, their collars. We dared not meet the eyes of the mistresses. I had thought that Darla, who was large and strong, was the fiercest, the mightiest, the most formidable of women, the bold and daring leader of a dangerous band of Panther Women, women to look up to, women before whom other women might kneel in fear, women not unlike the masters themselves, women not unlike men, but here was mighty Darla, naked, on her knees, chained and shackled, her ankles bound together with her own talmit, begging to be sold. Darla, I then realized, was a woman, and perhaps not so different from other women. Who knew what her thoughts had been, and her dreams? Perhaps she did have something in her of the woman, the blood, the instincts, the hopes, the needs, the fears, the desires, the longings, of the woman, the secret understanding, however hysterically denied, of her true place in nature, out of which she could not be herself. It was as though some image, some proud, contrived, clay encasement of a reality had finally broken apart, separating, revealing, hitherto hidden within, something quite unlike the image, or encasement, something not hard but soft, not artificial but real, not false but true, and needful. Yes, I thought, she was a woman, a true woman, but, as yet, was incomplete, for she had no master. How I remembered much of this from my former world, when I had lain in my bed for hours at a time, restless and miserable, knowing myself a slave, but a slave without a master. So, I thought, the sorry wallet has been opened, and it contains a coin of gold; the dingy wrapper has been unrolled, and within it we find rare silk; the uninspiring amphora has been unsealed, and within it we find a splendid wine, the sort men might prize, and for which they might bid, and heatedly. Yes, I thought, regarding Darla, a collar might look well on her neck. Yes, I thought, it belongs there.

Tuza then was no longer laughing but, furious, she freed her switch from her belt, rushed upon Darla, and switched her, again and again. Though we were not struck, Tula, Mila, and myself cringed, reacting to each stroke, for we had felt the switch of Tuza, and well knew its air-parting hiss, its crack, and sting.

"Please stop, please stop, Mistress!" cried Darla. I supposed it was the first time she had ever been switched.

"Do not call me 'Mistress'!" screamed Tuza, and gave her another stroke. "You are free, free!" she screamed, striking her twice more.

"Sell me," begged Darla.

"No," said Tuza.

"We sold Donna!" said Darla. "You helped me defeat her. You became second! We sold her together!"

"I have something else in mind for you," said Tuza. "Do you think I would permit you the ignominy, the degradation, the raptures, of the kajira?"

Darla, laying on her side, miserable, her body well inscribed with the bright records of Tuza's displeasure, looked up at her, confused, and frightened.

"Put her on her knees, that she may hear her fate," said Tuza.

Hiza and Emerald positioned Darla before Tuza.

"Prepare to hear your sentence," said Tuza.

Darla looked up at her.

"You have been defeated," said Tuza.

"Treachery," said Darla.

"No more than when we leapt upon Donna in her sleep, and bound her," said Tuza.

"I am not to be sold?" said Darla.

"No," said Tuza.

"What then?" asked Darla, trembling.

"I am now ready to pronounce your sentence," said Tuza.

"I am free," said Darla. "Let me speak."

"Speak," said Tuza.

"It was I," said Darla, "who in disguise at a trading point on the Laurius became first apprised of solicitations by the employer, seeking informants and scouts, to investigate rumors of a great ship being built near the headwaters of the Alexandra. He found few who would essay this task, for a great raiding party had recently been decimated in the northern forests. Many sent had failed to return, and those who had returned had nothing of substance to report. Ships sent to the mouth of the Alexandra had discovered nothing, and some apparently had fallen to pirates. It took me little time to discover that the employer had considerable, if finite, resources at his disposal. Indeed, he had, in the absence of other intelligence, organized a small army, recruited from a dozen cities, to close the mouth of the Alexandra, to prevent the exiting of this ship, should it exist. But even for his resources, this would be an expense which might ruin cities, and leagues of cities. He was thus in desperate need of intelligence. He must discover if the ship existed, and, if so, ascertain its location. Once this was done a stout raiding party might attack and destroy the ship, and withdraw with little, if any, loss. The mouth of the Alexandra then need not be closed, and its numerous guardians, in effect an army, might be paid and dismissed. Men talk much in their cups and I, posing as a free brothel mistress, shopping for brothel slaves, in various taverns, learned these things. It was then only necessary to contact the employer, and convince him that we might serve his purpose. Who would suspect a handful of Panther Women? Indeed, who might even know they were about? We know the forests, and their ways. We can move as quietly as the night. We can live off the land, like the beasts. We can hunt like the panther, and strike like the ost. We could well succeed where men, unfamiliar with the woods and woodcraft, would be likely to fail. Too, Panther Women do not range that far north, and it is late autumn. We would not be anticipated. Few would think of us, at all, if they did, certainly not that late in the season. Would we not be ideal for his purposes? So I must contact the employer and did so, with a hurled, note-bearing knife, cast from the darkness, which lodged itself in the center pole of his tent, not two horts from his head. By means of this device I conveyed our proposal and specified, as well, a secret meeting place, should he be interested. He was. And your wallets bulge with gold, a pittance compared to what we will receive upon our return and our imparting of our information. And it was I who brought you through the forest, for many days, far from our range, to spy upon the mysteries of the Alexandra. We have done our work well. We located the ship, and we have determined it might soon depart its wharf. Accordingly we must hurry to the Laurius, make our report, and gather in our riches. I have done much. I have led you well. Much skill and risk were involved in this. Free me and return to me the talmit of command."

Tuza looked at Darla, thoughtfully. Then she said, "Relieve her ankles of the knotted talmit, with which we have bound them together."

Hiza untied the talmit from Darla's ankles, and handed it to Tuza.

"These chains and shackles, as well!" said Darla. She moved

her knees. She pulled at her wrists, behind her back, held in the cuffs, attached to the waist chain. How well secured she was, I thought. How helpless we are in such things!

Tuza spread the talmit out.

Darla made as though to rise.

"Stay on your knees," said Tuza, and she then wrapped the talmit about her own brow.

"I do not understand," said Darla.

"When a Panther Woman has been found displeasing to her leader," she said, "it is our way that she be punished, and you have not been found pleasing to your leader."

"Sell me," begged Darla.

"Prepare to hear your sentence," said Tuza.

"Sell me," begged Darla, "to anyone, even a woman, if you so hate me."

"You will be driven from the camp," said Tuza. "Get her on her feet."

Hiza and Emerald lifted Darla to her feet.

"Relieve me of my chains, my shackles!" cried Darla.

"Get out," said Tuza, lifting her switch.

"Free me!" wept Darla. "Give me a weapon, if only a knife!"

"Away, slut," snarled Tuza, lifting the switch.

"I am helpless," said Darla. "I am naked. I cannot use my hands. I am shackled. I can barely move. The beasts will have me."

Tuza turned back to face Hiza and Emerald. "So it is," she said, "that the talmit may pass from one to another in the band. It is not uncommon. Surely such things are familiar. Do not concern yourselves. It is our way. Let the strongest and wisest, the fiercest, the most clever, rule. She is not needed. She could not be trusted. She betrayed, and sold Donna. We can find our way back. There will be more gold for all of us. Gather your weapons. We are breaking camp."

"Have mercy!" begged Darla.

"Must you be switched from the camp?" inquired Tuza.

Darla backed away, in misery, but she stopped, at the edge of the camp.

"Bundles up," said Hiza, and Tula, Mila, and myself, on our rope, bent down, and lifted our bundles to our head, steadying them with our hands.

Darla fell to her knees. "Do not leave me here," she begged. "Take me with you! Have mercy! You are now the mighty, indisputable, and noble leader. I acknowledge it. Take me with you, if only as bearer of burdens! Keep me if you wish. Sell me if you wish! Take me with you! I beg mercy!"

"Who begs mercy?" said Tuza.

"I beg mercy!"

"Who?" inquired Tuza.

"Darla begs mercy!" she wept.

"Darla," said Tuza, "the properly deposed, worthless, meaningless slut?"

"Yes," said Darla, "Darla, the properly deposed, worthless, meaningless slut begs mercy!"

"If you attempt to follow us," said Tuza, "your throat will be cut."

Darla then collapsed, weeping, at the edge of the camp. She lay in the dirt, sobbing.

"Prepare to trek," said Tuza, lifting her hand.

We steadied our bundles. When she lowered her hand, and indicated the trail ahead, we would move. The first step is taken with the left foot.

"Seize them!" I heard. A woman's voice.

We looked about, startled, wildly, to our right. A woman had emerged from the forest, pointing toward us. She was a sturdy woman, but one clearly worthy of a slave block. Her hair was black, and undone. She was barefoot. She wore a brief tunic, of bright scarlet. In the forest that would be easily marked. She was collared. There seemed much motion behind her, rapidly moving shadows amongst the trees. I saw the gleam of a weapon.

"Seize them!" she cried again, standing, pointing to our group.

"Donna!" cried Tuza.

Chapter Thirty-Eight

"Do not move," said the fellow. "Hold the beast!"

Axel tightened his grip on the leash of Tiomines. "Steady," he said to the sleen.

We were ringed with spears.

Our attention, I fear, had been on our own business, pursuing a small group, some four or five, of Panther Girls. These were suspected of spying on Shipcamp, doubtless to report to some larger body.

The newcomers had moved with stealth, and were suddenly, too suddenly, upon us.

"Be silent!" warned the fellow who seemed to be their leader, his hand warningly before his mouth.

I doubted that we, back in the forest, were now more than some two hundred paces from our quarry. Axel, clearly, was primarily concerned to establish its existence, numbers, and direction, following which he would consider his possible course of action, either to attempt to deal with it, saving at least one prisoner who might be later interrogated at Shipcamp, or, if it seemed prudential, to withdraw and, by means of the whistle of summoning, draw on additional forces, those come from the ships, who were, as far as we knew, ignorant of the location of, even of the existence of, Shipcamp. If these additional forces were beyond the reach of the whistle, so far that not even their larl might take note of the signal, I was to return to Shipcamp, and bring men, following the river west. He, with Tiomines, would retain contact with the quarry. It had apparently been the speculation of Axel, or, more likely, that of Tyrtaios, that

Panther Girls, if they were in the vicinity, might note the fled slave, and, naturally, would not be averse to acquiring her. Such obviously have value. They may be sold. In this way, following the scent of the fled slave, it was possible that one might locate the Panther Girls. Indeed, the slave, if encountering Panther Girls, might even have been foolish enough to call herself to their attention, perhaps hoping to elicit aid, perhaps hoping, even, to be enlisted as a member of their band, and not simply taken in hand as she would be, as the slave she was. To be sure, there had apparently been some sort of contact between Asperiche and Axel. I must remember to beat her. Whereas Axel had all this clearly in mind and had explained it to me, my own interest here was not identical with his. It was not that I had the least interest in a fugitive slave, who might have been any slave, for are they not all the same, but rather that I had thought it would be a pleasant outing, an amusement, a bit of sport, to pursue the little beast, to let it run awhile, and then catch it, rope it, and return it to her masters, the Pani. Certainly I had no intention of being a courier to Shipcamp. To be sure, the entire matter was moot at the moment.

"If you release the sleen," said the fellow, "it will be killed."

"Steady, Tiomines," said Axel, softly. The beast, in its single-mindedness, seemed to regard the newcomers as no more than a distraction. It was ready to resume the hunt.

I knew enough of sleen to know that any well-trained animal, which I took Tiomines to be, could be set upon anyone but its master, or Use Master, with as little as a word, or gesture, whatever the "kill" command might be, usually a word, as a word need only be heard and a gesture must be seen. Whereas Tiomines could doubtless, in one savage rush, reach the leader and tear off an arm or head, it would be his last attack. He would be transfixed by more than one spear before he could feed. Axel did not wish to lose the sleen. Too, I would not have given much for our chances either, had he been foolish enough to set Tiomines on the newcomer.

There were, as I counted, eleven of the newcomers. It is well to know exact numbers in such matters. Their leader was a large, spare man, clad in the wool of the bounding hurt, stained brown and black. He was bearded, wore a dagger and sword, and carried a spear, a hunting spear. His men were similarly clad. Two carried crossbows, quarrels resting in the guide. Three others carried nets.

"How is hunting?" inquired Axel, pleasantly enough. The party, indeed, seemed to be a hunting party. On the other hand I saw no tabuk, dangling from poles, nor skins slung over the shoulders of any of the fellows.

I wondered how long they had been out.

I would not have expected to encounter hunters in this vicinity, unless they were from Shipcamp.

These did not seem to be from Shipcamp.

Indeed, we were far from Shipcamp.

"What are you doing here?" asked the newcomer.

"Hunting," said Axel.

"And what have you taken?" inquired the newcomer.

"Nothing, as yet," said Axel.

"Perhaps," said the fellow, "it is you who have been taken."

"Our friend here," said Axel, roughly shaking the fur at the base of the neck of Tiomines, "could kill at least one of you."

"Perhaps, more," said the newcomer. "But it would be a shame for such a fine animal to die."

"I would suggest," said Axel, affably, "that you do not interfere with our hunt."

"Nor will you with ours, I trust," said the fellow.

"One supposes not," said Axel. "I wish you well."

"Tarry a bit," said the newcomer.

"You have the spears," said Axel.

"Aeson comes," said one of the fellows.

Arrivals were approaching from the direction of the river, which was south of our position. I suspected the several newcomers, of which the approaching fellows were doubtless a part, had originally crossed the river to the east. None of them had the caps common with mariners, so I supposed they must have come from the south, and then crossed the river, perhaps having come from as far away as the basin of the Laurius.

I counted four more of the newcomers, also armed with spears. That would make fifteen.

On a leash, held by one of the men was a tall, striking, dark-haired woman, her neck encircled with a typical band, clad in a brief, brightly scarlet slave tunic, slit at the sides. Two tarsks, I thought, of good Brundisium silver.

The fellow who held the leash approached, and stood near the leader. The slave then knelt at the leader's side, her head down.

"Head up," snapped the leader.

Instantly she raised her head.

"What do you think," asked the leader.

"Not bad," said Axel. That seemed a tepid appraisement. I wondered if he had his mind on Asperiche.

The leader looked at me, questioningly. Clearly he was pleased with the slave, and wished to show her off.

"Excellent," I said.

"What is on your neck, Donna," asked the leader.

"A slave collar, Master," she said.

"And what does that mean?" he asked.

"That I am a slave, Master," she said.

"What is on your left thigh, Donna?" he asked.

"A slave brand, Master," she said.

"And what does that mean?" he asked.

"That I am a slave, Master," she said.

"And what is the nature of your garment?" he asked.

"It is the garment of a slave," she said.

"And why are you clad in such a garment?" he asked.

"It is appropriate that I be placed in such a garment," she said, "as I am a slave."

"This," said the leader, indicating the slave, "was once a Panther Girl."

"She does not look like a Panther Girl," said Axel.

"She has been trimmed, exercised, dieted, and such," said the leader, "brought to prime selling condition."

"Please do not sell me, Master," she whispered.

I gathered she had a standing permission to speak, as she had not been cuffed. This is not uncommon, that a slave might have a standing permission to speak. To be sure, such a permission is easily revoked, and then the slave will be expected to ask permission before speaking.

"She is too soft, too feminine, too attractive, too desirable, too beautiful to be a Panther Girl," said Axel.

"They learn the collar," he said.

"Of course," said Axel.

"They want it," said the leader.

"True," said Axel.

"We have here," said the leader, indicating the slave and Tiomines, "two beautiful animals."

"The sleen is on a scent," said Axel. "He is restless."

"You can cancel the hunt," said the leader.

"It would not be wise without meat," said Axel.

"Would you be interested in a trade?" asked the leader.

"Please, no, Master!" whispered the slave, who dared not raise her voice.

I was surprised at the remark of the leader, as a sleen, a trained sleen, is commonly worth several slaves, just as a tarn is commonly worth several more. To be sure the slave was unusually beautiful. She now, head down, trembled at her master's thigh. I thought of another world, one on which beauty was seldom for sale, except on its own terms. I wondered if there was all that much difference, between a woman selling herself for her own profit, or being sold by another, for another's profit. In both cases she was sold. In the first case, she was her own merchant. In the second case, the merchant was another. Perhaps it was a prejudice of my caste, but it seemed to me that in the second case the transaction was less hypocritical, less deceitful, more open, and honest. So let her be openly put up, and openly bid upon. Surely the leader of the strangers could not be serious, if he were suggesting a straight exchange, a single, kneeling, scarlet-clad beauty for a trained sleen. On Gor beauty is cheap. It is well within the means of most.

"The sleen is on a hunt," said Axel.

"Perhaps he is hungry," said the leader.

"He may eat later," said Axel. "I wish you well."

"Remain where you are," said the leader. He then pointed to the sleen, and gestured to one of his men, a gesture of which Axel and I took uneasy note, and then turned to the fellow, Aeson, who had come from the direction of the river.

"She has located them for us," said Aeson. "They are only yards from the river. An altercation of sorts has apparently taken place in their camp. There are only three Panther Girls.

Other than this there are only a single, shackled prisoner, a stripped female, and three kajirae, tunicked, coffled in rope.

"Who, Donna, is the prisoner?" asked the leader of his slave.

"I do not know, Master," she said. "Please do not rid yourself of me, Master."

"I thought," said he, "you said there would be two kajirae with the band."

"They must have acquired another," she said.

I did not react to this remark, but had little doubt as to the likely identity of the unexpected kajira in the coffle.

"Here, friend," said one of the leader's men, returned to the group, and cast a large slab of meat, it looked like bosk meat, before Tiomines.

"No!" said Axel.

But Tiomines had snapped it up, and gorged it down. In feeding, there is little difference between a domestic and a wild sleen.

Spears pressed against Axel's tensed body.

"Surely you do not wish your beast to go hungry," said the leader.

Whatever marked stick we might have had to cast in this game, I feared, was no longer within our grasp.

Tiomines looked up at Axel, expectantly, ready to resume the hunt.

"Your beast is not in danger," said the leader.

"You are hunters," I said, "but it does not seem that you are after tabuk, tarsk, bosk, or panther."

"Perhaps not," said the leader.

"What then?" I asked.

"Perhaps women," he said.

"I know something of such matters," I said. "One hunts women where there are women, where game is plentiful, in cities, towns, even peasant villages, on traversed roads, on caravan routes, on pilgrimages to the Sardar, and such, not in the wilderness of the northern forests, not on the scattered, rocky skerries of Torvaldsland, not in the frozen expanses of Ax Glacier, not in the scalding wastes of the Tahari, far from caravan routes and oases."

The leader smiled.

"Perhaps you search for a Ubar's daughter, one fugitive, perhaps from Ar herself?" I asked.

"No," he said.

"I find it hard to believe that you have come this far, surely at the cost of time and coin, for a handful of Panther Girls who, as they are Panther Girls, are likely to be less appealing than your average she-tarsk."

The kneeling slave stiffened.

"What of Donna?" he asked.

"She is beautiful," I admitted.

The slave subsided.

"You change them," he said. "You put them in a collar, and they learn they are women." He then looked down at the scarlet-tunicked slave. "Are you a woman?" he asked.

"Certainly, Master," she said, puzzled.

"Do you like being a woman?" he asked.

"At one time I dreaded it, and hated it, and loathed it, and did my best not to be a woman, but a sort of man, one who hated men, and pretended not to want to be a man, but yet wanted to be a man, but then in my deepest heart I knew I was a woman, and wanted to be a woman."

"And now?" he asked.

"Now," she said, "I am a woman, and want to be a woman, and am fulfilled as a woman, and rejoice in being a woman. I would not want it otherwise, even if it could be so. If it were not so, I could not be what I am, and should be, in the order of nature, the slave of a master."

"It seems," said he, "you are helpless in the grasp of your hereditary coils."

"I have been given to myself," she said.

"But it is I who own you," he said.

"It is in being owned," she said, "that I am given to myself. It is in being owned that I am myself."

Many chains bind a slave, of course, and not all are of iron.

"Surely you know, Master," she said, "that we are your slaves, and want your collars."

"Be silent," he said, "and put your head down."

"Yes, Master," she said.

I noted that Tiomines had now gone to his belly, and put

his snout on his forepaws. This, too, was doubtless noted by Axel.

"But the others," I said, "surely they are not like this one."

"What of that, Aeson?" inquired the leader.

"There are three," he said.

"Pot girls?" asked the leader.

Aeson shrugged, noncommittally.

After all, one man's pot girl may be another man's pleasure slave.

"The prisoner?" he asked.

"She looks well, shackled," said Aeson.

"What of the slaves?" asked the leader.

"They are all acceptable as kajirae," said Aeson, licking his lips.

"Excellent," said the leader.

"May I speak, Master?" asked the slave.

"Yes," he said.

"Two will sell well," she said. "The prettiest is a blonde, Emerald. A brunette, Hiza, would look well on the block, but her hair is too short."

"It will grow out," said the leader.

A slave's hair, like every particle of her body, belongs to the master. Most masters prefer hair "slave long" on their properties. Much may be done with it in the furs. It may also figure in their discipline, as in being tied to a ring, and such. As slaves are commonly vain of their beauty, as other women, even extraordinarily so, a grievous discipline, which most girls will attempt to evade at almost any cost, is shaving their head. Their hair, of course, is not discarded. The wigs of many free women are often from the hair of slaves, though it is certified as having had a free origin. Too, woman's hair is excellent for catapult cordage, as it retains its strength and tensility indefinitely, and that under a variety of weather conditions and temperatures.

"There should be two others," said the slave, "Darla and Tuza. Let them be pot girls."

"It is they who deposed you," said the leader.

"Pot girls," she said.

"That is for men to decide," said the leader.

"Yes, Master," she said. "The two slaves would be Tula and Mila."

"There is a third," said Aeson.

"I do not know her," said Donna.

I was reasonably sure I knew her, particularly as Tiomines had brought us to this point.

"Is the sleen dead?" asked Axel.

Tiomines now lay at his feet.

"Look closely," said the leader. "You can see him breathe."

"The meat was drugged," said Axel.

"We have work to do," said the leader. "We cannot have him rushing amongst the prey, nor either of you, as well."

"We are also interested in this group," I said. "Let us join forces."

"That would be an excellent idea," said the leader, "if we needed you. But we do not need you."

"I am sure," I said, "you did not venture this far north merely to snare three or four Panther Girls, perhaps poor ones, for the slave block."

"Perhaps not," he said.

"The prey," said Aeson, "seems overconfident. We noted no guards, or scouts."

"Good," said the leader, "it was then not necessary to subdue, or kill, them. There is always some risk in that, particularly in daylight hours."

"It is my impression." said Aeson, "that they will soon be breaking camp."

"Good," said the leader.

Doubtless this intelligence was welcomed, particularly given the absence of guards or scouts in the area. Let them then be busy, thonging their sandals, checking their weapons, packing their gear, covering their fire, lading their slaves, and such. They would then be less likely to anticipate visitors.

"We are ready, are we not?" asked the leader.

"Yes," said Aeson.

"You understand," said the leader, turning to Axel and myself, "that we will not brook interference."

"We will remain here, quietly," said Axel.

"I am sure of it," said the leader. "Bind them."

Our wrists and ankles were then well-corded.

The leader then looked to the men about. They nodded. Two raised their spears, a common signal of readiness before an engagement. The three with nets lifted them, shook them a bit, and spread them a little. Nets are often used in Gorean hunting. Smaller nets can be cast; larger nets may be spread between poles or trees, to intercept driven game.

"You have done well, Donna," said the leader to his slave.

"A slave is pleased, if her master is pleased," she said.

"This is a day to which you have looked forward," he said.

"Yes, Master," she said.

"She tracked them like a sleen," said Aeson.

"A she-sleen," said a fellow.

"Quite so, Genak," said Aeson, regarding the slave.

It was surely true, whatever might once have been the case, that the slave was now incontrovertibly, and manifestly, female, indeed, helplessly and desirably so. It was hard to believe she had once been a Panther Girl. But are not all women pretty much of a muchness when stripped on a sales block? Is there that much difference, then, between a Ubar's daughter and a barbarian recently brought from the sordid towers of an abused world, one recently removed from her slave capsule and branded?

"Today, lovely, tunicked Donna," said the leader, "you will sip from the cup of vengeance."

"Perhaps, Master," she said.

"A wine sweeter than ka-la-na," he said.

"I do not think it will be bitter," she said.

"You were betrayed," he said.

"Yes, Master."

"And sold."

"Yes, Master."

"Doubtless you will be pleased to see them bound naked to selling poles on the coast," he said.

"Why do you think they have been careless, why have they posted no scouts or guards?" she asked.

"They are stupid," he said.

"I do not think they are stupid," she said.

"They are thoughtless," he said.

"In the sea," she said, "perhaps there are currents, stirrings, and movements of which there is little evidence on the surface. Behind mountains there may be mountains. Who knows about the depths of the sea, the farther mountains?"

"A trap?" asked the leader, warily.

"Perhaps," she said, "but for whom?"

"No animal lays a trap for itself," said the leader.

"Many do," she said.

"What animal would do that?" he asked, scornfully.

"One who wishes to be caught," she said.

"Absurd," he said.

"Yes," she said, "it is absurd."

"Let us make haste," said Aeson.

"Bind her, hand and foot," said the leader, indicating the lovely, scarlet-clad slave, to one of his men.

"Rather, Master," begged the slave, "let me accompany the masters."

"You wish to see the acquisition?"

"Yes, Master."

"I do not want Genak encumbered with a leashed slave," he said.

"Let me go, unleashed," she said, "that I may lead the masters directly to the prey. Let me announce the acquisition."

"You would like to do that, would you not?" he asked.

"Yes, Master," she said.

"Then it would be yours," he said.

"Yes," she said, "in a way."

"You are a pleasant piece of slave meat," he said. "I would not care to lose you."

"You have tunicked me, Master, so that I might not escape, but would stand out in the forest."

"And should you slip your tunic," he laughed, "your sweet, pale body would stand out, as well."

"I know escape is impossible for me," she said, "as I am marked and collared, but I do not care to escape my master. I do not wish to do so."

She pressed her cheek to his thigh.

"There is another reason I placed you in a scarlet tunic," he said.

333

"Master?"

"It proclaims to all the world," he said, "that you kick, moan, and squirm well."

She put her head down. "I am my master's slave," she said.

"Relieve her of the leash," he said. "And let her lead the acquisition."

The fellow who was called Genak, in whose care she had been, unbuckled the leash from her neck.

She sprang up. "Follow me, Masters!" she said, in exhilaration.

Chapter Thirty-Nine

"Prepare to trek," had said Tuza, and she had lifted her hand.

We had steadied our bundles. When she lowered her hand, we would move, making the first step with the left foot.

We had then heard a wild cry from our right, from amongst the trees. Tuza had not even lowered her hand. "Seize them!" we had heard, a woman's voice.

She appeared to be a slave, but there were men behind her, seemingly several men.

"Seize them!" she had cried again, standing, pointing to our group. What exultancy, what triumph, had there been in that voice!

"Donna!" had cried Tuza.

Darla turned about, in her shackles, and fell. I saw a fellow bending over her, quickly lacing her ankles together. Emerald turned about and fled toward the river. Hiza sped down the back trail. A large fellow followed Emerald. I saw nothing of Hiza. Turning about I saw Tuza standing, stupefied. Her hands were raised, over her head. A hunting spear was at her breast. Her weapon belt was being cut from her. Emerald was now in the river, in the water to her waist, facing back toward the shore, facing her pursuer, so close to her. Her dagger had been drawn. She struck at the fellow but he seized her wrist, and disarmed her. They stood facing one another, apart. She rubbed her wrist, which must have been painful. He slipped her dagger in his own belt. She then, wildly, tried to throw herself upon him, striking him with her small fists. But both her wrists were caught. She struggled, squirming, held, pitting her woman's strength against his. I feared for her. Did she not know the danger in which she stood? What if the master found her behavior displeasing? He held her until she stopped struggling, knowing herself helpless. He then released her, and indicated that she should precede him to the shore. But she disobeyed. She spun about, suddenly, to plunge away, into the river, to swim, but her pursuer was too close to her. He seized her by an ankle, and drew her to him, and then seized her hair and forced her head under the water. Her small hands were helpless on his wrist. I feared he would drown her. Then, after a time, he pulled her head up, out of the water, and she looked at him, turning her head as she could, sputtering, coughing, water in her eyes, his hand tight in her hair, gasping for breath. "No!" she begged, as her head was again forced under the water. Again, I feared she would be drowned. The next time he drew her head up, free of the water, he released her hair. They stood in the water, she half bent over, looking at one another. He then gestured toward the shore, as he had before, and this time she, head down, frightened, obedient, waded to the shore. Shortly thereafter, approaching from the east, I saw Hiza, the upper part of her body wrapped in a slave net, stumbling toward the camp. Behind her there were two men, one of whom was prodding her to greater haste with the butt of a hunting spear. Mila, Tula, and I had been, I am sure, in the first moment or two, as startled, and frightened as the mistresses, the woman's cries, the men like rapid shadows amongst the trees, moving toward us. Two of us had screamed. I fear I was one of these. The other may have been unable to make a sound. We had spun about, to our right, confused, in alarm, trying to discern what was occurring, our burdens tumbled away. Surely it was natural for us, then, desperate and frightened, in our consternation, to wish to withdraw from what it might be, not clearly understood, so menacing, that was rushing upon us, but we were in our neck rope. Tula tried to dart away, but was held to us. Mila and I were jerked from our feet, and Tula, too, fell. We were tangled with one another. I feared I might be choked. Tula sprang to her feet. Mila and I, too, leaped to our feet. All of us were looking about, wildly. The rope was on our neck. How could we run? Which direction might we run? Where could we run? Confused, frightened, looking about, we knew not what to do. Our first impulse had been to run, but we had impeded our own efforts. Did we think we could slip the neck loops? But how foolish it would have been, too, to try to flee. Did we not know what we were, that we were kajirae, only kajirae, roped domestic animals? But when things occur suddenly one has no time to reflect. I doubt that any animal would have behaved much differently from how we did. But then, almost immediately, Tula, wild-eyed, looking about, a rope burn on her neck, turned to us. "We are fools," she said, falling to her knees. "Kneel!" she hissed. We then knelt, as befitted what we were. "It is not Panther Women," said Mila, observing the pandemonium in the camp about us. "It is men!" "Yes, men, men!" said Tula. "They will know what to do with us!" "We must obey with perfection," said Mila. "They will have it so," said Tula, joyfully. I was frightened, seeing strange men in the camp. Yet I knew that as slaves we belonged to men; it was men who were our appropriate masters.

Tuza, weaponless, had been put to her belly in the center of the camp. Soon, in virtue of the keys surrendered by Tuza, Darla, now relieved of her impediments, and her ankles freed of the ankle shackling, lay beside her. Then Emerald, at a gesture from her captor, put herself in place, prone, beside Tuza and Darla. Hiza next, now freed of the capture netting, was flung to the ground, belly down, to Emerald's left. All were women, disarmed, prone, before men.

Two of the raiders then strode toward us, who were aligned, kneeling. We quickly straightened our bodies, and lowered our heads. Our hands, palm down, were on our thighs. It is a lovely position, and, of course, a common submission posture. We kept our knees tightly closed. We dared not be taken as pleasure slaves. How much we would then be at men's mercy! To be sure, a portion of my training, and doubtless of that of Tula and Mila, as well, had been that of the pleasure slave. It is assumed that any woman sold off the block is, or may be expected to make, a suitable pleasure slave. Even laundresses, mill girls, water bearers in the fields, and such, are not likely to be unfamiliar with what is expected of a pleasure slave. Certainly in the slave house I had served as such a slave. Some of the men, in assessing my promise, had even had me kneel before them in the position of the pleasure slave, my knees spread invitingly before them. How I had sensed then, even before being so commanded, sometimes to my embarrassment, my receptivity. Soon, sometimes to my shame, I had wanted their arms about me. Many times they made me beg. Men are cruel. I was changed, I knew, after my time in the slave house. How much I was then a slave! Not every slave, I knew, is sent to the slave house.

"Look up," said the large, bearded fellow, whom I took to be the leader of the intruders.

"What do you think, Aeson?" he asked.

"My original conjecture is confirmed," he said. "Acceptable, all of them."

"And as kajirae?" asked the bearded fellow.

"Yes," said Aeson.

He did not know, of course, that I was a barbarian. Yet, what difference should that make? Certainly many barbarians were taken for the markets, and thus deemed suitable for kajirae. I recalled a given master, perhaps the first who had ever looked upon me, though I could not be sure of that. What woman knows if the man who looks upon her, perhaps casually, perhaps appraisingly, is a master? How I hated the brute who had first discerned me in the aisle of the large emporium, he who had brought me to the degradation of the collar, for which I had yearned, he at whose feet I longed to lie, a submitted, nude, and collared slave.

"You may lower your heads," said the bearded fellow, the leader.

We lowered our heads.

I felt a boot-like sandal, with its high, wide thongs, thrust between my knees, and then they were forced apart. I kept my head down. I did not dare meet the eyes of a master.

I did not know what man had forced my knees apart. I thought it likely that it had been the leader, but it may have been the other, perhaps prompted by a cursory glance or gesture.

The two men then turned away.

I knew in what position I now knelt. Only I had had my position so adjusted. I wondered if I were attractive. I had not thought myself particularly so on Earth. I had not regarded myself much different from other women. Could it be, I wondered, that I possessed attractions of which I was unaware? Perhaps I was not as plain as I had thought. But I had been, I realized, chosen for the collar. Certainly not all women were. What had slavers seen in me, which I had not been aware of in myself? Perhaps I was more attractive than I thought, with all the attendant dangers that that might mean on Gor, a world on which men were masters and some women were their slaves. Had it been thought, long ago, that I might, at least eventually, do well off the block? In any event, I had apparently been favorably assessed. Certainly I had been brought to Gor. I had been put in the collar. I was both thrilled, and terrified. I had been found acceptable for a Gorean slave girl. I had been administered the stabilization serums which on Gor, of course, are administered even to slaves. It is desired by the masters that we retain our energy and vitality, our needs and passion, our attractiveness and desirability, our helplessness and responsiveness, our youth and beauty, doubtless not for our sake, as we are only slaves, but for their sake, that we may be more pleasing to them. On my world I supposed this might count as a gift beyond price, concerning which murders might be done, and wars fought. Here, as we were not free, it was little more in our case than a procedure or device to improve slave stock. I wondered what would be the case if a woman, say one of my world, had a choice in such matters. Certainly I knew what the political and ideological prescriptions would be on my old world. She would be expected to prefer decrepitude, withering, aging, and death to a collar on her neck, and a master in whose arms she would be no more than a begging, enraptured chattel. Let other women see these things as they will. Let them make what choice they would. I had had no choice. It was put on my neck. But it belonged there. I had known since puberty, even before I knew of collars, that one belonged on my neck. And when I learned of collars, stunned, startled, and almost fainting, almost losing consciousness, in my junior year in high school, that there should even be such things, I knew that I belonged in one, and wanted one. I wanted to love and serve, selflessly and choicelessly, to belong, to be owned, to be possessed, to be subject to the rope and chain, to be subject to the whip, to be mastered. I wanted to be a slave at my master's feet! How such thoughts tormented me! How I tried to fight them, and thrust them from me! How terrible I must be! Could I be so degraded a creature? Surely I was alone, terribly alone. Surely I was utterly different from tens of millions of other women? I must fight myself. I must not be myself, but another self, an external, dissatisfying, foreign self demanded of me! How I struggled to fulfill stereotypes alien to my deepest heart, to accept values which were not my own, to comply with rules and commands which would deny me to myself! Then I had found myself lying on a warehouse floor, with others, naked, bound hand and foot. Then a fellow's foot had turned me over, and I looked up at him, bound, helpless at his feet. I was to be taken to the markets of Gor.

I kept my eyes down.

Well was I aware of the position in which I knelt.

I was uneasy.

I could not help how I felt. I feared my belly had become the belly of a slave.

The leader, with some of his men, was now by the four prone prisoners.

"Remove their necklaces, the armlets, bracelets, and such," said the leader, "all ornaments."

Some of the armlets and bracelets, I was sure, were of gold.

Then, at another word from the leader, the hands of the prisoners were pulled behind their back, and their wrists were laced together. So slender a bond would hold them helpless, as it would me. A man, I was confident, might have torn apart such a feeble restraint. Was this, I wondered, a mere convenience, such lacing being at hand, or was it intended to be informative, as well, reminding the proud Panther Women that they, too, were women.

"No, please, no!" whimpered Tuza, as her skins were cut away. Darla needed not be subjected to this attention, of course, as she had been similarly served, following Tuza's victorious usurpation of leadership. Then the knife continued its rude work and Emerald and Hiza lay at men's feet, no different from other free women, perhaps more refined, gentler creatures, who might, say, have been driven from sacked, burning cities, snared on bridges by soaring tarnsmen, netted on outings, lured into taverns, seized from caravans, gagged and abducted in darkness from inns, taken in raids on the baths.

"Neck-rope them," said the leader.

"We will need rope," said a fellow.

"It is at hand," said the leader, nodding toward us with his head.

In a moment, Tula, Mila, and I had been freed of the neck rope, which had for so long held us together, like tied kaiila.

Freed of the rope I was suddenly excited and elated. What now might prevent my escape? I must strive mightily not to convey the least inkling of the ferment within me. I continued to kneel, docilely, though my heart was pounding, and my blood racing. How stupid they were! They did not know, of course, that I was from Earth. Put my knees apart, would they! I was not within walls, I was not chained. Few were about; the forest was dark, and wide. It would be easier to slip amongst the trees here than at Shipcamp.

It was with satisfaction, I am sure, that Tula and Mila, as well as I, observed our rope being knotted about the necks of the prone prisoners.

"Get them on their knees, as is appropriate for such," said the leader.

The Panther Women whimpered and wept as they were dragged by their hair to their knees before the leader. Tears coursed their cheeks, their lips trembled. Then they were kneeling before the men, their wrists bound behind them, in coffle.

"Behold," said the leader, "Panther Girls!"

"They look like slaves to me," said a fellow.

"Where now," said the leader, "are your pride, your weapons, your golden ornaments?"

"They are not in evidence," said a fellow.

"Nor will they be," said another.

"Behold Panther Girls," said the leader, "as is appropriate for them, as they should be, helpless, naked, and bound."

"Release us," said Tuza. "You are ignorant, you would grasp lightning. We are in the employ of others, numerous and dangerous others. We have our mission. We must return to the Laurius. Free us, immediately!"

"You see, Master," said Donna, who was standing to the side, in the background, in her scarlet tunic, "it is the very group you seek. I thought so. It is admitted! I found them for you. We have been successful."

Darla turned angrily to Tuza. "You stupid she-tarsk," she said.

"There are forces involved," said the leader to Tuza and Darla, "which you do not understand, nor, fully, do we. But somewhere, perhaps faraway, there is to be a contest, one on which the fate of worlds may hang."

"They were certainly well-paid," said a fellow. "Their purses were heavy with gold."

"No heavier than ours, I wager," said the leader.

"You were hired to seek us out?" said Darla.

"Yes," said the leader. He then turned to Tuza. "You spoke of a mission," he said. "What is it?"

"Nothing," she said, sullenly.

"Kill her," said the leader. A knife leapt from its sheath.

"No!" said Tuza. "I speak, I speak! We were sent to the forest to discover if rumors concerning a great ship being secretly built high on the Alexandra might be true, and, if true, to determine the location of this ship and its state of readiness to depart. It was planned then to dispatch a small, but swift, terrible force, perhaps only two hundred men, to destroy this ship before it could reach Thassa."

"I have heard such rumors, of such a ship," said the leader, "but I know nothing of such a ship."

"We have seen it," said Tuza. "Release us, you will be well paid."

"We are already well-paid," said the leader.

"What is to be our fate?" asked Darla.

"It is to be taken under consideration," said the leader.

"I do not understand," she said.

"Donna," called the leader.

The dark-haired, striking, scarlet-tunicked slave approached, and stood before the prisoners. She carried Tuza's switch.

"I trust you remember me," said Donna, tapping the blade of the switch in the palm of her left hand. "You, Darla and Tuza, set upon me, bound me, and took me to the coast, where you sold me."

Neither Darla nor Tuza responded. They did not meet her eyes. Both, I think, were angry, to be addressed by a slave.

"But," said Donna, "I saw Darla stripped, and belly-braceleted, and shackled. I gather then that loyal Tuza betrayed her new leader, as she and Darla did Donna, their former leader." She then turned to Emerald and Hiza. "And you," she said, "stood by while I was deposed, just as, I would suppose, you did when noble Tuza put noble Darla aside, even to chains."

"We could not interfere," said Emerald. "Darla and Tuza are stronger, quicker. They would kill us."

"Tuza drugged Darla," said Hiza.

"What a brave way to challenge for leadership," said Donna. "Are javelins in the forest no longer in order; are sticks no longer available to draw a killing circle, a circle of decision, in the camp?"

"Away, slave!" said Tuza.

"You are in the presence of free persons," screamed Darla. "Kneel, as befits a slave!"

But Donna remained on her feet. "This is Tuza's switch," she said. "I remember it well. I felt it often enough on the trek to the selling poles."

"She does not kneel," said Tuza, frightened.

"She is to be freed, for finding us," Darla whispered.

"It is her reward," said Tuza.

"Of course," said Darla.

At that point the leader gave a great laugh, and stepped forward. He put out his hand and Donna immediately surrendered the switch to him, and knelt at his side.

"Do you wish to be freed?" he asked, looking down at her, possessively.

"No, Master," she said. "Please do not free me!"

"Have no fear," he said.

"Would you free me, Master," she asked, "if I begged to be freed?"

"No," he said.

"Good," she said.

"You are too beautiful, too exciting, too desirable, to be freed," he said.

"I hope to please my master," she said.

She then held his leg, and licked his thigh.

"Slave!" said Tuza.

"Disgusting!" said Darla.

"I am a slave," she said. "It fulfills me to lick my master's thigh."

"Yes," whispered Emerald, softly.

"Who knows," said Donna to Tuza and Darla, "the time may come when you two will beg to lick a master's thigh."

Emerald moaned, softly.

"What is wrong with you?" Hiza asked Emerald.

"Do not be concerned, Hiza," said Donna. "There is a nice turn to your belly, and, in time, your hair will grow out."

"I cut it short!" she said.

"Who knows?" said Donna. "A master might not permit that."

Hiza shrank back a bit in her bonds, and pulled at the laces confining her wrists behind her back.

"Perhaps," said Donna, "you will long for longer hair, that you may be more pleasing to him."

The leader then motioned that Donna should rise. She did so. He then returned the switch to her.

This was regarded with some apprehension by the prisoners, as the switch may easily be taken not simply as an instrument of improvement, and such, but a symbol of authority.

"Put them in close shackles," said the leader, "and then free their hands. Keep the rope on their necks. If they attempt to remove it, cut off their hands."

Shortly thereafter the ankles of each prisoner had been shackled. The play of chain would allow them only small steps. Their hands were then freed. They remained kneeling, in coffle.

Donna stood over them, switch in hand.

"Do you think it wise," said Tuza, rubbing her wrists, "that we should be granted such freedom? We are Panther Women."

"Do you still think you are Panther Women?" asked Donna.

"Of course," said Tuza.

"Interesting," said Donna.

"Are we not?" asked Tuza.

"No," said Donna.

"You would dare to grant us the freedom of our hands?" said Tuza.

"Yes," said Donna.

"But why?" asked Tuza.

"That you might busy yourselves about the camp," she said.

"I do not understand," said Tuza.

"There are many things to do," said Donna. "Water is to be fetched, berries are to be picked, wood is to be gathered, the fire is to be tended, meals are to be prepared, the camp is to be tidied, soft boughs are to be gathered for the men to recline upon, many things."

"You cannot be serious," said Tuza.

"We are free women," said Darla.

"We dare not go into the forest shackled, naked, and unarmed," said Tuza. "There are wild tarsk, sleen, forest bosk, panthers!"

"A man will accompany you," said Donna. "He will protect you. Your lives will be in his hands, completely."

"Give us clothing," said Tuza. "Men look upon us with impunity."

"It is much like being a slave, is it not?" asked Donna.

"Give us back at least the shreds of our forest raiment, that it be resewn, that we may be covered," said Darla.

"You would be again presumptuously and arrogantly garmented in the skins of beasts, as though you were men, proud hunters and rovers?" said Donna.

"Please," said Tuza.

"You are no longer entitled to such pretenses and posturings," said Donna. "Your garmenture henceforth, if garmenture is permitted to you, will be in accord with your sex."

"Not the bundling absurdities inflicted on allegedly free women!" said Tuza.

"No!" cried Darla. "You would not dare to put us in such degrading garments, so enveloping, so cumbersome, so abundant, so hobbling, so layered, with hoods and veils, the garments of small, soft creatures of interest to men, educated, perfumed, pampered, and refined, meaningless, weak little animals, conforming little animals, mindlessly trapped in the cages of convention."

"When such come to us, we sell them," scoffed Tuza.

"Men like them," said Darla. "They crawl nicely under the whip. They are pretty in chains."

"They are not large, strong, hard, and coarse," said Tuza.

"Do you think me hard and coarse?" asked Donna.

"No longer," said Tuza, scornfully. "Now you are soft!"

"I like being soft," said Donna.

"Slave!" said Tuza.

"And you, too, are soft," said Donna.

"No!" said Tuza and Darla.

"Regard yourself in a mirror, your reflection in still water," said Donna.

"Do not put us in the garmenture of the women of the cities," said Tuza.

"We will not wear such degrading, colorful, cumbersome, lengthy, inhibiting, silken things, the vanities and affectations of weak, meaningless women," said Darla.

"Then, go naked," said Donna.

"No!" wept Tuza.

"We might wear such things, perhaps for a time!" said Darla.

"Surely," laughed Donna, "you do not think we carry about the wardrobes of free women in the forest."

"Cruel slave!" said Tuza.

"Such things were never an option," wept Darla.

"Certainly not," said Donna.

"You are clothed!" said Tuza.

"If you can call it that," said Darla.

"My master has permitted it," said Donna. "Do you like it? Is it not attractive? It is easy to move in such a garment."

"It is scarcely a scrap of cloth," said Tuza.

"It is enough for me," said Donna. "It is appropriate for me. I am a slave."

"Clothe us!" begged Tuza.

"With what?" asked Donna.

Tuza, turning, on her knees, pointed to us. "There!" she said.

"But there are only three tunics there," she said.

"One for me," said Tuza, "one for Darla, and let Emerald and Hiza cast a moistened pebble for the last."

"You would be willing to wear the rags of slaves?" asked Donna.

I doubt that Tula and Mila, any more than I, were pleased at this turn of discourse. Perhaps slaves are not permitted modesty, but few of us are without it. It is perhaps a bit like curiosity, which is supposedly unbecoming to a kajira, but who of us is without it? Certainly few of us would relish public nudity. Indeed, that is sometimes used as a discipline, sending us on errands so, and such. Our garmenture is precious to us, and we strive to be worthy of it. Indeed, Gorean slaves, even pleasure slaves, are often clothed far more modestly than many free women of my former world. Much of this is cultural, of course. A simple example would be veiling. Statistically, few women on my former world veil their features, but, on Gor, free women, particularly of upper caste, commonly veil themselves in public. On Gor a woman's lips are commonly regarded as sexually stimulatory. Thus veiling is common. On the other hand, slaves are not permitted veiling. They may not conceal their lips. Their lips, in all their erotic provocativeness, are to be publicly visible. They are slaves. Interestingly, nudity is not that unusual on Gor amongst manual laborers on hot days. It is more familiar than, and one thinks less of it than, the occasional, usually rare, public nudity of female slaves. Even paga girls are normally clothed, save in the alcoves. In private, in the confines of her master's domicile, of course, the slave may or may not be clothed. Some masters like to have a slave clothed, and others not. If she is clothed, of course, then the master may have the pleasure of removing the clothing. My own tunic, for example, like many, had a disrobing loop at its left shoulder. This is convenient for most men, as they are right-handed. Others, it seems, enjoy seeing their property about, clad only in its collar.

"But," said Donna, "you have not earned a tunic."

"We are free women," said Darla.

"I think it is time for us to be about our work," said Donna. "I think the first thing for us to do will be to gather soft boughs for the masters, that they may the better rest upon retiring. Then we may draw water, and fetch wood."

"Never!" said Tuza.

Then she cried out with pain as Donna savagely struck her, four times, with the switch she carried. Tuza bent down, low, her body trembling, her hands over her head, her hair to the dirt, and began to cry.

Two or three of the men about looked over, but none made any attempt to interfere.

Donna gave Tuza two more strokes.

I was in consternation. I was frightened. A slave is not to strike a free person. A slave's hands, and ears, and nose may be cut off. It is often regarded as a capital offense.

"A free woman has been struck!" Darla shouted to the men about. "A free woman has been struck by a slave, by a slave!"

The leader, who was in converse with two of his men, turned about, annoyed. "Beat her," he said.

"Bend over," said Donna to Darla, "grasp your right wrist with your left hand, head to the dirt!"

"Please, no," said Darla.

Donna then struck her four times, with measured strokes.

"But we are free women," wept Darla.

"Perhaps you are not free women," said Donna.

"But we are free women!" cried Tuza.

"If you are free women," said Donna, "you are captures, and, if so, you will not be the first free women to have felt the switch of a slave. It will help you to learn discipline, and prepare you for the collar."

"I will not be collared," cried Tuza. "I will never wear the collar!"

"You may not have the opportunity," said Donna.

"What?" said Tuza.

"Well, Mistresses," said Donna, turning to Emerald and Hiza, "do you wish to feel the switch?"

"No," said Emerald.

"No," said Hiza.

"Then kiss it," said Donna, "to show your fear of it, and your respect for it."

"Never!" said Hiza.

The switch was then thrust to her lips, and Hiza, sullenly, kissed it. "Lick it, as well," said Donna, not pleasantly.

I then watched the small, soft tongue of Hiza applying itself reluctantly, but obediently, to the supple instrument of discipline and authority.

The switch was then held a few inches before the face of Emerald, who bent forward and kissed it, and then, unbidden, licked it, carefully, delicately, tenderly. Emerald, I thought, is already in the collar.

How she might have driven a man mad with passion.

What a fine price she might bring!

"Like slaves!" said Tuza, regarding Hiza and Emerald with contempt.

"You, next," said Donna to Tuza, and the switch was thrust against her lips.

"No!" said Tuza.

"Now," said Donna.

Tuza then, as had Hiza and Emerald, kissed the switch. She was not required to do more. Perhaps it was felt that a tongue such as hers was unworthy of the switch.

"Mistress," said Donna, to Darla, and Darla, then, as had Tuza, kissed the switch. She, too, was not required to do more.

"Suppose," said Donna to the prisoners, "it had been not I, but a male who had held the switch."

I saw from the reaction of Tuza and Darla that they had some sense of what the difference would have been. Are not men the natural masters? Too, men are seldom patient with us. Emerald trembled, and the knees of Hiza moved, uneasily in the dirt.

Memories flooded back upon me, as I had witnessed the preceding ritual. I recalled a warehouse, on a far world, when not a switch, but a whip, had been held before me, as I had lain on my back, bound helplessly, and I had lifted my head a little, and kissed it. "La Kajira," I had said, as I had been bidden. At the time I did not know what it meant. I would soon learn. Those are commonly the first Gorean words a barbarian must utter. She will later learn their meaning. "I am a kajira," "I am a female slave," "I am a slave girl." Let us suppose a city has fallen, buildings are roaring with flame, blood is in the streets, walls collapse, the air is thick with choking, stinging smoke. Perhaps a free woman flings herself to her knees, before the reddened sword of a helmeted enemy, ready to strike, drunk with the lust of killing and looting. The blade is poised. She throws back her hood and tears away her veils, and her mouth is exposed to the conqueror. "La kajira!" she cries. "I am a slave girl!" This formula, once spoken, is irrevocable. She is then a self-pronounced slave. A quick, abrupt gesture of the sword and she must disrobe, immediately, completely. Her hands are then tied behind her, and she must hurry behind her captor, struggling to keep up, later to be penned with other slaves amongst whom, as she lacks the brand and collar, she is unlikely to be well treated. Her first sale, as her captor may wish to put her up for sale, might occur that very night, following her marking and collaring. Her life has changed.

Donna then stepped back.

"On your feet, dear, noble Mistresses," she said. "There is work to be done. First you will gather boughs, to make soft beds for the masters. I have seen promising boughs near the edge of the camp. That will make things easy for you. You will not even need a guard."

The prisoners rose to their feet, in their rope coffle. Then, following a gesture of the switch, they began to move toward the side of the camp, away from the river. I saw, with some satisfaction, they did not know how to move in coffle. Even slaves know that, especially, I supposed, slaves. "Stop, stupid Mistresses!" called Donna. "Left foot, the first step is with the left foot! Do you know nothing? You are being marched. Later, in gathering boughs, you may move independently. We will begin again. Now, move!"

The four prisoners then, with short steps, and a rustle of shackle chains, began to move again, carefully, slowly, toward the edge of the camp.

"Better," said Donna.

They must pass amongst the men to exit the camp. I saw their bodies tighten. Their heads were up, and they looked straight ahead. This is common in coffle. The attention of coffle beasts is not to rove about. They are not free persons. Too, in this way they are less likely to make eye contact with a free person. With the prisoners, however, I expected that this behavior was less to be attributed to the customs and decorum of the coffle, instilled in coffle beasts, than an apprehension of the gauntlet through which they, coffled, were passing. Certainly they knew they were under the scrutiny of men, though the scrutiny, for the most part, seemed to be relatively casual. It was not as though they were prize kajirae, four-or-five-silver-tarsk girls, perhaps even some gold-piece girls, say, being disembarked from slave wagons, whose arrival in a city had been long awaited, perhaps even having been heralded by a great number of wall bills.

"Oh!" cried Emerald, startled. She almost fell. "Ai!" gasped Hiza, the last in the line. Kajirae, of course, are familiar with such attentions, and may not object. Emerald and Hiza, on the other hand, were free women. I supposed Emerald and Hiza would be the first to be put upon the block, if that were the fate in store for them.

"Harta, faster," said Donna.

The prisoners, with their short steps, tried to hasten.

Tula, Mila, and I exchanged pleased glances. It gave us great pleasure to see our former mistresses so discomfited.

"Let them do our work," whispered Tula.

Yes, I thought, "our work," the work which befits such as we, the work which is ours, fit for Tula, Mila, and myself, the work of slaves.

I hoped the mistresses would also be made to bear burdens. Such may be done in coffle. I trusted that Tula, Mila, and myself would not be the only pack animals in camp.

I noted that the coffle had now exited the camp. It was from that direction that the earlier attack had sprung.

I looked about.

The men paid us little attention.

No longer neck-roped, there was nothing to keep me from slipping away into the forest. How much the masters took us for granted. Did they not know we might bolt as quickly as graceful tabuk, disappearing amongst the trees? I must wait my chance. I did suppose that, as in the march to Tarncamp, we might be secured at night. Still, it should be easy, sooner or later, preferably sooner, for me to complete the escape I had planned, and boldly ventured upon. The masters did not know me. They did not even know I was a barbarian. Had they known that they would doubtless not take me so much for granted. That was their mistake. I was not a Gorean girl. I was from Earth. I would escape!

At this point we heard the screams of women from the forest, the prisoners, I supposed, these coming from the direction they had exited the camp. Some sort of commotion was there. I did not know what was going on. Men rose up, seizing weapons, turning to face the sound. We heard a breaking through branches, cries of fear and misery, these again, I supposed, from the prisoners. "Slower, go slowly!" cried Donna. "Together, move together, step, step!" I saw the shackled prisoners then, on their neck rope. It seemed they could not move quickly enough to regain the camp, perhaps the protection of the men's spears. How helpless they were, how distressed, frightened, and frantic, trying to hurry, impeded by their closely chained ankles. Then near the edge of the camp they fell, tangled together, weeping. Donna stood between them and the forest. "Get up," she said. "Move slowly, to the center of the camp." I did not know what was in the forest. I took it Donna could see it. She kept herself between the forest and the prisoners. How brave she was. The leader went to her, with his spear, and thrust her behind him, and to the side. Then he, too, backed away, slowly.

Then I saw it.

Tula screamed.

"Sleen, sleen!" she cried.

It was a large, long, agile, sinuous, six-legged thing, brown with patches of black, massive, like an immense furred lizard, low to the ground for its size, its belly almost in the leaves, a large, broad, triangular head.

"Do not strike it," called the leader. "It is not wild. See the collar, the leash!" Then he cried out, in alarm. "Do not touch the leash, Aeson. You are not the use master. Let it alone."

"Is it hunting?" said a fellow.

"It was," said the leader.

The huge beast crouched there, at the edge of the camp, looking about. Then it shook its head, vigorously, as though to rid himself of some clinging parasite. It rose up a bit, and then sank down again. For such a large animal, seemingly agile, and sinuous, it had seemed momentarily unsteady.

I did not understand this.

"Kill it!" cried Tuza.

"It is a beautiful beast, do not harm it," said the leader.

"It is recovering," said one of the leader's men.

"How much did you give it?" asked the leader of one of his men.

"Enough to hold a sleen until morning," said the fellow.

"I think not this sleen," said the leader.

"It is a wondrous and mighty beast," said the fellow who had been addressed as Aeson.

The muzzle of that broad head then lay upon the leaves.

Its eyes were half closed.

"Let it alone," said the leader.

"Look at the nostrils," whispered Aeson.

"Yes," said the leader.

"It is taking scent," said Genak.

I then saw the round eyes of the beast open widely. A low sound, a growl of sorts came from that monstrous form.

"It has taken scent," said a fellow.

The long, pointed ears of the beast then lay back against the sides of its head.

"Kill it!" begged Tuza.

Suddenly Tula and Mila, who were with me, withdrew from my side, backing away. I did not understand this. I suddenly found myself alone, no one within several feet of me.

"Is it hunting?" asked the fellow who had asked this before.

"It is, now," said the leader.

I saw the eyes of the beast fasten upon me. It crouched down. "No!" I said.

"Do not move!" said the leader to me.

"She was a runaway!" screamed Tuza. "Kill her, before the beast goes mad in the camp."

"Remain perfectly still," said the leader to me.

The beast now crouched down, eyeing me, just a few feet from me. It began to growl. It scratched dirt, deeply furrowing it. Clearly it was becoming excited. Its tail began to lash.

"It is going to attack," said a man.

"Do not move," said the leader. "Remain perfectly still."

Suddenly the beast, with a spattering of dirt behind it, rushed forward and I screamed and felt that broad snout thrusting against me, excitedly, prodding and rubbing. I put my hands before my eyes, and the snout, pushing here and there, explored me. My tunic was ripped on the side. There was saliva from its jaws on my thigh, and under the softness of its jaw's fur, the jaws rubbing against me, I felt the curved knives of fangs.

The beast then, as though satisfied, circled me twice, and then crouched down, eyeing me, clearly ready to spring.

"Do not move," the leader cautioned me. Then he turned to Aeson. "The beast is impatient," he said. "Free and bring the guests from our camp. Hurry!" The leader then turned again to me. "The sleen is uncertain what to do," he said. "This is dangerous, very dangerous. The use master is not present. It is he who must restrain the beast. Only he will know the signals. Only he can handle the leash with impunity."

"In the wild," said a fellow, "when the hunt is done, the sleen attacks, kills, and feeds."

"The use master is being fetched," said a man.

"How much time is there?" asked a fellow.

"I do not know," said the leader. Then he said to me, "Do not move."

Then the sleen turned about, and faced the edge of the camp, the direction from which he had emerged from the forest, put back his head, and howled.

"It is announcing the end of the hunt?" said a fellow.

"No," said the leader. "That is not in the training."

"What then?" asked a man.

"It does not understand the absence of the use master," said the leader. "It has not encountered this situation before. It does not know what to do. It is puzzled, and frustrated."

"The hunt is done," said a man.

"It always feeds at the end of the hunt," said a fellow.

"Blood will tip the scale," said a man.

"How long does she have?" asked Genak.

"It depends on the animal," said the leader.

The beast had turned away from me. It could not see me. Was this not my opportunity? Would there be another? I turned about, and fled toward the river. I heard a scrambling in the dirt behind me, and stopped suddenly, almost falling, for the beast was now before me, between me and the river, head down, snarling.

"It is going to feed!" I heard.

Someone screamed, perhaps Tula.

"Back away, slowly," called the leader, soothingly. "Return to where the sleen found you, where you were before, exactly. I recommend you kneel there, and remain extremely quiet."

"It is fortunate he did not stop her by cutting or tearing her, and smell or taste blood," said Genak.

"That would have been the end of things," said a man.

I now knelt where, and as, I had been told.

"You disobeyed," said the leader.

"Forgive me, Master," I whispered.

"What you did was stupid and foolish," he said.

"Yes, Master," I whispered.

"She is a barbarian, Master," said Tula. "She knows no better."

"If you try to rise to your feet now," said the leader to me, "the beast may well attack."

"How much time does she have?" asked a man.

"Very little, I would suppose," said the leader.

"There is one way to make sure of one's prey," said a man.

"Certainly, kill it," said another.

"See the beast," said a fellow.

It was crouched down, trembling, ears back, the tail lashing back and forth. Clearly it was growing excited. My bolting had apparently ignited or stirred the whole animal.

"She should not have run," said a man.

"See the beast," said another. "It will not be long now."

"The hunt is done, it wants to feed," said another.

"Training is fragile," said a man. "Blood will have its way."

"Kill it, Master, I beg of you!" called Donna.

"Be silent," he said.

"Please, Master!" she wept.

"This beast is a prize animal," he said. "It is worth five, perhaps ten, of her."

"Please," she cried.

"This is a worthless piece of collar meat," he said, "sleen prey, thus a fled kajira. To see her torn to pieces will be an excellent example for other slaves."

She sank to her knees, weeping.

Did I think I was still on Earth? I was only a Gorean slave girl. In the market I would be worth far less than such a beast.

"It tenses!" whispered a man.

I bent down quickly and put my head down to the dirt, and my hands on my head. How can one prepare oneself for the claws, anchored in one's body, holding one, and then the fangs, mounted in that massive jaw, the tearing and feeding?

Then I heard a man's voice. I did not recognize it. It spoke softly. "Gently, gently, noble friend," it said. "Well done, well done! Easy, easy, fellow, the hunt is done. It is over. It is finished, well finished. Are you hungry, friend? Here is meat, much meat!"

Chapter Forty

"It worked out well," said Axel. "The foolish barbarian, naive little fool that she is, was picked up by the Panther Girls, as we had hoped. Thus, following her trail, Tiomines led us to our true quarry, those who would spy on Shipcamp."

"It was a gamble," I said. "Keep your voice down."

"The Panther Girls were greedy," he said. "They could not resist bending down and picking up a coin in the leaves."

"It was their mistake," I said.

"Else we might not have made contact with our spies."

"Surely you recognize that we are prisoners, as much as they," I said.

"The fugitive is apparently a barbarian."

"That is my understanding," I said.

"Barbarians are stupid," he said.

"Ignorant," I said. "Not stupid."

"It is well known," he said, "that barbarians are selected for stupidity, passion, and beauty."

"Not at all," I said. "And I am of the Slavers."

"Of the Slavers, yes," he said, "but surely you did not deal with barbarians, but with superior stock, Gorean girls, civilized, intelligent, lovely creatures to be captured, marked, and collared."

"I have had some dealings with barbarians," I said. I did not go into these matters. Axel need not know of a strange, gray world, of unusual ships of metal voyaging on dark seas, and secret slave routes. Many hazards were involved. In particular, there were the technology laws of Priest-Kings, and the ruthlessness with which they were enforced. Accordingly, slaves and other materials from the gray world, the Polluted World, must be smuggled to Gor. Such goods were contraband. To be sure, once they were delivered to Gor, no interest seemed to be taken in them, unless they were somehow in contravention of the laws of Priest-Kings. A coffle of a hundred naked, neck-chained beauties from the Polluted World might be marched openly between cities, whereas a small communication device, or a weapon small enough to be held in one hand, capable of emitting small metal projectiles, would court the conflagration of the Flame Death, which some have witnessed, for it is not a myth.

"They are all stupid," said Axel.

"Not at all," I said. "Barbarians are selected with several criteria in mind, surely beauty, and helpless responsiveness and passion, but also high intelligence, often quite high intelligence. No one wants a stupid slave. They do not sell well. The intelligent woman is quick to understand what has become of her, that she is now a slave, and must obey instantly and with perfection. It is almost never necessary to beat her, though she understands it will be done to her, and routinely, if she is not fully pleasing to her master. Too, interestingly, the intelligent woman is likely to be much more in touch with her deepest self, her needs, her profound wants and heart, than a stupid woman. The stupid woman often struggles to be what she was told she was, or should be; seldom, in the beginning, does she, the victim and dupe of a mechanistic conditioning program, its unquestioning puppet, dare to open herself to the liberating revelation and discovery of what she truly is. She often strives to perpetrate an externally imposed stereotype rather than acknowledge a reality, often preferring to ignore nature in favor of convention and artifice, often preferring lies to truth, slogans to history, clichés to biology, and ideologies to blood. Who is it who deems reality unlawful? Those who somehow profit from its denial? Why should it be incumbent on a particular form of life to betray itself? We do not ask that of the kaiila or sleen. Who could benefit from the denial of nature but the unnatural, the fearers of nature? To be sure, all, sooner or later, learn their womanhood. The major difference is that the highly intelligent woman of the Polluted World has often arrived on Gor with, so to speak, a collar already on her neck. She wants to be a woman, to be owned, to be at the mercy of men, to be her master's slave.

"Are not barbarians frigid?" he asked.

"Not at all," I said. "Touch one, and see her squirm, and beg."

"I suppose it might be nice to have one or another in one's pleasure garden," he said.

"I suppose," I said, "but I have heard they also make nice private slaves, as well. It is said they are commonly devoted."

"One must beware of caring for a slave," he said.

"Of course," I said. How preposterous was such a notion!

"You seem to know something of barbarians," he said. "How is that possible?"

"I have heard things," I said.

"I would prefer a Gorean girl," he said.

"Asperiche?" I asked.

"She might do," he said. "In any event," he said, "we have located our spies."

I glanced to the river, where the prisoners, each bearing two leather sacks of water, dangling from the ends of a curved-branch yoke on their shoulders, were climbing up toward the camp from the river bank. Donna, with her switch, was supervising them.

"For all the good it does us," I said. "We have been forbidden to leave the camp."

"They seem to have an interest in them, as well," said Axel. "I am not sure what it is. It may not be easy to bring them back to Shipcamp."

"It seems our friends might object," I admitted.

"Too, it would be difficult to move them," he said, "as they are close-shackled."

"A woman's ankles look well," I said, "shackled."

"To be sure," he said, "but it is difficult, in the light of such impediments, to move prisoners rapidly."

"The key must be somewhere in the camp," I said.

"Be at your ease," he said. "Consider Tiomines."

"Quite," I said. The massive brute lay curled about itself, sleeping. Axel could have reached out and touched him. Sometimes sleen can be not only affectionate, but possessive. I suspected it would be worth someone's life to attack Axel, if

Tiomines were about. To be sure, I was not within the shield of those claws and fangs. I wondered if our relative freedom, and even our lives, might not have something to do with the presence of Tiomines, who was not only dangerous, but, happily, valuable.

"Tula is a good cook," said Axel. "Is Asperiche better?"

"I would suppose not," I said. "But one can always buy them some instruction."

"One does not buy a slave for cooking," said Axel, "but for the furs."

"Of course," I said.

"What do you think of the prisoners?" he asked.

"As females?" I asked.

"Of course," he said. "They are women, what else?"

"Emerald," I said, "would sell well, and it is easy to think of Hiza being turned on the block. I do not think Darla and Tuza would do as well."

"Perhaps not," said Axel, "but all women have possibilities. Nature has seen to it. Put them in a collar and see what happens."

It is true that the collar can do wonders for a woman. I thought of Donna, the slave of Genserich, who was the leader of the strangers. How owned she was! What a superb possession!

"What of the others?" asked Axel.

"Tula and Mila," I said, "are fine stock, even excellent. Either or both might be chained behind a rich man's palanquin."

"What of the other," he asked, "the one they call Vulo?"

It was she on whose scent Tiomines had been set. She was the fugitive from Shipcamp.

"I had not much noticed," I said.

"It is she whom we sought," he said.

"I merely accompanied you for the sport, for the pleasure of the hunt," I said.

"I recall," he said. "But what do you think of her?"

"She is a barbarian," I said.

"Even so," he said.

"I suppose she is passable," I said.

"You would rate her below Tula and Mila?" he said.

"Tula and Mila are quite good," I said.

"Of course they are," he said. "But how would you rate her?"

"Inferior," I said, "of little interest."

"You are mad," he said. "Look closely. See the slave. See what is collared there. Consider the curves of her, the sweetness of the bosom, its small, but delicious amplitudes, scarce concealed within the tunic, the narrowness of the waist, the width of the love cradle, the softness of the shoulders, the rounded forearms, the small wrists, fit for bracelets, the slender thighs, the rounded calves, the trim ankles, can you not see them, too, in shackles? And consider that soft gloss of swirling, dark hair, and the face, framed within it, the exquisiteness of its features, their delicacy, the depth of her eyes, the soft lips, whose attentions a master might command."

"I suppose she is adequate," I said.

"I would think so," said Axel.

"She is a barbarian," I said.

"That is true," said Axel.

"And so," I said, "she is of no interest whatsoever."

"Certainly she is of some interest," he said.

"Perhaps to some men," I said.

"But not to you?"

"Certainly not," I said.

To be sure, the slave, even unscrubbed and uncombed, even in her soiled, rent tunic, was far different from the frightened girl I had watched being vended months ago in Brundisium. Her posture and carriage were now those of a slave. No longer was there a pound on her which was not well placed. Perhaps a silver tarsk, I thought. Ah, I thought. See her walk past that fellow. She does not even know she is needful. She is restless, and does not even understand it. Or does she, and is she afraid? Does she know that what smolders in her belly are slave fires, put there by men, and that, in time, they will grow, and rage, and she will find herself their prisoner, ready to beg relief from men, in time, from any man? Perhaps a silver tarsk, and, say, twenty copper, or even, perhaps, a bit more, I thought.

The leather sacks of water brought from the river by the prisoners had now been hung on branches at the edge of the camp, and the prisoners were being conducted into the forest, presumably to gather wood for the night fire. They were accompanied by Donna, with her switch, and two men, with spears. We had heard the roar of panthers in the forest.

We watched the coffle disappear in the shadows, accompanied by Donna, and its guards.

"The slaves are going to the river," said Axel.

"Water has already been fetched," I said.

"I think," said Axel, "they are being permitted to bathe, to launder their tunics, or such."

"They may run," I said.

"Nonsense," said Axel. "There is no escape for a kajira. They know that. By now even the barbarian will know that."

"I hope so," I said.

Axel looked after the prisoners, who had entered the forest, with their accompaniment, presumably to gather wood.

We heard the roar of a panther, but it was far off. Too, the coffle and Donna, in whose charge it was, were accompanied by two guards.

"I would suppose," said Axel, "that the prisoners will be collared."

"Do you doubt it?" I asked.

"I am not sure of it," he said.

"You think they will be freed?" I asked. It seemed absurd to think of freeing a woman, certainly once you had a chain on her.

"Certainly not," he said.

"Then?" I said.

"I fear so," he said.

"I see," I said.

"They are free, and share no Home Stone," he said.

"That would be a waste," I said.

"We do not know what the gold given to Genserich was intended to buy."

"I see," I said.

Chapter Forty-One

I stood waist-deep in the water.

Tula, Mila, and I rejoiced to have the opportunity to clean our bodies, to wash away, even in the chill, moving water, the sweat, grime, and dust of the trekking. Whereas the mistresses had occasionally availed themselves of the river to cleanse themselves, we had not been allowed to do so. We had been kept filthy, and roped. Free women, for whatever reason, are commonly cruel to slaves. Men are much kinder to us. They are our natural masters. They even like us, at least as pleasure objects and slaves. We had submerged our bodies fully several times, and washed our hair as we could. It was sopped and clinging, about our shoulders. We had removed our tunics at the water's edge, and, kneeling there, had soaked and rinsed them, twisting what water we could from the cloth. As only small pebbles and gravel were about, we could do little more. Then, laying the tunics out to dry, we had waded into the water. Several of the men had come down to the shore, to watch. There was nothing furtive, or clandestine, about this. They enjoyed looking upon us, and so looked upon us. Similarly we were neither surprised, nor shocked, at this attention. As we were slaves, our bodies might be looked upon with the same freedom as those of verr or kaiila, though we were well aware that looking upon us would be likely to provoke interests and excitements quite other than those likely to follow upon the scrutiny of those other beasts.

"See how the men look upon us," said Tula, pleased.

"Of course," laughed Mila. "There are collars on our necks."

How different we are, I thought, from those precious, glorious free women, at least of the high castes, in the cities, of whom I had often heard, who might faint with mortification should a sudden breeze disarrange a veil, or attack a fellow suspected of considering an ankle, or hire public avengers to respond to an inadvertent jostling in a public place. To be sure, it is probably a matter of degrees and extent. Free women on my former world, for example, while more open with respect to their bodies than their Gorean sisters, even to the extent of commonly forgoing facial veiling, would be unlikely to consider bathing naked before men. Certainly I would not have considered such a thing. It would have been unthinkable. But now I was on Gor, and, as Mila might have noted, there was a collar on my neck. I was now a collared beast, no different from other collared beasts, and might be bought and sold as such.

I wondered if anyone could be more woman, or female, if not in her collar.

Whereas there are doubtless terrors associated with the collar, there is also a certain freedom, from our own self-imprisonments. Certainly a thousand frustrations, fears, lies, and conflicts were avoided. I had the sense that wars were done and, in losing, I had won. I had come home to myself, and could not again leave myself, even if I had wished to do so, but I did not have that wish. I was choiceless, and would have it no other way. It would have been my choice to be choiceless. How free I then was! Everything was now objective, and natural. I was in my place, and I wanted to be there, for in it I was myself, and fulfilled. I loved being a slave. It was what I was!

We have our feelings and emotions, deep and profound feelings and emotions. I wonder if a woman can even have such feelings and emotions if she is not aware of how vulnerable and helpless she is, if she is not in a collar. They may do with us as they please. We are to be done with as they please. We are collared.

How helpless we are!

But we are not without our weapons, those of our wit and beauty. And such weapons are not inconsiderable.

Perhaps that is one reason free women hate us so.

Some men were watching.

We were slaves.

I recalled a man, one seen long ago, a man whom I had seen somehow, even so long ago, on a far world, as a master. I recalled I had lain at his feet in some large structure, stripped and bound. He had later looked upon me, appraisingly, in an exposition cage in Brundisium, and had then taken his leave, abandoning me, leaving me separated from him, behind bars, a chattel, caged. He had scorned me on the dock at Shipcamp. How I hated him! And I remembered how Donna had knelt beside Genserich and licked his thigh, beautiful, loving, obedient beast that she was. I would have loved to kneel beside his thigh, that master first seen on a far world, and so express my slave's devotion, hoping not to be cuffed away, to the side.

How glorious, how wonderful, to have a master to serve!

He had no interest in me.

But other men would, I knew.

Had not Master Genserich or Master Aeson kicked my knees apart, that I might understand I was, in that camp, a pleasure slave?

We have our power, our beauty, our wit, our intelligence, and may use it to our advantage. So, too, might a free woman. But how limited, and confined she is! Are not we, with our training, half-naked in our tunics, a thousand times more desirable, in our animal way, than the free woman? Does she not know that in any war of attractiveness, she is far outdone by the slave? When the heat of their manhood is upon them is it not we whom they seek, whom they buy, whom they bid for in the markets, whom they chain to their couch?

I wished that that master, who had had no interest in me, might now look upon me.

Some men were, why not he?

It would be pleasant to make him suffer.

How long ago it seemed that he had first looked upon me! At that time I did not even know that there was a world, Gor. I had, of course, heard rumors of such a world, but who had not? But, of course, it did not exist. And then I had found myself on a slave block, under torches, naked, being vended in Brundisium!

I wished he was watching me. How I would make him suffer!

I submerged my head in the water and lifted it up, almost

immediately. I thrust my wet hair back about my head, and, keeping my hands behind my head, put my head far back, and lifted it to the late-afternoon sky, my back arched, the water streaming from my body, sparkling in its droplets falling to the river.

How I hated him!

I wondered if he were watching, from the shore, if he saw me, as I was now.

I hoped so.

I would make him suffer!

I thought that I had even now improved on my block measurements.

Was he watching?

I would make him suffer.

I thought I might go for even a silver tarsk, now, in open bidding.

Was he watching?

Let him suffer!

Now I would follow Tula and Mila to the shore, and don my freshened, still-damp tunic. It would cling nicely to my body. I would not notice that of course. Then I would fasten the disrobing loop, slowly, modestly, carefully.

I wished that he whom I hated might be on shore, watching me, not that it made any difference to me.

He had scorned me on the dock at Shipcamp, and I would scorn him here, but not, of course, to the extent of risking a beating.

I had apparently lost consciousness shortly after hearing certain words, following which I had sensed, rather as though I might be somewhere else, that the sleen had not attacked me, that it might have been soothed, that it might now be gone. Certainly I no longer felt the heat of its breath on my back, nor was I any longer half-choked in the stifling reek of it, emanating from that deep, cavernous, fanged maw. Then clearly the beast had been pacified, and was being fed. I heard its feeding, the voracious tearing of the meat, the sound of its gorging, and it was then, I think, that I lost consciousness.

Tula and Mila were with me when I opened my eyes.

They kissed me. "You are alive, Vulo," had said Tula. Mila gave me water from a metal cup.

"There was a sleen," I said.

"There is nothing to fear from it now," said Mila.

"Unless you run again," said Tula. "Then it might kill you."

"The hunt is done," said Tula.

"But you have been caught," said Mila.

I was then very afraid.

But there would be little in this camp, I thought, from which my scent might be taken.

Might I not run again?

I was sure the sleen had been somehow set on my track from Shipcamp. They would take me back there. I had run. What, then, would be done with me there?

I must run again!

Once I was roped, and leashed, I would be helpless.

"There were two with the sleen," said Tula, "the use master and another. They were hunting together. We thought them with the captors, but they did not attack with them. It seems they were guests, with the sleen, in the camp of the captors. Apparently the sleen escaped. It is fortunate for you it was recovered."

I did not think it likely that the captors were from Shipcamp. I had seen none of them before. Indeed, I was not sure they had even known of the existence of Shipcamp. The two who had been with the sleen, on the other hand, must be from Shipcamp. I had been the quarry of their sleen. Their relationship to the captors, if any, was not clear to me. I suspected they might have fallen in with one another in the forest.

I had not even obtained a good look at the sleen's use master, let alone his fellow, as by the time of his arrival, I was kneeling, bent down, my head to the dirt, my hands over my head, expecting the momentary attack of the sleen. I had not even raised my head, so terrified I had been, when the beast had been withdrawn, and had begun to feed, and I had lost consciousness.

"You may only be whipped," said Tula.

"You are very pretty to be put to leech plants or fed to sleen," said Mila. "Men hate to lose a pretty slave. They have many uses for them."

"Too, you are a barbarian," said Tula. "That is clear from your accent. And barbarians are stupid. It might be thought you did not know any better."

"This time," said Mila, meaningfully.

"And allowances might be made for you," continued Tula.

"Once," said Tula.

"Who were with the sleen?" I asked.

"Those two, across the camp," said Tula.

Tula and Mila helped me to my feet, for I still felt unsteady.

"What is wrong?" asked Tula.

"Are you going to faint?" asked Mila, anxiously, tightening her hold on my arm.

"No," I said. "No!"

"Do you know them?" asked Tula.

"One," I said.

"Is he your master?" asked Tula.

"No," I said, "he is not my master, and I am not his slave!"

"I only asked," said Tula.

"You could do worse," said Mila. "Look at those arms, the hands, the shoulders, the power, the virility of that body."

"He could break one of us in two," said Tula.

"He could nurture, protect, and master a slave," said Mila. "I would be well pleased if his coin could take me off the block."

"Not I!" I said.

"I would love to crawl naked and collared at his feet, cleaning them with my tongue, any time," said Mila.

"Not I!" I said.

"Surely he is handsome," said Tula.

"Not at all," I said.

"I cannot even look at him," said Mila, "without feeling my bondage."

"It is he whom I fled," I said.

"Then he is your master," said Tula.

"No, he is not!" I said.

"Then you know he is your master, and you want him as your master!" said Mila.

"No, no!" I said.

"He is not the sleen master," said Tula. "Thus he must have hired the sleen and its master."

"You were the beast's quarry," said Mila.

"He came to seek you!" said Tula.

"Perhaps," I said, off-handedly.

I feared I might fall, seeing him here, in the camp, so close, only some yards away.

Then I stood very straight, and stiffly.

"He is an oaf," I said. "But, yes, doubtless he has come to seek me."

"So far through the forest, and its dangers," said Tula.

"He must want you very much," said Mila.

I swelled with pride. Had it not been my knees, and not those of Tula and Mila, which Genserich or Aeson had forced apart, so that I must kneel in the position of the most owned and desirable of slaves, the pleasure slave? How vulnerable is a woman so positioned! And I had been unable to subdue or ignore the feelings which I had experienced, being so placed, so as a slave, before a man. How can one help being heated, and excited? How can one help being aware of the changes in one's body, the readiness of one's belly?

"Perhaps," I said.

"But why, then, has he not put you in his bracelets?" asked Tula.

"I do not know," I said.

"I do not understand," said Mila. "He has paid you no attention. He has not even looked in our direction. I am not sure he knows you are in the camp."

"Could there be no other reason you were sought?" asked Tula.

"Perhaps," I said, falteringly. I suddenly realized that I might have been sought simply as a fled slave, only that. I was well aware of the security within, and about, Shipcamp, the guards, the prowling larls, and such. It seemed clear that there were secrets about Shipcamp which the Pani were concerned to protect. To protect the camp, deserters might be pursued, or fled slaves. Indeed, I had gathered that our captors' interest in the mistresses might have some relationship to these matters. It seemed they had spied on Shipcamp, and the captors had been concerned to intercept them, presumably before they might report their findings.

"It is all very strange," said Tula.

I did not think it so strange, but, if there were secrets concerning Shipcamp, I thought it best to remain silent.

"Where are the mistresses?" I asked.

"They have been sent out again, with the scarlet-clad slave and two guards, to gather wood."

I recalled that their first errand with this object had been interrupted by the appearance of a collared sleen approaching the camp.

"There are boughs at the edge of the camp," I said to Tula and Mila. These had been earlier gathered by the mistresses, but had not yet been strewn for the comfort of masters.

"So?" said Tula.

"They may not be suitable," I said.

"The slave, Donna, will have seen to that," said Tula.

"Nonetheless," I said.

"Beware of walking amongst the masters," said Tula.

"You are a clever one," smiled Mila.

"Or one very stupid," said Tula.

"I will only be a moment," I said.

"Beware of meeting the eyes of masters," said Mila.

"I am not afraid to do that," I said. To be sure, much depends on the time, the place, the situation, and the relationship. For example, eye contact between a private master and his slave is commonly as easy, pleasant, thoughtless, natural, welcome, and familiar as that between free companions. On the other hand in, say, the street, eye contact between a slave and a free person, say an unknown male, or, particularly, a free woman, is rare, unless commanded. Some men enjoy a certain amount of boldness in a slave; it is easy to put her to her knees again, and if it becomes too much, it is easy for the whip to take it out of her.

I took only a few steps, when I stopped, for the sleen, reclined, had lifted its head, and looked at me.

I remained very still.

The beast then put its snout down on its paws, and closed its eyes.

I realized then it no longer had any interest in me.

I continued to walk toward the heap of boughs. My small journey would take me, inadvertently, past two fellows, one, the sleen master, who was sitting cross-legged, and the other, his fellow, who was lying on his stomach. They were chatting. As far as I know neither had noticed me. But they would. I would see to it.

How I hated the boor who had scorned me in Shipcamp, and who ignored me now.

How I hated him, and wanted to throw myself before him, begging to be accepted as his slave. It was permissible; there was already a collar on my neck! In the cities, I had heard that even free women sometimes knelt before a given male, and begged his collar. Even free, they were women; and how much more a woman they would be in a collar! I recalled that long ago, on my former world, that I had felt the desire to throw myself to my knees before him, but I had turned, and fled away, in consternation.

Had I been a free woman it would have been easy enough to call myself to their attention. Might not the hem of a robe brush a foot? One might even loosen a sandal strap, and request its adjustment, that one need not bend down or go to one's knee in public, unthinkable for a free woman. One might even, in seeming to stumble, kick dirt upon one in passing, an accident pertaining to which a free woman might legitimately express regret, or even, less pleasantly, trip against them, and then execrate them for being in one's way, or such. Doubtless there are thousands of ways in which a woman may call herself to the attention of a man, even if one is an exalted free woman. After all, beneath all their veils and robes, they, too, are women. To be sure, few of these subtle stratagems, so to speak, would be at my disposal. For example, the hem of my tunic was high on my thighs, and I was barefoot. Too, I did not think it wise to initiate a physical contact with a free person. Too, it might be noted, realistically or not, that accidents are seldom accepted on the part of a slave. For example, if a slave should spill a beverage, or drop a utensil, while serving, let alone break a plate or a bowl, she may expect a whipping.

His hand whipped out and seized my ankle. I froze in place, frightened. "Master?" I whispered.

I could not even kneel, as I was held.

"Girl," he said, "go to my pack, at hand, that with two black straps. Open it, fetch forth a flask, bring it here, and then approach those two fellows playing stones, and invite them to be our guests."

I could not even say, "Yes, Master," so startled I was, so commanded, but, when released, I hurried to do his bidding. We had not made eye contact. He had not even looked at me. Any passing bared ankle, it seemed, would have served as well. A moment later I had brought him the flask, which he accepted, without looking at me. He then rose up, to sit cross-legged, like his friend. Gorean males commonly sit cross-legged, whereas Gorean women commonly kneel. "Masters," I said, kneeling, to the two fellows I had learned were Aeson and Genak, "those masters," and I indicated the sleen master and his fellow, "invite your presence." They looked to the side, and the sleen master's fellow lifted the flask, invitingly. "Good," said Aeson. They scooped the stones into a small bag, and rose up. "Paga?" called Genak. "Yes," said the sleen master. "We have paga, too," said Genak. "Bring it!" called the sleen master. Genak went to a case at the side of the camp, from which he drew forth four metal cups, and a large bottle which, in its net and sling, was half full, with some amber fluid. I rose up, and turned away, but was arrested by a sharp voice, which called, "Kajira!" Instantly I turned about, and knelt, waiting to be commanded, as the slave I was. "Stupid kajira," said the voice, "do you expect us to serve ourselves?" It was Genak. "No, Master!" I said. "She is a barbarian," called the sleen master. "Oh," said Genak.

Shortly thereafter the four fellows were sitting together, drinking and talking. The strangers were from the basin of the Laurius. I also learned that there was a town there, on the Laurius, called Laura, which interested me, for it is a name I was familiar with from my former world, and, indeed, it had been given to me in Tarncamp. I was now Laura, if it pleased masters. In this camp, however, I was called Vulo. I knelt back from the men, as was fitting. I was to be unobtrusive, and yet at hand, to serve. The flask was finished in one round, but I replenished the small metal cups more than once, pouring from the bottle, it suspended in its carrying net, slung on its strap about my shoulder. It is easy to tip the bottle in such a net, which supports it, and the sling allows it to be carried about, from place to place. I was also interested to learn that the sleen master and his fellow presented themselves as from a small village near the mouth of the Alexandra, which I knew to be false. I was accounted for as having fled from a beached ship on the coast. There were secrets, indeed, I gathered, pertaining to Shipcamp. It apparently did not occur to the free persons, happily, to look into these matters by interrogating me. I would have tried to lie well, but had little doubt that two or three judicious questions might elicit responses from me in virtue of which the entire fabrication I was trying to construct would collapse. I would not know the names of ships, or captains, or types of ships, or what they carried, or what I might be doing on such a voyage, and so on. I did know my collar was a plain one. Normally a collar is engraved in such a way that the slave may be identified. A typical collar might read something like "I belong to Achiates of Jad." Sometimes the slave's name also appears on the collar, as in something like "I am Gail. I am the property of Publius Major of Brundisium." In any event, my collar was unmarked. I did know that some of the slaves in Shipcamp, who were private slaves, had collars which did identify their masters. Most slaves hope one day to be the single slave of a private master. Few desire to be one of a hundred or more in a rich man's pleasure garden, or to be a city slave, or a slave owned by a business, such as a mill or great farm.

As the conversation continued to wend its way about through a miscellany of apparently random topics, certain things began to become clear to me. One was that there seemed to be no relationship between the fellows who had captured the Panther Women and the sleen master and his fellow. They were not part of the attacking force, or somehow in league with it. Indeed, I suspected they might be only too willing to leave the camp, but that that option might not really be theirs. If they were guests, it seemed they were not the sort which might come and go as they pleased. Further, whereas the conversation seemed casual and pleasant, on the part of the sleen master and his fellow, I began to sense it might not be as idle as it might seem on the surface. Why should they, out here in the forest, be discussing tunes, czehars, flutes, kalikas, and such? Aeson and Genak, I think, drank more than the sleen master, and his fellow. The sleen master, as it was hot, opened his shirt, and it was then noted that about his neck, on a slender strap, hung a whistle. "That," said Aeson, thickly, pointing to the whistle, "is how you control the sleen. It conveys the signals."

"No," said the sleen master.

"No?" said Aeson.

"No," said the sleen master, who had identified himself as Axel of Argentum. "Tiomines, like most sleen, responds to verbal commands."

"Which are secret, and pertinent, to the given animal?" said Aeson.

"Surely," said Axel of Argentum.

"What is the whistle about then?" asked Genak.

"It is a tune whistle," said Axel. "See the tiny holes. It is a pleasure to occasionally while away the time with it in a camp."

"Play us a tune," said Aeson.

"See how it is bent," said Axel. "It is defective. I would have it repaired."

"Try it," said Aeson.

"Even when new," said Axel, "not everyone could sound it, and it is now broken."

"It requires strength to sound it?" asked Aeson.

"Yes," said Axel.

"Nonsense," said Genak. "Even a slave could sound so little a thing."

Axel laughed and slipped the whistle, on its strap, over his head. "Let us see," he said, motioning me to him. I approached him, and knelt, the large bottle supported in its net, the sling running from my left shoulder to my right hip. As I am right-handed, I would guide the neck of the bottle with the left hand, and lift and tip it with the right hand. Axel handed me the whistle. It was bent. It did have tiny holes in its barrel. It was not large. It was about two horts in length, perhaps a little longer.

"Blow it," said Aeson.

I did not think it would be difficult to sound it. I was uneasy about calling attention to myself, when its blast was heard. To be sure, I had been commanded. Master Axel, nor the others, seemed concerned that its blast might be heard outside the camp. We were deep in a lonely, and unsettled, wilderness. And certainly the area about the camp had been routinely scouted, and guards posted.

I blew very softly on the whistle, hoping that whatever sound it might make would be scarcely noticed. Surely it would be enough for them to hear even a tiny note. If they wanted some great blast let it be sounded by some free person, not one whose body was subject to the lash. But no sound came from the device.

"See?" said Axel.

"Blow harder," said Aeson.

I then tried, again and again, to sound the whistle, but I heard nothing.

"Even when new," said Axel, "it required strength to sound it, and it is now broken."

As he extended his hand, I gratefully returned the whistle to him, and rose up, backed away a pace or two, and again knelt, where I had positioned myself for the masters' convenience. The bottle in its net was now light, as the liquid was mostly gone.

"I doubt I could sound it myself," said Axel.

Then he put the whistle to his lips, and, as far as I could tell, exerted great force on the tiny device.

"Let me try," said his fellow, whom I had resolved to hate with all my might.

It pleased me considerably that even he, so large a man, was unable to bring any sound from that recalcitrant, small object.

The whistle was then handed about to Aeson and Genak, but each, to their surprise, and chagrin, fared no better.

I glanced to the side, and noted that Tiomines, the hunting sleen, had awakened. His head was up, and those two large, pointed ears were erected. He growled, a noise more puzzled than anything else.

"The sleen is restless," said Aeson.

"Steady, friend," said Axel soothingly to the beast, which then, again, put its head down on its paws, and closed its eyes.

Axel slipped the whistle, on its strap, again, about his neck.

"The instrument is worthless," said Aeson. "Throw it away."

"Better to repair it," said Axel.

"Buy another," said Genak.

"I like it, I am fond of it," said Axel.

"Paga!" said Aeson, looking to me.

I rose up, to serve him. There was little left. No more than a quarter of a cup for each was practical.

I made it a point to stand quite close to the sleen master's fellow, he who had accompanied him on his hunt, the hunt in which I had been the prey, which had ended with my capture.

How I hated him!

But might he not have sought me?

Was it only as a fled slave that he had sought me? I did not know. Did his neglect of me in the camp seem too studied? Why was he here? How was it that he, who had first looked upon me, on a far world, and had looked upon me as a man looks upon a slave, the first time to my knowledge that I had been so looked upon, so obviously, and had doubtless figured in my selection for Gorean bondage, had been in Brundisium, and in Shipcamp, and was now here in the forest? Surely he must remember me, I thought. Am I so little, so meaningless to him, that I am only another item of cargo, another naked woman dragged to a sales block? Is this all a coincidence? Does he truly not remember me, me, in whose dreams he has so often appeared, with his insolence and arrogance, and authority, with his whip and chain?

I recalled the dock in Shipcamp.

Had he truly not recognized me, kneeling at his feet, he who had brought me to a collar, yet a collar I coveted?

So he despises me, I thought; so he scorns me, I thought. So then let him find himself where he is, within inches of me, no longer a free woman of Earth, but now, thanks to him, no more than a collared, barefoot, tunic-clad Gorean kajira, a beast who may be bought and sold, one which now, thanks to him, exists only for the service and pleasure of men. Let him feel my collared presence and, should he heat, and squirm, and sweat, let him keep well in mind that he does not own me!

I stepped back, with a swirl of the tiny tunic.

Aeson rose up, took the empty bottle, in its net, from me, wished the sleen master and his fellow well, and wandered away. Genak lay down where he was, and was soon asleep.

"Tal," said the leader of the attackers, who now stood over the sleen master and his fellow.

"Tal, noble Genserich," said Axel.

"I trust you enjoy the hospitality of the camp," said Genserich.

"We have just been drinking with two of your fellows," said Axel.

"I know," said the leader.

"We must be leaving presently," said Axel.

"You realize," said the leader, "that you will spend the night on a chain."

"Why?" asked Axel.

"To protect you," said the leader. "There are dangers in the forest." He then turned away.

I, too, expected to spend the night on a chain, or roped helplessly, as I had been on the trek to Tarncamp from the coast. But I was a slave. Such things are not unusual where a slave is concerned. Some believe that a slave is chained at night, or caged, or kenneled, that she not escape, but others believe it is largely to prevent her theft. I think the explanation is even simpler; it is to remind her that she is a slave.

I stood a few feet away.

"I must see to Tiomines," said Axel. He then rose up, and went to the sleen.

I looked to his fellow, who was sitting, cross-legged, regarding me. I boldly returned his regard.

What had I to fear? He did not own me.

He indicated, with a slight movement of his right hand, that I should approach. I did so. But I remained standing. Let him consider that.

"Why did you stand so close to me?" he asked.

"Surely Master does not mind the proximity of a slave," I said.

"Do I know you?" he asked.

"Do you?" I asked.

"What is your name?" he asked.

"Surely you know," I said.

"What is your name?" he asked.

"Margaret Alyssa Cameron," I said. "Perhaps you recognize the name?"

"No," he said.

"Perhaps you remember me from a large store, in a great city, on a far world, when you first laid eyes upon me?" I said.

"No," he said.

"Or from an exposition cage in Brundisium?"

"No," he said.

"Or, say, from a wharf, a dock?" I said.

"That is it!" he said.

Could he really not remember that it was he who had brought me to the collar?

Had it not been for him I would not now be on this world, half naked, with a marked thigh and an encircled neck, at the mercy of masters.

"What did you say your name was?" he asked.

"Margaret Alyssa Cameron," I said.

"That was your free name," he said.

"Yes," I said.

"Then it is no longer your name," he said.

I was silent.

"Is it?" he said.

"No, Master," I said.

"Surely you are aware," he said, "that as a slave you have no name, any more than any other beast, save as masters might choose to name you."

I remained silent.

"That is true, is it not?" he said.

"Yes, Master," I said.

"What are you called?" he asked.

"Here I am called 'Vulo'," I said.

"Amusing," he said.

"I have been named 'Laura'," I said.

"I know," he said. Of course he would know. That was the name under which I would have been hunted.

"Master has captured me," I said.

"You have an accent," he said.

"I am a barbarian," I said.

"Your accent may improve later, and, in time, might even be lost," he said, "unless a master would prefer for you to retain at least a trace of it, as a charming feature."

I was very angry, standing before him.

"Those of your sex," he said, "commonly have an excellent aptitude for the acquisition of languages."

"May I withdraw?" I asked.

"No," he said. "That is because, over countless generations, you have been traded about, exchanged, captured, carried off, and so on, with the result that you must learn, and quickly, the language of your possessors, your captors, masters, and such. Those with the highest skills in such matters would be the most likely to survive, to please, to be used for the purposes of reproduction, and such."

"How is it," I asked, "that Master accompanied Master Axel of Argentum in his hunt?"

"I was bored," he said. "I thought the pursuit of a foolish slave might provide something in the nature of a diversion."

"Only that?" I asked.

"Of course," he said. "What else?"

"It made no difference that it was I?" I asked.

"Of course not," he said. "Why should it?"

"You would have followed any," I asked, "as easily, as willingly, as diligently?"

"Of course," he said.

I turned out my hip, and straightened my shoulders, as I had been taught in my training. A girl has powers.

"I think, rather," I said, "Master finds this slave of interest."

"Does your body mark well under the attentions of a slave whip?" he asked.

"Master does not own me," I said.

"What a vain little piece of collar meat you are," he said. "How are you different from hundreds of others, similar, and better? You are scouted, observed, researched, inquired about, filmed and photographed in various lights, at various times of day, in various locations, against various backgrounds, engaged in various activities, in various garmentures. These pictures and reports are assessed. Points are assigned. You are even examined while asleep in your own bed. You are stripped and photographed, variously. Your measurements are taken, in detail, your bosom, waist, thighs, wrists, ankles. In this way, in your sleep, as you are gently sedated, you are measured variously, for example, your neck for the collar, your wrists and ankles for wrist and ankle rings, and so on. Then you are reclothed, and in the morning, you awaken, refreshed, and know nothing of all this. If you are found satisfactory, your name is entered on an acquisition list. You are then, unbeknownst to yourself, a Gorean slave girl. It only remains then that you be harvested, perhaps months later. Thus, small, vain kajira, you see there is nothing of particular interest or nothing special about you."

"I see," I said. I wondered if he were trying to convince me, or himself.

"You pose prettily," he said.

"Am I to understand that Master finds me of no interest?" I asked.

"Yes," he said, "of no interest."

"Master does not want this slave?" I asked.

"No," he said. "The slave is common meat, even inferior stock."

"Yet I was selected," I said.

"It seems so," he said.

"I have been found of interest by others," I said.

"Oh?" he said.

"Yes," I said, "Master."

"Why are you standing," he suddenly said, angrily. "Kneel, put your head to the dirt!"

Instantly, I knelt, my head to the dirt. How pleased I was!

"You should be lashed!" he said.

"You do not own me," I said. "You do not own me!"

He rose up, angrily, and kicked dirt upon me, and turned away. I remained as I was. I recalled that it had been my knees and not those of Tula or Mila which had been forced apart by the boot-like sandal of Genserich, leader of the captors, or his seeming lieutenant, Aeson. I knew I was slave enough to be of interest to a man. I have made him squirm, I thought. I have made him cry out. I have made him sweat. Let him be restless. Let him turn and roll angrily in his sleep. Let him see if he can cast from his thoughts the image of a certain dark-haired, collared barbarian. It was for her, was it not, that he essayed the dangers of the forest. Surely there was no simple diversion in this. He may not even have been authorized to leave Shipcamp. Were there not Pani guards set at the perimeters to prevent such departures? He may have followed me even from

Brundisium. He may have sought me in Tarncamp, and then, later, encountered me in Shipcamp. How arrogant the masters are, I thought. So we are nothing to them, are we! Are we truly to suppose that one slave is no different to them from another? Do they think slaves are unable to recognize interest, heat, passion, desire, possessiveness, need, drive, the lust to own, to collar, and master? Emotions, I was sure, despite any denials which might be proffered, had seethed within him. Had I not glimpsed, be it only for a moment, the eruption of his interest, scarcely controlled, hinting at the volcano of his wanting? Now, scornful Master, I thought, I have power. I am near, and you want me, but you cannot have me! At night you will even be on a chain! Now you are mine! I can tease and taunt you as I want, and I need fear nothing from you. Not only was I not his, but he and Axel of Argentum, his fellow, were prisoners here, it seemed, as much as I. He had scorned me. Now it was my opportunity to scorn, and torture, him.

I then became aware, lifting my head a little, that Donna, two guards, and the four prisoners, the Panther Women, Darla, Tuza, Emerald, and Hiza, had returned to the camp. The prisoners were struggling, bent over. Each, on her back, bore a large bundle of firewood. It pleased me to see the proud Panther Women laboring, as might common slaves.

I heard a panther roar, from somewhere in the forest.

"Get up," said Tula to me.

"I have not been given permission to rise," I said.

"It is all right," said Tula. "We are in the keeping of Donna. She is first girl. We may bathe."

I rose to my feet and looked about, and saw him whom I hated across the camp. I smiled, and tossed my head, and turned away. I am sure he saw me, but he had given no indication of that. I wondered if he were truly indifferent to me. Could that be? Might I be wrong? I did not think so. I thought he wanted me, and could not have me. I was pleased.

I then accompanied Tula to the shore of the Alexandra, where Mila was waiting for us.

Chapter Forty-Two

It was the morning of the day following the capture of the Panther Women, the appearance of the sleen in their camp, my experience with the beast, and its recovery by the sleen master. Too, of course, I had discovered that the sleen master had not been alone, but, to my astonishment and consternation, to my outrage, humiliation, fear, and fury, I now helplessly caught, to my hatred and relief, to my fear, misery, and joy, was accompanied by another, one whom I well knew, even if it were not one by whom I was well known.

How angry I was that he had found me, and how I had longed to see him again, and how I had feared I might never see him again!

How pleased I was to have been caught.

But of course I had not wanted to see him again, for I despised, and hated him, such a ruthless, uncaring, thoughtless, uncompromising brute, and master!

How terrifying it would be to be owned by such a man, to be his, to be done with as he pleased!

Why had he not bought me?

Surely I was not expensive, might I not be within his means? Did he not want me?

I hated him.

I wanted to be at his feet, head down, naked and collared, my lips pressed to his sandals, hoping to be found acceptable, even pleasing.

Was I truly nothing but another slave to him, merely another piece of meaningless collar-meat, to be indifferently fetched from a pen, or block, by a coin?

How I hated him!

How I wanted his collar!

Then I was afraid. What if he were companioned? Might he buy me for his companion? Would she sense that I was his slave? How cruel she would be to me! Might he keep me to the side, in rented space, in a girl stable, to be used when convenient?

Or would he want me, at all?

Was I truly so inferior, such common stock?

I loathed the thought of his touch.

How I would struggle to resist him!

How I would cry out, and whimper, begging for his least touch!

I wanted to be at his feet, alone there, where I belonged, in the place of a slave.

He and Axel of Argentum seemed to be free enough in the camp. Certainly they moved about as they wished. I did note they carried no weapons. Too, I had gathered they might have spent the night on a chain. All that was done with Tula, Mila, and myself was a simple rope ankle-coffle. A long rope had been looped and knotted about our left ankles, and then the rope was tied at each end to a tree. As it was fastened, Tula, had she desired to do so, could not reach the tree to her left to undo the knot, as the rope, knotted about the tree to her right, would not permit her to do so; similarly, I could not, had I desired to do so, reach the knot to my right to undo it, as the far knot on the left would not permit me to do so. Thus neither Tula nor I could free the rope of the two trees to which it was tied. Mila, of course, was between us. I supposed we might have tried to chew through the rope, which was not, as far as I knew, cored with wire, but this did not seem practical. Two guards were posted, and moved, from time to time, about the camp. What if, in the morning, the rope had been found damp, or partially bitten? Too, the forest is likely to be particularly dangerous at night. Twice I had heard the territorial roar of a forest panther, happily far off. But I had also heard, at about the second Ahn, the movement of some beast near the camp's periphery. It may have been only a tarsk. I did not know. Fires were tended through the night. The prisoners' night, I might mention, was less pleasant than ours. In addition to their ankles remaining shackled, and their neck-coffle being fastened to a tree, their wrists were bound behind their backs. Tula had prepared the supper yesterday evening. I had gathered that free women, at least of the upper castes, were commonly useless in the domiciles. It is not a matter of accident, I gathered, that slaves, in their training, are often taught something of cooking, marketing, sewing, the care of leather and silver, dusting, scrubbing, laundering, and such things. Interestingly, slaves often take a homely pleasure in such things. They realize such tasks are not demeaning to them, but appropriate to them, as they are slaves. Also, as slaves, they take pleasure in serving, and wish to please their masters. Too, most like a well-kept domicile. Beyond this, hanging on its peg, is always the whip.

Tula, Mila, and I had served the men. Tula seemed particularly attentive to Aeson, and Mila to Genak. Tula had approached Genserich, but she had been warned away by Donna. I made it a point not to serve, or approach, either the sleen master or his fellow. I hoped that would be obvious to one of them in particular. In serving, I think I walked well, knelt well, and served well, with suitable slave deference. When addressed I spoke as was appropriate, softly, respectfully, submissively, and clearly, for good diction is expected of a slave. Indeed, as slaves, we would not have dared to be otherwise. "You are a barbarian," observed a fellow. "Yes, Master," I had said. "Forgive me, Master." He had then turned to the fellow beside him. "What do you think?" he asked. I felt myself studied. "A silver tarsk," said the other. I did not look about, but I hoped that another present had heard that. It was more than twice what I had sold for in Brundisium. "You may withdraw," said the fellow. "Thank you, Master," I said, and rose to my feet, backed away, and then turned, and went again with the bowl ladle, its handle wrapped in cloth, to the cauldron over the fire. As I mentioned, I avoided the sleen master and his fellow, in the serving. I am not sure they noticed this. They seemed pleasantly enough engaged, in bantering with the men of the attackers. In any event, neither summoned me to him. That was all right. There was no reason to do so, of course. I did not mind. I was

pleased. Tula and Mila would do quite as well. When the men
were finished, Donna, Tula, Mila, and I, so instructed, surprised,
knelt to one side. We discovered that we, though slaves, were
to be served by the prisoners. This well outraged the shackled
mistresses, for they were free women. Too, though they were
free, they had not yet been fed. For this service, they, though
remaining shackled, were removed from the neck rope, that
their serving might be the more easily accomplished. Darla and
Tuza would serve Donna, who was first girl, and Emerald and
Hiza would serve Tula, Mila, and myself. Tuza, smugly, a small
smile about her lips, approached Donna. In a moment Donna
cried out in pain, and leaped to her feet. "It is an accident!" said
Tuza, now alarmed. "I will show you another accident, dear
Mistress!" cried Donna. Her switch was like a nest of striking
snakes, so swiftly did it strike, again and again. I could scarcely
follow the flash of the leather. Tuza, shackled, helpless, was
on the ground, rolling, and weeping. "Mercy," she begged.
"Mercy!" "Stay as you are!" snapped Donna, "as you are, on
your back, hands at your side!" Donna then threw down her
switch and seized up the fallen bowl-ladle and made her way
to the cauldron. "Please, no!" wept Tuza. "Stay as you are," said
Donna. "Do not move." "No, please, no!" begged Tuza. Then
the scalding contents of the brimming bowl-ladle were dashed
onto her body, and she shrieked in misery. "It is an accident,"
said Donna. Tuza, weeping in misery, with a rattle of chain,
crawled away. Donna then resumed her place. "Serve me," she
said to Darla. "Of course," said Darla. It might be noted that the
men did not much notice, and they certainly did not interfere
in the altercation which took place between Donna and Tuza.
Doubtless that was to be expected. Masters seldom interfere in
such matters, for example, in the squabbles of slaves. If there is
more than one female slave in a camp, in a household, or such,
one is almost always appointed "first girl." Otherwise one
might have chaos. The first girl stands in the place of the master.
It is her task to keep order amongst the other slaves, and she
answers only to the master. I would suppose that most "first
girls" are judicious and fair but some, doubtless, abuse their
authority, have their favorites, distribute ornaments, cosmetics,
silks, candies, pastries, delicacies, and such selectively, and

make life miserable in a variety of ways for others, less favored, with respect to work assignments, discipline, and such, which matters are largely in her hands. It is not well for a first girl to take a dislike to one. Such dislikes may be diversely motivated, but a common one is jealousy. A particularly attractive slave is perhaps most in jeopardy. She may be frequently caged. If the household is large she may be kept hidden from the master. She is not likely to be a stranger to the first girl's switch. Most first girls are responsive to flattery. The favorites are often sycophants. Some first girls seem to think they are free women, until they kneel before the master. And it is well-known how free women feel about slaves, view them, and treat them. One constraint on the first girl is that she may be changed, and then find herself, so reduced, only one slave amongst others, now defenseless, without protection amongst those over whom she may have been accustomed to tyrannize. Most slaves, as I may have noted, desire to be the one slave of one master, a private master. Emerald and Hiza served Tula, Mila, and myself without incident. Both seemed to be seriously shaken. Doubtless they had profited vicariously from the lesson which Donna had administered to the unwise and errant Tuza. Too, I supposed that it must be difficult for them, free women, to be stripped and shackled before us, tunicked slaves, serving us as though we might be free and they the slaves. Emerald leaned forward, and whispered, "What is it like to be a slave?" "Perhaps you will learn," I said to her. Hiza looked angrily at me. "And perhaps you, as well," I said. "Never!" she hissed. And then she turned back to me, and said, "I am afraid." I touched my collar, without really thinking about it. "That is appropriate," I said, adding, "Mistress."

After we had been fed, the prisoners were returned to the neck rope and allowed to feed themselves. I do not think there was all that much left by then, as nothing was saved for the next day. The prisoners were then taken to the edge of the camp where they relieved themselves, and then their neck rope was fastened to its tree, and they were put prone to the ground and had their hands tied behind their backs.

"What is to be done with us?" had asked Darla, shortly after her hands had been fastened behind her, trying to look up, of Genserich, who was nearby, observing the securing of the prisoners.

"You will learn tomorrow," he had said.

I was thinking of escaping, but then the rope was looped about my left ankle.

And now it was that day, tomorrow, so to speak, the morning of the day following the capture of the Panther Women, that following my menacing at the jaws of a large sleen, and its fortunate, if somewhat belated, restraint by the sleen master. Too, of course, it was the day following the arrival in camp of another, one who had apparently accompanied the sleen master and his beast, Tiomines, in what had proved to be a successful hunt, the quarry of which had been a barbarian slave.

I wiped the slave gruel from my lips with the back of my right forearm. I held the bowl in my left hand and went to the river to rinse it. Afterwards I stood for a little time on the shore, thinking of running. But it was light, and there were men about. And at night, one is on the rope. I understood that Genserich had some interest in Tiomines, and so I did not think he would permit the sleen to hunt me, for he might then lose the beast. It would be best, of course, if Tiomines would be conducted back to Shipcamp. No other hunting sleen were about. I looked across the water. I knew little of the south shore of the Alexandra. I did know that in the vicinity of Shipcamp, across the river, there were some buildings, including a mysterious stockade, where, it was rumored, prize slaves were housed, under great security, presumably to be boarded on the great ship, shortly before its departure.

I looked back to the camp.

I had been caught.

What chance has a girl if a sleen is on her scent?

I did not think they could catch me again, as, if all went well, there would be no sleen.

My vanity had been stung by the ease with which Emerald had captured me in the forest. Surely I had been an easily snared "vulo." How could I forget that? And she was not even a man! But I reminded myself that I, even had I wished to be so, could not have begun to be a match for her. How large, stern, severe, and powerful she had seemed, so different from myself. How formidable she had seemed, in her freedom, her pride, her size and sturdiness, in her rude skins, in her barbaric ornaments, with her dagger and spear. And I was slight, small, weak, and defenseless, and feminine, fit on this world to be only a female slave. The others, too, had seemed so large, so powerful, so forceful, so mannish, like women who were not women, but men. But then how small, weak, and female they had proved to be when compared not to me, but to actual men. Their skins gone, their ornaments removed, put to their knees, shackled, on a rope, how suddenly female they were. And now they were frightened. No longer did they seem proud Panther Women, but rather, now, only women, the captures of large and powerful men.

I must return to the camp.

It would not do, to be missed, at least not for too long.

I had been caught, first by the Panther Women, and then by the attackers, as simply one slave amongst others, as might be one kaiila amongst others, and then, I suppose, in a sense, by the sleen master and his fellow. Certainly the sleen had found me, and held me in place, doubtless expecting the hunters to be at hand, but they had not been. Happily, they had managed to arrive in time, moments before, it seemed, the sleen would feed.

I turned about, and, again, looked across the river. It was broad at this point, shimmering in the morning light. But, too, I was sure it was deep, for I knew it had been well sounded, and frequently, by the men in small boats. These had now been recalled, as the departure of the great ship was imminent, but would doubtless precede her in the voyage downstream. The channel of a river can be treacherous, in its turns and depths. Debris can accumulate. Bars can be formed overnight. I knew charts had been prepared. Following a false channel one can run aground.

A bird skimmed its surface, fishing. The forest looked small, on the other side.

I recalled the serving of yesterday's evening.

I had ignored him. Let him be stung by that, ignored by a slave! But he had not interjected his will, summoning me to him. I should have had to obey. The lash is not pleasant. But he had not summoned me to him!

Why had he not done so?

Could it be that he, truly, did not want me, that I was nothing to him, only another slave?

Had he truly pursued me only for pleasure, only for the hunt, as one might pursue any animal, a verr, a tabuk?

I did not think so.

Not at all.

I think he wanted me.

He would not have me. If he scorned me, I would scorn him, by flight, by departing. Next time there would be no sleen.

I would have my revenge. Let him hunger for a slave who was indifferent to him, one he might desire but who did not desire him, one who would be forever beyond his grasp, one whom he would never have, one who loathed him, who despised him, who found him repulsive, who hated him, who scorned him, whose most dreaded fate would be to fall into his hands.

Yes, Master, I thought, want me, dream of me, long to own me, long to have your name on my collar, your bracelets on my wrists, long to fling me as a rightless chattel to your slave ring, but it will not be!

I hate you, I hate you!

I must get back, I thought.

There was a stirring in the camp above, and so I turned about, and, carrying my now-rinsed gruel bowl, climbed up the slope to the camp.

Chapter Forty-Three

"Something is going on," I said to Axel.

"Yes," said Axel.

"Let us inquire," I said.

"Apparently it has to do with the Panther Girls," he said.

"I think so," I said.

The Panther Girls had been knelt near the center of the camp. Men were gathered about. We saw Genserich. Even the camp slaves, Tula, Mila, and the other, were present, kneeling to the side.

"Is it true," I asked, "that you can set a sleen on any quarry?"

"Most sleen," he said, "with the 'Kill Command'."

"Tiomines?" I said.

"Yes," he said.

"Bring Tiomines," I suggested.

"Why?" he said.

"He is our only weapon," I said.

"It is not ours to interfere," he said.

"Bring him," I said.

Axel slapped his right thigh, sharply. "With us, fellow," he said. The sleen immediately sprang up, and, a moment later, rubbed his muzzle against the side of Axel's leg.

"What are you going to do with us?" begged Darla.

She and the three other prisoners, Tuza, Emerald, and Hiza had been knelt, as noted, near the center of the camp. As before they were stripped, shackled, and on their neck rope. Too, now, though it was well into the morning, their hands were still tied behind their backs.

They were frightened. They had not been fed.

Perhaps, I thought, uneasily, their captors did not wish to waste food.

Genserich stood before them, regarding them, his arms folded across his chest. Most of his men were gathered about, save for one or two on guard. His slave, Donna, was behind him, kneeling, on his left, a common position in which a slave heels her master.

"Welcome," said Genserich to Axel and myself, acknowledging our presence. "Tal," we responded.

"We are free women," said Darla. "Remove from our bodies these hideous impediments, return to us our clothing, feed us, give us our weapons, let us go on our way."

Clearly, I supposed, they were still free. Certainly she had spoken without permission. A free woman, of course, may speak when, and how, she wishes, as she is not a slave.

"You were carrying gold," said Genserich, "and doubtless expected to acquire more. You were spying in the forest. You admitted learning of a great ship, its apparent readiness for departure, and your intention to inform others of this, with the expectation that a small force, say, some two hundred men or so, would be soon dispatched to attack and destroy this ship, withdrawing almost immediately."

"Yes," said Darla. "We have told you so much. Now let us go."

"Who is your employer?" inquired Genserich.

"We do not know," said Darla. "We did not need to know his name. Gold was enough."

"I am sure that is true, Master," said Donna.

"And who is your employer?" asked Darla boldly, looking up.

Genserich laughed, and slapped his thigh. "Gold was enough," he said.

I was puzzled by these things, though I had gathered, long ago, from Tyrtaios, that titanic forces might be involved in these matters, and that one, or more, worlds, in their way, might hang in some delicate balance. Certainly there had been an attack on Tarncamp some weeks ago, when I and others had been on timber duty in the forest. It had been beaten away. Some force, obviously, was interested in the ship, and concerned, for some reason, that it reach the sea, whence it might embark on some mysterious venture, perhaps even seeking, as some feared, the World's End. Some other force, apparently, wished to destroy the ship, thus precluding its voyage and any possible influence it, and its complement, troops, or such, might eventually bring to bear on certain distant, critical events.

"You may keep the gold," said Darla. "Free us, that we may make our report."

"We already have the gold," said Genserich.

"Free us, then," she said, "that we may make our report."

"There is some urgency in this?" he said.

"Yes, noble Genserich," said Darla. "An army is being maintained, at great expense, at the mouth of the Alexandra, to prevent the ship from reaching the sea. If the ship can be located and destroyed before its departure, this force need no longer be maintained in the field."

"But, I take it," said Genserich, "funds have already been allotted to maintain this force for some time, if not indefinitely, at the mouth of the Alexandra."

"One supposes so," said Darla.

Genserich laughed, and so, too, did the men about him.

"And such funds," he said, "devoted to, but not expended on, the closure of the Alexandra, might then find their way into diverse wallets."

"Perhaps," said Darla.

"I now see the urgency," said Genserich.

"Free us," said Darla, "and you might share in the employer's good fortune."

"He is a thief," said Genserich.

"Perhaps not," said Darla.

"A thief," said Genserich.

"He may only wish to conserve the funds which have been entrusted to him."

"For himself," said Genserich.

"Free us," said Darla.

"I do not know your employer," said Genserich, "or who, or what, stands behind him, but I doubt he would happily welcome us into his confidence. Rather, with such intelligence at our disposal, and our possible use of it, I suspect our lives might stand in some jeopardy."

"Allow us to make our report," said Darla. "We will be well paid. We will share our gains with you."

"You are generous," said Genserich. "What do you think those on whom you have spied would pay for you?"

"Surely not as much!" she said.

"I fear," said Genserich, "that your employer must continue to maintain, presumably at considerable expense, his men in the field, at the mouth of the Alexandra."

"Not if we make our report!" she said.

"No," said Genserich, "not if you make your report."

"Free us!" demanded Darla, pulling at her bound wrists, fastened behind her.

"But," said Genserich, "you will not make your report."

"I do not understand," said Darla.

"For what do you think we were hired?" asked Genserich.

"I do not know," said Darla.

"That your report not be made," he said.

"Free us, free us!" cried Tuza.

"Be silent, girl," said Genserich. "Another is speaking for the prisoners. Not you."

Tuza drew back, angrily.

I noted she had not been cuffed. To be sure, she was free.

"And it was for that purpose," he said, briefly glancing behind him, and to his left, where Donna knelt, in her scarlet tunic, "that a given slave, a former Panther Girl, indeed, one once of your own band, was obtained, that she might abet our search."

"I found them for you, Master," said Donna. "I was sure I could."

"We found her in a low market, for cheap, inferior slaves," said Genserich. "She still thought herself a Panther Girl, despite being neck-ringed, and pretended to angry resistance, and defiance. The whip quickly took that out of her, and she understood, trembling and weeping, that she was now a slave. After that, well-worked and, when it amused us, lengthily caressed, she began to learn her collar. Soon enough she was at my knee, whimpering."

"Disgusting slut!" exclaimed Darla.

"But she was quite pleased when she learned the reason for her purchase, and eagerly led us in our quest to intercept the now-so-called 'band of Darla', which had been hired to conduct its secret reconnaissance in the northern forests.

"Slut!" screamed Darla. "You betrayed us!"

"It was I who was betrayed," she said, "—Mistress."

"You have had your revenge!" said Darla. "We are now stripped and shackled, kneeling and helpless, bound, in the power of men!"

"We are women," said Donna. "We should be in the power of men."

"I hate men!" screamed Darla.

"Because you are not a man," said Donna.

"I do not understand," said Darla.

"Be what you are," said Donna. "You will then know the joys of being the surrendered slave of your master."

"No, no, no!" screamed Darla.

"Yes," breathed Emerald, pulling at her bound wrists.

"We put her in the scarlet tunic," said Genserich. "A former Panther Girl, she well understood how this would mark her out, how conspicuous it would make her, and how it would make clear that although she might be in the forest she was no longer of the forest."

"A slave's garment!" said Darla.

"I love it," said Donna. "In it I am myself, and more free than I ever was!"

"Our mission was secret," said Darla, angrily. "How did you learn of it?"

"Much is apparently at stake," said Genserich. "If there are two large and complex forces involved, it is not unlikely that each has spies in the camp of the other, perhaps even highly placed spies."

I was interested to hear this. I had not thought much of this before. It did not seem unlikely, however. I glanced over at Axel, but his attention was on Genserich.

"You see," said Genserich, "I cannot release you, for then you would hasten to the Laurius, to deliver your report."

"Then hold us for a time," said Darla. "And then release us. I am sure the ship will depart the wharf soon. Once it does so, there would no longer be point, or advantage, to our report."

"I have not been paid to release you," said Genserich.

"Not the collar!" cried Darla.

"No, no!" cried Tuza, despite the monition earlier accorded her.

Emerald and Hiza were silent.

I had earlier sensed that something would be done with the prisoners today. The attackers would see no point in remaining here. I supposed it most likely the prisoners would be collared and sold. That is the common fate of a female prisoner, and surely, now, it was clear that the Panther Women were such prisoners. Axel, as I recalled, had been less sure of this.

"You know too much," said Genserich. "I have been paid to kill you."

"No, no!" cried Donna, aghast.

I recalled that Axel, earlier, had remarked that we did not know what the gold given to Genserich was intended to buy.

"No!" cried Darla.

"We are women, spare us, spare us!" wept Tuza.

"Now you are women?" said Genserich.

"Please, Master," wept Donna. "Do not hurt them!"

"Mercy!" wept Emerald.

"Please, please!" said Hiza.

"It will be quick," said Genserich.

"Prepare to set the sleen on Genserich," I whispered to Axel.

"Do not be foolish," he said. "Do you want to die?"

"We are women!" cried Darla.

"But free women," said Genserich.

"The sleen," I whispered to Axel.

"No," he said. "Wait!"

"Now," I said.

"Wait," he said.

"Please," cried Darla, "let it be the collar!"

"You are free," said Genserich. "Surely you would not accept the indignity of the collar, of being sold?"

"Yes," said Darla, "yes!"

"Be merciful, Master!" begged Donna.

"Mercy!" cried Tuza.

"Please, Master!" cried Emerald.

"'Master'?" said Genserich.

"Yes, 'Master'!" she cried.

"And what of you?" Genserich inquired of Hiza.

"Master!" she wept.

Genserich stepped back, and surveyed the prisoners.

"Pronounce yourself slave," said Genserich.

"I am a slave!" said Darla.

"I am a slave!" said Tuza.

"I am a slave, Master!" said Emerald.

"I am a slave, Master!" said Hiza.

The women were now, legally, slaves. Such words cannot be unsaid.

"You may beg collars, as the slaves you are," said Genserich.

"As the slave I am, I beg a collar, Master," said Darla.

"As the slave I am, I beg a collar, Master," said Tuza.

"As the slave I am, I beg a collar, Master," said Emerald.

"As the slave I am, I beg a collar, Master," said Hiza.

"Are you Panther Girls?" asked Genserich.

"No, we are slaves, Master," said Darla.

"Thank you, Master!" cried Donna.

"We have been paid to kill them," said Genserich, thoughtfully.

"Surely, Master," said Donna, "you were paid to kill free women, not slaves. Free women are gone, slaves remain. Now there are only beasts. Surely one would no more kill a slave than a verr, a tarsk, a kaiila."

"What think you, Aeson?" asked Genserich.

"If we had not apprehended them," said Aeson, "we would have been unable to kill them."

"True," said Genserich.

"It is similar," said Aeson. "You failed to cut their throats while you had the chance, while they were free."

"An oversight," said Genserich.

I doubted that.

"Now," said Aeson, "if we kill them, we are merely butchering beasts. We were not paid for that."

"Genak?" inquired Genserich.

"Please, Master," said Donna to Genak.

"It seems a shame to waste slaves," said Genak. "The two on the end," he said, indicating Emerald and Hiza, "suitably dieted, exercised, and trained, might plausibly be chained to a slave ring. The other two might do as pot girls, kettle-and-mat girls, field slaves, mill girls, that sort of thing."

"Even they," said a fellow, eyeing Darla, "might learn their womanhood."

She looked down, frightened.

"It is within every woman," said another.

"I need not learn my womanhood, Master," said Emerald. "I know it well. I have fought it for years."

"That battle is now over," said Genak, as he surveyed the kneeling slave.

"Yes, Master," she said.

"The employer is dangerous," said Genserich. "He is unlikely to be satisfied."

"Let us take them back to the Laurius," said a fellow, "and turn them over to the employer, that he may do with them as he wishes."

"Good," said more than one man.

"He will kill them!" said Donna.

"Possibly," said a man.

"Please sell us, Masters," begged Darla. "There are selling poles on the coast. Bind us to them, and sell us to the crews of passing ships."

"They watch for such things, as they pass," said Tuza.

"It was done with me," said Donna.

"We might claim we failed to find them," said a man.

"Some lies are justified in honor," said Genserich, "and some are not."

"Surely, Master," said Donna, "honors may war with honors."

"It is dishonorable to lie," said a man.

"Not more dishonorable than the slaughter of helpless slaves," said another.

"The house of honor is large," said a fellow. "Its turrets are clear, but only a fool would claim to know its every brick and stone."

"The matter is delicate," said Genserich.

"No!" said Donna.

"Such lies are perilous," said a fellow. "They hang by many threads, and if one breaks, it is found out."

"True," said another. "The risk is too great."

Tuza put down her head, and moaned.

"I will do it," said a fellow whipping out a dagger. He rushed forward, and thrust Genserich to a side. The men about were confused, startled. This, clearly, they had not anticipated. The former Panther Girls, now slaves, Darla, Tuza, Emerald, and Hiza screamed, and tried to pull back. Donna, too, cried out in fear. Tula, Mila, and the other slave, called Vulo here, kneeling to the side, did so, as well. Before Genserich could regain his feet, the fellow's hand was in Darla's hair, and his blade was at her throat. I saw a drop of blood at its edge. She dared not make the slightest move or sound.

"The matter is not yet decided, Rorton," said Genserich, angrily. "Sheathe your dagger, and return to your place."

"I know weakness when I see it," he said. "I declare myself first."

"Mutiny!" said Aeson.

"If you would be first, let us do contest," said Genserich.

"The employer has placed me amongst you," he said, "to report independently to him, which I will. Perhaps there are others, as well. I do not know. He has paid his gold, and I will see that it has not been paid in vain. These women must be silenced, free or slave, for the information they bear."

"Put away your dagger, Rorton," said Genserich. "And that will be the end of it. We will deliberate further on the fate of the slaves."

"Deliberation is weakness," said Rorton. "We know what is to be done, and it wants only the doing." He looked about, menacingly. "Do not interfere," he said. "Draw no weapons, place no quarrel."

The men about looked to Genserich, and to one another. Indecision was in their eyes, and in their mien.

Rorton, clearly, could move his blade across Darla's throat before anyone could so much as draw a dagger.

"The matter has not yet been decided," said Genserich.

"I have decided it," said Rorton. "The employer is not to be crossed with impunity. Perhaps you have the wish to die, but I do not."

"But you may die," I said.

He looked at me, wildly.

"I do not fear to cross the employer, whoever or whatever he may be," I said. "I do commend the employer, however, for having the foresight to put an agent, or agents, in place to further assure the success of his plans."

"This one is first," he said. Darla's eyes were wide. She remained absolutely still.

I hoped I could count on the support of Axel.

"If you draw the blade on her throat," I said, "the sleen will be set upon you."

"Surely not!" said Rorton.

Axel put his head down, close to the shaggy, massive head of the beast. His lips moved, but what was communicated I could not hear, but the beast's response was instantaneous. Its ears flattened themselves against the sides of its head, and it crouched down, and began to growl.

"It is the command of preparation, of readiness," I said.

"Kill the beast!" cried Rorton to Genserich, and the others.

"It is a valuable animal," said Genserich.

"Kill the strangers, both of them!" said Rorton.

"Are they not our guests?" said Genserich.

"Kill them!" demanded Rorton.

"I do not think it would be wise to attack a sleen master in the presence of his sleen," said Genserich.

"Perhaps you would like to do so," said Aeson.

"The employer will be displeased," said Rorton.

"Employers are often displeased," I said. "Let us suppose that a displeased employer will have you killed. That may or may not be the case. I do not know. If it is the case, your choice is simple. You may choose to die now, or later."

"Put away your dagger, Rorton," said Genserich.

Rorton looked to Axel. "You will not release the sleen!" he said.

"But I will," said Axel.

Rorton stepped back, away from Darla, and returned his dagger, angrily, to its sheath.

Darla sank to the ground, unconscious.

"Who is first?" asked Genserich.

"Genserich is first," said Rorton.

Three or four men gathered about Rorton. "Kill him," said Aeson.

"No," said Genserich. "He was faithful to his fee."

"Be faithful to yours," said Rorton. "The women must be killed."

"Please, no, Master!" said Donna.

"Only a fool and a weakling attend to the words of a slave," snarled Rorton.

"And only a fool or weakling ignores right and truth, regardless of by whom it is spoken," said Genserich.

"Kill them," said a fellow.

"No," said another.

"They are mere slaves," said a man.

"They possess knowledge," said a man.

"So now do we all," said a man.

"We beg mercy of our masters," said Tuza.

"We are slaves," said Emerald. "Show us mercy, Masters!"

"Mercy, Masters!" wept Hiza.

"Deliver them, as slaves, to the employer," said a man. "He may then do with them what he wishes."

"Good," said a man.

"Yes," said another.

"No, Master," begged Donna.

"Be silent," said Genserich.

"Let us count," said a man.

"Yes," said another.

"Count, tally," said another.

"No," said Genserich. "I am leader, I am first."

"Then lead," said Rorton.

"We will sell them," said Genserich.

"No!" cried Rorton.

"Thank you, beloved Master!" said Donna, joyfully.

Genserich looked down upon her, angrily.

"Forgive me, Master!" she said. She had been warned to silence. I noted he did not strike her. Was he such a fool, I wondered, as to care for a slave? I feared so. Even strong men may have their weaknesses, their absurd flaws.

"We remain divided!" said Rorton.

"I am first," said Genserich.

"You fear the sleen!" said Rorton.

"Of course," he said. "What fool would not?"

"It may be killed," said Rorton.

"Of course," said Genserich.

"Then kill it," said Rorton.

"No," said Genserich. "It is beautiful."

"It is hideous and dangerous," said Rorton.

"And beautiful," said Genserich.

I, and surely Axel, who knew more of sleen than I, realized it would not be difficult to kill the sleen. A swift, unexpected blow across the back of the neck with a gladius would sever the vertebrae.

Genserich looked down at the collapsed, unconscious form of Darla. As she lay in the neck rope, her legs drawn up, I did not think she was all that unattractive. "Awaken the slave," he said.

Aeson went to the slave, and rudely kicked her, twice, in the thigh. She stirred, and opened her eyes. "Up, slut," he said, "kneel up."

"Yes," she said, "—Master."

Aeson seized her by the hair, that her face be held in place, and slapped her twice, first with the flat of his right hand, and then the back. She looked up at him, frightened, not understanding.

"You dallied too long in saying 'Master'," said Aeson.

"Forgive me, Master," she said.

"Align them, with perfection," said Genserich.

"Knees even," said Aeson, "back on heels, back straight, belly in, head up, hands, palms down, on thighs!"

"What of their knees?" inquired a fellow.

"Let them remain closed," said Genserich.

"They may be split later," laughed a man.

"Of course," said Genserich.

"Kill them now," said Rorton. "It is best."

The slaves paled, but did not break position. They knew themselves, as all slaves, in the absolute power of masters.

"You understand," said Genserich, "that you are to obey instantly and unquestioningly?"

"Yes, Master," they said.

"And," said Genserich, "will you strive to be pleasing to your masters, and fully so, in all ways?"

"Yes, Master!" said Darla.

"Yes, Master!" said Tuza.

"Yes, Master!" said Emerald.

"Yes, Master!" said Hiza.

"There," said Genserich, turning to his men, "they are slaves who are concerned to be pleasing. It is clearly dishonorable to slay such a slave."

"That is true," said a man.

"It is a turret in the house of honor," said another. "It is not only clearly visible, but conspicuous. It is uncontestable."

"Hold!" said Rorton. "The question is not whether or not they are slaves, or, if slaves, pleasing or displeasing slaves. The question is independent of status and condition. The question is one of knowledge, whoever it is borne by, free or slave. The knowledge they bear is their doom."

"That is what was at issue," said Genserich. "It is no longer at issue. I have decided it. They will be sold."

Donna leaned back in relief, but was wise enough not to speak.

"We have not decided it," said Rorton.

"I have decided it," said Genserich. "And I am first."

"Now," said Rorton, turning away.

"He had best be killed," whispered Aeson.

"No," said Genserich.

"There may be others with him," whispered Aeson.

"And who shall we kill?" asked Genserich.

"I do not know," said Aeson, looking about.

"Gather gear, prepare packs," said Genserich. "We are going to break camp."

"Prepare to trek," called Aeson. The cluster of men then broke apart, withdrawing from the place of deliberation, in which had been considered the fate of four women, who were no longer Panther Women.

"Remove the shackles from the slaves," said Genserich. He looked about, at the forest, and river. "I am not comfortable here," he said, glancing uneasily at Axel and myself. "We will wish to move swiftly."

Aeson drew a key from his wallet, and bent to undo the shackles on the four neck-roped slaves. They remained in position. They had not been given permission to break position.

Axel and I stepped back, preparing to withdraw.

"Hold," said Genserich. "I fear I must prevail upon you to accompany us."

"Surely," I said. "You are trekking to the coast, to selling poles. Our village lies to the west, true, but on the Alexandra. We will accompany you for a time. We will be grateful for your company. Return to us our weapons."

"I think not," said Genserich.

"How not?" I asked.

"Do you think I do not know a prime sleen, a tracking sleen, when I see one?" said Genserich. "No such animal would be found in an Alexandra village. It is too expensive. There would be no use for it, no point. I do not know who you are, or your business, but you are not villagers. I would suppose you are in league with those of whom we have heard, those of the camp of the great ship."

"If so," said Axel, "we can be of no interest to you. Give us back our weapons, and we will be on our way."

"The sleen," said Genserich, "was clearly hunting the slave, Vulo. Consider her flanks, her figure, her face. That is no village slave. She fled the camp of the great ship, and you were sent to retrieve her."

"Then," said Axel, "give her to us, and our weapons, and we will be on our way and concern you no longer."

"Give away a prime slave?" said Genserich. "You must be mad. We took her, and the others, when we captured the camp."

"I have my eye on the one called Tula," said Aeson, "and Genak, I suspect, would not object to having the one called Mila at his feet."

"What of the one called Vulo?" I asked. "Doubtless she is for Genserich."

"Are you interested?" he asked.

"Certainly not," I said.

"Perhaps at one time," said Genserich. "But I have a slave who juices quickly, and cuddles well, whose belly pleasantly warms my feet on cold nights."

Donna, nearby, put down her head, shyly.

"And the girl, Vulo?" I asked.

"We will tie her naked to a selling pole on the coast," he said, "and see what she will bring."

"She sold for less than a half tarsk in Brundisium," I said.

"You know that?" he said.

"Yes," I said.

"Clearly she is worth more now," he said.

I noted that three or four men were gathered about Rorton at the edge of the camp.

"I see nothing," said Axel, "to prevent us from slipping away into the forest."

"Nothing but a spear in the back," said Genserich. "Too, I would not care to be you in the forest without weapons. Too, your sleen is a dangerous beast and you will have little with which to feed it. If I were you, I would regard its imminent hunger with apprehension."

"Too," said Aeson, "surely you have heard the roar of panthers in the night. It is possible they are curious, and are closing in."

"Let us go," said Axel. "We will risk the forest, even unarmed and with Tiomines."

"There may be enemies about," said Genserich. "You appeared in the forest. There may be others. You might well be enemies."

"We are not your enemies," I said.

"Nor, I wager, our friends," said Genserich. "We cannot risk your contacting others, and following us."

"I see," I said.

"You are an excellent commander," said Axel.

"I am sorry," he said.

He and Aeson then turned away.

I looked at Axel. I saw that he would make away, at the first opportunity. Too, I saw that he was fully confident that I would accompany him. And why should I not accompany him, my friend? It was no longer practical for him to return with the quarry, and, in fact, he had not sought the quarry itself, but the Panther Women to which the quarry, luckily, had led us. Nor was it practical to return with the Panther Women either, for they were in the keeping of Genserich and his band. And he did have the assurance that they would be unable to report back to their employer, whoever or whatever he might be, with an intelligence which might prove threatening to the great ship and its projected commission, errand, or charge. That should be enough for Tyrtaios, and Lord Okimoto. And for my part, the hunt had been successful. The quarry had been run to ground and trapped, and that was all that I had been interested in; and that was all that mattered. I had had the sport of the hunt, and I had been concerned with nothing more. It had been a pleasant interlude, a diversion from the routine of Shipcamp. I told myself all this. On the other hand, though it was no more than a sop to my foolish pride, I did not much care to depart without that for which I had come. All I had cared for, of course, was the mere capture of the quarry, which objective had obviously been attained, but, for some reason, the victory seemed, if not empty, at least incomplete. Obviously I had no interest in the slave herself, in the slave as a slave. She was nothing. But might not pride be involved? Would Tyrtaios, or Lord Okimoto, or others, believe I had truly captured the quarry? Why should they believe me? Would they believe me? There was a simple way, of course, to convince them of my veracity.

"Forget her," said Axel. "Put her from your mind."

"I was merely looking toward the river," I said.

"We must watch our opportunity," he said.

"Of course," I said.

"There is going to be trouble here," he said.

"Rorton?" I said.

"Of course," he said.

"You suspect mutiny?"

"Of course," he said. "And it would not be well for us to mix in such matters. We could easily be slain by either side. We must take our leave as soon as possible."

"Genserich must be aware of the danger," I said.

"He could kill Rorton, but who else?" asked Axel. "And to strike at Rorton might well ignite the mutiny. This would not be wise to do without the advantage of numbers, and the numbers, I gather, are not clear."

"True," I said.

"Genserich is clever," said Axel. "He is breaking camp, and thus reaffirming his authority, while on the outlook for dissent. Too, on the trek, men strung out along the trail, it is difficult to conspire."

I looked across the camp.

"Conspiring may already be afoot," I said.

"Packs are being arranged," said Axel.

"Where are our weapons?" I asked.

"I have looked about," he said. "I have been unable to locate them in the camp. I suspect, thus, they are concealed outside the camp, to be retrieved when we depart."

"Donna is watering the slaves," I said.

"Please, Mistress," begged Tuza, "food!"

"That is up to the masters," said Donna.

"It would be well for the slaves to be fed," said Axel, "lest they lag on the trail, or faint."

"There is always the whip," I said.

"Even so," he said.

I looked about the camp. Some men were attending to the site. Boughs which had formed bedding were discarded. The fire was being covered with care. Some leaves and branches were being scattered about. There would be little evidence, particularly to an untrained eye, that men had camped here. Elsewhere, bundles were being closed and corded, which would presumably be borne by slaves.

"Dear guests," said Aeson, approaching us, carrying two small, black, metal pails. "We will soon march. We would the slaves were fed."

"We are free men," said Axel, sharply.

"So are we," said Aeson, evenly.

"Masters often feed slaves," I said. "It is one of the pleasures of the mastery, and helps the slaves, as other animals, to be clearly aware of their dependence on the master, even for their food."

I took the two small pails from Aeson, and handed one to Axel. Aeson then turned away.

"Why did you do this?" asked Axel.

"I think it is a test," I said. "Are we to be troublesome, or accommodating?"

"I see," said Axel. "They will be less on their guard."

"One might hope so," I said. To be sure, I was not optimistic in the matter. Besides, I thought it might be useful, in a way, to assay the responses of a slave. Also, I thought it might be interesting, to have her before me, obedient, kneeling, in her collar. Certainly she was a long way, now, from the aisle of a large emporium on a far world, in her strange garments, where she had not even had enough sense to kneel.

"You feed the four, not yet collared," I said. "I will feed the others."

"I thought so," said Axel.

I supposed his remark was motivated by the fact that it would take longer to feed four than three, particularly when the four had their hands tied behind their back. Thus they might try to get their face into the pail, as might a tarsk, or, more likely, given the size of the pail, be fed by hand, a cupped-hand of slave pellets being poured into the up-turned mouths. What other consideration might have motivated Axel's remark, to the effect that he had anticipated this division of the task?

Tula, Mila, and the other slave, here called Vulo, were kneeling, waiting. Doubtless they, too, as the other slaves, were hungry. One of them did not look too pleased. This pleased me. Let her try now, if she would, to avoid me. Here she was called Vulo. It was my understanding that she had been given the name 'Laura', either in Tarncamp or Shipcamp, presumably Tarncamp, perhaps named for the town on the Laurius, to the south, though, as I also understood it, that was a familiar barbarian female name, which might be bestowed on any barbarian slave, or, even, if one wished, on any slave, even a Gorean slave, if one wished to let her know how meaningless and unimportant she was. In any event, the name 'Laura' had been given to the barbarian, and it was the only name she had, a name given her at the pleasure of masters, a slave name.

"May I feed myself?" inquired Tula.

"Certainly," I said.

"Thank you, Master," she said, and dipped her two hands into the small pail.

"May I feed myself?" inquired Mila.

"Yes," I said.

"Thank you, Master," she said, and, putting two hands into the pail, carefully drew out two handfuls of the pellets.

I did not doubt but what the slaves were hungry.

"May I feed myself?" inquired she called Vulo, acidly.

I looked down upon her, kneeling before me, she looking up,

in the slight tunic, and collar, and she knew herself scrutinized, as a slave is scrutinized.

"May I feed myself?" she repeated, as before.

"No," I said.

Tula and Mila gasped, and then smiled, feeding.

"Shall I cast a handful of pellets on the ground for you," I asked, "and then you may, head down, not using your hands, feed?"

"Please do not," she said.

"Perhaps you would prefer to be fed by hand?" I asked.

"I am very hungry," she said.

"Would you prefer to be fed by hand?" I asked.

"Yes!" she said, shortly.

"You may then beg," I said.

"I beg to be fed by hand," she said.

I then, a pellet at a time, fed her, she reaching, delicately, to obtain the pellet.

"Keep your hands on your thighs," I cautioned her.

"Yes, Master," she said.

"I do seem to recall you," I said, "now that I think of it, from an emporium, faraway."

"I thought Master might," she said. "May I have more?"

"Yes," I said.

"But then," I said, "you were not kneeling, in a slave tunic, and collar."

"Please, Master," she said.

"I like you better as you are now," I said.

"Please, Master," she said.

I fed her, one after the other, two more pellets.

I then put a few in the palm of my hand, and let her take them from my palm. The pellets were dry, but her mouth and lips, and tongue and teeth, moving and nibbling, were moist. It was an interesting combination of sensations. Her head was down, over my palm. Her hair fell about her shoulders. It is no wonder that slaves are sometimes fed by hand. There are many subtle pleasures associated with the mastery.

"Kneel back," I said.

She did so.

"I am still hungry," she said.

"You have had enough," I said.

"Please," she said.

"We must be careful of your figure," I said.

"Please," she said.

"No," I said.

"As Master wills," she said.

I then addressed myself to the other two slaves. "Be about the business of the camp," I said.

"Yes, Master," they said, and rose up and departed, leaving me alone with the other slave. Both seemed pleased, for some reason. Tula went off to the vicinity of Aeson, and Mila somehow found herself in the proximity of Genak.

"Who owns you?" I asked.

"Surely Master knows," she said.

"Your collar is unmarked," I said.

"I am a camp slave," she said, "owned by the Pani."

"You were a fool to run away," I said. "Why did you run away?"

"It seems," she said, "because I am a fool."

"You have been a nuisance," I said.

"Forgive me," she said, "for any inconvenience I may have caused Master."

"You are a mediocre slave," I said.

"Not every man finds me so," she said.

"Ordinary, quite average," I said.

"I suspect Master did not always find me so. If I am not mistaken, I owe my presence on this world, and my collar, to Master."

"So do many others," I said. "And many better."

"It was my knees which were forced apart by Master Genserich or Master Aeson," she said.

"You do not know by which one?" I asked.

"No," she said, "I kept my head down. I am a slave."

"I trust you understand that," I said.

"It has been well taught to me," she said.

"The other slaves' knees were not forced apart?" I said.

"No," she said.

"I gather you find that noteworthy," I said.

"Perhaps," she said.

"Are you a vain slave?" I asked.

"Are not all slaves vain?" she asked.

I supposed that was true, for they were women. And why should women not be vain, as they are so precious, desirable, and beautiful? How can men not lust for them, and make them slaves? What pallid, inert fool would not wish to own one? Whose blood would be so weak that he would not see them as the natural property of men? And what woman was more entitled to her vanity than the female slave, the female of females, selected by connoisseurs for the block? It was no wonder free women hated her so. Was her very presence not a reproach to less attractive women? Was not the collar itself a badge of her quality, the brand seared into her thigh an indelible certification of her desirability? Does her very presence not say, "I have been found exciting, attractive, desirable, and beautiful, so much so that men will have me in a collar"?

"Are you a saucy slave?" I asked.

"No, Master," she said.

"A whip can quickly take that out of a slave," I said.

"Yes, Master," she said.

My hand moved to the disrobing loop on her tunic. A jerk would drop it to her thighs, and, should she stand, it would be about her ankles. Girls are taught to step gracefully from such a tunic. I did not doubt but what she would do so, as well. It might be interesting to see.

"Do not strip me," she said.

"Why not?" I asked.

"You do not own me," she said.

"You might look well without your tunic," I said.

"You do not own me," she said.

"You are a camp slave," I said, "and I am of the camp. It may be done with you as I please."

Surely she had seen girls on the dock hooted at, seized, and caressed as workers pleased, and, often enough, as a joke, stripped on the boards. Some rushed away in tears, but others posed provocatively, and then fled away, laughing. The public taking of a slave had been forbidden by the Pani. There were slave houses for such things. If paga was prohibited on the dock, for fear it might compromise or slow work, it was not surprising that the "ka-la-na" of the collar girl should be prohibited, as well.

"We are not in the camp," she said.

"It does not matter," I said.

"Please do not strip me," she said. "Have you not done enough? I am before you on my knees!"

"Where you belong," I said.

"You have made me beg to eat from your hand as a slave."

"As the slave you are," I said.

"Yes," she said, "as the slave I am!"

"You understand you are a slave?"

"Yes, Master."

"Have you any doubts on the matter?"

"No, Master."

"Are you modest?" I asked.

"A slave girl is not permitted modesty," she said.

"So, are you modest?" I said.

"No!" she said. "But please do not strip me."

"Very well," I said.

She seemed startled, and then angry, furious. I smiled, and turned away, to return the pail, and the remaining pellets, to Aeson.

"I hate you!" she called after me.

Bundles were laid in a line, and ready to be distributed. I noted there were seven.

The hands of the former Panther Girls had been unbound, but they remained kneeling, on the neck rope.

Perhaps they envied the other slaves their tunics. I considered removing the tunic from one of the other slaves. That can be useful as a discipline. But, too, not removing a slave's tunic, when she expects to be stripped and boldly surveyed, perhaps for the pleasure of a master or to conjecture a likely block price, can be disconcerting, even dismaying, if not insulting, to a slave. Is she not worth regarding? Is she of so little interest?

"Please approach," called Genserich to me, from across the camp.

In the hands of Genak, who stood beside him, with some others, there were two lengths of cord. Axel was with them.

"Do not resist," said Genserich to Axel. "The sleen might be agitated."

Axel's hands were tied behind his back.

411

I submitted, similarly, and Genak, with the second length of cord, was tying my hands behind me. A rope was then put on our necks, to keep us together.

The sleen gave no more thought to this than to other events in the camp. I was confident, however, that if Axel had cried out, or fought, the sleen, perhaps startled or confused, might have become active, presumably to the end of its own destruction and, most likely, that of some others.

"Please, forgive us, noble guests," said Genserich, "but we would not wish to risk losing you in the forest. I am sure you understand."

"Quite," said Axel.

"Be ready," called Aeson to those about. "We depart shortly."

I saw one of Genserich's men approach, from outside the camp. He bore two light hunting spears, and two belts, with swords and daggers, presumably those of Axel and myself.

"Get away from me," I said, suddenly, angrily.

She was near to me, too near.

I had not commanded this.

"Ah," she said, sympathetically, "poor Master is helpless, as helpless as a slave."

I tried to tear apart my wrists, but the several twists of the cord only ground the more deeply into my wrists.

"And he is on a neck rope," she said.

How close she was to me!

"Away!" I told her.

"Do not be afraid, noble Master," she purred. "The proximity of a lowly, mediocre kajira, an ordinary, average kajira, a meaningless collar girl, one of no interest to you, will be without effect; doubtless it will not even be noticed."

I did not speak.

Her head was lifted to mine. She brushed back her hair, behind her shoulders. I supposed they teach them that.

I feared her lips, those soft lips, those of a female slave, a property girl, goods which exist for the pleasure of men, might touch my face.

There was little I could do, bound as I was, should this take place, save perhaps cry out with rage.

But they did not, but were less than a hort away.

"Fortunately I am of no interest to handsome Master," she said. "Otherwise he might find my presence disturbing."

"Away," I said.

"Am I too close to Master?" she asked. "I trust not."

I did not respond to her.

"There is nothing to fear," she said. "I am less than nothing, only a lowly, unimportant kajira."

"Beware," I said.

"Surely I must kneel to beg forgiveness," she said, and she swiftly knelt. "Behold," she said, "I am at your feet. I kneel. I humbly press my lips to your feet. I humbly press my lips to your calf. I cling to your leg. I beg forgiveness for being of no interest to Master. I kiss and lick your thigh, hoping that you will forgive my mediocrity, my ordinariness, my lack of interest."

"Away!" I cried. She might have melted a stone. I would have fought a hundred men to get a chain on her. What I would have given to have her leaping, frightened, to the snap of my whip.

She sprang up, backed away, and laughed. "You did not expect this," she said, "long ago, in a great store, on a far world! But I am now collared. I have learned much. Be miserable, mighty Master! I am Mistress! I am kajira!"

"She-urt, she-tarsk!" I said.

"But not your she-urt or she-tarsk!" she laughed.

I struggled with the cords on my wrists.

"Clearly," she laughed, backing away another step, "Master finds a slave of interest!"

"No!" I cried, in fury.

"Do you think a slave does not know when a master finds her of interest?" she said.

"I would that I had you in my collar!" I said.

"But you do not," she said.

"I would treat you as you deserve, and then cast you into the markets!"

"How fortunate for me," she said, "that I do not belong to Master."

She then spun about, laughing merrily, and hurried away.

Tula and Mila, to one side, watched her, frightened.

"That slave," said Axel, looking after her, "is a bold slave."

"Too bold," I said.

"It is easy to be bold with a fellow who is helpless," he said.

"Too easy," I said.

"As I recall," he said, "you regarded her as inferior, and of little interest."

"And I do so regard her now," I said.

"You did admit, as I recall," he said, "that she might be of some interest, to some men."

"I suppose so," I said.

"But not to you?"

"No," I said.

"I watched," remarked Genserich, who was nearby.

"Why did you not interfere?" I asked.

"I thought she might do well as a torture slave," he said. "It could make a difference in her price."

A torture slave, as is well known, is a slave trained to arouse, humiliate, frustrate, and then deny a male prisoner. Some captains, commanders, Ubars, and such, utilize the services of such a slave, usually for the pleasure of witnessing the discomfiture and misery of some hated enemy. Irons, knives, and cords are not the only means by which a helpless enemy may be tormented.

"But I do not think she is in her heart a torture slave," said Genserich. "Few women are, particularly when collared."

"Then she must hate our friend very much," said Axel.

"Yes," said Genserich, "or something."

I did not understand this qualification. I did find it amusing that the slave might hate me. It is pleasant to take such a woman and caress her into weeping, begging submission, and then do with her what one wishes.

Genserich turned to Aeson. "Call in the guard," he said, "align and burden the slaves, we march within the Ehn."

"Noble Genserich," said Axel, "a moment."

"Speak," said Genserich.

"About my neck," said Axel, "as is known to several, say, Aeson and Genak, and some others, hangs a small musical instrument, a whistle, which few can sound. As you are a large, strong fellow, and leader, he of most prowess we must assume, I wager that only you, of all in the camp, could sound the instrument."

"Are you mad?" said Genserich. "We must march."

414

"I wager you cannot sound the instrument," I said.

"And I that you can," said Axel.

"You are both mad," said Genserich, and he turned away.

"It would be most impressive to the men could you do so," called Axel.

But Genserich was then busied elsewhere.

"That was a rather far-fetched, and somewhat desperate, plan," I said to Axel.

"True," said Axel. "Have you a better?"

"No," I said.

"Perhaps you might recommend that I have Tiomines chew through the cords?" said Axel, unpleasantly.

"Is that practical?" I asked.

"Certainly," said Axel, "first rub the cords with tarsk grease, and then be prepared to lose at least one hand."

"You need not be disagreeable," I said.

"You are in an ill humor from the attentions of the slave," he said.

"Not I," I said.

"Your position," said Genak, "will be between the new slaves and the others."

"Rather," I said, "let it be behind all the slaves."

"Very well," said Genak.

"You wish to be behind a certain slave," said Axel, "she who is last in line."

"Yes," I said. "And let her know that I am behind her, and observe each step she takes."

"Hopefully she will bear her burden gracefully, and well," he said.

"I trust so," I said.

"And if she does not?" he said.

"That would be called to the attention of Genserich," I said, "with suitable repercussions to her pretty hide."

"Then you admit she has a pretty hide?" he said.

"It will do," I said.

"I think it is quite pretty," he said.

"It will do," I said, "for that of a slave."

"Slaves have the prettiest of hides," he said.

"At least the most visible," I said.

"I fear the question is moot," he said. "Would that we were not bound."

"What is it?" I asked.

"Look ahead," he said.

Blocking the projected exit from the camp were six men, two with leveled crossbows, quarrels waiting in the guides, like patient snakes. "Hold," said Rorton, raising his hand, palm forward.

The attackers had an original force of fifteen men. Six were before us, in a menacing posture, including Rorton. Two guards were to be recalled from the forest, and one of Genserich's men had gone to bring them in. There were only two crossbows amongst the attackers, and it seemed that both of these were at the disposal of Rorton. This left six facing six, save that the men of Genserich lacked the readiness of the guide-set quarrel, poised to be instantly flighted. I did not know the likely allegiance of the three out of the camp. I did know that there had been uneasiness amongst several of the men at the decision of Genserich to spare the former prisoners. Neither Axel nor I, bound and on our rope, would be likely to figure in any resolution of what might be in the offing.

"Stay where you are, and reach for no weapon!" said Rorton. "The first to draw a weapon or lift a spear dies."

"Put aside your weapons," said Genserich. "Take your place in line."

Rorton laughed.

"The step has been taken," whispered Axel to me, "from which there is no return."

"Let us parley," said Genserich.

"Lay down your weapons," said Rorton.

"To die in our place?" asked Genserich.

Men looked at one another, tensely.

"We are six, you are six," said Genserich.

"Three others will join us," said Rorton. "They are with me."

"That I would hear from their own mouths," said Genserich.

"Put aside your weapons," said Rorton.

"Men do not choose doom lightly," said Genserich. "Your quarrels may find two, but then it is four to six. Those are not terrible odds, when the alternative is sure death. How many will die on each side?"

"None need die," said Rorton. "Set aside your weapons."

"Set aside yours," suggested Genserich. "Then this matter has not occurred."

The fellows with Rorton looked uneasily to one another.

"It has occurred," said Rorton.

"What do you want?" asked Genserich.

"Seven slaves, and the gold," said Rorton.

"Be with us and you will have your share, both of the selling price for the slaves, and your share of the gold," said Genserich.

"Who would not prefer it all?" he asked.

"Who, indeed?" said Genserich.

"I will be first," said Rorton.

"Let us do contest," said Genserich.

"Do contest!" suggested one of Rorton's men.

"Do contest!" called Aeson.

"We are men," said Rorton, "neither sleen, nor panthers."

"In such a way, only one dies," said Genserich.

"Do not draw your weapon!" said Rorton.

"I draw it," said Genserich, and very slowly eased the blade from its sheath. Neither bowman loosed his quarrel.

"I am not your match," said Rorton.

"Then take your place in line," said Genserich.

"No!" cried Rorton wildly, and whipped out his blade.

At that moment there came from our right a plunging through brush and leaves.

One of Genserich's guards broke into the camp, and with him was the other guard, and the fellow sent out to call them in.

"Larl, larl!" cried the man.

"Do not be foolish!" said Genserich. "There are no larls within a thousand pasangs of the forests. It is far beyond their range."

Axel and I exchanged startled, elated glances.

"I saw it!" said the fellow who had gone out for the guards.

"I, too!" cried the second guard.

"It is approaching!" cried the first guard.

"It is a large panther," said Genserich.

At that moment, to the right, high above the brush, higher

than the blade of a war spear, we saw a broad, wide, triangular-shaped head.

Two men cried out with misery. Slaves screamed in terror.

"Do not attack it!" I cried. "It is a domestic beast! There are men with it!"

"Two, three hundred!" called out Axel, in an authoritative voice.

"Cut us loose," I said, "now, if you would live. We may be able to save your lives."

"We are officers from the camp of the great ship, of which you have heard," said Axel, taking some liberties with the truth. "You are intruders, you are caught, trapped! A hundred bows are drawn, a hundred shafts set to the string. Cast down your weapons, free us, immediately, if you would live."

At this point, the larl crouched at the edge of the camp. It was a gigantic creature. Even crouching its head was as high as that of a tall man.

The hair on the back of the neck of Tiomines began to bristle. His ears flattened back. He began to growl. "Steady, friend," said Axel, as his hands were being freed.

I did see one or two men with the beast, behind it, in mariner's caps. Too, I saw a helmet. That pleased me. In this situation it was better to know the spear than the sea.

The larl, as it was a bred beast, was larger than the usual wild larl to the south. It may have weighed as much as a dozen panthers, three forest bosk.

This sort of thing is common with bred animals, where the largest and the fiercest, and the most dangerous, may be bred, again and again, increment by increment, with the largest, the fiercest, and most dangerous. The same is true of domestic sleen. The wild sleen is agile and dangerous, but it is seldom a match for the bred sleen.

My hands were being freed.

Aeson freed us of the neck rope.

"My weapons!" I demanded.

They were hurried to me.

I saw Axel cinching his belt about his waist. He then accepted his hunting spear, handed to him by Genak.

"How did they find us?" asked Aeson.

"We summoned them," I said, "yesterday evening. You, Genak, Axel, and I, with the whistle."

"It made no sound," said Aeson.

"None we could hear," I said, "but one easily detected by many animals, by the panther, the larl, the sleen. Did you not note the reaction of Tiomines?"

"I did," said Genak, wryly.

"I do not care to repeat myself," said Axel. "You are surrounded. There are more than two hundred men about. Must the larl be loosed amongst you, scattering bodies and blood as far as the river? Must a hundred, two hundred shafts, leap from the forest, seeking hearts? Look. I lift my hand. When I lower it, a wind of death will spring from the forest, a raging blast of feathered death. You will all be dead in an Ihn. Cast away your weapons and kneel!" Axel's lifted hand trembled, and his eyes glittered with a fierce, feral blaze. I thought he was doing quite well. I was about ready to cast away my own weapons. Asperiche, I thought, would have been proud of him. I must beat Asperiche, I thought. She has obviously been too free with her smiles.

"See?" I said. "He is only too ready to lower his hand! In the name of the Priest-Kings, if no other, save yourselves!"

Genserich looked about, wildly. Clearly it was difficult to see into the shadows of the forest, which were well nigh impenetrable.

For all he knew, an indefinite number of bowmen might be concealed in the shadows, and greenery.

Too, there was the larl.

"I urge you," I cried. "Your position is hopeless!"

"I will lower my hand!" cried Axel. "I am eager to do so!"

"Wait!" I said, doing as well as I could, but with little hope of outdoing Axel. "Do not act now! You know the fever to which you are subject. The blood lust is upon you!"

"It is not!" cried Axel, wildly, with an excellent imitation of a fellow on whom might rest the flames of blood lust.

"We were treated as guests!" I cried.

"But not well treated," he said.

"Show them mercy!" I cried.

"They deserve none!" he said.

"Wait!" I said.

"No!" he said.

"Please!" I said.

"I will count three," said Axel, eyes blazing. "One! Two!"

"Cast away your weapons, kneel!" commanded Genserich.

His voice, and the authority it bore, brooked no insubordination. Even Rorton, and his cohorts, obeyed.

"On your bellies, facing the river, your hands crossed behind you!" said Axel. Then he turned to the forest. "A few of you come forth to secure the prisoners; the rest of you remain where you are, bows drawn. Fire at the first indication of the least resistance."

Shortly thereafter the band of Genserich was helplessly trussed, hand and foot.

"You may sit up," said Axel, affably.

"Where are the others?" demanded Genserich.

"What others?" asked Axel.

"The hundred, the two hundred others," said Genserich.

"I may have miscounted," said Axel.

"One hundred, two hundred!" said Genserich.

"I did not know for sure," said Axel. "It was an estimate."

"There are no more than twenty here," said Genserich.

"I count seventeen," said Axel. "Still you are outnumbered."

"We are finished," said Rorton to Genserich. "You were tricked. You are a fool!"

"We mean you no harm," I said.

"Do not be sure of that," said Axel.

"The beast heard you yesterday evening," said the leader of the newcomers, who was the second in command, it seems, of one of the coastal ships, of the sort which had brought men to Tarncamp earlier. In his group, counting himself as one, there were ten mariners, and five mercenaries. The larl had been turned over to them by Pani, with two trainers, who had accompanied them. It may be recalled that this arrangement had been put in place by either Tyrtaios, or Lord Okimoto, to support Axel, and take action, if he were fortunate enough to make contact with the Panther Women. "We followed the beast," he said, "but it was slow going in the night, and we did not anticipate fifteen men here. We expected a small group of Panther Girls, and perhaps one or two mercenaries."

"That was what Tyrtaios anticipated," said Axel. "He did not expect a sizable party of armed men."

"The larl must be returned," said one of the two trainers. "It has done its work."

I was sure I knew why there was concern to return the larl. The great ship would soon begin its journey to the sea. There was housing for such beasts within its great hulk.

"Dally a bit," said Axel. "We may have need of it here."

"What for?" asked the trainer.

Axel gestured to the prisoners, "Why, to feed, of course," he said.

"No!" cried Donna. "No!"

"Do not fear," said Axel. "You are a slave. You will not be eaten unless perhaps you are displeasing in some way."

She would know that, of course. Accordingly her concern was not on her own behalf, but on behalf of another.

"Wretched Genserich!" snarled Rorton. "It is you who have brought us to this!"

"Stop her!" cried Axel, and Donna had scarcely reached the edge of the camp, her scarlet tunic bright against the green, when she was seized.

"Bind her, hand and foot," said Axel, "and throw her here." He indicated a place at the feet of Genserich. "It is where she belongs," he said.

Soon she lay at her master's feet, as helplessly trussed as he. "Forgive me, Master," she said, "I have failed you."

"Serve your new master well," he said.

She wept, her tears falling into the dirt.

"Did you hear me, worthless slut?" he said.

"Yes, Master," she wept. "I must serve him well. I am a slave."

"I am first here," said Axel to the mariner who was leader of the newcomers. "It is yours to abet me, and act in my support."

"How is it that you are first?" asked the mariner.

"I am a high officer amongst remote forces," said Axel. I could see why Asperiche might be taken with the fellow.

"I thought you were a sleen master, put out to locate spies for us," said the mariner.

"Do you think such a weighty task would be entrusted to one who was not a high officer?" inquired Axel.

"I would have supposed so," said the mariner.

"It was not," said Axel. "You may address me as 'Captain'."

"Yes, Captain," said the mariner.

"You have been paid, I take it," said Axel.

"Yes," said the mariner.

"But not enough," said Axel.

"Oh?" said the mariner, interested.

"You see those four slaves," said Axel, "those on the neck rope, who have not yet earned tunics?" Here he indicated Darla, Tuza, Emerald, and Hiza.

"Yes," said the mariner. "Two are passable."

"Those four were the spies," said Axel, "once Panther Girls."

"We were to capture them," said the mariner.

"Others have saved us the trouble," said Axel, indicating Genserich and his band, clustered about, bound and helpless.

"They are ours!" said Genserich.

"You are ours," said Axel, "and so what was yours is now ours."

"Sleen!" said Genserich.

"What is to be done with them?" asked the mariner.

"They are to be slain!" said Rorton, struggling.

"We give them to you as a bonus," said Axel, generously.

"My thanks, Captain," said the mariner.

"Kill them!" cried Rorton.

"Dead slaves are worthless," said a fellow.

"What is your home port?" inquired Axel.

"Brundisium," said the mariner.

"I supposed so," said Axel. "Good. I suppose you have marking irons, and collars, on your vessel."

"Of course," said the mariner. "In our business, we commonly pass selling poles."

"How long will it take you to reach Brundisium?" asked Axel.

"We are days from the coast here," said the mariner, "and then, once we reach the coast, and are under sail, depending on the winds, it will be ten to fifteen days."

"Excellent," said Axel.

"Why, excellent?" asked the mariner.

"It will give you time to deck train the new slaves," said Axel, "helping them to understand, and well, the nature of their new lives."

"That is true," said the mariner.

Also, of course, within this interval, the great ship would presumably be abroad on Thassa, and any intelligence borne by the slaves would be outdated, irrelevant, and useless, even should they dare to impart it.

"What of the other slaves?" asked the mariner.

"Do not be greedy," said Axel.

"What of the larl?" asked one of the two trainers. "Some haste is involved in these matters."

"There are fifteen prisoners here," said Axel. "Doubtless they should be stripped, if they are to be eaten."

"Not at all," said one of the trainers. "Organ meat is of most interest, and clothing may be torn through."

"Too, removing the garmenture of the prisoners would take time," I pointed out.

"Let us feed them one at a time to the larl, say, one each day," said Axel.

"One each day!" said the trainer, in exasperation.

"Who shall be first?" asked Axel.

"What of this fellow?" I said, indicating Rorton.

"Urt!" cried Rorton.

"An excellent choice," said Axel.

"Matters press," said one of the trainers. "We have no time for this. They are helpless. Cut their throats, and cast them in the river. I wish you well!" He then, with his fellow, turned about, and uttered something to the larl, which suddenly, even eagerly, bounded away, taking its way east, along the river. The two trainers then followed its track. The larl moves swiftly, and, like the sleen, has excellent night vision. I had no doubt it had received permission to return to its housing. No longer was it slowed by stumbling men, as it had apparently been the preceding night.

"I am pleased the beast is gone," said the leader of the mariners. "It is a fearful thing to be in its vicinity. I long for the deck of the ship."

I nodded. So, too, I thought might a tabuk be uneasy in the company of a panther, a verr at the side of a sleen. I had no doubt the larl was well trained, but it had two trainers, not one, surely for some reason, and I knew that the training of such beasts might suddenly snap, unexpectedly vanish, and be as naught. The seemingly most placid, and tame, of such beasts carries within its pelt, and surely not far beneath the fur, the ancient blood and antique heritage of Gor's most fearsome land predator.

"What is to be done with the prisoners?" inquired the mariner.

Axel whipped out his knife.

"Please, no, Master!" wept Donna, twisting in her bonds.

"Be silent!" said Genserich. "Do not plead! Do not shame me! This is a matter amongst men. You are to the side, as a stone, a beast."

"Forgive me, Master!" she said.

"There are fifteen," said the mariner. "Do you wish us to participate?"

"No," said Axel. "What I have to do will take little time."

"True," said the mariner. "Fifteen throats may be cut within a single Ehn."

"Marshal your men for withdrawal," said Axel. "Take what you want of their weapons and goods, and cast the rest at the river's shore."

The mariners and their five mercenaries rummaged through the packs, and relieved the bound prisoners of their wallets and whatever paraphernalia they deemed worth gathering in.

"Strange," said the mariners, "the leader's pouch is the least heavy."

"That is interesting," said Axel.

A few javelins, and blades, harnessing, goods, and such, apparently of little interest, were removed from the camp, and, following Axel's instructions, left by the shore of the river, in the mud, some one hundred paces away.

"I wish you well," said the leader of the mariners.

"And I, you," said Axel.

We then watched the leader of the mariners, with his men, and attending mercenaries, and four neck-roped slaves, leave the camp.

We did hear the crack of a strap, and a cry of pain, from the darkness of the forest. We did not know who was struck. On the trip to the coast I supposed, sooner or later, each of the slaves would become familiar with its admonitions. It is helpful in teaching a woman that she is a slave. I was confident that long before they could reach a sales block in Brundisium the matter of the great ship would be resolved in one way or another. An armed force, I had gathered, waited at the mouth of the Alexandra, to prevent the great ship from reaching the sea.

"We must finish our business here," said Axel, lifting his dagger, catching the early afternoon sun on the blade.

Donna wept in her bonds, at the feet of Genserich.

"Be done with it quickly," said Genserich.

"Who will be first?" inquired Axel, surveying the prisoners.

"I," said Genserich. "I am first here."

"Why not this fellow?" I asked, indicating Rorton.

"No!" he said. "Genserich is first."

"I thought you wished to be first," I said.

"Genserich is first," he said.

"Very well," said Axel, and he bent to Genserich, and Donna shrieked in misery.

With a few swift strokes, he cut Genserich's bonds away.

"Master!" cried Donna.

"What are you doing?" said Genserich.

"Cutting your throat," said Axel, "but I missed. I am apparently little better at this than estimating arrayed forces in the field."

"I do not understand," said Genserich, struggling uncertainly to his feet.

"You might have killed us, but did not," said Axel. "Now we might have killed you, but do not. Some weapons, and goods, are at the river shore. They should be enough to get you somewhere. Free your men, but do not fetch your things yet. We wish to be first away. Surely you understand."

"Indeed," said Genserich.

I glanced across the emptied camp at the three slaves. Seeing themselves observed by a free man they knelt, immediately. Tula and Mila seemed beside themselves with relief. Did Tula's eyes seek out Aeson amongst the prisoners; and was Genak the possible object of Mila's bright regard? The other slave, in contrast, seemed alarmed. I regarded her with a grim satisfaction, and she trembled in her place. How attractive, and helpless, are women on their knees, where they belong. I was well pleased that there were two sexes in my species, and that they were so different.

"I took the liberty, earlier," said Axel to Genserich, "of emptying your purse." He then handed Genserich a small but weighty sack of coin. "Do not fear," he said. "Our friends from the coast have done well enough here, in both coin and weaponry. Too, they have acquired four slaves, at least two of whom should do well off the block. Accordingly I retained your fee from the Laurius and the original fee gold dispensed to four women who no longer have need of it, and, as slaves, may now own nothing, not even a collar on their necks or a copper tarskbit."

"My thanks," said Genserich.

"Free us!" demanded Rorton, struggling.

"I was dispatched," said Axel, "to reclaim a slave, but there are two others in this camp, whom I now declare unclaimed."

Whereas cities have laws, and most castes have caste codes, there is only one law which is generally respected, and held in common, amongst Gorean municipalities, and that is Merchant Law, largely established and codified at the great Sardar Fairs. According to Merchant law an unclaimed slave, one legally subject to claimancy, may be claimed, and then is the property of the claimant.

Axel went to the kneeling Tula and Mila, seized them by the hair, and pulled them to the prisoners. There he flung Tula down before Aeson, and Mila before Genak.

"I claim her!" cried Aeson.

"Master!" said Tula, kneeling with her head to the dirt before him.

"I claim her!" said Genak.

"You are my master!" cried Mila, kneeling before him, her head to the ground.

Axel then turned to me. "As you know," said Axel, "time presses and a rendezvous is imminent."

I recalled the departure of the larl and its two trainers.

"I will gather our gear," I said.

"To me, Tiomines!" said Axel, sharply, and the large, low, sinuous beast, with a growl and a turn of its long spine, was at his side.

"Free us, free us now!" cried Rorton.

Genserich looked to Axel.

"You may free your men," said Axel, "but keep them from the shore until we are clear of the camp."

"I understand," said Genserich.

He then unbound his lieutenant, Aeson, and Genak, as well, which two then turned to others, who, in their turn, set themselves to free others. I saw Rorton freed. He sprang up, and glanced to the shore. Genserich, to my annoyance, bent to Donna. "Oh, no, please, Master!" she protested. "I am a slave. There are free men to be freed." But he, nonetheless, bending down, freed the slave, who, dismayed, but laughing, wept with happiness. Then she was at his feet, covering them with kisses. At least she, I thought, understood the protocols in such a situation. Genserich seemed a good commander. Surely he could not be such a fool as to care for a slave. Still, she looked well in her collar. But then what woman does not? Too, of course, his men were being freed, so he need not concern himself further with that matter, and perhaps he did not trust another to unbind his slave. After all, she was beautiful, and she would be unable, as any slave, to resist any handling or caressing to which she might be subjected. Men are often proprietary where a slave is concerned; after all, they own her. To be sure, there was also an implicit lesson in this, a common Gorean lesson, that whether the slave is bound or free, chained or not chained, fed or not fed, beaten or not beaten, is not up to her but to her master, for she is his belonging.

I regarded Axel.

"You will be taking the barbarian back with you," I said.

"Of course," he said.

"I will bind and leash her," I said, "and we will be on our way."

"Where is Rorton?" he asked.

"I do not know," I said, looking about.

"Beware!" screamed Axel.

Genserich spun about, startled, twisting to the side, Donna screaming, and the blade of the flung javelin, a flash of steel, tore through the collar of his tunic, leaving a tatter of cloth and a line of blood between his neck and shoulder, and lodged twenty paces beyond, quivering in a small Tur tree at the camp's edge.

"Kill!" cried Axel to Tiomines, pointing toward Rorton. "No!"

Rorton cried, and turned about, slipping, to run. Rorton had run no more than five steps before the weight of Tiomines struck against him and sent him rolling down the slope toward the shore. In an instant the sleen was on him, biting, and feeding.

Slaves screamed.

"Call him off!" I cried to Axel.

The sleen was dragging the body about, and shaking it, which, I gather, opens, tears, and loosens meat. In its eagerness, by the shore, its fur was covered by mud. Twice it was half in the water. Rorton's head hung by skin to a part of the body.

"Call him back!" I said to Axel.

"No," said Axel. "It is in its frenzy. It will not hear. It will not respond. Do not approach it, lest you, too, be seized and torn."

"Is it always like this?" I asked.

"No," he said. "Sometimes there is a simple bite through the back of the neck, and then the feeding. Do not interfere with the feeding. The tamest of sleen are extremely dangerous when feeding."

"Have you seen this before?" I asked.

"Once," he said.

"It is ugly," I said.

"Sometimes it is less so," he said. "It is never pretty. It is a long time since Tiomines had a kill."

"How long will he be like this?" I asked.

"Until his hunger is satisfied," said Axel.

The sounds of the sleen's growling, and feeding, though at the shore, carried to the camp.

"Winter is coming," said Axel. "There will be ice in the river. You are aware of the urgency. We must to Shipcamp."

"We need the sleen," I said.

"We will have him," said Axel. "The sleen is voracious. It feeds quickly."

I could see Tiomines, by the shore, lift his head, and look about. He shook his head, and blood spattered about, even into the water.

"It will not be long now," said Axel.

In a few Ehn Tiomines was ascending the slope to the camp. There seemed nothing unusual about his mien. He might have been returning from drinking at the river. Men parted, warily, to let him through. He approached Axel as usual, and, affectionately, rubbed his bloodied muzzle and fangs against Axel's thigh. "Good, lad," said Axel. The beast then, seemingly content, drew to one side, and lay down.

"We will attend to the body," said Genserich.

"What is left of it," said a man.

"Leave it for urts," said Aeson, "or cast it into the river, for eels, for river sleen." The river sleen is a small animal, seldom more than two or three feet in length, including the tail. Few weigh more than two or three stone. It is not to be confused with the common sleen, or the aquatic sleen, the sea sleen, which are large animals.

"No," said Genserich.

"Why not?" asked Aeson.

"He was of the band," said Genserich.

"Have it as you will," said a man.

"I will," said Genserich.

"Genserich is first," said Aeson.

"Is there challenge?" inquired Genak, looking about.

"No," said more than one man.

"Who is first?" asked Aeson.

"Genserich," said the men.

"We will now attend to the body," said Aeson. "Rorton was of the band."

"Your hospitality, such as it was," said Axel to Genserich, "has been acknowledged. You have been repaid with your lives. I trust that is sufficient. We have business, and cannot dally. We must away, immediately. Fetch your weapons, and supplies, and do not attempt to follow us. That would mean your death."

"I wish you well," said Genserich.

"I wish you well," said Axel to Genserich, and the others. "Tiomines," he called, slapping his thigh, and the brute shook its fur, still wet and muddy from the shore, and padded softly to his side. For its weight the sleen steps lightly. This has to do with the softness and width of the paws, like broad, velvet cushions from which knives might spring, curved knives, for anchoring prey. Axel then turned to me. "We have no time to spend here," he said. "We are much delayed. The matter is urgent. We may already be too late. We leave now."

"I shall bind and leash the barbarian," I said. I looked about. "Where is she?" I said.

"Master!" cried Tula. "She is gone!"

Chapter Forty-Four

I dared not move east along the river, for that would lead me to Shipcamp, and I feared to go west, for the intruders had gone west, toward the coast. And there might, for all I knew, be others, coming and going on those trails. Nearer the coast, too, there might be villages. I was terrified to cross the river, but I would wish to do so, sooner or later, to move south. It was already late autumn, and I was well aware of the lightness and flimsiness of the bit of rent rep-cloth I wore. Already, at night, more than once, cuddled in the leaves, I had longed for my kennel blanket. The leaves of the Tur trees had begun to turn. Once there had been a dusting of snow, the specks bright in the sunlight between the trees. I was very much afraid the weather might suddenly change. I knew there was eagerness at Shipcamp to bring the great ship to Thassa before the possibility of ice in the river. There seemed no immediate danger of that, but others knew more of such things than I. Many, I knew, thought it madness to take the great ship, or any ship, abroad on Thassa this late in the season. I had gathered it was seldom done. In such seasons Thassa grows capricious and turbulent. There is the wind, the cold, the storms, the mighty waves, the torrents of icy rain. Even coast vessels, seldom out of the sight of land, would seek their harboring before the onset of winter. I must move south. I resolved to go far enough inland to elude pursuit, and then, when sure of my escape, somehow cross the river, perhaps stealing a boat, perhaps building a raft, bound with vines, or even clinging to debris. I was wary of the water itself, as I did not know what might lie within it. I did know that the dreaded

431

river tharlarion which infest, and terrorize, the Cartius and Ua rivers did not range this far north. I must be careful not to return inadvertently to the vicinity of Shipcamp as I had before. I still did not understand how that could have come about. I did know that a small unevenness in one's pace, a tiny difference in the stride of one foot as opposed to the other, common in almost anyone, save perhaps those trained in a measured stride, such as warriors, might result in one's eventually describing a vast circle, but I did not think I had covered so many pasangs as to make that plausible. Too, what of the time of day, and the sun? And certain stars? Could one not gather one's directions from such things? How incomprehensible it all was. I remembered my terror, and dismay, when I beheld the wands marking the perimeter of Shipcamp. I had returned! How had it come about? Certainly I would not be so foolish as to repeat that mistake, however it had come about.

I looked up, through the trees. The sun was high.

Tula, Mila and I, and, I think, others, as well, even the men, had been startled when Master Axel had suddenly cried out, and Master Genserich, warned, had moved in such a way, so quickly, so suddenly, spinning about, as to avoid receiving a cast javelin in his back. As it was he was wounded only slightly, I think at the shoulder, near the neck. One of Master Genserich's own men had attacked him. Almost at the same time, Master Axel, his mien terrible, had cried out and loosed his hideous beast, setting it on the assailant. Tula, Mila, and I, and others, too, I think, had screamed with horror. It is not a pleasant thing to see. Tula had covered her eyes, and, in a moment, or two, sick, Mila and I had turned away. I had thought the sleen a domestic, well-trained beast, at least in the presence of its master or trainer, and it seemed so in the camp, and I had even stood close to it from time to time, without much fear, once even daring to touch it, but what I had beheld then was nothing which spoke of control, domesticity, restraint, or subordination. It spoke, rather, of the darkness of the forest, and the horrors which might lurk within it.

But at the same time, given the consternation about, the commotion in the camp, the attack on Master Genserich, and his narrow escape, the attack of the sleen on the assailant, and the tearing and feeding of the sleen, the attention of all, or the thought of all, on such things, I realized that the dark hand of chance had opened the door to my departure. No one would miss me, not for a time. This was my opportunity, terrible as it was, come unexpectedly. The attention of everyone was elsewhere. Even those at my side were distracted. Tula had her head down, her eyes covered; and Mila was sunk to her knees, shuddering, turned to the side.

I swiftly slipped away.

I looked back, once.

I shuddered.

Nature had designed the sleen. I did not think that even the Priest-Kings of Gor would have dared to do so.

I continued on, moving inland.

Interestingly, as I hurried away, I did not much fear being hunted again by the sleen. This had little or nothing to do with its recent kill, the interval which might be required for it to return to normality, its satiation and possible somnolence after feeding, or such, not even with the paucity of scent which might linger in the camp. Indeed, how could it be given my scent, rather than that of Tula, Mila, or others? Perhaps from a section of rope which had encircled my neck in the night, from footprints mingled with others, perhaps from trying various scents and rejecting all but one? Might it not even follow one of the slaves disappeared earlier with the intruders, on the trek to the coast? No, my confidence in this matter, though it was not an unqualified confidence, had more to do with Shipcamp.

At the time I had fled Shipcamp, I knew the great ship was being readied for its journey downriver. Indeed, I had been grateful to have been afforded the opportunity to gather Tur-Pah so close to the wands when I had, this facilitating my flight, for one of the reasons I wished to escape, and soon, was to avoid incarceration, with others, within those mighty timbers when her mooring lines were freed. What escape then for a hapless kajira helpless in such a floating, and perhaps doomed, prison?

My speculation then that I would not be pursued again by the sleen was primarily based on the likelihood of the great ship's imminent departure. The possibility of this event had seemed to loom over events here by the river. I recalled that the larl and its trainers had been anxious to leave, and had sped away at the first opportunity. Too, I was sure that Master Axel would wish to return quickly with the sleen to Shipcamp, and, happily, doubtless, too, the monstrous brute with him whom I hated with such vehemence. How dismayed I had been when the intruders had invaded the camp, allies, it seemed, of Master Axel and the brute with him, and they had been freed! I had earlier been much delighted to take my vengeance on the brute who had so ignored and scorned me, when he was bound and helpless. I had delighted myself with his tormenting. I had taunted him with a slave's body he could not possess. With what diligence and pleasure I had employed the soft arsenals at the disposal of a slave, her closeness, her breath, her smiles, her expressions, her lips, her postures, her attitudes, her words, and touch, to my advantage. I had made him suffer in my pretense of solicitude. Poor Master, indeed! Let him squirm, and sweat, and strain at his ropes! How helpless he was, and how gratified I was, to afflict him with impunity. Let him pretend I was nothing! I had made him suffer. Let him pretend, too, I was of no interest to him! I had given the lie to that, and before others, to their amusement. I was not his. He could not own me, he could not buy me! How cleverly I had subjected him to the honey of my vengeance. I had then taken my leave of him, leaving him behind me, humiliated, furious, helpless in his bonds. We were soon to trek, and I was to bear my burden. He had arranged, bound, the monster, to have himself placed behind me, and I knew then, to my great uneasiness, I would be under his constant surveillance. So I must walk before him, bearing my burden, keenly aware he was there, unable to see him, and walk as I must, as what I was, a slave. But the trek was arrested by mutiny within the band, and in the course of this mutiny, intruders from the coast had located the camp. Shortly thereafter he and Master Axel, who were apparently in some way in league with the intruders, had been freed, and I had trembled in terror. Soon I had seen his eyes, those of he whom I hated, upon me, and as those of a displeased master on a slave. Had I ever been so aware of my half-nudity and the light metal circle fastened about my neck? I knew then that I must escape as soon as possible, at any risk. With a blow he could break my neck. His strength might pull the limbs from my body. My opportunity soon occurred, unexpectedly, with the attack on Genserich and the loosing of the sleen on the ill-fated assailant.

I paused amongst the trees, listening, looking back. There was no sign of pursuit.

I continued on.

I had escaped.

Chapter Forty-Five

"No!" said Axel. "Let her go!"

"No!" I said. "She cannot be far. Use Tiomines!"

"He is not ready for another hunt," he said, "not for Ahn. Too, the kill is recent. He remembers the blood. It will be difficult to restrain him, for perhaps a day. I do not know. He would now be as likely to kill and eat the slave, as hold her for us."

"Keep him leashed!" I said.

"I cannot hold him if he rushes upon her," he said.

"We two together," I said.

"We might be unable to do so," he said. "Too, frustrated, he might turn upon us and rend us."

"I will risk it," I said.

"I will not," he said.

"Axel!" I said.

"If Tiomines were leashed," said Axel, "and all went well, she might keep ahead of us for two or more days."

"She does not have such a start," I said.

"It is not clear we could even give Tiomines a usable scent," he said. "He might follow the wrong slave."

Tula and Mila had left with Genserich's band, and Darla, Tuza, Emerald, and Hiza, were on their way to the coast.

"We could then revise the hunt," I said.

"We do not even know where to search for scent," said Axel. "We do not even know what direction she went."

"The attempt is to be made," I said.

"Do you not understand?" he said. "We must get back. Indeed, the ship may have left by now."

"Not yet," I said.

"You do not know that," he said.

"No," I said.

"It will take days to reach Shipcamp," he said. "We must leave immediately."

"The slave!" I said.

"Forget her," he said. "The forest will claim her. You left with me. Return with me. We will report on the capture of the spies."

"Go on, without me," I said.

"I do not choose to do so," he said.

"What does it matter?" I asked.

"Tyrtaios would not be pleased," he said.

"Go without me," I said.

Behold, his blade was half drawn from the sheath. I stepped back, and mine was free of its housing.

"I could set the sleen on you," he said.

"I know little of sleen," I said, "but I do not think that would be practical. We have been as fellows, for days, close to Tiomines, our scents mingled. We have both fed him. Such a command would do little more than confuse him."

"You know more of sleen than I had supposed," he said.

He thrust his partially drawn blade back in the sheath, resignedly. I then returned mine, as well, to its housing.

"I have no wish to kill you," he said.

"Nor I you," I said, "friend."

"It seems I have lost you in the forest," he said.

"Do you think Tyrtaios will believe that?" I asked.

"No," he said.

"I wish you well," I said.

"You will never find her," he said.

"For millennia, without sleen," I said, "men have trailed women, the most delectable of quarries."

"You have had some experience in this?" he said.

"It is in my caste training," I said.

"It would be better to have a sleen," he said.

"Much," I said, "but I have no sleen."

"You do find the slave attractive," he said.

I shrugged. "Somewhat," I said. "It might be interesting to see what I could get for her in a market."

"That is your only interest in her?" he asked.

"Certainly," I said.

"Fortunately for you," he said, "she is not a Panther Girl, familiar with the forest, adept at concealing her presence, and trail."

"True," I said.

"She is a barbarian," he said.

"True," I said.

"That should make things easier," he said.

"No more so than for a Gorean girl," I said, "provided she is from the cities."

"For your sake," he said, "let us hope she is as ignorant and untutored, as clumsy and naive, as inept and foolish, as lost and helpless, as easy to follow, as she is beautiful and desirable."

"You find her so," I said, "beautiful and desirable?"

"Yes," he said, "do you not?"

"Perhaps I will one day consider the matter," I said.

"I do not think you will find her," he said.

"Perhaps not," I said.

"There are better trackers than you in the forest," he said.

"Oh?" I said.

"Wild sleen, panthers," he said. "They will find her first."

I supposed that might well be true.

"I wish you well," he said. He then turned about, and strode away. Tiomines looked at me, as though puzzled, and then padded softly after him.

Chapter Forty-Six

By evening I was quite sure I was not followed.

A loose tracking sleen, if preceding its hunters, would have found me by now. I had also lingered twice to determine if a leashed sleen, in the keeping of a hunter, or hunters, might be seeking me. It seemed reasonably clear, given the intervals involved, that that was not the case. My conjectures concerning the urgency of a return to Shipcamp, the great ship poised for departure, seemed well warranted.

I found it hard to grasp my feelings.

In one sense I was muchly pleased to have escaped the camp and be, as far as I could tell, without pursuers. My original flight, disrupted by Panther Women, and fearfully terminated by the foiling arrival of a menacing hunting beast, had now been resumed. I was now successful. I was now muchly relieved. In particular, I had escaped a fearsome man, a large, impatient, powerful brute before whom I doubted I could now find the strength to stand upright, before whom I would now tremble in terror. Originally it seemed I might have been unimportant to him. I had been merely scorned and ignored, and, to my chagrin and fury, treated with contempt and indifference. But now, matters had muchly changed. Now, whereas he might continue to view me with contempt and scorn, as a worthless and meaningless slave, no longer would he be likely to ignore me, or treat me with indifference. Things were now muchly different. It was he on whom I had, in the way of a slave, well avenged myself. But then, soon after, he was no more at my mercy, helplessly roped by the strength of men. I had not anticipated that. What a transformation of fortune was there! He was then free, and armed. I had seen his eyes on me in the camp, those of a master who looks upon a slave who has been less than pleasing. He well remembered what I had done, how I had treated him, how I had humiliated him and made a fool of him. I had been profoundly alarmed. I must run! I must escape! And now I had run, and had escaped. Surely I must be overjoyed. Was I not now safe? Yet, strangely, I did not feel elated. How pleased I should be that I had escaped from the brute I hated, and now so terribly feared, but, too, strangely, and piercingly, I felt alone and incomplete, even lost, with each step, apart from him, apart from his attention, his size, power, and presence, almost as might, I supposed, a kajira separated from her master. Could it be I was somehow his, I asked myself, that I belonged to him as an object to its owner, as a slave to her master? Had I not sensed such things before, of this callous, uncompromising, dominant brute, many times? Could I return, somehow, retrace my steps, seek him out, put myself to his feet, begging forgiveness as a penitent slave? Then I cried out in fury that such thoughts could even occur to me. I hated him, hated him! Was he not the monster who had brought me to the marking iron and collar, the longed-for, ecstatic degradation of bondage, and had then dismissed me, as he must have a thousand others, processed like cattle for the girl markets of Gor? How I hated him, but even on Earth I had sensed, in the profound female of me, that I belonged in a man's collar. Then I did my best to thrust such thoughts from my mind.

How different were the men of Gor from so many of the men I had known on Earth! So many of the men of Earth had disappointed me; so many seemed pathetically devirilized, so reduced and robbed of their masculinity. Did they not know they were men? Did they think we longed for "persons," neuters, identicals, or imitation women? Were they ashamed of their blood? Did they fear it? Why did so many strive to diminish and betray themselves in order to please and satisfy those pathological ideologues who feared and hated them? What rewards, I wondered, could repay them for this reductive, stunting, biological treason? On the other hand, I had met many Gorean men, masculine, powerful, and formidable, before whom a woman knew herself as, and could be but, a slave. On Earth it was hard for a woman to be a woman. On Gor, collared, and put to her knees, she had no choice, nor wanted any. How could we be happy, if not in our place, at the feet of our masters? I hated him, yes, but I had wanted, too, to be owned by him. Even from the first time our eyes had met, on a far world, I had sensed I was appropriately a rightless belonging, and wanted to be his. I think women understand what I am saying. Perhaps so, perhaps not. Perhaps some have dreamed of the man who will look upon them, find them acceptable, and put them in his collar.

Then I struggled again to put such thoughts from me.

I was pleased. I had escaped. I was at last safe. But the forest seemed dark, lonely, and cold. How could one be safe within it, unarmed, and unprotected? I did not even know how to make a fire. Amongst those dark trees and shadows might lurk life forms, prowling and hungry. I had escaped, yes, but into what had I escaped?

Had something moved, in the darkness to my right?

I hurried on.

Suppose I managed to cross the river, and make my way south, what then? Had I then escaped, truly?

Could I escape? I was even a barbarian, who might still be betrayed by her accent, and doubtless, indefinitely, by her ignorance of any number of things, such as customs, sayings, legends, stories, histories, festivals, and heroes.

I touched the disrobing loop at my left shoulder, all that kept the tiny garment on me. I touched my collar, which I could not remove. And seared into my left thigh, just beneath the hip, was a small, lovely mark, a kef, which, to any who might gaze upon it, would show me kajira.

It is said that there is no escape for the Gorean slave girl. She is marked, collared, and distinctively garbed. There is no refuge for her, no safe haven, nowhere for her to run. Her nature, condition, and status are unquestioned in custom and institutionalized in law. Society accepts her with the same unquestioned equanimity that it accepts other domestic animals. She is a familiar, recognized, sanctioned, accepted, welcomed, desired, even treasured, component in the culture.

Certainly there is no doubt that she is an attractive and valued commodity, a vendible convenience and delight, surely a decorative and useful article of commerce. The culture and society wants its kajirae, and will have them. And the kajira herself well knows what she is, and what is expected of her, how she must behave, act, speak, and be. She has her place in society, and well understands it. It is as clear and fixed as the collar on her neck, the mark on her thigh.

How lonely it was in the forest!

Is it an escape, I wondered, to be dragged down by beasts, and eaten? Is it an escape, I wondered, if one starves, or freezes to death? Is it an escape, I wondered, if one manages to do nothing but change collars?

I no longer feared being captured by Panther Women. I now understood they seldom ranged this far to the north. Those whom I had earlier encountered were unusual, a small group bent on the business of espionage.

Too, what if I should encounter Panther Women, others, south of the river? I was not such a woman. I lacked their size, their power, their skills, their hatred, their masculinity, their ferocity. They would see me as worthless and despicable, as no more than another of the smaller, weaker, softer, more feminine women they despised, women whose wrists seemed made for slave bracelets, whose necks seemed made for the collar. Men do not hate women such as I, but Panther Women, for some reason, do. Why should that be? It is not our fault if men prefer us to women who are large, ill-tempered, cruel, belligerent, and gross, whose bodies might not interest a tharlarion. Were we the less women for our needs, our passion, our attractiveness, our beauty, our desire to love, and serve? I did not think so. Surely we had a right to exist, even though we were the sort men would buy and sell, the sort men fought to bring to the block. No, I knew enough now of Panther Women to avoid them. If I were not killed, I would be beaten for my beauty, if it were that, and then sold, if only for a sack of arrow points.

It was growing dark.

In my haste to escape the camp, I had stolen no food. Much had happened suddenly. In the confusion, I had darted away, precipitously. Who knew when such an opportunity might again present itself? Even a handful of gruel, softened in a pool, would have been more than welcome. It is not as though a girl who is not shopping can simply carry a basket or sack about with her. As is well known, the slave is a belonging, and can own nothing. She is not entitled to a free person's accouterments, say, a purse or wallet. The slave tunic, like most Gorean garments, lacks pockets. Tunics are inspected occasionally, and, if an internal pocket is discovered, or an open hem, where, say, a candy, let alone a tarsk-bit, might be concealed, the girl must expect to be punished, and, quite likely, severely. Few slaves are so stupid as to expect patience or indulgence from a master. They are, after all, slaves.

I carefully avoided a patch of leech plants.

I was wiser now in the ways of the forest.

I wondered how it had come about, once, that I had inadvertently returned to Shipcamp. That still struck me as incomprehensible. In any event I was not likely to repeat that mistake. I was wiser now in the ways of the forest.

I lay on my belly and drank from a small stream. Its current told me the direction of the Alexandra. By such simple things one may orient oneself. I was wiser now in the ways of the forest.

Too, now that I was sure I was not followed, I might look about, to assuage my hunger.

Soon, about the trunk of a tree, one of two so adorned, or afflicted, I saw, at a height I could reach, thick and coiling, a nest of Tur-Pah. I tore a length of it from the trunk about which it clung, its tiny, sharp roots anchored in the bark, and pulled away several of the heavy fleshy leaves. One would prefer Tur-Pah, certainly on a cool night, boiled in Sullage, or in some stew, or even fried, salted, and honeyed, but, too, it is often, perhaps most often, eaten raw. It is the basic ingredient in most Gorean salads.

I fed well.

I suppose a man, such gross beasts, would have wanted a great deal more, hot food, meat, and such, but I was content. Why should I not be? The fleet, graceful tabuk, for example, is not the ponderous, clumsy, lumbering, shaggy bosk, not the gigantic, tearing, voracious larl.

I now had no fear, at least at present, at least until winter, of starving in the forest. Other than Tur-Pah, I could recognize the leafage which betokened Suls, usually found in the open, in drier, sandier soils, and was familiar with a number of edible nuts and berries, such as ram berries and gim berries, the latter common at this time of year. Even the horrid sip root was edible, despite its bitterness.

I looked about.

I knew I must, even if I crossed the river, avoid villages, and certainly cities. I could not well walk into a village clearing, or through the gates of a town or city, and say, "Tal, I am a female slave. Who will put a chain on me?"

Escaped slaves I knew were commonly returned to their masters, as a courtesy, but sometimes there would be some negotiations having to do with a capture fee. My collar, of course, was a plain collar. I might then invent a master, and claim that I was attempting to return to him, not that that would keep the ropes off me. In problematical situations, escaped slaves are commonly publicly exhibited for a time, chained under a pertinent notice and then, if not claimed, auctioned, or delivered to the finder. Sometimes a slave is tortured and, in this case, she is likely to acknowledge herself the slave of anyone whom the magistrate might suggest, perhaps a relative in another village. To be sure, a slave is seldom subjected to any grievous torture, as it might lower her value. An exception is when her testimony is to be taken in a court of law. Then any slave, male or female, will be placed on the rack, the theory being that this will guarantee a veracious testimony, even from the lips of a slave. What it commonly guarantees is that the slave, howling in misery or screaming through tears, will tell the judge whatever he wishes to hear.

I stopped, suddenly, in the dusk. Something was moving, nearby. I remained perfectly still. Then I heard it no more.

I wondered if it had been with me for some time.

But perhaps I had not heard it, at all.

I was now familiar enough with the forest, of course, to realize I should seek shelter before the fall of darkness. Though both sleen and panthers hunt when hungry, they prowl most frequently in darkness.

Both the sleen and the panther can leap well over their

length, and may be found on stout branches several feet above the ground, but neither is a climbing animal, as one commonly thinks of climbing animals, probably because of their weight, which would render many branches precarious, either because of a bending, wavering instability or the possibility of breakage.

But it was not practical for me to climb in this area.

The trees about were like lofty, isolated, living columns, separated by wide corridors of leaves. They foliaged in canopies high above the ground. It had been similar, often enough, on the march from the coast to Tarncamp. This arrangement is a consequence, one supposes, of a competition for light, a contest possibly spanning centuries of seasons. Yet, as noted earlier, a forest is not uniform, and there are forests within forests. Nor is the terrain itself uniform, for there may be streams and basins, and clearings, and meadows, elevations, canyons, and depressions, brush, thickets, even jumbles of rocks, from ancient glaciers, and weathered, winter-and-ice-cracked hills of stone.

From where I stood, in the dusk, I could see a large, fallen tree, its trunk black in the light, its exposed roots extended like claws, lying athwart a low sloping outcropping of rocks. I was sure I could wedge myself between the rocks and the tree, but, upon investigating, I found, to my delight, behind the tree, something much better, an open, narrow space between two large rocks. One could enter or leave this opening at either end, and, though the opening was quite narrow, it was large enough for me to enter, and, at the same time, I was sure, too narrow to admit either a sleen or panther. How frustrated they would be, did they discover me, that they could not reach me! In time a panther would look for new game. A sleen would presumably discount my presence, unless he had been following my trail. If he had been following my trail, he would presumably, after a time, depart, allowing me, sooner or later, to leave the shelter, after which, perhaps several Ahn later, he would pick up the trail again. Such things are tenacious. Further, if foresters, or independent huntsmen, were in the vicinity, my shelter would be as invisible to them as it had been at first to me.

Chapter Forty-Seven

I was furious with the girl. Did she not know she was in a collar? Was she unaware she was marked?

Would that I had had the senses of a Tiomines.

So she had sported with me, humiliating me before Genserich and his men, even before slaves! So then I would sport with her, and she would not soon forget the sport, might I find her!

Twice she had fled!

Did she think such things might be done with impunity?

Did she think the band about her neck, lovely as it was, was no more than a free woman's decoration, a bauble to be put on and taken off? Did she not understand its nature? Did she not understand its meaning? It was a slave collar, and locked on her. Did she think the beauty mark on her thigh was only a beauty mark? It was a brand, as well, seared into her pretty skin, identifying her for all to see, as kajira.

I would have given much for the services of Tiomines, now well on his way to Shipcamp.

I had anticipated difficulty in picking up the foolish slave's trail, which might have begun anywhere, but, eventually, from stirred leaves, a dislodged stone, a broken twig, a bent branch, such things, I had expected to be able to do so. As trackers went, I was not inept, and I had had training in such matters, common for those of my caste. As yet, however, I had failed. I had followed several trails, made by light, bared feet, but none had been hers. One would follow a trail, and then, to my frustration, it would return to camp. Donna, the slave of Genserich, and the camp slaves, Tula, Mila, and even she in whom I was interested, had left trails, in gathering wood, berries, and such, which, followed, would merely return to the camp. I had not located a single trail, which clearly left the camp, and had not returned. No one, it seemed, had seen her leave the camp. I had even traversed the shore of the Alexandra, for a pasang or more, both east and west, given the possibility that she might have waded, before returning to the land. Additionally, footprints would not be as clear now as one might desire, given the drying after the rain. Wind, too, may stir leaves, as well as a small, passing foot. Meanwhile, the little fool would be moving farther and farther away.

Axel had said to forget her but I, for some reason, though she was only a slave, did not wish to do so. He had suggested that the forest would claim her. I supposed that that was the case. How calm he had been! I wondered if he would have been as indifferent if, say, an Asperiche had been at issue. To be sure, she, too, was only a slave. "The forest will claim her," he had said. Yes, I had no doubt he was right in that. Sooner or later, it seemed certain that her foolish and ill-advised flight, so pointless and futile, would be abruptly terminated, beneath the teeth and claws of a panther or sleen. I gave her no more than four or five days, if that. Sometimes a panther, if it has fed recently, will shadow a new quarry for two or three days, keeping it under surveillance, so to speak, until its hunger prompts it to feed anew.

I supposed I should return to Shipcamp, like Axel. When the great ship cast its moorings, I was to be aboard her.

Already I might be too late.

I then sat in the old camp, cross-legged. I recalled how she had looked, in the water, bathing. I recalled her about the camp, in a dozen ways, fetching water, assisting Tula, tending the fire, serving the men. How was she different from others? To be sure, she was no longer the frightened girl sold in Brundisium. She now moved well. They learn such things. I wondered if they knew the effect such small things might have on a male. I supposed so. She seemed to serve well, at least others, as the slave she was, obedient, docile, compliant, attractive, beautiful, timid, hoping to please, realizing the lash might respond to the least imperfection of service. I now knew she had been in the slave house, though I had never found her there personally, not that I had looked for her, nor that it would have mattered to me, one way or the other, if she had been there or not. You must understand I was not much interested in her. Nor was I now. Had I found her there, in the darkness, in the light of the lamp, on her chain, I doubted that I would have condescended to put her to use. Doubtless I would have passed her over, in favor of other slaves, better slaves. Yet I had little doubt but what the slave house had changed her. It does that to a woman. She would no longer be able to help herself. By now, despite any pretense she might make to indifference, or disinterest, and despite any asseverations to the contrary, there would be combustible tinder beneath that tiny, flimsy tunic, which might be ignited by a glance, or touch. We make them slaves; they soon learn to beg. I did not now think, all in all, that she was all that inferior as slave stock, at least considering that she was only barbarian collar meat. Axel, I recalled, had not despised her, not wholly. I imagined her, exhibited naked on the block, in chains, dancing to the flute and tabor, to the snap of the auctioneer's whip, her belly promising untold pleasure to the master who would buy her. No, I thought, she was not all that unattractive, not really. Perhaps, I thought, she might bring as much as two and a half. It was hard to tell. I recalled the first time I had seen her, long ago, in the aisle of the huge emporium, startled, frightened, clearly a slave but not yet collared. I recalled, with amusement, those outlandish, concealing garments she had worn.

How dared she, a slave, so conceal herself? Surely she should have been stripped and lashed! Why did those of the polluted world not assess their women, and divide them into the slave and free, and see to it that those who were slaves, and should be slaves, were dressed accordingly, as what they were, slaves? Surely that would be pleasant, to see them so distinguished. Why should they be permitted the audacity of indiscriminately mingling amongst free women? Did they not know they were slaves?

But then are not all women slaves, bred so over a thousand generations?

But I gathered she did not know at that time that she belonged in a tunic and collar, in which she would soon find herself, a Gorean slave.

I pondered, sitting alone in the camp.

As each Ahn passed I realized the chances of locating the slave before some beast of the forest were rapidly diminishing.

Why should I care?

But I did not know where to look.

A hundred men might have combed a thousand pasangs.

I was only one man, who had perhaps followed a hundred false trails.

Even had I Tiomines at my disposal it was not clear I could have given him an unambiguous scent.

There is a game, called Blind Kaissa.

It is played in the training of high officers, in Ar, in Treve, in Kasra, and Jad, even in far Turia.

It is played much like ordinary Kaissa save that there are two boards, separated by a vertical screen, precluding each player from seeing the moves of the other. An arbiter is at hand who can see both boards. It is his role to warn against illegal moves, and to announce captures, threats to the Home Stone, and such. In this manner, as neither player can see either his opponent or his opponent's moves, a premium is placed on intuition, sensitivity, reading the character and nature of the opponent, and probable conjecture. Such situations are not unprecedented in war, where one may not know the position of the enemy, the forces at his disposal, his plans, where he might strike, and so on. One gambles. On the board one may lose pieces; in the field one may lose cities.

I granted that the slave was highly intelligent. Were this not so she would not, in all likelihood, have been collared. But I also supposed she would be ignorant of woodcraft, and untutored in techniques of evasion. Not being a Panther Girl I doubted she could read signs, even something as obvious as territorial spoor markings. I would suppose her capable of little more than making a fire. Surely she would know enough to do that, as it is easy enough to construct a fire drill or find fire rocks and strike them together over dried leaves. In most camps, of course, a simple fire maker is used, which is more convenient. A free person will retain the fire maker, and the slave, who has usually arranged the materials for the fire, will tend it once it is burning. A slave is seldom permitted to handle such a device. Too, of course, she is not permitted to touch a weapon. This can be a capital offense. I supposed she would be unlikely to move east on the Alexandra for in that direction lay Shipcamp and if she moved west that would put her in the wake of the mariners and mercenaries who had surprised Genserich's camp. She would, presumably, initially, try to set a difficult trail away from the river, which one might depart from in any direction, and then, later, return to the river. She would wish to cross the river, sooner or later, and then move south, particularly given the lateness of the season.

It was a gamble, surely. How soon, and where, might she return to the river? I had no way of knowing, but there are likely moves in the game. Certainly the opponent has objectives, and is playing to win. By now, given the recency of her flight, and the likely prompt detection of her departure, she would doubtless anticipate an immediate pursuit, if one were to be made. Accordingly, if her backtrail remained empty, that would be taken to mean either that no pursuit was in progress or, more likely, that her flight had been successful. If it were not successful, presumably, given the recency of her flight, and a prompt pursuit, a tracker or trackers would be close behind her, perhaps only some Ehn away. Judicious observations at various intervals would be quite sufficient to establish that this was the case, or not the case. By now, she would be confident that it was not the case. She might then be willing, I supposed, to terminate her venturing away from her likely goal, and turn back to seek it, the river. Presumably, alone, and particularly vulnerable to the elements, she would wish to cross the river as soon as possible. How fortunate, I thought, that we give them so little to wear.

So, lacking sleen, and having no viable trail to follow, I rose up, gathered my pack and weapons, and went to the river.

Chapter Forty-Eight

I crouched in the bushes, elated.

There was a seeming movement to the side, and I glanced to my right, quickly. But it was only a rustle, and shadows, stirred by the wind in the brush. I had sensed, from time to time, I might be accompanied in the forest, but if something was there, as I supposed it was not, I did not think it was concerned with me. Certainly it had given no threatening evidence of its presence.

Through the branches I could see the broad, shimmering vista of the Alexandra before me. There were no signs of patrols from Shipcamp along the shore nor of the small sounding boats which might be testing the river or preceding the slow, stately journey of the great ship to the sea. Either the ship had not yet reached this point, perhaps still moored upriver, or had already passed. I saw no advantage in delaying my crossing, supposing that I could manage it. I must manage it, somehow. Making it sooner, rather than later, also minimized the danger of being detected by our visitors from the coast, who had so discomfited Genserich and his band, and left with four stripped, neck-roped slaves, once Panther Women. They would have already passed this point.

I had planned astutely, and had carried out my plan flawlessly. I congratulated myself on my cleverness. How clever was Margaret Alyssa Cameron! Then I lifted my hand and, with my fingers, touched my collar. How absurd was that thought! Who was this Margaret Alyssa Cameron? I was not Margaret Alyssa Cameron. She was a free woman. I was a slave. I was not she. I was Laura, so named at the pleasure of masters, a slave, like many others, of Pani Warriors. I was a slave. I knew that. It was indisputable. The former Margaret Alyssa Cameron no longer existed; she who had once been she was now Laura, merely another Gorean slave girl.

Even on Earth I had sensed myself a slave. And here there was no ambiguity about the matter. Here it was so not only in the aching, longing reality of the heart, desiring to belong to and serve a master, but in the full, implacable reality of fact, truth, and law. I was rightless goods, merchandise, a slight, collared, curvaceous beast, subject to purchase and sale, and knew myself such!

But I was no ordinary slave. I was an extraordinarily clever slave. I had escaped. I had eluded the masters.

I looked across the Alexandra.

How bright, how clever, how superior, I was! I had eluded the masters. What slave can manage that?

And they said there was no escape for the Gorean slave girl! But I had escaped! They would never recapture me! I could not be recaptured. I was too clever for them!

But what could I do, marked, tunicked, and collared, easily identifiable, female and slave, where could I go?

But the difficulty now was to manage the crossing.

I glanced to my left, and my attention was suddenly arrested, fearfully so, in a moment of terror. For an instant I could not move. Again, as I had long ago, on the first day of my escape from Shipcamp, I thought I saw a beast's head in the shadows, looking at me, a large, broad, motionless head. I had then regarded it with greater care, and found that it was no more than a misconstrued pattern in the forest, an artifact of perception, a misinterpreted mixture of brush and branches, light and shadow. It was no more than the creature of my fear.

I laughed with relief.

But then it emerged the brush, crouching, no taller than my waist. My eyes grew wide; my hand was raised before my mouth. I could not move. It was to my left, and between me and the river. Strangely it did not seem attentive to me. Rather it was looking beyond me, though, when I dared turn, I could see nothing there.

Then the beast stood up fiercely, like a threatening, pulsating mountain, broad and braced, seething, its chest expanded, its paws spread, stood up to each tiny increment of its height, lifted its large, shaggy head angrily to the afternoon sky, and roared, a terrible roar, much like those we had heard when in the camp of Genserich, but then far off, and then closer. From such a sound, even were the monster caged, I think uneasy, awed men might back away and women flee. Then from my right I heard, unmistakably, from within the brush somewhere, an answering, rumbling growl. I had occasionally sensed I might have shared the forest with some unseen companion, like a shadow amongst the trees, but I had dismissed this apprehension as, Ahn after Ahn, even following investigations, I had detected nothing. Too, if there were any warrant for my fears, why had I not, in all this time, if it were a predator, been attacked? To bring down, and feed upon, a prey such as I might be, an unarmed kajira in the forest, would pose no difficulty to any likely predator. I lacked the stealth and speed of the tabuk, the horns of the forest bosk, the tusks of the tarsk boar. But clearly, now, there was not one, but two beasts, that which had emerged from the brush of the riverside, where, suddenly disturbed, it might have been drinking, and the other, still unseen, in the brush to my right.

I remained perfectly still. I think this was less wisdom than a consequence of the fact that I found myself unable to move. I suppose I was too frightened. But, too, more consciously, I did realize, even if I felt I could move, any swift movement on my part would be likely to trigger the pursuit response common in most predators. And turning one way, away from one beast, even had I the agility and speed of the small, graceful tabuk, might have brought myself within the compass of the other. It seemed to me that my body, denying me the capacity for motion, possibly expressed a rationality deeper than one rationality itself might have recognized.

I then saw the second beast. Its mottling would have rendered it almost invisible in the lights and shadows amongst the trees, its common background. There was tall grass and brush here, however, near the river. Seemingly it had availed itself here of this natural cover. However, that might be, the grass now parted like a curtain as it pressed it aside. Half of it was then clearly visible. Its belly was low, but its head was up. It snarled.

The jaws were half open. I had seen such teeth before, fangs, pierced and strung on necklaces and armlets of Panther Girls. It was clearly vicious, and determined, this beast, but, too, it was smaller than the beast which had appeared from the side of the river.

The larger beast roared, again, but the smaller beast held its ground, crouched down, snarling.

I suddenly felt miserably sick and helpless.

I now had some sense of what was transpiring. The smaller beast had been following me, seemingly content, at least for the time being, for some reason, to do no more than keep me within its range. I had been unaware of its presence. I was unclear as to why, if it were about, it had not attacked. And, in following me, the smaller beast had strayed into the range of the larger beast. The panther, like the sleen, is highly territorial. The defense of territory selects for size, power, and ferocity. The Ubarship of a territory is not easily won, nor easily maintained. Territory, obviously, contains game for harvesting. If carnivores such as the panther and sleen were permissibly gregarious, the game within a territory would be soon depleted, and starvation would ensue. Larls may pride but they usually frequent, as well, areas where game is abundant, and the prides themselves can be competitive. Larls, as noted, do not frequent the northern forests. It would not be practical for them to do so. Claiming and maintaining a territory can also figure in successful mating, as females of various species will seek out territory masters, and present themselves, wooing and seducing, for acceptance or rejection. Males without well-established territories often remain unmated. In this sense, in several species, the primary competition seems not so much directly for mates, as for food, and survival, for the achievement of territory, a consequence of which is likely to be access to one or more females, depending on the species.

The first beast then roared, again, terribly.

I supposed these threatening displays were intended to be intimidating. Surely they seem so. The hair on my forearms and on the back of my neck rose. It is clearly in the interest of the territory master, wherever possible, to avoid combat. If it can bring about the backing down, or withdrawal, of a challenger, frightening the challenger, convincing the challenger that the challenge is ill-advised, the territory master survives unscathed, and the challenger, as well, who may then try elsewhere, perhaps with better fortune. If combat actually occurs, as it might, one or both animals may be killed, and, if not, both may be weakened, bled, and impaired, with the consequence that the territory master is more vulnerable and the challenger is less well equipped to initiate a new challenge elsewhere.

Despite the fearful roar of the larger beast, the smaller animal did not retreat, but, rather, came into view, fully, parting the grass, moving through it, and, to my uneasiness, came about me, not taking its eyes from those of the larger beast, and crouched down, tail lashing, growling, between the larger beast and myself.

Then, to my further bewilderment, and trepidation, the larger beast moved about me, so that, now, it was behind my position, between me and the forest, and the smaller beast now placed itself between me and the river. Any thought that I might have had of reaching the river or slipping back into the forest, eluding the beasts as they concerned themselves with one another, was gone. They then began, each threatening and snarling, again and again, regarding one another, to traverse the perimeter of the circle in which I found myself the reluctant, trembling center.

I stood there, watching, moving as little as possible.

I could not understand why the smaller animal did not make away. I thought it no match for the larger beast. Then, sick, I thought I understood. Even a small sleen, I knew, will defend its food dish in the face of a larger animal. There are many animals, even animals commonly loyal, and friendly, between whom and their food it would be unwise, even dangerous, to place oneself. One does not attempt to remove a haunch of tarsk from even a pet sleen, once it has been given to him. It is then his. Few animals will surrender their food to another. Nature has apparently not favored that behavior.

I suspected the smaller animal, though it was certainly large enough, and fearsome enough, had been with me since yesterday, when I had fled the camp of Genserich. If it had kept itself with me, as a subtle, lengthy, softly treading, breathing shadow, always nearby, there must have been a reason. The likely reason then became disturbingly clear to me. The panther, the sleen, the larl, seldom feed daily. Indeed, they may go days between meals. The smaller beast, I suspected, for some reason, was saving me. It had not yet been ready to feed.

Suddenly the larger beast, as though some spring in that great body had been released, charged, scrambling, through the center of the circle, and I was buffeted, spinning, to the side, for it struck me in its passage, I felt its ribs, and it hurled itself on the smaller beast which was rolled to its back, and then, in a moment, they were rolling about, biting, and tearing at one another. I could scarcely follow their movements, so rapid they were, so swift and fierce was the tumult of their engagement.

Then I saw the larger beast rear up from that loose, spattering tangle of fur and blood, its jaws on the throat of the smaller beast, and, itself rent, torn, and bloody, its flanks and shoulders red with the furrows of claw marks, it lifted the smaller body half from the ground, and shook it, and shook it, long after it was without life, repeatedly, meaninglessly, in the pointless, spasmodic frenzy of the kill. It then lay down, its scarlet-flowing jaws still clenched on the throat of the smaller beast, whose body now lay across its paws. It was breathing heavily. An ear was half torn away. I could see bone at the side of its face. It was looking toward me. I did not know if it saw me or not.

I was lying on my belly, where I had fallen, near the center of that circle whose periphery had been recently trodden by two dangerous beasts.

I felt my hands pulled behind me and I heard the click of slave bracelets. Then a leash collar was buckled about my throat.

"Kill it, please, kill it, Master," I begged.

"No," he said.

"It is dangerous!" I said.

"It is not dangerous now," he said. "Perhaps later it will be dangerous."

I recognized the voice.

"You are fortunate you were not eaten," he said. "I might not have arrived in time."

"I think I was followed since yesterday," I said.

"Quite possibly," he said. "A panther not driven by hunger will often linger in the vicinity of prey, or follow it, at a convenient distance."

"How did you find me?" I asked.

"I speculated you would regard your escape from the camp as successfully accomplished, not irrationally, and would then, too soon perhaps, return to the river. I thus kept to the shoreline. To be sure, some fortune was involved. I feared, naturally enough, you might be tracked by panthers, or sleen, and thus, when I heard a particular roar, a typical roar of warning, of territorial claimancy, I conjectured a territorial intrusion might have occurred, either deliberately or inadvertently. In any case, I decided to investigate."

"Did you see it all?" I asked.

"Yes," he said.

"But you did not intervene."

"It was not necessary," he said. He then stood up, and stepped back. "You are in the presence of a free man," he observed.

"Forgive me, Master," I said.

I then struggled to my knees, and knelt before him, looking up at him, a Gorean master, my hands braceleted behind me, his leash collar buckled about my throat, the leash itself, twice looped, in his hand.

"Perhaps you thought you had escaped," he said.

"Yes, Master," I whispered.

"Did you escape?" he asked.

"No, Master," I said.

"Why did you run away?" he asked.

"I beg not to speak," I said.

"Very well," he said.

"Thank you, Master!" I whispered.

"On your feet, kajira," said he.

I rose to my feet, and stood before him, head down.

"Are you a slave?" he asked.

"Yes, Master, I am a slave," I said.

"You understand that, fully?" he asked.

"Yes, Master," I said. Had I not known this, since puberty?

"You have been displeasing," he said.

"Forgive me, Master," I whispered.

His hand reached to the disrobing loop at my left shoulder.

"Oh, yes, Master!" I said. "Please, Master!"
"You have been displeasing," he said.
"Master?" I said.
"You will be lashed," he said.
"No, Master!" I said. "Please, no, Master!"

Chapter Forty-Nine

I leaned back against the tree, and listened to the crackle of the small fire, in the tiny camp on the way back to Shipcamp.

I idly reached for the leash, and tugged twice, which activated the metal ring on the leash collar, lifting and dropping it twice, signaling the slave that she should approach, which she did, on all fours.

"Please me," I said.

"Yes, Master," she said, bending over me.

Later she lay beside me, her head at my thigh.

I had seen fit to deny her clothing.

"Keep me," she whispered.

"You are a camp slave," I reminded her, "at Shipcamp, and are the property of Pani masters."

"Will Master return me to Shipcamp?" she asked.

"A caught slave," I said, "is to be returned to her masters."

"I am afraid," she said.

"As well you might be," I said.

"What will they do with me?" she asked.

"I do not know," I said.

"I do not want to die," she said.

"I do not think they will kill you," I said. "They bought a large number of women and, I think, not primarily for the use of mariners and mercenaries, but for sale, or use as trade goods, somewhere, where I am not sure, presumably wherever the great ship makes its eventual landfall, doubtless one of the farther islands, for who would dare venture beyond them?"

"I heard," she whispered, "they seek the World's End."

"That would seem madness," I said. "No ship has ventured much beyond the farther islands and returned."

"There is a man called Tersites," she said, "a master shipwright, he is supposedly determined."

"I think he is mad," I said.

"It is said he thinks of the World's End," she said.

"I think that may be to dismay strangers, perhaps to obscure an actual destination. In any event, there are many rumors. Who knows what courses might be plotted in the privacy of a secret chartroom?"

"Perhaps the ship has departed," she said.

"That is possible," I said, uneasily.

She rose on her elbows. "Then you could keep me!" she said.

"I will sell you at the first opportunity," I said.

"I do not think so," she said.

"Why not?" I asked.

"I think Master is fond of Laura," she said.

"Laura is a slave," I reminded her.

"Even so," she said.

She then lay beside me again. I felt her breath on my thigh. And then her lips.

"Laura loves Master," she said.

"Laura is a liar," I said.

"Slaves are not permitted to lie," she said.

"I think I will sell you to a woman," I said.

"Do not!" she said. "I am a man's slave, and would be yours."

"Do not fear," I said. "I cannot sell you. I do not own you. You belong to Pani."

"I see," she said.

"Do you really think the Pani want us to sell, or trade?" she asked.

"Certainly," I said.

"Why?" she asked. "We are very different from their Pani women."

"What does it matter?" I said. "It is always a pleasure to see pretty slaves on the auction block, regardless of their skin color, their hair and eye color, and such."

"Perhaps we might have some value as exotic goods," she said, "something unusual, or different."

"Also," I said, "I do not think there were many Pani women for sale in Brundisium."

"I saw few in Tarncamp, or Shipcamp," she said.

"I suppose," I said, "that there are Pani kajirae, captures in war, and such, but the usual arrangement seems to be in virtue of contracts of some sort, which may be bought and sold, the woman accompanying the contract."

"How is that different from the collar?" she asked.

"It seems to have something to do with prestige, or such. The status is putatively higher. One would expect such women to be treated with more esteem and deference than a common slave. One would not expect them to be collared, or publicly stripped, or such. Too, they are often highly trained, in music, singing, dancing, conversation, the serving of tea, the arranging of flowers, and such."

"But they still go with the contract," she said.

"That is my understanding," I said.

"I saw two of them," she said, "in Shipcamp. Both were beautiful."

"So, too," I said, "are most common slaves, let alone women purchased for the Pleasure Gardens of Ubars, high merchants, and such."

"Am I beautiful?" she asked.

"Yes," I said.

"Thank you, Master!" she said, softly, gratefully.

"You have improved in the collar," I said. "It has that effect on a woman."

"I think you like me," she said.

"You do have a hot, active little belly," I said.

"I think Master followed me north from Brundisium," she said. "I think Master sought me in Shipcamp, and perhaps in Tarncamp. Master pursued me into the forest with Master Axel, and his beast. And when others returned to Shipcamp, Master did not do so. He followed me, and recaptured me."

"I was well paid to come north," I said. "I joined Axel for diversion, and a pleasant hunt. I later followed you because you had annoyed me in the camp of Genserich, and I decided to get my leash on you, and make you pay."

"You have made me pay well, Master," she whispered.

"You are attentive, and juice nicely," I said.

"I love Master!" she suddenly wept.

"With what love?" I asked.

"With the deepest and most profound of loves," she said, "the helpless, abject love of a slave!"

I took her by the hair, my hand tight in its rich, dark, glossy loveliness.

"Hurt me," she said. "Show me that I am a slave, and that you own me."

She winced.

I relaxed my grip. "But I do not own you," I said.

"Buy me," she begged.

"Only a slave begs to be purchased," I said.

"I am a slave!" she said.

Ritual phrases are often required of a slave. One of the most common is, "Buy me, Master." Sometimes along the side of a road, where a number of slaves, neck-chained, may be knelt for inspection and possible sale, the slave is expected to lift her head and, as she is examined, utter the phrase, "Buy me, Master." This phrase is not that unusual on slave shelves, and such, as well.

"I remember," she said, "the first time I saw Master."

"And I you," I said.

"I was free!" she said.

"No," I said, "you were merely a slave, not yet collared."

"No!" she said.

"Do you think I cannot recognize a slave when I see one?" I asked.

"I was free!" she said.

"As free as a woman such as you could be," I said, "one not yet taken in hand by a man, and put to his feet, stripped and collared."

"How you looked at me!" she said.

"The chain," I said, "is made for women such as you."

"Fully clothed," she said, "I felt naked before you."

"And so I perceived you," I said, "as you might appear, exhibited on the block for the consideration of buyers."

"I fled," she said.

"You were well and carefully scouted," he said, "as I explained to you in the camp of Genserich, in a number of venues, in a number of garmentures, and such."

"And even, sedated, in my own bed, it seems," she said, "stripped, variously positioned, photographed, measured in considerable detail, and such."

"Of course," I said.

"Were you involved in this?" she asked.

"Yes," I said. "But do not concern yourself. You awakened later, pleasantly enough, and knew nothing of what had taken place."

"But it had taken place!" she said.

"Certainly," I said.

"It seems we are carefully selected," she said.

"Yes," I said, "but also with an eye to the future. What will she be like when she has learned her collar? What will she be like once she is the victim of the raging slave fires we will build in her belly? What will she be like once she has been trained to please men? What will she be like when she has suitably dieted and exercised?"

"I see," she said.

"Your body, for example," I said, "is more of a slave's body now than it was on Earth."

"I am pleased if Master is pleased," she said, moving more against me, the she-tarsk, with the maddening softness of her.

"Your Gorean is coming along nicely," I said.

"We must strive to learn the language of our masters," she said.

"Why did you run away?" I asked.

"Please do not make me speak," she said.

"Very well," I said.

"I fear the men of Gor," she said.

"But they stir your belly, and you suddenly become acutely aware, as you were not before, of your sex."

"Yes," she said. "It suddenly becomes meaningful. It suddenly seems the single most important thing about me, that I am not a male, but a female."

"I understand," I said.

"That is because there are men here," she said.

"There are men on your former world," I said.

"How is it," she said, "that Gorean men are so different from those of my former world?"

"I do not think they are so different," I said. "They are of the same species."

"It is hard to believe," she said.

"There are different roads, different paths," I said. "Much depends on which one takes."

"My former world," she said, "is filled with unhappiness, misery, and hatred."

"Much depends on the road one takes," I said.

"Few find their own way," she said. "Most take the road they are told to take."

"And few will try another," I said.

"Herds," she said, "ask no more than to be driven."

"It seems so," I said.

"Even if to the slaughter bench," she said.

"There is profit in this, of course," I said, "for those who drive the herds."

"I do not think the men of Gor herd," she said.

"No," I said, "it is not in their culture."

"The men of Earth herd," she said.

"Not all of them," I said.

"Where are the masters?" she asked, bitterly.

"Here and there, doubtless," I said.

"Where are the slaves?"

"Here and there, doubtless," I said.

"I knew none," she said.

"You may have," I said. "You may have known women who, unbeknownst to yourself, and concealed from the world, were their master's slave, even to nudity, the whip, and collar."

She lay back, her shoulder against my thigh.

"Master has a slave, Asperiche," she said.

"Yes," I said.

"I hate her," she said.

"It is not your concern," I said.

"Is she better than Laura?" she asked.

"A thousand times," I said.

"I find that hard to believe," she said.

"Oh?" I said.

"You did not follow her from Brundisium, into the labors and dangers of the northern woods," she said. "You did not risk your life to pursue her in the forest!"

"It is growing late," I said.

"What is Laura to you?" she asked.

"No more than a foolish slave, a capture, to be returned to the Pani," I said.

"After what you have done to me?" she said. "After what you have made me feel?"

"You are a slave," I observed.

"I hate you," she wept.

"You are, of course," I said, "a nicely curved piece of collar meat."

"Can she lick the whip as well as Laura?" she asked. "Can she belly and crawl as well as Laura? Are her lips as warm, and begging, on your thigh as those of Laura?"

I was silent.

"I am sure she is very nice," she said.

"She is hot, and lovely," I said.

"But perhaps not the slave for you," she said.

"A slave is a slave," I said. "They are interchangeable."

"Master has the advantage over me," she said.

"How is that?" I asked.

"A slave," she said, "must tell the truth."

"I see," I said.

"Is that why one slave sells for more than another, why one slave's price might purchase a ship, and another a wooden bowl and spoons, why one slave is bartered for a city, and another for a she-tarsk, why one girl is purchased to be chained at the foot of a Ubar's throne and another to carry water in the fields or quarries?"

"Kneel, turn about, put your head to the leaves," I said.

"Yes, Master," she said.

She did not sound displeased.

"You obey promptly and well, Earth woman," I said.

"I am no longer an Earth woman," she said. "I am now a Gorean slave."

"You are far from the aisle of that great emporium where I first saw you," I said.

"Yes, Master," she said.

"Did you expect to find yourself one day as you are now?" I asked.

"No, Master," she said.

"But you are now here, as you are," I said.

"Yes, Master," she said.

I then put her to my pleasure.

Chapter Fifty

He took no chances with me.

On the return to Shipcamp I was stripped, which is a common way to return an escaped slave to masters. This not only designates the slave as having been errant or displeasing, but marks her out, as well, for attention. A tunicked slave amongst tunicked slaves might attract little attention; she might even slip away again; a naked slave amongst tunicked slaves, on the other hand, is quickly noticed. Nudity, in its way, makes escape less likely. Further, in the trek to Shipcamp, my hands were braceleted behind me, and I was kept on the leash, usually, in more dangerous areas, following him, led, but in more open areas often forced to precede him, almost like a slave on promenade. At night my wrists would be braceleted about a small tree, I placed either on my belly, my arms forward about this living stanchion, or on my back, my arms back, above and behind me.

I was muchly used, for slave purposes, on the trek back to Shipcamp, especially in the evening and night, but, sometimes, during the day, as well, when, his need upon him, as it seemed so frequently to be, he would throw me to the leaves.

Often enough, as well, I would creep to him, whimpering.

Never as a free woman had I suspected how grievous, irresistible, and even painful might be a slave's needs, how helpless she would be in their grip. I supposed even on Earth I would have been ready to yield to a master, hoping to be found pleasing. But on Gor, once I was in a collar, half naked, with a slave brand seared into my flesh, and knew myself an object, a domestic animal, only goods, these feelings and needs became far more acute. Then I had been, at Shipcamp, chained in the slave house. There I had begun to sense the ecstasy, and the terror, and the helplessness, of one in whom slave fires had been ignited. Then, after my recapture, in the arms of my captor, for whose touch I had longed even as long ago as my former world, when I had seen him but once before my acquisition, these fires had begun, perhaps to his amusement, to blaze in such a way that I found myself their prisoner and victim. Doubtless this was due in part to his ruthless skill in setting such fires in the belly of a slave, but, too, I would have been almost helpless before him, even had I been a free woman, on my former world, for he, so severe, virile, confident, and strong, was the most exciting and attractive man I had ever seen, and here I was before him not as a free woman, but, on this rich, green, savage, perilous, exotic world, his world, Gor, a slave.

And, to my fear, chagrin, and humiliation, given what had been done to me on this world, I found myself disturbed, considering what almost any man might now do to me, now that I was a slave, and not simply he for whose collar I longed with such excruciating desire. I did not doubt now but what I could not help responding, and as a slave, to the touch of almost any of these arrogant, conquering Gorean males. In setting slave fires in a woman's belly they well know how to make her a slave.

"The wands, Master," I said.

"The larls are in," he said.

"Sometimes they are," I said. I had depended on that, in my original flight.

"More likely our approach has been noted," he said. "Surveillance may be intensified."

"I am to be turned over to Pani?" I said.

"Of course," he said.

"What is to be done with me?" I asked.

"You will learn," he said.

"I returned to the wands before," I said, "inadvertently."

"Perhaps not so inadvertently," he said.

"I do not understand," I said.

"Look there," he said, "through the trees."

"The ship, the great ship!" I said.

"We are in time," he said. "It has not yet left."

It was hard to see through the leafage but, clearly, the great ship was still at its moorings.

"There is not much time," he said.

"Master?" I said.

He pressed aside a branch, and pointed toward the dock. "See the high pole north of the dock, across from the stern of the ship.

"Yes, Master," I said. I was sure that pole had not been there when I had been employed about the dock.

"At its height," he said, "on its line, is the ready banner."

He indicated a long, tapering, triangular swirl of bright scarlet silk. It could be seen from a great distance.

"Final preparations are being made," he said. "When the banner is lowered, the moorings will be cast, and the voyage begun."

"How long is it flown?" I asked.

"I had heard three days," he said.

"But one or two days may have already passed," I said.

"Yes," he said. "We will learn."

"Perhaps it will leave today," I said.

"No," he said. "It will leave in the early morning, to make the most of a day's light."

"Perhaps then tomorrow?" I said.

"Perhaps," he said, letting the branch fall back into place. "I do not know."

"Tal!" called a cheery voice.

"Axel!" said my captor.

"I see you have her," said Axel. "Good! Doubtless, a barbarian, she was an easy catch. Come within the wands. We wish to loose the larls again."

I felt the tug on my leash ring, and I stumbled after my captor.

Shortly thereafter we were within the perimeter of Shipcamp. There, near the wands, doubtless waiting, was an unusually lovely slave. She, as I, was dark-haired and dark-eyed. "Master!" she said, delightedly, and knelt quickly before my captor, kissed his feet, and lifted her head happily to him. "We feared for you!"

"What are you doing here?" asked my captor.

"I brought her," said Axel.

"So you came, perforce?" asked my captor.

"Of course, Master," she said, smiling. "What could I do? He is a free man."

"So this is Asperiche?" I said.

"Yes," said my captor, indicating with a gesture that Asperiche might rise.

"She is very lovely," I said.

"So this is Laura?" said Asperiche.

"Yes," said my captor.

"And she is very lovely," said Axel.

"Oh?" said Asperiche.

"Certainly," said Axel.

"I had expected her to be different," she said.

"How so?" asked Axel.

"More beautiful," said Asperiche.

I knew I was not the sort of girl who went for a handful of silver, or even a piece of gold.

Still I thought I was beautiful enough. Some men had seemed to think so. Surely I was popular in the slave house.

Asperiche regarded me. I straightened my body. She walked about a bit, partly behind me, and then, again, was before me. "But, yes, you are pretty, Laura," she said. "And you look well, on a leash, braceleted."

"Thank you," I said.

"You are short of clothing," she observed.

"Yes," I said.

"I am tunicked," she said.

"Rather briefly," I said.

"My master enjoys exhibiting me," she said. "I am the sort of slave masters enjoy showing off, the sort they relish displaying."

"You have a beautiful figure and face," I granted her.

"You must be very stupid," she said, "to run away. You are kajira. Do you not know that there is no escape for a kajira? But then you are a barbarian, and all barbarians are stupid."

"I am not stupid," I said.

"Surely you must feel stupid," she said, "to be led back here on a leash for all to see, naked and braceleted, like a tethered verr."

"I do feel stupid," I said.

"You did a very stupid thing," she said.

"Yes," I said. "I did a very stupid thing."

"Perhaps you are not stupid," she said. "Perhaps you were only a fool."

"I was a fool," I said.

"Perhaps you are no longer a fool," she said. "Perhaps now you know you are a slave, and that there is no escape for you."

"Yes," I said, "I now know I am a slave, and that there is no escape for me—Mistress."

"'Mistress'?" she said.

"Yes," I said, "for you are superior to me. You are a private slave, and I am only a camp slave."

"We are both only slaves, Laura," she said.

"I want to be a slave!" I said.

"We all want to be slaves," she whispered.

"Enough of the meaningless chatter of bond sluts," said Axel. Then he turned to my captor. "I will report the capture of the slave to the magistrates," said Axel. "You will see to her keeping."

"I will do so," said my captor.

"May I accompany Master Axel?" inquired Asperiche.

"Yes," said my captor, "heel him closely and well."

"I shall," she said, happily.

How willingly and light-heartedly, I thought, did the slave follow Master Axel. Surely my captor must have noticed this. Would he not be concerned? I was made uneasy. Aside from raids, warfare, and such, the exchange of kajirae normally takes place in a civilized manner, with negotiation, and buying and selling, and such. But, occasionally, I knew exchanges took place by means of the negotiation of blades, particularly on the open road or in the fields, outside walls, beyond the jurisdiction of archons and praetors. I supposed the weapon skills of my captor and Master Axel would be similar. Few men, I was sure, saving perhaps workmen, some mariners, and such, had been hired north without the assurance that they possessed one or another of the dark skills. Some here, I speculated, might even be of the caste of Warriors, though in such a case, perhaps renegades or exiles, possibly men who had fared badly in city revolutions, even men who may have forsworn Home Stones or betrayed codes, desperate men, dangerous men. And I did not see my captor as one with whom one might trifle with impunity. Was he not concerned with the behavior of his slave? What master would not be? Had Asperiche been sold? No, she had knelt before my captor, kissed his feet, and addressed him as 'Master'. Might my captor be thinking of ridding himself of her? Might he be interested in some other slave? Might I be she? But Asperiche was beautiful! But Gorean males, depending on their means, may have more than one slave. The pleasure gardens of Ubars and high merchants might house innumerable slaves, even slaves purchased by agents, slaves of whom their masters might not even be aware. I had heard of a Mintar of Ar who owned more than a thousand slaves, though most were chained in his mills. There were city slaves, too, of course, in the high cities, in their brief gray tunics and gray metal collars. I hoped my captor wanted me. How I would strive to please him, in all the ways of the meaningless, abject slave! How I longed to be the single slave of a private master! I did not think it could be borne, that I might share my master with another. I trusted that lovely Asperiche would not be the cause of bloodshed between Master Axel and my captor. It is strange, I thought, how Gorean masters, before whom we are negligible, at whose feet we are nothing, who hold us in the lofty contempt of a free person, will kill for us. Are we then so meaningless, truly? But, I thought, Master Axel and my captor are friends. Surely they would not draw steel on one another. But Asperiche was very beautiful. Even on behalf of lesser women, I supposed, edged steel might suddenly divide friends. But perhaps my captor was not determined to retain Asperiche. Was she not a bauble, as any slave, which might be bestowed as a master might wish? But my captor, I was sure, would need a slave. He was such a man. I wondered if many of the males of my world could even understand such a thing, that there are men so powerful, so masculine, so virile, so lustful, so passionate, so dominant, so uncompromising, so demanding, that they will make women slaves, for they will choose to have them as such, as properties, as the goods and animals they will then be. They will choose to own their women, categorically and absolutely. We are their rightless belongings. I supposed few males of my former world, that tepid, gray world, could even understand such a thing.

And few women of my former world, I supposed, had ever found themselves the object of a passion so intense, so fierce, and demanding, that it could be satisfied with nothing less than their absolute possession, their ownership, with nothing less than their being the belonging of their master. Presumably they could not even understand such passion, such desire, until, perhaps, they found themselves collared, and the object of it. Let them then understand that they are owned, as any object may be owned, wholly and without qualification; let them then strive to be a suitable belonging, an acceptable belonging; let them then strive to be pleasing, fully pleasing, and in all the ways of the slave, for the whip is not pleasant.

"Master Axel," I said, "reports my capture to my Pani masters."

"Yes," said my captor.

"And you are to see to my keeping?" I said.

"Yes," he said.

"As is appropriate for my captor?" I said.

"It is to be expected," he said.

"So I am to be returned to my kennel?" I said. This was the long, low, log-built building, which I shared with several others, in which we would be chained at night.

He looked at me. I could not read his expression.

"I trust I will be permitted a tunic," I said.

"It is not likely," he said.

"Then I would be humiliated before my sister slaves," I said.

"They did not run away," he said.

We noted a female slave passing, carrying, on her head, a basket, filled with damp male tunics. She was presumably returning either from the river or from one of the laundry troughs, filled with rain water.

"She is shackled!" I said.

"Some are," he said. "She is probably from one of the port cities. There they know something of Thassa. There is a rumor abroad, hopefully false, that mad Tersites and the Pani intend to take the great ship past the farther islands, seeking the World's End. It is little wonder then that the slim, lovely ankles of some kajirae, most likely those who would be most aware of the dangers of such a voyage, are now graced by ankle rings, linked by less than a foot of slave chain."

"I see," I said.

"Do not be concerned," he said. "The ankle rings are lovely, and the chain is not heavy. It is girl chain. The whole arrangement is quite attractive."

"You enjoy seeing us in chains, do you not?" I said.

"Certainly," he said. "A woman is lovely in chains."

"I see," I said.

"Whereas the chaining is effective, as it would be in the case of any animal," he said, "one must not overlook the aesthetics of this, and the psychology. The obdurate, unyielding metal affords a lovely contrast with the soft, vulnerable, helpless flesh it impounds; how it lies against it, and such. Consider the colors, the textures, the differences in the substances involved. Consider its weight on her limbs. Even the sounds of the links moving against one another can be an informative, illuminating music. Is a woman not beautiful in chains? Indeed, most chainings are designed to enhance a woman's beauty, such as the sirik. And much, too, is psychological. After all, chained or not, there is no escape for the slave. But seeing her so helplessly confined, and so vulnerable, pleases the male, who naturally relishes having so beautiful and desirable a beast before him, at his mercy. And, too, of course, it has its psychological effect on the female, making it absolutely clear to her that she is a slave, wholly and helplessly at the mercy of masters, as she wishes to be."

I did not respond to my captor. He need not know how sexually stimulatory to me was the leash in which I found myself, proclaiming me a leashed animal, the slave bracelets which confined my hands behind my back, the weight of chains that I had occasionally worn, even the chain on my ankle in the kennel. How I was stimulated by the bars of a cage, by ropes on my body, by the commands of a master, by the lightness and brevity of a tunic, by my nudity! And my bondage itself, the very condition itself, as I had anticipated even on my former world, that I would be owned and must obey, was a joy to me. How I then pitied free women, and began to understand why they hated us so. We were the most joyful, and truest of women, the slaves of our masters.

"You will return me to my kennel," I said.

"No," he said.

"I do not understand," I said.

"You will be kept in another way," he said.

"Please," I said, "keep Laura—keep her for yourself!"

"I do not own you," he said.

"She would be yours," I said, "your slave!"

"I thought you hated me," he said.

"I love you!" I sobbed.

My left cheek, my head struck to the side, stung with the sudden, fierce, angry, open-handed slap of his smiting right hand, and I might have reeled and fallen, save that his left hand, its grip close to the leash collar, held me upright, in place. Tears streamed from my eyes, and my cheek burned with pain. He relaxed his grip, enough that I could get to my knees, and I knelt before him. I must look up at him, for the leash was pulled up, taut, and tight, gripped in his fist. "Forgive me, Master," I said.

He looked down upon me, with a savage, angry, ferocious light in his eyes, with all the contempt with which the free may regard a slave.

"Even a beast may love her master," I said.

"Do not dare speak of love, you blasphemous she-tarsk," he said. "You are not a free woman but what you should be, a meaningless slave. You are an article to be used, an object purchased for work and pleasure, for inordinate raptures of unspeakable pleasure, to be derived from your body whenever and however a master might please."

"So use me!" I begged.

He drew back his right hand, again, angrily.

"Please do not strike me, Master!" I said.

He lowered his hand, but he kept the leash taut. I was unable to lower my head.

"Does Master not want Laura?" I asked.

"You should be fed to sleen," he said.

"You muchly caressed me in the forest," I said. "You made me such that I could not help but respond to you as a slave girl to her master."

"As you would do to any man," he said.

"We are slaves," I said.

"There was no other at hand," he said.

"Yes, Master," I said.

He relaxed the leash, and I put down my head, gratefully.

"I thought Master might want Laura," I said.

"Laura," he said, "is worthless."

"Still," I whispered.

"We must see to your keeping," he said.

"Buy me," I begged.

He laughed, but I did not care. In begging to be bought, one acknowledges that one can be bought, and thus acknowledges that one is a slave. But I did not care. I was a slave. I had known this from long ago, from the time transforming changes had occurred in my body, a consequence of which was my realization that I belonged in a man's collar.

"Who would want a worthless slave?" he said.

"I think many men," I said.

"Your face is acceptable," he said, "and you are not badly curved."

"Surely," I said, "there is a slave ring anchored in the floor of your hut, to which I might be chained."

"To the same ring to which Asperiche is chained?" he said.

"If it be Master's wish," I said.

"I do not chain just anything to a slave ring," he said.

"I am sure many men would find me acceptable at such a ring," I said. "And was it not Master who brought me to the collar?"

"You are an insolent she-sleen," he said.

"The whip will teach me timidity and deference," I said.

"On your feet," he said.

I rose up, and stood before him, head down.

"I am not to be returned to my kennel?" I said.

"No," he said.

"And I am not to be taken to your hut?"

"No," he said.

"I do not understand," I said.

He then turned about, and I followed, on the leash. He began to descend toward the river. On the way, we passed a number of slave girls, several of whom smiled contemptuously as I was led by. "Fool," said one. "Caught slave," said another.

At the shore I looked across the broad Alexandra. The remains of the framework in which the great ship had been built were to my left, and, a hundred paces or so to my right, was the eastern end of the long dock at which the great ship was moored. North of the dock, amongst some of the shops, and workers' huts, I saw the high pole at which was flown the long, some yards long, unfurled, wind-whipped, scarlet triangle of silk, which I had been informed was the "ready banner," the banner that was put in place three days before departure. But neither, at that time, my captor nor myself knew when it had been hoisted into place. He would doubtless soon learn, whereas I, if I were to inquire of a free person, might be cuffed. Curiosity, as it is said, is not becoming in a kajira.

Standing at the edge of the shore, I could see, across the river, some of the buildings, and the mysterious stockade, which had excited my curiosity in the past. I gathered that there might be special supplies stored there, even treasure. One story was that slaves were held there who were too beautiful to risk holding in Tarncamp or Shipcamp, for fear men might mutiny to claim them. I thought it quite possible that high slaves might be housed there, and perhaps unusually beautiful slaves, or exotics, or such, but I did not think there would be that much difference between one girl on a block and another. Unusual prices are usually the results of unusual goods, or unusual market situations. One would expect, for example, that an unusual dancer, a trained physician, the daughter of a defeated general, or such, might go for more than another slave, even if the other slave might, for most intents and purposes, be an equivalent, even a better, buy. For example, two of my friends, sister slaves, kennel sisters, Relia and Janina, I thought, were quite beautiful. I did not expect many slaves to be more beautiful than they. Too, men may see beauty differently. One man's pleasure slave may be another man's pot girl, or kettle-and-mat girl.

At the edge of the shore, there were several small boats tied in place, to stakes anchored in the beach, some, long boats, propelled by several oars, and others, smaller boats, propelled by a pair of oars. These boats sufficed for traffic across the river. They were not equipped with the weights and cords, the water-tight cabinets for marking tools and charts, used by the fellows who regularly plotted, and sounded, the river's sometimes treacherous depths and channels.

"Master?" I said, gazing across the broad, shimmering waters.

"Oh!" I cried, taken by the hair and flung down, on my back on the beach. I squirmed, trying to avoid the pebbles.

"Master!" I said.

But several coils of rope were tying my ankles together and then more rope was being tied about my calves and thighs. I was then put to my stomach, and I felt the small key inserted into the locks of the slave bracelets, and they were removed and, I suppose, placed in his wallet or pack. Then my hands were tied behind my back, and more coils of rope, as I was being positioned, rolled, and turned, were being put about my body, binding my forearms in place, and reaching, in coil after coil, even to my shoulders. These were no lovely, silken cords, supple, delightful cords, bright with color slave cords, suitable for the attractive binding of a secured, helpless slave, but were a common, coarse ropage, the same, it seemed, as that which tethered the boats in place. "Please, Master!" I begged. I squirmed, swathed in the coarse constraints. I was uncomfortable. "Please, Master," I said, "the ropes are coarse. They scratch. I am tightly bound. I can hardly move." He had left the leash collar and leash on me, and now, by it, pulled me to a sitting position on the beach. "Please, free me, Master!" I said.

"You are a she-tarsk," he said. "Does a she-tarsk object to being bound as what she is, a she-tarsk?"

"Master!" I said.

Then he pulled me to my feet by the leash under my chin, and I could not stand upright, as I was bound, my ankles closely crossed, save for his left hand on my arm, and his right hand on the leash, close to the collar.

"I am only a female slave," I said. "I am much smaller and weaker than you. Please show me mercy!"

He then scooped me up, lightly, and carried me to one of the nearby small boats, one with two oars, and put me on my back, roughly, on the boards, at the bottom of the boat. The lower part of my body would then be between his feet, and partly under his seat.

He must then have freed the boat from its mooring, for he was wading beside it, thrusting it into the river, and then he entered the boat, took his seat, freed the oars, set them in place, and began to row.

As he was rowing he was facing me, naturally, and the closer shore. He could not see where the small craft was going without turning about. I, on the other hand, as I was situated, might I struggle to a sitting position, could see around him to the opposite shore.

I tried to struggle up a bit, to see, but his foot pressed me back to the boards. Yes, I thought, angrily, curiosity is not becoming in a kajira! So I lay back on the boards. I looked up. The sky was quite blue, and cloudless.

We had been some Ehn on the water, when I realized he was looking at me.

"You are a pretty package, partly tucked beneath the thwart," he said.

"Where are we going?" I asked. "What are you going to do with me?"

He smiled.

"Yes, yes," I said, "but we are curious!"

"But it is not becoming, is it?" he asked.

"No, Master," I said. I roiled in frustration, with helpless frustration. The boards were rough, and hot from the afternoon sun. Our lives, our destinies, our fates, are in the hands of the masters! Do they think we have no interest in what is going on, in what is to take place, in what is to be done with us? I twisted futilely in the ropes, unanswered, uninformed.

"What is wrong?" he asked.

"How you torture us!" I said.

"How so?" he asked.

"Where are we going, what is to be done with me?" I cried.

"You are in a collar," he said.

"Yes, Master," I said.

"One does not explain things to beasts," he said. "Do you understand?"

"Yes, Master," I said. There are many sorts of things involved in this practice, of course. For example, in not explaining things to a slave it is made further clear to her, as if she needed further proof, that she is negligible, that she is a slave, an animal, a beast. Would one, for example, feel it incumbent on one to explain things to a sleen, a kaiila, or verr? Too, of course, if the slave is kept ignorant, or uninformed, one has much more control over her. She is more helpless, more at one's mercy. But surely, too, the masters enjoy treating us as the slaves we are, in their thousand small ways. Is it not part of the pleasures of the mastery, finding amusement in keeping us in ignorance, in frustrating our desire to know? Why should we know, we are slaves! It is a small thing, but it is very real. So let us suffer in our unease, our anxiety, and our helpless frustration. Let it be so; we are slaves! But, too, I wondered, lying before him, bound, do we not want it so, and is it not pleasant in its way, finding ourselves helplessly subject to this deprivation and torment; is it not a reassurance to us that we are truly what we wish to be, slaves.

In a few more Ehn, I felt the bottom of the boat grate against the shore. The oars were drawn inboard, and my captor left the boat, and, wading, drew it high, onto the beach.

As I lay supine, apparently as my captor wished, I could see little but the inside of the boat, and the sky.

I did realize we were now on the southern shore of the river. So, I thought, I have, at last, managed to cross the river!

He then reentered the boat and undid the ropage which had bound my ankles and legs. The coils were then, in their several loops, cinched up, closely, about my waist. He lifted me over the side of the small craft and set me, standing, on the beach. I could feel the sand, and gravel, beneath my bare feet.

This was the first time I had been in a position to see the southern shore this closely. Some small boats were tied up on the shore, rather as they had been on the opposite shore. To one side, there was a steep wooden stairway, with broad steps, leading up from the beach to the level, where I could see something of the higher parts of the walls, and the roofs, of several small buildings, and the carved points of the palings of the stockade.

At the head of the walkway were two guards, who apparently recognized my captor.

I did not know his status at Shipcamp. I did not think he was a high officer, as there were few such, and most such posts were held by Pani. I did not think him a common member of the mercenary infantry, nor of the tarn cavalry. Yet he was recognized here, in an area prohibited to most, and had apparently experienced no difficulty in accompanying Master

Axel into the forest. There might then be, I realized, groups within groups, or groups apart from groups.

A tug on my leash ring informed me that I was to follow my captor, who, to my relief, chose to avail himself of the wooden walkway.

As I climbed the steps of the stairway I wondered a little at the breadth of the steps. Then, to my unease, I realized the likely explanation for the width of the plankings. Such a footing would be suitable for conducting coffles of bound, blindfolded slaves.

I was soon at the height of the stairway, on the broad, wooden platform from which the stairway descended. At each side of this platform was a post to which was attached a slave ring. I was knelt near the post at the right and my leash was looped about the slave ring. My captor and the two guards then withdrew some paces, where they conversed together. In a few moments my captor had returned to my side, and the two guards were making their way toward the stockade.

My leash was unlooped from the ring. "On your feet, slave girl," said my captor.

I struggled to my feet.

"Back on your knees," snapped my captor, "and rise, properly."

"Yes, Master," I said.

I then rose, gracefully, as I had been taught, and stood before him, gracefully, and submissively, my head down.

Men may require different things from a slave, but, unless one has reason to believe otherwise, or has been instructed otherwise, the slave is to be softly spoken, deferent, docile, obedient, and submissive, quite submissive, utterly submissive. She is not a free woman; she is a slave, a belonging.

"You are a poor slave," he said.

"Forgive me, Master," I said.

At the gate of the stockade, I think that signs of some sort might have been exchanged. In any event, the gate was opened.

I felt a tug on the leash ring.

Shortly thereafter I was at the gate. One of the guards regarded me. "The slut has good legs," he said. "It is hard to see much more," said the other.

"Do not fear," said my captor, "the ropes will soon be off."

I looked back, from this height, across the river. Even the great ship looked small. I could detect the "ready banner" on its line, like a tiny, fluttering scarlet thread in the distance.

"Enter," said a third guard, who was within the stockade. "Nicely marked," he said, as I passed.

My brand was the small, tasteful, but unmistakable "Kef," the "staff and fronds," beauty subject to discipline. There are many slave brands on Gor, but the "Kef," is the most common. The joke is that it is the common brand for the common girl, but I knew that some of the highest, most expensive, and most beautiful girls wore it. In any event, it is a beautiful brand, and is commonly thought to muchly enhance the value and beauty of the goods it marks. "Kef," I am informed, is the first letter in the Gorean word, 'Kajira'. Whereas I now speak Gorean, as I must, as it is the language of the masters, I have not been taught to read the language. This sort of thing is not that unusual. Barbarian slaves, and illiterate slaves, usually extracted from the lower castes, are commonly kept illiterate. Would one teach a sleen, a kaiila, a verr, to read? Similarly, such slaves may be used to carry messages they cannot read. An additional security is that the message is often put in a sealed message capsule tied about the slave's neck, the message being inaccessible to the slave, as she is back-braceleted. A slave may not be taught to read without her master's permission. In any event, I am illiterate in Gorean. Does that not make me more a slave?

As I entered the gate, I could see, toward the rear wall of the stockade, something like a barracks or kennel, not unlike my kennel at Shipcamp, and, before it, within the palings, a clearing, which I supposed might function as an exercise yard, an inspection yard, a sales yard, or such. Near the gate, within it, to my right as I entered, was a low, flat, round tank, presumably for water, and a feed trough. I supposed their nearness to the gate was for the convenience of masters, to facilitate their replenishment, supplies being brought from the outside. In the yard, too, I saw what I took to be several kajirae. At least they were stripped and collared, and, I did not doubt, marked, as well. They turned about, and regarded me. I noted the height of the palings. I had not realized they were so high. They were at least twice the height of a male, and each was wickedly pointed.

So, I thought, these are the special slaves, the precious slaves, those which might precipitate mutinies, which might cast woe and discord amongst the men of Tarncamp or Shipcamp. Yes, I thought, they are beautiful, but I did not think them that extraordinary, or different. I had seen many slaves in Tarncamp, and particularly in Shipcamp, where I had been housed, which seemed to me their equals, if not superiors. If that were the case, I thought, there must be more involved than what was circulated in the rumors, rumors perhaps deliberately circulated, in the camps. But what then could be the real reason for the isolation of these slaves?

The two guards who had been stationed at the head of the stairway, leading upward from the shore, withdrew, presumably returning to their post. The third guard, the interior guard, then lowered the two closing beams into their brackets. As the beams were heavy their lifting and lowering was managed by a system of counterweights. I also noted that there was an arrangement for chaining them in place, which chaining might be secured by a massive padlock. Now, however, the loops of heavy chain, and the padlock, now open, reposed on a large hook, to the right of the gate, as one would look outward.

I looked about the interior of the stockade, at the slaves I could see. I supposed there might be others in the kennel. Perhaps only so many were allowed into the sunlight and fresh air at a time.

My captor began removing the ropes from my body, and then, even, my hands were unbound. I felt the welcome air on my body. I rubbed my wrists. So, I thought, I had been bound as a she-tarsk. I might thank my captor for that. I still wore the leash collar and leash.

"Genuinely acceptable," said the guard.

I was standing well, as I had been taught, as a slave. I had not thought much about it. After a time one does not. After a time the kajira stands, walks, sits, moves, kneels, reclines, and such, with grace. As kajira, she is to be beautiful. She is given no option in this matter. There is always the whip. She is not permitted the awkwardness, the clumsiness, the crudity of movement, the carelessness of movement, the slovenly posture of the free woman. I suppose it is rather like a dancer. I had erred earlier, by the post at the head of the stairway, but it had been difficult to rise to my feet, bound as I was. Happily I had not been punished, but given the opportunity to rise again, more properly.

"Usually we remove their tunics when they enter," said the guard.

"She is a fled slave," said my captor.

"I see," said the guard.

Fled slaves are, as suggested earlier, commonly returned naked to their masters. Nudity, in its way, as earlier noted, makes escape less likely. Shortly after my capture my clothing had been removed. I now suspected that a similar consideration explained the absence of clothing on the kajirae incarcerated within the stockade. Are they truly so special, I thought, that this precaution seemed advisable, or is it a part of a plan, designed to enhance the aura of specialness and mystery with which it seemed this place was perhaps deliberately imbued?

"What is her name?" asked the guard.

"'Laura'," said my captor.

The guard then removed a marking stick from his wallet and I felt its soft point pressing into my left breast. I looked down at the markings, which, to me, were unintelligible. "There," he said, "'Laura'."

"The others are not inscribed, as nearly as I can tell," said my captor.

"The others are prize slaves," said the guard. "This will distinguish this one from the others."

"It is interesting," said my captor, "that it would require a marking to make that clear."

"I grant you," said the guard, "you have a beauty here."

How pleased I was to hear this unsolicited, casual appraisal. What woman, slave or free, does not wish to be beautiful?

If only my captor might see me so, I thought. How I had hoped he might find me of interest, the sort of interest a man feels for a woman he might buy. He had, of course, well pleasured himself with me, and frequently, on the return to Shipcamp, as a master may well pleasure himself with a slave. But, too, he had well taught me, with his perfunctory use of me, and his indifference, though I was crying with need, surrender, and helpless passion, that I was a meaningless pleasure object.

What was he to do? In the forest I was the only slave available to him. I was no more than a local convenience for his lust, a convenience no farther from him than the length of my leash. How could I interest him, as a slave desires to interest a master? Had I been a free woman, perhaps I might have tortured him, and made him long for me, flirting, approaching and then backing away, demanding attentions and bargains, teasing, and taunting, implicitly bespeaking my favors, and then, perhaps with feigned surprise or scorn, withholding them. Might I not make my companioning, if I were interested in such, a prize in a game many might play, and from which, at my whim, I might withdraw? Might I not sell myself, on my own terms, as I saw fit, to the highest bidder, for station, and wealth? But there is no hurry in such matters. Lure, seem to promise, and then deny. What powers are at the disposition of the free woman! Is it not a pastime most pleasant, one of the more diverting of sports, and one which, with its anecdotes, stories, and amusements, is twice delightful, once in its enactment, and then, again, in its recounting? Accounts of such exploits surely afford the gist of many a meeting amongst oneself and one's free sisters. Who is the most skillful player, she with the most victories, the most discomfited, shattered swains, she who is to be most admired, the most emulated, and perhaps the most envied? But I was not such a woman. I was a slave. No such tactics, pleasantries, and stratagems could be mine. We are at the disposal of the free. We must obey, instantly, and unquestioningly. A simple word, a gesture, a snapping of fingers may command us. Did I not learn that in the forest? We hasten to do the biddings of our masters. It is our hope that we will be found pleasing, fully pleasing, and, if not, we must expect to be punished. So the games of the free woman are far from the slave. Nor would I have cared for them. But, too, such games can be dangerous. Gorean men do not enjoy being trifled with. The same free woman who may have taunted with her veil, and the glimpse of a slippered foot, may later find herself stripped and collared, at the feet of some fellow who was wearied of her nonsense. Why do they behave so, I wondered? Do they want the collar?

"A common, mediocre slut, average collar-meat," said my captor.

"But there are other matters involved," said the guard.

"Political matters?" said my captor.

"Perhaps," said the guard. "Is the banner still flying?"

"Yes," said my captor.

"Water her," said the guard, gesturing to the tank at the side. "Then secure her as you will within. I will send a slave to feed her shortly."

I was then led to the tank.

"On all fours," said my captor. "Drink."

I went to all fours at the edge of the tank and put down my head, and drank. The leash went up, from the ring on my leash collar, to my captor's hand. I was well aware of how I had been positioned, and was drinking. Might not a leashed sleen or verr be watered similarly? In such small ways may a slave be reminded that she is a beast, to be sure one of a sort likely to be of interest to men.

I was then taken to a ditch near the wall where I relieved myself.

"Now," said he, "again, on all fours, and into the kennel."

He then walked beside me as I made my way, on all fours, into the darkness of the kennel.

I recalled that my "keeping" was in his charge.

It took a little time for my eyes to adjust to the dimness of the kennel, which was of stout planking, and logs.

There were empty blanket spaces but, too, there were several slaves within. As nearly as I could tell none were secured.

My attention, when my eyes became better accustomed to the light, was arrested by one slave who sat to the side, her head down, her long black hair over her knees, about which she had forlornly clasped both arms. She seemed an image of hopelessness, and misery. What struck me most about her was that she, of all the slaves in the stockade, was gowned. The gown was sleeveless, of course, for she was a slave, but its length, if she were to stand, must have fallen almost to her ankles. It was a slave garment, but it was not a tunic, not the common, brief garment in which masters place their girls to remind them that they are slaves and which, to the pleasure of men, leaves little doubt as to their purchasable charms, or the far more scandalous common camisk, outlawed in public in certain cities, both garments for which a slave will be grateful, and beg piteously to be permitted. Rather it was the sort of slave garment in which a matron might insist her slaves be clothed if she was entertaining her sons. I was sure it was the only garment the slave wore. Too, it would doubtless lack a nether closure. The only slave garment I knew which was permitted a nether closure was the Turian camisk. I did not understand why this slave, and not the others, was permitted a garment so tasteful and modest. A slave walked past her and said something to her, which caused her to raise her head, angrily. Two of the other girls laughed. The gowned slave, obviously, did not stand high in the kennel order. Surely, I thought, her gowning would be likely to produce contempt and amusement amongst her kennel sisters, if not actual envy and hostility. Perhaps, I thought, it is a joke that she is so garbed, a mockery of sorts. I wondered about the gowned slave, apparently so alone, and despised. What of nudity to mark out prize slaves, and diminish the possibility of their flight, I asked myself. Why is she not stripped, as the others? Then I realized she was more marked out, or as marked out, as the others. In such a gown she stood out prominently amongst them, and even amongst tunicked or camisked slaves. And, if she should slip it away, she would have no other, and would then be as easily noticed as any other stripped kajira.

"Oh!" I said, thrust back, sitting, against the back wall of the kennel. My captor tossed a bundle of chain on the boards beside me. The leash collar was unbuckled from my throat and put to the side, with the coiled leash. To my dismay a heavy metal collar was placed about my throat and snapped shut. There was a ring in the back of the collar and, in a moment, by a chain and two snap locks I was fastened to a heavy ring behind me, set deeply in the logs of the kennel. Then manacles were snapped about both my right wrist and left wrist, separately, and by these, and chains and rings, my hands were chained, one on each side, to wall rings. I could not even feed myself. Then my ankles were grasped and each, in turn, was encircled with iron, independently shackled, and, by chains run to floor rings, one on the left, and one on the right, I was fastened in place.

My captor then retrieved the leash and leash collar, stood up, and looked down at me. I could not well see his expression, as he was outlined against the light from the opened door of the kennel behind him.

I shook the chains in misery, looking up at him, unbelievingly. I tried to lean forward but was held by the wall collar.

"Now, slut," he snarled, "escape!"

"I did a foolish thing," I said. "It was terribly foolish. I am sorry."

"What did you think to accomplish?" he asked. "You were tunicked, half naked in a scrap of rep cloth, and collared. You were marked. Where would you go, what would you do?"

"I was upset," I said. "I was not thinking clearly."

"There is no escape for such as you," he said.

"Need I be chained so heavily?" I asked.

"Be pleased," he said, "that you are not placed in close chains."

"Yes, Master," I said.

"In your chains," he said, "which please me, as in them you are eminently locatable, be instructed, barbarian slut. Learn from them. In them ponder the futility of escape."

"Yes, Master," I said. I had indeed been the fool. I had learned there was no escape for the Gorean slave girl.

He made as though he would turn away.

"Master!" I cried.

"Yes?" he said.

"I know I cannot escape," I said.

"Good," he said.

"But I do not wish to escape," I said.

"Oh?" he said.

"No!" I said.

"Why?" he said.

"Because I want the collar!" I said. "It belongs on me! I fought this for years, but it is true. Some women desire more than anything to be a slave, and I am one! Call me shamed and degraded, if you wish, but it is true, as true as my sex and the color of my eyes. And what is wrong with being what you are, and want to be? What have females been to males, and women to men, for thousands of generations? Have we not been fought for and led away, on ropes, haremed and herded, bargained for and exchanged, bought and sold, for millennia? Have not the attractive been chosen and the masters the choosers? Have we not been bred together, male and female, man and woman, for countless millennia as master and slave? Is this not in the hereditary coils of our very being, that we should be at our masters' feet? Surely I am a slave! I have known this from childhood. In how many dreams and irresistible thoughts did I kneel before a master! I am a slave! It is what I am in my heart, and desire to be. I ache for the ruthless domination of a master. I belong in a man's collar, his to do with as he wishes! Despise me, hate me, denounce me, if you wish, but I want to kneel, and be collared, and be owned! I want a master!"

"Worthless slut," he said.

"Buy me!" I begged. "Own me! Be my master!"

"I?" he asked.

"I want you as my master!" I said.

"A slave's wants are meaningless," he said. "She is a slave."

"Yes, Master," I wept. How true that was!

"She goes where she is sold. She does not choose the chains which will weight her fair limbs."

"No, Master," I said.

"Any man will do for you," he said.

"I must serve any man who owns me to the best of my ability," I said, "I go with the coins that will buy me, but I desire you as my master, and have, from the first moment I saw you, long ago, on Earth, in the great emporium."

"You turned about, and fled," he said.

"I was terrified," I said. "I did not know what to do! Never before had I been so looked upon, looked upon as a slave!"

"You looked well in the warehouse," he said, "on the floor, naked, bound hand and foot, at my feet."

"We are slaves," I said. "We want masters."

"Do you think you will escape now?" he asked.

"Do you think I can escape the iron on my neck and limbs?" I asked.

"Why did you run from Shipcamp?" he said.

"Please do not make me speak," I said.

"Do you wish to be shoulder-and-belly lashed?" he asked, loosening the leash strap.

"No, Master!" I said.

"Speak," he said.

"Please," I begged.

"Must a command be repeated?" he asked.

"No, Master," I wept. "I longed for you, so longed for you, and then you observed me in the exposition cage in Brundisium and turned away, and then, to my hope and joy, I encountered you on the dock at Shipcamp, but you scorned me. Walked away! I was nothing! I was scorned! I was miserable, distraught, devastated, furious, helpless, my hopes vanished, my world collapsed! All the seething obstinacy my world had conditioned into me erupted; all the lies and falsities of my former world reasserted themselves, proclaiming nature a mistake and her repudiation a necessity and virtue, reasserted themselves hissing and shrieking, in all the pervasive, manufactured din contrived to drown out the songs of nature, the messages of the hereditary coils, the voice of reality. So I decided to show the masters! I would run, I would escape! They would never catch me! And I would hate you, hate you with all my heart, for you had scorned me! And I knew I must flee at the first opportunity, as who knew when the great ship might depart? Who could escape if chained in one of its holds, abroad on deep, fierce Thassa? So it was with great anxiety that I awaited my opportunity. Then, when it came, I seized it."

"Why did you return to Shipcamp?" he asked.

"I was lost, confused," I said. "Surely it was not intentional."

"You were hurrying back to your chain," he said.

"No!" I wept.

"It was the same with the Panther Girls who prematurely relaxed their vigilance in the forest."

"Surely not!" I said.

"So," he said, "you would like me as your master?"

"Yes," I said. "Buy me! Buy me!"

"No," he said.

"But did the trek to Shipcamp mean nothing, what you did to me, what you made me feel?"

"No," he said.

"I see," I said, and then, apprehensive, added, "—Master."

"There was no other at hand," he said. "I told you that before."

"You well sported with a capture," I said.

"Of course," he said.

It was as I had feared. I meant nothing to him. But what more, I asked myself, could a slave expect of a free man?

Even in my training we had been taught that we were nothing, only slaves.

"Master!" I said.

"Do not escape, slut," he said. Then he turned away.

"Master!" I sobbed.

He did not look back.

I saw the gate of the stockade open and close, the two beams lowered into place.

I leaned back, in misery, against the wall of the kennel.

"You are well chained," said the gowned slave. "One might think you were important."

"I am not important," I said.

"That is true," she said.

"She is a barbarian," said one of the girls.

"That is obvious," said the gowned slave.

Doubtless this had been clear from my accent.

"You are so clever," said another girl, sneeringly.

"I could have had you boiled in tharlarion oil," snapped the gowned slave.

"Be careful or they will take your gown away," laughed another girl.

"Her vanity is exceeded only by her addled wits," said another girl.

"She is mad," laughed another.

"I am not!" cried the gowned slave.

"She thinks she is important," said another.

"I am important," said the gowned slave. "I was important."

"Who are you?" asked another of the girls.

"No one," said the gowned slave, angrily.

"She is mad," said one of the girls, "with all her airs. That is why they have named her 'Ubara'."

"That is cruel," I said.

"It is a joke," said one of the girls.

"I hate barbarians!" cried the gowned slave.

"They are stupid and ignorant," said a girl, "but why would you hate them?"

The gowned slave was silent.

"What is your name?" asked one of the girls of me.

"Laura," I said.

"That is a pretty name," said one of the slaves. "But as you are a barbarian, why did they not give you a barbarian name?"

"I think it is a barbarian name," I said.

"That is a well-known town on the Laurius to the south," said a girl.

"Perhaps it is a coincidence," I said, though I doubted that. Certainly I had found occasional words in Gorean which were words also in my native language, or very similar to such words, perhaps influenced by them or derived from them. I supposed Gorean, like most complex languages, may have borrowed from many tongues. Certainly it seemed to me that Goreans, or most of them, were clearly human, and, doubtless, directly or indirectly, owed their origin to my native world, Earth. Perhaps, I thought, the clue to the mystery might lie in the distant, formidable Sardar Mountains, of which the legendary or fabled Priest-Kings were supposedly denizens. In any event, much in these matters was obscure to me.

"Perhaps," said the girl.

"You are very nice looking, Laura," said another slave. "Why are you so chained? Do they think you are going to leap over the stockade wall? What did you do?"

"I ran away," I said.

"You see," said a girl who had earlier spoken, "barbarians, they are stupid."

"We are not stupid," I said. "We may be ignorant. We might do foolish things."

"Such as run away?" said one of the girls.

"Yes," I said.

"Ubara!" called a male voice, from the clearing outside the kennel, within the stockade.

The gowned slave, whether or not her wits were addled, or whether or not she was mad, must have been subjected to discipline, for she sprang up, and hurried outside and knelt before the guard, putting her head down to his feet, then lifting it, to attend his words.

I was startled at seeing the gowned slave outside the kennel, in the light. Before she had been much in the darkness of the kennel, away from the door. Now I saw that she was an incredibly beautiful woman, with a face and figure that might bring as much as a piece of gold off the block. She had long, dark hair, and a smooth olive skin. She might be mad, I thought, but she was such as one might expect to find chained beside a Ubar's throne. She might be an admiral's woman, or the slave of a polemarkos. If all were such as she, I thought, then the stockade might well be what it was rumored to be, a holding area for unusually beautiful slaves, prize slaves. Her appearance and mien suggested that in the days of her freedom, for I supposed she had once been free, she might have been of high caste. A slave, of course, has no caste. She is property, an animal, a beast.

"No!" she cried. "I will not!"

"You will not?" inquired the guard.

"Of course, I will obey, Master!" she cried. "But do not make me do this! Do not so humiliate and insult me, I beg of you! I am a high slave! I was of high caste! I might bring gold! I would be worthy of sandals!"

"Fetch a bowl," he said. "Go to the feed trough, fill it, and feed the barbarian slave."

"Please, no!" she begged.

"Now," said the guard.

"Yes, Master," she said.

Several of the slaves in the kennel, and some of those outside, laughed delightedly, apparently gratified by the discomfiture of the lovely, olive-skinned slave.

In a few Ehn, obviously fuming with displeasure, but holding a small bowl, which she had dipped briefly and angrily into the feed trough, the gowned slave, apparently named 'Ubara' as an insult or joke, entered the kennel. Several of her kennel sisters laughed.

"She-sleen!" said the gowned slave.

"Feed the barbarian, low slave!" laughed a girl.

"The mad one, in her lovely gown, worthy of a high merchant's companion, is least amongst us!" said another.

"She waits upon a barbarian," said another. "Let her pride absorb that!"

"Forgive me, Mistress," I said to her. "It is not my doing."

Even in the light I could see that the gowned slave had dark

493

eyes, matching the sable crown of glorious hair which swirled about her shoulders and down her back. When she had exited the kennel I had seen that the hair, despite its length, had been cut in the "slave flame." That is unusual. The "slave flame" is usually used with medium-length hair, just behind the shoulders. Her eyes, she was now close to me, were deep, and beautiful, but, I saw, too, they were now dark with anger. I did not doubt but what it might take gold to bring such a prize from the block.

"There," said the gowned slave, placing the bowl on the planks before me.

"Mistress," I said, "I cannot reach it."

"Unfortunate," she said.

As I was chained, I could not even bring my hands together, nor could I lift them to my mouth.

"You should not have run away," she said.

"I am hungry, Mistress," I said.

"Then eat," she said.

"Please, Mistress!" I said.

"The ship will leave soon," she said. "I have heard the ready banner is flying. Perhaps they will feed you on the ship."

"Feed her, low slave!" said one of the girls.

"We will call the guard!" said another.

"Do not call the guard," said the gowned slave, obviously frightened. "I am teasing. It is only a merry jest."

"Feed her," said another.

"I shall, you she-tarsks," said the gowned slave.

I did not think the gowned slave had addled wits, or was mad. In any event, I saw no indication of this. If anything, I saw high intelligence and cleverness. She did carry herself aristocratically. Her origins, I gathered, were mysterious. I did not doubt she might have been of high caste. That she should feed me was intended, I gathered, to insult her, to humiliate her, and help her better understand that she, identically with the others, was a slave. Surely that was not so hard to understand. Did she not know there was a collar on her neck? And I did not doubt but what beneath that gown there was a searing furrowed into her left thigh, just beneath the hip. Perhaps she did have airs, or pretensions. Perhaps she did suggest terrors she was in no position to inflict. Perhaps she did pretend she had once, if not now, been important. Perhaps she did despise the other slaves as inferiors. Perhaps she did not even recognize herself as a slave, or think of herself as a slave. Perhaps she thought of herself as wholly other than the others, as though she might be free, and they mere slaves. Did she think to put herself on the free side of the immeasurable chasm that separated persons and citizens from properties and beasts? Such things, doubtless, would make her resented amongst her chain sisters, but, too, they would not seem to me indications of madness, and certainly not, if there were any ground for possible airs or pretensions.

The gowned slave put her hand behind my head, holding it in place, and thrust the small bowl to my lips.

"Feed, barbarian she-tarsk," she said.

I choked a little, and I felt some of the gruel run beside my mouth.

"There," she said, "it is done," and drew the bowl away.

I recalled the quick, superficial descent of the bowl into the feeding trough. The bowl was small, of plain, unglazed, baked clay, and was chipped, and there had been very little in it, presumably by the gowned slave's intent, and part of what there was had been removed with the bowl.

She stood up, and, with her finger, several times, wiped some gruel from the bowl, which adhered to her finger, which she would then suck away. Then she turned away to return the bowl somewhere outside.

I was still very hungry.

"We saw, Laura!" said one of the slaves.

"You were not well fed," said another.

"Call the guard, and complain," said another.

"No," I said, "he is a master." I did not wish to be lashed.

"We will back you," said another girl. "Call out!"

"No," I said.

"Then we will do so," said another.

"Pretty Ubara then will be stripped and lashed, tied in the doorway," said another.

"It will not be the first time," laughed another.

"No," I said, "do not do so! Please do not do so!"

"What is going on?" said the guard, entering, holding the

gowned slave roughly by one arm. She seemed small and distraught beside him, so held.

"Ubara did not feed the barbarian!" said a girl.

"No, she ate her food!" said another.

"Speak!" said the guard, shaking the miserable gowned slave by the arm, almost causing her to lose her footing.

"I fed her well, as commanded!" said the gowned slave, frightened. "A full bowl, as commanded! I did not eat her food."

So, I thought, beauty, for all your having possibly been of high caste or whatever, and for all your pretensions and superiorities, you are now only a frightened slave, and a liar.

The guard dragged the gowned slave before me. "Speak," he said to me. It was clear he held the beautiful, olive-skinned slave in contempt. To him, I saw, she was no more than another slave, and perhaps one that was less than pleasing. I did not think he would find her stripping and lashing amiss. Perhaps it was he who had put her in the gown, to signal her out for envy and derision. It is the masters, of course, who decide whether or not a slave is to be clothed, and, if clothed, how, and to what extent. Such small things, as many others, help the slave to keep well in mind that she is a slave.

"I was fed, Master," I said. "I am content."

Several of the slaves in the kennel cried out in protest. The gowned slave, her arm released, regarded me with surprise, and then, as the guard withdrew, with contempt.

"You did not inform on me," she said.

"No," I said.

"You were afraid to do so," she said.

"No," I said.

"Why did you not have her beaten?" asked a girl.

"She was afraid," snarled the gowned slave.

"No!" I said.

"Then why?" asked another slave.

"The whip hurts," I said.

The gowned slave, her face contorted with fury, bent toward me. "You are a fool," she whispered. "I owe you nothing!"

"I expect nothing, and want nothing, from such as you," I said.

"From such as I?" she said.

"You may or may not have been born to high caste," I said, "but I see little of high caste about you. You may be beautiful, but you are small, petty, cruel, pretentious, self-centered, and a liar, and most obviously, now a slave."

"Silence, slave!" she hissed.

"A slave may speak so to a slave," I said.

"I am not a slave!" she cried.

"Slave!" I said.

The gowned slave then threw herself upon me, screaming, striking, biting, and scratching, and the other slaves about leapt to their feet, and rushed toward us, to protect me, and, as they seized her, the gowned slave had seized my hair, and shook my head, violently, and I had pulled back, with a rattle of chain, that I not be strangled in the wall collar, and the gowned slave's hands were pulled apart, away from my hair, and she wept with pain, as she was dragged back, away from me, by the hair.

"Release me!" she demanded, but two girls held her arms, one on each side, and another had her hair pulled back so tightly that the gowned slave's head was facing the ceiling of the kennel. Other slaves were crowded about, angrily, and some others had entered from the clearing outside the kennel.

"I hope you marked her," said a slave to the gowned slave, "that your nose will be cut off!"

"No, no!" cried the gowned slave. "She is not marked, not marked!"

"Who are you that you would attack a chained slave?" asked a slave.

"She is not marked!" cried the gowned slave.

I was scratched but, as it turned out, superficially. I did not think any damage had been done. I was more angry than anything else. My assailant's blows, dealt with the sides of her fists, happily, had been administered only with a woman's strength, and my rescuers had been upon her almost as soon as she had hurled herself upon me. The bites about my shoulder had not drawn blood. I did taste blood, but I had inadvertently bitten my own lip in the tumult.

"Cut off her nose!" said a slave of the gowned slave.

"No!" she wept.

Masters, as is recognized, seldom mix in the altercations of slaves. On the other hand, they are very much concerned with maintaining the value of the goods involved. Nothing is to be done to a girl which might reduce her value on the block. For example, the supple, broad-bladed, five-stranded slave whip designed to punish an errant slave, and well, is also designed in such a way that it will leave no lingering residue of its attentions. Happily for women, and, I suppose, for their owners, if they are owned, it is very rare that their disagreements, unlike those of men, result in any permanent injuries or disablements. Amongst free women who may tear veils or lose slippers, or amongst slaves, who may rend or lose a tunic, not much is likely to take place which could not be reduced to unpleasantries such as insults, scratchings, bitings, and yanked hair.

"Cut off her ears, too!" cried another slave.

"No, no!" wept the gowned slave.

She was then forced down to her knees.

She struggled but was helpless in the hands of her chain sisters, two of whom maintained their grip on her arms, one on each side.

"Would that we had a dagger," said one of the slaves.

"The guard has one," said a slave.

"Call him!" said another.

"No, no, no!" begged the gowned slave.

"Leave it to Laura!" said a girl.

"No!" begged the gowned slave. "No! Not to her!"

"Beg her forgiveness!" said one of the girls holding the gowned slave's arm, the left arm.

"She is a barbarian!" protested the gowned slave.

"Now!" cried a girl, and, taking the gowned slave's head by the hair, with two hands, forced it down to the planks before me.

The gowned slave howled with misery. "Forgive me, forgive me!" she wept.

"Call her 'Mistress'," said another girl.

"Mistress!" wept the gowned slave.

"I am not 'Mistress'," I said. "Let her up."

It was permitted to the gowned slave that she might raise her head, but she was held on her knees, helpless, as before, before me.

"Bespeak your contriteness," said a girl. "Beg her forgiveness, as what you are, a lowly, miserable slave."

"That is not necessary," I said.

"Now," demanded one of the girls.

"I am not injured," I said.

"I am contrite, Mistress," said the gowned slave. "Please forgive me, Mistress."

"I forgive you," I said.

"We do not!" said a slave, angrily.

"Please, let her alone," I said.

"Are you important?" asked a slave of the gowned slave.

"No, Mistress," she said.

"What are you?" asked another.

"A slave, Mistress," she said.

"What sort of slave?" asked another.

"A meaningless slave, Mistress," said the gowned slave.

"Are you better than we?" asked a girl.

"No, Mistress," said the gowned slave.

"Are you less than we?" asked another.

"Yes, Mistress," said the gowned slave.

Several of the slaves laughed. "She speaks truly," said one of them.

"Remove her gown," said a girl.

"No!" begged the gowned slave.

"The guard will not permit it," said a slave.

"Go, see!" said a slave, and another slave hurried from the kennel.

"No, no!" said the gowned slave.

In a moment the slave who had rapidly exited the kennel returned, beaming. "It may be done!" she shouted.

"No!" wept the gowned slave, but then, in a moment, she was as stripped as the others. She was then dragged toward the door. There the light was better. "The mark of Treve!" cried a slave, pointing to the thigh of the held slave.

So, I thought, she is branded. I knew little of Treve, other than the fact that it was reputedly a bandit city somewhere in the vastness of the mighty Voltai mountains, far to the south.

"I hope masters burn a dozen brands into her leg," said a slave.

"Yes," said another.

"Let her alone," I said. "Please let her alone."

The slaves then went about their ways. She who had been gowned then crept back into the darkness of the kennel, and lay on the planks, her head down on her arms.

A slave approached me. "Are you all right?" she asked.

"Yes," I said.

"The gate is opening!" called a girl.

"Keep back," said the guard.

Four men entered, two bearing small boxes, and two, together, bearing a long chain with collars.

"What is it?" asked a girl.

"A coffle chain," said a girl.

"We are going to be moved!" said a slave.

"Is the ready banner down?" called another.

"I cannot see," said a slave.

"What is in the boxes?" called a girl, from the kennel doorway.

"I do not know," said a girl, from the clearing.

"I can see through the gate!" called a girl. "Across the river! I cannot see the ready banner! It is down!"

"Get back!" ordered the guard. There was a snap of his whip.

"The ship departs tomorrow!" cried a girl, frightened.

"Back, back!" said the guard. I heard the snap of his whip, twice more. "Into the kennel!" he said. There was another snap of the whip, and the slaves who were in the clearing, hurried back into the kennel. They left the door open, and were clustered just inside, looking out.

"I do not want to sail to the farther islands," said a girl. "It is too late in the season. Thassa will not permit it."

"I have heard the World's End," said another.

"That is absurd," said another. "That would be madness."

"I do not want to go to the World's End," said a girl.

"We will go where we are taken," said another.

"Have no fear," said another. "That cannot be the destination."

"The men are going," I heard. "The guard is closing the gate."

"To the feed trough!" called the guard.

The slaves then hurried to the trough, with the exception of she who had been gowned, who remained prone on the planking inside the kennel, to the left of the door, and one other, who lingered by me. "I will bring you something," she said.

"Thank you," I said.

The slaves were crowded at the trough. They were permitted to use their hands. After a time she who had volunteered to feed me entered the kennel. She carried the small, simple bowl which had been earlier carried by the slave who had been gowned. She held it to my mouth that I might feed, and, with a finger, as I could not do so, wiped what had clung to the bottom and sides of the bowl into my mouth.

"Thank you," I said.

She then returned the bowl to the feed trough in the clearing, and returned.

"I am very grateful," I said.

"You did not want Ubara hurt," she said. "Why?"

"She is a slave," I said.

"Do not expect her to be grateful," she said.

"I do not," I said.

"I do not know why Ubara is as she is," said the slave.

"Perhaps she was once free," I said.

"So, too, were we all," said the girl. "There are no bred slaves here, save that we are women."

"You think that women are born slaves?" I said.

"We are not complete until we are the slaves of our masters," she said.

"Even Ubara?" I asked.

"She fears greatly that for which she most longs," she said.

"Do you think she would make a good slave?" I asked.

"She is very beautiful," she said.

"But surely more is required," I said.

"She has not yet learned her collar," she said.

"I see," I said.

"Men can teach it to her," she said.

"I have learned my collar," I said.

"But you ran away," she said.

"I now know my collar," I said, "and want it, and love it."

"Even though you will be despised by free women?" she asked.

"Let them be themselves," I said, "and let us be ourselves."

"They are the mistresses," she said.

"Why do they hate us so?" I asked.

"It is we whom men strip and collar, and bind, and buy and

sell, and raid for, and capture, and put to their feet, and want," she said.

"I feel sorry for free women," I said.

"Do not feel sorry for them," she said. "They have the switch and whip."

"How deprived, and lonely they must be," I said, "in their pride and misery."

"They envy us our collars, and our joy," she said.

"I fear so," I said.

"Have you been mastered?" she asked.

"I am a slave," I said. "Any man can master me."

"But perhaps you hope for a given master?" she asked.

"Oh, yes!" I breathed. "But why do you ask?"

"You are well chained," she observed.

"I do not understand," I said.

"Think," she said. "You have not only been put naked in a high-security stockade, but chained, by the neck, and hand and foot. You are held to the wall, and you cannot even bring your hands together before your body or bring your legs together. Surely you are aware of your vulnerability, and how you might be caressed with impunity."

"Yes," I said, frightened.

"What do you think the point of all this is," she asked, "the meaning of such a chaining?"

"I think," I said, "to instruct me."

"How so?" she asked.

"To convince me of the futility of escape," I said.

"Perhaps," she said. "What else?"

"That I may better know myself a slave?" I said.

"Doubtless," she said. "And, too, does your utter helplessness and complete vulnerability not arouse you?"

I dared not respond.

"But there is more meaning here," she said, "than you understand, and perhaps more than he who chained you understands."

"I do not understand, at all," I said.

"There is no slave in this stockade," she said, "who is not lovely, who would not be an excellent buy, who would not be a prize to remove from an auction block, and yet you are the only one who is chained."

"Perhaps they fear I will try to escape," I said.

"By leaping naked over the palings?" she asked.

"No," I said.

"If that were all," she said, "a single ankle chain would do. It would hold you in place very nicely, in utter helplessness, while you await the convenience of masters."

"I cannot understand you," I said.

"What sorts of things are secured?" she asked.

"I do not know," I said.

"Prizes, treasures, valuables," she said.

"It seems so," I said.

"And what is secured with great care," she asked, "with heaviness and authority, even immoderately?"

"I do not know," I said.

"Something which is important to one," she said, "something one does not wish to risk losing, something which one wants, something which one desires, something which one refuses to give up, something which one is determined to possess."

"Surely not!" I said.

Chapter Fifty-One

"We leave in the early morning," said Tyrtaios, angrily.

"I understand," I said.

"Surely you understand the importance of the secret cargo we boarded some nights ago, and disguised in the hold," he said.

"I understand it is important," I said, "but I do not understand why it is important, or how it is important."

"Worlds may hang on its delivery at the World's End," he said.

"It seems unlikely to me," I said, "that the ship, mighty as it may be, will reach the World's End, if such a place exists. What is such a ship, even so stout and strong, in the merciless grip of Thassa?"

"Doubtless it will be grievously tested," said Tyrtaios.

"Consider the season," I said.

"Do you fear to sail with her?" asked Tyrtaios.

"Of course," I said, "as might any rational individual, understanding what is involved, but I am prepared to do so."

"You know the risks," said Tyrtaios.

"Of course," I said.

"And there are more," said Tyrtaios.

"I understand," I said.

"Much may be risked where much is to be gained," said Tyrtaios.

"I understand," I said.

"Would you not wish untold wealth, the command of fleets and armies, your choice of women?" he asked. "Do you not want a ubarate, or ubarates? Perhaps you might be given Cos or Tyros, Ar or Turia, a dozen cities?"

"I find this hard to believe," I said.

Angrily, he drew from his wallet a double tarn of gold, and hurled it against my jacket, where I caught it, and regarded it, incredulously. Many Goreans have never seen such a coin, and some doubt that it exists. "It is yours," he said, "and it is nothing. Do you understand?"

"I understand," I said.

"I and my principal are displeased with you," he said.

"How so?" I asked.

"Few know of this, the secret cargo, and those who do are important, so important that they must be relied upon, or eliminated. And you, like an enamored fool, rush into the forest on the track of a meaningless chit, even a barbarian."

"I thought it would be a pleasant diversion," I said.

"Seek your diversions less distant," said Tyrtaios.

"I accompanied Axel of Argentum," I said.

"He was sent to locate spies," he said.

"They were located," I said, "and are unlikely to report their findings, or, in any event, in time for their intelligence to be meaningful."

"You should have remained in Shipcamp," he said. "What if the ship had departed? What if you had been killed by beasts in the forest? What if you had been captured by enemies, and tortured, and had revealed the existence of the secret cargo?"

"Fortunately those things did not take place," I said.

"It is feared," he said, "that you are unreliable."

My hand went to the hilt of my blade.

"Do not be stupid," said Tyrtaios.

"Forgive me," I said.

"You could have had a dozen quarrels in your back an Ahn after your return to Shipcamp," he said.

"I see," I said.

"You did a foolish and stupid thing," he said.

"Obviously," I said.

"Have I seen the slave?" he asked.

"I do not know," I said.

"She must be very beautiful," said Tyrtaios.

"Not particularly," I said.

"I understand you have placed her in the stockade," he said.

"Yes," I said.

"That is reserved for special slaves," he said.

"She has been breast-marked with her name," I said. "That will distinguish between her and the special slaves."

"Why did you take her there?" asked Tyrtaios. "That is a maximum-security facility."

"She ran away," I said.

"Why did you not have her fed to sleen?" he asked.

"She is nicely curved," I said.

"The two major housing areas for kajirae on the ship," he said, "are on the Kasra and Venna decks. The stockade girls will most likely be housed on the Venna deck, and the more common slaves in the Kasra area."

"Then she will doubtless be chained in the Kasra area," I said.

"You pursued her in the forest," said Tyrtaios.

"I accompanied Axel of Argentum," I said, "who was dispatched to locate spies, Panther Girls. She was, so to speak, to lead us to them, assuming she might fall to them, a naive barbarian, as a capture slave."

"Which occurred," said Tyrtaios.

"Yes," I said.

"You should have remained in Shipcamp," he said.

"Forgive me," I said.

"What is the slave to you?" he asked.

"Nothing," I said. "She is only a slave."

"She is not yours," said Tyrtaios. "She is a camp slave, a common camp slave. She was even chained for a time in the slave house."

"I understand that was the case," I said.

"She must then be comely," he said.

"Doubtless some would find her so," I said.

"What about her belly?" he asked.

"She has little to say about such things," I said.

"Her needs have been ignited?"

"Quite," I said.

"If she were not to be sold for three or four days," he said, "would she be scratching at the sides of her kennel?"

"Yes," I said.

"Do you find her of interest?" he asked.

"She is a barbarian," I said.

"Do you find her of interest?" he asked, again.

"Not particularly," I said.

"And yet you pursued her into the forest," he said.

"For the sport of the chase," I said.

"And you captured her?"

"Yes," I said, "to the west, near the Alexandra."

"In returning to Shipcamp," he said, "did you put her to frequent and rich slave use?"

"Yes," I said. "There was no other at hand."

"And did you have her whimpering, and begging, at your feet?"

"Yes," I said.

"A slave is nothing," said Tyrtaios.

"True," I said.

"There is nothing to choose from amongst them," said Tyrtaios. "One is no better or worse than another. They are animals, goods, properties, objects, beasts," he said. "They are little different from she-urts, to which they are inferior."

"True," I said.

"Yet you pursued her into the forest," he said.

"For sport," I said, "for sport."

"And you have housed her in the stockade."

"She had run away," I said.

"Would you like to own her," he asked, "to have her at your feet, in your collar, helplessly yours, your slave, under your whip?"

"She is a barbarian," I said.

"We fear," said Tyrtaios, "that this slave is of some interest to you."

"No," I said.

"That she is a distraction, that she may compromise your value to our cause."

"You need have no fear on that score," I said.

"The cause is all-important," said Tyrtaios.

"Certainly," I said.

"It was not for nothing that we paid you two golden staters," he said.

"I understand," I said.

"Also," he said, "you know a great deal, which knowledge is a dangerous burden."

"I understand," I said.

"It is rather like carrying a live ost in your hand," said Tyrtaios.

"You may rely on me," I said.

"As you are honorable?" asked Tyrtaios.

"No," I said. "As I am fond of gold, and am reluctant to feel the fangs of an ost in my palm."

"I think you may easily dispel our uneasiness, and reassure us of your good will, reliability, and fidelity," said Tyrtaios. "My principal has suggested a simple test to clarify matters."

"Oh?" I said.

"By means of which you will prove your worthiness, your dependability, your resolve, and loyalty."

"Speak," I said.

"Is your dagger sharp?" asked Tyrtaios.

"Yes," I said.

"And its edge?" he asked.

"It can wound the morning mist," I said. "It can draw blood from the fog."

"Good," said Tyrtaios.

"What is the test?" I asked.

"Before the great ship leaves in the morning," he said, "before the stockade slaves are boarded, you are to cross the river, enter the stockade, and cut the throat of a certain slave. Do you understand?"

"Yes," I said.

Chapter Fifty-Two

It was damp, and chilly, on the plankings. I had slept but little. In the kennel in Shipcamp, we had had blankets. If these slaves were so special, I thought, why are they not better cared for? Is it to impress upon them that they are, however special, only slaves? Even had I a blanket, I could not have well covered myself, chained as I was. I wondered how early it was. The door to the kennel was shut. I thought I could see a sliver of light, lamplight, through the crack, at the bottom of the door. Last night I had heard the two beams dropped into place which sealed it, from the outside. I thought it must be very early.

I heard a girl to my left, somewhere, moan in her sleep.

I had run away. I had been punished, lashed, near the shore of the Alexandra by my captor. I did not know if I were to be further punished, or not, and, if so, how. They tell us little.

I had heard yesterday afternoon that the ready banner had been lowered. The ship, then, must be on the verge of beginning the descent of the Alexandra. The stockade slaves, I supposed, would have to be transported across the river. I supposed a boat, or boats, would be waiting. I had seen various boats on both the north and south side of the river.

"They are coming for us!" I heard, a slave's voice, frightened, from somewhere in the darkness.

I had heard nothing.

I did see part of the sliver of light blocked, from the outside.

Then, clearly, I heard men outside, and men's voices. A moment later, one after the other, I heard the two beams outside removed from their brackets.

The door was then swung outward, and I could see four or five men outside, with the guard, who held a lamp, upraised. I heard, too, a rattle of chain.

"Slaves outside!" I heard. "Stand, single file, facing the gate, tallest girl first, in order of height."

It was not yet dawn.

The order of marshaling was a common one, in which a slave line is organized in terms of height, in descending order. Goreans tend to have a sense of proportion and harmony, of propriety, and beauty. This tendency may be expressed in innumerable ways, from the design of cities to the bright colors of buildings and walls, and porches and pillars, from long garden paths, a pasang in length, characterized by a planned music of scent as well as a scenic melody of blossoms, to the shaping of vases and lamps, from the boss on a shield or a clamp on a kaiila harness to the intricate, subtle carving which might be lavished on the handle of a common tool or a humble wooden spoon.

I was then alone in the kennel. The door had been left open. Outside I could see the lamp, and, in the light and shadows, the men and slaves. The slave who had been gowned was toward the rear of the line.

I watched as the slaves were coffled. Then I learned what had been in one of the two small boxes brought yesterday afternoon to the stockade. The wrists of each slave were drawn behind her, and braceleted. It then, a bit later, became clear what had been the contents of the second small box. It contained slave hoods. One by one the slaves were hooded. How helpless one is in a slave hood, how confused and disoriented, how much at the mercy of the masters!

I saw the gate to the stockade opened. Two men were outside, with torches.

"Prepare to move," called the guard, the lamp held over his head.

"No, no!" I heard. "Please, Masters! Do not take me away, Masters!"

It was the voice of she who had been gowned. How frightened she sounded. What did she so much fear? Where did she think she might be taken? Presumably to the ship. Possibly elsewhere? What did she think might be done with her? Did she think her fate might be different from that of the others? Was there something special about her? Was she not merely another slave?

"Where are you taking us?" cried a slave.

"They will take us to the ship!" said another.

"The great ship!" said another.

"No!" said another.

"Not to the ship!" cried another slave.

"I do not want to go to the World's End!" cried a slave.

"Beat us, sell us, take us elsewhere!" begged a slave. "But do not take us to the ship."

"Have mercy on us!" cried another. "We are slaves!"

"Forward," said the guard. "Step carefully."

"Masters!" I called.

I was not sure, fully, what was going on. It did seem that the ready banner was down, and the great ship might soon depart.

Certainly the girls in my kennel at Shipcamp had feared to be placed on the great ship, and it seemed the stockade slaves had similar trepidations.

It seemed reasonably clear to me, certainly highly probable, that slaves, both here and at Shipcamp, were to be embarked on the great ship. Were they not slaves, goods, to be sold or traded at the World's End, or the farther islands, whatever might be the destination of that mighty frame now poised for its journey downriver to Thassa?

Why, I wondered, had they been hooded? Surely it was not necessary for purposes of security. They were back-braceleted and coffled. I supposed it might be to make clearer to them that they were slaves. But then I thought it might be more likely that they might be hooded that their faces might be concealed. If so, it did not seem likely that the fear was their beauty, and its possible effect on strong men, for, although they were beauties, it seemed there were many in Shipcamp who were their equals, if not superiors. So, I thought, the hooding must be that they not, or one or another of them, be recognized. But what difference would it make, I asked myself, if one slave or another might be recognized?

I saw the coffle begin to move slowly toward the stockade gate. The left arm of the lead girl was held by one of the fellows who had accompanied the guard. The guard himself, with his lamp, was to the left of the coffle. The two fellows with torches had turned about, and were moving toward the broad stairway leading down to the river, that which I had ascended yesterday.

"Masters!" I called out, plaintively.

But no one turned about.

The coffle proceeded on its way.

"Masters!" I cried.

If Shipcamp were abandoned, and, with it, the stockade and buildings here, on the south side of the Alexandra, what of me? Had I been forgotten? I could not free myself.

"Masters!" I cried. "Masters!" I shook the chains. I pulled at them, futilely.

Then I was alone, not only in the kennel, but in the stockade. I had run away.

Was this my punishment, I wondered, to be left behind, alone, chained, without food and water?

Better, I thought, the brief attentions of sleen or, more lingeringly, those of leech plants.

"Masters!" I screamed. "Please, I am here! Do not leave me! Do not leave me! Have mercy on me!"

I pulled at the chains, again and again. "Masters!" I cried. "Masters!"

Tor-tu-Gor, Light-Upon-the-Home-Stone, the common star of two worlds, Earth and Gor, was rising.

It was a cold, damp morning.

In a few Ehn I could see the points on the palings, and, later, in the grayness, the clearing beyond the door of the kennel, with the food trough to the side and near it the catchment, the small reservoir or water tank, where I had been permitted to drink yesterday, though only on all fours, and leashed. I could see that the gate had been left open. Doubtless that was because they thought the stockade was empty.

"Masters!" I wept. "Masters!"

Then I was very frightened, for I smelled smoke. The torch, I feared, was being set to the local buildings. Probably the stockade, too, then, would be burned. I wondered if, too, across the river, Shipcamp was to be destroyed.

Men would be setting such fires, which would spread from building to building, and, possibly, to the stockade. Possibly the stockade itself had already been set afire, from the outside. I heard the crackling of flames. I called out, again and again, shrieking for attention, but if any heard me I received no indication that they had done so.

How I cried out! How helpless I was in the chains. I felt heat behind me, so anomalous and frightening in the cold morning. The back wall of the kennel might be aflame. Through the door I saw smoke, billowing like dark, ugly, suffocating clouds, and then there was a sudden gust of wind, which tore apart the smoke, and flung before it a shower of sparks, and then more sparks began to fall about, the wind softening, in the clearing, these now descending like hot, bright rain. I began to choke. I pulled, weeping, at the chains, coughing.

A large, dark figure appeared in the doorway. I saw it outlined, black, with flames bright behind it. It coughed, and cast about. I think it had one hand before its face. "Master!" I cried. It felt its way, through the smoke, uncertainly, toward me. I could hardly keep my eyes open, for burning tears, for the stinging of smoke in my eyes. I was aware of a key being forced into locks. A beam, burning, dropped from the ceiling to my right. Then, by a powerful hand grasped on my wrist, I was jerked to my feet, and dragged, stumbling, from the kennel, out, into the clearing, and then I was pulled across the clearing and out the gate.

"Master!" I wept, my hand imprisoned in his grip.

We stopped several paces from the gate, and I sank to my knees, gasping for air, on the grass between the stockade gate and the head of the stairway leading down to the river, and he was crouching beside me, his head down, coughing. It was he who had chained me there, to whom my keeping had been allotted.

The air seemed acrid with smoke. Behind us the stockade and kennel was aflame. I could see across the river, and Shipcamp, too, was aflame. There was a crash behind us where, I conjectured, the roof of the kennel had collapsed.

"Master has risked his life to save the life of a slave," I gasped.

"You are valuable," he said.

"Valuable to Master?" I said.

"Certainly," he said. "You might bring two silver tarsks off the block."

"You risked much for two silver tarsks," I whispered.

"I would have done as much for a tethered verr," he said, "or an urt on a neck string."

"A slave is grateful," I said. "May her lips not repay Master?"

"Do you wish to be cuffed?" he asked.

"No, Master!" I said.

"A slave," he said, "has nothing, nothing with which to either pay, or repay. One simply takes from her whatever one might wish, whenever one wishes it, and however one wishes it."

"Yes, Master," I said.

He rose to his feet, looking across the river.

I remained kneeling. It is seldom wise to rise to one's feet in the presence of a master, if one has not received permission. I did go to all fours, which seemed acceptable for a beast, and joined him, in looking across the river. "Shipcamp is afire," I said.

He looked down upon me, and reached into his wallet. He flung me a small handful of wadded cloth. "Put it on," he said.

"Yes, Master!" I said, gratefully.

"I had little time," he said.

In a moment I had pulled on the tunic, and fastened the disrobing loop at the left shoulder.

"It is too long," he said, "but it can be considerably shortened later."

I thought it already short, quite short.

"A slave thanks Master for the privilege of a garment," I said. How strange, I thought, remembering my former world, that a girl would be almost tearfully grateful for so tiny a bit of cloth, in which she was next to naked, a Gorean slave tunic. A Gorean free woman, I thought, might almost die of shame at the mere thought of being placed in such a garment, but would learn to prize it soon enough if she were collared.

My rescuer, whom I shall choose to refer to as my "captor," for it was he who had captured me, and he in whose keeping I remained, suddenly looked about, to his right.

"On your stomach," he said, "hands behind your back."

Instantly I was prone, as directed. A Gorean master is to be obeyed instantly, and unquestioningly.

"Look toward the river," he said.

I turned my face, on the grass, toward the river, which was to my left. I felt my hands fastened behind me, in slave bracelets.

"Ho!" said a voice. "What have we here?"

"On your feet," said my captor, and I rose to my feet, and kept my head down. "A slave," he said.

Two men had approached; each carried a torch. They had doubtless been firing the buildings and stockade.

"The ship will soon depart," said one of the men. "Where did you get her?"

"The stockade," said my captor.

I felt a thumb push my head up.

"She is pretty," said the second fellow with a torch.

I put my head down again. It is usual for a slave girl, if she is permitted to stand, to stand so before free persons, humbly, head down, self-effacingly, respectfully.

"The stockade girls are being boarded," said the first fellow with a torch. It was still burning. I could hear it crackle.

"She should have been put in the coffle, stripped, braceleted, and hooded," said the second fellow.

"She was housed in the stockade, but she is not a stockade girl," said my captor.

"A runaway?" asked the first fellow.

"Once," said my captor.

"Stupid slut," said the second fellow.

"She is a barbarian," said my captor, I thought unnecessarily.

"Why is she clothed?" asked one of the men.

"I prefer to get her to the ship without incident," said my captor. "It will delay things if she is jeered, accosted, or beaten."

"She should have been fed to sleen," said the first fellow.

"Come now," said my captor. "Look at her. Surely you can think of something better to do with this than feed it to sleen."

"Yes," said the first fellow, "but there is no time. There are boats waiting. You had best come with us."

"We will follow, shortly," said my captor. "I wish you well."

"And we you," said one of the men, and then they began to descend the long stairway leading down to the beach. We watched them. They extinguished their torches in the water. Behind us the stockade was raging with flame.

"We had best descend the stairway," said my captor. "There will doubtless be others."

"May I speak?" I asked.

"Yes," he said.

"A slave is grateful that Master has seen fit to save her life," I said.

"It is not saved yet," he said, "or mine."

"I do not understand," I said.

"It is political," he said. "Do not concern yourself with it."

"Please, Master," I said.

"It is not pleasant to carry a live ost in one's hand," he said.

"I do not understand," I said.

"Surely you do not think it would be pleasant, do you?"

"No, Master," I said.

"Step carefully here," he said. "The steps are broad, but, as you are braceleted, it would be well to exercise caution."

"Yes, Master," I said.

"Do you not know how to follow a man?" he asked.

"Forgive me, Master," I said.

"No!" he said, suddenly. "Precede me. I wish to keep my eye on you."

"I welcome the scrutiny of Master," I said. "I hope he finds a slave pleasing."

"I do not wish you to escape," he said.

"I fear Master is not candid," I said, "as I am braceleted."

"Keep moving," he said, "or I will use my belt across the backs of your thighs."

"Yes, Master," I said.

"Do not think," he said, "that I find you of interest."

"Yet Master risked his life for me," I said. "And he pursued me in the forest. And I think he followed me from far Brundisium."

"I came for sport, and gold," he said.

"And perhaps for a slave," I said.

"It is an unwise slave who tempts the lash," he said.

"Forgive me, Master," I said, contentedly.

He growled with anger.

"Here," he said at the foot of the stairway, "move to the left, toward the small boats."

But near the foot of the stairway there were several men,

mostly mercenaries. Some were entering boats, long boats, six- or eight-oared, and small boats, two-oared, thrusting oars outboard, and some were partly in the water, preparing to launch the boats, and several were about, with weapons, supervising the beach.

It was chilly on the beach, and there was fog, flat about the surface of the stirring water, and in the sky there was smoke, drifting westward, toward Thassa. Here, close to the river, no sparks fell. Across the river one could see Shipcamp afire.

"Hold!" said a mercenary, a large fellow, bearded, with a helmet crested with sleen hair.

"Yes, Captain?" said my captor.

"We have received the signal from the dock," he said. "The first whistle has been blown."

"I see," said my captor. "Then we must hurry to our boat."

"Take your place there," said the mercenary, indicating an eight-oared craft.

"My accouterments," said my captor, "are in the far boat, there, along the shore."

He pointed west along the shore, where, to be sure, there were some small boats.

"What are you doing here, on this side of the river?" asked the captain.

"Fetching a slave," said my captor, indicating me.

"She is a camp slave," said the captain. "Ship her here," he said, indicating the specified craft. "It makes no difference."

"No," said my captor. "She is a private slave."

"That is a camp collar," said the officer.

"It has not yet been changed," said my captor.

"Put her here," said the officer, unpleasantly, indicating the same vessel he had earlier suggested.

"She was privately purchased by a high officer," said my captor, confidentially.

"Who?" asked the captain.

"Others are interested in her," said my captor. "It will not do to make that public until her collar is changed."

"Am I to believe that?" asked the officer. I noted that some three or four of his men had now, perhaps sensing some difficulty, approached more closely.

"She is to be unobtrusively, privately, delivered," said my captor.

"Seat her there, on a thwart there!" said the captain, pointing to the designated vessel, angrily.

"Of course, as you will," said my captor. "But may I inquire your name?"

"Why?" asked the officer, warily.

"I will not have this on my head," said my captor. "I must report it."

"To whom?" asked the captain.

My captor leaned forward, and said, softly. "To Lord Okimoto, lord in Shipcamp, high lord of the Pani."

"Ah," said the officer. "Proceed."

"My thanks, Captain," said my captor, and he hurried west, toward the small boats drawn up, tethered, some one hundred paces or so to the west.

"Hurry!" called the captain, from several paces behind. "We are expecting any Ehn now the signal that the second whistle has sounded; then we must leave." I supposed a keen ear could hear the whistle from across the width of the Alexandra, but those on this side of the river were apparently reading a flag signal, or such, informing them of the state of departure.

"There should be only one boat here," said my captor, uneasily, "my boat," as we approached two, small, two-oared boats. There were two I now saw, farther west on the beach.

He reached into the boat and gathered up a pack.

"Master!" I cried.

From the trees and brush nearby an armed figure had emerged. "I have been waiting for you," he said. "Tyrtaios feared this."

"Tyrtaios," said my captor, "is very clever."

"I think so," said Axel of Argentum.

"He leaves little to chance," said my captor.

"Very little," said Master Axel.

My captor put down his pack on the beach, and stepped away from it, and away from the small boat.

"We trekked together in the forest," said my captor.

"True," said Master Axel.

"What are you doing here?" asked my captor.

"Surely it is clear," said Axel.

"It seems," said my captor, "that indeed I hold a live ost in my hand."

"I do not understand," said Axel.

"It is unimportant," said my captor.

"You were to cut the throat of the slave, and report to the ship," said Axel.

"I forgot," said my captor. "Or I did not wish to dull the edge of a fine dagger, or I preferred to avoid the task of cleaning the blade, or such."

"Or such, I think," said Axel.

"I thought you were my friend," said my captor.

"It seems," said Axel, "that your head has been turned by a slave."

"I have occasionally thought of her at my slave ring," said my captor.

"Master!" I cried.

"Be silent," snapped my captor. There was about five or six paces between the two men. That, I supposed, would give each the time necessary to draw a blade, and, unrushed, begin with care to attend to the exigencies of private war.

"It is then the sword?" said my captor.

"It is only necessary," said Axel, "that you cut the throat of the slave and return to the ship."

"I do not choose to do so," said my captor.

"So it would seem the sword," said Axel.

"Yes," said my captor.

"You would risk your life for a slave?" asked Axel.

"For sport," said my captor.

"I see," said Axel.

"We are one to one," said my captor. "I am not unskilled."

"Nor I," said Axel. "Nor are many who have taken fee north."

"It is strange to me," said my captor, "that Tyrtaios would trust this business to one man."

"Not strange," said Axel. "Few are to know of these things."

"He deems one man sufficient," said my captor.

"Apparently," said Axel.

"It still seems strange to me that you would be alone," said my captor.

"I am not alone," said Axel. He then, without turning his

head, gave a soft, low whistle. A moment later, its belly almost on the ground, with a quick, serpentine twist, the long body of the hunting sleen, Tiomines, emerged from the brush.

"It seems," said my captor, "that one man was not deemed sufficient."

"I think one would do," said Axel.

"But noble Tyrtaios wishes an additional assurance," said my captor.

"Possibly," said Axel.

"Or you?" said my captor.

"It is true," said Axel, "that I do not know the nature of your skills."

"Tiomines, old friend," said my captor. "Surely you remember me from the forest."

"I returned first to Shipcamp," said Axel. "We have been separated for days. The interval is sufficient."

"I see," said my captor.

"It is only necessary, if I wished," said Axel, "that I engage you defensively. It is difficult to penetrate an exclusive defense. If your skills are such as I suppose, you will know that. And, in the meantime, Tiomines may attack. If you turn to defend yourself against him, you will be open to my blade."

"If you set the sleen on me," said my captor, "he is likely to reach me before you, and I might then strike him before you can reach me. I will be sure to have his body between us. Then, again, it is one on one."

"The force of his attack, even if struck to the heart, a difficult blow, would carry you to the ground, where you would be an easy mark," said Axel.

"Possibly," said my captor. "Such things are difficult to tell."

"True," said Axel.

"So the game is to be played?" said my captor.

"Obviously," said Axel.

"I am sorry," said my captor.

"So, too, am I," said Axel.

"May I secure the slave?" asked my captor.

"Certainly," said Axel.

"I will not run away!" I said.

"No," said my captor, "you will not."

Axel withdrew a few paces.

He had no crossbow, nor was one at hand. His dagger remained in its sheath, as did his sword, the gladius.

How confident he is, I thought.

My captor drew a short lace from his wallet, and pointed to the beach. "On your belly, cross your ankles," he said.

My ankles were bound. I could not rise to my feet. As soon as he rose from my side, I twisted about, to see the men, propping myself up on my left elbow.

"Do not fight, Masters!" I begged.

"You were told to be silent," said my captor.

"Forgive me, Master," I said.

I watched.

They seemed to measure one another, warily. Neither had unsheathed his weapon.

"Are you ready?" inquired Axel.

"Yes," said my captor.

I struggled against the bracelets, against the lace which fastened my ankles together. I could not rise to my feet. I lay to the side, on my side, where I had been left. A slave, I must await, helpless, the outcome of the doings of men. Would it not be the same with kaiila, or verr?

I became aware of men calling out, from down the beach, by the stairs. I could not make out what they were saying. I twisted about. Some were pointing to the great ship.

"The second whistle must have sounded," said Axel. "There is little time."

On the hill, behind us, the buildings were burning, and the stockade. I could see smoke billowing, too, from Shipcamp, across the river. To my horror, I saw, too, across the river, that the dock was afire.

"This is your last chance," said Axel, menacingly.

"I welcome it," said my captor.

"Cut her throat, and return to the ship," said Axel.

"I decline," said my captor.

How swiftly, with so little sound, two blades left their sheaths! Tiomines began to growl.

Down the beach, behind us, the last of the boats were making their way across the river.

"Why do you sheath your sword?" asked my captor.

"The game is done," said Axel.

"I do not understand," said my captor.

"I have learned," said Axel, "what I came to learn, that you are not the creature of Tyrtaios."

"I do not understand," said my captor.

"Nor am I," said Axel.

"It seems betrayals are afoot," said my captor.

"On the great ship," he said, "unbeknownst to most, contraband is stored."

"Two great boxes, disguised," said my captor.

"To be secretly disembarked at the World's End," said Axel.

"I gather so," said my captor.

"It is rumored some contest is to take place at the World's End, on which may hang the fate of worlds."

"I have heard hints of such from our friend, Tyrtaios," said my captor.

"But it seems cards may be marked, or dice weighted," said Axel.

"Possibly so," said my captor.

"What is in the great boxes?" asked Axel.

"I do not know," said my captor.

"Surely something which might secretly and unfairly alter the outcome of a world's games."

"I fear so," said my captor.

"And in whose favor?" he asked.

"I do not know," said my captor.

"But it is unlikely that the great ship will reach the World's End," said Axel. "No ship has hitherto done so. Were it possible it would have been done a thousand times."

"Perhaps," said my captor, "Thassa has her secrets as well as her ferocities."

"The knowledge we bear is dangerous," said Axel.

"It is the ost," said my captor, "borne in the palm of one's hand."

"Tyrtaios?" said Axel.

"Yes," said my captor, "our friend, Tyrtaios."

"We must begin our trek south," said Axel.

"I would give you Asperiche," said my captor, "if you would

find her of interest, but, I fear, she is already housed in the great
ship."

"Not in the great ship," said Axel. "But in the small boat."

He then went to one of the two small boats drawn up on the
beach, that other than the one my captor had apparently used,
from which he had removed his pack. There was a tarpaulin
there and he flung it aside. Within, bound hand and foot, briefly
tunicked, was the unconscious form of Asperiche.

"Tassa powder," said Axel.

I had heard of Tassa powder in my slave training. The
instructresses had delightedly informed us of its properties. It
is a powder which may be undetectably added to any beverage,
most commonly Ka-la-na, with the result that the individual
who partakes of the beverage is soon rendered unconscious.
The length of the unconscious state is partly determined by
the individual involved and partly by the amount of the drug
administered. The approximated weight of the individual
involved and the desired length of the unconscious state are
used to determine the dosage. It is a favorite of slavers. The
delight of my instructresses, in regaling us with accounts of
its effects, had to do largely with its administration to free
women, who might sip it discreetly behind their veil in some
assignation or tête-à-tête, in their rich robes of concealment,
and later awaken naked and in chains, perhaps in sight of
some flaming brazier from whose burning coals protrude
marking irons.

Axel lifted Asperiche from the boat and put her half in the
chill water, at the beach's edge, and she began to cry out, and
shudder, and was then lifted up, wide-eyed, and placed on her
back, not far from me. She was bound with thongs. I was not
pleased to see her here, so close to me. She was very beautiful.
She belonged to my captor.

"Untie her," said my captor. "See to whose feet she runs."

Axel unbound Asperiche, and she looked at my captor,
frightened. "Forgive me, Master," she said. And then she ran
to Axel of Argentum, knelt, and put her head down to his feet,
trembling.

"Here," said Axel, who drew from his wallet a small coin, a

yellow coin, a gold tarsk, perhaps from Besnit or Harfax, where such coins are popular, and tossed it to my captor, who caught it. "Is that enough?" inquired Axel.

"I would give her to you, in friendship," said my captor.

How pleased I was that he was ridding himself of her! But would he want me?

"No, no," said Axel. "Is it enough?"

"Yes," said my captor. "It is more than enough. It is several times her value. She is yours."

Asperiche had her head to Axel's feet, and was sobbing, with relief, and joy.

How, I wondered, could my captor bring himself to give up that beauty, for any amount of gold? To be sure, she, as I, was a property and would go for whatever coin or coins might be agreed upon by masters.

How joyful was Asperiche! She had found her master. But I had not found mine.

"Free my ankles," I said, "and see to whose feet I run!"

Axel undid the small lace with which my ankles had been tied together, and I, tunicked, my hands braceleted behind me, sped to my captor, knelt, and put my head down to his feet.

"I would that I was yours," I said.

"You are," said Axel. "He is your master."

"He is not my master!" I said.

"He bought you yesterday, from the Pani," said Axel.

"Master?" I said.

"Yes, worthless slut," he said, angrily. "I own you!"

I was then, suddenly, terrified to learn that I was his, that I belonged to him. He owned me, as a pair of sandals or a sleen might be owned. I had been shaken with the very sight of him long ago, in the great emporium, when I, who had so frequently fantasized myself a slave, and had profoundly sensed I was a slave, and I belonged in the collar, had found myself, for the first time in my life, to my trepidation and consternation, looked upon, regarded as, what I had so often conjectured myself to be, a slave, looked upon, regarded, literally, as a slave. I had fled in terror. Then I recalled how helplessly I had lain at his feet, naked and bound, in the warehouse, with other women. In the exposition cage in Brundisium, I had had the bars between us, so I was not so frightened. But he had turned away, and I had felt not so much relieved, but rejected. When I was sold, I could not well see the crowd. On the block, turned and exhibited, naked, under the torches, I had wondered if he were out there, somewhere, in the crowd. I did not think he had made a bid on me. Then I had been sold, as it turned out, to an agent for Pani, for forty-eight copper tarsks. I had not seen him, again, until the dock at Shipcamp, when I had been scorned at his feet. In anger, misery, and humiliation, I had fled, to be captured by Panther Women, who, in turn, had fallen to Genserich and his band. My captor and Master Axel had earlier been apprehended by Genserich. Both Genserich and Master Axel had independently sought the Panther Women, Genserich from the south, from the vicinity of the Laurius, to preclude their reporting to forces gathered at the mouth of the Alexandra, and Master Axel, from the north, to locate them as spies and summon assistance, were he successful, and it needful, from mariners and mercenaries come from the coast, placed there by those of Shipcamp, should the occasion arise, to cut off the escape of possible spies. Master Axel had somehow managed to contact this latter group, bringing it into play. Eventually Genserich, his task accomplished, although scarcely as he had anticipated, returned to the coast, the captured Panther Women in his custody, and Master Axel, with the sleen, Tiomines, had returned to Shipcamp, to report the outcome of his pursuit, which outcome would assure that the security of Shipcamp was, as yet, unbreached. My captor had accompanied Master Axel, he said, for sport, but did not accompany him back to Shipcamp. Rather, as I had again fled, distressed and frightened, for I had richly humiliated him in his helplessness, not anticipating that he would soon be free to deal with me, he followed me in the forest. Was that for sport, or vengeance? In any event I was soon captured, to be returned to Shipcamp and my masters, the Pani. In the return to Shipcamp he had well revenged himself on me for the indignities to which I had subjected him, and had soon, in his vengeance, stirred my slave fires almost to the point of madness. No longer did I fear he would touch me, but only that he might not touch me. How I wanted to hate him, who was so uncaring and cruel, but I soon hoped for permission to lick and kiss his feet. Returned to Shipcamp, I had been placed in the stockade, a facility of maximum security. Why had that been? As the great ship prepared for its departure, Shipcamp was fired, and the buildings and stockade on the south side of the river, as well. He had rescued me from the burning stockade, at no little danger to his own life. Perhaps he would have done as much for a tethered verr or urt. I did not know. I thought perhaps he would. But did he, too, I wondered, care for me, or, better, more likely, want me, for I now knew myself a comely slave. Perhaps he saw me from a commercial point of view, merely as an item he might sell, on which he might make a profit. I did not know. Or did he buy me to ventilate on my collared flesh all his scorn and hatred of me, recalling my public humiliation of him, when he was helplessly bound in the camp of Genserich. What amusement that provided for the men of Genserich!

"Be kind to me, Master," I said.

"You are a slave," he said.

"Forgive me, Master," I said.

"Behold!" said Axel, pointing across the river.

The great ship was moving away from the flaming dock.

Smoke billowed from Shipcamp, as well as the buildings and the stockade on our side of the river.

"The voyage is begun," said my captor.

"There are forces massed at the mouth of the Alexandra to stop her," said Axel.

"Straws might as well struggle to impede the rolling of a dislodged boulder," said my captor.

"Thence it is to raging Thassa," said Master Axel, "and its winter."

"I do not think it will reach the World's End," said my captor. "But, if it should, a strange cargo, contraband, may tip the balance in the scale of war, the stakes perhaps two worlds."

"Is there no way in which this may be drawn to the attention of the Pani?" asked Axel.

"It is too late," said my captor. "The voyage is begun."

The large vessel was now in midriver. I marked a slight adjustment of the large, single rudder. Most Gorean vessels with which I was familiar were double ruddered, with two helmsmen.

The vessel was six-masted but no sail was set. She would be carried by the current.

"Tal," said my captor, half moved from his place of stand, by the rough caress of the sleen's snout, and the brush of its long, furred body.

"He is fond of you," said Axel.

"I did not think so before," said my captor.

"We were together in the forest," said Axel.

"He was prepared to attack," said my captor. "Did you not note the menace of the growl?"

"You know little of sleen," said Axel. "The growl was one of recognition."

"It sounded threatening enough," said my captor.

"Only to one unfamiliar with sleen," said Axel.

"He would not have attacked me?" said my captor.

"No," said Axel.

"You knew this?" said my captor.

"Of course," said Axel.

"I did not know it," said my captor.

"Neither did Tyrtaios," said Axel. "Else others might have been consigned to accompany me."

"You said the interval of separation had been sufficient," said my captor.

"I wanted you to believe that," he said.

"I see," said my captor.

"The sleen is a terrible beast," said Axel, "but, too, it has a long memory, and it is capable of affection."

"There is much I do not know of sleen," said my captor.

"That was fortunate for me," said Axel.

"How did you know I would not do the bidding of Tyrtaios and join the ship?"

"I did not know," said Axel.

I shuddered.

"I would have known," said Asperiche. "He is mad to possess this slave."

"No!" said my captor.

"He followed her from Brundisium, and sought her for days in Tarncamp," she said, "before finding her in Shipcamp."

"Silence," said my captor.

"It is my master, noble Axel of Argentum," she said, "who should silence me, if I am to be silenced, not you, Master. You are not my master. You sold me," and here Asperiche looked pleasantly at me, smiling, "—for a gold tarsk."

"Far more than you are worth," snapped my captor.

"Not more than I was worth to Axel of Argentum," she said.

"His aberrations are of little interest to me," said my captor.

"My judgment is notoriously suspect," said Axel.

"Master!" protested Asperiche.

"But she does have lovely ankles," said Axel.

"I have always found then so," said my captor.

I glanced at my ankles. I was told they took shackles, and thongs, well.

"What if I had done as you seemed to wish," said my captor, "slain the slave and rejoined the ship?"

"You would not have rejoined the ship," he said. "I would have struck you down from behind, you unsuspecting, as you entered the boat."

"Why?" asked my captor.

"That Tyrtaios have one less minion at his disposal," said Axel.

"You would have permitted me to slay the slave?" asked my captor.

"I would have attempted to intervene," he said.

"Honor?" asked my captor.

"You have heard of that?" asked Axel.

"It is within my recollections," said my captor.

"I suspected so," said Axel, "from the forest. But, too, aside from questions of honor, there are better things to do with a slave, I am sure you will agree, than cut her throat. We have two lovely slaves here. It would be absurd to slay them. It would be a waste. Slaves have their uses."

"Slave uses," said my captor.

"Certainly," said Axel. "And if one does not want one, give her away, or sell her."

I was suddenly frightened. For all my fear of him, I did not want my master to sell me. And yet I knew he could do so. I must try so to please him that he would not wish to do so.

"On your feet," said Axel to Asperiche, who leapt up.

"Rise," said my master, and I, too, stood.

The two men then regarded us, and we stood as slaves, regarded. I recalled that Axel had spoken of two lovely slaves. Asperiche had her head lifted, so I, too, lifted mine. The men were obviously comparing us, as properties.

"Nice," said Axel. "But mine is better."

"Obviously," said my captor.

I jerked angrily at the slave bracelets which confined my hands behind my back.

"I think, however, Master," said Asperiche, "that we must admit that Laura, for a barbarian, is attractive."

"Many barbarians are attractive," said Axel. "It is only that they are stupid."

"May I speak, Master?" I asked.

"No," said my master. "Barbarians," said my master, "are not simply found under a veil when a city is falls or a caravan raided. They are selected for beauty and intelligence."

I straightened my body, and lifted my head a little more.

"And passion," he added.

I reddened. I could not help the nature of my belly, the needs of my body, the helplessness of my responses to a man's touch. But why, I asked myself, should I be embarrassed by, or shamed by, or disconcerted by, signs of, and the obvious consequences of, health, life, hormonal richness, and vitality? Had not nature made me so, designed me to be a yielded, surrendered slave in the arms of masters? And in the collar, and in bondage, and on Gor had not nature liberated me a thousand fold to be myself? In a natural world does not nature thrive?

"Both are excellent slaves," said Axel.

"One at least," said my master.

"Put either one of them in with a crowd of free women, all stripped," said Axel, "and one would see her as the slave."

Perhaps that was the case, I thought. I did not know. Certainly I was a slave. I had often thought that my master, when he had first seen me on my former world, had seen me as such, and immediately, even without thought, as a slave.

Both men then turned to the river, and we two, slaves, standing, followed their gaze. The great ship was nearly out of sight. Momentarily it would reach a bend in the river, and we would no longer be able to follow its course from our vantage point.

"Tyrtaios would have paid well," said Axel.

"Gold, women, fleets, cities, a ubarate or ubarates," said my master.

"We might have been mighty men," said Axel, fondling the shaggy, lifted head of Tiomines.

"It is quite possible," said my master, "that the World's End would never be reached."

"Thassa," said Axel, "is treacherous, deep, and cruel."

"It is a voyage, as no other," said my master.

"Tersites," said Axel, "would challenge the winds and the sea, fearful Thassa, in the fiercest and most ruthless of seasons."

"He is mad," said my master.

"Perhaps, it is so," said Axel, "of all who, so to speak, build great ships."

"Do you trust Tyrtaios?" asked my master.

"No," said Axel. "He would be as likely, when he had of us what he wanted, to pay with steel as gold."

"Still," said my master, "we might have been well rich."

"Then it seems our desertions were ill-advised," said Axel.

"Masters may have sacrificed much," said Asperiche.

"And have little to show for it," said Axel.

"Two slaves!" laughed Asperiche.

"Your slave is insolent," said my master. "Does she have permission to speak? Have you suffered her to speak?"

"She has always spoken freely before me, owned or not owned," said Axel. "I enjoy having her speak her mind."

"I see," said my master. I did not think he would be as permissive as Master Axel.

"It makes it all the more pleasant then," said Axel, "to bring them again to their knees."

"I see," said my master, with satisfaction.

"A privilege not granted is not much missed," said Axel, "but a privilege granted is more missed when it is withdrawn."

"Of course," said my master.

As is well known we speak well, and love to speak. It is one of the delights of our being. Accordingly few things more impress our bondage upon us, and with greater keenness, than the fact that our speech, as other aspects of our being, is subject to our master's will. Unless we have a standing permission to speak, which might, of course, be rescinded at any time, we are commonly expected to request permission to speak, and are not to speak without such permission, which permission might or might not be granted. How painful it is, and how frustrating, to wish to speak, to desire fervently to do so, and not be permitted to do so! But it is not we, but the master, who will decide these things. They do not always wish to hear us speak, and then we may not do so.

Perhaps, I thought, lovely Asperiche could thus be well reminded that she is a slave. The whip, too, of course, is useful in this regard.

The great ship of Tersites was no longer in sight.

"We will trek," said Axel. "I think it best to do so separately."

"I agree," said my master.

"Axel," said my master.

"Yes?" he said.

"Genserich," said my master, "speculated as to the possibility of two large and complex forces, each of which might well have spies in the camp of the other, perhaps even highly placed spies."

"I recall," he said.

"I think you are such a spy," said my master.

"Possibly," he said.

"For whom do you work?" asked my master.

"I do not know," he said.

"You are hired through agents," said my master.

"Of course," he said.

"To what end?" asked my master.

"To inquire into the doings of Tyrtaios, and others," he said, "to see if deceit is practiced, to see if there is treachery amongst the Pani, to see if the cards are marked, the dice weighted."

"And it is so?" said my captor.

"As you have confirmed," he said.

"And what is to be done?" asked my master.

"Nothing now," said Axel. "It is too late. The ship is upon the river."

We looked after the ship, which was now gone from sight. There was only the empty river, quiet in the morning sun, and the cries of some birds, fishing, skimming its surface, sometimes diving under the water, and there was smoke, here and there, drifting about. It seems there had been fires in the vicinity.

"Are you a spy?" asked Axel.

"No," said my master.

"I wish you well," said Axel.

"I, too, wish you well," said my master.

Asperiche hurried to me and kissed me. "I wish you well, Laura," she said. "And you are very beautiful."

"I wish you well, Asperiche," I said, kissing her. "And you are very beautiful." I could not hold her, as my hands were braceleted behind me.

"Hoist my pack," said Axel to Asperiche.

"Yes, Master," she said, happily, and slung it about her shoulder.

Shortly thereafter Axel made his way up from the bank, south, into the forest, heeled by his slave. Tiomines rubbed his snout, head, and coat against the thigh of my master, and then, turning about, padded away, in the wake of Axel and his slave, Asperiche.

My master turned to face me.

"No," he said. "Do not kneel. Turn away."

I felt the key inserted into the bracelets, and they were removed from my wrists. I then turned about, to face him.

He pointed to the ground, and I knelt.

"Do you think you are a tower slave?" he asked.

"I do not know what sort of slave I am," I said.

"Get your knees apart," he said. "Widely! More widely!"

"Yes, Master," I said.

"Do you now know what sort of slave you are?" he asked.

"Yes, Master," I said. There was now no doubt about that. I was frightened, but excited and thrilled, as well. How frightening it is to be wanted, wanted not as a free woman is wanted, but wanted as a slave is wanted, to be wanted with all the power and force, and uncompromising authority, that a slave is wanted! And yet, too, what woman would wish to be less wanted? What woman does not wish to be so desired that she will be collared and possessed? A slave is many things to her master. Among them is his beast and pet, his plaything. I hoped he would not be difficult to please. I did not wish to be whipped.

"I grant you a standing permission to speak," he said.

"Thank you, Master," I said. "I thank you for saving my life. I thank you for freeing me of the bracelets."

"You will wear them frequently," he said.

"As Master wills," I said.

"Do you think to escape?" he asked.

"No, Master," I said. "I am collared, tunicked, and marked. There is no escape for me."

"Do you fear me?" he asked.

"Yes, Master," I said. How small, helpless, and weak I felt, kneeling before him. I was a scion of a far world kneeling before a Gorean master.

"It is well," he said, "that a slave fear her master."

"Yes, Master," I said.

"You well humiliated me in the camp of Genserich," he said, "with the tortures of the provocative slave girl."

"Forgive me, Master," I said.

"The men of Genserich were much amused," he said.

"I was angry," I said. "You had turned away from me! You had scorned me. I hated you. I wanted to make you suffer! I wanted to have my vengeance on you!"

"You do not seem so forward, so bold, so impudent, so insolent now," he said.

"I am not, Master," I said. "Is it true you bought me?"

"Yes," he said.

"May I inquire for what sum?"

"You vain she-tarsk," he said.

"Master Axel paid a gold tarsk for Asperiche," I said. "Perhaps you were as keen to buy Laura."

"Do not flatter yourself," he said.

"What did you pay?" I asked.

"The standard Pani price for changing the collar of a camp slave," he said. "Two silver tarsks."

"There was no bidding or negotiation?" I said.

"No," he said. "They assumed, of course, that I would participate in the voyage. Otherwise they would not have sold you, and, I suppose, would have slain me."

"That is more than forty-eight copper tarsks," I said.

"More than four times as much," he said, "as Brundisium counts tarsks." I knew there were considerable differences in coinages from city to city. Gorean polities are fiercely independent, and many are substantially isolated from the others. That is why money changers commonly rely on scales, at least for gold and silver. For example, in some cities there are eight tarsk-bits to a copper tarsk, and in others, such as Brundisium, a major commercial port, a hundred tarsk-bits to a copper tarsk. These divisions, it seems, might facilitate subtle distinctions in pricing and trading.

"What would I go for on the open market?" I asked.

"It would depend on the market, and season, and the supply, and such," he said. "There is no simple answer to that. But I would suppose, in an average market, you might go for two and a half silver tarsks."

"So much?" I said.

"Possibly," he said.

"It seems then," I said, "that I have become more beautiful."

"Women do, in the collar," he said.

"And how high might you have gone if the bidding were close, and fierce?"

"That is my business," he said.

"As high as a gold tarsk?" I asked.

"Do you think me weak?" he asked.

"Not at all," I said.

"I could have bought you in Brundisium," he said. "I might have kept you for myself, even before Brundisium."

"But you did not," I said.

"No," he said.

"Why did you not do so?" I asked.

"I do not know," he said.

"I do not understand," I said.

"What had happened?" he asked. "What had you done to me?"

"Nothing, Master!" I said.

"Was there some spell in this, some drug?" he asked.

"No, Master," I said.

"Why was it that I wanted you so?" he asked.

"I do not know," I said.

"To be sure," he said, "I thought you would look well in ropes, and a collar. Else you, a confused Earth slut, knowing nothing of your place, and your nature, would not have been brought to Gor. You should have been left to pine and languish in your shallow, tepid world, left, if anything, to the timid, polite, fumbling attentions of psychologically emasculated pseudomales, conditioned from infancy to disown their own nature, and deny their own blood, the creatures of a pathological world where nature and truth are against the law, against laws brought into being by those who would deny both truth and nature."

"It is a great honor," I said, "for a woman of my world, such a world, to be adjudged worthy of a Gorean collar."

"'Worthy'?" he said.

"Forgive me, Master," I said.

"Do you think you, a woman of your world, any woman of your world, is worthy to be the slave of a Gorean male?"

"No, Master," I said. "We, the women of my world, so taught and conditioned, so shallow and trivialized, are not even worthy to be the slaves of Gorean males."

"Still," he said, "you look well on the block, and in chains."

"It is our hope that our masters will be pleased with us," I said.

"One does not need a worthy slave," he said, "only a beautiful slave, however unworthy, from whom we will require much work and from whom we will derive much pleasure."

"Yes, Master," I said.

"It is common, of course, for a man to desire a slave," he said.

"And for a slave to desire a master," I said.

"You know I followed you from Brundisium," he said.

"On the dock at Shipcamp," I said, "seeing you, I had hoped for as much."

"'Hoped'?" he said.

"I wanted you as my master," I said, "from the first moment I fled from you."

"Liar!" he said.

"No, Master!" I said.

"I do not understand these things," he said angrily, his fist

clenched. "Am I a fool, a joke, a weakling, a traitor to codes?"
He looked down at me, and I was frightened. Why was he angry,
so angry? I feared his fury? What had I done? Did this have to
do with him, or with me, or both? How dark was his visage,
how twisted his frown!

"You are a mere slave," he said, "a mere slave!"

"Yes, Master," I said, uncertainly.

"You are worthless," he said.

"Yes, Master," I said.

"No different from countless others," he said.

"Yes, Master," I said, frightened.

"And yet," he said, "how I have fought the wanting of you!"

"Master?" I said.

"How I tried to drive the thought of you from my mind!
What storms of hate and denial I invoked to banish you from
my heart! Was not the thought of you, or your image, in the
corners of darkened rooms, in clouds, everywhere, in rain, in
shimmering leaves, in high, green, bending grass? What had
you done to me, you, merely another meaningless Earth female,
branded and collared, brought to our markets? Yet I would
own you! I was driven to own you, and be your master! What
tides and currents bore me to seek you out! Do you think I can
forgive you what you have done to me, you only a slave and I
a free man! So I have followed you, and I have pursued you,
from a far world, from Brundisium, even into the dark, green,
trackless terrors of the northern forests, to get a chain on you,
to get you to my feet, as mine! Can you wonder why I hate you
so, hate you for what you have done to me, for what you have
made me?"

"On the great ship," I said, "I have heard there are two major
holds for housing the public slaves, the Venna hold and the
Kasra hold."

"So?" he said.

"In which hold would I have been housed?" I asked.

"The Kasra hold is on a lower deck," he said. "The better slaves
are housed on the next deck, the Venna deck, in the Venna hold.
Asperiche, were she a public slave, would have been housed in
the Venna hold, and you in the Kasra hold."

"I see," I said.

"Does it make no difference to you," he asked, "what you have made me, what you have done to me?"

"Naturally I am concerned," I said. "You hold the whip."

"What power," he said, angrily, "lies in that small, soft, curved body of yours, in an ankle, a shoulder, the movement of a hand, a lifting of the head, a glance, the soft, brightness of eyes, the tremor of a lip."

"A slave cannot help what she is," I said.

"Is it nothing to you," he asked, "that you have wrenched my heart, that you have tormented my nights and distressed my days, that you have half torn me out of myself with desire?"

"A slave does not object to being wanted," I said.

"What power you have!" he cried, angrily.

"I have no power," I said. "I am before you, on my knees."

He howled with rage, and seized up his pack, and from it, to my alarm, drew forth a whip. He hurled it from him, perhaps fifty or more feet. "Fetch it," he said, "as a whip is fetched!"

I crawled to the whip on all fours, and put down my head, and took the long handle, it is made to be held in two hands, just behind the blades, in my teeth, turned about, and returned to him, on all fours, and lifted my head to him, the whip between my teeth.

When he had taken the whip from me, I knelt, in position, back on heels, back straight, belly in, shoulders back, head up, hands down, palms down, on my thighs, my knees spread, as befitted the sort of slave I had learned I was.

"I think," I said, lifting my head to him, "Master cares for a slave."

He lifted the whip, and I feared he would strike me. His hand wavered, with anger, and then he lowered it. His scowl was fierce. I had not meant to anger him. I had not meant to insult, or demean, him. Was it so unthinkable that a free man might care for a slave? Was he to be ridiculed by his peers, and scorned by free women? If a man might care for a sleen or kaiila, why not for a female slave? But no, I thought, the female slave is different. She is to be despised, scorned, and held in contempt, for she is a female slave.

He thrust the whip roughly to my lips.

I was frightened.

Surely that was not the action of one who might care for a slave. How foolish had been my remark. Did I not know I was a female slave?

"Have you not been trained?" he asked.

I began to attend to the whip, kissing and licking it. I did this softly, slowly, tenderly, carefully, humbly, deferentially, and, I fear, seductively.

When he drew back the whip, I leaned back, and waited, in position.

If a girl does not do this well, she must expect to be whipped.

To my relief, he replaced the tool of discipline, unopened and unapplied, back in his pack.

The ritual of kissing the whip can be a lovely ritual. In it, one acknowledges one's submission, one's subjection to the mastery. It can be very beautiful. The whip itself, of course, is a symbol of the mastery. As the whip, however, had been so rudely put to my lips I had no difficulty in gathering that my supposition that a master might care for a slave had borne little resemblance to reality. Indeed, that action had been more an expression of annoyance, or contempt, an indication that a master might disapprove of, and fail to tolerate, an unwarranted presumptuousness on the part of a property, a mere beast.

I should have known better.

"Do you think a slave is to be cared for?" he asked.

"Forgive me, Master," I said.

"A slave," he said, "is to be dominated, mastered, used, worked, and put to one's pleasure, until she weeps and screams with need."

"Yes, Master," I said.

"You should be whipped," he said.

"Lash me then," I said, "that I may the better know myself yours."

"I have said things I did not wish to say, but had to say," he said. "I have spoken truths which have alarmed and shamed me. I have acknowledged a mighty wanting of you, fierce as the tides of Thassa, and as irresistible and inalterable, that I have fought to free myself from this inexplicable, terrible wanting, and have failed to do so. My intentions vanished like smoke, my resolve collapsed. I must have you. I would not rest until you were mine. I must own you. And you, stupid Earth slut, dare to speak of caring? Rather, tremble, and speak of owning, mastering, and possessing, yes, possessing, as any object, article, or animal may be possessed. For that is what you are, and only that, an object, article, and animal, and that is what you will be, that, and only that, in my collar! Yes, you are desired, you are wanted, but you are desired, and wanted, as what you are, a slave, a worthless, meaningless slave!"

"Yes, Master," I said. I saw that he would be my master. But what slave would want it otherwise?

"Do you wish to be a free woman?" he asked.

"No, Master," I said. "I am a slave. It is what I want to be."

"That is unfortunate," he said. "If you wished to be a free woman, it would be pleasant to keep you as the most abject of slaves."

"I think, Master," I said, "that such a woman would soon beg to be kept as your slave, and fear only that you might sell her."

"It is interesting," he said, "the effect of a collar on a woman."

"We belong in it," I said.

"I hate you," he said.

"I will try to please you," I said.

"I will own you as few slaves have been owned," he said.

"And it is thus that I would be owned," I said.

"I have waited long," he said, "that you would be mine."

"And I," I said, "that I would be yours."

"We shall trek," he said.

"Yes, Master," I said.

He turned about, and suddenly stiffened. His head was up. I looked, too. He shaded his eyes. I did not see it immediately. Then I saw it. It was a dot in the sky, in the distance. "Into the brush," he said, curtly. I rose to my feet, and hurried into the brush to the side, from which, earlier, Master Axel had emerged. My master seized up his pack, and, in a moment, had joined me. We crouched down.

"He is probably back scouting," he said, "looking for stragglers, deserters."

"Perhaps only to see if the ship is followed?" I said.

"Remain motionless," he said.

I regretted that my tunic was white. How much better would

have been the skins of Panther Women which would have blended with the background, the branches, the shadows, and foliage.

He removed his dagger from its sheath, and held it, lightly, by the tip of the blade.

"Do not move," he said.

I had seen men playing near the dock, hurling knives into an upright plank or post. A tiny circle is drawn on the target, and the winner is he whose blade comes closest to the center of that circle.

Some Ihn later we saw the shadow of the giant saddlebird pass.

"He is gone," I said.

"No," he said.

"Where is he?" I asked.

"Upriver, circling Shipcamp, the ruins of the dock, of the stockade, who knows."

"Would it not be best for us to be on our way?" I said.

"Not yet," he said.

"He is on tarnback," I said. "He could not follow us in the forest."

"If he detects us," he said. "He could report our existence, our approximate location."

"Do you think he will land?" I asked.

"I do not think so," he said. "Stragglers, deserters, fugitives would be dangerous men."

"He may land," I said.

"It would be for the best if he does not," he said.

"You would kill him?" I said.

"Or he us," he said.

"I am afraid," I said.

"Let him be afraid," he said.

"Where is he?" I asked, again.

"I do not know," he said.

Four Ehn or so passed.

I looked up, frightened.

"Do not move!" he said.

There was a blast of wind which shook the brush about us. The great bird had descended, not yards from us, on the beach.

I had never been this close to a tarn before, not even on the training field east of Tarncamp, en route to Shipcamp. How small the man appeared next to this terrible, winged monster, its broad wings restless, its head, with its fearful beak, high above the beach, moving alertly about, the large, wicked, round, shining, black eyes.

The rider descended the mounting ladder, and looked about himself, warily.

I saw my master half rise, and his hand drawn back, the knife held lightly by its tip. The usual cast with such a knife is overhand, with a powerful snap of the wrist. But the distance, I feared, was much too far for either accuracy or a suitable penetration. The men near the dock, who played the knife game, sometimes gambling on its outcome, threw not even half the distance.

"He does not wear the gray of the Pani's cavalry," I said.

"He would be of the cavalry, but not on the cavalry's business," said my master.

"On whose business then?" I asked.

"On that of the Shipcamp conspirators," said my master. "Better then that the uniform not be worn."

"What is he doing?" I asked.

"I fear," said my master, "searching for me. It is I who carry the live ost in my hand."

"I do not understand," I said.

The tarnsman made his way to the two small boats tied up on the beach. He examined them, but, one supposes, found them of little interest, two boats left there, apparently abandoned on the beach. He did lift and cast aside the tarpaulin which had been in the boat brought by Axel, which had covered the unconscious form of Asperiche. He then threw three oars out into the river, and, with the remaining oar, punched an opening in the bottom of each boat, following which he thrust them out into the current, and then hurled the last oar after them. He then turned about, and, again, regarded the beach, east and west, and then, again, he looked out, into the brush, to the south.

I muchly feared he would see us.

"We should have freed the boats," said my master.

"They would seem abandoned," I said. "They lack goods, and supplies; they give no indication of preparation for flight."

"Let us hope he judges the matter so," he said.

"Do you recognize him?" I asked.

"No," said my master, "but I fear it is a man of Tyrtaios."

I shuddered. "I have heard him spoken of," I said. Men usually spoke of him in whispers.

"My absence on the great ship may have been noted," he said.

"Surely not so soon," I said.

The tarnsman then climbed the mounting ladder, and drew it up, fastening it in its place.

He gave one last, long, sweeping glance about him.

"What a fool I am," whispered my master.

"My master is no fool," I said. I had long sensed he was a man not only of formidable size and strength, and virility, and desire, but of formidable intellect, as well. I would have been frightened to lie to him, not simply because I was a slave but because I had the sense I would be helplessly transparent to him, that he could simply look through me and immediately discern in me the least particle of deceit or dissimulation. Also, he might, without a second thought, put the liar's brand in my thigh, marking me as a mendacious kajira.

The tarnsman drew on one of the straps, threaded through its ring, and the huge bird screamed, and smote the air with those great wings, scattering sand and pebbles about, and was into the air, low, several feet over the river.

"No," said my master, "a fool! Did you not see he carried, slung at the saddle, a crossbow, and quarrels?"

"I did not notice," I said.

"If our tarnsmen had been about," he said, "that fellow could not have come within fifty pasangs of Shipcamp. He would have been slain over the forest or the river."

"I do not understand," I said.

"Our tarnsmen," he said, "are differently armed. They carry the short, horn-reinforced saddle bow. It is a powerful bow, capable of rapid fire, like any string bow, and is designed for use from a saddle, which it may easily clear, from any side, or front and back."

"I did notice," I said, "the broad leather pad before the saddle, and the rings at the saddle's side."

"What do you think they are for, pretty barbarian?" he asked.

"I do not know, Master," I said.

"The pad," he said, "is useful for stretching a stripped captive over, on her back, belly up, her wrists crossed and tied to a ring on one side of the saddle, and her ankles crossed and tied to a ring on the other side."

"I see," I said, uneasily.

"She may then, in the leisure of flight, if the tarnsman wishes, be caressed into submission."

"I see," I said.

"At the conclusion of the flight," he said, "she is ready for the iron."

"Doubtless," I said.

"And the rings on the side of the saddle," he said, "and they are on both sides, are useful for tying stripped women."

"I see," I said.

"It is not unusual for tarnsmen to raid for females," he said.

"To be made slaves?" I said.

"Certainly," he said, "is that not what females are for?"

"Some, at least," I said, "surely."

"Such as you," he said.

"Yes, Master," I said, "such as I." Even as a young girl, I had longed for a master, and the chains of a slave.

"I am pleased," I said, "that the tarnsman withdrew."

"And I, as well," he said.

"You were too far away to strike him," I said. "You would have had to rush upon him, sword drawn, and hope he had no time to react."

"I had the knife," he said, puzzled.

"I have seen the men play by the dock," I said. "He was too far away, and the penetration, at the distance, would be insufficient, even if the blade reached him."

"I had no idea," he said, "that you understood so much of these things."

"I watched," I said.

"And now," he said, "you will watch again."

"Master?" I said.

"Stand before that tree," he said, "face me, and do not move."

"This tree?" I said, uneasily.

"That will do," he said.

"Should I not face the tree," I asked, "and my arms be bound about it, that I may be conveniently whipped?"

"You are not to be whipped, kajira," he said, "at least not at the moment, however richly your smooth skin invites the lash."

"What is Master going to do?" I asked.

He strode away from me.

"Am I as far now," he called, "as was the tarnsman on the beach?"

"Farther," I called back. "What is Master going to do?"

He slipped his dagger from the sheath.

"Do not, Master!" I cried.

"Do not fear," he said. "How could the blade even reach you from this far, and, if it could, how could it produce an efficient wound?"

I saw his hand draw back.

"Do not!" I cried.

"Remain in place," he said. "Do not move. You are in no danger, unless you move."

"Please, no, Master!" I called.

"The blade," he said, "will enter the wood three to five horts from your throat, on the left. If it is easier, close your eyes."

I closed my eyes, trembling. It seemed I had them closed for a long time, though I would suppose the interval was actually quite short. I had just decided that he, mercifully, had decided not to cast the knife after all, when there was, close, to my left, at the level of my throat, a sudden, firm, unmistakable sound, like the slap of metal driven into wood, followed by the tremor of a briefly quivering blade.

I opened my eyes just long enough to catch sight of the handle still vibrating, a hand's breadth from my throat, and then, I fear, I slumped into unconsciousness at the foot of the tree.

Chapter Fifty-Three

"It is my hope," I said, "that Master's slave has pleased him."

"In two days," he said, "we should reach the Laurius. We will avoid Laura, for I fear partisans may linger there. We will cross the Laurius by ferry, inconspicuously with others, at one point or other, and continue south, eventually to reach the Vosk, following which we will seek Victoria."

I was on my master's blanket. My left ankle was shackled, and a light chain ran from the shackle ring to a small tree, about which it was locked. I was naked, as my master commonly kept me.

"Is Victoria not a market town," I said, "a major market for slaves, wholesale and retail? Are not many slaves disposed of there? Do not buyers come there, even from far beyond the Vosk basin?"

"It is the major slave market on the Vosk," he said.

"A slave is uneasy," I said.

"As well she might be," he said.

"I have tried to be pleasing to my master," I said.

"Of course," he said, "you are a slave."

"I gather," I said, "you are in need of funds, and have little to sell."

"I have you, of course," he said.

"A slave is well aware of that," I said.

"Do you know what this is?" he asked.

He had drawn a yellow disk from his wallet, which was as large as his palm.

"It is like a coin," I said, "but it is too large."

He held it toward me.

"May I touch it?" I asked, warily.

"Take it," he said.

"It is heavy," I said.

"It is a coin," he said. "It is gold, a double tarn, from the mint of the state of Ar."

He held out his hand, and I hastily, with relief, returned the coin. "It must be valuable," I said.

"Yes," he said. "Many laborers might not earn its equivalent in years. There are merchants who have never had their hands on such a coin. Certainly it is the first I have seen. It was given to me by Tyrtaios to hint at the riches which might accrue to one enleagued with him."

"My master is not destitute," I said.

"No," he said.

"He could buy many slaves such as Laura," I said.

"Dozens," he said.

"It is my hope that he will not do so," I said.

"Please me," he said.

"Yes, Master," I said.

I lay beside my master, my head at his thigh, on his blanket. My ankle was still clasped in its close-fitting shackle, the shackle chain running to the small tree, about which it was fastened.

"By the river," I said, "Master spoke strangely, spoke of holding a live ost in his hand."

"Do you know what an ost is?" he asked.

"It is a tiny, brightly colored serpent, commonly orange," I said, "which is venomous."

"It is the smallest, and deadliest, snake on Gor," he said. "It moves quickly, and can hide almost anywhere. Its bite is lethal, unless the limb can be cut off within a few Ihn. It is an unpleasant death. It ensues within a few Ehn. The victim commonly cries out with joy, to die, rejoicing that the pain will end."

"I fear Master is in danger," I said.

"I bore the burden of knowledge," he said, "of knowing fearful and important things, though I did not fully understand them. To protect this knowledge, and prevent its revelation, men would kill. Few are permitted to bear this knowledge, and, I fear, few for long. Even now I suspect several who had, of necessity, some sense of these things, having been utilized in certain actions, deliveries, and concealments, have been done away with, even creatures other than ourselves. That is what is meant, that knowing such things is dangerous, as dangerous as might be the carrying of a live ost in one's palm."

"It has to do," I said, "with the contents of two large boxes, heavy, which it required several men to lift and carry."

He looked at me, sharply.

"Two such boxes, concerning which the contents were obscure," I said, "were disembarked from the galley which brought me and others north. They were carried overland, through the forest, at least as far as Tarncamp."

"Beyond," he said, "to Shipcamp, thence to be secretly stored on the south side of the river. They are now on the great ship, disguised as common goods."

"The ship is departed," I said, "and, I fear, from what I have heard, even should it reach Thassa, it will never reach the World's End."

"The danger to the world, or worlds," he said, "is that it might reach the World's End."

"You have done your work," I said, "for well, or ill. The ship has departed. You could now cry out your knowledge to all the world, with impunity."

"Those who bear the knife in these matters," he said, "are few, and those few are now, doubtless, on the ship."

"The ship is departed," I said. "It cannot be recalled. The game has begun. The tarn is aflight. Your knowledge makes no difference now."

"I should have spoken," he said.

"To whom?" I asked.

"Yes," he said, thoughtfully, "to whom?"

I went to my knees, and took up his right hand, gently, opened the fingers, and kissed the palm of his hand. "See, Master," I said, "I kiss the ost from your hand."

He then seized me, and threw me under him, with a rattle of chain.

* * * *

"Do you know my caste?" he asked.

"The Slavers," I said. "Surely Master is of the caste of Slavers."

"I am of the Merchants," he said. "The Slavers is a subcaste of the Merchants. It is merely a question of the goods with which one deals. The Slavers deal with soft, living goods."

"I would rather," I said, "Master dealt with leather or iron, fruit or grain, copper or tin, verr or kaiila."

"You can see," he said, "why a fellow might prefer buying and selling women."

"I suppose so," I said.

"But I am now thinking," he said, "of other goods, perhaps ka-la-na or silk."

"I am pleased to think so," I said.

"But I do not understand why that is so," he said, thoughtfully.

"Long ago," I said, "Master suggested that my return to Shipcamp was not inadvertent, or accidental, but was rather an expression of my desire to be recaptured, to return to a chain, that I needed, and wanted, the collar, so to speak."

"I think that is clear," he said.

"But I had no understanding of that," I said.

"And rejected the very thought," he laughed.

"I understood very little of myself," I said.

"Few of us do," he said.

"And you spoke of the Panther Women who prematurely relaxed their vigilance in the forest," I said.

"Unhappy with themselves, without masters," he said, "they became careless, and soon found themselves kneeling naked before men, with the collars for which they had hoped fastened on their necks."

"And what of you, Master?" I asked.

"I do not understand," he said.

"You may have labored in the tasks of the Slavers for the pleasantries of the merchandise, but I think there was more involved, for you seem now to be thinking of dealing with other goods. Indeed, I suspect I know why you followed the Slavers' trade, a dangerous trade surely, with its alarming hazards, and even to another world."

"Oh?" he said.

"You were looking for a particular slave, your slave," I said.

"And you think I have now found her?" he said.

"It is my hope that you have done so," I said.

"I have owned several women," he said. "What of Asperiche?"

"She is a beauty," I said.

"Far more so than you," he snapped.

"Doubtless," I said. "Why then did you let her go, and keep Laura?"

"She-tarsk," he snarled.

"Asperiche is lovely," I said. "But I think you would rather have Laura, not Asperiche, for whatever reason, if the choice were to be made, crawling naked through the leaves, begging for your touch."

"You should be lashed," he said, angrily.

"Master may do with me as he pleases," I said. "I am his slave."

"You are a worthless she-tarsk," he said. "You are of no interest. You are nothing!"

"I have some finite value," I said, "even in silver. And I find it hard to believe that I am of no interest to Master, who pursued me even from Brundisium, and risked much to follow me in the forest, even on the brink of the great ship's departure."

"You are nothing!" he said.

"Yes, Master," I said, "as I am a slave."

"You are a homely she-tarsk!" he said.

"I am a beautiful slave, Master," I said. "I know that now. And I know I have become more beautiful in the collar, as I have found myself as a woman, and slave. I have seen the eyes of men on me. Do you think a slave does not know when men ache to have her in their arms? I am nothing for you to be ashamed of. I know I am beautiful."

"Yes, you slut," he cried, leaping to his feet, "you are beautiful!"

"A slave is pleased," I said, "if her master finds her pleasing."

"You are the most exciting and beautiful woman I have ever seen!" he cried, enraged. "From the first moment I saw you I wanted you as you are now, naked, on my chain, possessed, mine, my property, my slave!"

"I waited years for you!" I wept.

"And I years for you!" he said, angrily.

549

"Do not be angry with your slave," I said. "She is wholly at your mercy. She is yours."

"I must hate you!" he cried.

"No!" I cried. "Love me!"

"Love?" he said. "For a slave!"

"Forgive me, Master," I said.

He seemed beside himself with fury. He strode to his pack, tore it open, and drew forth the whip, shaking its blades free.

"I love you, Master!" I said. "Please do not beat me!"

He held the whip, two hands on the staff.

"May not even a she-sleen love her master?" I said.

He lowered the whip, and turned abruptly away. He replaced the whip in his pack, seized up his blankets and drew them to the side. He then drew them angrily about himself, and lay down. I tried to crawl to him, but the impediment on my ankle prevented this. I reached out, agonizingly, across the leaves, toward him, but could not reach him.

"Please forgive Laura, Master," I wept. "Let his slave please him."

"I will sell you in Victoria," he said.

Chapter Fifty-Four

In the damp, cold morning, north of the Laurius, the turning leaves overhead, I awakened, and found myself warm, covered with his blanket.

"Master," I said.

He was leaning over me. I reached up, and put my arms about him.

"I have decided not to sell you in Victoria," he said.

"Why?" I asked.

"It would be a bother to have to buy you back," he said.

"A slave begs use," I whispered.

And to my petition he acceded.

The chain and shackle were in his pack.

Over my tunic, I wore his jacket.

"Prepare to trek," he said.

"Whence, Master?" I inquired.

"Victoria," he said.

"If I am not to be sold," I said, "why are we going to Victoria?"

"It is the town of my Home Stone," he said.

"You have a Home Stone?" I said.

"Of course," he said.

"I do not have one," I said.

"Certainly not," he said. "You are a slave, a purchasable beast. Beasts do not have Home Stones."

"I see," I said.

"Victoria is one of the greatest of the river ports," he said. "A hundred galleys come and go each day."

"It is very busy," I said.

"In it there are many slaves," he said.

"I wear a camp collar," I said.

"It will not be recognized," he said. "It will be removed."

"And I will then have a new collar?" I asked.

"Certainly," he said. "Why do you ask?"

"I thought," I said, "Master might free me."

"Free you?" he said.

"Yes," I said, "and then petition for my Companionship, which offer I might then accept or refuse, as I might please."

"Are you mad?" he said.

"Surely," I said, "just as Companions may become slaves, so slaves might become Companions."

"Only a fool," said he, "frees a slave girl."

"That is a saying, is it not?" I said.

"Yes," he said.

I had known that, of course.

"Do you think I am a fool?" he asked.

"No, Master," I said.

I regarded him.

"I am then to be collared anew?" I said.

"Certainly," he said, "you are a slave."

"You will not free me?" I asked.

"No," he said. "You are not a free woman. You are a slave. The collar belongs on your neck."

"I see," I said.

"One collar or another," he said.

"But not necessarily yours," I said.

"Certainly not," he said. "You are the sort of woman who should be in a collar, one who belongs in the collar. Any man's collar would do for you."

"But you will keep me in your collar?" I said.

"Yes," he said.

"That is the way you want me?"

"Yes," he said, "that is the way I want you, and that is the way I will have you."

"Collared?" I said.

"Yes," he said.

"A vendible, meaningless slave?"

"Certainly," he said.

"You will keep me then?"

"Until I tire of you, and sell you," he said.

"I see," I said.

"I trust it is not hard to grasp," he said.

"I have nothing to say about this?" I said.

"No more than a verr, a tarsk, or kaiila," he said.

"I will try to be pleasing to my master," I said.

"Of course," he said. "You are a slave."

"I thought I might be special to you," I said.

"How could a slave be special?" he said.

"I do not want to be sold," I said.

"You have nothing to say about it," he said.

"I will try to be such that you would not wish to sell me."

"Perhaps I will not wish to sell you," he said.

"I hope that you will not do so," I said.

"You are, of course, I grant it, the sort of slut who looks well at a man's feet," he said.

"It is my hope that I will be pleasing to you," I said.

"You will be so or you will be punished," he said.

"Could you whip me," I asked, "if I was not pleasing?"

"Certainly," he said, "and promptly, and well."

"And what will my collar read?" I asked.

"What pleases me," he said.

"I cannot read," I said.

"And you will not be taught," he said. "It pleases me that you should be illiterate. It will give me more power over you."

"I will not even be able to read my own collar?" I said.

"No," he said. "But I will tell you what it says."

"And what will it say?" I asked.

"Perhaps," said he, "that you are a worthless she-tarsk."

"And whose worthless she-tarsk?" I inquired.

"Mine," he said.

"Surely the name of my master is to be put on my collar," I said.

"It will," he said. "It will clearly identify you as my property."

"What will it read, Master?" I asked.

He then told me what the collar would read, and I, for the

first time, was apprised of the name of my master, which name, for obvious reasons, must not appear here.

"It is a beautiful name," I said.

"It is not a beautiful name," he said. "It is a strong name."

"In any event," I said, "it is the name of my master."

"Do not forget it," he said.

"I am unlikely to do so," I said, "as it will be locked on my neck."

"You may now lick and kiss my feet," he said, "and thank me for the privilege of wearing my collar."

"A slave," I said, kneeling, and pressing my lips to his feet, licking and kissing, again and again, "thanks her master for her collar."

"Continue," he said. "It is pleasant."

"I am yours, submitted and owned," I said. "I would have it no other way."

"It will be no other way," he said.

"Yes, Master," I said. How fulfilled I felt at his feet. What a joy it was to acknowledge myself a slave, at the feet of her master. What free woman can understand this, I wondered. What free woman can understand what it is to surrender themselves wholly, to abandon themselves unqualifiedly to love and service, asking nothing but hoping to give all? But perhaps, I thought, many free women can understand this, some surely, for what is a free woman but a slave, lacking her collar?

"More," he said, "exquisite, shapely kajira."

"Yes, Master," I whispered.

I do not know then what mad impulse seized me. I looked up, brightly, pertly.

"What is it?" he asked.

"I would have this no other way," I said. "But what of Master?"

"I do not understand," he said.

"Perhaps Master would prefer to free me, as I earlier suggested, and then petition for my Companionship, which I might then, should it amuse me, or should the whim possess me, refuse."

"Do not sport with me," he said.

"Then, I gather," I said, "it is your intention to keep me as a slave."

"Do you truly think," he asked, "I would let a slave off her chain, any slave, and, in particular, a slave such as you?"

"I do not know," I said, and then, thinking it wise, added the word, "—Master."

"You are too slave to free," he said. "You are too beautiful and exciting to free."

"Oh?" I said.

"And every corpuscle in your body is a slave corpuscle," he said.

"Yes, my master," I said.

"You are a slave," he said.

"Yes, my master," I said.

"And you have not been pleasing," he said.

"It is my hope that I have not been displeasing," I said.

To my consternation he pulled me to my feet, removed his jacket from me, and yanked loose the disrobing loop on my tunic. It fell about my ankles. He then took a long thong and bound my wrists together. He then threw me to my knees, again, and, with the free end of the thong, tied it about the base of a tree, a yard or so away.

"Master?" I said.

"What are you?" he asked.

"A slave, Master," I said.

"Are you sure of it?" he asked.

"I do not know!" I said.

"You will soon be sure of it," he said.

"What is Master doing?" I asked, looking over my shoulder. I saw him yank the whip from his pack.

"Please do not whip me!" I begged.

And then he whipped his slave.

After that he put me to my back and drew me, by the ankles, from the base of the tree, so that my bound wrists were high above my head, following which I was used for slave pleasure.

He then cuffed me, twice.

My head snapped back and forth. He was not easy with me.

After that he untied my wrists, and tossed my tunic to me, which I donned. He then gave me the jacket, as he had before.

I would then be warmer.

"Do you now think you will be freed, curvaceous slave?" he asked.

"No, Master," I said.

I was then in no doubt as to my bondage. I now knew myself a slave, only that. I had been displeasing, and had been punished, "promptly, and well." If I had had any doubts as to my bondage they were dispelled. The matter was transparent, and simple. I was a slave, only that. I had been displeasing, and had been put to the leather. There is no answer to the whip; leather is irrefutable.

Interestingly, though I much fear the whip, and would do much to avoid it, I was not displeased to have felt it then.

It was then good for me. I should have been punished, and had been punished.

I was reassured that I was a slave, and his slave.

I was pleased to belong to such a man.

I was grateful, and proud, to be the slave of such a man.

I considered him.

I wondered if any of the men of my world, so many of them weakened, reduced, crippled, confused, conflicted, taught to doubt themselves and deny their own blood, could even begin understand such a man. Let them tremble and hide, and fear even to think of such; let them denounce such men, if it pleases them, and in denouncing them denounce themselves, if there yet remains any such self within them to denounce.

But Goreans were clearly human.

Are they not our brothers, and twins?

Are they so different? I did not think so. Is it only that they have failed to sully soil and water, refused to create poisoned atmospheres, refused to reduce and shame themselves, had no interest in ascending prescribed treadmills, placed in the midst of nothing, leading nowhere?

Can the steps of a false journey not be retraced?

It is possible to live against nature, and accept the inevitable consequences; it is also possible to live with nature, and enjoy her bounties. Flowers and stars are not evil.

"Prepare to trek," he said.

"Yes, Master," I said.

He handed his pack, now closed, to me. "Follow me," he said, "two paces behind, on the left."

"Yes, Master," I said.

"In two days, with some fortune," he said, "we should reach the Laurius."

"I am a slave," I said. "I cannot match the pace of Master."

"Then three days," he said. "It does not matter. We can think of things to do on the way."

"I fear for the great ship," I said.

"By now," he said, "it has either been destroyed at the mouth of the Alexandra, where it debouches into Thassa, or it is somewhere abroad on Thassa, its course set for the farther islands, and, I fear, beyond, to the World's End."

"And what of the mysterious cargo?" I said.

"It is the time of winter on broad, rolling, thundering Thassa," he said, "a time of cold and ice, of impenetrable fog, and short, dark days, of storms, of waves as high as flighted tarns and as mighty as clashing mountains, and it will go down with the ship."

"But what if the ship does not go down?" I asked.

"Then, I fear," he said, "it will reach the World's End, and find its employment."

"One pertinent to worlds?" I said.

"It is thought so," he said.

He then turned about, and strode through the trees, and I hurried behind him, carrying the pack.

I was very happy.

I was now content with my master. I had been well taught that I was his. No longer was there the least doubt in my mind of this.

He was Gorean. He was the sort of man by whom a woman would hope to be purchased, one who would be a strong and fine master, one who would protect her, and care for her, and master her, and never let her forget she was his slave. There are such men, who so lust for, and desire, a woman, that nothing less than her absolute possession will satisfy them. She is to be owned. She is to be their belonging. They will have her, and keep her, on their terms, on their terms alone, on the terms of the master, as their rightless, helpless slave.

There are such men, and they are our masters.

I was content. I was happy. I followed my master.

About the Author

John Norman, born in Chicago, Illinois, in 1931, is the creator of the Gorean Saga, the longest running series of adventure novels in science fiction history. Starting in December 1966 with *Tarnsman of Gor*, the series was put on hold after its twenty-fifth installment, *Magicians of Gor*, in 1988, when DAW refused to publish its successor, *Witness of Gor*. After several unsuccessful attempts to find a trade publishing outlet, the series was brought back into print in 2001. Norman has also produced a separate, three installment science fiction series, the Telnarian Histories, plus two other fiction works (*Ghost Dance* and *Time Slave*), a nonfiction paperback (*Imaginative Sex*), and a collection of thirty short stories, entitled Norman *Invasions*. The *Totems of Abydos* was published in spring 2012.

All of Norman's work is available both in print and as ebooks. The Internet has proven to be a fertile ground for the imagination of Norman's ever-growing fan base, and at Gor Chronicles (www.gorchronicles.com), a website specially created for his tremendous fan following, one may read everything there is to know about this unique fictional culture.

Norman is married and has three children.

OPEN **(1)** ROAD

INTEGRATED MEDIA

Open Road Integrated Media is a digital publisher and multimedia content company. Open Road creates connections between authors and their audiences by marketing its ebooks through a new proprietary online platform, which uses premium video content and social media.

Videos, Archival Documents, and New Releases

Sign up for the Open Road Media newsletter and get news delivered straight to your inbox.

Sign up now at
www.openroadmedia.com/newsletters

FIND OUT MORE AT
WWW.OPENROADMEDIA.COM

FOLLOW US:
@openroadmedia and
Facebook.com/OpenRoadMedia

www.ingramcontent.com/pod-product-compliance
Lightning Source LLC
Chambersburg PA
CBHW032255020726
47495CB00001B/109